THE
COMPLETE
YES PRIME
MINISTER

THE COMPLETE
YES PRIME
MINISTER

*The Diaries of
the Right Hon. James Hacker*

EDITED BY
JONATHAN LYNN & ANTONY JAY

BBC BOOKS

BBC EDITION

The BBC TV series *Yes Prime Minister* were written
by Jonathan Lynn and Antony Jay and
produced by Sydney Lotterby.
The part of *James Hacker* was
played by Paul Eddington, *Sir Humphrey
Appleby* by Nigel Hawthorne and *Bernard
Woolley* by Derek Fowlds.

Photographs of Harold Wilson on
page 101 from The Hulton Picture Company

Published by BBC Books
An imprint of BBC Worldwide Ltd.
Woodlands, 80 Wood Lane
London W12 0TT

First published in two volumes in 1986 and 1987
This paperback edition first published 1989

Reprinted 1989 (three times), and 1990 (four times), 1991,
1993, 1994, 1996 (twice), 1997, 2000 (twice), 2001, 2003, 2007, 2008, 2009

© Jonathan Lynn and Antony Jay 1986, 1987, 1989

ISBN 9780563207733

Typeset by Phoenix Photosetting, Chatham
Printed in Great Britain by
Cox & Wyman Ltd, Reading, Berkshire

Contents

Editor's Note

Hacker's unexpected elevation to the Premiership, which occurs at the end of the first chapter of this volume, created almost as many problems for his editors as it did for Britain. He was determined that his diaries should portray his period in office as a series of triumphs, even though the task would have defeated a far more skilful diarist. History dealt somewhat roughly with Hacker as Prime Minister; but readers of his full diaries will see some justice in this, since Hacker as an author dealt even more roughly with history. It may be that the office of Prime Minister encouraged in him – as in others – a progressive separation from reality, and a breaking down of the barrier between fact and imagination as he dictated, alone with his customary glass of Scotch and his cassette recorder, a version of the day's events in which he relived his successes and reinterpreted his failures.

Grateful though we are for the honour of editing and transcribing these extensive tape recordings, we were astonished to discover that, at times, Hacker seems to have decorated and rearranged past events in order to present himself in a favourable light. Indeed, surprising though it may be to a modern reader, he seems positively confident that this goal can be achieved. We cannot believe that any politician would rearrange past events deliberately in order to distort the historical record, and so we have had to assume that Hacker had some strange defect of mind that frequently led him to ask not 'What did I do?' but 'What is the most impressive explanation of my actions that cannot be disproved by published facts?'

The reader of political memoirs will know that most politicians' memoirs are models of fairness and accuracy, suffused with generosity of spirit, making no attempts to justify past errors. Politicians generally write of their colleagues with a warmth and admiration which is only equalled by their modest deprecation of their own contribution to government. They seldom try to pretend or suggest that every measure they proposed turned out to be successful, nor do they claim to have warned against every decision that led to disaster.

Politicians are a noble breed of men, who by their dedication and selfless public service have made Britain what she is today.

Indeed, the sad task of the editors of most political memoirs is to compel the politicians, who have the deepest reluctance to comply with this demand, to inject sufficient controversy, distortion and malice into their books for the publisher to have a chance of selling the serial rights to the *Sunday Times*.

Why was Hacker different? Perhaps the most likely explanation is that elevation to high office actually made him come to see language in a different way. Politicians are simple, direct people. They are accustomed to saying what they mean in a straightforward manner. But prolonged exposure to the Civil Service, as personified by Sir Humphrey Appleby, may have led Hacker to see language not as a window into the mind but as a curtain to draw across it.

Hacker devoted a great deal of time to talking into his cassette recorder. It would hardly be an exaggeration to say that he had a sort of love affair with it. Finally it was the only thing in the world that was willing to listen to him uncritically. And not only would it listen – it would repeat his own ideas and thoughts to him, a quality that Prime Ministers find very reassuring.

Hacker's recollections would thus be a very imperfect record of his period at Number Ten Downing Street were it not for the other documentation which has so generously been made available to us. Once again we have made copious use of the voluminous Appleby Papers, which contain Sir Humphrey's private diaries, letters and memoranda, and we would like to express our gratitude to his widow, his trustees, his executors, and the Public Record Office which has generously released all possible documents under the Thirty Year rule. We are especially grateful also to Sir Bernard Woolley GCB, formerly Hacker's Principal Private Secretary at Number Ten Downing Street and eventually Head of the Home Civil Service, who has again given us his own recollections and checked this volume for historical accuracy, a thankless task indeed. The responsibility for all errors, whether of omission or commission, remains entirely our own.

Hacker College, Oxford　　　　　　　　　Jonathan Lynn
May, 2024 AD　　　　　　　　　　　　　Antony Jay

1
Party Games

December 6th

Sir Humphrey's up to something. When I saw him yesterday at the Department of Administrative Affairs he was in a sort of dream and he seemed quite unable to concentrate on my problems with the Eurosausage, which is the latest idiotic standardisation fight that I have to have with our European enemies. [*Or European partners, as Hacker referred to them in public – Ed.*]

But more of that in a moment. Sir Humphrey normally has a real zest and enthusiasm for bureaucratic battles, and he has been strangely subdued recently. No doubt he's plotting something. I suppose I'll find out soon enough – if not, I'm in trouble!

Meanwhile, today was mostly spent on routine business. I was wading through some Cabinet Defence Papers in the office this morning when Bernard interrupted me.

'Excuse me, Minister, but I'm afraid you have to deal with something that is much more urgent.'

I asked what.

'Your Christmas cards, Minister. They cannot be postponed any longer.'

Bernard was right. Getting the Christmas cards out *is* much more important than reading Cabinet Defence Papers – unless you're the Secretary of State for Defence, I suppose.

[*Hacker, like many politicians, was apparently unable to distinguish between 'Urgent' and 'Important'. Bernard had described the Christmas cards as the former. Hacker assumed that he meant the latter. On the other hand, the possibility exists that Hacker was right in describing the Christmas cards as more important. As a mere member of the Cabinet his influence over defence matters would be negligible. So would the information contained in the papers he would be shown – Ed.*]

Bernard had laid out large piles of DAA[1] Christmas cards along

[1] Department of Administrative Affairs.

the conference table. The piles were all different sizes. Clearly they were divided for a reason.

Bernard proffered the reason. 'They're all clearly labelled, Minister.' He strolled along the table, casually indicating each pile in turn as if he were reviewing a Guard of Honour. 'These you sign Jim. These you sign Jim Hacker. These, Jim and Annie. These are Annie and Jim Hacker. These, love from Annie and Jim. These Mrs Hacker should write, and you should append your name.'

I spotted two more piles. 'What about those?'

'Those are printed. And those have cyclostyled signatures, so you needn't write anything. Just check to whom they're being sent, to make sure they're not going to people to whom you should have sent a *personally* signed card. You know,' he added in explanation, 'signed Jim, or Jim Hacker, or Jim and Annie, or Annie and Jim Hacker.'

There was yet another large batch at the end of the table, subdivided into several more piles. 'What are those?'

Bernard was completely in command. 'Those are the constituency cards. Your election agent dropped them off this morning.'

I hadn't realised that they were divided up into different sections like that. But of course, constituency mail is considered political, not governmental. The Civil Service would never help with that, because it mustn't take sides in party politics. At least, that's their excuse.

However, Bernard was more than happy to explain about the constituency Christmas cards. 'Those you sign Jim, these Jim Hacker, these Jim and Annie, these love from Annie and Jim . . .'

I told him that I'd got the gist. But it was clearly going to take up much of the day. What a bore.

In fact, I hadn't yet been shown the full magnitude of the task. Bernard suddenly produced a bulging carrier bag.

'And Mrs Hacker left these,' he murmured sympathetically. 'Your personal cards. But it won't take too long. Only eleven hundred and seventy-two.'

I was appalled. 'Eleven hundred and seventy-two?'

'Apart from', he added, 'the cards that are waiting for you at Party Headquarters.'

My heart sank. Party Headquarters. I'd forgotten about all that. I didn't sign any Party Christmas cards last year. But last year I wasn't Party Chairman. This year I am.

I started signing the cards. To my surprise I noticed that there were two kinds: DAA cards and House of Commons cards.

Bernard explained. 'Departmental cards bestow a slightly higher status on the recipient than a mere House of Commons card.' Quite right too – a departmental card can only be sent by a member of the Department, whereas a House of Commons card can be sent by any ordinary backbencher.

I asked why we didn't send departmental cards to everyone.

'They cost 10p more, Minister.'

'But aren't people who get mere House of Commons cards going to be offended at being downgraded?'

'No, Minister, we've worked it out quite carefully. For some people you can get away with a House of Commons card if you sign it Jim instead of Jim Hacker, or Jim and Annie instead of Jim and Annie Hacker, or add "with love", or sign it instead of cyclostyling, or . . .'

I silenced him with a look.

There was one card I particularly resented sending. It was to the EEC Agriculture Commissioner in Brussels. I would rather have sent him a redundancy notice. He's even worse than his colleagues, and I can't speak any worse of anybody than that. He's the fool who has forced through the plan to standardise the Eurosausage. By the end of next year we'll be waving goodbye to the good old British sausage, and we'll be forced to accept some foreign muck like salami or bratwurst in its place.

Of course, they can't actually *stop* us eating the British sausage. But they can stop us calling it a sausage. It seems that it's got to be called the Emulsified High-Fat Offal Tube. And I was forced to swallow it. I mean, it is a perfectly accurate description of the thing, but not awfully appetising. And it doesn't exactly trip lightly off the tongue. It sticks in the throat, as a matter of fact. There's going to be frightful trouble over it.

But it's my job to implement EEC regulations. And, in exchange for getting a new deal on farm prices and on Britain's reduced contribution to the community budget, a concession had to be made. The PM didn't seem to mind, nor did the FO, nor did Agriculture – presumably because I'm the one who is to be landed with trying to sell this to the British people. It could ruin my career.

Bernard asked me what the EEC has against our sausage. Apparently he doesn't read the papers he puts into my red box.[1]

'Didn't you read this analysis?'

'I glanced at it, Minister, but I'm afraid it rather put me off.'

I re-read it, there and then.

[1] The official briefcase containing government papers, which members of the government are given each evening and weekend as their homework.

```
                            - 3 -


    a lack of healthy nutrition.  The average British

    sausage consists of:


                32 %  ..... Fat

                 6 %  ..... Rind

                20 %  ..... Water

                 5 %  ..... Seasoning, preservatives

                            and colouring

                26 %  ..... Meat

    The 26% meat is mostly gristle, head meat, other

    off cuts, and mechanically recovered meat steamed

    off the carcass.
```

I felt slightly sick. I had had one for breakfast.

Bernard read the analysis. 'Perhaps the EEC Commissioner is right about abolishing it.'

Bernard sometimes misses the point *completely*. 'He *may* be right,' I explained wearily, 'but it'll be dreadfully unpopular with the voters.' Bernard nodded gloomily. 'Ah well,' I added, 'it seems we'll just have to grit our teeth and bite the bullet.'

[*We have kept Hacker's mixed metaphors in the text of this document because we feel it gives an insight into the mind of one of our great national leaders – Ed.*]

Bernard tactfully suggested that I should send Maurice a Christmas card, nonetheless. I toyed with the idea of wishing him an offal Christmas and a wurst New Year, but Bernard advised me against it.

[*One of the reasons for trying to maintain impenetrable secrecy around Government Ministers is that without it many would make themselves laughing stocks within days or – at most – weeks. Bernard's advice in this case was clearly wise – Ed.*]

I asked Bernard what Christmas presents it would be appropriate to give to the Private Office.

Bernard said that it was entirely up to me. But he recommended bottles of sherry for the Assistant Private Secretaries, large boxes of House of Commons mints for the Diary Secretary and the Correspondence Secretary, and small boxes of House of Commons mints for the rest.

'What about the Principal Private Secretary?' I asked absent-mindedly.

'That's me,' he replied, slightly startled.

I explained that I knew who he was. But I wondered what I should give him.

'You don't have to give me anything, Minister.'

'I know that,' I said with real warmth. 'But I'd *like* to.'

Bernard seemed quite touched. 'Oh, Minister,' he replied.

'Well?' I asked.

'Well, anything really.'

He obviously didn't want to say. But I had *no idea* what he'd like.

'Such as?' I prompted.

'Really,' he said, 'I'd like a surprise.'

I still didn't have a clue. 'What *sort* of surprise should I give you?'

'Well,' he said cautiously, 'a bottle of champagne is the customary surprise.'

I spent the rest of the day signing these bloody cards. I was supposed to have a big meeting with Humphrey, but it was cancelled because he had some unexpected meeting with Sir Arnold.[1] I think Bernard knows that there's something going on with Sir Humphrey because I got one of his less-than-completely-straightforward replies when I asked him if the meeting was about something I should know about.

'Well,' he answered evasively, 'I'm sure that if, you know, it's about something you should know, assuming that, you know, you *didn't* know about it already, then, obviously, *when* you can know will be when Sir Humphrey really knows.'

'I don't like being kept in the dark,' I complained.

'Well, quite honestly, Minister, Sir Humphrey may not know what it's about. Only Sir Arnold may know what it's about. And they do have meetings that aren't just about this Department.'

Bernard may be right. But Sir Arnold always makes me feel nervous. The Cabinet Secretary is, in some ways, the most powerful man

[1] Sir Arnold Robinson, the Secretary of the Cabinet.

in the country. He's the Prime Minister's right-hand man. He controls Cabinet Agenda. He can control access to the PM.

[*Sir Humphrey Appleby's meeting with the most powerful man in the country was to have a momentous effect on the future of them all: Hacker, Appleby and Bernard Woolley. A note of the meeting has been found among Sir Humphrey's private papers – Ed.*]

Had an astonishing and nerve-wracking meeting with AR[1] today. The CS[2] fixed me with an eagle-eyed stare.

'Humphrey,' he murmured, 'I've been giving some thought to the matter of early retirement.'

I was shocked. I had no wish to retire. I couldn't see what I'd done wrong. But he seemed very firm. 'The time has come, Humphrey. Enough is enough.'

I told him that this was a bit of a bombshell.

'I'm well aware of that, Humphrey,' he replied firmly, 'but no one is indispensable.'

I was hesitating, wondering whether I should launch into a defence of my own recent conduct, pointing out that there were severe limits to one's achievements when one has a Minister such as Hacker to contend with, when Arnold added: 'Don't try to persuade me, Humphrey, the die is cast. I shall retire six months early, in the New Year.'

I reflected how fortunate it was that thirty years of training in Civil Service methods had triumphed over my initial impetuosity. So long as there is anything to be gained by saying nothing, it is always better to say nothing than anything.

But why was Arnold taking me into his confidence? The answer became clear immediately. 'My successor, Humphrey, has to be someone who can be firm with our political masters.'

I hastened to agree. We can't put up with too much nonsense from that lot. I said as much. But we both agreed that Sir Arnold's successor, while not putting up with any nonsense, had to be tactful, suave, charming and emollient. But, above all, he has to be *sound*. There was no doubt in my mind that I embodied all the necessary qualities in full measure. And indeed, Arnold went on to say that it is his heavy duty to convey a recommendation to the Prime Minister as to which of the present Permanent Secretaries best meets these stringent criteria.[3]

He came to the point. He remarked that in his job, the problem isn't really finding the answers. It's finding the questions. 'We need the man who can find the key questions.'

[1] Sir Arnold Robinson.
[2] Cabinet Secretary, the same AR.
[3] A small committee, including the Permanent Secretary of the Treasury and the Head of the Civil Service would have made this recommendation. In practice, the Prime Minister was likely to follow Sir Arnold's recommendation, especially if Sir Arnold ensured that his colleagues endorsed it.

So this was it! This was my test. As I'd been given no warning of this oral examination I had to think fast. Fortunately I collected my thoughts in a matter of moments, and the key question popped into my mind.

But it had to be asked with taste and discretion. So I remarked that I was changing the subject completely, and then enquired what he intended to do when he retired.

Arnold was delighted. He congratulated me on asking such a good question. But it was immediately clear to me that there would be ways in which he might serve the country [*i.e. jobs that Sir Arnold might pick up – Ed.*] that his successor as Cabinet Secretary might persuade him to undertake [*i.e. slip his way – Ed.*]

It transpired that Sir Arnold had given this matter some thought already, and had been offered the Chairmanship of Banque Occidentale, plus directorships of BP and IBM.

However, I made careful notes of a few other ways in which Sir Arnold suggested that he could serve his country, and which were on his mind. The Chairmanship of the Royal Opera House Trust is coming up next year, and the Chancellorship of Oxford. We agreed that the Deputy Chairmanship of the Bank of England would be a challenge, as would being Head of the Security Commission. And the Presidency of the Anglo-Caribbean Association would also give Arnold a chance to be of service. Especially in the winter months.

I assured Arnold that any successor worth his salt would be able to arrange those matters satisfactorily. I could tell that Arnold found my positive approach extremely reassuring.

However, it transpired that he had other matters on his mind as well. He was concerned that certain advice that he might have given the Prime Minister in the past could, if it comes out, be misinterpreted. [*In other words, could be understood perfectly – Ed.*] Naturally we are, all of us, in the Service, concerned that advice that one has given could be misunderstood if it were to come into the public domain.

Arnold was particularly concerned because it appears that papers exist recording his reasonable and sensible advice to use troops during strikes, and suggesting the equally reasonable precaution that such troops should be armed. Of course, taken out of context [*i.e. placed in the correct context – Ed.*] such information could be damaging to him.

He has also, in the distant past, suggested we ensure that sanctions against Rhodesia [*as it then was – Ed.*] never happened, and in the recent past he proposed negotiations with South Africa about reactivating the Simonstown naval base. This was all perfectly sensible strategically, and of course would be a great help with the Falklands. But it could be an embarrassment for somebody in line for the Secretary-Generalship of the Commonwealth. And I was able to confirm that Arnold *would* be in line for the Secretary-Generalship of the Commonwealth.

He was gratified, especially when I told him that in my opinion the right successor would see no problem in keeping the relevant files under wraps.

So we reverted to the original subject of discussion, namely Arnold's retirement. He told me that he could now see his way forward to placing my

15

name at the head of the list. Good news – and better news followed at once, as careful questioning elicited the hint that there would be no other names on that list.

As I left, on cloud nine, Arnold mentioned that he had already accepted the Presidency of the Campaign for Freedom of Information. I was rather stunned. But then I quickly saw the wisdom of it. The Campaign is always very popular with the Opposition. And today's Opposition is tomorrow's government. Also his Presidency of the Campaign will ensure that the Freedom of Information is not abused. Hopefully he will be in a good position to help keep those files of advice given to the PM – and to Ministers – under wraps.

We drank a toast to the continuity of sound government, and to freedom of information – whenever it's in the national interest.

[*Appleby Papers/PPC/MPAA*]

[*Hacker's diary continues – Ed.*]

December 9th

The day began with a frightful misunderstanding about Humphrey's future. The resulting embarrassment could have been ghastly, but for the fact that I covered up the situation with my customary skill.

He came in to see me first thing this morning. He told me that he had very grave news, and he said it in a profoundly sepulchral tone. In fact, the misunderstanding that ensued came about entirely because he speaks in gobbledegook instead of plain English.

Later today I asked Bernard what Humphrey had said, and he remembered it perfectly. Apparently Humphrey had said gravely that 'the relationship, which I might tentatively venture to aver has not been without a degree of reciprocal utility and even perhaps occasional gratification, is approaching the point of irreversible bifurcation and, to put it briefly, is in the propinquity of its ultimate regrettable termination'.

I asked him if he would be so kind as to summarise what he's just said in words of one syllable.

He nodded in sad acquiescience. 'I'm on my way out,' he explained.

I couldn't believe my ears. Did he mean what I thought he meant?

'There comes a time,' he continued, 'when one must accept what fate has in store, when one passes on . . .'

'Passes on?' I interrupted softly, aghast.

'. . . to pastures new,' he continued, 'perhaps greener, to put oneself finally at the service of one who is greater than any of us.'

I was shattered. I told him I was frightfully sorry. He thanked me. I

16

asked him if his wife knew. He said that, apparently, she had suspected for some time. I asked him when they had told him. He said this afternoon. Finally, I asked him how long they'd given him.

'Just a few weeks,' he said.

I was appalled. And very moved. It did strike me at the time that he was being awfully brave, but . . . I just thought he was being awfully brave.

'Humphrey, you're being awfully brave,' I said.

'Well, I am a little anxious, I must admit – one is always frightened of the unknown – but I have faith. Somehow I'll muddle through.'

I was overcome. Overwhelmed. In fact, I am not ashamed to admit that I wept. Fortunately, Humphrey couldn't quite see that, as I had the good sense to cover my eyes with my handkerchief.

But he certainly noticed I was upset, and he asked me what the matter was. I was hopelessly inarticulate. I tried to explain how sorry I was, that we'd had our ups and downs but they were nothing really. Then I sort of noticed Humphrey eyeing me as if I were emotionally unstable.

'Minister, don't take on so,' he remonstrated. 'We'll see each other regularly – once a week at least.'

I thought I'd misheard him. But he was smiling a confident smile. My brain was in a whirl. What could he possibly mean? Had I totally misunderstood him?

'I haven't told you where I'm going yet.'

I goggled at him.

'I've been appointed Secretary of the Cabinet.'

I *had* totally misunderstood him. 'Secretary of the Cabinet?'

'Yes.' Now he looked as confused as I must have looked. 'Why, what did you think I meant?'

I could hardly tell him, could I? 'I thought . . . I thought . . .' Then I gave up and tried to explain it all away by hinting that I wasn't quite myself, tired, overwrought, that sort of thing. I've honestly never been so embarrassed in the whole of my life.

Sir Humphrey's sympathy, unlike mine, is to be avoided at all costs. 'I'm so sorry,' he murmured. 'Perhaps as Cabinet Secretary designate I should suggest to the Prime Minister some lightening of the load.'

That'll teach me to have kindly feelings towards him. I'll never make *that* mistake again! I hastened to reassure him that I was absolutely fine. I congratulated him warmly, even effusively, on his elevation. I may even have been too effusive, but I don't think so. I even

17

flattered him a little, by asking how I would manage without him.

'You'll probably manage even better without me,' he replied with uncharacteristic honesty. I was about to agree enthusiastically, but I realised, just in time, that it would be a little tactless.

Also, it was already clear to me that Humphrey, when it was time for a reshuffle, would inevitably be advising the Prime Minister on his Cabinet colleagues. The PM would be bound to question Humphrey about me.

So I gave him a lot of soft soap about how wonderful he'd been, how I had tremendous admiration for all he'd done, wonderful work in the highest traditions of the service. Fulsome twaddle, but he lapped it up and told me I was too kind. Too true!

Carefully, I gave him the chance to reciprocate, by saying that in my opinion we'd done a pretty good job together. 'I couldn't have wished for a better Minister, Minister,' he said. Jolly nice, that. And I think he means it. Humphrey's pretty devious but I've never caught him out in an actual lie.

[*Sir Humphrey Appleby's diary reveals a somewhat different view of the conversation that Hacker describes above – Ed.*]

I told the Minister that I had to pass on to pastures new, and put myself at the service of the PM. I tried to express it with a sadness that I did not feel, in order that Hacker should not perceive the sense of delight and relief that I was experiencing now that my sentence of several years' hard labour with him was nearly over. I had not been expecting to be paroled.

He reacted in a way which genuinely makes me wonder if he is emotionally unbalanced. He seemed to be weeping. He is obviously a serious hysteric. This had not been clear to me until today.

It took him some time to understand my new job, so upset was he at the thought of losing me. But then he grovelled in a deeply embarrassing fashion. He asked if I'd be doing for the Prime Minister what I did to him. He must have meant *for* him. [*We don't think so – Ed.*] He smarmed and greased his way through a bootlicking speech about how much he admired me and how wonderful I'd always been. Perfectly true, of course, but his motives were completely transparent.

He invited me to return the compliment. The best I could manage was to assure him that I couldn't have wished for a better minister. He seemed positively thrilled. Remarkably, he still takes everything I say at face value.

We agreed that I'd tell the DAA staff of my departure on Friday evening, just before my new appointment is promulgated. Then I can bid them all farewell at the Christmas drinks party.

Hacker said that that will certainly make it a happy occasion. Obviously he means for me. Of course it will be sad for him.

[*Appleby Papers 928/2033/NT*]

[Hacker's diary continues – Ed.]

December 18th

This has been a highly dramatic weekend. It all started on Friday evening. We had a little drinks party in my offices at the end of the day. We had all the chaps from my private office and Humphrey's private office in for some Christmas cheer, plus Roy my driver and a couple of messengers and cleaners. These are egalitarian times.

I gave them all their House of Commons mints, or bottles, and they all seemed pleased though not a bit surprised. Then we all had a few drinks, not too much, and I proposed Humphrey's health in a charming speech which, though I say it myself, went very well. He complimented me in turn and we all drove home.

SIR BERNARD WOOLLEY RECALLS:[1]
Hacker's diary is a less than accurate account of that Christmas party. I remember it well. It was the usual initial embarrassment – all of us standing around in a inarticulate circle, clutching sticky sherry glasses, in a freezing room because the central heating had already been turned off for the Christmas break. As at all office parties, we had nothing to say to each other socially, and foolish grins predominated until we realised that the Minister was, predictably, getting drunk.

He poured lavish drinks and finally asked us all, not once but several times, if we were having a good time.

I recall that he asked Sir Humphrey if he were looking forward to the Cabinet Office. Sir Humphrey enthused, but added kindly that everyone was still very excited over the vexed question of the Eurosausage.

'Ah yes,' slurped the Minister, 'the Eurobanger.'

Sir Humphrey was unable to resist a little joke at Hacker's expense and replied that surely the Eurobanger was NATO's new tactical missile.

'Is it?' asked Hacker, confused, not getting the joke. This increased the general embarrassment factor tenfold.

Then, at last, the moment we all dreaded: Hacker's speech of farewell to Sir Humphrey. Hacker's belief, revealed in his diaries, that he made a charming speech which went well is a startling example of self-deception even by his own unique standards.

He began by saying that he had to say 'a few words' – always an understatement, I fear. He babbled on about how Christmas is a special time for us all, peace and goodwill to all men and so forth, and how it is always a pleasure to have a little seasonal get-together for those who serve him. He clumsily amended 'serve' to 'help'.

He thanked them all for their help, 'everyone from the Permanent Secretary right down to my messenger, my driver, the cleaner . . . not *down* to, that is, at least only down in the sense that Humphrey's up here on the fourth floor, oh no! we don't have any élitism here.'

[1] In conversation with the Editors.

19

He must have noticed that we were staring at him in some disbelief, as he hastened to explain himself still further. 'We're all equals,' he said with transparent dishonesty. 'A team. Like the Cabinet, except that we're all on the same side. No backstabbing, no leaking to the press.' Realising that he was being quotably disloyal to his Cabinet colleagues, and that even though he was arguing that we were all on the same side with no backstabbing or leaking there might nevertheless be amongst the gathering an unofficial spokesman or an informed source, or perhaps a feeling that *he* was being a bad team player by criticising his Cabinet colleagues, he added, 'I mean, the *Shadow* Cabinet'. Then he retracted even that. 'No. No. *Must keep politics out of it*. Peace and goodwill. Even towards one's officials, especially those who are leaving. So . . . to Humphrey.' He raised his glass unsteadily.

It is hard to describe the sense of relief that swept around the frozen room as Hacker finished his speech. We sipped our drinks and Sir Humphrey replied briefly and elegantly thanking everyone for their hard work over the past years. He remarked that such an occasion engenders a certain emotional ambiguity and personal ambivalence, because though honoured by the cause of his departure he was saddened by the fact of it.

He added that he was particularly sad to leave the service of a Minister without parallel in his experience. Perhaps it was this remark that Hacker mistook for a compliment.

We all agreed that an absolutely unique partnership had come to an end.

[Hacker's diary continues – Ed.]

I sent our detectives home early, before the party. They shouldn't have gone off duty, but I insisted. Season of goodwill and all that. So they weren't on hand when the police stopped me. I don't know why they did. I was driving perfectly safely. I was going slowly and carefully home to the constituency. I do dimly remember being overtaken by a middle-aged lady on a bicycle, which may suggest that I was overdoing the safety bit, but that is hardly a reason to accuse me of drunken driving. I mean, there's nothing wrong – I mean morally, of course, not legally – with being drunk. The danger comes if you're *dangerous* with it, which I never am.

Anyway, a couple of bobbies appeared from nowhere in a panda car, but when I mentioned that I had a Silver Badge[1] there was no more trouble. I don't think Annie's much of a driver, but in the circumstances I had to let her drive the rest of the way home.

[Our researches have not revealed the notebooks of the policemen who stopped Hacker that night. But we were fortunate enough to find, in the Home Office files, a letter from the Commissioner of Police in which their report was quoted. We reproduce it opposite – Ed.]

[1] See page 22 below.

NEW SCOTLAND YARD

BROADWAY. LONDON. SW1H 0BG

Permanent Secretary
Home Office
Whitehall
London SW1

19 December

Dear Richard,

We regret to inform you that the Rt Hon James Hacker, MP, Minister for
Administrative Affairs, was stopped while driving home on Friday night.
He was driving at approximately nine miles an hour, and his breath smelled
strongly of alcohol. Since he immediately produced his Silver Badge
my two officers did not breathalyse him, a serious error which I can only
put down to inexperience.

They reported that when they approached Mr Hacker he began the conversation
with the words 'Good evening, Cinstable, Happy Chrostmas.' When asked
why he was driving so slowly he replied, 'I didn't want the kerb to
hit me.' Mrs Hacker, who had apparently not been drinking, offered to
drive the rest of the way home.

I would be obliged if you would make the Minister aware of the seriousness
of this matter and warn him that, in the event of a further breach of the
law, his Silver Badge will afford him no protection. For my part, I shall be
disciplining the detectives responsible for his 'protection', and ensuring
that in future they understand that their job includes protecting politicians
from themselves.

Yours sincerely

December 20th

Imagine my surprise when after the next Cabinet meeting – Humphrey's first as Cabinet Secretary – he buttonholed me as we were leaving the Cabinet Room and asked me if I'd pop over to his office and have a word with him.

I congratulated him on the conduct of his first Cabinet meeting and asked him how it felt, sitting there at the PM's right hand.

He ignored my question, asked me to take a pew and, absolutely without any warning and not even pausing to offer me a drink, told me that he wanted to have a word about a traffic incident.

Well, a nod is as good as a wink. I realised at once that it must be my little incident to which he was referring.

'I've had a report from the Home Office. Of course, it's entirely your affair . . .'

I interrupted him firmly. 'Precisely,' I said.

'But,' he continued, 'the Home Office take a very grave view. They feel that Ministers should set an example. There's a lot of damage to police morale if people get away with things just because they happen to hold an office of trust, however temporarily.'

The threat in the last two words was unmistakeable. I could hardly believe my ears. Two days as Cabinet Secretary and he was really getting rather uppity.

'Humphrey,' I asked with some incredulity, 'are you trying to tell me off or something?'

He backtracked immediately. 'Minister! Far be it from me. I am only the servant of the members of the Cabinet. A humble functionary. But I have been asked to reassure the Home Office that it will not occur again.'

I knew I was untouchable. 'What do they give us Silver Badges for then?' I enquired loftily.

'To get police co-operation, to let us pass through police cordons and security barriers and so on. Not to protect drunks who drive cars.'

I rose above it. 'Humphrey, I am not going to be lectured by functionaries, not even those as humble as your good self. I am a Minister of the Crown.'

'Of course, Minister,' he replied pleasantly, 'I will inform the Crown of the incident, if that is your wish.'

That was *not* my wish, as he perfectly well knew. I started to explain that I was speaking purely technically when I said I was a Minister of the Crown, but he interrupted me to add that his proper course was actually to inform the Prime Minister. At which point I decided that, thinking it over, he could feel free to tell the Home Office that I'd taken the point.

He thanked me politely. I asked if the Home Secretary knew. It would obviously be rather humiliating if the rebuke had been authorised by one of my colleagues.

Humphrey said no. 'This came straight from the Permanent Secretary of the Home Office.'

I was relieved. 'So there's no need for the Home Secretary to be . . . I mean, one doesn't want one's . . . colleagues (I nearly said enemies) to know?'

Humphrey guessed what I meant. After all, my views on Ray have not exactly been a closely guarded secret. 'I think the Home Secretary is not in a position to take advantage.'

I wondered why not. I suddenly realised that Ray hadn't been at Cabinet. Then Humphrey showed me the headline in the *Standard*.

The long and the short of it is that the Home Secretary, having personally initiated the 'Don't Drink And Drive At Christmas' campaign, and having ordered a get-tough policy from the police, was picked up pissed in his car in his own constituency.

How had he got into such a situation? I asked Humphrey why his security man hadn't been with him.

'Apparently,' replied Sir Humphrey pointedly, 'he'd given him the slip. You know how cunning these drunks can be.'

It transpired that the Home Secretary had been rather less lucky than me. He'd collided with a lorry that was full of nuclear waste. Then, as if that wasn't unlucky enough, he rebounded off the lorry

23

and smashed into a car which was being driven by the editor of the local newspaper. Fat chance of hushing *that* up. So naturally it leaked out. [*The story, not the nuclear waste – Ed.*]

That was the end of Ray. By the end of the day he would be out of office.

I looked at Humphrey. 'What'll happen to him?'

'I gather,' he replied disdainfully, 'that he was as drunk as a lord – so after a discreet interval they'll probably make him one.'

SIR BERNARD WOOLLEY RECALLS:[1]

I well remember the dramatic events of two days later. I had called at the Minister's London flat, to collect him for a dinner to which I had to accompany him.

He was late home from the office. Annie Hacker was writing her Christmas cards, and asked me if I could put stamps on them while I was waiting.

I explained that I was not able to. Not, I hastened to explain, because the task was beyond me, but because I guessed that the cards were being sent to constituents. Such Christmas cards were considered political activity rather than government business, and of course as a Civil Servant I was not allowed to help with the Minister's political activities.

'I'm only asking you to lick some stamps,' she said plaintively.

I explained that it would be government lick. [*Bernard Woolley's cautious and pedantic attitude is seen clearly here, and doubtless explains his relatively quick rise to the highest reaches of the Civil Service – Ed.*]

Mrs Hacker found an ingenious solution to her dilemma. 'Suppose all these cards were to journalists?' she asked.

'That would be all right,' I confirmed.

'They're all to journalists,' she said firmly, and of course I could not doubt her word. So I settled down on the sofa to lick stamps, reflecting privately that licking is an essential part of relationships with the press. [*Doubtless Bernard Woolley and Mrs Hacker were pleased to be only licking journalists' envelopes, for a change – Ed.*]

We discussed the opinion polls which had been released to the newspapers that morning. The Minister had been absolutely delighted with them. It seemed that the Home Secretary's misfortune had done the Government no harm in the country, even though he was the Deputy Leader of the Party.

We discussed the inevitable reshuffle, although Mrs Hacker seemed uninterested. The only thing that concerned her was the fact that Hacker might get Northern Ireland, but we agreed that the Prime Minister did not appear to dislike Hacker enough for that. Most people, of course, found Ulster a dead end, though there was always the possibility of finishing up there in a blaze of glory. [*We feel sure that Sir Bernard intended no puns here – Ed.*]

Eventually we switched on the television news. Like most Government wives, Annie Hacker liked to watch the news because it was her best chance of finding out where her husband was.

[1] In conversation with the Editors.

We were astonished by a newsflash, reporting that Number Ten Downing Street had just announced that the Prime Minister was to retire in the New Year.

According to the press release, the Prime Minister did not wish to serve through another Parliament and therefore was resigning now in order to give his successor a good run up to the next election. A historic day.

[*Hacker's diary continues – Ed.*]

December 22nd

When I got home Annie and Bernard were there, apparently poleaxed by the news of the PM's resignation. I knew already – the PM had held an emergency Cabinet meeting late this afternoon, to tell us. You could have knocked all twenty-four of us down with the metaphorical feather.

Annie asked me why he'd resigned. That was the question we were *all* asking. He had said, to us and to the press, that he'd done it so as to give his successor a good run up to the next election. So that's obviously not the reason.

There have also been some amazing rumours flying around Whitehall. The left are saying the PM's a secret CIA agent. The right are saying that he's a secret KGB agent.

Bernard and I discussed these rumours. Bernard had heard something quite different. 'Minister, I've heard that there is £1 million worth of diamonds from South Africa in a Downing Street safe.[1] But of course,' he added, 'it's only a rumour.'

'Is that true?' I asked.

'Oh yes,' he said authoritatively.

I was amazed. 'So there *are* all those diamonds in Downing Street.'

Bernard looked surprised. 'Are there?'

I was confused. 'You said there were,' I said.

'I didn't,' he replied indignantly.

'You did!' I wasn't going to let him get away with it. 'You said that there was this rumour. I said, is it true? And you said yes!'

'I said yes, it was true that it was a rumour.'

'No, you said you'd heard it was true.'

'No, I said it was true that I'd heard it.'

Annie interrupted us. 'I apologise for cutting into this vital discussion, but do you believe the story about the diamonds?'

I don't, and nor does Bernard (it transpires). It's not impossible,

---

[1] Similar rumours circulated in Whitehall at the time of the surprise resignation of Mr Harold Wilson, as he then was.

but it's never been officially denied so I think we can discount it. The first rule of politics is Never Believe Anything Until It's Been Officially Denied.

We discussed the likely possibilities. It was clear that there wouldn't be a general election. Our party has quite a big majority. All that will happen is that the party must choose a new leader.

Annie asked me if I wanted the job.

I hadn't really thought about it. There's no chance. It'll either be Eric [*Eric Jeffries, the Chancellor of the Exchequer – Ed.*] or Duncan [*Duncan Short, the Secretary of State for Foreign Affairs – Ed.*]. I started to explain why to Annie. 'You see, it *would* have been Ray, he was Deputy Leader, but as he's had to resign from the Home Office . . .'

I stopped dead. Suddenly I understood. *That* was why the PM resigned! He had always hated Ray. And Ray was his natural successor. So he had just hung on long enough to make sure that Ray didn't get the job.

[*The Prime Minister had probably learned this trick from Clement Attlee, who unquestionably hung on as Prime Minister until Herbert Morrison was out of the running. It has also been suggested that Harold Wilson chose the time of his own surprise resignation to coincide with a period of Denis Healey's unpopularity with the Left of the Labour Party, thus ensuring the succession for James Callaghan. Of course, there is no evidence for this allegation – Ed.*]

I explained this to Annie and Bernard. Bernard was touchingly pleased that the Prime Minister's press statement had been true. 'So the resignation *is* to give time for the new leader to be run in before the next election.'

'Now that the Home Secretary's been run in already,' said Annie with a quiet smile.

Naturally we started to discuss the two likely candidates. They had both buttonholed me after Cabinet this afternoon.

'Eric wants me to support him,' I told them. 'I think he could be the man for the job, he's been quite a successful Chancellor. I've already indicated that I'm on his side.'

Annie was surprised. 'But what about Duncan?'

Duncan is indeed a very real possibility. I nodded. 'Perhaps he should get it. He's done quite well at the Foreign Office, after all. Yes, he could be the man for the job. I think perhaps I'd better give him my support.'

'So you're supporting Eric *and* Duncan?' she enquired innocently.

I was indignant. It's obviously a very difficult choice. 'Look,' I told her, 'if I support Duncan, and *Eric* gets it . . . then, that's it, it's all over for me. But if I support Eric, and *Duncan* gets it . . . that's it too.'

'Then don't support either of them,' she suggested.

If only it were that simple. 'Then, *whichever* of them gets it, that's it!'

She understood. Then she asked me which one I actually am going to support. I told her.

I'll support Eric.

Or Duncan.

December 23rd

Eric wasted no time in lobbying me. I was in my office at lunchtime when he phoned and said he was popping over for a drink.

Eric's a charming man. Tall, elegant, greying hair, with an incisive, intelligent manner. Quite an appealing party leader to offer the electorate, I think. They never see the other side of him – mean-spirited, devious and malicious. He'd hardly set foot in the room when he started rubbishing Duncan.

'Duncan's so divisive. So it really wouldn't be for the good of the party, or the good of the country.'

I still haven't made up my mind and I was struggling to find a way to avoid committing myself. I was starting to say that I didn't see how I could offer Eric my public support, when he explained his position more fully.

His argument, quite simply, is that my support would be crucial for him because I'm universally popular. I must admit that I can see the truth of this. He also emphasised that I have a good public image and that I'm regarded as sound by everyone.

I explained my problem. Well, at least, I didn't explain that I was undecided because of my legitimate anxiety about backing the wrong horse. But I did explain, fully and frankly, that as Chairman of the Party I have to look impartial. [*We note that Hacker's definitions of 'fully' and 'frankly', though in general use in politics, would not correspond with definitions found in the* Oxford English Dictionary – *Ed.*]

Eric played on my feelings of party loyalty. He reminded me that we are both moderates, that we've always had the same objectives for the Party, and that if Duncan got it it would be a disaster.

I knew he'd say all that. But then he surprised me. 'I'll tell you one thing,' he said firmly, 'I wouldn't keep Duncan at the Foreign Office. I'd be looking for a new Foreign Secretary.'

The inference was clear. He means me! This is very exciting! But it's still dangerous – what if he were to lose the race? However, I must seize my opportunities. So in conclusion I said to Eric that although I must *appear* impartial I would find ways of hinting at support for him. In a completely impartial way, of course.

So I think perhaps I'll be supporting Eric.

December 24th

Duncan came round to see me at the flat last evening. I got the impression that he'd heard about my little chat with Eric.

Duncan is very different from Eric. Also very bright, he is not devious, malicious or treacherous – he is a straightforward, heavy-handed bully. I began to explain that I ought to be impartial, or at least *look* impartial, as Chairman of the Party.

He brushed that aside in his usual offhand manner. 'As Chairman of the Party you carry more weight than before. And you haven't got any real enemies. Yet.'

The threat was unmistakable. Then he went on to explain what a catastrophe it would be if Eric got into Number Ten. I nodded, which I felt could be interpreted as full agreement, but in fact could also be taken merely as an indication that I could hear what he was saying.

Then, like Eric, he tried the loyalty gambit. He bared his teeth in what he thought was a warm and friendly smile. 'Jim, we're on the same side, aren't we?'

I said yes, as I felt that a yes could simply mean that as members of the same party we must be on the same side. [*Not necessarily – Ed.*] I was scrupulously careful not to tell lies. [*There is, of course, a significant difference between not telling lies and not telling the truth. 'The truth' in politics means any statement that cannot be proved false – Ed.*]

'Good,' said Duncan. But I'm afraid that he could see my support for him was less than wholehearted, because he added: 'I'm going to win, you know. And I never forgive people who let me down.'

Really, Duncan's not awfully subtle. I pointed out that if I gave him my support I couldn't make it too public.

'It doesn't have to be public,' he answered, 'just as long as everybody knows. Then, when I'm in Number Ten and Eric's in Northern Ireland,' here he chuckled maliciously, 'we know who'll be the next Chancellor, don't we?'

Another job offer! He means me! But, predictably, he couldn't finish the conversation without a threat. 'Unless you fancy Northern Ireland yourself?'

I think perhaps I'll be supporting Duncan.

[*There the matter rested until after the Christmas break. Hacker gave himself a well-earned holiday, and even stopped dictating his notes for his diary. There are one or two undecipherable, slightly slurred cassettes that may have been dictated over the festive season, but we have ascribed their lack of clarity to a faulty cassette recorder.*

Early in the New Year Sir Humphrey Appleby met Sir Arnold Robinson for lunch at the Athenaeum Club. Appleby refers to the lunch in his private diary – Ed.]

It was my first meeting with Arnold since he retired from the Cabinet Office and took on his other onerous duties. I asked him, mischievously, how things are at the Campaign for Freedom of Information. 'I'm sorry,' he said, 'but I can't talk about that.'

Fair enough. Arnold wanted to know whether the new PM was likely to be our eminent Chancellor or our distinguished Foreign Secretary. [*Sir Humphrey used irony extensively, even in his private notes – Ed.*] Funnily enough, this was what I wanted to discuss with Arnold: who, in his opinion, should get Number Ten?

He takes a fairly dim view of them both. He's right, it is a difficult choice, rather like asking which lunatic should run the asylum.

We both agreed that they would present the same problems. They are both interventionists and they would both have foolish notions about running the country themselves if they became Prime Minister.

Arnold asked me if we had any allies. [*Allies, that is, in helping to find a third, more suitable candidate for Number Ten – Ed.*] There is the Chief Whip, of course. He is worried that whichever gets the job will antagonise the other one's supporters and split the party. A very real fear, in my view.

As this could lead to a period of real instability and change [*two things that the Civil Service wishes to avoid at all cost – Ed.*] it is clearly advisable to look for a compromise candidate.

We agreed that such a candidate must have the following qualities: he must be malleable, flexible, likeable, have no firm opinions, no bright ideas, not be intellectually committed, and be without the strength of purpose to change anything. Above all, he must be someone whom we know can be professionally guided [*manipulated – Ed.*], and who is willing to leave the business of government in the hands of the experts.

Only one person seemed to have all these qualifications . . . Hacker! But the idea of his becoming Prime Minister seems, on the face of it, completely laughable. And, what is worse, it would be difficult to achieve.

Nonetheless, we felt that it should be seriously considered for several reasons. Many of the government would welcome a less interventionist leader. The real obstacle will undoubtedly be the two front-runners for the job, but Arnold feels that they might be persuaded to stand aside.

The key to this lies in their MI5 files. I have not yet had a chance to glance at them but Arnold advised me that one should always send for the MI5 files of Cabinet Ministers if one enjoys a good laugh. [*The Cabinet Secretary is the centre of all security operations, and the Cabinet Office contains rooms full of top-secret security information – Ed.*]

BW[1] joined us for a brief cup of coffee, as he had some final DAA files for me to look at. We wished each other a Happy New Year, and then I raised the matter with him.

He was quite astonished when I asked him what he would think of his present master as the next Prime Minister. In fact, he seemed unable to grasp the question for some moments. He kept asking if I meant Mr Hacker, *his* Minister?

AR wanted to know if BW was suggesting that JH was not up to the job of PM. BW seemed unable to frame an appropriate reply. So we explained that there is a considerable body of opinion that can see many advantages in such an appointment. Advantages for Britain. [*By which Sir Humphrey meant advantages for the Civil Service, which in his view represented all that was best about Britain. It is also worth noting that Sir Arnold Robinson's statement that there was a considerable body of opinion in favour might not have been true at that moment, but would definitely have been true by the following morning – Ed.*]

We concluded the meeting by giving BW some firm and clear advice as to what Hacker should not do in the next few weeks if he was to succeed. Essentially, Woolley has to ensure that his Minister does nothing incisive or divisive in the next few weeks, avoids all controversy, and expresses no firm opinion about anything at all.

Bernard felt that this would be no problem. He believes that this is probably what Hacker was planning to do anyway.

[*Hacker's diary continues – Ed.*]

January 2nd
There was a drinks 'do' at the FCO[2] this evening. It was for our European friends. With friends like them . . .

I met an EEC official who seemed awfully Teutonic, and I asked him where he was from.

'From Brussels I have just arrived,' he told me.

I was surprised. 'You're from Belgium?'

'Brussels is in Belgium. That is correct.' The Teutonic mind!

Bernard came to the rescue. 'I think the Minister is asking if you are Belgian?'

The official nodded and smiled. 'No, I am German.'

'And what are you at the EEC?' I asked pleasantly.

'I am still German.'

I reminded myself that patience is a virtue. 'I *know* that,' I said, and looked to Bernard to rescue me again.

[1] Bernard Woolley.
[2] Foreign and Commonwealth Office.

'I think the Minister means,' said Bernard carefully, 'what is your job?'

'Ah,' said the Kraut. 'I am a Chef du Division.'

'It's a sort of Assistant Secretary,' Bernard whispered to me.

I wondered, to Bernard, if our German friend (as I have to call him) can help us with our sausage problem. Bernard nodded, and asked him *exactly* what his job is.

He was only too happy to explain. 'My job is concerned with the Common Agricultural Policy. I have to see that the farmers are paid enough money to produce more food.'

This came as a considerable surprise to me. I thought we were producing too much food in the EEC – hence the surpluses. I said as much.

The German nodded significantly. 'Too much food to *eat*, yes!'

I was baffled. 'What else is food for?' I asked him. His eyes lit up with pleasure.

'We do not produce food for eating. Food is a weapon!'

I couldn't exactly see what he meant. 'A weapon?' I said. 'You mean . . .' I searched for the right response, but answer came there none. 'You mean . . . what *do* you mean, exactly?'

It was obvious to him. 'Food is power. Green power.'

I asked if he meant that we fight the Russians with food. He became impatient, and explained that we don't fight the Russians. They are our friends, our customers. We fight the Americans!

I asked him to expand on this theme. He was delighted. His eyes gleamed as he discussed his nation's favourite pastime. 'It is a war,' he began. 'A trade war. Using food we can increase our spheres of influence over Third World countries. You should have seen Dr Kissinger's face when we threatened to sell wheat to Egypt.' He chuckled merrily. 'He wanted Egypt to himself. You see, if the Third World switches from American to European wheat, the US President loses millions of votes in the vest.'

It took me a moment to realise that he was speaking geographically, not sartorially.

'The *Mid*-vest,' he explained. 'So. The Common Agricultural Policy gives us great influence over America, you see? Last war, guns. This war, butter.'

'It's better, butter,' I remarked facetiously and laughed a little. He did not get the joke. [*Such as it was – Ed.*] So I asked what, *precisely*, he did in the food war.

'I ensure that our farmers are subsidised to produce all the food

31

that they can. We have underground silos bursting with agricultural missiles.' We were standing by the buffet, and he started to set up a dinner-table battlefield as an illustration. 'We move a division of butter to Bangladesh, we threaten Egypt with three brigades of wheat. But it is a decoy, you see,' he cried triumphantly. 'We have six airborne divisions of beef waiting to fly into China. Then . . .'

He suddenly paused, and then burst out laughing. Bernard and I stared at him, bemused. Finally I asked him what the joke was.

'It's better, butter,' he chortled. 'Very funny. Very funny.'

Bernard took me by the hand and led me quietly away to another part of the reception, where he presented me to a Monsieur Jean Penglet, who is also a Chef du Division in Brussels.

I speak no German, but I tried out a little French on Monsieur P. 'Vous parlez anglais, Monsieur Penglet?' I enquired poetically.

'I do,' he replied with cool politeness.

'And what do *you* do?' I asked.

'My job,' he said with a patient smile, 'is to deal with food surpluses.'

'You mean, export them or store them?'

He was confused. '*Non* – I pay farmers to see that all surplus food is destroyed.'

Now I was confused. 'Destroyed?' I repeated.

'But of course,' he said with a patronising Gallic shrug. 'Don't you know the Community produces too much food?'

I kept my temper.

'But look, sorry, I don't want to appear dense but that chap there' – I pointed to our humorous friendly German – 'pays farmers to *produce* surplus food. Green power, he says.'

'I know,' he nodded. 'He does a good job. Food is a weapon.'

This was making less and less sense. 'Then *why*,' I demanded, 'do you pay people to destroy it?'

There was no contradiction as far as our French friend was concerned. 'All weapons must be made obsolete. Then you can pay people to produce more. Simple.'

'Can't you just go on storing it?'

He thought that was a silly idea. '*Non*, it is cheaper to destroy the food than to store, liquefy or dehydrate.'

'Or send it across the world?' asked Bernard.

'Exactly.'

The whole Through-The-Looking-Glass approach was becoming clear to me. 'And', I said, 'I suppose you can't sell it at the market price because then the price would fall and the farmers would not make enough money.'

The Frenchman was delighted that I understood. 'Exactly.'

I decided to sum up. 'So, *he* pays French farmers to grow too much food – *you* pay the same French farmers to destroy it!'

He was grinning now. 'Exactly.'

There was just one thing left that I didn't understand. 'Why,' I asked, 'don't we just pay the farmers to sit there and not bother to grow the food at all?'

The Frenchman was offended. 'Monsieur Hacker,' he replied snootily, 'French farmers do not want to be paid for nothing. We do not want charity.'

[*Hacker's xenophobia[1] is clear from the above passage. This unattractive ability to see Germans and Frenchmen only in national stereotypes was both a personal weakness and a political strength. We shall see how it became his trump card at a crucial moment in his climb up the greasy pole – Ed.*]

January 3rd

I didn't get to the office till late afternoon today. And, although I had lots to do, somehow I just couldn't concentrate. I felt overwhelmed by the complete futility of it all, of everything we do, in the face of an EEC bureaucracy even more pointless than our own home-grown variety.

I sat behind the desk, musing, lost in my thoughts. Then I realised that Bernard was standing in front of me, trying to attract my attention in his characteristic way.

'Um,' he was saying hopefully.

I stared at him gloomily. 'What's it all *for*, Bernard?' I asked. 'What are we all doing? What's the point of it all?'

He looked momentarily nonplussed. 'I didn't read theology, Minister.'

I tried to explain my concerns to him. 'What I mean is, Bernard, the *waste* of it all. Paying a lot of people to produce masses of food. Paying another lot to destroy it. And paying thousands of bureaucrats to push paper about to make it all happen. Doesn't the futility of it all depress you?'

'Not really,' he replied, slightly puzzled. 'I'm a Civil Servant.'

'But when it's all so pointless? I entered politics to make people's lives happier.'

[1] Hatred of foreigners.

'Oh but they are, Minister.' He was concerned about me now, trying to cheer me up. 'Busy people are much happier than bored people.'

'Even if the work's futile?' I asked despairingly.

'Oh yes,' he replied encouragingly. 'Look at your private office. They're all much happier when you're here and they're busy.'

I couldn't see what he meant. I pointed out that the work in my private office has a purpose.

Bernard sort of disagreed. 'Well, most of it is drafts for statements you don't make, speeches you don't deliver, press releases nobody prints, papers nobody reads, and answers to questions nobody asks you.'

This comment, not without truth, made me even more depressed. I told Bernard that he was saying my job is as futile as the EEC.

He denied this, emphatically. 'Not at all, Minister. You went into politics to make people happy. You are making people happy. You're very popular in the private office. And everywhere else, of course,' he added hastily.

We sat in the conversation area, and discussed the race for the Premiership. 'Bernard,' I began, 'I've been talking to Eric and Duncan. I think I've promised to support Eric's candidature.'

'I see,' he said with interest.

'And then,' I continued, 'I think I promised to support Duncan.'

Bernard looked approving. 'That sounds very even-handed, Minister.'

He'd missed the point. I explained that I can't exactly keep my promise to both of them.

He didn't seem to think that this was anything to worry about. 'They were only political promises, Minister, weren't they?' I nodded. 'Well then,' he said, 'it's like your manifesto promises, isn't it? People understand.'

He's probably right about that. But there is another problem. I'm not sure, now that I think back on my conversations with Eric and Duncan, that either of them made any categorical promises to *me*.

I confessed this to Bernard, slightly concerned that it would make me seem a little inept. But Bernard felt that if they'd made no promises to me, then I didn't really have a deal with either of them. Even if he's right, I still have to decide which of them to support. It's not just a question of picking the winner, because my support may tip the balance. 'So the question is, Bernard, do I want to be Foreign Secretary or Chancellor of the Exchequer?'

I must say, I was genuinely surprised by his reply. 'Neither.'

'Neither? Why not?'

'They're both such terrible jobs.'

I thought at first that Bernard was being rather silly. After all, he was talking about two of the top three jobs in the Cabinet. I explained to him that as he was just a Civil Servant he didn't really understand politics.

He looked contrite and apologised.

'To be a success in politics, Bernard,' I continued, 'you have to be in the limelight. You have a very high political profile if you're the Chancellor. That has to be good for votes. Do you see now?'

It turned out that he saw only too well. He saw lots of things that I hadn't seen. I felt rather embarrassed that I'd patronised him, but I hoped he hadn't noticed.

'The Chancellor is Mr Killjoy,' said Bernard. 'Raising taxes on beer and cigarettes goes down awfully badly with the electorate.' He was right. 'And, Minister, have you considered working with the permanent officials of the Treasury? I believe I'm right if I suggest that you sometimes felt that Sir Humphrey, when Permanent Secretary here, did not always lay all his cards on the table?'

Good old British understatement. But I pointed out to Bernard that, nonetheless, I usually got my way. [*Here Hacker's capacity for believing his own fantasies, essential equipment for all politicians, is clearly shown – Ed.*] Bernard asked me if I had no fears at all about handling the officials at the Treasury.

I was about to reply none, when I realised that I'm not an economist, which meant that they could run rings round me. Also, it suddenly occurred to me that no new economic policy has any visible effect for at least two years – which means that for the first two years as Chancellor you are, in effect, paying for the mistakes of your predecessor. And no one realises that when the economy goes wrong there is *nothing* you can usually do about it. Especially as our economy is governed by the American economy over which I, as Chancellor, would have no control.

Bernard concurred, and added that the grapevine thought that there were shockwaves coming from America.

It was now perfectly clear to me that I shouldn't become the next Chancellor. 'There's no escape in that job, is there?' I said to Bernard.

'No, Minister. Unless, of course, you were sent to the Foreign Office as a punishment.'

35

I couldn't see what he meant. 'A punishment?'

'The Secretary of State for Foreign and Commonwealth Affairs is an even worse job.'

So that's what he meant. No longer so willing to dismiss Bernard's view out of hand, I stopped to consider this. Did he simply mean that there are no votes in foreign affairs?

'It's not just that, Minister. The Government has to be nice to foreigners but the electorate want you to be nasty to them. For instance, they resent foreign aid to less developed countries while there is unemployment in the Midlands.'

My constituency's in the Midlands! [*The fact that Bernard Woolley gave this example was hardly coincidental – Ed.*] And, once I started to think about it, there are a variety of reasons for avoiding the FO. The Secretary of State for Foreign Affairs has to go gadding about the world, while all the rest of the Cabinet are involved in the nuts and bolts of government policy. The unemployed would see pictures of me on the news eating fancy meals in our Paris Embassy while their hospitals are being closed.

And in terms of world politics, the Foreign Office is virtually irrelevant. We have no real power, we're just a sort of American missile base, that's all.

Bernard commented that the Prime Minister would send the Foreign Secretary out on all the tricky foreign missions – but would go abroad personally and take the limelight if there was any glory to be had.

Nothing new in that. It's the same for the Chancellor. Everyone thinks that Chancellors lose elections but that the Prime Minister wins them. Chancellors never get the credit, only the blame.

I sighed deeply. 'It's a choice between the devil and the deep blue sea,' I told Bernard.

He had an unusual twinkle in his eye. 'Unless . . .' he replied hesitantly . . . 'um, there is, of course, one other option.'

I couldn't think what.

'Do the middle job.'

'No, Bernard,' I said. 'Home Secretary? Don't be daft. Be responsible for all the muggings, jailbreaks and race riots? Thanks a lot.'

'No, Minister, be the one who takes all the credit.'

At first I didn't see what he meant. Then I saw! *Prime Minister!* Bernard is even more ambitious for me than I am for myself! It was more than I had dared hope for, or even think of. But now that Bernard has suggested it to me, I can't get it out of my mind.

I asked him modestly if he was serious. He confirmed that he was. 'Why not, Minister? Now that you've considered the various possibilities, it does all seem to be pointing in one direction.'

The major problem is that I'm literally up to my neck in the Eurosausage. [*Not literally, we presume – Ed.*] But if that problem could be solved . . .

Anyway, I thanked Bernard. I told him that it had been a most useful conversation and that I would have to consider whether or not my candidature was a serious possibility.

Bernard said that, of course, it was not for him to say, being a mere civil servant. But he suggested that I should consider asking my Parliamentary Under-Secretary[1] to stand in for me at tomorrow's Guildhall ceremony. It seems that there is likely to be an anti-government protest in the street on arrival, and he suggested that this might not be the time to be seen in a controversial context or hostile environment.

He's absolutely right, and I followed his advice. I told him that he was getting more like Sir Humphrey every day.

'Thank you, Minister, I see that as a compliment.'

'You must have very good eyesight,' I joked. But he was right. It was.

[*While Bernard Woolley, acting on Sir Humphrey's instructions, was planting the seed of Prime Ministerial ambitions in the fertile and plentiful soil inside Hacker's head, and ensuring that Hacker avoided all controversy, Sir Humphrey himself was not idle. He telephoned Jeffrey Pearson, the Chief Whip, and invited him to a secret meeting at the Cabinet Office. There is no record of this conversation in Sir Humphrey's private papers, perhaps because of its sensitive nature and security implications. Jeffrey Pearson, being a politician, had no such scruples, and the conversation is reported in his elegant memoirs* Suck It And See – *Ed.*]

I got a phone call from Sir Humphrey Appleby, the Cabinet Secretary, asking how the race for the leadership looked from the Whips' Office.

He knew the grim prospect only too well. If Eric got Number Ten there would have been a split in the party in three months. If Duncan, there would have been a split in three weeks.

He gave me some startling information. He revealed that there were security question marks over both candidates. I pressed him for details but he said that he could say no more. The only person he could disclose this to,

[1] Hacker's junior minister.

in the PM's absence,[1] and since it was essentially a party matter, was the Chairman of the Party. [*Jim Hacker – Ed.*]

He had invited Hacker to a meeting in the Cabinet Office, and wanted me to be there also. Naturally I accepted. He also asked me to suggest a compromise candidate. My first thought was that it could be any one of half a dozen.

Sir Humphrey asked if I'd considered the Party Chairman himself. The idea of Jim Hacker as Prime Minister, though it struck me as ludicrous at first, rapidly became an idea that was really no worse than any other. After all, who *is* fit for the job? You never know, till you suck it and see.

Sir Humphrey pointed out that there have been less likely Prime Ministers. I wonder who. [*Extensive research suggests that Sir Humphrey must have been referring to the Marquis of Bute – Ed.*]

[*Hacker's diary continues – Ed.*]

January 4th

I got a message to see Sir Humphrey urgently, in his office. To my surprise Jeffrey Pearson, the Chief Whip, was also there. A big burly man, with twinkling eyes just visible behind huge heavy-framed glasses topped by a shiny bald head which reflected the overhead chandelier. I felt I should have brought my sunglasses.

Humphrey was at his most courteous. 'So good of you to call, Minister. I have a problem. I need your help.'

'Can't you run the country on your own?' I asked.

He was not amused. 'Yes, it *is* rather a grave matter, I'm afraid.'

I became grave at once.

'It's about the leadership election. The PM felt that he had no alternative but to call you in.'

So it was *that* bad. I nodded, and waited. Then he said something that I couldn't quite get the hang of – perhaps I wasn't concentrating properly.

[*Sir Humphrey's remarks that Hacker couldn't follow are recorded in a minute, reproduced opposite, which Sir Humphrey sent to the Prime Minister shortly after the meeting with Hacker – Ed.*]

[1] The Prime Minister, having announced his resignation, went abroad on what were ostensibly goodwill visits to friendly countries. In reality he was setting up a lucrative lecture tour and some profitable consultancies.

70 WHITEHALL, LONDON SW1A 2AS

Memorandum

To: The Prime Minister
From: The Secretary of the Cabinet

> I informed Mr Hacker that there are certain items
> of confidential information which while they are
> in theory susceptible of innocent interpretation do
> nevertheless contain a sufficient element of ambiguity,
> so that, should they be presented in a less than
> generous manner to an uncharitable mind, they might
> be a source of considerable embarrassment, and even -
> conceivably - hazard, were they to impinge upon the
> deliberations of an office of more than usual
> sensitivity.

[Hacker's diary continues – Ed.]

Jeffrey Pearson explained that Humphrey was talking about security.

'Security?' I repeated, puzzled. 'What do you mean?'

'Secrets,' he said.

I tried to conceal my impatience. Obviously I know what security *means*. But what did Humphrey mean? Exactly.

'I'm not allowed to know,' said Jeffrey.

'Why not?' I asked.

'Security,' he replied.

I turned to Humphrey for clarification. For once, he obliged. He explained to me that, as in the Prime Minister's absence I was deputising on party matters, he needed me to look at the Security file on the Chancellor of the Exchequer. He was not allowed to give me the whole file, but only to show me the relevant items.

39

He then showed me some astonishing pieces of paper. Reports on Eric from the Security officers, from the Special Branch, an interview with his driver, and a confidential memo from the PM himself.

I really can't go into the details here. This information is dynamite, and if the wrong person were to get their hands on this cassette [*Hacker always dictated his diaries into a cassette recorder – Ed.*] it would be disastrous for Eric. Suffice to say that Eric had never struck me as a sex maniac or a dirty old man, and I simply can't imagine how a workaholic like him finds the time for everything that I read about today.

Sir Humphrey has an explanation. 'My experience is that people who are highly active in one area of life tend to be equally active in all the other areas.'

'I mean, to look at him you couldn't think that he went in for . . .' I was stuck for a sufficiently delicate phrase.

Sir Humphrey supplied it. 'I believe the current expression is horizontal jogging, Minister.'

I pointed out that all of this horizontal jogging had happened a while ago, and none of it proved conclusively that Eric had breached security.

Humphrey readily agreed. 'That's why the PM thought it all right for him to be Chancellor. But in view of the Yugoslav one . . . and the South Africans . . . not to mention the shady lady from Argentina . . . and it's thought that she's just a cover, by the way.'

This was even more mind-boggling. A cover? What on earth *for*? If these 'ladies' are a cover story, I can't imagine what his real requirements are.

Nor can Humphrey, apparently. But it is clear that Defence or the Foreign Office might be a little too delicate for such a minister. And if Eric became PM he'd be head of the Security Services as well. I could see why old Humphrey was worried. It would be unthinkable.

'So,' I said, 'what you're saying is, it's got to be Duncan.'

Sir Humphrey hesitated. Then he reached across his desk for another Top Secret file. 'I was coming to that,' he replied carefully. 'This is the Foreign Secretary's file.'

Another staggering pile of paper! More from the Special Branch. And from the Fraud Squad, and the Inland Revenue. Secret auditors' reports. Letters from the Bank of England Foreign Exchange Division.

It took longer to read and grasp the essentials of this file. I wondered if everything revealed in it could be technically legal.

Sir Humphrey nodded judiciously. '*Technically*, maybe. But it certainly ruled him out of consideration for the Treasury.'

I suddenly got a little paranoid. I wonder if there were reports like this on me in the Cabinet Office. [*Definitely – Ed.*] Not that anyone could suspect me of this sort of impropriety. [*This is almost certainly true. Hacker's private life was fairly dull – Ed.*] I asked Humphrey how they found out so much about Duncan's finances.

He evaded the question. 'Let's just say it's all been gone into quite enough.' Like the shady lady, I suppose.

I suppose that MI5 is behind all these investigations. Though Sir Humphrey's line on MI5 is that it doesn't exist. 'We do not admit that it exists. But if it did exist, which of course it does not, its title would actually be DI5. Which, since it does not in any case exist, is never used.'

I don't believe a word of that. I'm sure MI5 exists. [*Hacker was right. Sir Humphrey was giving Hacker the official disinformation, which is devised to try to confuse MI5 watchers – Ed.*]

I must admit that I was totally amazed by everything I'd read about my colleagues Eric and Duncan. I turned to the Chief Whip. 'Isn't this amazing?' I said.

He was now looking irritable as well as shiny. 'I don't know,' he snapped. 'I haven't seen it.'

I apologised and turned back to Humphrey. 'Humphrey,' I said, 'I don't want you to think me stupid . . .'

'Perish the thought, Minister,' he replied, a little slow on cue, I thought.

'But,' I went on, 'why is the Chief Whip here if he's not allowed to see these classified files?'

Jeffrey gave me the answer himself. 'We, the Party, dare not risk these scandals coming to light – if they are as embarrassing as you both seem to think. It could be a deep embarrassment to both the country and the Party if either of them were Head of Government. We don't want to be caught with our trousers down.'

Not like Eric. I didn't say that though, it was all far too serious. I simply remarked that the situation was serious.

'Very serious,' agreed Jeffrey.

'Very serious,' echoed Sir Humphrey.

We gazed thoughtfully at each other. 'So,' I asked, 'what *could* happen if either of them were elected PM?'

'Something very serious indeed,' replied Sir Humphrey carefully.

'Very serious,' agreed Jeffrey.

'I see,' I said, and waited.

'Serious repercussions,' mumbled the Chief Whip.

Sir Humphrey nodded. '*Serious* repercussions,' he emphasised.

'Of the utmost seriousness,' added Jeffrey, clarifying the situation.

'In fact,' said Sir Humphrey seriously, 'I would go so far as to say that it could hardly be *more* serious.'

We all fell silent. So I decided to sum it up. 'I think we're all agreed then,' I said. 'This is serious.'

They nodded. We were all in agreement.

The question was, what should happen next? Jeffrey had an answer. 'We've got to have another candidate. Quick.'

'The Chief Whip,' murmured Humphrey, 'wondered if you had any ideas.'

'As you're the Party Chairman,' explained Jeffrey.

Naturally Bernard's words were ringing in my ears. Why not go for the top job? Be the one who gets all the credit. But I couldn't suggest myself right away. They might think that I had delusions of grandeur. So I assumed a look of studied thought.

'It's pretty difficult,' I said. 'We're looking for someone pretty remarkable – a potential Prime Minister. Someone's who's sound.'

'Flexible,' added Sir Humphrey.

'Yes,' I agreed. 'And normal,' I remarked, bearing Eric's predilections in mind, and knowing that I was unassailable on that score.

'And,' Jeffrey reminded us forcefully, wearing his Chief Whip's hat, 'someone who's acceptable to both wings of the Party.'

'And someone who understands how to take advice, Minister,' concluded Humphrey.

The Cabinet Secretary and the Chief Whip looked at me politely, waiting for my suggestion. But I was not willing to suggest myself, just in case I'd misread the signs.

Finally Jeffrey spoke. 'Have you considered doing the job yourself?'

I pretended to be completely astonished. '*Me*?'

'Why not?' enquired Sir Humphrey.

'Wouldn't you want to be Prime Minister?' asked Jeffrey.

I decided to be modest. I explained that I'd love it, but that I was not sure that I actually could do it.

Humphrey seemed to accept this *far* too easily. 'Perhaps this was not a good idea after all,' he said, turning to Jeffrey.

I was forced to ask Humphrey what he meant. 'Perhaps you do not feel, Minister, that you are absolutely Prime Ministerial calibre.'

I told Humphrey, very firmly, that I think that there is no doubt about *that*. Modesty forbids, but I have absolutely no doubt about my ability to do the job.

But Jeffrey said there was a fly in the ointment. 'You are a bit of an outsider. Unless you can stage-manage some sort of public success in the next few days.'

I suggested that I merely start campaigning, and let people know I want the job.

'Quite the reverse, I think,' said Jeffrey. 'Better to let people know you don't want it.'

I wondered if that would be enough. Jeffrey and Sir Humphrey were quite sure it would be provided that I let *everybody* know that I don't want it. Jeffrey offered to manage my campaign. If anyone asks me, I am simply to say that I have no ambitions in that direction.

And if anyone tries to trap me by asking if I'd *refuse* to stand, Humphrey advised me that on previous occasions a generally acceptable answer has been that, while one does not seek the office, one has pledged oneself to the service of one's country and if one's colleagues persuaded one that that was the best way one could serve, one might reluctantly have to accept the responsibility, whatever one's own private wishes might be. (I wrote it down at the time.)

Finally, we got to the question of the election. It seemed to me that it would inevitably be a three-way election. But the Chief Whip thinks differently. He wants an unopposed election. Unity always goes down well with the public, and the Party would welcome a little unity too.

But there are two more flies in the ointment, namely Eric and Duncan. I suddenly realised the relevance of the Security files – my two opponents have to be persuaded to withdraw. I asked Jeffrey if he was planning to have a word with them both.

'I can't.' He was insistent. 'I haven't seen the files.'

I asked Humphrey.

'No, Minister. It is an internal party matter. It would be most improper.'

The full horror of it now dawned upon me. They wanted *me* to force Eric and Duncan to withdraw. They want me to tell one of my colleagues that he's a swindler and the other that he's a pervert. I refused.

Humphrey said that I needn't say that at all, not in so many words. 'You can just let them know you know something.'

It seemed hopeless. 'They'll tell me to mind my own bloody business.'

Jeffrey intervened. 'If they do, you must say that as Party Chairman it's your duty to see that, if they stand, this information reaches those who need to know. The Party executive, its major contributors and elder statesmen. The Palace, perhaps. You must tell each of them that he has no alternative but to pull out and support someone who will . . . protect him.'

I could hardly believe my ears. Jeffrey wanted me to *protect* them?

Humphrey concurred, remarking that their private lives are nobody else's business as long as security is not involved.

I didn't quite have the stomach for this talk. Regretfully I told Humphrey and Jeffrey that I wouldn't . . . *couldn't* do this. But Humphrey wasn't prepared to listen. He told me that, now that I know about them, I have no choice.

'As no one else knows that I know,' I said firmly, 'I intend to forget all about it.'

Then Humphrey dropped his bombshell. 'That would be very courageous of you, Minister.'

I was appalled! Courageous? I don't want to do anything *courageous*! That's the kind of thing that finishes careers.

Sir Humphrey remained calm. 'If something were to happen and later it were to emerge that you had had the information and suppressed it . . .'

I interrupted. 'Do you mean you'd leak it?' I was aghast!

Humphrey did not answer my question. 'It would be seen as covering up for your chums. Greater love hath no man than this, that he should lay down his career . . .'

I told him to stop threatening me.

He tried to soothe me. 'No, Minister, I'm helping you.'

Jeffrey mopped his shining forehead and blotted the top of his head. 'You see, Jim, there is one other quality that Prime Ministers need. The killer instinct.'

He's right. The killer instinct. But do I have it? We'll see. Now that I know about Eric and Duncan, I have no choice but to stab them in the back.

Or the front.

Oh my God!

January 5th
Believing that there is no time like the present I rang Duncan this

morning. I told him that I had something urgent to discuss with him about the contest for the Premiership. I refused to be drawn on the phone. Indeed, I could hardly have said what I had to say over the phone. But I tried to sound cheerful so that he'd think I had good news.

He cancelled some appointments and showed up here at the flat after dinner. I poured him a small Scotch and me a large Scotch, and we sat in front of the fire. I'd warned Annie and Lucy[1] to make themselves scarce.

Duncan was unusually cheerful. He raised his glass. 'Here's to Number Ten, eh?'

'Thanks,' I said, without thinking. He gave me a funny look. I corrected myself somehow, drank up my Scotch and poured myself another biggie. I turned from the sideboard to see Duncan eyeing me with suspicion.

'What's up, Jim?'

'Duncan, I have a . . . a problem.'

'You're not going to support me?'

The conversation was getting out of control and it had only just begun. I drank my next large Scotch, and told him that some information had come my way. Serious information. To do with his personal financial operations.

Of course he pretended he didn't know what I meant. So I referred to the collapse of Continental and General, which he said was just bad luck, and I mentioned earlier transfers of funds to Directors' nominee companies, to which he replied that there was nothing wrong with that.

I replied that technically there wasn't, but if you looked at it in conjunction with a similar case at Offshore Securities . . .

I let that remark hang in the air, unfinished.

Duncan swallowed. 'Where did you get all this?'

I didn't answer. But I indicated that, if he stayed in the running for PM, I would be obliged to share my knowledge with senior members of the party, the Revenue, the Fraud Squad, and so forth. 'Not that it would matter if it's all above board,' I added innocently, 'and I'm sure it is if you say it is. But the Americans would also have to know. And Her Majesty . . .'

He took a drink and considered his position. 'There was nothing improper,' he said. Not a very convincing denial.

'Fine,' I said cheerfully. 'If that's what you say, I'll feel free to talk

[1] Hacker's daughter.

about it to them all. Bring it all out in the open.'

He panicked. 'Hang on! Financial matters can be misinterpreted. People get hold of the wrong end of the stick.'

I sipped my drink and waited. It didn't take long. It transpired that, acccrding to Duncan, he didn't really want Number Ten at all. He said he'd never wanted it really. He felt the Foreign Office was a much better job in many ways. He wanted to assure me that he had only wanted Number Ten to keep Eric out. 'I just want to make one thing clear – I won't support Eric!' he insisted hotly.

I suggested that Eric might not get it. 'How would it be if you transferred all your support to someone else?'

Duncan looked blank. 'Who?'

'It would be a question of finding someone who recognised your qualities. Someone who'd want you to stay on as Foreign Secretary. Someone who would be discreet about Continental and General. Someone you trust. An old friend.'

I thought for a moment I'd overplayed it. I'm an old acquaintance of Duncan's but scarcely an old friend. And clearly there's no one he trusts. No one at all.

But he sat there, staring at me, and I smiled back at him, and gradually I saw it dawning upon him.

'Do you mean – you?' he asked.

I pretended surprise. 'Me? I have absolutely no ambitions in that direction.'

'You do mean you,' he observed quietly. He knows the code.

Perhaps I do have the killer instinct.

January 6th

Today I dispatched my other colleague and rival. It's all proving much easier than I thought.

Eric came for a drink at the House.[1] This time I found I was able to come to the point much more quickly. I have tasted blood now. I certainly believe that, having killed once, it's much easier for a murderer to kill again.

Anyway, I told him what I knew, roughly. He went pale and downed his Scotch. I offered him another.

'Yes please,' he said quietly. 'I need a stiff one.' Actually, that doesn't seem to be his problem. I asked him if he realised that his position was . . . serious.

---

[1] of Commons.

Grimly, he said that he saw that only too well. 'And,' he said, eyeing me bitterly, 'you're not going to help me, right?'

'Yes,' I said.

He was confused. 'Yes you are or yes you're not?'

'Yes,' I said, and hastily added: 'Yes I'm going to help you. But not to get elected Prime Minister.'

'You said you were.'

Really, how could he not see that things are quite different now? I patiently pointed out that my offer to help him predated my knowledge of the shady lady from Argentina. And others.

'Look, Eric, as Party Chairman I have my duty. It would be a disaster for the party if you were PM and it came out.' I realised that there was an unintentional innuendo there, so I hurried on. 'I mean, I wouldn't care to explain your private life to Her Majesty, would you?'

'I'll withdraw,' he muttered.

About time too, I thought. If he practised withdrawal a little more often he wouldn't be in this predicament now. But I told him reassuringly that we would say no more about it. To anyone.

He thanked me nastily and snarled that he supposed that bloody Duncan would now get Number Ten.

'Not if I can help it,' I told him.

'Who then?'

I raised my glass to him, smiled and said, 'Cheers.'

The penny dropped. And so did his lower jaw. He was staggered! 'You don't mean – you?' he gasped.

Again I put on my surprised face. 'Me?' I said innocently. 'Our children are approaching the age when Annie and I are thinking of spending much more time with each other.'

He understood perfectly. 'You *do* mean you.'

This *is* fun!

January 9th

Events are moving fast. Although Eric and Duncan are both out of the running, no one knows that but me, Humphrey and Bernard. The trouble is, although they're out of the running, I'm not yet *in* the running. I do need some sort of public success to swing the party *my* way at the crucial moment, so that the others can plausibly drop out.

My big problem remained. I was stuck with the awful Eurosausage hot potato, and somehow I've got to pull something rather good out of the hat. Or out of the delicatessen.

47

But we took a big step along that path today and, I must say, to give credit where credit is due, old Humphrey was quite a help.

Apparently Maurice, the European Commissioner who landed me with this mess, was in London yesterday. And Humphrey found out that his flight was delayed and managed to fix a brief meeting with him.

I was summoned to an urgent meeting in Humphrey's inner sanctum at the Cabinet Office. The only problem was that it was all arranged at such short notice that I only got there moments before Maurice himself arrived. So I had no idea what Humphrey's strategy was, or what I was to say or anything. Humphrey simply whispered to me that he hoped to persuade Maurice to solve our little sausage problem, that I was to leave the talking to Humphrey but give him support when he asked for it.

Maurice arrived all smiles. 'Jeem, to what do I owe zis pleasure?'

Of course, I didn't know the answer to that. But Humphrey rescued me at once.

Sitting us all down in his conversation area, Humphrey began by explaining (wholly untruthfully) that I had asked him to arrange the meeting to see if he could help us with a problem. Of course, it wasn't a *real* lie, more a white lie really – the whole convention of our government is that when Civil Servants think of a good idea they give the credit to the Minister. Quite right too – we take the blame for all their mistakes, we certainly deserve the credit for their occasional good ideas!

Anyway, I nodded, and echoed that we had a problem. Maurice said of course he'd help.

'The problem is,' said Humphrey smoothly, 'that the EEC is becoming very unpopular over here.' He turned to me. 'Isn't that so, Minister?'

No problem there. 'Yes,' I said.

Maurice knows this already. 'And you want to restore its image?' he asked.

'Yes,' I said, jumping the gun.

'No,' said Humphrey firmly.

'No,' I corrected myself hastily, resolving not to speak again until it was quite clear what Humphrey wanted me to say.

Humphrey continued. 'The problem is that the Minister feels there would be more votes – that is, he would be better expressing the views of the British people – by joining the attack on the EEC rather than leaping to its defence.'

He looked at me. I was happy to agree with that. Furthermore, it was actually true!

I was surprised how much this threat upset Maurice. It can't have been news to him. But he seemed quite appalled. 'But . . . your government is committed to support us,' he expostulated, glaring at me.

I wasn't quite sure how to answer this, as I hadn't yet got Humphrey's drift. But Humphrey came to the rescue again.

'The Minister's point, as I understand it, is that the government's commitment is to the concept and the treaty.'

'Treaty,' I repeated firmly.

'But it is not committed,' Humphrey was quite adamant here, 'to the institutions. Or to the practices. Or to individual policies. You were giving me an instance, just now, weren't you, Minister?'

He looked at me. This was my cue. But I couldn't imagine what he wanted me to say. He must have seen the panic in my eyes. 'About food production,' he hinted.

I suddenly saw the plan! 'Yes.' I fixed Maurice with my tough gimlet-eyed gaze. 'I discovered recently that one of your staff spends all his time paying people to produce food, and the man in the next office spends all his time paying people to destroy it.'

Maurice was outraged. 'That's not true.'

Humphrey and I were surprised. A barefaced denial? How could this be, we'd had the story from the horses' mouths.

'Not true?' queried Humphrey.

'No,' said Maurice. 'He's not in the next office. Not even on the same floor.'

'The Minister has hundreds of similar examples of the EEC's nonsensical behaviour,' continued Humphrey inexorably.

'Hundreds,' I agreed, trying to remember another.

'And the nub of the problem, Maurice, is that the Minister is beginning to think that some member of the Cabinet ought to start telling the British people about them.'

Maurice was angry now. 'But that would be intolerable,' he cried. 'Even the Italians would not stoop so low.'

I saw my chance, and went for the jugular. 'The Italians are not being asked to redesignate salami as Emulsified High-Fat Offal Tube.'

Our cards were on the table. Was Maurice going to pick up the ball and run with it? Yes, he grasped the nettle with both hands. [*Yet again Hacker's mixed metaphors give us a special insight into the*

49

quality of intellectual coherence in the mind of one of our great national leaders – Ed.]

'What', enquired Maurice carefully, 'are you proposing? After all, we are committed to harmonisation. We cannot call it the sausage. What do you suggest?'

I had no idea at all. What do you call a sausage if you can't call it a sausage? The whole point was that we *should* be able to call it a sausage. But I should have realised – Humphrey had thought ahead.

'Politics is about presentation. Can't we call it the British Sausage?' he murmured.

A brilliant idea. Maurice tried it out in a few of the EEC languages. 'Saucisson anglais . . . Salsicce inglese . . . Britischerwurst.' Dreadful show-offs, these Continentals. 'Mmm, yes, I think we could recommend that to the Commission.'

Of course he could. It was an offer he couldn't refuse.

We wrapped up the meeting, all agreeing furiously that the EEC is an absolutely splendid institution. I even kissed Maurice on both cheeks.

After he left, I had a long think. Humphrey and Bernard suggested that I call a press conference of all the European correspondents, to tell them that I've solved the Eurosausage problem.

But I have a much better idea. Solved problems aren't news stories. For the press, bad news is good news. So why should I give them such a non-story? A solved Eurosausage problem is not going to catapult one into the leadership of the Party – the public doesn't even know the problem exists, so why should they care if I solve it? No, I've decided that tomorrow I shall give them news of a disaster. They'll love that. Then when I give them a triumph a few days later I'll be a hero.

January 10th

Today I held an off-the-record, non-attributable briefing with the European correspondents.

The lobby system really is invaluable. The hacks are keen to get a story, yet lazy enough to accept almost anything that we feed them. I told them that we had a big problem coming up with Brussels. Since they'd be hearing about it anyway some day soon, I told them I'd level with them now and give them the whole embarrassing story. They lapped it up!

'Brussels', I said, 'is going to make the British sausage illegal under EEC regulations.'

Bernard looked very worried, and passed me a hurried note reminding me that the EEC plan was not to illegalise the British sausage, but merely to prevent us *calling* it a sausage.

I crumpled up his note decisively. Bernard just doesn't understand politics. [*Though he did understand the difference between truth and falsehood – Ed.*]

I threw the meeting open to questions. The first question picked up the same point. 'What do you mean, *illegal*?'

I qualified my answer. 'Effectively illegal,' I replied. 'Pork sausages will have to be seventy-five per cent lean pork, and beef sausages too.'

Somebody from *The Sun* asked if beef sausages will have to be seventy-five per cent lean pork, too. Typical lobby correspondent. If he was the sole entrant in an intelligence contest, he'd come third.

I explained that insisting that sausages contained seventy-five per cent lean meat would put them in the luxury foods bracket. The implications for the average wage-earner were all too clear.

One of them asked when this was to be promulgated. I told him: next month. Then, cunningly, I added that the EEC will probably deny it at the moment. In fact, they will probably try to tell the British press that they are only discussing changing the name of the sausage.

Finally, one of the reporters asked me what the government is going to do about it. I looked despairing, pathetic and helpless, and told him that I had no idea, that it is a big problem, and that I wouldn't pretend that we have an answer.

Then I sent them all out into the waiting room so that the Press Office could ply them with drinks. As they left, Bernard cornered me. 'Minister! You realise the press will be printing something that isn't true?'

'Really?' I smiled at him. 'How frightful!'

January 12th

It all went like clockwork. The story about the outlawed sausage has been all over the front pages for the last two days. It's caused a major political storm. All the commentators and pundits have been saying that, with the government and the party leaderless, the sausage could be a banana skin.

Everyone's been saying that the succession is also unclear. Jeffrey has been quoted all week as an Unofficial Spokesman, an Informed Source, Feelings in the Party, Sources Close to the Leadership, and as a Growing Body of Opinion. His fingerprints are all over the stories in the press saying that the party is increasingly troubled by the fact that the two obvious candidates for the leadership represent the extreme wings of the party.

I've been leaking a little myself, to the effect that pressure is mounting for both Eric and Duncan to withdraw in favour of a compromise candidate. Unfortunately, the lobby correspondents to whom I've been chatting have not had the sense to name me as the aforesaid compromise, but have foolishly added their own comments to the effect that none of the contenders has so far caught the public imagination. It is astonishing how you have to spell *everything* out to journalists. And not only can't they draw the simplest conclusions, they can't even quote me correctly: I actually said 'moderate' not 'compromise'.

I've planned a big press turnout for my constituency speech tomorrow night. BBC News and ITN are going to be there. Bernard asked me why they were so interested in fire and safety policy in government.

I didn't answer. But I'm sure he will not be surprised if I talk about other issues as well.

[*Hacker's big speech did indeed attract a full press, radio and TV turnout. 'Sources Close to the Minister' had hinted that he was going to make a major policy speech, and it was clear to all in Fleet Street that this meant that he was mounting a bid for the leadership. Much was to hang on how well Hacker's speech went that night. The result was exactly as Hacker had hoped and planned, as can be detected from the triumphant tone of his diary – Ed.*]

January 13th
I have a feeling that tonight I clinched the leadership of the Party and, if I did, it's only a matter of time before I'm in Number Ten. Today was Friday the thirteenth, and thirteen is my lucky number. [*But perhaps not the United Kingdom's – Ed.*]

There were several bursts of applause during my speech, some lasting for up to half a minute, and at the end I sat down to cheers and a standing ovation. The last part of the speech really got them going. I think I might have a future as a major demagogue.

[*The original typescript of the speech has been lost, so we cannot publish it in full. However, we can reproduce a transcript of the last section of it – taken from the BBC Nine O'Clock News recording. Audience reaction is marked – Ed.*]

THE ATTACHED TRANSCRIPT WAS TYPED FROM A RECORDING AND NOT
COPIED FROM AN ORIGINAL SCRIPT. BECAUSE OF THE RISK OF
MISHEARING THE BBC CANNOT VOUCH FOR ITS COMPLETE ACCURACY.

'NINE O'CLOCK NEWS' 'NEWSNIGHT'

TRANSMISSION: JANUARY 13th

ACTUALITY:

THE RT HON. JAMES HACKER MP: I'm a good European.
I believe in Europe. I believe in the European ideal!
Never again shall we repeat the bloodshed of two World Wars.
Europe is here to stay.

      But, this does not mean that we have to bow the knee
to every directive from every bureaucratic Bonaparte in
Brussels. We are a sovereign nation still and proud of it.
(APPLAUSE)

      We have made enough concessions to the European
Commissar for agriculture. And when I say Commissar, I use
the word advisedly. We have swallowed the wine lake, we
have swallowed the butter mountain, we have watched our
French 'friends' beating up British lorry drivers carrying
good British lamb to the French public.
We have bowed and scraped, doffed our caps, tugged our
forelocks and turned the other cheek. But I say enough is
enough! (PROLONGED APPLAUSE)

- 1 -

BRITISH BROADCASTING CORPORATION

(CONT) The Europeans have gone too far. They are now threatening the British sausage. They want to standardise it - by which they mean they'll force the British people to eat salami and bratwurst and other garlic-ridden greasy foods that are TOTALLY ALIEN to the British way of life. (CRIES OF 'HEAR HEAR', 'RIGHT ON', AND 'YOU TELL 'EM, JIM')

Do you want to eat salami for breakfast with your egg and bacon? I don't. And I won't! (MASSIVE APPLAUSE)

They've turned our pints into litres and our yards into metres, we gave up the tanner and the threepenny bit, the two bob and half crown. But they cannot and will not destroy the British sausage! (APPLAUSE AND CHEERS)

Not while I'm here. (TUMULTUOUS APPLAUSE)

In the words of Martin Luther: 'Here I stand. I can do no other' (HACKER SITS DOWN. SHOT OF LARGE CROWD RISING TO ITS FEET IN APPRECIATION).

[*The following day Hacker was interviewed by Ludovic Kennedy, the well-known television interviewer. We have been fortunate in obtaining the complete transcript from BBC Television, and reproduce it below – Ed.*]

---

[1] Sixpenny piece.
[2] Threepenny piece
[3] Two shilling piece.
[4] Two shillings and sixpenny piece.

BRITISH BROADCASTING CORPORATION

THE ATTACHED TRANSCRIPT WAS TYPED FROM A RECORDING AND NOT
COPIED FROM AN ORIGINAL SCRIPT. BECAUSE OF THE RISK OF
MISHEARING THE BBC CANNOT VOUCH FOR ITS COMPLETE ACCURACY.

TRANSMISSION: JANUARY 14th

ACTUALITY:

KENNEDY: Your speech was strong stuff, Mr Hacker.

HACKER: Well, it's something I feel very strongly
about. In fact, I sometimes wonder whether you media people
really appreciate how strongly the rest of us feel about our
country and our way of life. We love it and we're proud of it.

KENNEDY: So you're at odds with Government policy
over the EEC?

HACKER: I'm very happy with Government policy,
Sir Ludovic. Sorry. Mr Kennedy. It has never been Government
policy to abolish the British sausage. Sausages are not just
good to eat, you know. They're full of top-quality nourishment.

KENNEDY: Brussels has denied ever wanting to
abolish the British sausage.

HACKER: Well, they would, wouldn't they? They
know what they're up against. They know the strength of British
public opinion.

KENNEDY: Minister, your speech certainly got a
lot of coverage and a lot of praise. Was there any significance
in its timing?

- 1 -

55

BRITISH BROADCASTING CORPORATION

```
HACKER:          (CONT) What do you mean?

KENNEDY:         With your Party looking for a new leader.
After all, your name has been mentioned by a few people.

HACKER:          Quite a lot of people, actually. But
no.  Absolutely not.  I have no ambitions in that direction.

KENNEDY:         You mean, you wouldn't let your name go
forward?

HACKER:          Well, Ludo ... all I've ever wanted to do
is serve my country.  I've never sought office.  But I suppose
that if my colleagues were to persuade me that the best place to
serve it from was Ten Downing Street, then I might reluctantly
have to accept the responsibility, whatever my own private
wishes might be.

KENNEDY:         So, if you're not in the running, who
will you be voting for?

HACKER:          Well, of course, it's too early to say.
But what I will say is that I see this as a time for healing.  A
time to stress what we agree about, not what we disagree about.
We need to see the good things in our opponents, not to keep
looking for their faults.  There's good in everyone, you know,
Ludo.

KENNEDY:         Except the French.

HACKER:          Except the Fre ... No, even the French.
```

[*Hacker's diary continues – Ed.*]

January 18th

I've been too anxious to do anything these last three days. Even making notes for the diary was too great a strain. But today I made it! I'm it! I'm in! I did it! I got it! I won!

I'll try to recount the last events of the leadership campaign in a coherent manner.

The committee held the annual meeting today. The ad hoc party leadership committee, that is. Eric and Duncan withdrew after the success of my speech put me unexpectedly at the front of the race. Of course, rather than vote for each other, they now both promised to put their weight behind me. As I've got them both by the balls, this was no surprise to me, though it impressed everyone else no end!

So today the only issue was whether or not the Parliamentary Party was going to put up another candidate to oppose me. If so, we would have had to have an election.

I called both Eric and Duncan this morning, to check that they were supporting me. They were both slightly equivocal. It was still possible for them to withdraw and support someone else. In which case I'd *probably* have won the election, but the agony would have been prolonged by another two or three weeks – and who knows what might have happened in that time? If a week is a long time in politics, three weeks is an eternity.

Then I went to Humphrey's office and we waited, all through lunch, Humphrey and me. Would the phone never ring? There were two phones on his desk. I asked him which one they'd ring on.

'This one, probably,' he replied. Then, after a moment's thought: 'Or this one. Either, really.'

I was none the wiser. Even that information was denied me. I told Humphrey that I'd just sit and relax. As I sat his intercom buzzed, sending me three feet into the air. Bernard had arrived.

'Minister,' he told me reverently, 'the Palace has been on the phone.'

'The Palace?'

'They're checking with all the possible candidates, to see if they'd be free to kiss hands[1] at five o'clock. That's only in the event of an unopposed recommendation, of course.'

I told Bernard that I thought I could probably make time for it.

We sat and waited. And then I made a spontaneous and generous suggestion which I think I regret already. I asked Bernard to be my Principal Private Secretary at Number Ten, should I become PM.

His reply was characteristically ambiguous. 'Oh Minister. Gosh!' But he smiled and went a little pink.

Pleased, I turned to Humphrey, whose face had turned to stone. I asked him if that would be all right.

'The Prime Minister's word is law,' he replied bleakly.

[1] The formal expression of allegiance to the Sovereign by a newly appointed Prime Minister.

GO TO WORK ON A SAUSAGE !

Perhaps he's right. On second thoughts, I was hasty. I'm not actually sure that Bernard is up to it, he is so naïve. But I'm sure he'll manage somehow and he is very loyal and he never plots against me. [*Hacker's calling Bernard naïve in this context shows a remarkable lack of awareness of Bernard's true loyalties, divided as they were – equally – between Hacker, his political master, and Sir Humphrey Appleby, his Civil Service master – Ed.*]

I think I could have done better than Bernard [*Hacker was correct – Ed.*]. Still, I've done it now.

At that moment, with Bernard all dewy-eyed with gratitude, the phone rang. I grabbed it. Nobody there. Humphrey coolly picked up the other one. 'Yes?' he said. 'Yes . . . yes . . . yes he's here . . . I'll tell him.'

He rang off. I looked at him. I couldn't speak. But written all over my face was the question: was it me? Was I unopposed? Had I reached the top of the greasy pole at last?

'Yes – Prime Minister,' said Humphrey. And I fancy that he looked at me with new respect.

2
The Grand Design

January 23rd

The last few days have been overwhelmingly exciting. I went to the Palace and kissed hands. The next morning I moved into Number Ten. I'd read in the memoirs of past Prime Ministers that the staff line up in the front lobby, and in the long corridor inside it that leads down to the grand central staircase, and applaud the incoming Prime Minister. I wonder why they didn't applaud me. [*This accolade is only granted, traditionally, to a Prime Minister who had just won a general election – Ed.*] I hope this does not bode ill.

It took a day or two to move in. The PM lives in the flat 'above the shop', and the whole building is extremely confusing. From the outside it looks like an average size Georgian terrace house – but inside it is absolutely huge, a small stately home, a mini palace.

This is because it is, in reality, two houses. Not two houses side by side (the Chancellor of the Exchequer lives in Number Eleven), but two houses that almost back on to each other, joined by corridors, stairwells and courtyards. Each house has five or six floors, and the house at the back has large, elegant staterooms for entertaining my subjects. [*Hacker was plainly suffering from delusions of grandeur, and was confusing himself with the monarch – Ed.*]

The main problem in finding one's way around Number Ten is that, because it is two different houses, because of subsidence during the war,[1] and because the ground slopes away towards the back, it's almost impossible to know what floor you're on once you're upstairs.

But my confusion on moving in was like nothing compared to my state of mind today, my fifth day in office, on being taken into the top-secret operations room below the MOD.[2]

It looked just like you'd expect: maps of the five continents, girls at video terminals, officers at desks. I was shown around by the Chief of

[1] World War II.
[2] Ministry of Defence.

the General Staff, General Sir Geoffrey Howard, a tall dapper chap with sandy hair, bushy eyebrows and a brisk commanding voice. Sir Humphrey and Bernard were hovering about, as always.

Naturally, my first question was about the Hot Line. The General looked puzzled.

'Which one?'

'To Russia.'

'Ah. That's in Downing Street,' the General told me. I glanced at Bernard. Why hadn't I been shown it? He looked surprised – perhaps he hasn't been shown it, either.

I continued: 'So if there's an emergency, can I get straight through to the Soviet President?'

'Theoretically, yes,' General Howard replied cautiously.

'Does that mean no?'

'Well, it's what we tell journalists. In fact, we did once get through to the Kremlin, but only to a switchboard operator.'

'Couldn't the operator put you through?'

'We couldn't find out, she didn't seem to speak much English.'

'How often is it tested?'

The General looked blank. Testing had clearly not occurred to him.

'They try not to test it too often,' Humphrey intervened smoothly. 'It tends to create unnecessary panic at the other end. And panic is always a good thing to avoid where nuclear weapons are concerned, don't you think?' I certainly do.

The General walked me over to a telex machine.

'Now this –' he said meaningfully, '*is it*!'

'Is it?' I asked.

'Yes,' he said.

'Good,' I replied, encouragingly. Then I realised that I was going to get no further clue as to what he was talking about. 'Er . . . *what* is it, exactly?' I enquired casually, with what I hoped was a knowledge-able air.

'It's the trigger, Prime Minister,' Sir Humphrey murmured.

I felt a sudden chill. 'The trigger?'

'Yes. The nuclear trigger . . . the button.'

'This?' I couldn't believe it. I stared at the innocent-looking telex machine.

'Indirectly, yes.' The General could see my concern. 'It's simply a telex link to HMS Northwood. You would send a coded signal, you see. Then the telex operator at Northwood sends out an authenti-cation signal.'

'So he knows it's from you, you see,' added Sir Humphrey softly.

'And when the instruction has been authenticated, and a target indication been made, Northwood would send the command to one of our Polaris submarines, and they'd actually press the button.' The General seemed quite satisfied with all this.

It all seemed so simple, so cut and dried. I give the order, they carry it out. My mouth felt all dry, but I had to find out more.

'They'd do it . . . just like that?'

'Just like that.' General Howard was visibly proud.

'When I say so?'

'When you say so.'

'But wouldn't anyone . . . *argue* with me?'

General Howard was shocked. 'Of course not. Serving officers obey orders without question, Prime Minister.'

I swallowed. 'But supposing I get drunk?' I asked, jokingly. Humphrey replied, rather too seriously: 'On the whole, it would be safer if you didn't get drunk.'

'Yes, but . . . seriously,' I asked 'what happens if I go off my rocker?'

'I think the Cabinet might notice.' Sir Humphrey was trying to sound reassuring.

I wasn't reassured. I don't think one can count on the Cabinet noticing that kind of thing. For a start, half of them, if not exactly off their rockers themselves, are not exactly what you'd call well-balanced.

I had to know more. 'Supposing I gave the order to press the button, and then changed my mind?'

'That's all right,' said the General with a chuckle, 'no one would ever know, would they?' Everyone else chuckled appreciatively.

I tried to chuckle too, but somehow I just couldn't. Instead, I asked how many actual bombs we have.

'Four Polaris submarines,' said the General. 'Sixteen missiles on each. Three warheads per missile.'

Mental arithmetic has never been my strong point and I didn't like to fish out my pocket calculator. Bernard saw my problem and spoke up. 'One hundred and ninety-two actual bombs, Prime Minister.' Obviously he'd been told before.

One hundred and ninety-two nuclear bombs! It doesn't bear thinking about! And Humphrey piled on the pressure, pointing out that each has at least five times the power of the Hiroshima bomb.

They all waited for me to speak. But I felt quite overwhelmed by the horror and the insanity of my new responsibilities.

The General looked at me with sympathy and understanding. 'I know what you're thinking,' he said. 'Not very many.'

That wasn't *at all* what I was thinking! I told him sharply that one hundred and ninety-two bombs seemed plenty to me. He didn't agree. 'Not with twelve hundred Soviet missiles trained on Britain, waiting to retaliate instantly.'

Twelve hundred? I felt I should assume a stiff upper lip. 'Ah well,' I remarked, 'Britain's always fought against the odds, haven't we? The Armada, the Battle of Britain . . .'

Even as I spoke I realised that the notion of fighting bravely against the odds is completely irrelevant in the context of nuclear war.

But General Howard saw this as an opportunity to put in a plug for Trident. He pointed out that we would have much more fire power at our disposal when it is delivered. And therefore we'd have a much greater deterrent.

'Meanwhile,' I said, 'thank God we've got our conventional forces.'

They all looked at me, slightly sceptically.

'Prime Minister,' said the General stiffly, 'our conventional forces could hold the Russians for seventy-two hours at most.'

'At most?'

'At most.'

The General was standing at attention. It looked most odd in his civilian suit. As a matter of fact, I thought irrelevantly, all these men around me were unmistakably soldiers, even though none of them were in uniform. Unless you call baggy blue pinstripe suits a uniform.

I forced myself to consider the ghastly implications of the latest piece of information that I'd just taken on board. 'So, in the event of a Russian attack, I would have to make an instant decision, would I?'

Generally Howard shook his head and smiled. 'No, Prime Minister. You'd probably have twelve hours.'

Twelve hours? That's what *I* call instant. I asked him if we shouldn't do something about that.

The General agreed emphatically. He thinks we certainly should do something about it. But, he informed me bitterly, the military has been told by the politicians for thirty years that this country can't afford the conventional forces to do the job.

Sir Humphrey, at my shoulder, nodded.

'Conventional forces are terribly expensive, Prime Minister,' he explained. 'Much cheaper just to press a button.'

January 24th

I had a sleepless night last night. My visit to the MOD had unsettled me quite profoundly. I couldn't get those figures out of my head. My powers of concentration are pretty remarkable [*we believe Hacker intended no irony here – Ed.*] but today I found it hard to keep my mind on my work.

'Seventy-two hours,' I found myself murmuring in the middle of a meeting with Bernard.

'Um, Prime Minister?' He was trying to bring me back to what we'd been discussing. 'Isn't seventy-two hours a bit generous for a meeting with the New Zealand High Commissioner?'

He was being facetious, I suppose. He could see I was thinking about the length of time that NATO forces could hold the Russians. I asked him if we could persuade the Americans to strengthen *their* conventional forces.

Bernard felt that it wouldn't really help. 'Apparently the American troops in Germany are all so drug-ridden that they don't know which side they're on anyway. And on the last NATO exercise the US troops dispersed and picnicked in the woods with lady soldiers.'

I asked him about the other NATO armies. He said they were all right on weekdays. I asked him to make himself clear.

'The Dutch, Danish and Belgian armies all go home for the weekend.'

This was the most extraordinary thing I'd heard yet. 'So,' I followed through with my usual relentless logic, 'if the Russians are going to invade we'd prefer them, on the whole, to do it between Monday and Friday.'

He nodded.

[*In fact, even if Warsaw Pact forces had invaded between Monday and Friday it would hardly have helped the NATO forces. The NATO barracks were so far behind their forward positions that the invaders would have, in any case, reached those positions first – Ed.*]

'Is this widely known?' I asked, amazed.

He could see I was thinking of the Russians. He explained that if he knew it, the Russians certainly do. 'The Kremlin usually gets NATO defence information before it filters through to us at Number Ten.'

I summed up. 'So it all comes back to Trident.'

'When it comes,' he agreed.

'When it comes,' I mused, wondering when that would really be.

'If it works,' Bernard added.

If it works? What did he mean?

Casually, he told me. 'Frequently, Prime Minister, when new weapons are delivered the warheads don't fit the ends of the rockets. That's what happened with Polaris. You know the sort of thing. It's all in the files.' He flipped through a file. 'Wiring faults, microchip failure. Ground-control transmitter on a different frequency from the receiver on the missile.' He looked up at me apologetically. 'We didn't have the means of delivering Polaris for some years. Cruise is probably the same. Trident might be too.'

I told him that I considered this absolutely intolerable, that we should take the manufacturers to court.

Bernard shook his head sadly, and explained that it is impossible for us to risk the publicity. And he's right of course. Security makes it impossible. And the manufacturers know it.

I asked him about changing manufacturers.

'Oh we do.' He sighed. 'All the time. But the trouble is that all the manufacturers know it too. That's why that torpedo landed on Sandwich Golf Course.'

I thought I'd misheard him. A torpedo on Sandwich Golf Course? Why hadn't we seen that in the papers?

Bernard knew all about it. 'There was a cover-up. The members just found a new bunker on the seventh fairway the next morning.'

I didn't know whether I was more concerned about the cover-up or the malfunctioning torpedoes. I asked Bernard why even our torpedoes don't work. He reassured me. Apparently it's only the *new* ones that don't work. All the others are working fine – the ones that were designed during World War II.

But these are forty years old. Why, I wanted to know, do they work better than our latest weapons? The answer was so obvious that I should have thought of it myself: the old torpedoes had lots of testing. We can't afford to test modern weapons properly – partly because it's too expensive and partly because if there *is* a nuclear war it won't last long enough for weapons tests.

I wondered what other revelations lay in store, now that I was entitled to know all our military secrets. I decided I'd better find out. 'What else don't I know about the defence of the United Kingdom?' I asked Bernard.

'I don't know, Prime Minister. I don't know what you don't know.'

I don't think he was being insolent because he went on to give me some useful advice. If I want another view, I might find it valuable to have a word with the Government's Chief Scientific Adviser. Apparently he sees the problem rather differently from the MOD.

I told Bernard to get him in at once. Bernard was hesitant. 'A late drink may be better,' he advised. 'Better not to let the Cabinet Office know. Sir Humphrey gets rather upset – he doesn't regard the Chief Scientific Adviser as one of us.'

I looked up the Chief Scientific Adviser in *Who's Who*. Professor Isaac Rosenblum. DSO at Arnhem. How could Humphrey not trust a man who fought on our side at Arnhem, and who was decorated by His Majesty for bravery?

'I'm afraid that it doesn't make up for his speaking with an Austrian accent,' Bernard remarked. 'And he certainly didn't go to Oxford or Cambridge. He didn't even go to the LSE.'

One of Bernard's little jokes. I think.

January 25th

Tonight I asked Professor Issac Rosenblum up to my flat for a late drink. And now my mind is reeling. It's not very often in politics that you meet, and talk to, a genuine intellectual. I used to be a poly-technic lecturer, and you don't get very many intelligent conversa-tions in academic life either. [*Hacker, it seems, regarded polytechnics as part of academic life – Ed.*] There are a *few* intellectuals in both walks of life, of course, but politicians never dare own up to it and academics prefer gossip anyway.

Professor Rosenblum is a small wiry elderly man. He is in his mid-seventies, lean, bright-eyed, and with a mind like a steel trap. I felt like an undergraduate at a tutorial. But I certainly learned a thing or two, and I believe that tonight's discussion will have a decisive effect on the future of my government and of this country. There will be changes made. [*Hacker was so excited when dictating this entry into his diary that he completely forgot about the Civil Service – Ed.*]

He popped in to Number Ten this evening, long after Humphrey had gone home.[1] I arranged with the security people that he should be allowed in through the back door, as there's always press watching the front.

He began by asking me if I believed in the nuclear deterrent.

'Yes,' I said.

'Why?' he asked.

I didn't quite know what to say. I mean, everyone believes in the nuclear deterrent. I asked him to repeat his question.

'Why?' he asked again.

[1] 6 pm.

65

'Because . . . it deters,' I replied, weakly.

'Whom?'

I'd never before met anyone who spoke in such short sentences. You never find *them* in politics, nor in academic life either. But I couldn't see quite what he was driving at.

'I beg your pardon?' I asked.

'Whom?' he asked again. He could see I didn't understand. He clarified his question. *'Whom does it deter?'*

It seemed obvious to me. 'The Russians. From attacking us.'

'Why?' There it was again, that irritating little word. Why *what*? I played for time. 'I beg your pardon?' I asked.

'Why?'

Why does the deterrent deter the Russians from attacking us, that's what he was asking. 'Because,' I replied firmly, 'they know that if they launch an attack I'd press the button.'

'You would?' He sounded surprised.

'Well . . .' I hesitated, 'wouldn't I?'

'Well . . . *would* you?'

'In the last resort, yes. Definitely.' I thought again. 'At least I *think* I definitely would.'

His questions continued relentlessly. I had to think carefully. [*Hacker was out of practice at this – Ed.*]

'And what is the last resort?'

'If the Russians invade Western Europe.' That at least seemed quite obvious.

Professor Rosenblum smiled. 'But you would only have twelve hours to decide. So the last resort is also the first response, is that what you're saying?'

Was that what I was saying? It seemed crazy.

The Chief Scientific Adviser stared at me critically. 'Well, you don't need to worry. Why should the Russians try to annex the whole of Europe? They can't even control Afghanistan.' He shook his head. 'No. If they try anything it will be salami tactics.'

[*Salami tactics was the description customarily given to 'slice by slice' manoeuvres, i.e. not a full scale invasion of the West, but the annexation of one small piece at a time. More often than not, the first steps would not be annexation of land but small treaty infringements, road closures, etc. – Ed.*]

Rosenblum stood up. He paced enthusiastically up and down my living-room, a glass of orange juice in hand, expounding an assortment of defence scenarios. First, he postulated riots in West Berlin, with buildings in flames, and the East German fire brigade crossing the border to help. He stopped pacing, stared at me, and asked me if I'd press the button in such circumstances.

Obviously the answer was no. Rosenblum nodded. He seemed to agree. Then he asked me if I'd press the button if the East German *police* came with the fire brigade. Again I shook my head. How could I start a nuclear war because of such a small territorial infringement?

Rosenblum started pacing again. A little smile was now visible around the corners of his mouth. 'Suppose the East Germans send some *troops*. Then more troops – just for riot control, they say. And then the East German troops are replaced by Russian troops. You press the button?'

Russian troops replacing East German troops in West Berlin? Would I start a nuclear war? I don't see how I could. I shook my head again.

The Chief Scientific Adviser smiled, and suggested cheerfully that the next 'slice' would be that the Russian troops don't go. They would be 'invited' to stay, to support the civilian administration. Then the civilian administration might close the roads and Tempelhof Airport. West Berlin would now be cut off. [*West Berlin was an island of the West German Federal Republic, sixty miles inside the border of the German Democratic Republic. 'Democratic', in this context, naturally means communist – Ed.*] Would I *now* press the button? he enquired.

I didn't know. I told him I needed time to think.

'You have twelve hours!' he barked.

I felt totally panicked. Then I reminded myself, and him, that he was inventing all this, and I relaxed.

He shrugged. 'You are Prime Minister today. The phone might ring now, from NATO Headquarters.'

The phone rang! It shook me to the core. Bernard hurried across my study and answered it. 'Hello. Yes?' He turned to me. 'NATO Headquarters, Prime Minister.'

Was a nightmare coming true? Then Bernard went on. 'Are you willing to address NATO's annual conference in April?'

I *thought* I was – but by then I was no longer sure of anything. I couldn't reply.

'Yes,' said Bernard into the phone, and rang off.

Professor Rosenblum turned to me again. 'Right,' he began. 'Scenario Two. Russian army manoeuvres take them "accidentally" on purpose across the West German frontier . . . is *that* the last resort?'

'No,' I replied. It didn't seem to be.

'All right,' he continued with great enthusiasm. 'Scenario Three. Suppose the Russians *have* invaded and occupied West Germany, Belgium, Holland and France. Suppose their tanks and troops have reached the English Channel. Suppose they are poised for an invasion, is *that* the last resort?'

I stonewalled. 'No.'

'Why not?' he demanded. *'Why not?'*

My mind was a fog. I was trying to see sense in all this. 'Because,' I fumbled, 'because . . . we would only fight a war to defend ourselves. And how can we defend ourselves by committing suicide?'

'So what *is* the last resort?' smiled the little old Professor. He shrugged, sat down and settled back into the overstuffed chintz armchair by the fire. 'Piccadilly? Watford Gap Service Station? The Reform Club?'

I stared at him, trying to put my thoughts in order. 'If you put it like that,' I said to him, 'the nuclear deterrent makes no sense. Is that what you're saying?'

Professor Rosenblum shook his head. 'No – I'm not saying that. If either the Russians or the Americans have the bomb, the other side must have it too. And we might as well keep Polaris, just in case.'

I didn't yet understand what exactly he was proposing.

He spelt it out to me. 'Cancel Trident. Spend the £15 billion you will save on conventional forces. Because you wouldn't really press the button, would you?'

'I might,' I said carefully, 'if I had no choice.'

He sighed. 'But we've been through this. They'll never put you into a situation where you have no choice. They'll stick to their salami tactics, remember?'

'So,' I took a deep breath, 'what happens if we divert £15 billion from Trident. What do we spend it on – tanks?'

'No. We spend it on ET.'

What on earth could he mean? Extra-terrestrials?

He saw what I was thinking, and smiled. 'ET stands for Emergent Technology. Smart missiles. Target finding. Infra-Red. The ET needs to be operated by a large conventional army.'

And then I got my inspiration! I suddenly saw what to do. Everything fell into place. It is ridiculously simple, but *completely workable*. First, we cancel Trident. We don't buy Cruise either. Then we introduce conscription, which will not only solve our defence problems by giving us a large conventional army, it also solves our unemployment problem! Excited, I explained my thoughts and Bernard raised a worry. 'Isn't conscription a rather courageous policy, Prime Minister?'

Bernard was quite wrong. Conscription would certainly be a courageous policy in times of full employment – but nowadays it would give young people something to do.

In fact, there are other definite plusses. Conscripted young people would be learning trades and skills. They'd even learn to read – the army never discharged anyone who was illiterate. In fact, we will be able to give our young people a comprehensive education, to make up for their Comprehensive Education.

We shall call the whole thing National Service, just like they used to – to remind everyone that the young people will be out in the country, serving the community and the nation.

It's a great policy. A new deal for Britain. I shall call it my Grand Design. Hacker's Grand Design. I already have notes for my House of Commons speech in which I shall outline the whole concept: 'From time to time, in our great island story, it falls to one man to lead his people out of the valley of the shadows and into the broad sunlit uplands of peace and prosperity.'

I wonder why I never thought of all this till tonight.

[*One reason, perhaps, was that Hacker and Professor Rosenblum had only just met – Ed.*]

January 26th

Things have really got to change round here, and I'm the man to see that those changes happen. [*After only a week in office Hacker appears to have slightly lost touch with reality – Ed.*]

A very busy morning was spent in Cabinet Committee and in appointing the remaining members of my government including some junior ministers. Then I went upstairs to the flat for lunch.

But there was none. As I came in Annie was putting on her raincoat. And she wasn't in too good a mood. When I asked her in a tone of only mild surprise if she was going off somewhere she reminded me that she was late for her Voluntary Services Committee. Whatever that is.

I asked her if there was any chance of some scrambled eggs or something. *Anything* really. She told me that there were eggs in the fridge.

I couldn't believe it. She wanted me to make lunch. I mean, it's not that I'm a male chauvinist or anything, but I am the Prime Minister and I do have plenty of other things to do. And as a politician I'm not really eligible to eat with all the Downing Street civil servants in the Cabinet mess.[1]

I can see her point. We did agree that she could carry on with her work if I became PM and we moved to Number Ten. She had been very opposed to the move here anyway, and I begin to see why. There's not much privacy. We were just discussing the eggs and I was fairly unhappy at finding myself cast as Mother Hubbard when there was a knock on the open door and a young woman messenger marched in with a Foreign Office Green Box.

'Foreign Office telegrams, Prime Minister,' she explained.

Annie was absolutely fed up. 'See what I mean?' she complained. 'It's bad enough living in this goldfish bowl anyway. I've got to be able to get out and live my own life. Every time I want to step out for some cigarettes I have to walk past a dozen journalists, a TV film crew, a bunch of messengers, housekeepers and policemen in the lobby, and fifty gawping tourists at the bottom of the street. There's no privacy *anywhere*!'

I pointed out that there is a back door. She thinks it makes virtually no difference which door we use. And there's total privacy up here in the flat. Or nearly total privacy. Well, *some* privacy, anyway.

'Our life's not our own any more.' She hammered home the point. 'What about the President ringing you in bed from the White House at two o'clock this morning?'

Rather foolishly I replied that it was only nine p.m. in Washington, which, I agree, hardly makes it any better from her point of view. I was about to explain that it was an important call to discuss my forthcoming visit to Washington when there was another knock on the door and in burst two sniffer dogs with tongues hanging out dragging a couple of police dog-handlers behind them. Apparently there was a bomb scare, and they had to search the place.

Annie looked at me and asked, 'Privacy?'

She wasn't being very reasonable, in my opinion. Surely she'd rather have security checks than be blown up. I told her that she could always have privacy if she went for a walk in the garden. I've never seen anyone out there at all.

'I've tried that,' she answered with defiance. 'About sixty people stare at you from the windows of Number Ten, Number Eleven, Number Twelve *and* the Cabinet Office. It's like exercising in a prison yard and being watched by the inmates and the warders. To think we

[1] Attached to the Cabinet Office.

70

actually have to pay rent for this place. They should pay us to live here.'

I must admit I share her resentment about the rent. I should have thought – I *did* think – that we would be given the place to live in, in view of the great personal sacrifice one makes for one's service to the nation. [*Many non-politicians do not see the acquisition of the greatest political power and patronage in the land solely in terms of 'great personal sacrifice'. And many others may wonder why Hacker imagined that, on attaining power, he should be entitled to live rent-free – Ed.*]

The dogs and dog-handlers left. I said to Annie: 'Look, it's actually a pretty nice place to live, at least it's quiet.' It was an idiotic thing to say – no sooner had I uttered it than the bloody brass band started playing on Horse Guards Parade, right outside the window.

She snarled at me. 'That's been going on since seven o'clock this morning.' True, but it *is* Horse Guards Parade out there, and they are the Horse Guards – they have to rehearse somewhere. Of course, I'm lucky, because I'm always up by 7 a.m. in any case.

I tried to calm her down. 'Be reasonable, Annie. A career of public service inevitably involves some sacrifice.'

She buttoned her coat up. 'Fine. I sacrifice my sleep. You sacrifice your lunch.' And off she went.

I ran after her. 'What did *you* have for lunch?' I called down the staircase.

'Half a Yorkie bar.'

Seething, I returned to the flat to look for the other half. I couldn't even find it. There were indeed some eggs in the fridge but I just couldn't face cooking. So I meandered gloomily down the stairs and mooched into my study. Hungrily I stood at the window, watching the military band marching up and down. I left a message in the private office that Bernard should pop up to see me as soon as he returned from lunch.

Forty-five minutes later he bounced in, cheerful and well-fed. I turned and asked him if he'd had a good lunch.

He was slightly surprised. 'Quite good, yes.'

'Where did you have it?'

'In the Cabinet mess.'

'Three courses?'

'Yes.'

'Wine?'

'A glass of claret, yes.' He paused, trying to understand what I was driving at. 'Um . . . if you're interested, Prime Minister, I had mulligatawny soup, followed by a veal chop with sauté potatoes and . . .'

'I'm not interested, Bernard,' I snapped. 'Do you want to know what *I* had for lunch?'

He sensed that I was upset, but still couldn't quite see why. 'Um . . . do you want to tell me?' he asked.

I smiled unpleasantly. 'Yes,' I snapped. 'Nothing.'

'Are you dieting, Prime Minister?'

I explained succinctly that I was not dieting. I expressed my total astonishment that there are facilities at Number Ten for feeding Bernard, and all the private secretaries, the whole of the Cabinet office, the press office, the garden-room girls,[1] the messengers . . . but not me. And I bloody live here!

Bernard asked if Mrs Hacker could cook for me. I reminded him that she has her own job. Then he offered to get me a cook. It looked a good offer – until closer examination revealed that I would have to pay for it. And, according to Bernard, the cost of a full-time cook would be between eight and ten thousands a year. I can't afford that. Trying to get himself off the hook, he suggested that I talk to the Cabinet Secretary – obviously he didn't want to get involved in a discussion when it wasn't in his power to change the system.

But I was very irritated. Still am, come to that. I turned back to the window and fumed silently.

Bernard cleared his throat. 'I think the Cabinet Secretary's due here in a few moments anyway. So shall we get on with the affairs of the nation?'

'Stuff the affairs of the nation,' I replied. 'I want a cook.'

Bernard promised that the matter would be looked into, and ushered in Malcolm Warren, the Number Ten press officer. He's a big bluff Yorkshireman, a career civil servant but with a sense of the way things are done in the real world. He was appointed by my predecessor in Number Ten, but I've kept him on because he has an iron grip on the lobby correspondents and the whole Whitehall public relations machine.

I asked him to be brief, as I was due to meet the Cabinet Secretary any moment.

'Certainly, Prime Minister. Two things. First, and most important, we should discuss your first TV appearance as Prime Minister.'

This is such a big and important subject that I asked him to postpone discussion of it for a day or two, until we have time to go into it thoroughly.

[1] The name given to the very high-class ladies of the registry and typing pool at Number Ten, who worked in a basement room that leads out on to the garden.

The other thing he wanted to discuss was my official Washington visit. Of course, that's much less important than my first TV appearance.

The one urgent point he wanted to raise was that an awful lot of press want to come with us to Washington. I think that's good. Malcolm was worried about the expense. But I explained to him that this would be a terribly important occasion. I shall be standing there, on the White House lawn, side by side with the President of the United States. There will be national anthems. Photographs of two world leaders together. He will tell the world about our happy relationship, our unity and resolve. He'll probably say a word or two about my own courage and wisdom and statesmanship. And it is essential that, if so, it is fully reported back here in Britain. This sort of publicity is vital to Britain. [*Hacker meant that it was vital to him – Ed.*] Vital to our prestige. [*His prestige – Ed.*] Our place in the world. [*His place in the history books – Ed.*]

Malcolm readily agreed, especially when I told him that, as a matter of policy, I intended that we should have no secrets from the press about this country's successes. I told him that we must be absolutely frank about my government's achievements. I want fearless honesty about every government triumph.

He understood. He raised the nit-picking point that, as I have only been in office for seven days, there aren't all that many triumphs yet. Perfectly true. But there will be.

I also gave him an idea for a good press story: I told him that I had had to make my own lunch today. I asked him if he knew. It appeared that he hadn't been informed of this. So I told him all about it. How there's no cook or housekeeper for the flat upstairs, how Annie has her own job, we can't afford staff, and that it looked as though I'd be washing the dishes and washing my socks.

He was a bit slow on the uptake. He couldn't see that there was a good press story in all this. I explained that he could do one along the lines of 'Jim Hacker's not stuck up. He can identify with the problems of ordinary people.' That sort of thing.

Malcolm wanted to think about it. 'We don't want you to seem *too* ordinary, Prime Minister, even though you are.'

Did he mean that the way it sounded? I don't think so, because he continued: 'What I mean is, that sort of publicity can be counter-productive. You remember when Jimmy Carter was attacked by a rabbit?'

I did vaguely remember. He looked a bit of a fool. Also there was that photo of him out jogging, lóoking as though he was on the point of total collapse. He probably thought it was a good idea to be photographed taking exercise – but it made the voters think that he was not long for this world. Lost him a lot of support. Maybe Malcolm's right to be cautious.

Malcolm amplified his point of view. 'Perhaps it's better that we build you up a bit – photos of you doing the washing might make you look a bit wet.'

I sent him out and Bernard brought Humphrey in. I told him I'd been thinking.

'Good,' he said encouragingly.

'I've been Prime Minister for a week now,' I said.

'And a very good Prime Minister you are too, if I may say so.'

I was pleased. It's always nice to have the approval of one's colleagues, especially if they are as hard-bitten as Humphrey. I told him that I wasn't fishing for compliments. But it *has* been going well, and I'm glad he recognised it.

However, we immediately uncovered our first mistake, or rather *their* first mistake, and a pretty serious mistake it is too. I remarked, casually, that it's nice to be able to reward one's old allies. 'Was Ron Jones pleased about his peerage?' I enquired.

'Oh yes,' said Bernard. 'He said his members would be delighted.'

I couldn't think what Bernard meant. 'Members?'

'The Members of his Union. The National Federation of . . .'

I suddenly saw what had happened. I was livid. 'Not *him*!' I yelled. 'I meant our backbencher. I wanted to offer the peerage to Ron Jones, not *Ron Jones*.'

'Ah,' said Bernard. A rather inadequate response, I thought.

We all sat and stared at each other. There was no going back on it now. Bernard tried to make the best of it. 'If it's any consolation to you, Prime Minister, I gather he was awfully pleased.'

I bet he was! Pleased – and amazed! I asked Humphrey what we could do about *Ron Jones's* peerage – could we give him one too? Humphrey thought not. 'With respect, Prime Minister, we can't send *two* Lord Ron Jones to the Upper House – it'll look like a job lot.'

But I've promised him an honour of some sort. We scratched our heads for a bit. Then Humphrey had an idea. As Ron isn't remotely interested in television, hasn't even got a TV set, we're going to make him a Governor of the BBC.

Then we passed on to important matters. I explained to Humphrey that we need a cook–housekeeper in the flat upstairs.

He suggested that I advertise. He was missing the point. I explained that we need a *government* cook–housekeeper.

Humphrey, as I expected after my talk with Bernard, was not entirely helpful. He said that it could be difficult to get a government cook–housekeeper as Number Ten is a private home which just happens to be in a government building.

I pointed out that I happen to live in it. And therefore – surprise, surprise! – happen to eat in it too. 'It is not unreasonable to want someone to cook my lunch.'

'No. But it's not possible,' said Humphrey categorically.

I've never heard anything so ridiculous. Humphrey was asking me to accept that I have the power to blow up the world but not to ask for scrambled eggs. [*It was not in dispute that Hacker had the power to ask for scrambled eggs – Ed.*]

I explored this nonsense a little further, taking it to its logical conclusion. 'Suppose I invited the German Ambassador to lunch?' I asked.

'That would be all right,' reflected Humphrey. 'Official engagement. Government hospitality will gladly provide five courses, with three wines and brandy. No problem.'

So what Humphrey was saying was that the German Ambassador's lunch is government business, but my lunch isn't. And not just the German Ambassador's, of course – *any* ambassador's.

So, there and then I told Bernard to get the diary out. Then I ordered him to arrange for me to have lunch with the German Ambassador on Monday, with the French Ambassador on Tuesday, and on Wednesday the American Ambassador. Then, not forgetting the Commonwealth, on Thursday I would lunch with the New Zealand High Commissioner. 'Bernard, how many countries are there in the United Nations?'

He knew the answer, of course. 'One hundred and fifty-eight.'

'Good,' I beamed at Humphrey. 'That'll keep me in lunches for about six months. Then we'll go round again.'

Bernard was hurriedly leafing through the diary. 'Prime Minister, you're not free for lunches with ambassadors every day. Sometimes you will have other official lunches.'

'Good news,' I replied. 'So much the better. We can just use ambassadors to fill up the blank spaces.'

Humphrey was looking worried, and remarked that the Foreign and Commonwealth Office might have views on this matter. [*This would undoubtedly have been the case. It has always been said that one*

Prime Minister's lunch with an ambassador destroys two years of patient diplomacy. The Foreign Office would have been unlikely to react favourably to such lunches – Ed.]

I didn't much care what the Foreign Office would say. 'It's quite absurd that there's no one to cater for me and my family.'

Humphrey couldn't see why. But then he wouldn't, would he? He gets his lunch in the Cabinet mess too. 'Prime Minister, it's the way things have been done for two and a half centuries.'

'Is that the clinching argument?' I demanded.

'It has been for two and a half centuries.'

Bernard, bless his heart, intervened in his usual pedantic and obsessive fashion. 'Um . . . with respect, Sir Humphrey,' he began disrespectfully, 'it can't have been the clinching argument for two and a half centuries, because half a century ago it had only been the clinching argument for two centuries, and a century ago only for one and a half centuries, and one and a half . . .' Humphrey was staring malevolently at him and he ground to a halt. But Bernard's logic was both as impeccable and irrelevant as always.

I stepped in hurriedly, to distract Humphrey and direct his wrath away from my loyal Private Secretary. 'Humphrey, I am not convinced. I want a cook and I want you to see that it's paid for.'

Humphrey was stony-faced. Stubbornly he turned to me. 'Then let me put it like this. How would you like the press to announce that your first act as Prime Minister was to give yourself an effective salary increase of eight to ten thousand pounds a year?'

I hadn't thought of that. But I couldn't see why we should tell them. Nobody would ever know.

Humphrey read my thoughts. 'We must tell them, by the way. We have no alternative. The Prime Minister's salary and expenses have to be published.'

'Isn't there any way we can . . . not refer to it?' I asked hopefully.

'Open Government, Prime Minister. Freedom of Information. We should always tell the press, freely and frankly, *anything* that they can easily find out some other way.'

I simply do not believe that there is no way to solve this problem. But I had to let it drop for today. Humphrey's position is that ever since Number Ten was first used as the PM's official residence, two hundred and fifty years ago, there has been no solution to this problem. And therefore, according to Civil Service reasoning, there never will be.

Humphrey changed the subject. 'Prime Minister, you said you had been thinking.'

'Yes, Humphrey,' I replied. 'We have agreed that things have been going well ever since I've been Prime Minister. So I have been asking myself: "How do I ensure that this run of success continues?"'

Humphrey gazed at me hopefully. 'Have you considered . . . masterly inactivity?'

Ridiculous. But I was patient with him. 'No, Humphrey, a Prime Minister should be firm.'

'Indeed!' he agreed. 'How about *firm* masterly inactivity?'

I could afford to be nice – after all, I'm in the driving seat now. 'No,' I smiled, 'but I *shall* be firm.'

'Good,' said Sir Humphrey.

'And decisive,' I went on.

'Absolutely,' agreed Sir Humphrey.

'And imaginative,' I added provocatively.

'I'm not so sure about imaginative.' I *bet* he's not!

'And above all,' I finished up, 'I must offer leadership.'

'Leadership.' He was at his most encouraging. 'Leadership, above all.'

'And as I'm the Prime Minister I have the power to do so, don't I?'

'Indeed, Prime Minister, you are the Prime Minister, and wherever you lead we shall obediently follow.'

So I told him my new policy. My Grand Design. 'I've decided to cancel Trident, spend the £15 billion on conventional forces and the ET,[1] bringing in conscription, and thus solve our defence, balance of payments, education and unemployment problems at a stroke.'

He gaped at me. I glanced at Bernard, who was watching his old boss with considerable interest.

I waited for Humphrey's response. But answer came there none. Not at first, anyway. He seemed absolutely poleaxed. I gave him a few moments to pull himself together and then, as I was getting bored with waiting, I told him to say something.

'I . . . er . . . where did this idea come from?' Not a very flattering question. But I reminded him that I'd been thinking.

'You can't do that!' he said with desperation.

At first I thought he was telling me that I can't think. Or mustn't think. But he went on to say that what I was proposing was completely revolutionary, an unprecedented innovation.

[1] Emergent Technology.

So the gloves were off! He meant that I could not pursue my policy. Well, in my opinion it is not up to him to say.

He clearly thinks it is. 'Prime Minister, you can't simply reorganise the entire defence of the realm, just like that!'

My answer was simple. 'I'm the Prime Minister.' Besides, he had said he would follow me. He had agreed that I should be decisive. He had agreed that I should offer leadership. So what was he complaining about? [*Presumably Sir Humphrey wanted Hacker to be decisive only if he took decisions of which Sir Humphrey approved. And leadership was only welcome if it went in the approved direction – Ed.*] 'Furthermore,' I added, 'I have the power.'

He didn't like that one bit. 'Yes – but only within the law and the constitution and the constraints of administrative precedent, budgetary feasibility and Cabinet government. What about your Cabinet colleagues, what do they think?'

I was obliged to admit that I hadn't told them yet. But I know they'll love it. They'll love anything that cuts unemployment. Half of them would even welcome inflation on those grounds. And I know that the Cabinet will be only too happy to have an extra £15 billion of Trident cash available for other public spending. Anyway, I'm the Prime Minister, what does it matter what they think?

'I appoint the Cabinet,' I said simply.

Humphrey smiled coldly. 'I'm sure you don't want to *dis*appoint them.'

Very droll, as he used to say so patronisingly to me. I didn't laugh. I didn't say anything. I just waited for him to capitulate. Unfortunately he didn't say anything either.

'Humphrey, you're very silent.'

'You've given me a lot to be silent about.'

'You mean, *you* think we should keep Trident?'

He could only answer that one way. 'It is not for me to say, Prime Minister.' Quite right. He's only a civil servant.

'Fine,' I agreed magnanimously, 'that's agreed then.'

Humphrey couldn't let it go. 'But since you ask my opinion . . .'

I was enjoying myself. 'Go on then.'

'Yes,' he said grimly, 'I do think we should keep it.'

I told him I couldn't see the sense in it. Humphrey, groping for my reasoning, asked if I was therefore going to buy Cruise missiles instead.

I told him that I intended that the UK should buy no more nuclear weapons.

He blanched. 'But Prime Minister – you're not a secret unilateralist, are you?'

I explained that I was nothing of the sort, that we still have Polaris, and that I have no intention of getting rid of that.

He relaxed a little. At least (in his view) I was not a security risk, just a loony. He tried to tell me Polaris is not good enough, that it's a ramshackle old system, whereas Trident is superb – faster, more warheads, independently targeted. According to Humphrey, Trident is almost impossible to intercept whereas the Soviets might easily develop a multi-layered ballistic missile defence system that can intercept Polaris.

'By when?' I asked.

'In strategic terms, any day now.'

I can spot an evasive answer at fifty paces. [*The more so since Hacker was himself a master of the evasive answer – Ed.*] I asked him by what year, precisely, this might happen.

'Well . . . 2020.' I smiled. 'But that's sooner than you think,' he added hastily.

'And you're saying that such a missile defence system could intercept all 192 Polaris missiles?'

'Not *all*, no. But virtually all – ninety-seven per cent.'

I took out my pocket calculator and did a few quick sums. I looked up at him. 'That would still leave five Polaris bombs which could get through the defences.'

Humphrey was triumphant. 'Precisely – a mere five.'

'Enough,' I reminded him gently, 'to obliterate Moscow, Leningrad and Minsk.'

'Yes,' he sneered, 'but that's about all.'

I wasn't sure I was understanding him correctly. 'I would have thought that that's enough to make the Russians stop and think.'

Humphrey's enthusiasm for Trident knows no bounds. 'But don't you *see*, Prime Minister – with Trident we could obliterate the whole of Eastern Europe!'

I don't want to obliterate the whole of Eastern Europe. I told him so. He nodded impatiently. He knew that. He thought I was missing the point. 'It has to be an effective deterrent, Prime Minister.'

'But it's a bluff,' I told him, 'I probably wouldn't use it.'

'They don't *know* that you probably wouldn't use it,' he argued.

'They probably do,' I said.

He was forced to agree. 'Yes . . . they *probably* know that you probably wouldn't. But they can't *certainly* know.'

79

He's right about that. But they don't have to certainly know. 'They *probably* certainly know that I probably wouldn't,' I said.

'Yes,' he agreed, 'but even though they *probably* certainly know that you probably wouldn't, they don't *certainly* know that although you *probably* wouldn't, there is *no probability* that you certainly would.'

Bernard was taking careful minutes. It's lucky he does shorthand and was able to reconstruct this conversation for me in writing by the end of the day.

But Humphrey could see that he was making no headway with his deterrent argument. So he made one attempt to persuade me to keep Trident, this time by flattering me and playing on my vanity. I can't imagine why he thought that would have any effect!

'Look, Prime Minister, it all boils down to one simple issue. You are Prime Minister, Prime Minister of Great Britain. Don't you believe that Britain should have the best?'

'Of course.'

'Very well.' He took that as a cue to rhapsodise. 'If you walked into a nuclear-missile showroom you would buy Trident – it's lovely, it's elegant, it's beautiful, it is – quite simply – the best. And Britain should have the best. In the world of the nuclear missile it is the Savile Row suit, the Rolls-Royce Corniche, the Château Lafite 1945. It is the nuclear missile Harrods would sell you! What more can I say?'

'Only,' I replied calmly, 'that it costs £15 billion and we don't need it.'

Humphrey shook his head sadly. In his view I had completely missed the point. 'You could say that about anything at Harrods,' he replied reasonably.

January 30th

Tonight we had a reception at Number Ten. Six-thirty to eight. My first party since I became Prime Minister, though many of the guests were hangovers from the previous regime.[1] As we were members of the same party, it didn't matter much.

I wasn't looking forward to it much, after a long and trying day. But, as so often happens, something truly unexpected emerged from a chance conversation. Among the guests was General Howard, who had showed me over the MOD a week or so ago. I buttonholed him. I told him that I had to sound him out on something, and that he was not going to like it.

[1] And a few *had* hangovers from the previous regime.

'Tell me the worst, Prime Minister,' he said stiffly.

So I did. I said that even though it would doubtless come as a severe blow to the services and would be most unpopular, I intended to cancel Trident.

He muttered something that I only half heard. 'Now hold on,' I said, 'don't jump on it too quickly, it's no use arguing, I . . .' And I stopped. I realised what I'd half heard. 'What did you say?' I asked, in case I was fantasising.

'Good idea.' Terse and to the point, as always. I wasn't sure I understood him correctly.

'You mean, you're in favour? Of cancelling Trident?'

'Of course.'

For the second time in just over a week, all my preconceptions about defence were stood on their head.

I stood there, gazing up at this imposing, sandy-haired, beetle-browed, six-foot-four giant. 'Why are you in favour?'

'We don't need it,' he replied briefly. 'It's a complete waste of money. Totally unnecessary.'

I could hardly believe my ears. The most senior army officer in the country agrees with me that Trident is a complete waste of money. I told him that I hoped to keep Polaris, keep the American bases, and strengthen our conventional forces.

'You're right.'

I wondered if he were a tame eccentric. 'Does the whole Defence Staff agree?'

He shook his head. 'No. The Navy want to keep it. It's launched from their submarines. Take away Trident and they've hardly got a role left.'

'So they'll resist it?'

'Yes, but the Navy resist everything. They nearly lost us World War I by resisting convoys.'

'And the RAF?' I asked.

'Well,' he replied dismissively, 'you can ask them. If you're interested in the opinions of garage mechanics. But I'm afraid they'd want Trident. Only they want it in the form of a missile launched from the air, like an Exocet.'

Suddenly it was all making sense to me. Why had I ever thought the Services would have a joint view of the matter?

General Howard continued to explain the RAF mentality as he sees it. 'They want the Bomb to be carried around in an aeroplane, you see. All they're really interested in is flying around dropping

81

things on people. Not that they're any good at it – I mean, they couldn't even close the runway at Port Stanley. They'd probably never even find Moscow. If they did, they'd probably miss.'

The problem is clear. How do I get the policy past the MOD if only the army is in favour of it? I put this to the General and he had a ready-made solution. 'The Chief of Defence Staff job is shortly becoming vacant. Technically it's the Navy's turn. But it's your decision. If you appoint a soldier . . .'

Delicately, he let his sentence remain unfinished. I already knew that he is the most senior soldier. So if I appoint him, I'll have the Chief of Defence Staff on my side. I don't know whether that'll be enough, or how the Navy will respond if I overlook their man, but it's obviously something I have to consider in due course.

[*Sir Humphrey Appleby also had a few words with General Howard at the reception at 10 Downing Street that evening. And their conversation, unlike General Howard's conversation with the Prime Minister, apparently changed the course of events. Sir Humphrey's recollections of that conversation are to be found in his private papers – Ed.*]

The General seemed unusually relaxed after a short talk with the Prime Minister, which I had been observing. When in due course I spoke to him, he remarked that he was pleased to have come across a Prime Minister with a bit of sense.

I asked which country was so blessed with such a leader. I knew, of course, that he was referring to Hacker, and my guess was that Hacker had not put him fully in the picture.

I was right, of course. The PM had spoken to General Howard about cancelling Trident, but *not* about reintroducing conscription. When I mentioned all the details the General was horrified, as I knew he would be.

Hacker wants conscription because it helps unemployment and therefore wins votes. The army does *not* want conscription, and has never wanted it. They are very proud of their élite, professional army. It is tough, disciplined, possibly the best in the world. The Chiefs of Staff do not want a conscripted mob of punks, freaks, junkies and riff-raff, a quarter of a million hooligans on its hands with nothing to do except peel potatoes at Aldershot. The generals are afraid that this would turn it into an ordinary army. [*Like the one that won World Wars I and II – Ed.*]

They are also worried about the new equal-opportunity legislation. In America it is well known that the NATO commanders don't know if the troops being posted to them are men or women. Not until they arrive. Sometimes not even then.

In view of the potential conscription General Howard felt that it would be better to keep Trident, with all its faults. He urged me to find some method of 'stopping' the Prime Minister from pursuing this unfortunate policy.

I explained that, unfortunately, Prime Ministers cannot be 'stopped'. But they can be slowed down. In fact, they almost invariably are – after a few months most new Prime Ministers have more or less ground to a halt.

My idea is to have a quiet word with the American Ambassador. General Howard approved.

[*Hacker's diary continues – Ed.*]

January 31st

Today there was good news and bad news. The bad news came first.

In my morning meeting with Humphrey, Bernard and Malcolm we went over the final preparations for my American visit. Malcolm is to make sure that the BBC News and ITN get really good positions on the White House lawn, so that they can get a close two-shot of me and the President.

I've also told him to ensure that there are good photo opportunities inside the White House as well. Shots of me and the President alone together.

I've given him a list of all the photo ideas that I've had: coverage of the start of the talks on the second day, coverage of the President saying goodbye to me, hopefully grasping my elbow with his left hand, the way he did with the West German Chancellor, it looked frightfully chummy.

I wanted him to arrange all of this with our Embassy, but Malcolm felt that it could be difficult. I must say, I don't know what we have all these Embassies for. Any time we need anything important for Britain [*i.e. for Hacker – Ed.*] they always make trouble.

It's not that I'm concerned with political advantage or vote winning, or anything like that. It's good for Britain to be seen by the rest of the world as an equal partner of the United States, that's all.

Humphrey was unwilling to discuss the publicity aspects any further. I wondered why. Instead, he showed me the Cabinet agenda.

You didn't have to be Hercule Poirot to see that the agenda had been tampered with. The discussion of the cancellation of Trident was conspicuous by its absence. I questioned Humphrey about this – after all, as Cabinet Secretary it's his job to draw it up.

'We were indeed going to discuss Trident, Prime Minister, but I thought perhaps it might be wiser to leave it a little longer. Go into it thoroughly, closer scrutiny, think through the implications, produce some papers, have some inter-departmental discussions, make contingency plans. We are discussing the defence of the realm.'

I can't believe that he still thinks these old devices will fool me. I challenged him, and he protested innocence. 'No, indeed, Prime Minister, but the Cabinet must have all the facts.'

I grinned. 'That's a novel idea.'

He was not amused. 'Important decisions take time, Prime Minister.'

I could see immediately what he was playing at: delaying tactics, the oldest trick in the book. The longer you leave things, the harder it is to get them off the ground.

But then came the bad news. It was a real bombshell. Apparently Humphrey has learned from the American Ambassador – informally – that the Americans would be very unhappy if we cancelled Trident unless we ordered another of their nuclear missiles instead.

At first I was defiant about it. After all, I have to think of what's best for Britain. But it seems they claim to have two reasons for their disquiet: the first is that they feel that they need our partnership and do not want to carry the nuclear burden alone. This is perfectly reasonable, but as we would still have Polaris they wouldn't be doing so. So the second reason is the real one: the little matter of losing billions of dollars of business and tens of thousands of jobs in the American aerospace industry.

The question is what – if anything – I can do about this American opposition to my Grand Design. I told Humphrey that I have no intention of changing my policy. The Americans will have to learn to live with it.

'As you wish, Prime Minister,' he said, 'but I thought if we kept your Trident proposal secret until after your American visit, it might save some embarrassment.'

I replied sharply that I didn't agree. 'If there has to be some tough talking, I might as well have it out with the American President when we meet.'

He shook his head sadly. 'Ah, well, that's the point. As you know, the agenda of your meeting must be agreed in advance. You can't just go all the way there for a chat.'

'Why not?'

'Well . . . you might not think of anything to say. And, if your Trident proposal were put to the Americans in advance, I understand there would be a slight change of plan.'

'What change of plan?'

'You would not be met by the President. You would be entertained by the Vice-President.'

I was thunderstruck. The Vice-President? I could hardly believe my ears. I thought he wasn't serious. But he *was*!

It's absurd. It's ludicrous. It's a total insult. Even Botswana was met by the President. [*Botswana had not just cancelled an order for Trident – Ed.*]

Humphrey tried to put it as nicely as he could. 'I'm sure they'd do it gracefully, Prime Minister. He'd have a diplomatic toothache, like Krushchev's. Or they'd explain that the President had catarrh, or bruised his thumb or something. Fallen asleep, perhaps.'

Humphrey knew as well as I that the whole point of the visit to the States was the PR value of being seen meeting the President. I asked him what choices we had. He advised me that in practice I have no choice at all. And that if I want to be entertained by the President I must leave Trident off the agenda.

This is a terrible blow. I have to raise it with the United States sometime. When better than while I'm there? But what must be, must be.

There remained the question of whether or not I should raise the Trident question in Cabinet. Humphrey advised me to leave it until my return, in case the discussion leaked to the US Ambassador. He could be right. Clearly someone has been leaking to him already on this subject. I wonder who.

'Anyway, Humphrey,' I said miserably, 'a new Prime Minister must show that he has arrived, show that there's a new mind and a firm hand in Number Ten. I must make my mark.'

And then Humphrey revealed the good news. It seems that I have accomplished something that none of my predecessors ever accomplished. A cook, no less! Seconded from the Cabinet Office canteen, to do our lunch in the flat when required. Except for weekends and bank holidays, of course.

This was gratifying. A place in the history books. I think that this shows that I have started the way I mean to go on. I am in charge, and the Civil Service can clearly see that there is a new mind and a firm hand in Number Ten.

I told Humphrey that, as far as Trident's concerned, I am not changing my policy and I am not changing my mind. In due course I shall lose it. [*Hacker presumably meant that he would lose Trident, not his mind – Ed.*] But in the meantime I see no harm in postponing the Trident discussion till I return from America, and I gave Humphrey my firm decision to leave Trident off the agenda for tomorrow.

He took it like a lamb. 'Yes Prime Minister,' he replied deferentially.

3
The Ministerial Broadcast

February 6th

I don't remember much about today. I got back from America last night and was in my study first thing this morning after a fairly sleepless night. But I needn't have hurried. I wanted to speak to Humphrey about something but he didn't seem to be around today. Bernard told me there wasn't much happening, and there were no appointments in the diary, so we spent some time reviewing what the papers had said about my American trip, and congratulating ourselves on the success of it. That's about it, really.

SIR BERNARD WOOLLEY RECALLS:[1]
The Prime Minister's recollection of his return from the United States is somewhat clouded by jet-lag, I fear. He was frightfully tired.

He lurched down the stairs from his flat and into his study, looking very white – except for his eyes, which were very red. He claimed that he was not jet-lagged, though he was concerned that he could not remember anything that the President said to him at the White House. Actually, this was not due to jet-lag – the President hadn't really said very much. Perhaps this was because the President was frightfully tired too.

Hacker yawned a lot and sent for Sir Humphrey Appleby, who had not been to Washington and was consequently very fresh and alert. Hacker, aware of his exhaustion, expressed concern that statesmen [*the word that politicians use to describe themselves – Ed.*] nowadays spend so much time jetting around the world, taking part in major negotiations that could affect the future of mankind when they are 'zonked', as he described it.

Sir Humphrey explained that this is the reason why such negotiations are nearly always completed in advance by humble servants such as himself. They could hardly be left in the hands of the 'zonked'.

Fortunately Sir Humphrey's comment passed unnoticed by the Prime Minister, who gently nodded off while he spoke. Perhaps this accounts for the Prime Minister's mistaken recollection that Sir Humphrey was absent that day.

[1] In conversation with the Editors.

We attempted to wake the Prime Minister. After some moments we succeeded. He opened his eyes, sat up slightly startled and said: 'Ah, Humphrey, good morning.'

Unfortunately Hacker had no recollection of sending for Sir Humphrey, nor could he remember why he had done so. I didn't know why either, because Hacker had fallen asleep before he told me. So Sir Humphrey left us. As he did so the Prime Minister nodded off again, and I left him to snooze in peace.

Much later in the day he buzzed down to me in the Private Office, and asked me to review with him the large backlog of work which he assumed – incorrectly – would have built up in his absence.

I was obliged to explain to him that there was no backlog, and that – contrary to public belief – he would have much less work to do now that he is Prime Minister and no longer has a department of his own.

The fact is that everything that one reads in the newspapers about how hard the Prime Minister has to work is rather a myth, generally put out by the Press Office. I listed the jobs for the Prime Minister that he actually has to do:

1. *Chair the Cabinet*   Two and a half hours per week.
2. *Chair two or three Cabinet Committees*   Four hours per week.
3. *Answers questions in the House*   Half an hour per week.
4. *Audience with the Queen*   One hour maximum (if she doesn't get bored before that).

This is a total of eight hours per week. Apart from that the Prime Minister has to read all the briefs, minutes, submissions, Foreign Office telegrams, and so forth. And the Private Office arranges to rush the Prime Minister from place to place, shaking hands with people. But in fact, although there are lots of things people want the Prime Minister to do, lots of things he should do, and any number of things he *can* do, there are very few things he *has* to do. After all, the Prime Minister is the boss.

[*In fact, there is much to be said for the system adopted by a United States President in the mid-1980s, of doing virtually nothing. This left time to think, if he felt up to it, or to sleep if he didn't – Ed.*]

In the absence of the expected backlog of work, the Prime Minister wanted to look at his press clippings.

He was delighted with the report sent to him by Malcolm Warren, the Number Ten Press Officer. Apparently in our absence the PM had been on all the TV news bulletins for three successive nights. There had been a special feature on *Panorama*. There were 1269 column inches in the nationals, and thirty-one photos. There were also sixteen radio reports.

I asked the Prime Minister if he regarded the Washington visit as a success. He did not understand my question – in his view, it was by definition a success if it achieved all this publicity.

My question related to possible agreements with the Americans. However, it seems that little progress was made on that front.

[*Later that day Bernard Woolley had a meeting with Sir Humphrey*

Appleby in his office. Sir Humphrey records the meeting in detail in his own diary – Ed.]

BW came to give me a report on the PM's Washington visit and confirmed that he had not mentioned his new defence policy to the President. This was a relief.

Nonetheless, we still have a considerable problem. By 'we' I mean all of us in the Cabinet Office, the Treasury, the MOD, the FCO and sundry lesser departments. The Prime Minister still wishes to cancel Trident and Cruise, continue with Polaris and bring back conscription to achieve a large conventional army.

BW, very properly in his role as Principal Private Secretary, defended the Prime Minister's ideas. He argued that to save money, reduce unemployment and make our defence credible is a worthy aim. I give him alpha plus for loyalty but nought out of ten for common sense.

He appears to believe that the purpose of our defence policy is to defend Britain. Clearly in this modern world this is an impossibility. Therefore, the only purpose of our defence policy is to make people *believe* that Britain is defended.

Some advocates of the deterrent theory understand this, but they assume that our defence policy is designed to make the Russians believe that we are defended. This is absurd. Our policy exists to make the *British* believe Britain is defended – the Russians know it's not.

Our defence policy is therefore designed to impress all those simple ignorant British citizens who shuffle in and out of houses, buses, pubs, factories and the Cabinet Room. We are trying to make them feel secure.

BW and the PM are seeking a better way, which is doubtless thoroughly laudable. But the very words 'better way' imply change, always a most dangerous notion.

At the moment we have a magic wand. It is called Trident. No one understands anything about it except that it will cost £15 billion, which means that it must be wonderful. Magical. We just have to write the cheque, and then we can all relax. But if people in the government start talking about it, eventually they will start *thinking* about it. Then they will realise the problems, the flaws in the reasoning. Result: the nation gets anxious.

BW was quite clear about these dangers after I had explained them to him. But he raised the question of the PM's impending television broadcast. He was concerned that the PM might want to use it to announce his new policy, immediately after discussing it in Cabinet and announcing it to the House. He might seek to use a TV appearance to open a national debate. This would be a bad precedent – one should not open a national debate until the government has privately made up its mind.

BW thinks that the PM has indeed made up his mind. If so, he must unmake it. I instructed him to see to it immediately.

BW was not sure that he could oblige, and loyally he pointed out that the PM is the PM, and, as such, he has certain rights and powers.

The PM's rights are obvious and generous. He gets his own car and driver, a nice house in London, a place in the country, endless publicity and a pension for life. I asked BW what more the PM wants.

'I think he wants to govern Britain,' he replied.

This must be stopped! He is not qualified.

[*Appleby Papers WB/CAA/400*]

[*Hacker's diary continues – Ed.*]

February 7th

I felt much more energetic today, and I also saw Humphrey for the first time since I'd been back, which was very pleasant.

But we began the day with a big meeting with Malcolm, to discuss my first broadcast on TV since I became Prime Minister. It raised a whole lot of interesting questions and problems that, as a mere Cabinet Minister, had never before confronted me.

The first question he raised was whether the broadcast should be an interview or to camera. I didn't understand the difference at first so I just said yes. But he explained that it had to be one or the other.

At first I suggested an interview, because I felt it might be less like hard work. But Malcolm immediately asked who I should like to be interviewed by. It seemed that the choice was between Robin Day, Brian Walden, Terry Wogan or Jimmy Young [*all well-known media people during Hacker's first term as Prime Minister although now, alas, forgotten – Ed.*].

'It depends, Prime Minister, whether you wish to be seen as a thinker, a man of power, the people's friend or just a good fellow.'

'All of them, really,' I said, but he misunderstood this and said that they wouldn't all interview me at once. I hadn't meant all of *them*, I'd meant that I wish to be seen to have all those qualities. Since I have them I couldn't see a problem.

Malcolm shook his head knowledgeably. 'An image is automatically created by the choice of interviewer. How do you wish to place the emphasis?'

I suggested that I should be seen primarily as a thinker. This, apparently, meant Brian Walden would talk to me. But Malcolm said there were problems associated with Brian Walden. 'He knows rather too much. He was an MP himself, don't forget.'

'Isn't that a help?' I wondered.

'No. Because if you don't answer the question, he asks it again. If you don't answer it a second time, he asks it a third time. Then, if you don't answer it three times, he tells the viewers you haven't answered it, and that you had three opportunities.'

On reflection, it seemed that Walden might not necessarily be the best choice. And perhaps, I thought, it would be good if my image were more the Man of Power rather than the Thinker.

Apparently this meant that I'd have to talk to Robin Day. But Malcolm said I would have to dominate him to get away with it. Dominating Day seemed a tall order, but clearly Malcolm felt that otherwise he might look more like a Prime Minister than I do.

Bernard Woolley felt that Robin Day was a little easier to handle since he got his K.[1] Be that as it may, I felt it would be better to take no chances. 'How would it be,' I asked, 'if I just opt for being a good fellow.'

'That means Wogan,' replied Malcolm. 'But you'd have to bandy words with him.'

I couldn't think what Malcolm meant. 'Bandy words?'

Bernard explained. 'You'd have to be witty.'

I could see no problem there. I've always been very witty. But Malcolm and Bernard were looking excessively gloomy. I couldn't see why, till Bernard suddenly said: 'Well . . . the trouble is, he rather goes in for insult humour.'

'Would he insult the Prime Minister?' I couldn't believe it.

'He insults everybody, if he feels so inclined.'

I had an idea. 'Perhaps *he'd* like a knighthood.'

Bernard didn't think much of that idea. 'Sir Terence Wogan? I hardly think so, Prime Minister.'

I was forced to agree that it would be a bit much, although a CBE would be okay and might ensure that he wasn't insulting.

Bernard was still unimpressed with the idea. 'Well . . . he's Irish. I'm not sure they really understand about honours. Also, being a Commander of the British Empire mightn't go down awfully well in Ireland. Especially in the peat bogs from which he emanates.'

It seemed to me that Bernard had a point. So it just left one option: I'd have to appear as the People's Friend, on the Jimmy Young show.

'There are problems with him too,' remarked Malcolm. 'You rather get shoved in between the record requests, the traffic news and the shopping basket.'

Bernard agreed. 'He's awfully chummy, but it can all look a bit lightweight. Furthermore, he's only on the radio.' [*How something can look anything on radio Bernard did not explain – Ed.*]

By this time I'd rather gone off the whole idea of an interview. It seems to me that it's much better for me to talk to the camera – then

[1] Knighthood.

I'll be in charge, not those failed MPs and jumped-up disc jockeys.

Malcolm suggested a party political. I thought that was a really crummy idea. Party politicals spell instant boredom. My whole idea is that it should be a Prime Minister addressing his People.

Bernard intervened. 'If you do that it will be a ministerial broadcast, and the Leader of the Opposition will want the right of reply.'

On the face of it, that is absurd. I said I wouldn't give a right of reply. Reply to what? I am Prime Minister, and I wish to speak to the people of my country.

Bernard was insistent that, constitutionally, we do have to give a right of reply. I asked him whose side he was on.

He was at his most punctilious and prissy. 'I am simply thinking ahead, Prime Minister. When you are the Leader of the Opposition, you will want the right of reply.'

I have no intention of being the Leader of the Opposition, at least not in the remotely foreseeable future. But I could see that I had to concede the point. So I told Bernard that I'd do it into the camera, like a party political.

'But you said they were boring,' he said.

I was getting fed up with him. 'I didn't say *I* would be boring, did I?' Silence. 'Do *you* think I'd be boring?' He made no reply. I should think not! It is highly unlikely that I would ever make a boring speech or broadcast, as he knows only too well!

Malcolm asked me if I'd done much talking to cameras. As I haven't, he offered to fix a rehearsal – an excellent idea.

Then he raised one final question. 'What is the broadcast to be about?'

I couldn't think what he meant for a moment. Obviously the broadcast is to be about me. I explained this to him, and he saw the point entirely. However, he wanted further clarification on one small matter of detail: what exactly was I going to say?

I couldn't see that this mattered much, but he wanted to know which policies I'd be referring to. I explained that it would be the usual: go forward together, a better tomorrow, tighten our belts, all pull together, healing the wounds, that sort of thing.

He was happy with that, but urged me to consider what I'd say *specifically*. My first thought was that I'd talk about specifically tightening our belts, healing specific wounds in our society.

But Malcolm pressured me to consider saying something *new*. I'd never considered that. Then, suddenly, I realised what an opportunity I have here: I shall talk about my Grand Design. I told

Malcolm that I'd let him have the text in due course. Meanwhile, he is going to find a suitable producer for the broadcast and set up a rehearsal. It all looks very promising.

February 8th
Tense meeting with Humphrey today. He had requested it for the earliest available moment today.

As soon as I was settled in my study I sent for him. He arrived almost at once. He must have been waiting downstairs for me.

'Ah, Humphrey,' I said. 'Here already?'

'Yes. I gather you want to discuss a television appearance.'

I was surprised that this was what he wanted to talk about. 'It's not that desperately urgent, is it?' I asked.

'Absolutely not,' he agreed. 'Not remotely important.'

I wasn't awfully pleased that my first TV broadcast should be described by Humphrey as not remotely important. He must have seen the expression on my face, because he hastily added that it was terribly important, but not a worry or a crisis.

It was quite clear that he wasn't worried about the broadcast *per se*, but about my Grand Design. He doesn't want me to mention it on the air.

I told him that I proposed to do just that and I asked him for his opinion.

'I think it is a mistake, Prime Minister.'

'The policy?' I asked. I was enjoying myself.

'No, no, announcing it on television. Precipitate. Premature. Perilous.'

He has an undoubted talent for alliteration when under pressure. I continued my little game. 'So . . . you do approve of the policy?'

He was trapped. He couldn't say he disapproved of both the policy and the TV announcement. It's not up to Civil Servants to approve policy. He hesitated. I waited. But of course, he was not lost for words for very long. 'I . . . er . . . I think the policy, is, er, interesting . . . imaginative . . . stimulating. A *most* stimulating approach. *Tremendously* refreshing to have a new mind on the old problem, challenging old ideas, questioning the whole basis of government thinking for the past thirty years.'

The implication was clear. If I was about to overturn all government thinking for the past thirty years, I must be a moronic idiot.

So I gave him the opportunity to express his opinion. 'You don't approve of the policy?'

As usual, he was less than frank. 'That's not true, Prime Minister. It's just that there are implications. Repercussions. Reverberations. Knock-on effects. We need time to sift and weigh the evidence. Examine the options. Test the arguments. Review. Research. Consult.'

I couldn't have been more helpful. I told Humphrey that he should press on with all those tasks, and, meanwhile, I would announce the policy in the broadcast.

'No!' he yelped. 'You can't. Not yet.'

'Why?' I wanted to know. He still hadn't come up with a reason.

'Well . . . we have to tell the Americans.'

Now I was angry. Suddenly I'd had enough. Only last week, before I went to America, he advised me *not* to tell the Americans. That's why I didn't do it while I was there. I faced him with this.

'Ah . . .' he replied carefully, 'yes, but that was before your visit. It was the wrong moment to talk to them.'

'And after I've got back,' I enquired with heavy irony, 'is the right moment to talk to them?'

He was defiant. 'Yes. But they will have grave objections. It will take many months of patient diplomacy. Delicate issues need sensitive handling.'

I decided it was time to remind Humphrey who was boss. 'Humphrey, who has the last word about the government of Britain? The British Cabinet or the American President?'

He sat back, crossed his legs, and considered the matter for a moment. 'That's a fascinating question, Prime Minister. We often discuss it.'

'And what conclusion do you come to?'

'Well,' he replied, 'I have to admit I'm a bit of a heretic. I think it's the British Cabinet. But I know I'm in a minority.'

I told Humphrey that I had news for him. From now on he is in the majority.

He was surprised. 'But you got on so well with the President.' He's right. I did. In fact, when we started our talks I read him my brief and he read me his, and then we decided it would be much quicker if we just swapped briefs and read them to ourselves. So we spent nearly all the time rubbishing the French. Terrific.

But now the honeymoon's over. I told Humphrey in no uncertain terms that from now on Britain will be governed in the interests of the British and not the Americans.

Humphrey wouldn't accept this. 'Prime Minister, are you sure you

93

can make that change without the approval of the Americans?'

I brushed his objections aside. I told him we would start to assert our independence with my Grand Design.

'Good, good,' he said. He was very unhappy. 'Excellent – but . . . not yet! It is my duty to speak up for the legitimate constitutional interests of the Cabinet. I'm their Secretary.'

A ridiculous ploy. 'You don't have to do that,' I pointed out. 'I appointed them. They are my government.'

'With respect, Prime Minister, they are Her Majesty's Government.' Now he was splitting hairs.

'With all due respect, Humphrey,' I said, putting him firmly in his place. 'I shall raise the policy formally with OPD[1] and then put it to Cabinet. I've sounded most of them out privately. They think it's a major contribution to the defence of this country, and, as such, very popular [*i.e. a vote-winner – Ed.*].

'With *great respect*, Prime Minister,' he was pulling no punches, 'it's not just a matter for the Cabinet. You know it must be announced to the House first. You are still a House of Commons man.'

I didn't need to be reminded of this. 'With the *greatest* respect, Humphrey,' I replied nastily, 'I'm announcing the Grand Design in the evening broadcast. I'll tell the House that same afternoon.'

'With the *greatest possible* respect, Prime Minister . . .'

I won't put up with that sort of insolence. 'You may regret that remark,' I informed him abruptly.

February 10th

Today we did the rehearsal for my television appearance. A very difficult and slightly embarrassing day.

We started with me sitting at a desk, talking to the camera. The script was on one of those autocue things.

We got off to a fairly bad start. I started the speech. It was the usual drivel. 'So let us be abundantly clear about this. We cannot go on paying ourselves more than we earn. The rest of the world does not owe us a living. We must be prepared to make sacrifices.' And so on. Cliché after cliché.

I demanded to be told who wrote this rubbish, and Bernard told me, in front of everybody, that I did. I couldn't believe it at first, but it turned out to be a rather old speech written when I was much less experienced.

Nonetheless, I had to explain that it wasn't drivel exactly (which

[1] The Overseas Policy and Defence Committee of the Cabinet.

I'm afraid it was) but that I felt we should be rehearsing with the draft of my actual broadcast.

Bernard seemed reluctant, because it was only a draft. I couldn't see that it mattered, since we were only doing a practice. Bernard said that it was highly confidential as it referred to my Grand Design, cancelling Trident, reintroducing conscription and so forth. I still couldn't see a problem – everyone in the room had been cleared.

So I insisted that they put the actual draft speech up on the autocue. I couldn't see why Bernard was being so unhelpful about it all.

Malcolm has found an ex-BBC producer called Godfrey Essex to advise me on the art of television. Very nice chap, I thought. Tall, slim, slightly grey, distinguished-looking with glasses – very experienced, with a gentle intelligent manner and a bow tie. While they changed the autocue I asked him how I was doing. He was extremely encouraging and said that I was pretty good.

But he raised an interesting point. The first of many, actually. He asked me if I'd be wearing my glasses.

I asked for his opinion.

'It's up to you,' he replied carefully. 'With them on you look authoritative and commanding. With them off you look honest and open. Which do you want?'

This was the first of many imponderables upon which I had to decide. I hadn't known this sort of thing mattered. I told Godfrey that I'd really like to look authoritative *and* honest.

'It's one or the other, really,' he said.

'Suppose . . .' I thought for a moment, 'suppose I sort of put them on and take them off while I talk?'

'That just looks indecisive.'

Well, I certainly don't want to look indecisive. That would be a travesty of the truth. I weighed up the pros and cons, unable to decide.

'What about a monocle?' suggested Bernard. I suppose it was one of his jokes.

I have left the decision about the glasses until the day of the recording.

The autocue was fixed, the new script in, and I began. Godfrey, Bernard, and Fiona – a charming make-up lady – all clustered around a monitor, watching me carefully. I felt as though I were a specimen under a microscope. It is a strange feeling, being watched so minutely.

I was pleased with the speech as it began. 'The Trident programme is too expensive. By cancelling it we shall release billions of pounds to fund an imaginative and radical attack on the nation's problems.'

Godfrey interrupted me. He told me it was *very* good, but he clearly had something on his mind. Bernard tried to talk to me as well, but I told him to wait.

Godfrey said that I was leaning forward too much, and that this made me look as though I was selling insurance. Trying to urge the customers to sign.

I tried a variety of ways of sitting, leaning and looking. I could tell that Godfrey didn't totally approve of any of them. Bernard and Malcolm had been off in a corner, and came back with a slightly different version of the speech: *We shall of course be reviewing a wide range of options over the whole field of government expenditure.*

'Bernard,' I exclaimed, slightly exasperated. 'That doesn't say anything.'

'Thank you, Prime Minister.'

He'd missed the point. 'Totally devoid of impact,' I explained.

'You're too kind,' he replied with a modest blush.

'No Bernard – *I don't like it*!'

He was surprised, and looked at it again to see how it could be given more impact. 'How about *urgently* reviewing?'

I scowled at him. He was a little edgy but stuck to his guns. 'I do really feel, Prime Minister, that it should be toned down a bit.'

I turned to Malcolm for his thoughts or guidance. He suggested: *The Trident programme is a heavy burden on your tax bill. £15 billion is a lot of money and we shall be looking at it very carefully to see if it merits the amount it costs.*

It obviously watered down the content somewhat but I accepted the compromise. I checked with Godfrey if it was okay to mention figures.

'Yes.' He was quite enthusiastic about figures. 'I mean, practically no one takes them in and those who do don't believe them. But it makes people think you've got the facts at your fingertips. Don't forget, people don't know you're reading them off the teleprompter.'

Good point. Apart from that his only criticism was that I was going a bit slowly. This was true – but I was going slowly because the teleprompter thing was going slowly. But I needn't have worried. He explained that it follows your speed – if you go fast, or slow, it just goes with you.

I tried it. Very slowly I said: 'The . . . Tri . . . dent . . . pro . . . gra . . . mme . . . is . . . aaa . . .' And then I speeded up abruptly:

'very-heavy-burden-on-your-tax-bill-Fifteen-billion-pounds-is . . .
a . . . lot . . . of . . . mo . . . ney . . . and . . . we . . .' I was going
dead slow again. And it worked. Very freeing, but quite difficult to
make it look natural, spoken rather than read. Still, I think I got the
hang of it pretty fast.

Godfrey picked up on another detail in that paragraph. 'I wonder if
you'd mind not saying "*your*" tax bill? It makes you sound as if you're
not one of the people. The ruler talking to the ruled. Them and us.'

Another good point. I should say *our* tax bill. I pay tax too!

Bernard was still worrying that this part of the speech was too
direct. I couldn't see any problem with that, till Bernard reminded me
that a lot of people's jobs in this country depend on Trident. He felt
that until there had been some consultation we shouldn't exactly spell
this out.

On reflection, I felt he might be right. Malcolm came up with an
alternative: *Defence expenditure is one of the areas which this
government will be examining closely to see if we can achieve the same
level of defence at lower cost.*

It seemed okay to me. But Godfrey said it was too long, and should
be said in two sentences. 'We find that if any sentence takes more
than two lines, when it gets to the end most people have forgotten
how it began. Including the person speaking it.'

So we split that bit into two sentences.

Godfrey was still worried about my position at the desk. Clearly I
had not yet arranged myself to his satisfaction. He told me that I was
starting to lean forward again.

I couldn't really help it. 'That's what I do,' I explained to him,
'when I want to look sincere.'

'The trouble is,' he replied, 'it makes you look like someone who
wants to look sincere. If you lean back, you look relaxed and in
control.'

I leaned right back. 'Not *too* far,' Godfrey said, 'it makes you look
as though you had a liquid lunch.'

We certainly don't want that! I sat bolt upright, wondering what to
do about looking sincere if I couldn't lean forward.

Godfrey had a solution. 'We'll underline the bits of the script
where you want to sound sincere. When you come to them you frown,
and say them a bit more slowly.'

So far so good. But then he started giving me acting lessons. He
told me my face was a bit wooden! Nobody's ever said that to me
before. I didn't quite know how to take it.

He explained that in normal speech people move their head and eyebrows and cheek muscles and so on. The teleprompter was apparently turning me into a zombie.

So I tried it again. My efforts to move my face seemed to provoke sniggers in the far corner of the room where the technicians were lurking. Godfrey told me I'd been doing it a little too much that time.

Bernard was still worrying about the relevant paragraph of the speech, which still read: *Defence expenditure is one of those areas which this government will be examining closely.* He still felt it was dangerously explicit. 'If you specify defence cuts it causes a lot of anxiety in places like Devonport, Portsmouth, Rosyth, Aldershot and Bristol.'

I suddenly saw his point. All those towns have marginal constituencies. I told him to tone it down a little. So we went on with another bit of the speech in the meantime.

It went like this. *You'll have heard a lot of nonsense from the Opposition. They say we waste money. They say we are selling out to the United States. I say, look at the mess they made when they were in power. Look at the damage they did to the economy.*

This time it was Godfrey who objected to the content of the speech. 'Prime Minister, if I might suggest – don't attack the Opposition.'

This was a very disappointing response. After all, those are the bits that the Party likes best.

But Godfrey's attitude was most interesting. His argument is that the Party will vote for me anyway. Attacking the Opposition will simply make the floating voters see me as an angry and divisive figure.

If he's right, we certainly don't want that. Godfrey also advised me never to repeat charges people make against me. It just gives more publicity to the criticisms. He also feels that people will think I'm really worried about the Opposition if I go out of my way to attack them.

So I couldn't see what I *could* say about them. His answer was simple. 'Don't mention them at all. Everything you say has to make you sound warm and friendly. Authoritative, of course, but loving. Father of the Nation. Try lowering the pitch of your voice.'

I found it enormously difficult to speak in a deeper voice. It sounded completely false, like a Paul Robeson impression. I'm told that I must take voice lessons from someone at the RSC[1] if I want to get it really right.

Anyway, in as deep a voice as I could muster I started on the next

[1] Royal Shakespeare Company, a theatrical production company which was highly regarded primarily for diction and voice production.

paragraph. *They reduced our gold resources, they destroyed our export trade, they concluded contemptible and infamous agreements . . .* I realised that all of this excellent knocking copy had to go as well. What a pity!

But Godfrey had a word with Malcolm and they slipped in an optimistic, positive piece about me and the future. I think he could be right that this is an improvement on saying negative things about the past: *We want to build a bright future for our children. We want to build a peaceful and prosperous Britain. A Britain that can hold her head high in the fellowship of nations.*

I thought it was rather good. I asked them where they had got it. It turned out they'd taken it from the last Party Political by the Leader of the Opposition. We'll have to paraphrase it.

Godfrey wanted to get back to the subject of my appearance. I prepared myself for more personal criticisms, but he wanted to discuss my clothes initially.

'What will you be wearing?'

'What do you suggest?'

'A dark suit represents traditional values.'

I said I'd wear a dark suit.

'On the other hand, a light suit looks businesslike.'

Another dilemma. To look traditional or businesslike. Again I wanted to look both. 'Could I have a sort of lightish jacket with a darkish waistcoat?'

'No, Prime Minister, that would just look as if you had an identity problem. Of course, you could try a tweed suit, which suggests the British countryside. Environment, conservation and so on.'

This sounded good too. But Godfrey had still more choices to offer. 'A sports jacket can be good – it looks informal and approachable.'

I explained to Godfrey that I am all of these things and have all of these qualities.

He was very good. He told me that I didn't have to make an instant decision, and gave me a list of pointers for when I had time to think about it. 'If you are all these things, then you should emphasise the one you're not. Or the one people are in danger of thinking you're not. So, if you're changing a lot of things, you want to look reassuring and traditional. Therefore you should have a dark suit and an oak-panelled background and leather books. But if you're not doing anything new, you'd want a light modern suit and a modern high-tech setting with abstract paintings.'

Fiona took Godfrey aside for a little word about my make-up. I had mixed feelings about it all. I must say, it is lovely to be fussed over and pampered, but I could hear the whole whispered conversation between them – which I think was not meant for my ears.

'Godfrey, are you happy about the grey hair or shall we darken it?'

'No, it's fine.'

'And the receding hairline?'

'Receding what?' I said, to indicate that I could hear them perfectly clearly.

Godfrey swung round. 'High forehead,' he said.

'Fine,' she said.

The next bit didn't please me all that much either, but Godfrey had warned me when he took on the job that he would have to be absolutely frank and honest with me or he wouldn't be of any help. He and Fiona stared at me in person, then at me on the monitor, then back at me again. 'Um, Fiona . . . can you do something about the eyes? Make them look less close-set?'

'Sure.' She could see no problem. Nor could I. 'And shall I lighten the bags underneath, and darken the pallid cheeks?' He nodded. 'The biggest problem is the nose.'

I intervened. 'The nose?'

Godfrey reassured me that there was no problem with my nose *per se*. It was just a lighting problem. There was a large shadow from somewhere, apparently.

I'd had enough of all this. I told them I wanted to get on with the rehearsal. But Godfrey asked Fiona if she had any other problems, reassuring me that all of this was in my interest: the better I look on television, the better chance I have of winning the next election. He's right, of course.

'There's just the teeth, of course,' said Fiona, and turned to me. 'Would you smile, Prime Minister?'

I smiled. They stared at me, gloomily. Then Godfrey sighed. 'Yes,' he said, in a tone of deep melancholy. And he strolled over to my desk. 'Prime Minister, how would you feel about a little dental work?'

I didn't feel very good about it at all.

But Godfrey was rather insistent. 'Just a little tooth straightening. People do pick on these things. And it did wonders for Harold Wilson. Look.' Fiona handed me two photos of Wilson, before and after his dental work.

I'll make an appointment for next week.

[*We have been fortunate to find the two photographs amongst Hacker's private papers, stored with the original cassette of this section of his diary. We reproduce them below – Ed.*]

So we began again. I sat back, but not too far back. I spoke in a deep voice, moved my face and eyebrows a little, and read at a variable speed: *We shall of course be reviewing a wide range of options over the whole field of government expenditure* . . . and I realised that this was exactly what I'd started out with!

I was getting irritated. I told Bernard that we seemed to be going round in circles.

'Prime Minister,' he said, 'I do think that this is the most suitable, most appropriate . . .'

'Most meaningless,' I interjected.

He begged leave to differ. 'Not exactly meaningless, Prime Minister. More non-committal.'

I was beginning to despair of ever getting it together. I asked Godfrey for his opinion on the material.

He wouldn't give it, of course. I don't blame him. It's not his problem. 'It's up to you, of course, Prime Minister,' he said, returning the ball firmly to my court. 'All I can say is that, if that's what you want to say, I suggest a very modern suit. And a high-tech background and a high-energy yellow wallpaper with abstract paintings. Everything to disguise the absence of anything new in the actual speech.'

I told him that I might go back to the original speech.

'Then,' said Godfrey obligingly, 'it's the dark suit and the oak panelling.'

Bernard was quite extraordinarily upset at my suggestion that I might go back to the old version. 'Prime Minister, I do earnestly beg you to reconsider.'

I decided that the moment had come to make my position plain. I told him, told them all, that as this is my first broadcast as PM it is imperative that it deals with an important subject. I can't just go on the air and waffle. My speech must have impact.

Bernard said that he agreed wholeheartedly (which he didn't, by the way) but couldn't I make a speech on a less controversial subject. I explained that, by definition, less controversial subjects have less impact than more controversial subjects.

'Surely some less controversial subjects have impact?'

'Such as?' I waited for his suggestions with interest.

'Well . . . litter!' Was he being serious? 'A stinging attack on people who drop litter. Or safer driving. Or saving energy. Lots of subjects.'

I made my own suggestion. I told him to save some energy himself.

Godfrey raised one final matter. The opening music. The same rules apply apparently: Bach for new ideas, Stravinsky for no change.

I suggested to Godfrey that it might be appropriate if we used music by British composers. Something that reflects my image. He seemed to like that idea. 'Elgar, perhaps?'

'Yes,' I said, 'but not *Land of Hope and Glory*.'

'How about the *Enigma Variations*?' said Bernard. I silenced him with a look.

[Three days later Bernard Woolley sent a note to Sir Humphrey Appleby, about the content of Hacker's television speech. Fortunately this came to light amongst the documents released under the Thirty Year Rule. We reproduce the original below – Ed.]

10 DOWNING STREET

From the Principal Private Secretary

February 13

Dear Humphrey,

I'm afraid the TV appearance looks unpromising.

The Prime Minister has ordered a dark suit and oak panelling. This means that he is planning to say something new and radical on the air, hence the need for a traditional, conventional, reassuring image.

I know that this will cause you some concern, but he is very keen on it.

Yours ever,

B.W.

[Bernard Woolley received this reply on the following day – Ed.]

70 WHITEHALL, LONDON SW1A 2AS

From the Secretary of the Cabinet and Head of the Home Civil Service

February 14

Dear Bernard,

The Prime Minister's intention to discuss his so-called Grand Design on television is a matter of the utmost concern.

The fact that he is very keen on it is neither here nor there. Things don't happen just because Prime Ministers are keen on them. Neville Chamberlain was very keen on peace.

This is precisely what we had hoped you would avoid.

Why has this happened?

Yours ever

AH

[Bernard Woolley immediately sent a brief note in reply – Ed.]

10 DOWNING STREET

From the Principal Private Secretary

February 14

Dear Humphrey,

The explanation is that the
Prime Minister thinks that his
Grand Design is a vote-winner.

The party has had an
opinion poll done. It seems that
the voters are in favour of bringing
back National Service.

Yours ever,
B. W.

SIR BERNARD WOOLLEY RECALLS:[1]

Yes, I remember that exchange of notes. Humphrey Appleby was not at all pleased that I had failed to have Hacker's speech watered down, in spite of my best efforts.

He asked me to drop in on him in the Cabinet Office, to discuss the situation. He was most interested in the party opinion poll, which I had seen as an insuperable obstacle to changing the Prime Minister's mind.

His solution was simple: have another opinion poll done, one that would show that the voters were *against* bringing back National Service.

I was somewhat *naif* in those days. I did not understand how the voters could be both for it and against it. Dear old Humphrey showed me how it's done.

The secret is that when the Man In The Street is approached by a nice attractive young lady with a clipboard he is asked a *series* of questions. Naturally the Man In The Street wants to make a good impression and doesn't want to make a fool of himself. So the market researcher asks questions designed to elicit *consistent* answers.

Humphrey demonstrated the system on me. 'Mr Woolley, are you worried about the rise in crime among teenagers?'

'Yes,' I said.

'Do you think there is a lack of discipline and vigorous training in our Comprehensive Schools?'

'Yes.'

'Do you think young people welcome some structure and leadership in their lives?'

'Yes.'

'Do they respond to a challenge?'

'Yes.'

'Might you be in favour of reintroducing National Service?'

'Yes.'

Well, naturally I said yes. One could hardly have said anything else without looking inconsistent. Then what happens is that the Opinion Poll publishes only the last question and answer.

Of course, the reputable polls didn't conduct themselves like that. But there weren't too many of those. Humphrey suggested that we commission a new survey, not for the Party but for the Ministry of Defence. We did so. He invented the questions there and then:

'Mr Woolley, are you worried about the danger of war?'

'Yes,' I said, quite honestly.

'Are you unhappy about the growth of armaments?'

'Yes.'

'Do you think there's a danger in giving young people guns and teaching them how to kill?'

'Yes.'

'Do you think it wrong to force people to take up arms against their will?'

'Yes.'

'Would you oppose the reintroduction of National Service?'

[1] In conversation with the Editors.

I'd said 'Yes' before I'd even realised it, d'you see?

Humphrey was crowing with delight. 'You see, Bernard,' he said to me, 'you're the perfect Balanced Sample.'

Humphrey really had a very fertile mind. It was a pleasure to work closely with him.

He had more suggestions to make. The Prime Minister was planning to make his broadcast in three or four weeks' time. The Cabinet Secretary urged me to tell Hacker that he should make the broadcast within the next eleven days.

I thought the Prime Minister might refuse. It was rather soon. Humphrey had foreseen this. He advised me to tell Hacker that I had just learned from the Joint Broadcasting Committee that the Opposition would have a Party Political in eighteen days' time, that Hacker was entitled to do his Ministerial first, but that if he didn't the first political broadcast of his Premiership would be given by the Opposition.

I wondered if Humphrey was telling me the truth. I challenged him on it. 'It will be,' he said with a smile, 'if you don't tell him till tomorrow morning.'

The reason for bringing Hacker's broadcast forward was to outflank him. He would not be able to use it to announce his new policy because within the ensuing eleven days he would have been able to squeeze in only one meeting of the Overseas and Defence Policy Committee – not enough to clear such a radical change of direction with his Cabinet colleagues.

His colleagues were largely in favour of the policy at that time. But only personally. Only politically. Not *officially*!

As responsible departmental Ministers their official reaction had to depend on the advice that they received.

[*Meetings at Whitehall were invariably minuted. Inter-departmental meetings were no exception. Everything had to be recorded on paper, as a record of what was decided and how it was to be acted upon. There was a wide measure of agreement that this was essential for the continuity of government. One meeting, however, was never minuted: this was the weekly meeting of Permanent Secretaries, which took place in the Cabinet Secretary's office every Wednesday, the day before Cabinet met. This was an informal 'keeping in touch' meeting, with no agenda.*

Fortunately for historians, Sir Humphrey did make private notes about some of these meetings, for his own purposes. He guarded them jealously throughout his lifetime. Lady Appleby has been good enough to make these notes available to us, and they include a record of the Permanent Secretaries' meeting on the morning of Wednesday 15 February – Ed.]

Very useful chin-wag this morning. Among those present were Dick, Norman, Giles and David. [*Sir Richard Wharton, Permanent Under-Secretary of the Foreign and Commonwealth Office; Sir Norman Coppitt, Permanent*

Under-Secretary of the Ministry of Defence; Sir Giles Bretherton, Permanent Under-Secretary of the Department of Education and Science; and Sir David Smith, Permanent Under-Secretary of the Department of Employment – Ed.]

We discussed the Prime Minister's so-called Grand Design. We agreed at the outset that the idea of abandoning Trident and Cruise missiles and of increasing conventional forces by means of conscription was both a novel and an imaginative proposal. [*From these two adjectives can be seen the depth of the contempt and animosity which those Civil Servants present at the meeting felt for Hacker's policy – Ed.*]

We agreed that as loyal Permanent Secretaries we have a duty to do everything in our power to assist its implementation.

Nonetheless, we suspected that our political masters may perhaps not have thought through all the implications. In view of this we discussed them at length, in order to be able to brief them when the PM raises the question tomorrow in Cabinet Committee.

Dick said that there were problems from the FCO point of view. The Americans simply won't stand for it. Not that British policy is determined by the Americans – Heaven forbid! – but, in practice, we do know that it is sensible to clear all new initiatives with Washington. Last time we failed to do so the results were unfortunate.[1]

I warned Dick that the Prime Minister might be somewhat hazy about the events at Suez, and therefore this argument might not worry him. Nor will he wish to look as though he is kow-towing to the Americans.

Dick raised one further point: cancelling Trident so early in his Premiership might look like weakness. Appeasement of the Soviets. Lack of courage and resolve. We agreed that this should form the basis of the Foreign Office view. The Prime Minister admires courage, from a safe distance. I enquired if Dick had been stating the views of the Secretary of State for Foreign Affairs. Dick was confident that these would be his views by tomorrow.

Norman was particularly concerned about the new policy, since it affects him most closely at the MOD. The Secretary of State for Defence is fairly confused at the moment – his special problem is that the advice from the Navy, Army and RAF is not always identical. There is underlying harmony, of course, but they have no one on whom to vent their warlike instincts except each other. However, the one thing that unifies the three Services is their implacable opposition to conscription. They have nothing against the young people of this country, but they do not want their skilled professional élite armed forces diluted by riff-raff. British officers are the best leaders of men in NATO. It is true that there are hardly any men to lead, which might be the reason why they lead so well.

I indicated to Norman that the Prime Minister might not take the opposition of the Service Chiefs as the clinching argument.

Norman felt that the argument should be kept simple: Trident is the best and Britain must have the best. This is an argument that could well appeal to the Defence Secretary. He is very simple himself and he will be able to follow it. We agreed that Norman would give him a little coaching.

[1] The Suez crisis, 1956.

The discussion turned to the DES. Giles felt that there could be problems with conscription from the educational point of view. Our educational system has been a triumphant success in turning out socially integrated and creatively aware children who are fully trained in the arts and techniques of self-expression. The DES has a proud record in this, and has done a first-class job. However, Giles felt that conscription would inevitably give publicity to the fact that many school-leavers cannot actually read, write or do sums. So the NUT[1] will be violently against its introduction.

Furthermore, there is a slight incidental risk that the Services might take over most of the Colleges of Further Education and use them for *teaching* purposes. We all agreed that such unnecessary interference would be rather shocking – a total distortion of their function.

I was concerned that, as conscription is not really an educational issue, it would be hard for Giles's Secretary of State to involve the NUT veto. Giles felt that, on the contrary, the NUT might veto his Secretary of State, making his life impossible.

I asked Giles what advice he proposed to give his political master. Giles remarked that although conscription is not what the DES call education, it would work very well in terms of actually teaching people things. So it's hard to oppose. Not that any of us want want to oppose it.

Norman wondered if the issue could not be raised that there has been a lack of reasonable time for deliberation. Fatal to rush things.

I suggested that there might be educational question marks about the credentials of the man putting the idea forward: Professor Rosenblum.[2]

Giles agreed enthusiastically. He felt it could be argued that Rosenblum's figures have come under severe critical scrutiny, or perhaps that he is academically suspect. He felt that this would be his Secretary of State's view, once the Secretary of State heard the facts. Indeed, Giles recalled that there is a paper coming out that criticises the whole basis of Professor Rosenblum's thinking. It will be coming out tomorrow morning. [*This technique is known in the Civil Service, as it is in football, as Playing the Man Not the Ball – Ed.*]

It so happens that this paper will be written [*Sir Humphrey made a slip here. He should have said* has been written *– Ed.*] by one of the Professors who was passed over for Chief Scientific Adviser. Not that he is jealous – he just feels that Rosenblum's influence may not be an entirely good thing.

We agreed that, to avoid hurting his feelings, it would probably be best if Professor Rosenblum does not actually see the paper. It should be submitted by Giles as personal advice to the Secretary of State. [*It is essential, if you play the man and not the ball, that you do not let the man know you are doing so – Ed.*]

We turned finally to the employment implications. It is a significant part of this scheme that National Service might involve young people in doing useful jobs in the community.

David felt that this was a jolly good idea, on the face of it. But it does create grave problems with the Unions. Once you start giving jobs to non-

[1] National Union of Teachers.
[2] See Chapter 2, page 65.

109

members of Trade Unions you are on a very slippery slope. Once you let a couple of kids do up the old folks' houses, you will have an uproar from all the bricklayers, plasterers, painters, plumbers, electricians and carpenters who ought to be doing it instead.

We agreed that community service can be very damaging to the community. However, it is likely that the Prime Minister will argue that if the kids were earning a living and the old people were pleased with the work, that would be all right. This argument is of course an over-simplification, but the Prime Minister never seems too worried about over-simplification.

David had an excellent idea. He felt that the Secretary of State for Employment might argue that the unemployed young people are now unfit, unorganised, undisciplined and untrained. They are a problem – but not a threat! Conscription would mean eventually releasing on to the streets an army of fit young people all trained to kill.

We unanimously agreed that this is a far-sighted and responsible attitude, and we encouraged David to ensure that his Secretary of State had taken the idea on board by tomorrow.

In my summing up we all agreed that there was no question of our trying to oppose the Prime Minister's policy, which we believe to be novel and imaginative. We are only opposed to precipitate haste.
[*Appleby Papers PA/121/LAX*]

[*Hacker's diary continues – Ed.*]

February 16th
Cabinet Committee this afternoon, and my colleagues responded to the Grand Design in a way that I did not predict.

It was last on the agenda. I told them that I intended to announce my Grand Design in my TV broadcast on Friday, and – if the Committee agreed – I would put it to full Cabinet on Thursday morning and tell the House the same afternoon.

There was a bit of a silence. I took it as general assent. So I was about to pass on to the next item when Duncan[1] spoke up.

'Prime Minister, I think it is an excellent plan,' he began.

'Good,' I said.

'The only thing is . . . cancelling Trident so early in your premiership could look like weakness to the Soviets.'

Humphrey grunted an impressed grunt, nodded thoughtfully, and turned to me with an enquiring expression.

I was a little taken aback. When last I spoke to Duncan he had been completely in favour. 'I thought you were in favour of the idea. It would surely enable us to *strengthen* NATO through credible conventional forces.'

[1] Secretary of State for Foreign Affairs.

Duncan nodded, but he didn't agree. 'Yes . . . But it could *look* like lack of courage. It might smack of appeasement.'

I told Duncan that I would record his view, even though he was in a minority of one.

I had spoken too soon. Hugh[1] piped up.

'Well, actually, Prime Minister, although I think it's an excellent plan too, the fact is that Trident is the best and Britain should have the best.'

I was astonished. 'But, Hugh,' I said, 'I thought you wanted to get rid of Trident. Pointless waste of money, you said.'

Hugh looked a little uncomfortable. 'Well, yes, I did say that, but now I'm not sure. I've been reviewing the papers. There's more to it than I thought.' I stared at him coldly. 'Um . . . I'm simply against making an early announcement, that's all.'

'I'm against making an early announcement too, Prime Minister.' Now Patrick[2] was lining up with Duncan and Hugh. I was speechless, so I asked him why.

'Because the whole plan is based on Professor Rosenblum's figures. And my information is that he is academically suspect. I've just received a high-powered paper that severely criticises the whole basis of his argument.'

'But, Patrick,' I said, with rising anxiety, 'you agreed that conscription will solve the whole youth unemployment problem, as well as give us meaningful defence forces.'

Tom[3] replied instead of Patrick. 'Yes, but it has since occurred to me that it will also create an army of fit, disciplined, organised young people wh ɔ will be released from the forces after two years, unemployed again but now trained to kill.'

I stared at him in disbelief. 'So you're against it *too*?'

He didn't answer directly. 'I'm against an early announcement. I think we need time to consider it all more fully.'

This entire conversation baffled me. Only a week ago they were all agreed that the policy was a real vote-winner. I shall have to think very hard about my next step.

Humphrey said that he'd minute the Committee meeting so as to leave the door open. Jolly helpful of him.

---

[1] Secretary of State for Defence.
[2] Secretary of State for Education.
[3] Secretary of State for Employment.

February 20th

Today I got a memo from Hugh at the MOD. They had an opinion poll done. It says that 73% of the public are against conscription.

This is deeply confusing. The Party's poll said 64% in favour!

And then the minutes arrived.

[*Sir Humphrey Appleby's minutes have survived the ravages of time, and are shown below – Ed.*]

Item 7, Grand Design   4.

It is clear that Cabinet Committee is agreed
that the new policy is an excellent plan, in
principle. But in view of the doubts being
expressed, it was decided to record that,
after careful consideration, the considered
view of the committee was that while
they considered the proposal met
with broad approval in principle, it
was felt that some of the principles
were sufficiently fundamental in principle,
and some of the considerations so complex
and finely balanced in practice that
in principle it was proposed that the
sensible and prudent practice would
be to subject the proposal to more detailed
consideration with and across the relevant
departments with a view to preparing
and proposing a more thorough and wide-ranging
proposal, laying stress on the less controversial
elements and giving consideration to the
essential continuity of the new proposal with
existing principles, to be presented for
parliamentary consideration and public discussion
on some more propitious occasion when the
climate of opinion is deemed to be more
amenable for consideration of the approach
and the principle of the principal arguments
which the proposal proposes and propounds
for approval.

[*Hacker's diary continues – Ed.*]

I read this passage over a few times. I think it simply means that the Committee didn't want me to refer to the Grand Design on TV on Friday.

I have no intention of abandoning my policy. But I'll have a fight on my hands, I can see that.

Meanwhile, I have instructed Bernard that on TV I'd better have a light suit, high-tech furniture, a yellow high-energy wallpaper background, abstract painting – and Stravinsky.

4
The Key

Dorothy Wainwright, my Chief Political Adviser, came to see me in the Cabinet Room this morning. She's a very attractive blonde of about forty, slim, efficient, and very hard-nosed.

When I say *my* Chief Political Adviser, it's hardly true. In fact she held that post for my predecessor, the previous Prime Minister, and it seemed a good idea to keep her on.

Humphrey Appleby had hinted that she wasn't awfully helpful – so it seemed an even better idea to keep her on! After all, I do need people who are not strictly within Humphrey's control. But since my first day here, when I asked her to stay, I've hardly seen her. So I was thoroughly surprised not only when she strode purposefully into the Cabinet Room, where I was sitting doing my paperwork, but also by her brisk opening remark.

'Look, Jim, if you don't want me as Political Adviser, I'd much rather you just said so.'

I was amazed. Why did she think I'd asked her to stay on? She was the only person that stopped my predecessor from losing all contact with the real world. But it seems that she has been given the impression that I've arranged for her to be kicked out of her office and banished to the servants' quarters.

'I used to be in the office next door to this room, didn't I?' Was it a rhetorical question or did it demand an answer?

I played safe. 'Yes.'

'And you asked for me to be moved to the front of the building, up three floors, along the corridor, down two steps, round the corner, and four doors along to the right. Next to the photocopier.'

This was news to me. I'd no idea where she'd been. 'I thought you were on holiday or something,' I explained. Actually, the job has been keeping me so busy that, to tell the truth, I'd hardly noticed she wasn't much in evidence. [*This was no coincidence – Ed.*]

'I might as well be on holiday,' she said sharply. 'I came back after your first weekend and found my office turned into a waiting room for Cabinet Ministers, officials and so on. All my things had been moved upstairs to the attic. Humphrey said it was on your instructions. Was it?'

I tried to think. Had I given such instructions? No, I hadn't. And yet . . . I *had*! 'You see, Dorothy, Humphrey came to me with a plan to rationalise things. Make better use of the space.'

She shook her head in silent wonderment. 'Don't you realise that the Civil Service has been trying to get me out of my office for three years?'

How could I have realised that? 'Why?'

'Because geographically it's in the key strategic position. It's the best-placed room in the house.'

'I don't see what difference that makes,' I said. 'You're still in Number Ten.'

'Just,' she said, tight-lipped.

'You get all the documents.'

'Some,' she acknowledged.

'We can talk on the phone,' I reminded her.

'When they put me through,' she said bitterly.

I thought she was being a bit paranoid and I told her so. Then she started talking about Albania and Cuba. She said Albania has very little influence on United States policy, whereas Cuba has a lot of influence. Why? Because Albania is remote and Cuba is near. She argues that, in Number Ten just as in the outside world, influence diminishes with distance. 'And I'm distant,' she finished balefully.

'You're not in Albania,' I said.

'No, I'm in the bloody attic,' she snapped. 'Look!' And she started to move things around on my desk. 'This desk is a plan of Number Ten. This file is the Cabinet Room, where we are now. Through the doors here' – she placed a book at one end of the file – 'is your private office. This ruler is the corridor from the front door – here. *This* corridor' – and she grabbed a paper knife and put it down alongside the file and the book – 'runs from the Cabinet Room and connects up to the locked green-baize door, on the other side of which is the Cabinet Office, which is this blotter, where Sir Humphrey works. This coffee cup is the staircase up to your study. And this saucer is the gents' loo – here. And *this* is – was – my office.' She put an ashtray down beside the file that represented the Cabinet Room. 'Now, my desk faced out into the lobby and I always kept my door open. What could I see?'

I stared at it all. 'You could see,' I said slowly, 'everyone who came in from the front door, or the Cabinet Office, or in and out of the Cabinet Room, or the Private Office, or up and down the stairs.'

She remained silent while I pondered this. Then, pressing home her advantage, she picked up the saucer and put it down again. 'And I was opposite the gents' loo. I *have* to be opposite the loo.'

I asked her if she'd seen a doctor about this, but apparently I was missing the point. 'The *gents*' loo,' she reminded me. 'Almost everyone in the Cabinet is a man. I could hear everything they said to each other, privately, when they popped out of Cabinet meetings for a pee. I was able to keep the last Prime Minister fully informed about all their little foibles.'

'Was that any of his business?' I asked.

'When they were plotting against him, yes!'

She's brilliant! No wonder Humphrey turned her office into a waiting room and banished her to the attic.

I buzzed Bernard. He appeared through the large white double doors from the Private Office, immediately.

'Ah, Bernard,' I said, 'I want you to put Dorothy back in her office.'

'You mean, take her there?' He pointed atticwards.

'No,' I said. 'I mean, take her to the waiting room, just outside here.'

Bernard was puzzled. '*Before* she goes back to her office, you mean?'

I was patient. 'No, Bernard. I mean the waiting room, which used to be her office, will again be her office.'

'But what about the waiting room?' he asked.

I told him to concentrate, listen carefully, and watch my lips move. 'The–waiting–room–' I said slowly and clearly, 'will–become–Dorothy's–office.'

He seemed to understand, but was still arguing. 'Yes, Prime Minister, but what about waiting?'

I lost my temper and shouted at him. '*No, Bernard, right away!*'

It *still* wasn't clear to him. Desperately he stood his ground. 'Yes, Prime Minister, I realise you mean at once, no waiting, but what *I* mean is, where will people wait if there is no waiting room to wait in?'

I saw what he meant. It was just a simple misunderstanding, that's all. But his question was still pretty daft. 'The whole building is full of waiting rooms,' I pointed out. 'All the state rooms upstairs, hardly ever used. And then there's the lobby, here!' I indicated my desk.

Bernard looked blank. 'Where?'

'There,' I said. 'Look. Between the ashtray, the cup and the saucer.'

He looked at the desk, then back to me, wide-eyed with confusion. 'Between the coffee cup and the saucer?'

He's so *dense* sometimes. 'The saucer is the gents' loo, Bernard,' I told him. 'Wake up!'

I sometimes wonder if Bernard's mind is agile enough for this job.

SIR BERNARD WOOLLEY RECALLS:[1]

Naturally I immediately acted upon the Prime Minister's instructions. I had no axe to grind, it was Sir Humphrey who had insisted that Mrs Wainwright was moved away from her strategic position overlooking the lobby outside the Cabinet Room.

The following day Humphrey phoned me and instructed me to explain myself or withdraw the instructions. I told him that there was nothing to explain – it seemed a matter of minor significance.

An hour later a note arrived from him, written in his own hand.

[*Sir Bernard was kind enough to lend us the note from Sir Humphrey. We print it below – Ed.*]

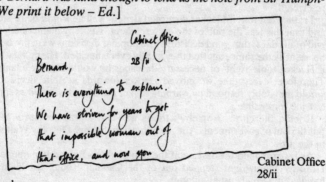

Cabinet Office
28/ii

Bernard,

There is everything to explain. We have striven for years to get that impossible woman out of that office, and now you snatch defeat from the jaws of victory.

The fact that the PM requested it is neither here nor there. You do not have to grant every little request from the Prime Minister. You have to explain that some of them are not in his own best interests. Most of them, in fact.

Our job is to see that the PM is not confused. Politicians are simple people. They like simple choices, and clear guidance. They do not like doubt and conflict. And that woman makes him doubt everything we tell him.

H.A.

P.S. Please destroy this letter immediately.

[1] In conversation with the Editors.

[*Fortunately for historians Sir Bernard did not obey Sir Humphrey's instruction to destroy the letter. Nor did he immediately withdraw the instructions to change Mrs Wainwright's office – Ed.*]

SIR BERNARD WOOLLEY RECALLS:[1]

No, indeed I didn't. I felt it was my duty to argue the Prime Minister's case. So Humphrey popped over to the Private Office to discuss it further. He wasn't pleased that I was taking an independent view.

I told him, quite simply, that Mr Hacker liked Mrs Wainwright. This argument did not impress him. 'Samson liked Delilah,' he commented. Fortunately, the Private Office was deserted. Humphrey had wisely chosen to come to talk to me at the end of the day when all the others had gone home.

I took a strong line with him. I told him that she was not dangerous, in my opinion. For a start, she didn't know very much of what was going on; we had always been careful to keep most of the important documents away from her.

This did not satisfy Humphrey. He reminded me, quite accurately, that we in the Civil Service were duty-bound to ensure the sound government of Britain. Whereas Mrs Wainwright's sole duty was to see that Mr Hacker was re-elected.

I rather felt that if Hacker governed Britain well he *would* be re-elected, and that this was the nub of the disagreement. Appleby maintained, to the end of his days, that good decisions and popular decisions were not only not necessarily the same, but that they hardly ever coincided. His belief was that if Hacker took 'right' or necessary decisions he would lose by a landslide. Therefore, every time we moved Hacker towards a 'right' decision, she would inevitably respond by warning him of potential loss of votes, making our job impossible.

Briefly, therefore, Appleby's thesis was that it was necessary to keep politics out of government. And, by extension, to keep Dorothy Wainwright in the attic.

As he explained this last point the double doors behind him opened and Dorothy Wainwright stepped out of the Cabinet Room. Sir Humphrey handled it with his usual aplomb.

'Ah, good evening, dear lady,' he said as he swung around. 'This is indeed a pleasure.'

She was unimpressed. 'Hullo, Humphrey. Waiting to see the Prime Minister?'

'Indeed I am, dear lady.'

'Why aren't you in the waiting room?'

He had no answer. I thought it was extremely funny but, as always, I had to hide my amusement.

Humphrey turned on me, determined to exert his authority some other way. He informed me that 'an alien' had been admitted to Number Ten the day before. The 'alien' turned out to be the Prime Minister's constituency agent, who had been allowed in without a security pass.

[1] In conversation with the Editors.

He was simply being petty. The policemen outside all knew the man. There was no risk. Nonetheless, Humphrey reminded me – in a slightly humiliating manner – that it was my duty to ensure that everyone who came to the front door must either show their Number Ten pass or have an appointment.

Mrs Wainwright was listening to this conversation, and it did nothing to improve her opinion of Sir Humphrey. 'Excuse me butting in, Bernard,' she said, 'but the Prime Minister asked me to make the necessary arrangements with you for moving my room back.'

I was embarrassed. Humphrey gave me a penetrating stare and waited for me to refuse her. I couldn't see how I could refuse, if the PM had made the request.

I tried to prevaricate, and told her that I just had to deal with Sir Humphrey's request concerning security passes. She said Humphrey's request could wait. He said that it couldn't. She said that it could!

Humphrey turned his back on her and walked into the Cabinet Room to see the PM.

I must say that in all my years in Whitehall I have never seen such direct rudeness as I saw when Sir Humphrey was faced with Mrs Wainwright. I wonder if it was because she was so forthright herself – she certainly didn't pull her punches, as Hacker's diaries reveal. Humphrey obviously disliked her very much indeed – and, if he didn't have cause to initially, he certainly had eventually.

[*Hacker's diary continues – Ed.*]

February 28th
I was dictating letters in the Cabinet Room today after a meeting with Dorothy. She was a little fed up that her office had not been moved back downstairs yet, but it was only yesterday that I gave the go-ahead for it. She felt sure there was opposition from the Civil Service and *I* felt she was being paranoid again.

No sooner had she left than I heard slightly raised voices in the private office. Then Humphrey appeared. 'I understand you are having second thoughts about our office reorganisation,' he said.

'No,' I replied. 'I've simply decided to put Dorothy back in her old office.'

'That, alas, is impossible.'

'Nonsense,' I retorted, and switched on my dictating machine preparatory to writing a letter.

But he didn't drop it. 'No Prime Minister, the whole reorganisation hinges on her moving out.'

I couldn't see why. I told him it was only a waiting room.

'Not *only* a waiting room,' he disagreed firmly, and strolled down the room towards me. 'A vital square on the board.'

119

'People can wait in the lobby,' I said, unaware that my dictating machine was recording us. 'Or the state rooms.'

'Some people, perhaps,' replied Sir Humphrey. 'But some people must wait where other people cannot see the people who are waiting. And people who arrive before other people must wait where they cannot see the other people who arrive after them being admitted before them. And people who come in from outside must be kept where they cannot see the people from inside coming to tell you what the people from outside have come to see you about. And people who arrive when you are with people they are not supposed to know you have seen must be kept somewhere until the people who are not supposed to have seen you have seen you.'

I couldn't possibly have remembered all that, and I had great trouble later today trying to decipher it. But the implications were clear: 'You mean while I'm quietly working away in here, there's an entire Whitehall farce going on outside that door?'[1]

'Prime Minister, Number Ten is a railway junction. It cannot work without its proper component of sheds and sidings and timetables. Mrs Wainwright's office is a vital shed.'

I challenged him. 'You want her out of the way.'

'Good heavens no, Prime Minister!'

'You think she's a nuisance. Be honest.'

'No, no. Splendid woman, Mrs Wainwright. Upright. Downright. Forthright.'

Sometimes Humphrey has a certain natural poetry. 'But a nuisance?' I asked again.

'Well,' he acknowledged cautiously, 'there have been occasions when her criticisms of the service have been, er, refreshingly outspoken. And when her conversations with the press have been . . . breathtakingly frank and full. And sometimes her requests for information and assistance could have been a touch less abrasive and persistent. But most of my staff who had nervous breakdowns in the past three years would probably have had them anyway.'

'But I find her advice valuable,' I reminded him.

'Of course, Prime Minister.' Humphrey's tone was now full of understanding. 'And you shall have it. On paper.'

'Where you can all read it?' I challenged him.

---

[1] Whitehall farce was a term used to describe a series of theatrical farces produced over a period of about twenty years at the Whitehall Theatre. Whitehall was also, of course, the street that connects 10 Downing Street to Parliament Square, and on which can be found a number of major government departments.

Immediately I realised I'd led with my chin. 'And why not?' he enquired. 'Will it be secret from me?'

Of course I had no answer to that. So I reiterated the main point of the argument. 'She needs to be where things are happening.'

'Think for a moment, Prime Minister. Is it fair to her?'

I couldn't think what he was driving at. 'All the rest of us in this part of Number Ten are career civil servants. Loyal. Trusted. True. Our discretion proved over many years. If just one temporary civil servant is from the outside, then whenever there is a security breakdown the finger of suspicion will be pointed at her. It is too heavy a burden for one lady to bear. However gracious.'

Is there any truth in this argument? It sounds plausible. It's certainly true that they'd take it out on her if they could! But I explained to Humphrey that she is valuable because of her *political* advice.

'Prime Minister,' he replied, 'you have the whole Cabinet to give you political advice.'

'They only advise me to give more money to their own departments. I need someone, Humphrey, who's on *my* side.'

Humphrey was now positively sweetness and light. 'But I'm on your side. The whole Civil Service is on your side. Six hundred and eighty thousand of us. Surely that is enough to be going on with?'

He seemed to be winning the argument. I should never have got into it at all. I should have just held firm to my decision. But it was too late now. I'd been sucked in to an argument I could never win. 'You all give me the same advice,' I said hopelessly.

'Which proves,' replied Humphrey with triumph, 'that it must be correct! So now, please, can we revert to the original reorganisation plan?'

I know when I'm beaten. I nodded.

Humphrey tried to sweeten the pill with a compliment. 'It's such a pleasure to have a decisive Prime Minister who knows his own mind.'

I asked Bernard to send for Dorothy. To my surprise she was waiting next door in my private office. She came right in. I waited for Humphrey to leave. He didn't. So I explained that I wanted a private word with Dorothy.

He still didn't leave. 'You can speak freely in front of me,' he smiled.

Dorothy could see which way the wind was blowing. 'The Prime Minister may be able to,' she snapped. 'I can't.'

'I'm sure you can,' Humphrey replied patronisingly.

This was a terrible situation, thoroughly embarrassing, and it really was my fault for not standing up to Humphrey properly. Dorothy turned on her heel and walked out. 'Bernard, perhaps you'll let me know when the Prime Minister is free.'

I stopped her, told her to come right back, and asked Humphrey to leave.

He didn't budge. 'If you think it's necessary, Prime Minister. But I understand you have only a few brief words to say and we have many other matters of moment to discuss.'

I couldn't think what. It was clear that Humphrey was determined to see that I denied Dorothy the office outside the Cabinet Room. While I was wracked with indecision, Dorothy turned on Humphrey.

'I'm sorry, Humphrey,' she said with steel in her voice, 'I thought I heard the *Prime Minister* asking you to leave.'

I kept silent. Humphrey realised that he had no alternative, turned and walked from the room. I signalled to Bernard to follow him.

The doors closed. Dorothy sat opposite me. She knew the whole situation only too well. She came straight to the point.

'He has no right to behave like this, you know.'

Trying to save face a little, I asked her what she meant. She explained that she meant barging in and out without so much as a by-your-leave, and telling me I couldn't spend too long talking to her.

'He is Cabinet Secretary,' I reminded her.

'Precisely. He's a Secretary.'

Now I felt I had to save Humphrey's face. 'He's the most senior Civil Servant.'

She smiled a wry smile. 'It's remarkable how people continue to consider you a civil servant when you behave like an arrogant master.'

Now I had to save *my* face again. 'I'm the master here,' I said in my best no-nonsense voice.

'That's right!' she said emphatically.

Encouraged, I told her that I am the Prime Minister, and that I shall be firm and decisive. As always. I told her that I wished to talk about her office, and that I've changed my mind.

She asked, impertinently, if I had done so firmly and decisively.

This was infuriating. I asked her precisely what her question meant. Unfortunately, she told me. 'Have you changed your mind or has someone changed it for you?'

I told her we need the waiting room. She asked why.

'Well,' I began, and realised that I was unable to reproduce Humphrey's argument. I'm afraid my version came out rather differently. 'Because, if people come to see people who people don't know people are coming to . . . that is, if people saw people before other people saw them seeing them . . . and *other* people see people . . . well, the whole ship goes off the rails.'

I ground to a halt, embarrassed. She gazed at me, her cool blue eyes appraising me. 'Did you work all that out for yourself?' she enquired.

'Look, be fair!' I defended myself as best I could. 'I can't go into everything. I have to rely on advice from my officials.'

She acknowledged the truth of this. But her view is that I have to rely on advice *not only* from officials. She believes that Humphrey is trying to shut off all my sources of information and advice except the Civil Service. And, furthermore, she insists he wishes to make himself the only channel for Civil Service advice.

This sounds a little fanciful to me. But she has more experience of Number Ten than I have, and I do know that she's on my side – or at least she's not on Humphrey's side, which may not be the same thing.

But how can Humphrey make himself the only channel for advice when I have the whole Cabinet every Thursday, and lots of Cabinet committees?

That's a question that I can answer for myself. My Cabinet mostly argue their Civil Service briefs. That's what I always found I was doing. And Humphrey meets their Permanent Secretaries informally the day before Cabinet – presumably they agree on their briefs. That's why I'm having such trouble with my Grand Design – the Civil Service is against it.

However, there is also the Think Tank.[1] I reminded Dorothy that they report to me.

She looked sceptical. 'I wouldn't be surprised if Humphrey suggests having them report to him instead. Then he'll ask for more space in Number Ten.'

'Why?' I asked. 'The Think Tank's supposed to be in the Cabinet Office.' [*The Cabinet Office was a separate building which adjoined 10 Downing Street. It was entered from Whitehall – Ed.*]

'He'll say,' predicted Dorothy, 'that they need more space. He'll gradually encroach on your territory here. Why? Because it will give him the right to treat Number Ten as his own, as well as the Cabinet Office. Then you know what he'll do? He'll start getting you out of the way.'

[1] The colloquial term for the Central Policy Review Staff, known for short as the CPRS.

123

I've begun to think that Dorothy is a little crazy. 'Are you suggesting,' I asked, 'that he wants to be Prime Minister?'

'No, no,' she said impatiently. 'He doesn't want the title or the responsibility. He only wants the power. So, having made himself the focus of all information and advice, he'll start encouraging you to go off on long overseas trips. Then he'll have to take a number of decisions in your absence – sorry, recommend them to Cabinet – and you'll have to follow his advice if you're not there. And Cabinet will follow his recommendations because they'll be getting the same recommendations from the Permanent Secretaries.'

This seems a hideous scenario. I really can't believe it. However, I think Humphrey has to be curbed a little and, on reflection, I think that tomorrow I'll give Dorothy her office back.

March 1st

Today I really was firm and decisive. What a feeling! I have established my authority well and truly.

First I summoned Dorothy. I told her, firmly and decisively, that I had changed my mind again! She was to get her office back.

Then I asked Dorothy for her advice about Humphrey. Not that I would necessarily have taken it! But I wanted to know if she was recommending that I sack him.

She shrank from such a response. But she wondered if I might want to clip his wings. And she had a very good suggestion as to how to do it. As well as being Cabinet Secretary, he is Joint Head of the Home Civil Service. He is responsible for the Personnel side – appointments and so on. Pay and Rations are in the hands of Sir Frank Gordon, Permanent Secretary of the Treasury. So the job of the Head of the Civil Service is effectively split between Sir Humphrey and Sir Frank.

Dorothy's suggestion, brilliantly simple, is to take Humphrey's half of the job away from him and give it all to Sir Frank!

The danger of such a move, of course, would be that it might make Sir Frank as powerful as Sir Humphrey is now. Would that be any better for me? Hard to tell. I don't know Sir Frank all that well. But I don't have to commit myself yet. All I had to do today was put the frighteners on Humphrey! And that I certainly achieved!

I sent for him. He arrived while Dorothy was still with me. I began by telling him that I had *definitely* decided to give her her old office.

He started to protest, but I wouldn't let him speak. He asked for a private word about it. Dorothy smiled unpleasantly and said he could speak freely in front of her.

He seemed reluctant. I asked him if he were about to dispute my decision.

'Not once it *is* a decision, no,' he replied carefully.

'Good,' I said, closing the matter. 'Now, I have another important matter to discuss with you.' And I indicated to Dorothy that she should now leave. She smiled sweetly at me, and departed in triumph.

Before I could mention my threat to give some of Humphrey's responsibilities to Sir Frank, he spoke up. And I could hardly believe my ears.

'I think we should think about the Think Tank,' he began. My God, had Dorothy *known* this was coming? Or was it an inspired guess, based on her knowledge of the man? In any event, I realised at that moment that I could no longer risk dismissing her fears as paranoia.

'Can't the Think Tank think about themselves?' I asked casually.

'I'm worried that their lines of communication are unclear,' he said.

I looked surprised. 'How can they be? They report to me.'

'Operationally, yes. But administratively they report to me.'

Humphrey was claiming that this was a serious anomaly. So I pretended to misunderstand him. 'I see,' I said. 'So you want them to report to my office administratively as well.'

He hadn't foreseen that interpretation. 'No, no!' he answered hastily. 'It would be quite wrong to burden your office with administration. No. I suggest they report to me operationally as well.'

I pretended to be open to this new plan. Inwardly I was seething. 'So they should deliver their reports to you?'

Humphrey clearly felt he'd won. 'Yes, well, just for checking and so on,' he replied, leaning back in his chair and relaxing a little. 'To see that you get them in an acceptable form.'

'Humphrey,' I said, smiling my most insincere smile, 'this is *very* generous of you. Won't it mean a lot of extra work?'

He assumed his brave, British, *Cruel Sea* look. 'One must do one's duty,' he grunted.

I decided to put Dorothy's theory to the test. 'But . . . gosh . . .' I said innocently, 'how will you manage for space?'

'I was just coming to that,' he said. 'We shan't be able to accommodate the extra staff in the Cabinet Office. But I think we can probably find a few rooms here in Number Ten.'

She was right again, damn it!

'Here?' I asked.

'Well, there is some space,' he explained.

'In that case,' I asked, 'why did we have to move Dorothy's office?'

He was only fazed for a moment. 'Well . . . if she's staying here we could move a couple of them into her new office. Her old office. Her old new office.'

'Go on,' I said, playing with him.

'Is that agreed?' he enquired.

'No, it's not agreed,' I replied pleasantly, 'but it's fascinating. Anything else you want to propose?'

'Just some overseas visits,' he said, producing some sheets of paper. I nearly fell off my chair. 'You ought to consider them.'

I read the list he gave me. It included a NATO conference, the United Nations Assembly, the EEC Parliament, negotiations in Hong Kong about the future of the colony, Commonwealth meetings in Ottawa, and summits in Peking and Moscow. I marvelled at Dorothy's knowledge of the system and the people who operate it.

But to Humphrey I said: 'If I'm away all this time, won't it mean an awful lot of extra work for you?'

'I think, Prime Minister, that it's very important for you to take your place on the world stage.'

'I agree,' I said enthusiastically. 'But it's asking too much of you. I really must try to lighten your load.'

He eyed me with much suspicion. 'Oh no, there's no need.'

I exuded crocodile sympathy at him. 'Oh, but there *is*, Humphrey, there *is*! I've been thinking too. On top of everything else, you're Head of the Civil Service, aren't you?'

He was evasive. 'Well, the Treasury handle pay and rations.'

'But you are responsible for promotion, appointments and so on. Isn't that a bit much for you?'

He laughed off the notion. 'No, no, not at all. Takes no time at all. A doddle.'

I was enjoying myself. 'The promotion and appointment of six hundred and eighty thousand people is a doddle?'

'Well, I mean, it's delegated,' he explained carefully.

I smiled cheerfully. 'Oh good,' I said. 'So if it's delegated anyway, there'd be no problem in moving it to the Treasury.'

He was getting rattled now. 'Quite impossible,' he replied firmly. 'The Treasury already has far too much power – er, work.'

I was relentless. 'You see,' I said, 'with you doing promotions and them doing pay and rations, the lines of authority are unclear. It's all rather unsatisfactory. A serious anomaly.'

Humphrey saw an opening. His eyes lit up. 'Well, in that case I could take over pay and rations too.'

Nice try, Humphrey, I thought. I shook my head sorrowfully. 'On top of all your other burdens? Plus these you plan to assume? No, Humphrey, I can't allow you to make that sort of sacrifice.'

He was getting desperate. 'It's no sacrifice. No trouble at all!'

For once in his life he was probably telling the truth. 'Humphrey, you are too noble,' I replied. 'But I can see through your arguments.'

He eyed me like a frightened ferret. 'You can?'

'You're trying to sacrifice yourself,' I said gently, 'to save me from worry, aren't you?'

He was nonplussed. He couldn't figure out the safe answer, the answer that would get him what he wanted. 'Oh,' he said. 'Er . . . yes. Um, no,' he went on. 'It's really *no* sacrifice,' he concluded.

I was now bored with my game. So I told him a final no.

But Humphrey needed to know the answers to his other proposals, chiefly those concerning the Think Tank.

'The more I think about it, Humphrey,' I said, 'the more I realise that you already have too much on your plate. In fact, I don't want to keep you here any longer when you must have so much to do in *your* office.'

He couldn't quite believe his ears. Had he been dismissed? I decided to clarify his position. 'You may now leave. If you're needed again in Number Ten, you'll be sent for.'

He stood up, then paused to correct me. 'You mean *when*.'

I smiled apologetically. 'I mean when,' I agreed. He turned towards the door. 'And if,' I added mischievously.

He froze for a moment, then walked to the doors. As he left the room I made sure that he heard me pick up the intercom and ask Bernard to get Sir Frank over to see me as soon as possible.

March 2nd

Sir Frank was tied up yesterday, so I spoke to him on the phone.

'Frank,' I said, 'I just want to sound you out about something. It's about Humphrey. I'm wondering if he's got too much on his plate.'

As I expected, Frank assured me that Humphrey could manage splendidly, is tremendously able, is not overstretched, and has everything perfectly under control with no problem at all.

Then I indicated that the reason I was asking was because of Humphrey's role as Head of the Civil Service. I wondered, I said, if Frank could do some of Humphrey's job.

It will come as no great surprise to any reader that Frank said not one single word more about Humphrey's great ability. Instead he remarked that such a proposal could make a lot of sense.

I asked him to come to meet me tomorrow and, meanwhile, would he note down on paper his precise thoughts as to whether or not Humphrey is overstretched and send them over to me.

An hour later his thoughts arrived, duly noted. These are they:

H M Treasury

Permanent Secretary

March 2

Dear Prime Minister,

When I said that HA was not overstretched, I was of course talking in the sense of total cumulative loading taken globally rather than in respect of certain individual and essentially anomalous responsibilities which are not, logically speaking, consonant or harmonious with the broad spectrum of intermeshing and inseparable functions and could indeed be said to place an excessive and supererogatory burden on the office when considered in relation to the comparatively exiguous advantages of their overall consideration.

Yours ever,

Frank

I read it carefully several times. My conclusion: he *could* do part of Humphrey's job.

March 3rd

Frank came to see me today. But we never had the meeting.

When he arrived. I instructed Bernard to see that Humphrey did not interrupt us. I wanted complete confidentiality.

Bernard said: 'I'll do my best.'

'Your best may not be good enough,' I told him. Oh, my prophetic soul!

I had seen Dorothy first thing this morning. She had reminded me that, technically, Sir Humphrey is supposed to phone us from the Cabinet Office before coming through the green-baize door to Number Ten.

I checked this with Bernard. He was hesitant. 'Perhaps that is right in theory, Prime Minister, but in reality it's just a formality.'

'Good,' I said. 'Humphrey likes formality.'

Bernard agreed, but with reluctance. 'Yes, Prime Minister, but as they say . . . it is a custom more honoured in the breach than in the observance.'

I really am fed up with Bernard, Humphrey, Frank, the lot of them. Why must they all express themselves in such a pompous and roundabout manner? All this rot about customs being honoured in the breach . . . Why do they distort and destroy the most beautiful language in the world, the language of Shakespeare? [*Hacker was apparently unaware that Bernard was quoting Shakespeare:* Hamlet, *Act I, Scene iv – Ed.*]

SIR BERNARD WOOLLEY RECALLS:[1]
That day was a turning-point in my life and my career. I had never realised that my new post as Principal Private Secretary to the Prime Minister gave me the opportunity to assert my strength and independence from my old boss. It came as a revelation, a blinding flash, the road to Damascus!

I had just shown Sir Frank Gordon into the Cabinet Room and returned to the Private Office.

I dialled Humphrey's number on the phone.

I heard Humphrey's voice, loud and clear. 'Yes?'

'Ah, Sir Humphrey,' I said.

'Yes,' he said again, and I realised that the reason his voice was so loud and clear was because it was right behind me. He had entered the room.

'Bernard here,' I said stupidly. Well, I was flustered.

'So I see,' he replied. I replaced the receiver.

'Just the person I wanted to talk to,' I said, still very worried by his close proximity to Mr Hacker's secret meeting.

'Well here I am, in person. Even better,' he said.

'Yes and no,' I said. I was chattering on meaninglessly, saying that I wanted to have a word with him, which was why I was telephoning him, why else? And finally I managed to say that the Prime Minister had asked me to

[1] In conversation with the Editors.

remind him that it might be more convenient if he were to phone through from the Cabinet Office before popping over to see us in Number Ten.

Humphrey assured me that it was not inconvenient.

'Yes it is,' I said.

'No it's not,' he said.

And, much too firmly, I said: 'Yes *it is*!'

He stared at me. Then, suddenly very cool, he asked if the PM was busy.

I had to say that he was. Humphrey wanted to know with what. I tried being vague, and muttered that he was doing his paperwork. Humphrey really frightened me, you know, in those days.

Humphrey said that if it was only paperwork he could pop in and have a word with the PM. I was forced to admit that the PM was doing his paperwork *with* somebody.

Sir Humphrey eyed me carefully. It was clear to him that I was being less than frank with him, and perhaps completely mendacious. 'You mean, he's having a meeting?' I nodded. '*With whom, Bernard*?' he rasped.

I think he knew already. It's been in the air for two days now. No sooner had I admitted that the PM was meeting the Permanent Secretary of the Treasury than Sir Humphrey was through the doors into the Cabinet Room like a ferret up a pair of trousers. I couldn't possibly have stopped him – my reflexes just weren't quick enough.

[Hacker's diary continues – Ed.]

However, immediately I started to talk seriously to Sir Frank Gordon, Humphrey barged in. I asked him what he wanted. I was not welcoming. He said he was checking to see if he could be of service. I asked him if Bernard had told him I was in a meeting. Bernard nodded vigorously in the open doorway. Humphrey admitted this was so.

'So what do you want?' I asked impatiently.

He clearly had nothing to say to me. He was just checking up on me. 'Well,' he said, 'since it was a meeting with one of my professional colleagues, I thought – *hello*, Frank – that I might have a contribution to make.'

He smiled effusively at Frank who, I noticed, hardly smiled back.

'I see,' I said. 'No, thank you.'

I waited for him to leave. He didn't move.

'Thank you,' I said, quite clearly.

'Thank *you*, Prime Minister,' he replied, and still didn't move a muscle. He just stood at the door, waiting, listening, defying us to divest him of any of his responsibilities.

'Humphrey,' I said, feeling the irritation rising in me, 'this is a private meeting.'

'Ah,' he said. 'Shall I shut the door?'

'Yes please,' I said. Imagine my amazement when he turned and shut the door from his side. 'No, Humphrey, from the *other side* please.'

He was angry and defiant. 'May I ask why?'

Meanwhile Frank was getting distinctly nervous. He rose and offered to leave. I told him to sit down, and Humphrey to leave.

Humphrey seemed prepared to pretend that he was the village idiot rather than leave. 'In what sense of the word do you mean leave?' he asked, as if it were a sensible question.

I shouted at him to get out. I told Frank to go as well – I was now too upset and angry to continue a rational conversation with him.

Bernard was creeping away. I shouted at him too, telling him to come back. We were alone together.

I asked him, 'Why did you allow Humphrey in when I explicitly told you not to?'

'I couldn't stop him,' he replied with a helpless shrug.

'Why not?'

'He's bigger than me.'

'Then,' I said with grim determination, 'he must be confined to the Cabinet Office.'

'How?' he asked.

It was obvious. 'Lock the connecting door,' I said.

'But he has a key,' whimpered Bernard.

'Then take his key away from him,' I said.

Bernard couldn't believe his ears. 'Take his key away from him?' he asked incredulously.

'Take his key away from him,' I repeated.

'*You* take his key away from him!' said Bernard.

I've never heard such impertinence and open defiance. '*What*?' I exclaimed.

Bernard took a deep breath, stopped, and tried again. 'I'm sorry, Prime Minister, but I don't think it's within my power.'

Bernard is very academic and well educated, but so inhibited and constricted and highly trained to do things the way they have always been done, that sometimes he can't see the wood for the trees.

'I'm giving you the power,' I explained. 'I'm authorising you.'

He appeared to be on the verge of a complete crack-up. 'But . . . I don't know if I . . . I mean . . . crikey. He'll go completely potty.'

I smiled at Bernard. And he smiled back at me. Then his smile faded and he licked his lips nervously. He still didn't quite have the courage, I could see. 'It's up to you, Bernard,' I said gently.

'Yes, but . . .'

'Freedom, Bernard,' I said softly.

'Yes, but . . .'

'I'm giving you the power, Bernard,' I reminded him gently.

'Yes, but . . .'

'You, alone, will have access to the Prime Minister,' I encouraged him cunningly.

But even that didn't quite convince him.

'But . . . but . . .' He was unable to formulate his objections. His whole world was being turned upside down.

'But me no buts, Bernard. Shakespeare.' I thought it was time for me to demonstrate a little learning.

But a little learning is a dangerous thing. Bernard immediately sought refuge in useless and irrelevant pedantry. 'No, Prime Minister, "but me no buts" is a nineteenth-century quotation, circa 1820. Mrs Centlivre used the phrase in 1708, I believe, but it was Scott's employment of it in *The Antiquary* which popularised it.'

I thanked Bernard, and asked if we could stick to the point. He misunderstood me – wilfully, I think – in a further attempt to evade the issue of Sir Humphrey's access.

'Yes – the point *is*, Prime Minister, that I think you are confusing Mrs Centlivre with Old Capulet in *Romeo and Juliet, Act III, Scene v* when *he* said, 'Thank me no thankings, nor proud me no prouds.'

I thanked Bernard again, and told him to say that to Sir Humphrey.

He looked blank. 'Say what?'

'Proud me no prouds, Sir Humphrey.'

'Yes, Prime Minister.' He was not looking at all happy. 'Um . . . there's only one problem: if I'm to deprive him of his key, what reason can I possibly give?'

I lost my temper. He's a born Civil Servant – the man can only see problems. But with every problem there's also an *opportunity*. 'For God's sake, Bernard,' I snapped. 'Find a reason!'

He retreated. 'Yes, Prime Minister. Thank you, Prime Minister.'

I beamed at him over the top of my glasses. 'Thank me no thankings, Bernard,' I said.

[*Dorothy Wainwright's memoirs*, The Prime Minister's Ear, *were a bestseller two or three years after the event described here. In this extract we see, from her point of view, what happened later that day when Bernard Woolley exercised the authority which Hacker had just given him – Ed.*]

I was just contemplating my hoped-for move back into my old office, when I heard Bernard's raised voice coming out of the Private Office on the other side of the lobby. 'I said *no*, Sir Humphrey,' he said – and then he said it again.

Intrigued, I popped in on the Private Office. Bernard was on the phone. His face was pink and he looked very agitated. 'I *did* say no,' he was saying. 'The Prime Minister is busy.'

Sir Humphrey, at the other end of the phone, must have offered to come to see Bernard because Bernard then said: 'I'm busy too.'

There seemed to be some abuse crackling down the line for a moment. Then Bernard drew himself up to his full five foot ten and a half, took a deep breath and said: 'Sir Humphrey, you may not come through. You do not have permission.'

Humphrey shouted, 'I'm coming anyway' – *that* could be heard across the room – and slammed down his phone. Bernard rang off and sank into his chair, half delighted, half appalled. He looked at me with a dazed smile. 'He couldn't believe his ears,' he said with delight.

'What did he say?'

'That he's coming anyway.'

'Are you feeling strong enough?' I asked with sympathy.

Bernard sat back and relaxed. 'It's all right, he can't come. I instructed Security to take the key from his office.'

At that moment the door flew open. Sir Humphrey strode in. He was angrier than I've ever seen him. There literally was steam coming out of his ears. [*Literally, there could not have been – Ed.*]

Bernard leapt to his feet. 'My God!'

'No, Bernard,' snarled Humphrey, 'it's just your boss.'

[*Technically this description may have been correrct, as Sir Humphrey Appleby was Head of the Home Civil Service. However, since moving to Number Ten Bernard Woolley no longer reported to Sir Humphrey. As the Principal Private Secretary to the Prime Minister he now had virtually as much power and influence as the Cabinet Secretary – hence the row – Ed.*]

'How did you get through a solid door?' asked Bernard.

'Where has my key gone?' asked Sir Humphrey.

'You must have a spare!' deduced Bernard.

'Where is my *key*?' snarled Sir Humphrey.

Bernard took his courage in both hands. 'I was instructed by the Prime Minister to have it removed.'

I thought I should come to Bernard's rescue. 'That's quite correct,' I added.

Humphrey turned viciously. 'Would you mind, *dear lady*?' he snarled. 'This has nothing to do with you.' He turned back to Bernard. 'The Prime Minister does not have it in his power to deprive me of my key.'

'It's his house,' said Bernard bravely.

'It's a government building,' said Sir Humphrey.

Bernard didn't panic or lose his nerve. 'I believe it is the PM's decision as to who comes into his house. After all, I don't give my mother-in-law the key to my house.'

I almost laughed out loud. The analogy caused Humphrey to look as though he might explode with rage.

'I'm not the PM's mother-in-law, Bernard.'

Bernard didn't reply. He didn't need to. He simply stood there in silence. After a moment Humphrey walked to the window and did some quiet slow deep breathing to calm himself down. Then he turned back to Bernard with a crocodile smile.

'Look, Bernard, I don't want us to fall out over this. It's so petty of the Prime Minister. You and I have to work together for some years yet. Prime Ministers come and go – whereas your career prospects depend on those who have power over promotions and appointments on a long-term basis.'

'Let's stick to the point,' I said abrasively, and Humphrey flashed another vicious look in my direction. If looks could kill!

Bernard, to his great credit, *did* stick to the point. 'I must insist that you tell me how you came in.'

Sir Humphrey immediately pursed his lips. It was his familiar *my lips are sealed* look.

'You must have a personal key,' said Bernard. Humphrey stayed silent. 'Are you telling me that you haven't?' Bernard asked.

Humphrey half-smiled. 'I'm not telling you that I haven't. I'm simply not telling you that I have.'

Bernard held out his hand. 'Hand it over!'

Humphrey stared at Bernard for a few moments, then turned on his heel and walked out. Bernard sat down abruptly and hyperventilated for a bit. I told him he'd done well.

He nodded. Then he reached for one of his phones. He called Security, told them to change the locks on the door connecting the Cabinet Office to the house, and told them to bring *all* the keys to him.

[*Later on the same day, 3 March, there took place the weekly meeting of the Permanent Secretaries in Sir Humphrey Appleby's office. A most instructive note was recently found in Sir Frank Gordon's private diary, relating to a brief conversational exchange that happened informally after the meeting – Ed.*]

On my way out Humphrey asked me about my meeting with the PM. Didn't tell him that it shuddered to a halt after Humphrey's unwelcome intrusion. Instead, told him it was v. successful.

He asked me if any particular subject came up. I asked him if there were any particular subjects he was interested in. H asked me if the PM raised the issue of Service appointments, or if the PM foreshadowed any redistribution of responsibility. Since nothing was discussed by the PM I merely hinted that the topics may have cropped up, and that we had had a wide-ranging discussion.

Interestingly, he asked if it had moved towards any conclusion. He must be v. worried. I said that there were arguments on both sides, perhaps tending slightly one way more than the other way, but certainly nothing for *me* to worry about.

[*Hacker's diary continues – Ed.*]

March 6th

My plan was a total success. Humphrey knows his place at last. As I suggested to Dorothy only a day or two ago, it was time to clip Humphrey's wings. [*Alert readers may recall that, in an earlier entry in this diary, Hacker acknowledged that the suggestion to clip Appleby's wings came from Dorothy Wainwright – Ed.*]

Apparently Bernard changed the locks on the door between Number Ten and the Cabinet Office, so that Humphrey *had* to seek permission. When Humphrey phoned for permission to come through this morning, Bernard denied it.

Shortly afterwards, he and Dorothy heard thumps and bangings on the other side, accompanied by shouts of suppressed frenzy: 'Open the door! Open the door!'

Humphrey then ran out of the front door of the Cabinet Office into Whitehall, round the corner, and up Downing Street to Number Ten. The two policemen wouldn't let him in because he had no appointment card and no Security pass – only a Cabinet Office Security pass.

Bernard had instituted new security rules last week, apparently on Humphrey's own instructions: *no one* may now be admitted unless they have the Number Ten pass or are on the daily list.

The policeman knows Humphrey well, of course, and apparently buzzed through to the Private Office for permission. But by then Bernard and Dorothy had come into the Cabinet Room for a meeting with me.

Humphrey must have run back into his office, jumped out of the window into the garden of Number Ten, run across the lawn and the flower beds and clambered up the wall cat-burglar style to the balcony outside the Cabinet Room.

Certainly the first I knew of all this was when I saw a muddy and dishevelled Sir Humphrey balanced precariously outside the French windows. I smiled and waved at him. He grasped the handle of the window and tried to open it – and immediately we were absolutely deafened by bells and sirens. A moment later uniformed police and dogs and plain-clothes detectives rushed into the Cabinet Room.

We all shouted above the din that we were okay, and that we didn't need protecting from the Cabinet Secretary, however angry he was or however hurt his feelings.

The sirens were switched off.

Sir Humphrey stepped forward and handed me a letter, in his own handwriting.

'Humphrey,' I said, 'what's this?'

He was speechless, fuming, fighting back tears, trying to retain his dignity. He couldn't speak – he just indicated the piece of paper. I read it.

Cabinet Office

Dear Prime Minister,

I must express in the strongest possible terms my profound opposition to the newly instituted practice which imposes severe and intolerable restrictions on the ingress and egress of senior members of the hierarchy and will, in all probability, should the current deplorable innovation be perpetuated, precipitate a progressive constriction of the channels of communication, culminating in a condition of organisational atrophy and administrative paralysis which will render effectively impossible the coherent and co-ordinated discharge of the function of government within Her Majesty's United Kingdom of Great Britain and Northern Ireland.

Your obedient and humble servant,

Humphrey Appleby

I read it carefully. Then I looked up at Humphrey.

'You mean you've lost your key?' I asked.

'Prime Minister,' he said desperately, 'I must insist on having a new one.'

I'm ashamed to say I played games with him. 'In due course, Humphrey,' I replied. 'At the appropriate juncture. In the fullness of time. Meanwhile, we have another decision to take. A more urgent one. About Dorothy's office.'

'Quite!' said Dorothy, aggressively.

Humphrey tried to brush this aside, as he always does. But I wouldn't let him. 'No, Humphrey,' I explained with great patience, 'it has to be resolved now. One way or the other. Like the question of your key, really.'

I could see from his face that the penny had finally dropped. While he wrestled with himself, I tried to give him a face-saving opening. 'I was wondering what your views were. They are, in a sense, the key to our problem. What do you think?'

He gave me what he hoped would seem like a considered opinion and a dignified compromise. 'I think – on reflection – that Mrs Wainwright *does* need to be nearer this room,' he said.

We were all relieved. 'So we'll move her back, shall we?' He nodded. 'At once?' He nodded again.

I told Bernard to give him the new key, I thanked him for his help and co-operation, and dismissed them all.

Later today, Bernard tells me, Sir Humphrey rang to ask if he could see me privately. I said 'Of course!' Bernard magnanimously invited him over. Humphrey entered my study deferentially, and asked whether the other matter was resolved.

Other matter? I couldn't think what he meant.

He cleared his throat. 'May I, er, enquire who is to be the Head of the Home Civil Service?'

'You – perhaps,' I said. He smiled. 'Or, maybe, Sir Frank,' I added. His smile faded. 'Or maybe . . . share it like now. I haven't decided yet. But whatever happens, it's my decision, isn't it, Humphrey?'

'Yes Prime Minister,' he replied, a sadder but wiser man.

5
A Real Partnership

March 9th

I staggered upstairs to the flat for lunch today. Fortunately Annie was home. She took one look at me and asked me if it had been a bad Cabinet.

'Got anything for getting blood off carpets?' I groaned as I slumped into my chintz flowered armchair with a deep sigh. [*We presume that it was not the armchair which was the possessor of the deep sigh – Ed.*]

'Whose blood?' asked Annie, as she picked up the decanter.

'Everyone's,' I told her miserably.

She asked me if I wanted a small scotch or a double. I settled for a triple.

The nub of my depression was a Treasury Paper that had just been presented to us. The financial crisis is much worse than any of us thought. No one saw it coming – least of all me – except one person: my predecessor, the last Prime Minister. No wonder he resigned unexpectedly!

Annie wasn't a bit surprised. 'I always thought,' she mused, 'that it was strange that he resigned to make way for an older man.'

I was slightly put out. 'I'm not older than him,' I said.

'Oh.' She gazed at me with sympathy. 'Maybe you just look it.'

I do *now*, I thought, that's for certain! I really don't know what I'm going to do about all the cuts that have got to be made in the Cabinet's spending plans. They weren't at all prepared for this. They all have ambitious development ideas, because I asked for them.

We heard the sound of leaden footsteps. Bernard appeared at the living-room door. Annie offered him a Scotch.

'Triple, please,' he replied bleakly.

Annie nodded sympathetically, and wisely kept silent.

'Bernard,' I said, 'Humphrey should have warned me this was coming.'

He sat on the sofa and sipped his drink. 'I don't think Sir Humphrey understands economics, Prime Minister – he did read classics, you know.'

'Well, what about Sir Frank? He's head of the Treasury.'

Bernard shook his head. 'I'm afraid he's at an even greater disadvantage in understanding economics, Prime Minister. He's an economist.'

Annie joined us, with a Perrier. 'Jim, if there's an economic crisis, can't the Cabinet see there've got to be cuts?'

'They can see that the other departments have got to make cuts. Not theirs.'

'That's rather selfish,' she remarked. Annie still seems to think that the Cabinet is full of team spirit. It's not. They're in a constant popularity contest against each other. And the quickest way to become popular is to spend money. Public money. This makes them popular with their Department, the Party, the House and the press. Cutting spending makes everyone unpopular. Annie didn't see why. Bernard tried to explain, but he rabbited on for ages in a totally incomprehensible way about hats, making everything as clear as mud.

SIR BERNARD WOOLLEY RECALLS:[1]
My explanation was crystal clear, as it happens. Mrs Hacker seemed to feel, as I remember, that the public would be *pleased* if spending were cut, because the public are the taxpayers. I explained that it was and is a question of hats. The voter, wearing his voter's hat, is always frightfully pleased when the Government pays for something because he thinks it's free! He doesn't realise that, wearing his taxpayer's hat, he's paying for what he's receiving in his voter's hat. And the Cabinet Ministers, wearing their Head-of-a-Department hats, are competing with themselves because, wearing their member-of-the-Government hats, they have to pull economic success out of the hat and yet allow the taxpayer, wearing his voter's hat, to think that the Government is spending someone else's money when it's *not*, it's spending *theirs*, and so they have to try and keep this under their hat.

[Hacker's diary continues – Ed.]

Annie asked me, 'Presumably you encouraged all those spending plans because you wanted to be popular?'

Yes and no was the only possible answer. Of course I want to be popular – nothing wrong with that, that's how you get elected, being popular is what democracy's all about. But I also thought we could afford it. I didn't know, and nobody had told me, of these looming

---

[1] In conversation with the editors.

problems with inflation, the sterling crisis and low productivity.

Annie asked what I was doing about it. 'Did you order a clamp-down this morning?'

'I can't order anything, Annie,' I explained miserably.

She didn't understand. 'He's only the Prime Minister, Mrs Hacker,' said Bernard. 'He doesn't even have a department of his own to clamp down on.'

Annie thought – still thinks, for all I know – that the Prime Minister is completely in charge. It's a fallacy. A leader can only lead by consent.

'So who is in charge, if you're not?' asked Annie, rather perplexed.

I was perplexed by her question. There didn't seem to be an answer. I thought for a bit. 'Nobody really,' I said finally.

'Is that good?' She was even more perplexed.

'It must be,' I replied hopelessly. 'That's what democracy is all about.'

'It's made Britain what she is today,' added Bernard with sincerity.

Annie contemplated what she'd just been told. 'So your Cabinet are in control, not you.'

She'd got completely the wrong end of the stick! 'No!' I said. 'Think back, Annie! I wasn't in control when I was a Minister, was I?'

'No,' she said, 'but I thought that was just you.'

Annie, like the press and the media, keeps harping on about 'control'. But the point about government is that no one has control. Lots of people have the power to stop something happening – but almost nobody has the power to *make* anything happen. We have a system of government with the engine of a lawn-mower and the brakes of a Rolls-Royce.

Of course I'd never say any of this in public. The electorate would interpret this as defeatism. It's not, though! It's the truth! And I am going to fight it. [*We do not believe that Hacker wanted his readers to believe that he intended to fight the truth – Ed.*]

We began talking about the further implications of this financial mess. Tomorrow I've got a deputation of backbench MPs coming to see me, about a pay rise I promised them. Naturally I'll have to tell them they can't have it now. They'll be furious. They'll say:

1. That I can't go back on a promise.
2. That they are shamefully underpaid.
3. That it's all very well for me because I get fifty thousand quid a year.
4. That it's not the money, it's the principle of the thing.

5. That it's not for them personally.
6. That I am striking a blow against the very foundations of Parliamentary democracy.

How do I know they'll say all that? Because that's what I said when I was a backbencher.

The only way to reply is to lie. I shall say:

1. That I sympathise deeply – which I don't!
2. That they certainly deserve the money – which isn't true!
3. That I shall make it my number one priority when the crisis has passed – which I shan't!
4. And that if MPs vote themselves a whacking great pay rise and then tell everyone else there's no money for pay rises, it doesn't do wonders for the dignity of Parliament – which it certainly doesn't!

I shall forbear to add that when anyone says, 'It's not the money, it's the principle,' they *mean* it's the money!

I explained this all to Annie. To my surprise she sympathised with them. 'Aren't MPs underpaid, in fact?'

I was astonished. Underpaid? Backbench MPs? I explained to Annie that being an MP is a vast, subsidised ego trip. It's a job that needs no qualifications, that has no compulsory hours of work, no performance standards, and provides a warm room, a telephone and subsidised meals to a bunch of self-important windbags and busybodies who suddenly find people taking them seriously because they've got the letters MP after their names. How *can* they be underpaid when there's about two hundred applicants for every vacancy? You could fill every seat twenty times over even if they had to pay to do the job.

'But you were a backbench MP only five years ago,' said Annie.

'I was an exception,' I explained. 'I was the cream. That's why I rose to the top.'

Annie wanted to know if I thought my answers would shut them up. I don't think so. They never shut me up. 'But,' I said to her with a shrug, 'there's no choice. The country just won't accept pay rises for MPs when we're cutting back on nurses and teachers.'

'Nurses and teachers?' Annie looked worried. 'That's much more serious, isn't it?'

Sometimes I think Annie has learned nothing about politics. 'No, Annie,' I said wearily, 'much *less* serious. Nurses and teachers can't vote against me till the next election – backbenchers can vote against me at ten o'clock tonight.'

March 10th

As I predicted, I had a very stormy meeting with my backbenchers. They said all the things I said they'd say and I said all the things I said I'd say, and they said that I should remember that I wouldn't be able to say anything to anyone if I lost the support of my own backbenchers.

I called Humphrey in afterwards. I told him that if I'd had some notice I might have softened them up a bit in advance.

He agreed that the lack of notice was regrettable.

Which meant that he hadn't taken my point. 'It's up to you, Humphrey,' I emphasised. 'You're Secretary of the Cabinet. You must insist we get papers circulated earlier.'

Humphrey hung his head. 'Alas! There are grave problems about circulating papers before they are written.'

So if the papers weren't written, *why* weren't they written? I scowled at Humphrey. 'Surely the Treasury must have seen this coming?'

'Prime Minister,' replied Sir Humphrey with a shrug, 'I am not Permanent Secretary of the Treasury. You must ask Sir Frank.'

'What would he say?' I asked.

Humphrey shrugged again. 'It is not for a humble mortal like me to guess at the complex and elevated deliberations of the mighty. But in general I think Sir Frank believes that if the Treasury knows something has to be done, the Cabinet should not have too much time to think about it.'

I was furious. 'But that's an outrageous view.'

'Yes,' he said with a smile, 'it's known as Treasury policy.'

'Suppose,' I asked, 'that the Cabinet have questions to ask?'

'I think that Sir Frank's view,' said Humphrey carefully, 'is that on the rare occasions when the Treasury understands the questions, the Cabinet does not understand the answers.'

I was getting furiouser and furiouser. 'Do you support this?' I asked bluntly.

Humphrey looked truly amazed. 'I, Prime Minister? I merely try to carry out the wishes of the Prime Minister and the Cabinet.'

I instructed Humphrey that it is my wish that, in future, all papers are circulated at least forty-eight hours before Cabinet meetings. I told him to tell Sir Frank.

Humphrey said he would do so with pleasure, and that he would seek an audience with him at once. He left.

The regal phraseology did not escape me. He clearly thinks Frank is getting too big for his boots. Unless . . . he is still worrying about my threat last week to make Sir Frank head of the Home Civil Service. Of course! That's why he's so disloyal to Frank at the moment.

I wonder if I should put him out of his misery. Do I gain anything by keeping them both in suspense? Yes, I gain an anxious and co-operative Cabinet Secretary.

[*Later that day Sir Humphrey Appleby met Sir Frank Gordon, Permanent Secretary of the Treasury, at the Reform Club in Pall Mall. Sir Humphrey made a note about the meeting in his private diary – Ed.*]

Frank and I discussed the late arrival of Treasury papers for Cabinet this week, and the short notice of the information concerning the economic crisis.

Frank expressed a hope that I had explained that the short notice was due to America's sudden change of policy over interest rates. I assured Frank that I defended him gallantly, leaving the Prime Minister in no doubt as to the real cause of the rush.

Frank was delighted with this reply. He is less subtle than I would have expected.

He was concerned that we do not lose the PM's goodwill at this time. With the financial crisis, we shall obviously have to bring in some form of pay restraint. Unfortunately, the MPs are being denied the pay rise they have been expecting just at the moment that Frank is due to bring forward the proposed Civil Service pay rise.

This is indeed awkward. Obviously one is not interested in the pay rise for oneself. The last thing Permanent Secretaries care about is the money. We could all have made a fortune if we'd gone into industry. Money is money, and service is service.

Nevertheless, Frank and I are both in full agreement that we owe it to our junior colleagues to do everything we can for them.

Ironically, trying to help them will involve raising our own salaries – about which we don't care at all – and then we get criticised for feathering our own nests. Still, that is just another cross we have to bear.

[*This passage from Sir Humphrey's diary is most intriguing. Was he really able to convince himself that in pushing for a large Civil Service pay rise, in which he and Sir Frank would get the largest cash sum, he was acting altruistically? Or was he so cautious that everything he wrote, even for his private diary, could withstand scrutiny if stolen and leaked? – Ed.*]

I urged Frank to put our pay proposal in fast, before any pay restraint begins. It is also clear that it must go in the night before next Thursday's Cabinet – if Ministers have two days to spend talking about it to back-benchers and political advisers they'll come up with all sorts of objections.

Frank was worried about bouncing Cabinet two weeks running. I assured him that there was no alternative.

Frank then suggested that it would be better if the proposal came from both of us. I can see why – there is safety in numbers. However, he gave as his reasons that we are effectively joint heads of the Civil Service.

Needless to say, this is not a view that I accept. The Cabinet Secretary is the *de jure* head of the Service. Frank chooses to believe that, as he looks after the financial side and I look after the Establishment side, we are both *de facto* heads of the Service.

He seemed eager to pursue this discussion, as if to prove a point. I simply avoided it by informing him that, in my view, I must remain aloof and judicial on the matter of Civil Service pay. I told him that it would be fatal, for the Service, if I lost the PM's confidence. [*Fatal for Sir Humphrey too, as he was well aware – Ed.*]

I encouraged Frank to make the running and assured him that when the time was ripe I would come down on his side.

Frank had another worry, this time quite legitimate. Quite rightly, he does not want the Cabinet to adjudicate on the claim.

We decided that it should be referred to an impartial committee, as usual. The question was: who should chair it? We agreed that Arnold[1] should be on it, but it seems improbable that the Cabinet will approve an ex-Civil Servant as an impartial chairman of a committee to decide upon Civil Service pay.

I suggested Professor Welsh. Frank has heard that he is a silly old buffer. Be that as it may, Welsh has asked me to put his name forward as the next chairman of the University Grants Committee. So he will understand what's required of him.

Frank agreed that Professor Welsh would be an excellent choice.
[*Appleby Papers BA/281/282*]

[*Hacker's diary continues – Ed.*]

March 15th

Only five days have elapsed since I instructed Humphrey to ensure that no more papers were bounced through Cabinet. On that very day we decided that MPs were not going to get their pay rise, and that the Treasury would be cancelling half our spending plans.

But what did I find on my desk today? A plan for a *Civil Service* pay rise!

Humphrey has had the temerity to suggest that because spending cuts mean a lot of extra work for the Civil Service, they deserve a pay rise for coping with them.

Ridiculous! And even if that were legitimate, how dare he try to get it through Cabinet tomorrow, after I told him to make sure that all Cabinet papers come through forty-eight hours in advance?

Humphrey claimed it was not his fault. 'Prime Minister, it is not for me to speak for Sir Frank.'

[1] Sir Arnold Robinson, the retired Cabinet Secretary.

'Speak for yourself,' I retorted. 'You're Cabinet Secretary. You're also Head of the Civil Service.'

'Am I?' Humphrey smiled. 'How gratifying.'

'At the moment,' I said significantly, regretting my momentary slip of the tongue.

'As Cabinet Secretary,' said Humphrey, 'I am most eager to reduce public spending, but as Head of the Civil Service I am responsible for the very real problems that will arise administratively if a pay rise does not come through soon. This is a difficult matter for me because I'm wearing two hats.'

'Isn't that rather awkward?' I enquired.

'Not if one is in two minds,' he replied smoothly.

'Or has two faces,' intervened Bernard, and I could see he instantly regretted it.

'Perhaps I should relieve you of one of them,' I suggested.

Humphrey panicked. 'Oh, no. No. I'm very happy with both of them.'

'Faces?' I asked with amusement.

'Hats,' he snapped.

'But,' I reminded him, 'you said you have very real problems.'

'The problem is low morale, which inevitably leads to the danger of a strike. Think of the effect of a strike of the computer men on the social services. Furthermore, we are already experiencing difficulties of recruitment.'

This was news to me. 'I thought you had about ten applicants for every place.'

'Yes,' he acknowledged with reluctance, 'but we are getting applicants of a very low quality, with very few first-class degrees. Most of them have lower seconds.'

Ridiculous intellectual snobbery! 'I got a third,' I remarked.

Humphrey hesitated, aware that he'd been less than tactful. Bernard tried to cover for him. 'A third's all right for a Prime Minister, but Sir Humphrey's talking about Civil Servants.'

Humphrey stuck to his guns. 'Non-cooperation by the Civil Service Unions brings government to a standstill.' Presuming that it was previously moving, I suppose. 'The FDA[1] has a huge membership now.'

'Including yourself?' I asked.

Humphrey assured me that even though he is a member of the union he will always cooperate with me to the same extent as usual.

[1] The First Division Association, the Union that represents the top Civil Servants in Whitehall.

Which is roughly what I'm complaining about.

I reiterated to him that I cannot possibly get this through, *even if I want to*. With the backbench revolt looming over the cuts, MPs will never okay a pay rise for the Civil Service. And the Cabinet is bound to resist.

Humphrey saw the point quickly. He suggested that we merely ask for Cabinet to agree, in principle, to look at the application. Then the matter could be put before an independent group of assessors to consider the claim in detail.

This seems a reasonable compromise. The only thing that puzzles me about it is that Humphrey's suggestion for chairman is Professor Welsh. I've heard he's a silly old buffer!

[*The Cabinet, the following day, did agree to look at the matter in principle, but made no other commitments. There the matter rested until the pay claim was worked out in detail. This was done in considerable haste, and only eleven days later the following letter was sent by Sir Frank Gordon to Sir Humphrey Appleby. Sir Frank was slightly less careful than Sir Humphrey about what he was prepared to put in writing. We found this personal, handwritten note in the Cabinet Office ourselves. Presumably it was carefully preserved by Sir Humphrey Appleby in case it should prove useful in his fight with Sir Frank for control of the Service. In the event, it was never shown to Hacker, but it reveals much about the way Civil Service pay claims were prepared in the late twentieth century. The complete note is reprinted opposite. – Ed.*]

H M Treasury

Permanent Secretary

2?/111

Dear Humpy,

I enclose the working papers. I'm sure that you will agree that, in all fairness, the most senior grades of the service who really bear the heat of the battle should receive the greatest increase.

This means that there is a simple

H.M. Treasury
March 27th

Dear Humphrey,

I enclose the working papers. I'm sure that you will agree that, in all fairness, the most senior grades of the service who really bear the heat of the battle should receive the greatest increase.

This means that there is a significant percentage increase for Under Secretaries, Deputy Secretaries, Permanent Secretaries, and those two jobs which bear the greatest burden of all.[1] It comes to about 43%, alas!

The enclosed papers are not for submission. The submission papers, which follow shortly, go up to Appendix Q, so there is little chance that the Cabinet will read them all. The one-page summary for the Cabinet[2] is more or less the same as last time. It is headed 'Comparable Jobs in Industry', and is also enclosed.

You will recognise that the salary comparisons are based on directors of BP and IBM. I think that there is no risk of their being challenged because, in line with our usual custom and practice, we do not mention them by name. They are referred to as 'typical industrial firms'.

Then we take our own new examples of increase from the lowest point of the incremental scale,
e.g.: £3.50 a week rise for a Messenger
£4.20 a week rise for a Registry Clerk
£8.20 a week rise for a Scientific Officer

For the most senior grade[3] in the Service it would be a rise of £26,000 per annum. It hardly seems necessary to mention that in the Janet and John Bit, firstly because it can be calculated by the Cabinet Members themselves should they desire to do so, and secondly because it only applies to the two top jobs mentioned above. If there is criticism it is, as we said, just another cross we have to bear.

Sincerely,
FG

[*Sir Humphrey sent a carefully worded reply – Ed.*]

---

[1] The two jobs being Cabinet Secretary and Permanent Secretary of the Treasury, which, coincidentally, were held by the sender and the recipient of this letter.
[2] Known in the Civil Service as 'The Janet and John Bit'.
[3] Sir Frank and Sir Humphrey only.

70 WHITEHALL, LONDON SW1A 2AS

From the Secretary of the Cabinet and Head of the Home Civil Service

March 27th

Dear Frank,

      I was glad to hear of your proposals for the Civil Service pay claim. Thank you for keeping me informed.

      Thank you also for not showing me the full details. It would be most improper if I had full knowledge, since pay is within your purview. Do you think we should volunteer to forego some of the pay rise ourselves? And you have not mentioned pensions.

      Are you quite sure that the Cabinet will not want to go through the proposals in much greater detail than the summary?

      As ever,

[Sir Frank replied to Sir Humphrey – Ed.]

March 27th

Dear Humphrey,

If our own pay rises are brought up we can volunteer to *defer* the rise. And get it back later, when the fuss has died down.

I have not mentioned pensions. I find it is better not to, ever since we got the inflation indexing through. It creates animosity, confuses things, and pensions are so difficult to put a real value on.

I see no likelihood of Cabinet Ministers going into this matter more deeply. Ministers are briefed by their own officials, and we all know where their loyalties lie.

Frank.

[*And Sir Humphrey replied to Sir Frank – Ed.*]

March 28th

Dear Frank,

I shall put the matter on the agenda last item before lunch. The agenda is full, so with careful management there will only be about five minutes left.

So if should all be plain sailing, but for the vigorous scrutiny of Professor Welsh!

As ever,
H.A.

[*Hacker's diary continues – Ed.*]

March 29th

I had a most interesting phone call from Dorothy Wainwright this morning. I had asked her to do a paper on the Civil Service pay claim. She wanted to give me an immediate response.

I asked her what her answer was.

'I haven't an answer, more a series of questions,' she told me. 'Not for you, but for Humphrey. The claim is self-serving and inappropriate, and significant for the questions it leaves unanswered. But please treat my questions as highly confidential, or else you'll never catch Humphrey out.'

I've locked the list of questions in my desk and taken the key. So I can't list them here, but I shall come back to this matter tomorrow.

[*Fortunately for Sir Humphrey Appleby, this phone call was overheard by Bernard Woolley. He was not eavesdropping. It is the Principal Private Secretary's duty to listen in on all telephone calls to or from the Prime Minister, in order to minute and witness what was said, to give the Prime Minister an aide mémoire, and to protect the Prime Minister against subsequent misrepresentation. In this instance, Dorothy Wainwright made a tactical error in not calling on Mr*

149

Hacker's private line. Better still, she could have spoken to him in person.

It is also true to say that Bernard Woolley had a duty to respect the complete confidentiality of the call. It might be argued that he stuck to the letter of the rules – but it is clear from this entry in Sir Humphrey's diary that Bernard Woolley did not stick to the spirit of confidentiality. But then, like all Private Secretaries, he did have a difficult dual loyalty to maintain – Ed.]

En route to the Cabinet Room through the Private Office I was halted by an anxious BW.[1]

He informed me that there had been movement. Specifically, movement on a matter on which the Civil Service hoped there would be no movement.

I refrained from pointing out that the Civil Service generally hopes that there will be no movement on any matter.

BW seemed unable or unwilling to express himself with even his usual clarity. He told me that it was in relation to a subject that is normally wholly and exclusively within the control of the Civil Service that developments have developed. I told him that he was speaking in riddles. He thanked me.

Most unusually for me I had been slow on the uptake. I realised that his lips were sealed, and that he must be referring confidentially to minutes that he was duty-bound to make of a confidential conversation between the Prime Minister and one of his confidential advisers.

I asked if this were so. He acknowledged with a nod.

I asked for the name of the confidential adviser. He told me that he was not at liberty to divulge her name. Very helpful.

I questioned him closely, to find out whether the confidential advice concerned the financial crisis or the PM's foolish nuclear strategy. BW hinted that the matter was even more important than either of the above.

I realised at once that he must be referring to the Civil Service pay claim. I asked him, and he refused to confirm or deny it. Quite correctly. [*It might be argued that this refusal to confirm or deny was less than correct, since Bernard Woolley had given a clear negative response to all of Sir Humphrey's other questions. The inference was therefore unmistakeable – Ed.*]

I asked BW for his advice. He advised me to consider my position very carefully, perhaps temporarily adopting a middle-of-the-road posture, while keeping my ear to the ground, covering my retreat and watching my rear. A little undignified but I took heed of his warning.

I thanked him for his help. He replied that he had not told me anything. I agreed, for it would have been most improper had he done so.

[*Appleby Papers 638/T/RJC*]

[*Hacker's diary continues – Ed.*]

March 30th

I studied the Civil Service pay claim in great detail when I rose early

[1] Bernard Woolley.

this morning and, armed with Dorothy's excellent questions, I was ready to raise hell with Humphrey. I was delighted that her comments were given to me in complete confidence – because I learned something important about Humphrey today: he is *not* always on the side of the Civil Service. With no prior knowledge of the awkward questions I raised he performed reasonably and helpfully, and impressed me more than somewhat.

I handed him the very bulky Pay Claim file when he came in. It's incredibly long and verbose – goes up to Appendix Q, I think. Thank God Dorothy's a patient reader. And a quick one.

I asked Humphrey what he made of it. He said it was too large for an instant judgement. I told him to read the excellent one-page summary at the front.

He did so. Then he looked up at me, and remarked that I was putting him in a very difficult position.

I got heavy with him. 'Look, Humphrey,' I reminded him, 'I appreciate that you have a loyalty to your colleagues but you also have a broader loyalty to the Cabinet and its policies.'

'I agree,' he said.

I was confused. 'You agree?'

'Yes,' he said.

I wanted to get this quite clear. 'You mean you agree with me?' I asked.

'Yes, I agree,' he repeated.

I still wasn't quite sure that he wasn't playing some verbal or linguistic game. I wanted to be quite sure where I stood. 'Who, precisely, do you agree with?'

'With you,' he replied.

I wanted to be absolutely sure. 'Not with Sir Frank?'

'No,' he said.

I summed it up. 'So . . . you're not arguing with me at all?'

'No,' he answered. 'Perhaps I haven't made it quite clear, Prime Minister – I agree with you.'

Well, you can imagine how completely flabbergasted I was. So I asked him for *his* view of this self-serving pay claim.

'It's not excessive in itself,' he replied, 'but at a time of national stringency it is neither wise nor in the national interest. I don't like to criticise my colleagues, but in my opinion Sir Frank, though no doubt acting from the best of motives, should have placed the good of the nation before the narrower sectional interests of Civil Servants. This claim raises serious questions.'

How interesting that he should use that phrase. I told him I'd made a note of some questions too. I handed Dorothy's list over to him.

He stared at it. 'Good questions,' he said quietly. 'Where did they come from?'

I wasn't sure that I cared for the implication of his question. 'They . . . occurred to me,' I said.

He glanced at the paper again. 'Yes. Well, they're *very* good questions.'

This was exactly what I – and Dorothy – had thought. So I asked Humphrey what we should now do about these questions. He said that we should ask them. I thought I *was* asking them, but his view was that I should ask them of Sir Frank. 'I think you should invite him here to discuss them. He may well have answers. Indeed, he should have answers. This is his job, after all.'

I realised that he was quite right. I told him to speak to Bernard and arrange such a meeting. And I told Humphrey that I genuinely appreciated his impartiality on this subject. After all, there's no doubt that Humphrey himself would do quite well out of this pay claim if it went through.

Humphrey thanked me, but explained that he saw the rewards of his job as the knowledge that one has been of service to the nation. I'm sure he was telling the truth. And of course, I see my rewards in exactly the same light. Nonetheless, one must give credit where credit is due – Humphrey was extremely fair-minded today.

After he left I asked Bernard how the FDA[1] worked. How, if they are all in the Union, can they bargain with themselves over their own pay?

I could have predicted the answer – Bernard said it's not so difficult if they simply wear two hats.

'All very well,' I said, 'but what happens when there is industrial action?'

[*This phrase must be the only occasion on which the Civil Service uses the demeaning word 'industrial' to apply to itself. Though it frequently describes itself as 'industrious' – Ed.*]

'It can be awkward,' said Bernard. 'The Secretary of our Union was on the Council of Civil Service Unions which planned the last bout of disruption – and at the same time, as Number Three at Swansea, his duty was to make contingency plans for frustrating the disruption.'

I asked what happened. Bernard said he was very successful.

[1] First Division Association.

I couldn't see how. 'He must have known the other side's plans,' I said.

'Which other side?' asked Bernard.

'*Both* other sides,' I answered logically. 'Whichever side he wasn't on at whatever moment he was on the *other* side.'

This presented no problem for Bernard. 'Yes,' he agreed, 'but he never disclosed the other side's plans.'

'To whom?' I was getting confused.

'To his own side.'

'*Which* own side?' I asked.

'Whichever side', explained Bernard patiently, 'that he was on at whatever moment he wasn't on the *other* side.'

I was now groping blindly through the fog of logic. 'Yes, but even if he never disclosed the other side's plans to his own side, *he* knew the other side's plan because he was on the other side too!'

Bernard contemplated this question briefly. 'Therefore I imagine', he replied, 'that he never disclosed to himself what he knew.'

I asked Bernard how such a thing was possible. It seemed all too easy to Bernard. 'He was a model of discretion,' he said.

To me the Number Three man at Swansea sounded like a model of institutionalised schizophrenia. But there remained one vital unanswered question, 'When there is a genuine conflict of interest, Bernard, which side is the Civil Service really on?'

This time he replied without hesitation. 'The winning side, Prime Minister.' And he gave me a winning smile.

[*Sir Humphrey, having been forced by events to side against the Civil Service pay claim proposed by Sir Frank, was left in something of a dilemma. It had been useful to him to appear more loyal than Sir Frank, and, in any case, since the Prime Minister had found some of the key questions, the claim was inevitably doomed and any wise man would have distanced himself from it. Now, however, he was obliged to find a way to make the Civil Service pay claim seem acceptable – partly because it would consolidate his position with the PM and with his colleagues in the Service, and partly because he wanted the money.*

Accordingly, he consulted his eminent predecessor Sir Arnold Robinson. One of the many jobs Sir Arnold had accepted on his retirement was the Presidency of the Campaign for Freedom of Information. Strangely, however, Sir Arnold did not report the events described in this chapter to the press, nor to the Campaign. Indeed, his private notes only came to light comparatively recently when, under the

153

terms of his will, his private papers were released from the strongroom of his bank in Woking thirty years after his death – Ed.]

We lunched in the Athenaeum. Humphrey was concerned that he had not been able to support Frank's case. Deeply distressing, no doubt, but one does not support proposals that are clearly going to be rejected.

The Wainwright female had given Hacker a list of questions, plus the suggestion that the politicians stop letting us handle our own pay claim and let a Select Committee of Parliament decide on them. An *appalling* notion! The next thing we'd have is politicians removing Civil Servants on the grounds of incompetence, which would be the thin end of the wedge.

It is true, doubtless, that some Civil Servants are incompetent, but certainly not incompetent enough for a politician to notice. A better idea might be that Civil Servants could remove politicians on the grounds of incompetence, although that is a sadly improbable notion because it would virtually empty the House of Commons, remove all the Cabinet, be the end of democracy and the beginning of responsible government.

It appears that Frank used the normal formula – comparable jobs in industry. And they need a rise of 43%. I made the following suggestions:

1. Since virtually all the relevant staff work in London, there should be a big increase in the London Allowance. Allowances rank as expenses. Because they do not count as a rise, they do not show up in the percentage calculations.
2. Introduce a Special Graduate Allowance for those with First Class Degrees, and Upper Second-Class degrees. (Oxford does not give Upper Seconds, so count any Second at Oxford as an Upper Second.)
3. Double the Outstanding Merit Awards, which *everyone* gets. Awards rank as Bonuses and, like Allowances, do not count as pay rises.
4. Items 1–3 bring the claim down to about 18% for the top grades. Therefore it should be calculated from 1973, which was the high point in percentage increases [*not in income – Ed.*]. And take the calculation to the end of two years from now, *i.e.* the *end* of this claim period rather than the beginning.

These four measures bring the percentage increase down to about 6%. But that *still* means that the Civil Service overall pay bill will be too high. The only option is to reduce the size of the Civil Service. Thus, a comfortable rise for individuals would be a smaller rise in the total bill.

Of course, *real* reductions in the size of the Civil Service would be the end of civilisation as we know it. The answer is much less worrying: stop calling some officials by the name of Civil Servant.

E.g. Turn all museums into independent trusts. Then all the staff stop being classified as Civil Servants. They will still be the same people doing the same job and still paid by government grants. But grants, like allowances and bonuses, do not count in the pay statistics. It will look like a cutback, a most impressive cutback, unless anyone enquires very closely.[1]

---

[1] This procedure was followed in the 1980s, leading the British public to believe that the Civil Service numbered 680,000, its smallest size for many years.

There is only one problem: setting up a sufficient number of trusts. But it may not have to be done at all. It must only be *planned* for some time in the next two years in order to be reflected in the statistics. If it subsequently does not happen, it will not be anyone's fault.

Appleby thanked me profusely. I indicated that I was always happy to oblige. [*Especially, we suspect, with the Birthday Honours approaching. Sir Arnold did have the GCB[1] conferred upon him in June – Ed.*]

I offered to discuss the matter also with Frank Gordon at the Treasury. Humphrey was adamant that I should not do so. Apparently Frank Gordon has a lot of problems coming up at the moment. He hasn't mentioned them to me. [*This was because Sir Frank did not yet know about them – Ed.*]

Finally I suggested one major reform to Appleby:

Members of Parliament can be very small-minded about Civil Service pay, and there is often a struggle to get an increase past the House. But if MPs' pay were to be linked to a grade in the Civil Service, then every time they vote for a Civil Service pay rise they will accidentally be raising their own salaries. We could also index-link MPs' pensions. This could save much unpleasantness all round.[2]

This was not done in my time in the Cabinet office because Mr Hacker's predecessor as PM felt it might motivate parliament to frequent inflationary increases in government spending. I hope that MPs would not be so self-seeking, but politicians are a very mercenary lot and we in the Civil Service must not judge everyone by our own high standards.

[*Hacker's diary continues – Ed.*]

April 3rd

A most interesting meeting was held today. Present were Sir Humphrey, Bernard, Sir Frank and Dorothy Wainwright. Oh, and me, of course. I learned that Humphrey is a loyal, unselfish servant. I'm not sure about Frank.

Frank began the meeting by asserting that Civil Service pay has fallen significantly behind comparable jobs in industry. When I asked which comparable jobs, he avoided giving me a specific answer, and said that it was quite a complex formula which has been generally accepted for some time.

I confronted him with facts. 'According to my figures,' I informed him, 'a Permanent Secretary is already getting something over forty-five thousand a year. And the Cabinet Secretary and the Permanent Secretary to the Treasury get over fifty-one thousand pounds.'

---

[1] Knight Grand Cross of the Order of the Bath.
[2] This provision was enacted in 1983 without any legislation and with the minimum of publicity: it was announced in late July, to coincide with the summer holidays of the few journalists who would have seen its significance.

Frank hedged. 'Maybe you're right,' he said with a weak smile.

Ludicrous! Doesn't he know how much he earns? Or has it temporarily slipped his mind, perhaps?

I turned to Humphrey, sitting on my right at the Cabinet table, and asked him for his view.

He was cautious. Rightly so. 'It's not for me to say really, Prime Minister. I have a vested interest and Sir Frank is in charge of Civil Service pay. Aren't you, Frank?'

At least Humphrey had the decency to declare his interest. Dorothy, sitting on my left, spoke next.

'May I ask a question, Prime Minister?' I nodded. She stared hard at Frank, across the table. 'Sir Frank, what deduction do you make for job security?'

He was startled. This was obviously a question he'd not been asked before and was not expecting.

Dorothy explained further. 'Top people in industry can get sacked. Pushed out in take-overs, their firms can go bust. But your jobs are guaranteed.'

He hedged again. 'Well, there are swings and roundabouts.'

'What about the roundabouts?' Dorothy asked acidly.

Frank explained that top Civil Servants may have guaranteed jobs, but they have great pressure and long hours.

'Don't they have those in industry?' Dorothy wanted to know. Then she looked at me and added: 'Anyway, industrial leaders have to take decisions and stand by them.'

This angered Frank. His cheeks acquired small pink spots. 'So do Civil Servants,' he retorted.

Dorothy turned on him nastily. 'Really? I thought that Ministers took the decisions.'

'And the blame,' I chimed in. 'That's the deal, isn't it?'

Frank didn't really know whether to answer all these rhetorical questions or not. 'Yes . . . well . . . Ministers do, of course, take the decisions,' he acknowledged. 'But Civil Servants have to decide how to carry them out.'

Dorothy went for the jugular. 'Like a secretary deciding how to lay out a letter?'

'Yes,' said Frank. 'No,' he said, changing his mind instantly. And he appealed for help: 'I think Sir Humphrey knows what I mean.'

Humphrey's eyes were firmly fixed on the blank sheet of paper lying in front of him on the table. 'Well, Frank, it's up to you, you're in charge of Civil Service pay.'

Dorothy passed me a note. It said *What about the service element*?

I stared coldly at Frank. 'What about the service element?' I asked.

'Service element?' he repeated. 'What do you mean, service element?'

I wasn't quite sure what I meant, or what Dorothy meant. I'm sure it didn't show, though. I turned casually to Dorothy and indicated that she might speak for me.

'There is a strong service element about the job,' she began briskly, 'which is rewarded by honours – CBs, KCMGs, knighthoods.'

'To an extent,' conceded Frank with caution.

Dorothy turned to me again. 'You see, Prime Minister, I wonder whether we shouldn't compare civil servants with directors of charities rather than industry. I think,' she was rustling through all her papers, 'that they get about seventeen thousand.'

I smiled. 'That's an interesting proposal.'

Indeed it was. Frank was looking panicked. Humphrey wasn't looking any too pleased either.

'I don't think . . . well, we'd never recruit,' said Frank in a voice that was noticeably half an octave higher. 'Morale would plummet . . . I'm sure Sir Humphrey would agree.'

Humphrey stayed silent.

I looked at him. 'Humphrey?' I enquired.

'Well, Prime Minister, my opinion is that . . .' he looked up at Frank, with a distinctly unsupportive look in his eyes, 'Sir Frank is in charge of Civil Service pay. Though I do think, Frank, that the Prime Minister is entitled to an answer.'

Frank was visibly startled by this reply. He tried another weak smile. Nobody else at the table smiled.

The question of index-linked pensions was also on Dorothy's notes. I raised it next. Frank dismissed that as completely irrelevant. 'Those were agreed a long time ago.'

'But they have a considerable value,' I asserted.

He was disparging. 'A value, yes. But modest.'

I picked up one of the papers in the superb brief that Dorothy had prepared for this meeting. 'I have an estimate here that it would cost £650,000 to buy back a Permanent Secretary's pension.'

Frank smiled again. 'That's absurd!'

'How would you value it?' asked Dorothy.

Frank was foolish enough to suggest a figure. 'About £100,000.'

I pounced. 'In that case, Frank, I'll make you an offer. The government will buy back your pension – and anybody else's who will

157

sell – at your valuation. We'll give you a hundred thousand, cash, in exchange for your pension rights. Is that a deal?'

Frank was now doing the well-known Civil Servant impression of a headless chicken. 'Well, I mean, no, I was talking off the top of my head, it could be, that is, I haven't calculated it myself.'

Dorothy threw another dart straight at the bullseye. 'The figure of £650,000 came from the Society of Insurance and Pension Actuaries.'

'Yes, but when it was agreed,' whined Frank helplessly, 'I'm sure it was nothing like that.'

Dorothy was relentless. She had yet another idea. 'What about having index-linked pensions as an *alternative* to honours? Every Civil Servant could choose which way he wanted to take his reward – honours or cash!'

'But that's preposterous!' shrieked Frank.

'Why?' asked Dorothy.

I wanted the answer to that question too. It sounded like a damned good idea to me. On my right, Humphrey was looking very tight-lipped and was conspicious by his silence. Even Bernard was turning pale. I was thoroughly enjoying myself.

It was left for Frank to defend the indefensible. 'Such a choice would, it would, it, er, it would put us, er, put *them* in an impossible position. I mean, what about those who already have honours?'

Dorothy, of course, had an answer to that. Clearly she had worked out every implication in advance. 'It's quite simple. They could choose whether to renounce their honour or renounce their pension index-linking.' She leaned forward and smiled cheerfully across me at Humphrey. 'What do you think, Sir Humphrey – or will you be *Mr* Appleby?'

Humphrey was not amused. He had expected Frank to perform better than this – his own salary increase and honours were now under attack. 'I'm sure Sir Frank has gone into this very thoroughly,' he said.

'Not thoroughly enough,' I said. 'Frank, you personally would make a lot of money out of this pay claim, wouldn't you?'

Frank spluttered with indignation. 'Prime Minister, that is not a consideration,' he said. Which means *yes*, presumably.

Dorothy treated Frank to one of her acid smiles. 'You mean you'd be happy to be personally excluded from this rise?'

Frank was speechless. She turned to Humphrey. 'I'm sure the Cabinet Secretary would be, wouldn't you, Humphrey?'

I was sorry for Humphrey, but he was in a rather awkward position.

He stammered and stuttered about precedents, and thinking of the service as a whole, and considering long-term points of view. Then suddenly he found a brilliant way out. 'Yes!' he said, suddenly and very firmly. 'I would agree to be excluded from the pay rise *if*, and only if, the government did believe that senior people should be paid less than their subordinates, and if they extended the principle to Cabinet Ministers and their junior ministers.'

Naturally I had no such intention. And anyway, my purpose was not to corner Humphrey, who had taken my side on this matter. So I thanked everyone and dismissed them.

I kept Humphrey back for a quick private word. I asked him if he thought we were a bit hard on Frank. 'On the contrary,' he said. 'Most proper and penetrating questions, if I may say so, even though I do not like to be disloyal to colleagues.'

It's clear he's never been a Cabinet Minister.

April 5th
Humphrey really came through today. He has been hard at work on a new, much smaller Civil Service pay claim. He wanted to explain why.

'I'm afraid I thought all along,' he told me, 'that at a time of stringency the Treasury claim was excessive, not in the nation's interest. Nice for Civil Servants, of course, but not something the Cabinet Secretary with his higher loyalty could recommend. *That* is why we don't let the Permanent Secretary of the Treasury be Head of the Civil Service.' I took the point.

He then offered me a much more modest submission which amounts to only 11% over two years, with the top grades rising only by about the average. The overall Civil Service pay bill would only go up by about 6% a year over a period, in Humphrey's scheme.

This is obviously much more reasonable, and I'm perfectly willing to okay it. He wasn't even asking for that at once. He said that obviously the lower grades will have to go through the normal procedures, but he suggested that the First Division claim should be processed with the utmost secrecy and speed.

The reason is that he fears that his scheme could backfire if there is widespread discussion of it. Many members of the FDA might want to make a bigger claim – I'm sure he's right, if Frank is anything to go by. So Humphrey wants no one to see it now, even advisers.

That's only acceptable to me if he can get his colleagues to accept such a small rise, a mere 6%. He says he can swing it if I guarantee support and co-operation over the secrecy. I guaranteed it. I got a real bargain there!

But there was one outstanding problem: Parliament. The backbenchers always hate Civil Service pay rises. Humphrey had a solution – a brilliant solution. It involves a major reform that will be universally popular. [*By universally popular Hacker was referring to Parliament and the Civil Service, not the British public. To him, the universe consisted of Westminster and Whitehall – Ed.*]

'Prime Minister, if MPs' salaries were linked to a grade in the Civil Service, then they wouldn't have to keep voting themselves their own pay rises. Everytime the Civil Service got one, they'd get one too. Automatically. And if their pensions were index-linked too, that would help.'

'It certainly would,' I agreed. 'Excellent. Thank you.' Humphrey really has been a tower of strength, and thoroughly self-sacrificing. 'What grade should a backbencher's be, do you think?' I asked him.

'I think, perhaps, a Senior Principal.'

I was surprised. 'Isn't that rather low?'

'Backbenchers are rather low,' he said with a mischievous twinkle in his eye.

'And to what grade should Cabinet Ministers be linked?' I asked.

'Under Secretaries?' suggested Humphrey.

'And the Prime Minister?'

'Well,' said Humphrey, 'at present you earn even less than I do, but I think you should grade yourself as a Permanent Secretary. And you, like me, could have an index-linked pension. And it could be calculated not on your years as Prime Minister, but as if you had been doing the job all your life and it was your retirement salary.'[1]

A very fair offer. I thanked him. He shrugged off my thanks. 'After all, Prime Minister, this is a partnership.'

'Indeed it is,' I agreed. 'A real partnership.'

'Yes Prime Minister,' said Humphrey. What a nice man he is, underneath it all.

---

[1] This has been the practice since the 1980s.

6
A Victory For Democracy

We had a drinks party at Number Ten tonight. Among the many guests was the American Ambassador. He cornered me in the yellow pillared room, and edged me towards one of the pillars.

'How are things in the White House?' I asked cheerfully.

He is a very tall, burly, amicable fellow. It's hard to believe that his words were threats. And yet . . . 'They've heard some talk about plans to cancel Trident, and coming on top of all this food war – er, that is this friendly rivalry from our European friends[1] it could just about blow the whole North Atlantic Alliance.'

One of those nice comfortable middle-aged ladies with those small silver trays of drinks passed by. I gratefully selected a Scotch. The US Ambassador waved her away.

'It's only a rumour, of course,' he continued. 'I can't personally believe the British Government would try to cancel Trident. But I know there's pressure on you.'

In reality, all the pressure to cancel Trident is coming from me. But I wasn't actually lying when I replied bravely, 'Yes, well, pressure's part of the job, isn't it?'

'But the White House has asked me to convey to you – informally, of course, not in my official role as Ambassador – that it might cause problems. The defence industries, you see, contain some of the biggest single contributors to party funds.'

This was the kind of American reaction that Humphrey had predicted. It was not news. 'Really?' I said, as if this were news.

The Ambassador came even closer to me. I'm sure he was only trying to be confidential, but it felt threatening. 'The White House would do a lot to stop cancellation. A lot!'

Again I was given a moment to think, this time by one of the ladies

---

[1] See page 31.

from Government Hospitality with a tray of mixed canapés. I took some brown bread with smoked salmon and asparagus rolled up in it. 'Delicious,' I said, and indicated to the Ambassador that he should enjoy our hospitality. He abstained.

'You can tell the White House, unofficially,' I said bravely, 'that you have made your point.'

'Unofficially?' He agreed to maintain the fiction. 'Fine. But the State Department and the Pentagon have other worries.'

'What about?' I couldn't think of anything else I'd done to offend the Americans.

The Ambassador sipped his Perrier. 'Well, you're aware of the East Yemen problem?'

I'd never heard of it. 'Absolutely,' I said. 'Big problem.'

The Ambassador seemed surprised at this response. 'Well, not at the moment, surely?'

'Not at the moment, of course,' I agreed hastily. 'But . . . potentially.'

'Right!' He was warming to his subject. 'And you know about St George's Island?'

Another place I'd never heard of. 'St George's Island?' I repeated, as if I were holding my cards close to my chest.

It didn't fool the Ambassador. 'It's part of your Commonwealth,' he explained.

'Oh, *that* St George's Island,' I said, as if everyone knew there were two.

'Well . . .' The Ambassador looked grim. 'It looks like the Communists might try and grab it.'

This sounded serious. 'Really?' I said. 'I'll speak to the Foreign Secretary.'

The Ambassador looked a little dubious. 'You think that'll do the trick?'

I didn't know, did I? For a start, I didn't know what trick was required. And speaking to Duncan rarely achieves anything anyway. So I prevaricated. 'Well, not in itself, perhaps – but . . .'.

'The White House,' interjected the Ambassador, 'is worried that your Foreign Office might not be tough enough about it. They might just sit by and watch. The White House think your Foreign Office is full of pinkoes and traitors.'

I laughed. 'They've read too many newspapers . . . I mean, detective stories.' Freudian slip.

'That's what I tell them,' agreed the Ambassador with a sigh. 'But the Pentagon say they've read too many NATO secrets in Russian files. Prime Minister, the White House would be very upset if the Reds got hold of a strategic base like St George's Island.' So it's a strategic base! 'There's a talk of putting tariffs on British car exports. No more Jaguar sales to the United States.' He *was* threatening me!

I tried to interrupt but he was in full swing. 'Of course, I'd oppose it. But who am I? And the White House might tax US investment in Britain. That would cause a real run on the pound. They could demote GCHQ[1] and upgrade the listening post in Spain instead. They might even leave Britain out of Presidential visits to Europe.'

These were all humiliating threats, but the last was catastrophic. [*This was because it would have been humiliating to Jim Hacker personally – Ed.*] I was virtually speechless at this onslaught.

'But as I say,' the Ambassador went on, hopefully misinterpreting my silence as a counter-threat [*Hacker was always a wishful thinker – Ed.*], 'I would certainly not recommend that sort of reprisal against our friend, and old ally.'

I couldn't think who he was talking about. 'Who?' I asked.

'You,' he said.

I was about to edge away to talk to one of my other 200 guests, when the ambassador took me by the arm. 'Oh, by the way, I take it your man at the UN won't be supporting the Arab resolution condemning Israel? That would really make the White House burst a blood vessel. Freedom and democracy must be defended.'

I agree, obviously, that freedom and democracy must be defended. So does any right-thinking person. Whether a UN resolution makes such a difference to the future of freedom and democracy is anybody's guess. But the whole conversation was very unsettling. I'll see Duncan tomorrow.

April 11th

I didn't sleep too well last night. The American Ambassador had really worried me. This morning, first thing, I told Bernard all about it.

I asked Bernard, what is the big problem we have in East Yemen? 'Um' he said. He added that he would try and find out. I told him of the US worries about St George's Island, and that the US felt the Foreign Office couldn't help because it's full of pinkoes and traitors.

'It's not,' said Bernard indignantly. 'Well, not full.'

[1] The top security radar espionage centre in Cheltenham.

Bernard said he'd arrange a meeting with the Foreign Secretary for this afternoon. 'You can get him to sort it out,' he said reassuringly. 'After all, they are on our side.'

'Who are?' I asked.

'The Americans,' said Bernard.

'Oh. *They* are, yes.' I said. 'I thought for a moment you meant the Foreign Office.'

[*It appears that Duncan Short, the Secretary of State for Foreign Affairs, was unable to see the Prime Minister that day. A meeting was arranged at 10 Downing Street for the following morning. However, shortly after the Foreign Office received from Bernard Woolley the urgent request for a meeting with the Prime Minister, a different meeting was arranged for the same afternoon – between Sir Richard Wharton, the new Permanent Secretary of the Foreign Office, and Sir Humphrey Appleby. Sir Humphrey makes a note about it in his private diary. – Ed.*]

Dick Wharton of the FO came to my office for a quick chat. He was worried. I couldn't think why. I had understood that he had the Foreign Secretary eating out of his hand.

Dick confirmed that the Foreign Secretary was completely house-trained. The problem, apparently, is that the Prime Minister is starting to mistrust Foreign Office advice when Duncan gives it to him. It seems that the PM is even questioning Foreign Office policy.

Dick is beginning to see a danger of the Cabinet pursuing its own foreign policy. This would be absurd. The country can't have two foreign policies!

It is true that the PM is gravely under the influence of the White House. Except when it comes to Trident, which is the only time that he should be!

Dick told me of two matters on the horizon, over which the PM might need a little guidance in the right direction.

1. *St George's Island.* Dick had to remind me where it was: one of those few islands in the Indian Ocean to stay in the Commonwealth after independence. It is democratic, has free elections, but there is a group of Marxist guerrillas in the mountains who are reportedly planning a coup.

These things happen, of course. But, according to Dick, the guerrillas are going to be helped by East Yemen – or, to give it its full title, the People's Democratic Republic of East Yemen. Like all People's Democratic Republics it is a communist dictatorship.

These guerrillas from East Yemen are Soviet-backed and Libyan-backed. The FO is planning for Britain to stay out of the situation, because:

a) We would only upset a lot of front-line African states if we got involved.

b) We don't want to antagonise the Soviets at the moment.
c) We have just landed a large contract to build the new St George's Island airport and harbour installation. If we back the wrong side we will lose the contract.
d) We don't mind whether the democrats or the Marxists win. It makes no difference to us.

The potential problem with the PM: He might get into one of his ghastly patriotic Churchillian moods. He might want to start some pro-British 'defending democracy' nonsense.

The Foreign Office solution: The PM must understand that once you start interfering in the internal squabbles of other countries you are on a very slippery slope. Even the Foreign Secretary has grasped that.

2. *The Israelis raided Lebanon last week.* It was a reprisal for the PLO bomb in Tel Aviv. The Arabs have put down a UN motion condemning Israel. Naturally we shall vote on the Arab side. But apparently the PM had indicated that he wants us to abstain. His reasons, as expressed to the Foreign Secretary, are unclear. But roughly:
a) the PLO started it this time;
b) faults on both sides;
c) concern about the Americans;
d) worries about the Holy Places.
The FO view is that points a) and b) are sentimental nonsense. With regard to c) the PM is dangerously sycophantic to the Americans as it is. As for point d), the PM should worry more about the oily places than the Holy Places.

The potential problem with the PM: Like all inhabitants of 10 Downing Street, he wants to take his place on the world stage. But people on stages are called actors. All they are required to do is look plausible, stay sober and say the lines they are given in the right order. Those that try to make up their own lines generally do not last long.

The Foreign Office solution: The PM must realise that as far as Foreign Affairs are concerned his job is to confine himself to the hospitality and ceremonial role.

[*Appleby Papers FO/RW/JHO*]

[*Hacker's diary continues – Ed.*]

April 12th

My meeting with Duncan was mysteriously postponed yesterday. He came along to Number Ten this morning.

I told him that the American Ambassador had had an 'unofficial' word with me the night before last.

'About what?' he asked nervously.

I sat back in my chair and watched him carefully. 'What do you know about St George's Island?'

Duncan's eyes moved shiftily from side to side. 'What do you know about it?' he asked. I didn't know whether he knew anything about it, or whether, like me, he was damned if he was going to reveal his total ignorance.

'You're the Foreign Secretary, not me.' I allowed myself to sound a little indignant. 'Do you think there's any danger of a Communist takeover?'

He still looked like a frightened rabbit. 'Did he say there was?'

'He hinted,' I informed him, and waited for Duncan's answer.

Duncan decided to take a firm, positive line. 'No. No danger at all.'

'Sure?'

I awaited definite assurances. I got them, but I didn't feel very reassured. 'Of course. The Foreign Office would have told me.'

'Are you sure,' I enquired, 'that they always tell you everything?'

'Everything they think I should know,' he said with a confident smile.

'That's what I was afraid of,' I retorted. 'But the White House is worried about it, apparently. And we mustn't upset them at the moment.'

'I'm sure we've got it all under control,' said Duncan with quiet confidence.

'Chamberlain was sure he'd got Hitler under control,' I reminded him. 'And Eden was sure he'd got Nasser under control.'

Duncan leapt belligerently to the defence of the Foreign Office. For Duncan, a natural thug, attack is always the best form of defence. 'Are you suggesting the Foreign Office doesn't know what it's doing?'

'No,' I said carefully, 'I'm suggesting the Foreign Office isn't letting us know what it's doing.'

Duncan said that this was an absurd accusation. 'I get full answers to any question I ask.'

'What about the questions you don't ask?' I countered.

'Such as?'

'Such as about St George's Island!'

He shrugged. 'Ah – well, I don't ask those.'

'Well, ask them,' I begged him. 'For me. All right?'

As if he'd do *anything* for me. He'll never forgive me. [*For becoming Prime Minister – Ed.*]

Duncan looked as though he was reluctant to ask the Foreign Office about St George's, though he said he would. But he admonished me. 'Don't forget that once you start interfering in the internal squabbles of other countries you're on a very slippery slope.'

I turned to the other matter the American Ambassador had raised. Was it true, I asked him, that we were proposing to vote against Israel in the UN again tonight?

'Of course,' he said, in a tone of slight astonishment that I could ask such a question.

'Why?'

'They bombed the PLO,' he said.

'But the PLO bombed Israel,' I said.

'But the Israelis dropped more bombs than the PLO did,' he said.

'But the PLO started it,' I said.

He was about to answer back again, but I stopped him with a gesture. I was getting tired of this. 'Anyway,' I said, 'it seems to me that they're both equally to blame.'

'Not according to my advice,' said Duncan with determination.

'Either way,' I said, fed up with the pros and cons and wishing to deal with known incontrovertible facts, 'I'm under a lot of American pressure about it. I want us to abstain tonight.'

Duncan looked genuinely anxious. And shifty. 'Oh, I don't think we could do that. The Foreign Office wouldn't wear it.'

I lost my temper. 'Are they here to follow our instructions, or are we here to follow theirs?'

'Don't be silly,' replied Duncan.

Obviously that's another question he doesn't ask.

April 14th

Two days have gone by. I've had no response from Duncan. It's making me edgy. I called in Humphrey after lunch for a discussion on Foreign Affairs – something we've never really had before.

We sat in the study, on either side of the fireplace, and had coffee while we talked. We had no agenda – I just wanted a chat really. But the afternoon certainly taught me a thing or two.

'Foreign affairs are so complicated, aren't they?' I began.

'Indeed, Prime Minister.' He took a chocolate digestive biscuit. 'That's why we leave them to the Foreign Office.'

I smelt a rat at once!

'So . . . do they know what they're doing?' I asked casually.

He smiled confidently. 'If they don't, who does?'

This hardly answered my question. I told Humphrey that I was worried about the Americans. It didn't seem to bother him at all.

'Yes, well, we're all worried about the Americans,' he remarked with a weary smile.

There is a general creeping anti-Americanism in opinion-forming circles in London – specifically in Whitehall – which worries me a little. But Humphrey can't just dismiss my worries so easily, he knows that I've got to do everything possible to keep in with them in the next few months if I'm to cancel a huge defence order for Trident.

Of course, I know what he'd suggest: don't cancel Trident! He's made his views perfectly clear on more than one occasion and I suspect he is doing everything possible to obstruct me in that area. In fact, this could account for his apparent unwillingness to help with this new American problem.

Nonetheless, I'm determined to cancel Trident and I have to be sure, therefore, that we don't upset the Americans any other way.

I came straight to the point. 'The American Ambassador mentioned something about St George's Island,' I said.

He looked surprised. 'Really?'

'Humphrey . . . do you know what's going on in that part of the world?'

'What part of the world is that?' he asked, staring at me with insolent blue eyes. Damn it, he realised that I didn't know exactly where it is!

Well, I *still* wasn't going to admit it. 'That part!' I said doggedly. 'The part where St George's Island is.'

'What part is that?'

I bluffed it out. 'If you don't know, Humphrey, I advise you to look at the map.'

'I do know, Prime Minister.'

'Good. Then we both know,' I said. I'm not sure that he was convinced. But I explained that the Americans fear that St George's will be taken over by Marxist guerrillas. He didn't seem to mind a bit. I wonder if he knew already.

'They think we ought to do something about it,' I continued.

Humphrey chuckled and shook his head sadly.

I admonished him. 'It's not funny, Humphrey.'

'No indeed, Prime Minister. Rather touching, actually.' Sometimes he is so superior I could wring his neck!

'It's *not funny*!' I said irritably.

The smile was wiped off his face instantly. 'Certainly not,' he agreed emphatically.

'It's a Commonwealth country. And a democratic one.'

'Yes, Prime Minister, but once you start interfering in the internal squabbles of other countries you're on a very slippery slope.'

Now I had proof that this conversation did not come as a surprise to him. That was exactly what the Foreign Secretary had said to me, word for word.

I turned to the matter of Israel. I pointed out that both sides were to blame, that the Middle East situation is a tragedy created by history, and that morally speaking we shouldn't condemn either without condemning both.

Humphrey didn't agree, which was no great surprise. 'Surely,' he argued, 'it's a question of maintaining our relationship with the Arabs. The power of Islam. Oil supplies.'

I tried to get him to understand. 'Humphrey, I am talking about right and wrong!'

He was shocked. 'Well, don't let the Foreign Office hear you,' he advised me with sudden vehemence.

I felt that I had to give him a basic history lesson. I reminded him that we in Britain are the flagbearers of democracy. We keep the torch of freedom alive. Our great duty, nay, our destiny, is to resist aggressors and oppressors and maintain the rule of law and the supremacy of justice. We are the trustees of civilisation. [*This was, presumably, the Churchillian outburst which Sir Humphrey Appleby had feared – Ed.*]

Humphrey agreed. Well, he had to! And he proposed a compromise: if I insist on an even-handed approach, the Foreign Office might agree to abstaining on the Israel vote, so long as we authorise a powerful speech by our man at the UN attacking Zionism.

I wasn't sure this was such a great idea either. 'Surely we should use the debate to create peace, harmony and goodwill.'

'That would be most unusual,' replied Humphrey, eyebrows raised. 'The UN is the accepted forum for the expression of international hatred.'

He seems to think that this is good. Presumably on the grounds that if we don't express hatred in a controlled environment we might all end up going to war again. But since there are sixty or seventy wars currently being fought in various parts of the world anyway, between member nations of the UN, I rather feel that expressing less hatred might not be a bad thing to encourage.

Humphrey would not budge in his approach to the defence of democracy or St George's. He made a couple of scathing references to what he called 'flagwaving and torchbearing'. He argued strenuously that defending democracy is not the priority if it harms British interests by upsetting those whom we wish to have as friends.

I was shocked. This is the voice of the people who appeased Hitler. The same Foreign Office, in fact, now I come to think of it.

But to my complete and total open-mouthed astonishment Humphrey defended the appeasers. 'They were quite right. All we achieved after six years of war was to leave Eastern Europe under a Communist dictatorship instead of a Fascist dictatorship. At a cost of millions of lives and the ruination of the country. That's what comes of not listening to the Foreign Office.'

I think that is one of the most shocking things Humphrey has ever said to me. I mean, he may be right, but it strikes at everything that we hold dear.

I challenged him. 'Humphrey, are you saying Britain should not be on the side of law and justice?'

'No, no, *of course* we should,' he answered emphatically. 'We just shouldn't allow it to affect our foreign policy, that's all.' He is completely amoral.

'We should always fight for the weak against the strong.'

'Oh really?' He was using his snide voice. 'Then why don't we send troops to Afghanistan, to fight the Russians?'

That was totally below the belt. I didn't bother to answer him. The Russians are *too* strong, obviously. In my opinion it didn't alter the validity of my argument, and I told him so. I instructed him to send assurances to the democratically elected Prime Minister of St George's Island that Britain will stand by him.

Humphrey stood up. 'Perhaps you wish to discuss this with the Foreign Secretary.'

'I'll tell him, if that's what you mean,' I replied coldly, and indicated that he could go. He had not been a great help. I sent for Bernard, and was forced to ask him a very embarrassing question. 'Where exactly is St George's Island?'

To my great relief and greater pleasure I realised that he didn't know either. 'Um . . . shall we look at the globe?' he said. 'There's one in your Private Office.'

We hurried down the grand circular staircase, decorated with photographs of past prime ministers, past the chattering tickertape, and into the Private Office. There were some clerks around. None of the other private secretaries were in there except Luke. He's the Foreign Affairs Private Secretary. He is the most Aryan-looking chap I've ever seen – tall, slim, blond – rather attractive actually, if he didn't have such a superior and patronising manner. Which really doesn't suit a man only in his late thirties.

He stood up as I came in, immaculate as ever in his perfectly pressed double-breasted grey-flannel suit. I wished him a good afternoon. He returned the compliment.

Bernard and I went straight to the globe, and Bernard pointed to a spot in the middle of the Arabian Sea – which is the part of the Indian Ocean which is close to the Persian Gulf.

'The Persian Gulf is the lifeline of the West,' said Bernard. 'Now look,' he went on, pointing to the land mass lying due north of the Arabian Sea. 'There is Afghanistan, which is now under Soviet control. If the Soviets ever took Pakistan . . .'

'Which they wouldn't,' interrupted Luke smoothly. I was suddenly aware that he had joined us at the globe and was standing right behind us.

'But if they did,' Bernard persisted, pointing to Pakistan which lies on the coast, south of Afghanistan and north of the Arabian Sea, 'the Soviets would then control the Persian Gulf, the Arabian Sea, and the Indian Ocean. And the Soviets have always wanted what they call a warm-water port.'

Luke smiled a superior smile. 'There's no risk. They wouldn't invade Pakistan and anyway the Americans have a fleet permanently stationed here.' He pointed to the Indian Ocean.

I turned to Luke and asked him, with his Foreign Affairs expertise, to tell me why the Americans are so worried about St George's. Is it because of the threat of Libyan and Soviet-backed guerrillas?

Luke said that we must remember that the front-line African states – and he pointed to the East African coast which also borders on the Indian Ocean – would be frightfully miffed if we interfered.

'Do they like Communist guerrillas?' I asked.

'They don't mind them,' Luke told me. 'Most of their governments started as Communist guerrillas. It can be argued that the guerrillas have the support of the people of St George's Island.'

'Who argues that?' I asked.

'The guerrillas,' said Bernard drily.

Luke emphasised that as we have a lot of trade with the front-line African states we don't want to upset them. When I suggested that we should be fighting for freedom and democracy on St George's Island, he sniggered and told me snootily that it's all rather more complicated than that, and that the Foreign Office took the view that we should do nothing. But the Foreign Office always takes the view that we should do nothing.

He then had the temerity to lecture me on peaceful coexistence. He said that the Americans can be too aggressive – well, we all know that. And he quoted his Permanent Secretary's view that the opposite of peaceful coexistence is warlike non-existence. The old FO appeasement line again.

Then, to my surprise, Bernard suddenly said that he wanted to have an urgent word with me about home affairs. I told him to wait but he started nodding and winking in a most peculiar way. At first I thought he was developing a nervous tick, then I realised that his back was to Luke and he was indicating that he wanted a private word with me.

We went into the Cabinet Room next door, and Bernard carefully shut the doors behind us.

'I don't want to be disloyal or anything,' he said in virtually a whisper, 'but I didn't really feel it was an awfully good idea to continue that conversation in front of Luke.'

'Luke? Why not?'

'Security,' whispered Bernard.

I was astounded. 'He's your colleague. One of my Private Secretaries. How could MI5 allow such a thing?'

Bernard corrected me hastily. 'No, Prime Minister, he's not that sort of security risk. It's just that he works for the Foreign Office.'

This was a revelation! I'd always thought that Luke worked for me. But it turns out that he is not only my man from the Foreign Office, he's also their man in Number Ten. In other words, he's a plant!

I understood this. But the implications were considerable. And worrying. It confirmed, definitively, what I've been suspecting for a while.

'Bernard,' I said, tiptoeing away from the doors in case Luke had his ear to them, 'do you mean that the Foreign Office is keeping something from me?'

'Yes,' he replied without hesitation.

'What?' I asked.

'I don't know,' he said helplessly. 'They're keeping it from me too.'

'Then how do you know?'

Bernard was confused. 'I don't.'

I began to get irritated. 'You just said you did.'

'No, I just said I didn't.'

What the hell was he talking about? I was now boiling with frustration. 'You said they were keeping things from me – *how do you know if you DON'T KNOW??*'

Bernard was beginning to look desperate. 'I don't know specifically what, Prime Minister, but I do know the Foreign Office always keeps everything from everybody. It's normal practice.'

'So who *would* know?' I asked.

Bernard thought for a moment. Then he gave me the full benefit of his education and training. 'May I just clarify the question? You're asking who would know what it is that *I* don't know and *you* don't know but the Foreign Office know that *they* know, that they are keeping from you so that *you* don't know but they *do* know, and all *we* know is that there is something *we* don't know and we want to know but we don't know *what* because we *don't know*.' I just stared at him in silence. 'Is that it?' he asked.

I took a deep breath. It was that, or grabbing him by the lapels and shaking him senseless. 'May *I* clarify the question?' I asked. 'Who knows Foreign Office secrets apart from the Foreign Office?'

'Ah, that's easy,' said Bernard. 'Only the Kremlin.'

[*Bernard Woolley sent notes to both Sir Humphrey Appleby and Sir Richard Wharton, asking for a meeting on the subject of St George's Island. Wharton's letter in reply was kept by Sir Bernard Woolley in his private papers and given to us for this edition of the Hacker diaries – Ed.*]

Foreign and Commonwealth Office

London SW1A 2AH

18ᵗʰ April

Dear Bernard

I shall be happy to attend your meeting tomorrow. This bit of bother on St. George's is getting to be a bit of a bore.

For your own background information, I believe that we made the real mistake twenty years ago when we gave them their independence.

Of course, with the wind of change and all that, independence was inevitable. But we should have partitioned the island as we did in India and Cyprus and Palestine and Ireland. This was our invariable practice when we gave independence to the colonies, and I can't think why we varied it. It always worked.

It has been argued by some people that the policy of partition always led to Civil War. It certainly did in India and Cyprus and Palestine and Ireland. This was no bad thing for Britain. It kept them busy and instead of fighting us they fought each other. This meant that it was no longer necessary to have a policy about them.

However, it's no use crying over spilt milk. The damage is done now.

See you at 3pm tomorrow.

Dick

[*The following day, after lunch, Bernard Woolley had a meeting with the two wiliest mandarins in Whitehall. They had a frank conversation, in which Woolley learned for the first time how the Foreign Office really works. Fortunately for historians, Sir Humphrey Appleby made a careful note of the meeting and it was preserved amongst his private papers. Thus, for the first time, the general reader can be given an understanding of the Foreign Office approach to world affairs from the 1930s onwards – Ed.*]

I attended the meeting at BW's request, first having had a private word with Dick Wharton. We decided that BW must be initiated into a full understanding of FO working methods.

BW began the meeting, which was technically about St George's Island, with his problem as he saw it: namely that the PM was completely in the dark. Dick said that this was good, and we began to encourage BW to see this not as a problem but as an opportunity.

This concept did not come easily to BW. He asked if there was anything else the PM did not know – a truly absurd question. I sometimes wonder about Bernard. Then he asked if there was something important that the PM doesn't know about St George's Island, and Dick correctly explained that the PM's proper course is to ask the Foreign Secretary to inform him of anything he needs to know. Then all that the FO has to do is ensure that the Foreign Secretary does not know the whole story either.

We were getting to the root of BW's problem. He was under the impression that the PM ought to know what is happening.

The basic rule for the safe handling of Foreign Affairs is that it is simply too dangerous to let politicians get involved with diplomacy. Diplomacy is about surviving till the next century – politics is about surviving till Friday afternoon.

There are 157 independent countries in the world. The FO has dealt with them for years. There's hardly an MP who knows anything about any of them. Show MPs a map of the world, and many of them would have difficulty finding the Isle of Wight.

Bernard was prepared to argue that MPs cannot be so ignorant. So Dick gave him a short quiz:

1. Where is Upper Volta?
2. What is the capital of Chad?
3. What language do they speak in Mali?
4. Who is the President of Peru?
5. What is the national religion of Cameroun?

Bernard scored nought per cent. Dick suggested that he stand for Parliament.

BW's problem is that he has studied too much constitutional history – or, at least, taken it too much too heart. He was arguing, not very articulately I may say, that 'if you've got a democracy, shouldn't people, sort of, discuss things a bit?'

We agreed that full discussion with the PM was essential. Therefore, Bernard argued, the PM should have the facts. There was the fallacy!

BW needs to understand the following argument clearly:

i) Facts complicate things.
ii) The people don't want them.
iii) All that the press, the people and their elected representatives want to know is Who Are The Goodies? and Who Are The Baddies?
iv) Unfortunately, the interests of Britain usually involve doing deals with people the public think are Baddies.
v) And sometimes British interests mean that we cannot help the Goodies.
vi) Therefore, discussion must be kept inside the Foreign Office. Then it produces one policy for the Foreign Secretary, which represents the FO's considered view, and he can act upon it. QED.

BW was concerned that the FO produces only one considered view, with no options and no alternatives.

In practice, this presents no problem. If pressed, the FO looks at the matter again, and comes up with the same view. If the Foreign Secretary demands options, the FO obliges him by presenting three options, two of which will be (on close examination) exactly the same. The third will, of course, be totally unacceptable, like bombing Warsaw, or invading France.

One further option is occasionally used: encouraging the Foreign Secretary to work out his own policy. The FO then shows him how it will inevitably lead to World War III, perhaps within 48 hours.

BW understood the idea, but – quite properly, since he is a Private Secretary at the moment – wanted to pursue the discussion from the point of view of the politicians. He remarked the Ministers are primarily concerned about the effect of policy on domestic political opinion. That's what they're good at, in fact. And the Foreign Office system does not really allow for this.

He was quite correct. The FO does indeed take a global view. It asks what is best for the world, whereas most Ministers would rather it asked: What is the *Daily Mail* leader going to say? This would be quite inappropriate for the

FO to consider: foreign policy cannot be made by yobbos like Fleet Street editors, backbench MPs and Cabinet Ministers. The job of the FO is to take the right decision, and let others sort out the politics afterwards.

Bernard was also concerned about what happens if the Foreign Secretary still will not accept the FO's advice after all the options have been presented. I explained to him that it is a free country, and the Foreign Secretary can always resign.

The whole basis of our conversation then took an unexpected turn. A Flash Telegram arrived. Dick read it, and informed us that East Yemen are preparing to invade St George's Island in support of the Marxist guerrillas.

BW thought this was bad news. It is, of course, moderately bad news for the government of St George's – but it's very good news for the guerrillas.

BW wanted to know, of all things, if it was good news for the islanders. I'm afraid he has been a Private Secretary too long – he is beginning to react like a politician.

Dick suggested, and I agreed, that we could do nothing to help the islanders. If they appeal to us, we shall give them every support short of help. If the Prime Minister insists that we help, then we follow the traditional four-stage strategy, the standard Foreign Office response to any crisis:

Stage One
We say that nothing is going to happen.
Stage Two
We say that something may be going to happen, but we should do nothing about it.
Stage Three
We say that maybe we should do something about it, but there's nothing we can do.
Stage Four
We say that maybe there was something we could have done but it's too late now.

[*Hacker's diary continues – Ed.*]

April 19th
Dramatic events today. I think I've had a major triumph.

It all came to a head this afternoon, when that insufferable young man Luke brought the old green box containing Foreign Office telegrams into the Cabinet Room.

Bernard wasn't there, for some reason. He'd left a message that he was at a meeting with Sir Humphrey.

I picked up the first telegram: it said there were troop movements in East Yemen. I looked at Luke. He said that this was not significant.

'But,' I told Luke, 'the American Ambassador mentioned something about East Yemen last week.'

'Really?' said Luke with a patronising smile. 'I'm surprised he's heard of it.'

I asked Luke why there were troop movements in East Yemen. He said that he presumed that they were just preparing one of their regular raids on West Yemen.

'Is there anything for us to worry about?'

'Nothing at all,' he assured me.

I sat back and thought. Then I said to Luke: 'The American Ambassador talked about St George's Island as well.'

'Really?' said Luke again. 'Educated man, for an American.'

'Is there a problem there?' I asked.

'No, Prime Minister, just the normal local squabbles.'

Luke was hiding something. I didn't know what. And, of course, the trick is not finding the right answers, it's finding the right questions. I didn't know what question I should be asking, the question that would oblige Luke to tell me what the FO was concealing.

'The American Ambassador seemed worried about a possible Communist takeover,' I said eventually.

'Americans always are,' he smiled.

And that seemed to be that. So I picked up the next telegram – and I did not like what I read! Apparently we voted against Israel in the UN last night. I showed it to Luke. He remained calm.

'Luke,' I said, 'I gave express instructions that we were to abstain.'

'I think not, Prime Minister,' he said with his usual smile. How dare he?

'I did,' I reiterated firmly. 'I told the Foreign Secretary I felt very strongly that we should not take sides.'

'That's quite right,' agreed Luke. 'The Foreign Secretary noted your very strong feelings.'

I was on my feet now, very angry indeed. 'Well, why did he do nothing about it?' I shouted.

'With respect, Prime Minister,' said Luke, manifestly lacking respect, 'he did do something. He asked our UN Ambassador whether we should consider abstaining.'

'And what did the Ambassador do?' I asked.

'He said no,' replied Luke.

I was appalled. It seems that the Foreign Office thinks it can simply defy the wishes of the Prime Minister.

Luke denied that this is what happened. He says that the FO takes full account of my wishes in coming to a decision. But events move rapidly. 'There were important factors in our relationships with the Arabs last night that were not known to you when you took your view. It wasn't possible to get through to you in time.'

Bloody ridiculous! 'I am on the phone, you know,' I said.

'It was not thought sufficiently important to wake you at three a.m.'

'It was extremely important,' I yelled at that supercilious snob. 'The White House will do its nut!'

Luke didn't look as if he cared all that much. 'Well, I suppose I could arrange for you to be telephoned before every UN vote. But there are two or three a night while they're in session.'

He was wilfully missing the point. I don't express a personal view about many UN votes, as he knows only too well. But when I do, I expect it to be acted upon.

It was useless arguing about the mistake. I considered the future. 'What can I do to reverse this?' I asked him.

'Nothing, Prime Minister,' he replied flatly. 'That would be embarrassing. Once government policy has been stated it can't be retracted.'

Perhaps he's right. All the more reason not to state a policy that hasn't been approved by the PM!

Then I had an idea – a great idea. One that, I now believe, will change history. At the time I didn't realise where it would lead. 'Luke,' I said, 'I'd like to talk to the Israeli Ambassador.'

He shook his head. 'I think not, Prime Minister.'

I could hardly believe my ears. Who does Luke think he is? I repeated that I wanted to talk to the Israeli Ambassador. Luke stuck to his guns, and repeated that in his opinion it would be rather unwise.

I pointed a forefinger to my mouth. 'Luke,' I said, 'can you hear what I'm saying? Watch my lips move. I – WANT – TO – TALK – TO . . .'

He got the point. Finally he understood that I meant what I said. Who put it about that all these Foreign Office types are bright? Expensively educated – yes!

Luke said that if that was my wish, then of course! I felt like a small child being indulged. 'I will contact the Foreign Secretary and Sir Richard, and then ring the Israeli Ambassador.'

'I don't want either of them,' I said, enjoying myself hugely with this whippersnapper. 'I just want the Ambassador.'

He began to get a little edgy. 'Prime Minister, I have to advise you that it would be most improper to see him without the Foreign Secretary present.'

'Why?' I asked. 'What do you think I want to talk to the Israeli Ambassador about?'

He paused, scenting a trap. 'Well, presumably the vote at the UN.'

'Really, Luke!' I admonished him, with apparent severity and complete humbug. 'That would be most improper.'

He was stuck. 'Oh,' he said feebly.

Now it was my turn to follow up a lecture on propriety with a patronising smile. This was fun! 'No, Luke, it's just that Lucy is thinking of spending her next university vacation on a kibbutz. Or perhaps, since she's at the University of Essex, I should say another kibbutz.'

'I see,' said Luke grimly.

I went on to explain that the Israeli Ambassador and I were at the LSE together, and I thought that Annie and I would get him round to the flat to give his advice on kibbutzim.

'Oh,' said Luke again.

I smiled at him unhumorously. Showed my teeth, really, that's all. 'Nothing wrong with that, I take it?'

'Um – no,' he said again.

I rubbed salt in the wound. 'Do we need the Foreign Secretary or Sir Richard to help choose Lucy's holiday place?'

'Um – no,' he repeated, completely defeated.

I told him to fix it for six p.m. this evening, and dismissed him with a regal wave.

At least I'd won one round. And I hoped that David Bilu, my Israeli friend, would be able to help me find some way of reversing Foreign Office reflexes in relation to Israel.

I didn't succeed. But I did find out something else, of much greater import.

David came at six, and we sat in the living-room up at the top. He accepted my apologies about the UN vote with equanimity. He said that the Israelis were completely used to it, and it happens all the time.

I assured him that I had told my people to abstain. He believed me. He nodded, his big brown eyes sad and full of resignation. 'It's well known,' he explained gently, 'that in the British Foreign Office an instruction from the Prime Minister becomes a request from the Foreign Secretary, then a recommendation from the Minister of State and finally just a suggestion to the ambassador. If it ever gets that far.'

He spoke such perfect English that I was amazed. Then I remembered he *was* English, and emigrated to Palestine just before it became Israel.

Thankful that my apology was over and accepted with such good grace, I stood up to pour him another scotch. I was just about to raise the subject of how to deal with the problem that he had just outlined so accurately when he dropped his first bombshell.

'Well, Jim, what are you going to do about St George's Island?'

Slowly I turned to face him. 'You know about that?'

He shrugged. 'Obviously.'

I brought the drinks back to the coffee table and sat down. 'That's not a serious problem, is it?'

He was astonished. His eyebrows raised themselves halfway to his curly greying hairline. 'Isn't it? Your information must be better than mine.'

'How can it be?' I asked. 'Mine comes from the Foreign Office.'

He sipped his scotch. 'Israeli Intelligence says that East Yemen is going to invade St George's in the next few days.'

So that was the connection! And I hadn't been told!

David Bilu explained that the FO have agreed with East Yemen that the British will make strong representations but do nothing. In return, the Yemenis will let the British keep the contract to build a new airport there, after they have taken over.

But that's only the start. Apparently David has been told by Israel's Ambassador to Washington that the Americans plan to support the present government of St George's. In battle! On the island! They intend to send in an airborne division backed up by the Seventh Fleet.

The Americans invading a Commonwealth country to protect freedom and democracy would be a profound humiliation for the British! The Palace would hit the roof!

'Why haven't the Americans told me?' I asked David. I didn't think he'd know. But he did.

'They don't trust you,' he replied sympathetically.

I was embarrassed. 'Why not?'

'Because you trust the Foreign Office.'

I could see their point. I couldn't really blame them. Then David offered me some great advice.

'Jim, you have an airborne battalion on standby in Germany that is not now wanted for NATO exercises.'

'How do you know?' I said.

'I know,' he said. He seemed very confident. 'And if you sent it to St George's it would frighten East Yemen off. They would never invade. But, of course, it's not for the Israeli Ambassador to advise the British Prime Minister.'

His eyes were crinkling humorously. I grinned back at him. 'And he wouldn't take your advice anyway,' I said, as I hurried to the phone to take his advice.

I told the switchboard to get me the Foreign Secretary and the Defence Secretary in that order. While I waited for them to be found, I speculated as to why the FO hadn't covered themselves on this. They usually do. I had been through all my boxes tonight, except one. So I rummaged about in it, and near the bottom was a very thick file labelled Northern Indian Ocean: Situation Report. I realised this was probably it. I counted the pages: 128. I *knew* that this was it! But I'll have to go through it with a fine toothcomb before tomorrow.

Duncan came through on the blower. I told him that I wanted the President of St George's Island to invite Britain to send an airborne battalion for a goodwill visit. As a friendly gesture.

He saw no objection. Of course not – he doesn't quite understand what's going on either. He did remark that 800 paratroopers armed to the teeth is an awful lot for a goodwill visit. I told him it's just an awful lot of goodwill!

Then Paul[1] came on the line. It's amazing how quickly the system can track us all down. I was inspired. I told him that as we have an airborne battalion on standby in Germany I want it sent off to St George's. He was a bit awkward. He wanted to know how I knew we had a battalion on standby. Bloody cheek! I told him I knew, that's all!

He wanted to know where St George's was. Extraordinary ignorance. I told him sort of between Africa and India and to look on a map. Not that it matters to him where it is.

He was also sceptical that it was for purely a show-the-flag goodwill visit. I assured him that we'd been invited, and told him to give orders to leave in six hours. I explained it was an instant goodwill visit.

Finally, I told him to tell the press that it is a routine visit. He amended it to routine surprise visit, which was all right with me. He asked how to explain it all, and I suggested he say that we were invited earlier but the NATO exercises prevented us accepting the invitation – and now they're not needed in Germany, they're going to St George's instead.

He was still stalling, this time on the ludicrous grounds that the story isn't true. I pointed out that nobody knows it's not true and in any case press statements aren't delivered under oath. I rang off after telling him they'd better be airborne by midnight or else.

[1] Paul Sidgwick, the Secretary of State for Defence.

182

Its now one a.m., as I dictate these notes. The troops did leave before midnight – I checked. I feel completely invigorated, not at all tired, fresh as daisy, very excited – quite Napoleonic, in fact.

I thanked David Bilu for his help. He was impressed. 'You won't only frighten the Yemenis, you'll terrify the Foreign Office,' he said as he departed discreetly into the night through a side door.

He's right. And I'm looking forward to it. The Foreign Office is a hotbed of cold feet.

April 20th
My victory was complete today. I didn't sleep well, I was too excited. So I was already busy in my usual place in the Cabinet Room when Humphrey arrived.

It hasn't taken long for the FO to let him know what was going on, for Humphrey came straight in to see me.

'I gather,' he said, in a voice pregnant with malice, 'that there's an airborne battalion in the air.'

'Sounds like the best place for it,' I said with a grin.

He stared at me coldly. 'I gather it's on the way to St George's,' he said.

'Yes, it's due to land in a couple of hours, actually,' I confirmed.

He was not mollified by my engagingly frank manner. 'Quite,' he said nastily. 'Isn't this all rather sudden?'

I nodded cheerfully. 'Yes, I had a sudden friendly impulse, Humphrey,' I said. 'I wanted to spread some goodwill.'

'There's not a lot of goodwill at the Foreign Office this morning,' he growled.

'Really?' I said, pretending innocence. 'Why not?'

'It could be construed as provocative, flying a fully-armed airborne battalion in to a trouble spot like that. Explosive situation.'

I picked him up immediately on the word explosive. 'But Humphrey, you told me there were no problems there.'

He tried to get out of this corner he'd painted himself into. 'Yes. No. There aren't. No problems at all. But it's explosive . . . *potentially*. Moving troops around.'

'Come, come, Humphrey.' I was openly amused now. 'We're always moving troops around Salisbury Plain. Is that potentially explosive?'

Bernard intervened, trying to save Humphrey's face. I think. 'There's a lot of unexploded shells on Salisbury Plain.'

I thanked Bernard for his contribution, and politely invited

Humphrey to explain precisely what the Foreign Office was worried about. I was fascinated to see how it would be argued.

'It's a very sensitive part of the world,' he began.

'But they've been telling me how stable it is.'

Again he was stuck. 'Oh, it is. Yes, yes, it is.' His eyes narrowed. 'But it's a very unstable sort of stability.'

Luke came in just then, with the box of Foreign Office telegrams. His lips were so tight-set that they had virtually disappeared. With frigid politeness he set the box down in front of me. I opened it. 'Ooh, rather a lot,' I said with feigned surprise. I looked at Luke for his comments.

'Yes, the, er, somewhat unorthodox visit to St George's seems to have stirred things up,' he said thinly. [*'Somewhat unorthodox' was Foreign Office code for 'irresponsible and idiotic' – Ed.*]

The first telegram contained the best news: East Yemen was moving its troops back to base. 'They decided not to invade West Yemen after all?' I said to Luke, who nodded grimly. I knew that he knew, and he knew that I *knew* that he knew that I knew.

The next telegram was from the White House expressing delight at our goodwill visit. I showed it to Humphrey.

'And look,' I pointed to the relevant passage. 'They say they have a whole airborne division ready if we want reinforcements.'

'Reinforcements of what?' he challenged me.

I was unmoved. 'Reinforcements of goodwill, Humphrey,' I said with charm.

Humphrey could contain himself no longer. 'Prime Minister, may I ask where the impulse for this escapade came from?'

'Of course you may, Humphrey,' I replied. 'It came from Luke.'

Humphrey didn't know whether to believe me or not. He turned to Luke, who had gone ashen.

'From *me*?' gasped Luke, horror-struck.

I produced the 128-page file, *Northern Indian Ocean: Situation Report*, and flourished it at him. 'You put together this masterly report, didn't you?'

Luke was beginning to panic. He swallowed. 'Yes, but it was arguing that we needn't do anything.'

I gave him a conspiratorial smile, told him he couldn't fool me, and that I could read between the lines. I told him that the one small paragraph on page 107 (which I know he'd only put in to cover himself, in the least obtrusive way possible) had made it quite clear that St George's needed urgent support. 'I took the hint,' I said. 'Thank you.

Reproduced by courtesy of The Gaurdian.

And I've given you full credit, and told the Foreign Secretary to tell Sir Richard Wharton that it was your prompt warning that sparked off the whole military manoeuvre.' This, at least, was true – I had told the Foreign Secretary to make it known that this was Luke's idea.

Luke was desperate, and so anxious to defend himself that he couldn't possibly think of blaming the Israeli Ambassador, the obvious tip-off man. 'No, no, it wasn't me,' he cried. 'You haven't!'

'And I don't think I'm giving away any secrets when I say you are to be rewarded,' I said in my most avuncular voice. 'You are being sent as ambassador to a very important embassy. Straightaway!'

'Which embassy?' Luke whispered, fearing the worst.

'Tel Aviv,' I said with delight.

'My God,' croaked Luke, a broken man. 'No! Please! You can't send me to Israel. What about my career?'

'Nonsense,' I replied briskly, knowing only too well that this would be the end of him. 'It's an honour. Promotion.'

Luke was trying anything to save himself. 'But what about the Israelis? You'll upset them. They won't want me, they know I'm on the Arabs' side!'

I didn't speak. I allowed the silence to speak for itself. Convicted

185

out of his own mouth. We all stared at Luke, and I heard the grand-father clock ticking. 'Not that I meant . . .' he said feebly, then stopped.

Bernard and Humphrey averted their eyes. They didn't like being present at the end of a colleague's career.

I answered him. 'I thought you were supposed to be on our side,' I remarked quietly.

Luke was silent.

'Anyway,' I said with a brisk smile, 'we need someone like you in Tel Aviv to explain to them why we always vote against them in the UN. Don't we, Humphrey?'

Humphrey looked up at me. He knew when the game was lost. 'Yes Prime Minister,' he said humbly.

7
The
Smokescreen

[*Some three and a half months after Hacker became Prime Minister he had to face his first Cabinet crisis, and the way in which he overcame it was a tribute to his increasing political skills. The crisis involved many issues simultaneously – his fight to save his Grand Design, threatened leaks, the threatened resignation of at least one and possibly two junior ministers, and his use of the powerful tobacco lobby in a fight to outwit the Treasury and obtain tax cuts to give him some short-term electoral advantage.*

The origins of the crisis may be seen in the notes of a meeting that took place early in May between Sir Humphrey Appleby, the Cabinet Secretary, and Sir Frank Gordon, the Permanent Secretary of the Treasury. There is no reference to this meeting in Sir Humphrey's diary but Sir Frank's notes were recently found in the Civil Service archives in Walthamstow – Ed.]

Lunched with Appleby at the Reform Club. Appleby was concerned because our new Prime Minister wishes to cut either taxes or public expenditure.

This should be resisted. Politicians are like children – you can't just give them what they want, it only encourages them.

Nonetheless, Appleby should not even have allowed it to get as far as

187

being a *Formal Proposal*. It should not have been allowed to get past *Informal Discussions*.

[*Sir Frank Gordon could not have been seriously worried. There are nine further preliminary stages after Informal Discussions and Formal Proposals. All eleven stages are as follows:*

1. *Informal discussions*
2. *Formal proposals*
3. *Preliminary study*
4. *Discussion document*
5. *In-depth study*
6. *Revised proposal*
7. *Policy*
8. *Strategy*
9. *Implementation plan circulated*
10. *Revised implementation plan*
11. *Cabinet authorisation*

Any competent Civil Servant should be able to ensure that if a policy is unwelcome, stage 11 will not be reached until the run-up to the next General Election – Ed.]

Humphrey is unduly relaxed about the matter, in my humble opinion. The possible tax cut is contingent upon Hacker's fantasy about cancelling Trident and switching to conscription to create large conventional forces. The Services will never wear it because, however much they dislike Trident, they hate conscription.

But my staff are horrified. There are waves of panic running through the Treasury. Giving away one and a half billion pounds of our money is unthinkable. [*Hacker was arguing that the money was the taxpayers', and that – in the event of a tax cut – the Treasury would merely* not *be taking it away from them. This has never been the Treasury view – Ed.*]

I indicated to Humphrey Appleby that Arnold[1] would never have allowed such a notion to become a Proposal. Appleby observed, with some justice, that Arnold was not at Number Ten with the present inmate.[2]

As Humphrey Appleby is relatively new to the job I made the following matters clear to him:

1) The entire system depends on the supposition that he can control the PM and that I can control the Chancellor.
2) For this control to be maintained there must be an agreeable mistrust between them.
3) Hostility between them would be preferable.
4) Tax cuts unite them. Politicians win votes with them.
5) Even *proposed* tax cuts unite them, because they give the promise of votes to be won.

Appleby was confident. One might almost say complacent. He is confident that the Prime Minister and the Chancellor will manage their hostility without our help. Eric,[3] he believes, will never forgive Jim for winning

[1] Sir Arnold Robinson, the previous Cabinet Secretary.
[2] Hacker.
[3] Eric Jeffries, the Chancellor of the Exchequer.

Number Ten, and Jim can never trust Eric again – after all, one never trusts anyone that one has deceived.

I have *ensured*, however, that Eric opposes any tax cuts. I used the usual bait – told him we needed the money for hospitals, schools and the old people. [*This argument was known in the Treasury as the Kidney Machine Gambit. It hardly ever failed. It was followed up with the suggestion that the incumbent would be known to history as The Caring Chancellor. This never failed – Ed.*]

Appleby still felt that I was overly concerned about a tax cut of a mere one and a half billion pounds. It is true that the amount is not much in itself. But I indicated that some of our senior colleagues are worried that he (Appleby) is not in control. This cut has been proposed far too soon. Is Appleby able to keep up Arnold's tradition – the iron fist in the iron glove? It would, after all, be a black day for Britain if the politicians started running the country.

[*Sir Humphrey Appleby did not seem unduly worried by Sir Frank's hints, anxieties and veiled threats. He records his own dry comments in his diary.*]

Frank was worried about Hacker's proposed tax cuts. They are serious, I know, but if I were in his shoes I should be much more worried about the state of the economy and low productivity. Of course, there's not much Frank can do about that. The British worker is fundamentally lazy and wants something for nothing. Nobody wants to do an honest day's work any more.

This afternoon I went to Lords. When I got there England were seventy for four. Another collapse by England. What with the state of the pound and the state of our batting one sometimes wonders whether England has any future at all.

Still, it was a delightful afternoon. Warm sunshine, cold champagne, and the characteristic smack of willow on leather – occasionally, anyway.

I was there on government business, of course, as the guest of Gerald Baron, Chairman of the British Tobacco Group. The BTG are national benefactors in my opinion. I took the opportunity to ask Gerald for more sponsorship for the Garden.[1] Gerald was fairly open to the idea, though he mentioned that the Minister for Sport might also drop in at Lords this afternoon, twisting his arm on behalf of Wimbledon, Brands Hatch or some snooker tournament. I don't know where we'd all be without the BTG.

I did notice, however, that Dr Peter Thorn, the Minister of State for Health, was again conspicuous by his absence. Apparently he's been got at by the anti-smoking lobby. Gerald asked me if Dr Thorn has much clout in Whitehall. I was able to reassure him on that score. Dr Thorn is only a Minister, and has no clout at all.
[*Appleby Papers WHS/41/DE*]

---

[1] The Royal Opera House, in Covent Garden, which was more or less run from the Cabinet Office.

[*Hacker's diary continues – Ed.*]

May 3rd

Humphrey and I had a meeting about a study paper that he had sent me on the subject of cancelling Trident and reintroducing conscription. It was very long, very full, very fat, and completely unreadable.

I showed it to him. He was pleased with it. 'Ah yes, we can't get enough papers on that,' he remarked smugly. 'We need lots of input. We don't want to make any announcements until we have examined every implication and ramification.' Familiar delaying tactics.

'This *is* going to happen, Humphrey,' I told him firmly.

'Oh yes, Prime Minister.' By *yes* he meant *no*. 'Indeed it is, beyond question, at the appropriate juncture, in due course, in the fullness of time.'

'No Humphrey,' I replied sharply. 'This century. This Parliament, in fact.'

He shook his head sadly. 'This Parliament? I'm not sure it would be fruitful. The time may not be ripe. It could turn out to be a banana skin.'

Perhaps his doubts are a reflection of the curious obstinacy that I am encountering from Eric. The paper shows that if my plan goes ahead we'll have one and a half billion pounds available for tax cuts. And the Chancellor, of all people, opposes it. How can he oppose such a chance to win popularity from the voters? The only possibility, according to Humphrey, is that Eric is being advised by the Treasury, which apparently doesn't believe in giving money back.

This is always hard for a non-Treasury man to understand. I explained that the money is not the Treasury's, it is the taxpayers'.

'That *is* one view,' Humphrey acknowledged. 'But it is not the view that the Treasury takes. Not once they have got their hands on it.'

'But if they don't need the money . . .' I began.

He interrupted me, puzzled. 'I'm sorry?' he asked.

'If they don't need it . . .' I reiterated, and was again stopped in mid-sentence.

'Taxation,' said Humphrey loftily, 'isn't about what you need. The Treasury does not work out what it needs and then think how to raise the money. The Treasury pitches for as much as it can get away with and then thinks how to spend it. If the government started to give money back just because we didn't need it, we would be breaking with centuries of tradition. What would happen to the British Navy, for instance?'

I couldn't see any relevance to the question. 'It would still be there. We still need a Navy.'

Humphrey explained that, as we only have four capital ships, we only would *need* four Admirals and one Admiral of the Fleet. Whereas we have a total of sixty Admirals. And tempting though it would be to do away with fifty-six of them, the effect would be to reduce the number of serving officers all the way down, until there was hardly anybody left in the Navy at all.

I felt this was a red herring. My conversation with Humphrey was completely circular. To summarise it: the Treasury is the most powerful department of government because it controls all the money. Every time you take away some of its money you take away some of its power. Therefore it resists. The only way to get the Treasury to agree to tax cuts is to get the Chancellor to agree. But the Chancellor won't agree unless the Treasury agrees. So how do you force the Treasury's hand? Only by forcing the Chancellor's hand. And how do you force the Chancellor's hand? Only by forcing the Treasury's hand.

Humphrey suggested that I try to persuade the Chancellor to give me his active support. He is my Cabinet colleague. That, briefly, is the drawback – I need help from somebody who is on *my* side.

We got nowhere. I'll have to give this a lot of thought.

May 10th
Today I saw the way to get my tax cuts. And the help is going to come from a most unlikely source: the Minister of State for Health. Not only is he an unlikely source of help, he doesn't even know that he's going to help. And I'm certainly not going to tell him!

This is how it happened. Dr Thorn came to see me. He had sent me a paper on cigarettes, apparently, and the power and influence of the tobacco lobby in this country. Unfortunately I hadn't had time to read it. He asked me for my reaction to it, so I asked him to summarise it in his own words.

'Those were my own words,' he said, slightly nonplussed.

Bernard came to the rescue, very skilfully. 'The Prime Minister often finds that a brief verbatim summary clarifies the emphasis and focuses on the salient points.'

'Salient points,' I echoed, to encourage Dr Thorn.

So he told me what he had in mind, I was staggered. His idea was for the government to take action to eliminate smoking. He had a five-point plan:

1. A complete ban on all cigarette sponsorship.
2. A complete ban on all cigarette advertising, even at the point of sale.
3. Fifty million pounds to be spent on anti-smoking publicity.
4. A ban on smoking in all public places.
5. Progressive deterrent tax rises over five years until a packet of twenty costs about the same as a bottle of whisky.

It is a drastic scheme. He claims it should reduce smoking by at least eighty per cent. Even ninety per cent, perhaps. He reckons it will drive the tobacco companies out of business.

I had no immediate answer for such radical proposals. Of course, it would have helped if I'd read his paper before the meeting, but one can't find time for everything! But he was very serious and I had to keep him happy. So I told him that obviously Ⅰ agreed with him, basically, that smoking ought to be stopped. No question. And I told him that we would definitely stop it in due course, at the appropriate juncture, in the fullness of time. I could see Bernard nodding with approval in the background. I'm getting very good at Civil Service stalling techniques.

Dr Thorn could see what I was doing, though. 'You mean, forget it?'

I assured him that that wasn't what I meant. And it wasn't! Well, not exactly! But we do have to be realistic. 'After all,' I remarked, 'we weren't born yesterday.'

'No.' He was very tight-lipped. 'And we didn't die yesterday.'

'What do you mean?' I asked.

'Three hundred people did die yesterday, prematurely, as a result of smoking. There are a hundred thousand deaths a year, at least.'

I tried to show Peter just how unrealistic he was being. If I took his proposal to Cabinet, the Treasury and the Chancellor would surely say that smoking brings in four billion pounds a year in revenue, and that we can't possibly manage without it.

Peter insisted that he wasn't unrealistic. 'I know you can't beat the Treasury with financial arguments. But this is a moral argument.'

And then my *brilliant* idea occurred to me! A way to beat the Treasury. With Dr Peter Thorn's help, but without his knowledge. And *not* on the issue of smoking, but as a means of securing the tax cuts that I want.

I was very careful. I didn't *exactly* tell Thorn that I'd support him. But I told him he'd made his case, and that we could give his plan a try. I told him I'd even read his paper. I added 'again' just in time.

He tried to pin me down on the issue of actual support for him. I explained that I couldn't give him *public* support – not yet. 'It would undermine my position if I took sides at this stage. I have to be seen as the impartial judge who is persuaded by the strength of the case.'

He said he saw the sense of that. He is a bit gullible. I must remember that, it could be dangerous. Or useful, come to think of it.

'But off the record,' I concluded, 'I'd like to see this pushed very hard. Very hard indeed. I'd like to see you make some speeches on it.'

Bernard looked alarmed, but Dr Thorn's face lit up. He flushed with pleasure, and thanked me profusely for my help. I thanked him for his cigarette paper. [*Presumably Dr Thorn understood that Hacker meant his paper on cigarettes – Ed.*]

After Peter Thorn left Bernard asked me if I were serious. He explained that it has been the practice in the past to discourage anti-smoking speeches by Ministers, and not to print or distribute their speeches if they make them. I asked Bernard if there had ever been a written directive on this. He said that it wouldn't be cricket, and that there was just a gentleman's agreement of the matter.

I instructed Bernard to check that Peter Thorn's anti-smoking speeches are printed and distributed, and to make sure that everyone knows. It is particularly important that the Treasury gets to hear of it all soon.

Bernard, of course, had no idea of my plan and he asked me if I thought I could possibly win this fight.

I smiled cheerfully. 'Some you win, Bernard, and some you lose. This one I shall definitely lose.'

Now he was completely baffled. 'Then why . . . ?'

I saved his breath for him. 'Because *when* I lose they'll have to give me something in return. If you were the Treasury, which would you rather give up – one and a half billion pounds of income tax revenue or four billion pounds of tobacco tax revenue?'

He smiled. 'I'd prefer the income tax cut.'

I nodded. 'And that, as you know, is what I've wanted all along.'

His face was full of admiration and respect. 'So you're using cigarettes to create a sort of smokescreen?'

'Precisely,' I said.

May 11th

Humphrey came to see me this morning. He was very tense. Clearly Bernard has been doing an excellent job of making sure that everyone knows about Dr Thorn's new policies.

'Prime Minister,' he began, 'I just wondered . . . did you have an interesting chat with Dr Thorn?'

'Yes. He has proposed the elimination of smoking.'

Sir Humphrey laughed derisively. 'And how, pray, does he intend to achieve this? A campaign of mass hypnosis, perhaps?'

I remained calm. I leaned back in my chair and smiled confidently at him. 'No. By raising taxes on tobacco sky high, and simultaneously prohibiting all cigarette advertising including at the point of sale.'

Humphrey chuckled confidently, but said nothing.

'Don't you think,' I asked, 'that his position is admirably moral?'

He was as superior as only Humphrey can be. 'Moral perhaps, but extremely silly. No one in their right mind could seriously contemplate such a proposal.'

'I'm contemplating it,' I said.

'Yes, of *course*,' he replied without a moment's hesitation, the patronising smile wiped instantly from his face. 'Don't misunderstand me, of course it's right to contemplate all proposals that come from your government, but no sane man could ever *support* it.'

'I'm supporting it,' I said.

'And quite right too, Prime Minister, if I may say so.' His footwork is so fast that one might be forgiven for not noticing that he totally reversed his opinion with each sentence he uttered.

I gave him the chance to come over to my side. 'So you'll support it?' I asked.

'Support it?' He was emphatic. 'I support it wholeheartedly! A splended, novel, romantic, well-meaning, imaginative, do-gooding notion.'

As I thought. He is totally against it!

'The only problem is', he continued, 'that there are powerful arguments against such a policy.'

'And powerful arguments for it,' I replied.

Oh, *absolutely*! But *against* it,' he persisted, 'there are those who will point out that the tax on tobacco is a major source of revenue to the government.'

'But there are also those who would point out that tobacco is a major cause of death from a number of killer diseases[1].'

---

[1] Cancers of the lung, larynx, mouth, oesophagus, pancreas, bladder and kidney; emphesyma and chronic bronchitis; coronary heart disease; strokes; peri-natal mortality; and smoking in pregnancy carries a higher risk of still birth. Also there were about 10,000 fires per annum, in the 1980s, attributed to smoking, causing about 250 deaths a year.

Humphrey nodded earnestly. 'Yes. Indeed. Shocking. If it's true. But of course, no *definite* causal link has ever been proved, has it?'

'The statistics are unarguable,' I said.

He looked amused. 'Statistics? You can prove anything with statistics.'

'Even the truth,' I remarked.

'Ye-es,' he acknowledged with some reluctance. 'But £4 billion revenue per annum is a considerable sum. They would say,' he added hastily, for fear of it being thought that he was taking sides in this dispute. *They* were clearly the Treasury.

I remarked that a hundred thousand unnecessary deaths a year – minimum – is a hideous epidemic. He agreed that it was appalling. So I went for the kill. 'It costs the NHS[1] a fortune to deal with the victims. So the Treasury would be delighted if we discouraged it.'

This was a tactical error. Sir Humphrey swung confidently on to the offensive. 'Now I think you're wrong there, Prime Minister.'

I couldn't see how I could be wrong. 'Smoking-related diseases,' I said, referring to Dr Thorn's paper which I had in front of me, 'cost the NHS £165 million a year.'

But Sir Humphrey had been well briefed too, by the Treasury and by their friends in the tobacco lobby. 'We have gone into that,' he replied. 'It's been shown that, if those extra 100,000 people a year had lived to a ripe old age, they would have cost us even more in pensions and social security than they did in medical treatment. So, financially, it is unquestionably better that they continue to die at about the present rate.'

I was shocked. I've been in politics a long time and not much shocks me any more. But his cynicism is truly appalling. [*Interestingly, Hacker was shocked by Sir Humphrey's cynical desire to encourage smoking, but was not shocked by his own self-declared plan to use the smoking issue merely as a way to force the Treasury into conceding income tax cuts. He had no more intention than Sir Humphrey of following Dr Thorn's advice. But he was able to convince himself, temporarily, that he was less hypocritical than his Cabinet Secretary. Of such self-deceptions are great political leaders made. Thus Hacker was able to conduct the argument with Sir Humphrey in moral terms – Ed.*]

'Humphrey,' I said, 'when cholera killed 30,000 people in 1833 we got the Public Health Act. When smog killed 2500 people in 1952 we got the Clean Air Act. When a commercial drug kills fifty or sixty people we get it withdrawn from sale, even if it's doing lots of good to

[1] National Health Service.

195

many patients. But cigarettes kill 100,000 people a year and what do we get?'

'Four billion pounds a year,' he replied promptly. 'Plus about 25,000 jobs in the tobacco industry, a flourishing cigarette export business which helps the balance of trade. Also, 250,000 jobs indirectly related to tobacco – newsagents, packing, transport . . .'

I interrupted. 'These figures are just guesses.'

'No,' he said, 'they are government statistics.' He saw me smile, and hurriedly continued: 'That is to say, they are facts.'

I couldn't resist it. 'You mean, your statistics are facts, but my facts are just statistics?'

Sir Humphrey decided it was time to tell another little untruth. 'Look, I'm on your side, Prime Minister. I'm only giving you arguments you will encounter.'

I thanked him, and told him that I was glad to know that I should have support such as his. I hoped that would bring the conversation to a close – but no! He was determined to give me *all* the arguments I shall encounter.

'It will also be pointed out that the tobacco industry is a great sponsor of sport. They give much innocent pleasure to millions of people, and you would be taking it all away. After all, where would the BBC sports programmes be if the cigarette companies couldn't advertise on them?' [*This was a slip of the tongue by Appleby. Until the late 1980s the BBC maintained the fiction that it did not screen advertisements. Of course, he must have intended to ask where BBC sports programmes would be if cigarette companies could not 'sponsor' the events that are televised – Ed.*]

I reiterated that we were discussing over 100,000 deaths each year. Humphrey agreed immediately.

'Yes, Prime Minister . . . but in a very overpopulated island. And there aren't enough jobs for everyone anyway. The benefits of smoking greatly outweigh the ill-effects: cigarettes pay for *one-third* of the total cost of the National Health Service. We are saving many more lives than we otherwise could because of those smokers who voluntarily lay down their lives for their friends. Smokers are national benefactors.'

'So long as they live,' I reminded him grimly.

'So long as they live.' He nodded. 'And when they die they save the rest of us a lot of money. And anyway, there's always more coming along to replace them. Not that any direct causal link has been proved, as I said before.'

This nonsense about no direct causal link was beginning to irritate me. I reminded Humphrey that the US Surgeon-General says that 'cigarette smoking is the chief avoidable cause of death in our society and the most important public health issue of our time'.

Humphrey dismissed the US Surgeon-General's report with a patronising smile. 'In his society, maybe. But do remember, Prime Minister, that Americans do love overstating everything, bless their warm little hearts.' He begged me to do nothing rash, to be very sure of my ground, and be very careful before I made any move. Of course, that's what he says about virtually everything.

Bernard interrupted us. It was time for Cabinet Committee, to be followed by lunch at the House – where the Minister for Sport wanted an urgent word with me.

The news is certainly getting round fast. I stared accusingly at Humphrey, pretending to be angry.

'Who tipped him off?' I enquired.

Humphrey and Bernard looked at each other. Then they looked at me. They remained silent.

'He's part of the tobacco lobby,' I said to Humphrey.

Humphrey pretended he didn't know. 'A member of your government?' he asked, with a feeble pretence of shock-horror.

This ploy was unworthy of Humphrey. *Obviously* the Minister for Sport has a vested interest in tobacco – all that sponsorship. Furthermore, this particular Minister for Sport [*Leslie Potts MP – Ed.*] is the Member for one of the Nottingham constituencies – and there are thousands of tobacco workers in Nottingham.

I told Bernard to tell the Minister I'd give him ten minutes at 2.30.

'With pleasure, Prime Minister.'

'Not with pleasure, Bernard,' I replied, 'but I'll see him anyway.'

At 2.30 we had our meeting. I have inherited Leslie Potts from the previous administration. He really is a dreadfully unappealing, unattractive figure. He is short, very thin, with bulging pop-eyes that seem to bulge even more than nature intended because they are so heavily magnified behind his inch-thick spectacles. He coughs and wheezes, his fingers are permanently stained yellow with nicotine, he chain-smokes and spreads ash all around him like an ancient volcano. His hair is greasy, his teeth are yellow, and he smells like a smoker's railway compartment, second class. I can only suppose that when my predecessor appointed him Minister for Sport he must have been giving a rare outing to his little-known sense of humour.

'Mind if I smoke?' rasped Potts.

I shook my head, whereupon a lit cigarette appeared instantly from inside his half-closed fist. He took a deep drag on it, coughed a bit, and asked about the rumour that I intended making a personal attack on the tobacco industry.

I gave a truthful but irrelevant answer. 'I haven't heard that rumour,' I said.

'Is it true?' asked Leslie, not deceived.

'The Minister of Health is considering the matter. No decision has been taken.'

'There's no smoke without fire,' said Leslie. He should know!

'Naturally you'd be consulted,' I said, in my most consultative voice. 'As Minister for Sport I realise that you have an interest in the matter.'

'I don't give a stuff about sport! I've got 4000 tobacco workers in my constituency. What about my seat?'

'What about your lungs?' I said.

'My lungs are fine,' he snarled.

'And he doesn't breathe through his seat,' said Bernard, not very helpfully.

'What did you say?' wheezed Potts.

'Oh,' said Bernard. 'Your seat. I see. Sorry.'

I tried not to laugh. I silenced Bernard with a wave and turned back to Leslie.

'I am aware, of course, that your constituency has a cigarette factory in it. But sometimes one must take a broader view.'

'Even *broader* than your seat,' added Bernard mischievously. I didn't dare meet his eyes – I might have burst out laughing.

Leslie Potts MP was not amused. 'It's not just *my* seat,' he snapped. 'There are marginal seats in Bristol, Nottingham, Glasgow, Basildon and Northern Ireland, all with tobacco works. And then there's all the brewery towns, which are owned by the tobacco manufacturers.'

'I can see there's a problem,' I acknowledged. 'But if something is right for the country, don't you agree that the government should do it regardless?'

There was no contest as far as Leslie Potts was concerned. 'Of *course* the government must do what's right – but not if it affects marginal constituencies! There's obviously a limit.'

I reassured him that no decision had yet been taken. And of course the decision he fears never will be – it's a *different* result that I'm after. But he wouldn't let it drop. He told me that, for the good of the party,

I couldn't interfere in the smoking issue.

I disliked being told what I can and can't do by junior members of my government! 'It's no good huffing and puffing at me, Leslie,' I complained.

'Sorry,' he said, waving away clouds of second-hand blue smoke.

'Weren't you.' I went on, 'a paid consultant for the British Tobacco Group?'

He drew himself up majestically to his full height of five foot two and a half, and replied in his most self-righteous tone. 'The fact that BTG paid me a small retainer is totally beside the point.' I managed to keep a straight face. 'They are a very generous corporation with a strong sense of responsibility towards the community. Look at all the money they give to sports. And now you're trying to stop them!'

I'd had enough of all this rubbish. 'Leslie,' I said firmly, 'they only give money to help sell more cigarettes.'

'No,' he insisted doggedly, 'they're doing it out of a genuine wish to serve the community.'

'That's fine,' I answered. 'In that case, they can go on giving the money anonymously, if they like.'

'Ah,' he said, and hesitated. 'Well . . . of course, they would be very happy to, provided they could publicise the fact that they were doing it anonymously.' He saw no problem there. 'Tell me, Jim, is it true that Peter Thorn is also trying to change the government health warning?'

I didn't want to reply, so I looked to Bernard for help. But Bernard was still not taking the conversation absolutely seriously. 'I believe,' he replied, deadpan, 'that Dr Thorn is proposing something like *Dying of cancer can seriously damage your health*.'

Leslie Potts was outraged. 'It's simply not true!' he exclaimed. I wonder if he believes it himself. By now I am really coming to believe that we must actually do something about this smoking and health problem – but not until the time is ripe, I think.

'Look, Leslie,' I said, 'if we do nothing there'll be a million premature deaths in this country over the next ten years – minimum.' I actually shocked myself as I uttered that statistic.

'I agree,' he answered desperately. 'A million deaths. Terrible. But they'll be *evenly spread*, not just in the marginal constituencies. Listen, Jim, there is no conclusive proof of any causal link between smoking and . . .'

I couldn't understand the rest of his sentence. It was lost in another paroxysm of coughing and choking. But I think I got the gist.

199

[*Meanwhile, an anxious correspondence was taking place between Sir Humphrey Appleby and Sir Frank Gordon, Permanent Secretary of the Treasury. Copies of the letters have been found in both the Cabinet Office files and the Treasury files, all now available to us under the Thirty Year Rule. As the discussion was in writing, both gentlemen were careful to express their enthusiasm for government policy. Their real feelings must be read between the lines – Ed.*]

70 WHITEHALL, LONDON SW1A 2AS

From the Secretary of the Cabinet and Head of the Home Civil Service

May 15 th

Dear Frank,

We are, of course, agreed that in an ideal world cigarette smoking would be discouraged. And we agree, obviously, that it is our duty to help the Prime Minister achieve his objectives. Nonetheless, we may have to help him understand that we are not in an ideal world and that he might be wise to reappraise not his objectives but his priorities.

He is unfortunately subject to silly pressure groups and fanatics such as the Royal College of Physicians. These fanatics want the Government to have a policy about smoking.

This is wishful thinking, I regret to say. It is not how the world works. Everyone outside government wants government policies. But none of us in government want them including, I venture to suggest, the Prime Minister when he fully understands the risks and the downside.

If you have a policy someone can hold you to it. And although the anti-smoking lobby see the whole matter in terms of black and white, merely preventing death and so forth, we know that the whole issue is much more complex than this.

As in all government, I'm sure that you agree that there has to be a balance. For instance the Minister of Health may be anti-smoking, but the Minister for Sport needs the tobacco companies.

It would be easier if the government were a team. But as, in fact, it is a loose confederation of warring tribes, it is up to us to find the common ground.

Comments, please.

HA

[The following day a reply was received – Ed.]

H M Treasury

Permanent Secretary   May 16

Dear Humphrey,

　　The Minister for Health wishes the smoking problem
dealt with by high taxation. The Chancellor, however, will
not let me raise taxes too high – he is concerned about his
own popularity with the electorate.

　　I must agree with him, for other reasons. The inflationary
effect of such a high rise in cigarette taxes would be
considerable.

　　Nonetheless, it must be admitted that there is a moral
principle involved. And we at the Treasury fully understand
and applaud the PM's concern. We earnestly believe in the
moral principle.

　　But when four billion pounds of revenue is at stake I
think that we have to consider very seriously how far we are
entitled to indulge ourselves in the rather selfish luxury of
pursuing moral principles.

　　As you recall, I have been worried about a suggested
income tax cut of one and a half billion, and that was in a
proposal that may not now happen. A cut of four billion would
be a catastrophe!

　　I suggest we get Noel's opinion and advice. I have copied
these letters to him.

Frank

*[The copies of the correspondence were sent to the DHSS[1] for the
comments of Sir Noel Whittington, the Permanent Secretary. Two
days later this letter was sent to Sir Frank, with a copy to Sir Humphrey
– Ed.]*

[1] Department of Health and Social Security.

Department of Health and Social Security

LP1

May 18th

Dear Frank,

There are several worrying implications raised by this potential cigarette tax increase:

1. It is not just a matter of revenue loss. There is also the question of scrutiny. If we 'took on' the tobacco companies they would put a host of people on to scrutinising everything we do. They would point out, publicly, any errors of facts, inconsistencies of argument, inaccurate or misleading published figures, and so forth. Of course, it is said that our work should be able to stand up to scrutiny. Quite right too! Parliamentary scrutiny and press scrutiny are to be applauded. But not professional scrutiny, which could take up far too much government time. It is therefore not in the public interest to provoke it.

2. The tobacco companies might attempt to embarrass us by threatening to drag up all the times we have accepted invitations to lunches and free tickets at Wimbledon, Glyndebourne, etc.

3. Where would the arts be without tobacco sponsorship? They would be at the mercy of the Arts Council!

4. Above all, and here I speak for the DHSS specifically, we must remind the PM that there is a moral issue here: Government must be impartial. It is not proper for us to take sides as between health and cigarettes. This is especially true in the DHSS, which is the Department

Cont.

2.

    of Health <u>and Social Security</u>. We have a dual responsibility.
What will happen, if we lose the tobacco revenues, to the
extra 100,000 people per year who would be alive and drawing
pensions?

    It is clear that we must, as always, maintain a balance. We
want a healthy nation, but we also need a healthy tobacco industry.

    We have a duty to be even-handed: tobacco sponsorship may
encourage people to smoke, but sponsored sport encourages them
to take exercise.

    In my view, the DHSS may already go too far on this anti-
smoking matter. We already devote one third of an Assistant
Secretary's time and half a Principal's time to reducing smoking.
Surely this is enough in a free society.

    In summation I make two suggestions:

    1) that Humphrey Appleby arranges for the PM to meet some
of the tobacco people. He would then see what jolly good chaps
they are, and how genuinely concerned about health risks. In
my view, there cannot be anything seriously wrong with BTG, for
instance: they have an ex-Permanent Secretary on their Board.
And it has been suggested that they could well need another, in
the fullness of time.

    2) I think we might raise some questions about our junior
Minister, Dr Peter Thorn. He is a highly intelligent, very
imaginative Minister. But he is inexperienced, and not at all
even-handed. Unfortunately, he comes to his post with severe bias:
he is a doctor and, as such, he is unable to take the broader
view. His <u>sole point</u> is keeping people alive. Seeing patients
die must have, regrettably, distorted his judgement. It is
understandable, of course, but emotional responses are a great
handicap to cool decision-taking.

    I look forward to hearing your conclusions. I think it
is vital that Sir Humphrey takes some immediate action.

*[Sir Humphrey considered this correspondence carefully, and made
the following note in his private diary – Ed.]*

[1] This suggests that hints had been dropped to Sir Noel himself.

Thursday 18 MAY

I shall be meeting the P.M. after the weekend, and must have a strategy on this tobacco matter.

I believe that the key lies in Noël's

I shall be meeting the PM after the weekend, and must have a strategy on this tobacco matter.

I believe that the key lies in Noel's comment that we are a free society. Therefore people should be free to make their own decisions. Government should not be a nursemaid. We do not want the Nanny State.

The only drawback to this view is that it is also an argument for legalising the sale of marijuana, heroin, cocaine, arsenic and gelignite.

My strategy, therefore, is as follows: When Hacker was Minister for Administrative Affairs[1] he accompanied me not only to Glyndebourne as the guest of the BTG, but also Wimbledon, Lords, the opera and the ballet.

At *The Sleeping Beauty* one might have thought he was auditioning for the title role. He has no interest at all in the arts, which is why using sponsorship to save the arts from the Arts Council is likely to be an unproductive line of argument. At the ballet he kept quiet, apart from his snoring. When Act IV of the Wagner started at the Garden he asked why they were playing extra time. And he referred to Act V as 'injury time'. A total philistine.

But I digress. It seems that he is implicated in receiving tobacco hospitality worth hundreds of pounds, if not thousands, from the BTG. If this were to leak, shocking though a leak might be, it could be a grave embarrassment for him.

[*Sir Humphrey overestimated his threat. At the meeting four days later Hacker was able to deal with it with an ease that surprised the Cabinet Secretary – Ed.*]

[1] See *Yes Minister*, Vols 1–3, and *The Complete Yes Minister*.

SIR BERNARD WOOLLEY RECALLS:[1]

The Prime Minister was in very bullish mood on the morning of 22 May. He informed me that things were going very well, and that he had the Treasury on the run. And the Chancellor.

I asked him if this was entirely to the good. After all, the Chancellor is a member of the Prime Minister's own government.

'Of course it's good,' he told me. 'He's got to be brought to heel. He's got to learn to co-operate.'

I asked him what he meant, precisely, by co-operate. He revealed that he defined co-operation as obeying his commands! 'That', he said, 'is what co-operation means if you are Prime Minister.'

It reminded me not a little of Humpty Dumpty.[2]

'The Chancellor wanted to be Premier, remember? He was the front runner. And I outsmarted him.' How well I remember this! The Prime Minister did a little dance of glee in front of his study windows. 'Now I'm outsmarting him again. He knows that if he loses £4 billion of tobacco revenue he'll either have to impose four billion more in other taxes, which will make him frightfully unpopular in the country, or cut £4 billion of government expenditure, which will make him even more unpopular in the Cabinet. They're all terrified about Peter Thorn's policies – loss of smokers' votes, loss of tobacco taxes, loss of jobs – it's wonderful! So I shall support Peter Thorn until I get the Treasury to stop obstructing me on the income tax cut of 1.5 billion that *I* want.'

[*Hacker's diary continues – Ed.*]

May 22nd

A good meeting with Humphrey. He began it by showing me some impenetrable piece of paper, always a good sign I now realise. He can no longer bamboozle me like that. It's merely an indication of his own insecurity. [*A sign of Hacker's growing awareness and administrative skill – Ed.*]

[*The piece of paper contained Sir Humphrey's comments on a submission concerning Dr Thorn's plans, which had been submitted by the DHSS. The entire submission survives. Sir Humphrey's comments are reproduced overleaf – Ed.*]

---

[1] In conversation with the Editors.

[2] 'When I use a word,' Humpty Dumpty said in a rather scornful tone, 'it means just what I use it to mean – neither more nor less.'

'The question is,' said Alice, 'whether you *can* make words mean so many different things.'

'The question is,' said Humpty Dumpty, 'which is to be master – that's all.'
Through the Looking-Glass, Chapter 5, by Lewis Carroll.

(1)

Notwithstanding the fact that the
proposal could conceivably encompass
certain concomitant benefits of a marginal
and peripheral relevance, there is a
consideration of infinitely superior
magnitude involving your personal
complicity and corroborative
malfeasance, with the consequence that
the taint and stigma of your former
associations and diversions could
irredeemably and irretrievably
invalidate your position and culminate
in public revelations and recriminations
of a profoundly embarrassing
and ultimately indefensible character.

I asked Humphrey for a précis. In one short sentence.

He thought for a moment. 'There's nicotine on your hands,' he said.

I couldn't think what he meant. I'm a non-smoker. Then I realised he was speaking not literally but figuratively. 'All the hospitality you have enjoyed at BTG's expense,' he reproached me in a sorrowful voice. 'Champagne receptions, buffet lunches, the best seats at sporting and cultural events.'

He seemed to think that the tobacco companies might release this embarrassing information to the press if I legislated against them.

But I can't see anything embarrassing about that. I've had drinks at the Soviet Embassy – that doesn't make me a spy. If that's the best idea Humphrey can come up with to block me, I may have to put Dr Thorn's proposals through after all! I think Humphrey may be losing his grip – it's the feeblest threat I ever heard.

Humphrey realised it himself, because he fell silent. 'Anything else?' I asked, hopeful that he'd do better.

'Yes, Prime Minister.' He was fighting on, but not looking too confident. 'It has been put to me that since smoking is not a political issue the government should not take sides.'

'You mean we have to be impartial?'

'Exactly,' he replied with gratitude.

'You mean,' I enquired innocently, 'impartial as between the fire engine and the fire?'

He hurried straight on. He knows when he's backing a loser. 'And there is a much graver objection. A large number of people, *eminent* people, *influential* people, have argued that Dr Thorn's legislation would be a blow against freedom of choice.'

I asked why. He rabbited on about how it is a serious attack on freedom to introduce penal taxation and prohibit the advertising of a product which is perfectly legal in itself. I told him this was complete and utter rubbish! We are not talking about prohibiting smoking itself. And I asked him if every tax increase is a blow against freedom?

He hedged. 'That depends on how big a tax increase.'

A fascinating answer. 'So,' I asked, 'is twenty pence a blow against freedom?'

He began to protest. 'Prime Minister . . .'

I brushed him aside. 'Is twenty-five pence? Thirty pence? Thirty-*one* pence? Is something a blow against freedom just because it can seriously damage your wealth?'

Rather good that, I thought! He didn't laugh though. He just remarked grimly that it was very droll.

So I took him through the freedom of choice argument. We agreed that advertising is essential if there is to be a free choice because free choice depends on full information. Therefore there should be advertising on both sides. Why, since the tobacco companies spend at least £100 million on advertising and promotion, shouldn't they pay an equal amount to advertise the arguments *against* smoking? This, I suggested to Humphrey, would be a point of view that would appeal to all those eminent and influential people who favour freedom of choice.

'Prime Minister,' he said, gritting his teeth. 'I do have to advise you that this proposal will cause grave difficulties. I foresee all sorts of unforeseen problems.'

'Such as?' I asked.

Humphrey was getting irritable. 'If I could foresee them, they wouldn't be unforeseen!' he snapped.

'But you said you could foresee them,' I reminded him cheerfully.

He was cornered. He had now reached his last refuge. 'Look, how about setting up an interdepartmental committee . . . a Parliamentary enquiry . . . a Royal Commission?'

I asked the question that I've been wanting to ask for days now. 'Humphrey, why are you so keen on the tobacco industry?'

He ignored the question. I knew he would, of course. 'Prime Minister, how about a Treasury Committee in the first instance?'

This was my opening. 'Don't talk to me about the Treasury,' I sighed sadly. 'They're blocking my plan for including a one and a half billion tax cut in my new defence strategy.' I sighed again heavily, theatrically, wondered if I were overdoing it a bit, then pressed on. 'Of course, if *only* the Treasury would show some flexibility . . .'

Humphrey saw the point immediately, or even sooner. 'Oh,' he said, brightening up considerably. 'Er . . . Prime Minister, I don't think they're fully committed to that other matter yet.'

'Really?' I pretended surprise.

'Absolutely not. Oh no. Flexible. I'm sure they could find a way.'

'Could they?' I asked with wide-eyed amazement. I should have got an Oscar for this one.

'The only stumbling block,' said Humphrey, adjusting rapidly to his new negotiating position, 'would be that if the anti-smoking proposals go through, the Treasury will be too busy working on those to look for a way to help with the other cuts.'

We were now talking in a code that we both understood. 'Well,' I said, 'the anti-smoking proposals don't have nearly such a high priority as defence.'

Humphrey now knew what deal I'd accept. The quid pro quo was acceptable to him, I could see. It's just a question of clearing it with the Treasury.

May 23rd

A slight complication developed today.

Peter Thorn came to see me in my room at the Commons. 'I've just had some very exciting news, Prime Minister,' he began. 'We have just got full backing from the BMA, the Royal College of Physicians, and eight other top scientific and medical colleges.'

My heart sank into my boots. I hadn't expected him to make so much progress so soon. I told him that this was excellent news, but that his legislation couldn't happen immediately.

'No,' he said, 'but their support only requires it to be announced as government policy within three months and a White Paper in a year. So that's bags of time.'

His enthusiasm was touching. I was genuinely sorry that I was about to ditch his scheme, particularly as I'd argued it so successfully with Humphrey that now I had even begun to believe in it myself.

I told him I'd encountered problems with the Treasury. He immediately saw the turn that the conversation was taking.

His eyes narrowed. 'It can't be anything you didn't know about before.'

'It's not as simple as you think, Peter.' I knew I sounded unconvincing.

Peter took a deep breath. And then he made a threat that was a *real* threat. 'Look, Jim, I really am serious about this. It's the one really important and worthwhile thing I believe I can do in politics. If you stall it, I shall have to resign. And say why.'

I told him to calm down, but he said he was perfectly calm already. 'Jim, the medical bodies are even more committed than I am. Perhaps I shouldn't have told them about your support, but they say they'll announce that you've capitulated to the tobacco companies.'

His strategy was all worked out. Clearly he was not a bit surprised by my new position on this matter – in fact, he must have been half expecting it.

I really didn't know what to say or do. But I was saved by the bell. The telephone bell, to be precise.

Bernard answered it. 'Excuse me, Prime Minister, could Sir Humphrey see you urgently, just for a moment?'

I asked Thorn to wait outside. Humphrey came bursting in with *good* news: he'd spoken to the Treasury first thing this morning and, surprise! surprise! they can encompass my income-tax cut. This is on the understanding that no further work would be needed on the anti-smoking proposal.

I briefly filled Humphrey in about the new complication – Dr Thorn's threatened resignation and the ensuing public condemnation of me by the entire British medical establishment.

Humphrey was worried – but only for a moment. Then he had a

brilliant idea, the kind of idea that makes him worth all the trouble he causes me – well, almost all!

'Prime Minister, you still have that government vacancy in the Treasury, don't you?'

It was genius, pure genius. It would be a big promotion, a very rapid promotion, for Peter Thorn. But why not, for such an able Minister?

We got him back in.

'Peter,' I said, 'I have just remembered that we still have a vacancy at the Treasury. I couldn't think how to fill it – but your work on this proposal, I have to tell you, has impressed me a lot.'

He was suspicious. Well, who wouldn't be? 'You're not trying to get rid of me?'

'Absolutely not. Quite the reverse.'

He was tempted. 'Well . . . it's a terrific step up.'

'But merited,' I said in my warmest father-figure voice. '*Thoroughly* merited.'

Thorn was torn. 'I don't see how I can take it if it means dropping the anti-smoking bill.'

'Peter, let me be absolutely honest with you. The bill would have been . . . will be . . .' I think I managed to correct myself without his noticing . . . 'very difficult to get through. The Treasury is the key place, the true stumbling block, not the Department of Health. It may take a bit longer, but if you're inside there, if you learn the ropes, there's a much better chance of a really foolproof watertight Act when it finally gets on to the statute books. Believe me.' It sounded so convincing an argument that I almost believed it myself.

Fortunately he bought it. 'So my proposals aren't dropped?' he asked, *wanting* the answer no.

'Absolutely not,' I said. I wasn't exactly lying – maybe I will come back to them in due course. In the fullness of time. When the time is ripe.

He only hesitated for a second. 'Okay,' he answered. 'I'll take the Treasury job. Thanks a lot.'

We shook hands and he left, walking on air. The great thing about being Prime Minister is that you can give people so much happiness and such a great sense of achievement.

May 24th
Peter Thorn's promotion to the Treasury left me with another vacancy, in the Ministry of Health. Clearly we now want to avoid a

Minister who will antagonise the tobacco lobby. So an obvious candidate sprang to mind.

I sent for Leslie Potts this morning. It didn't take him long to drive over from Marsham Street.[1] He wheezed into my study enveloped in his usual cloud of pollution, a lit cigarette clamped between his stubby yellow fingertips.

I welcomed him warmly. 'My dear chap, do come in. How would you like to be the Minister of Health?'

He was extremely surprised. 'Me?'

I nodded.

He coughed for a while, a good chesty wet rasping cough. Even *I* felt better after it.

'It is a considerable promotion' he said at last, eyeing me with caution and wondering what I was playing at.

'But merited,' I said warmly.

He thought for a moment, but could see no signs of a trap. Indeed, there were none. 'Well, of course, I can't refuse. Thank you, Prime Minister.'

I sent for Humphrey and introduced him to our new Minister of Health. Humphrey pretended slight surprise, even though it had been Humphrey's idea.

Meanwhile, Leslie thought he'd found the catch. 'Wait a minute,' he croaked suddenly. 'I don't want the job if it means attacking the tobacco industry.'

I was able to reassure him completely. 'No, Leslie, we in government have to be realists. I want you to work with the tobacco industry: they're nice chaps, caring people, fabulous employers, and they really want to help – I want you to work with them, not against them. All right?'

Leslie Potts looked pleased but, as he tried to reply, he was overwhelmed by a fit of uncontrollable coughing. He went purple, and struggled to say something – I simply couldn't tell what it was.

I turned to Humphrey. 'What did he say?' I asked.

'I think,' said Humphrey cheerfully, 'that he said "Yes Prime Minister".'

[1] Where the Department of the Environment has its headquarters.

8
The Bishop's Gambit

June 5th

Finished work by six p.m. tonight, except for my red boxes. So Bernard and I watched the six o'clock news. There was nothing new. But the media are making a big story out of a young British nurse called Fiona McGregor who is being held in the Gulf state of Qumran for the alleged possession of a bottle of whisky.

They've given her ten years' imprisonment and forty lashes, but apparently the sentence is not to be carried out till it is 'confirmed', whatever that means.

On the news they showed her mother and her MP (Stuart Gordon, one of our backbenchers) taking a petition to the Qumran Embassy. The officials refused to accept the petition.

The final item of this story was the official response from the Foreign Office, which said that the Foreign Secretary has described the incident as 'regrettable', but that no action is planned.

The news moved on to telling us that there has been another bad day for the pound. I switched off, and sent for Humphrey. When he came I told him that this situation with the nurse is a big worry. There's a lot of public sympathy for her.

He agreed.

'What's the best thing to do?' I asked.

'I'm sure the Foreign Secretary will advise you,' he said.

'He advises me to do nothing,' I said.

'I'm sure that's very good advice,' said Humphrey.

The usual obstruction from the FO. This has been going on too long already. 'If we don't do anything we look heartless,' I explained. 'We also look feeble. It doesn't do the government any good to look heartless and feeble simultaneously.' I turned to Bernard. 'What do you think, Bernard?'

Bernard perked up. 'Perhaps you could manage it so that you only look heartless and feeble alternately.'

I ignored him, and simply reiterated to Humphrey that we have to do *something*. My hope is that since I trounced Humphrey and his Foreign Office pal Dick Wharton[1] only recently, this time they may knuckle under with less pressure from me.

However, it doesn't look hopeful at the moment. Humphrey informed me politely that the Foreign Secretary doesn't think that we have to do anything. Well, *obviously* not – he's been told what to think by the Foreign Office, and the officials there do not know or care what the electorate wants.

Humphrey gave me the official view. 'The Qumranis are good friends of Britain. They have just placed a huge defence contract with us. They tell us what the Soviets are up to in Iraq. They even sabotage OPEC agreements for us. We can't afford to upset them.'

'I *know* all that, Humphrey,' I said wearily. Sometimes he talks to me as if I'm a complete idiot. 'But the point is, a British citizen is facing a barbaric punishment for a trivial offence in a foreign country. And the Foreign Office is there to protect British subjects.'

He shook his head and smiled sadly. 'They are there to protect British interests.'

'It's not in her interests to be flogged,' I said.

'It's not in our interests to prevent it,' he replied with sudden firmness.

I did not and do not accept this view. I have refused to accept it for days now and I still refuse. [*The Foreign Office would have been perfectly content for Hacker to refuse continuously to accept their view, for his refusal appeared to satisfy him emotionally, so long as this did not result in his forcing the FO to accept a change in policy – Ed.*] Humphrey argued that this is one of those little bush fires that flares up and dies down in a few days. The only mistake we can make is to put fuel on it. Statements, actions, ultimata, sanctions – they would all only make it worse. The Foreign Office wants me to sit back and do nothing.

He claims that the FO is doing something. Tomorrow, apparently, we are to deliver a strongly worded note of protest to the Qumranis.

'Why can't we do it now?' I asked.

'Because we haven't got their agreement yet,' he explained. 'We're talking to the Ambassador privately now. When they have approved the wording we shall hand it to them. Then,' he remarked smugly, 'we'll have done all we can.'

---

[1] The Permanent Secretary of the FCO.

213

It seems like a pretty odd way to protest. It's a purely diplomatic protest, for public consumption only. No teeth at all. And Humphrey thinks that this would be sufficient action to take on behalf of that poor girl. 'I suppose the Foreign Office thinks Pontius Pilate did all he could.'

To my surprise, Humphrey agreed enthusiastically. 'Yes indeed, Pontius Pilate would have made an excellent Foreign Secretary. You can't put the nation's interests at risk just because of some silly sentimentality about justice. If we took moral positions on individual injustices and cruelties we'd never have been able to hand Hong Kong over to the Chinese, or put Mugabe in power in Zimbabwe. Morality was what fouled up the Foreign Office's plans for a quiet handover of the Falklands to Argentina – they don't want to take any moral positions for a long time now.'

I sighed. He seemed to be right, in purely practical terms. There seems to be nothing we can do. 'It's very heartless,' I said gloomily.

Humphrey leaned forward encouragingly. 'It's safer to be heartless than mindless. The history of the world is the triumph of the heartless over the mindless.'

He'd won and he knew it. We all fell silent for a moment, then Humphrey rose and asked if he might leave as he had a dinner engagement. As he walked to the door I called after him that the Foreign Office will never get the Cabinet to agree to this policy.

He turned in the doorway. 'The Foreign Office never expect the Cabinet to agree to any of their policies. That's why they never fully explain them. All they require is that the Cabinet acquiesce in their decisions after they've been taken.'

And he was gone.

I stared morosely at Bernard. 'Bernard, is there anyone else in public life who is quite as spineless as our Foreign Office officials?'

Bernard was surprised. 'They're not spineless, Prime Minister. It takes a great deal of strength to do nothing at all.'

I'd never thought of it that way. 'Does it?' I asked.

'Yes, Prime Minister, that's why people regard *you* as a strong leader.'

Was this a compliment or an insult? It seemed that Bernard wasn't too sure either because he continued hurriedly: 'I mean, because you resist pressures.' Then he reminded me that I should get ready for the Reception tonight.

I asked him to give me a rundown of the list of significant guests. The most significant tonight were representatives of the Synod of the

214

Church of England. There is a vacancy in the diocese of Bury St Edmunds, and I have to make the choice between two names which they will be submitting to me.

But although, by tradition, they have to submit two names, they will be anxious that I don't pick the wrong one. I asked Bernard how I will know which to pick.

'It's like any Civil Service option, Prime Minister. It'll be a conjuring trick. You know, "take any card" – you always end up with the card the magician forces you to take.'

It was very bold of Bernard to admit this. So I asked, 'What if I don't take it?'

He smiled confidently. 'You will.'

We'll see about that, I thought to myself. 'Who are these clerical cards they're going to offer me, Bernard?'

'With the church,' he grinned, 'you're usually given the choice of a knave or a queen.'

[*Sir Humphrey Appleby's dinner engagement that evening was at the High Table of his alma mater, Baillie College, Oxford. There, by chance, the subject of Sir Humphrey's retirement impinged unexpectedly on the Prime Minister's forthcoming choice of a bishop. The conversation at High Table, which Sir Humphrey reports in his private diary, was of course not known to the Prime Minister – Ed.*]

We had the usual adequate dinner. As always the claret was better than the food, the port was better than the claret, and the conversation was better than the port.

The serious conversation, as always, began as we reached the port and walnuts. After the customary courtesies, the Master thanking me for coming to dine with them and my replying that it is always a pleasure to dine with old friends, the Master came to the point. He told me that he would be retiring in four or five years, roughly when I shall be retiring from the Civil Service.

The juxtaposition could hardly have been coincidental. So I was alerted for his next remark: 'The Bursar and I think you could be just the chap to succeed me as Master of Baillie.' Sweet words. Music to my ears.

However, it soon became clear that there is an obstacle. This obstacle is known as The Dean. Somewhat reluctantly, but without pulling any punches, the Master revealed that the Dean does not like me.

This astonishes me. Why should he dislike me, I've never done anything that he should be grateful for?

Nevertheless, it seems to be a fact. The Bursar's theory is that the Dean believes that I'm too clever by half. One would have thought that, at Oxford, to be called clever might be rather a compliment.

Apparently, the Dean also thinks I'm smug. I got that from the Bursar

215

too, who seemed to be enjoying the whole conversation a little too much for my liking.

The Bursar may have realised that I wasn't appreciative of his candour, because he told me that in his opinion it did not matter. I thought he was saying that it didn't matter what the Dean thought – but no, he was saying that it didn't matter that I am smug!

And he went on and on about it. He told me that it was perfectly obvious, and that furthermore I have a lot to be smug about. If he had £75,000 a year, a knighthood, an index-linked pension and a bunch of politicians to take the blame for all his mistakes, he informed me, *he* would be pretty smug too.

This remark was very revealing. Envy is at the root of the Dean's dislike for me, and the Bursar's belief that I am smug. There can be no other explanation. It is yet another cross to bear. But I shall do my best to bear it with grace.

The Master added that the Dean hates intrigue and does not like politicians. For a ghastly moment I thought that the Master was suggesting that *I* am a politician. I decided that we had spent enough time discussing their distorted vision of my personal qualities, and asked to know more about the Dean.

The Bursar explained that the Dean is paranoid that the Master and the Bursar are intriguing about this matter behind his back. Which is why they decided to discuss it with me while he's away. They made two matters quite clear: first, that they do *not* go in for intrigue; second, that the only way I can become Master of Baillie is if they can dump the Dean.

This could be a problem. The Dean is a lazy bugger. He only has to do four hours work a week, give one lecture and a couple of tutorials – and he has tenure for life. They say that he only has two interests: cricket and steam engines. He never has to read a new book or think a new thought, so being an Oxford don is the perfect job for him. Why would he ever move?

The Master and the Bursar have concluded that only a bishopric would get him away from Baillie and they were wondering about the Diocese of Bury St Edmunds, which is up for grabs.

It is a very appealing Diocese. It is one of the old ones, with a seat in the Lords. This, I know, would appeal greatly to the Dean. In *my* observation of him, his principal hobby is sucking up to the aristocracy.

Unfortunately, I'm not sure if I can do anything about getting Bury St Edmunds for the Dean. It's rather late in the day. Furthermore, as I explained to them, the Church is looking for a candidate to maintain the balance between those who believe in God and those who don't.

It comes as a surprise to many, including the Master and the Bursar, to learn that many people in the church do not believe in God, including most of the bishops.

Bury St Edmunds is sewn up. It has been arranged by the Church that Canon Mike Stanford will get the job. In theory Hacker has to recommend the appointment. But the Church customarily puts up the candidate they want plus an impossible second candidate, to ensure that the PM has no real choice.

Furthermore, the Dean has not done enough public service even to qualify for Bury St Edmunds.

But this is a serious matter for my own future, especially as there are no other dioceses coming free in the near future. Bishops don't retire as often as they should. The older appointees don't have to retire at sixty, and bishops tend to live long lives – apparently the Lord is not all that keen for them to join Him. Ὃν οἱ θεοὶ φιλοῦσιν, ἀποθνῄσκει νέος[1], which perhaps explains why bishops live to a ripe old age.

We concentrated on the only hopeful line of attack: more public service for the Dean. He is an expert on Islamic studies, and he loves the Arabs. One of his few good qualities. I had a flash of inspiration: I suggested that the Master gets his bishop to send him to Qumran to intercede on behalf of that nurse. They were delighted with the idea.

It is a situation in which we cannot lose. If he fails, he has at least tried. If he succeeds, he will be a hero. And if he doesn't come back he won't be missed.

I wouldn't want to go there, though. It's an awful country. They cut people's hands off for theft, and women get stoned when they commit adultery. Unlike Britain, where women commit adultery when they get stoned.

He might even come back with certain parts missing.

Look, no hands!

[*Appleby Papers 42/43/12 BD*]

[*Hacker's Diary continues – Ed.*]

June 6th

A meeting with Peter Harding, the Appointments Secretary. He's about sixty, and he's a quietly confident sort of chap. Very sound, apparently.

I was a little hesitant because I've never appointed a bishop before.
[*Recommended the appointment to the Sovereign – Ed.*]

There were two candidates. First, Canon Mike Stanford. Michael, I suppose, though it seems they all call him Mike. People never called bishops 'Mike' when I was a kid! Not in public, anyway. Perhaps he's called Mike because he's always on the radio.

Peter told me that Mike is a Modernist. This was new terminology to me. 'A theological term, Prime Minister. It seems that he accepts that some of the events described in the Bible are not *literally* true – he sees them as metaphors, legends or myths. He is interested in the spiritual and philosophical truth behind the stories.'

[1] Menander. Pronounced *Hon hoi theoi philousin apothneeskei neos*. Translation: Those whom the gods love die young.

217

I expressed it my way, to be sure I understood. 'You mean, he doesn't think God created the world in seven days, or that Eve came out of Adam's rib, that sort of thing?'

Peter was delighted. It seems it's that sort of thing *exactly*, which sounds very sensible. The only other things Peter said I need to know about Mike Stanford are that he went to Winchester and New College, Oxford, and his name is first on the list. 'And,' added Peter, 'he has an eminently suitable wife.'

'You mean she's devout and full of good works?' I asked.

He was surprised. 'No, I mean she's the daughter of the Earl of Dorchester.'

Now it was my turn to be surprised. So what? I wondered. I asked him who was second on the list.

'Well . . . second is Dr Paul Harvey.'

And I waited. But Peter seemed reluctant to say more.

'And?' I prompted him.

'Well, he's an admirable man,' said Peter. This was damning with praise if I ever heard it. Peter was staring at his shoes.

'But?' I wanted an explanation.

Peter sighed, then looked me straight in the eye. 'Of course, it's your choice, Prime Minister. But there is a suspicion that he tends towards disestablishmentarianism.'

'Ah,' I said knowledgeably, then realised to my embarrassment that I wasn't *absolutely* sure what he meant. I asked him for details.

'It's the view that the Church of England shouldn't be part of the state. Some people feel it should be separate, like Methodists or Catholics. They think ordinary people feel the established church is a club for the ruling classes, not a faith.'

He sounded like an awfully good chap to me, and I said so. But Peter maintained a pained silence. So I asked him what was the matter.

'Well, it's entirely up to you, of course, Prime Minister. But I suspect that Her Majesty might be a little surprised if you asked her to appoint a man who believes she should be made to break her Coronation vow to defend the church.'

Fair enough. But then why is he on the list at all? Peter prevaricated. He explained that Harvey is not *exactly* a *card-carrying* disestablishmentarian *yet*. It's just the way his mind seems to be moving. But as a result of the discussions his name emerged. His health may be suspect too. Also he's getting on a bit.

One thing is clear to me: someone is bad-mouthing him! Or else he was never a suitable candidate to start with. In any case, this is not what I call a choice. 'You're saying I can choose Canon Stanford or Canon Stanford,' I said to Peter.

'No,' he replied blandly. 'It's entirely your decision. But in this case, may I suggest, quite an easy one.' He refused to admit anything. His face was expressionless. 'Prime Minister, the Commission is offering you the two names which emerged.'

'Was there an open election?' I asked.

He tut-tutted impatiently. 'There *can't* be an open election. Bishops are seen as part of the apostolic succession.'

Not being a churchgoer, I asked for an explanation.

'It's God's will. When Judas Iscariot blotted his copybook he had to be replaced. They let the Holy Ghost decide.'

I was mystified. 'How did he make his views known?'

'By drawing lots,' said Peter.

'So can't we let the Holy Ghost decide this time?' I asked, looking for a way out of this awkward decision.

Peter and Bernard looked at each other. Clearly my suggestion was not on. Bernard tried to explain. 'No one', he said, 'is confident that the Holy Ghost would understand what makes a good Church of England bishop.'

I asked how this 'choice' emerged. Peter informed me enigmatically that soundings were taken.

'Peter,' I said with a smile. 'When I was a student I used to play poker. I can recognise a stacked deck when I see one.'

Bernard stood up, and reminded me that I was due to meet Sir Humphrey. He suggested that Peter and I continue the discussion tomorrow. Peter looked thankful and left.

While Humphrey came in and I poured end-of-the-day drinks, Bernard went off to get Mike Stanford's career details, having whispered to me that appointing Mike Stanford might be a bit of an own goal.

Humphrey and I wished each other Good Health and relaxed in the comfy study armchairs. I asked him what was *really* meant by a Modernist.

He misunderstood, and asked me whether I was referring to Shostakovich or Marcel Duchamp. I told him that I was referring to Mike Stanford.

As I expected, he knew exactly. 'In the Church of England the word Modernist is code for non-believer.'

'An atheist?' I asked with surprise.

'Oh no, Prime Minister,' he replied wickedly. 'An atheist clergy-man couldn't continue to draw his stipend. So when they stop believing in God they call themselves modernists.'

I was staggered. 'How can the Church of England recommend an atheist as Bishop of Bury St Edmunds?'

Humphrey crossed his legs and sipped his drink. 'Very easily,' he smiled. 'The Church of England is primarily a social organisation, not a religious one.'

This was news to me. But then I don't come from a very 'social' background.

'Oh, yes,' Humphrey continued knowledgeably. 'It's part of the rich social fabric of this country. Bishops need to be the sort of chaps who speak properly and know which knife and fork to use. They are someone to look up to.'

So that, I realised, is what Peter meant by Stanford having an emi-nently suitable wife.

I asked Humphrey if there are no other suitable candidates. He said that there aren't at the moment. Apparently there were a couple of better jobs available recently. I couldn't think what could be better than a bishop, other than a rook! But apparently the Dean of Windsor is a better job. So is the Dean of Westminster. Humphrey explained that such preferment enables one to be on intimate terms with the royals.

It was all becoming clear to me. 'So being a bishop', I summed up, 'is simply a matter of status. Dressing up in cassocks and gaiters.'

Humphrey nodded. 'Yes, Prime Minister. Though gaiters are now worn only at significant religious events – like the royal garden party.'

I wondered why cassocks and gaiters are now out of style.

'The church is trying to be more relevant,' said Humphrey.

'To God?' I asked.

'Of *course* not, Prime Minister. I meant relevant in sociological terms.'

What he was saying, in effect, is that the ideal candidate from the church's point of view is a cross between a socialite and a socialist.

Bernard came back with Mike Stanford's career details. He was right. They were very instructive. After he left theological college he became Chaplain to the Bishop of Sheffield. He moved on to be the Diocesan Adviser on Ethnic Communities and Social Responsibility. He organised conferences on Inter-faith interface, and interface between Christians and Marxists, and between Christians and the

Women of Greenham Common. [*This was a part feminist/part lesbian encampment of anti-nuclear/pacifist/Marxist women that stationed itself illegally outside the gates of an American airbase near Newbury, where Cruise missiles were kept. Only women and children were allowed to take part in the protest, which was against nuclear weapons, America and men, possibly in the reverse order. Nuclear missiles were seen as a form of phallic symbol. The Women were regarded by Freudians as suffering from a severe case of penis envy. Expressing support, even limited support, for the Women of Greenham Common was perceived as a 'progressive stance' – Ed.*] Subsequently Stanford became University Chaplain at the University of Essex, then Vice Principal of a theological college, and he is now the Secretary to the Disarmament Committee of the British Council of Churches.

There was one significant gap in his CV.[1] 'Has he ever been an ordinary vicar in a parish?' I asked.

Bernard was surprised by the question. 'No, Prime Minister. Clergymen who want to be bishops try to avoid pastoral work.'

'He's a high flyer,' remarked Humphrey.

'So was Icarus,' replied Bernard mysteriously.[2]

'Anyway, I don't want him if he's a political troublemaker,' I decided.

Bernard nodded wisely. 'What peevish fool was that of Greece who taught his son the office of a fowl.' I told Bernard to stop quoting Greek at me. [*Hacker was incorrect. Bernard Woolley was quoting Shakespeare's* Henry VI Part III – Ed.]

Humphrey responded with cautious agreement to my decision. He said that Stanford would have the added nuisance value of speaking with the authority of a bishop and as a member of the Lords.

'He's exactly the sort of person I don't want,' I explained 'It's no good all these bishops exhorting me to spend more on welfare. You can't always solve problems by throwing money at them, especially other people's money. What this country needs is a greater spirit of responsibility and self-reliance.'

Humphrey smiled at me. 'Isn't it interesting how nowadays politicians talk about morals and bishops talk about politics?'

He's right. Bernard gave us an example from Stanford's career. 'He designed a new church in south London. On the plans there were places for dispensing orange juice, and family planning, and organis-

---

[1] Curriculum vitae, i.e. the story of his life.
[2] Icarus was the son of Daedalus. He flew too near the sun and his wings melted. Thus he put himself out of the running by his ambition, like Canon Stanford.

ing demonstrations – but no place for Holy Communion.' He added, in all fairness, that there was a dual-purpose hall in which a service could be held.

I asked my two officials if the Church approved of this design.

'Oh yes,' said Humphrey. 'You see, the church is run by theologians.'

'What does that mean?' I asked.

'Well,' he smiled, 'theology's a device for helping agnostics stay within the church.'

'Perhaps I'm naïve,' I said, 'but . . .'

'Perish the thought, Prime Minister,' interrupted Humphrey.

Stupid flattery! Couldn't he tell it was false modesty? Of course I don't think I'm naïve. I waved him to shut up, and continued. 'I think the church should be run by simple men who believe in God, not worldly politicians seeking preferment.'

'You could argue,' said Humphrey amiably, 'that those who seek preferment feel that they can be of greater service to the community in a more important job.'

'That's hypocritical twaddle,' I said.

He shrugged. 'Just as you yourself only wanted to serve your country here in Number Ten.'

Suddenly I saw what he meant. He's right. But I still don't want Stanford.

Humphrey explained to me that I can turn both candidates down, although it would be exceptional and not advised.

'Even if one candidate wants to get God out of the Church of England and the other wants to get the Queen out of it?'

'The Queen,' said Humphrey, 'is inseparable from the Church of England.'

'Is she?' I asked. 'And what about God?'

'I think He is what is called an optional extra,' replied my Permanent Secretary, finishing off his drink.

June 9th

An interesting development about that nurse in Qumran tonight. There's been nothing from the Foreign Office for days. This is not really a surprise – the Foreign Office aren't there to do things, they are there to explain why things can't be done.

I was trying to explain this to Annie over dinner. She had difficulty in grasping the concept. She kept asking irrelevant questions like 'Don't they care?'

'No,' I said. She had difficulty in grasping that answer.

'Isn't that rather awful?' she asked.

Obviously it *is* awful. It's doing the government a lot of damage. Yet all the Foreign Office does is shrug its shoulders and say we mustn't upset the Qumranis. 'The FO simply can't see beyond its narrow selfish interests,' I said.

'It must be ghastly for her,' said Annie.

'Who?' I asked. Then I realised she meant that nurse. 'Yes,' I agreed.

Annie stared at me coldly. 'You don't care about her any more than the Foreign Office do.'

I don't think that's entirely fair. [*Not* entirely *fair, perhaps – Ed.*] Annie seemed to think that just as the Foreign Office is worried about its popularity with the Arabs, I'm worried about my popularity with the voters. That's not wholly true – but in so far as it *is* true, what's wrong with it? I'm an elected representative – isn't it right and proper that in a democracy I should be concerned with pleasing the electorate?

Bernard came to the flat. I was irritated. It doesn't seem possible any more to have a quiet drink with my wife without being interrupted. He was wearing his coat and was clearly on his way home.

He apologised for the intrusion, but said it was important. 'The Foreign Office have just rung to say that the Bishop of Banbury and the Church Missionary Society have announced that we are sending the Dean of Baillie College to Qumran on a mercy mission to plead for that nurse.'

This was good news. But I couldn't see why they were sending an Oxford don. Bernard explained that the man has faith in the Arabs.

'It's good to hear of a senior member of the Church of England who has faith in anything,' I said. 'But isn't this rather a hopeless journey?'

Bernard thought not. 'Although he's a Christian he's an expert on Islam. It's a faith to faith meeting.'

I smiled, and told Bernard to tell the Foreign Office that I'm happy to support the trip. Bernard shook his head vigorously. 'No, no,' he said, 'actually the Foreign Office want you to stop it. They're furious. They say it's a futile gesture and will only impair our relationships with a friendly country.'

This was really too much. I had no intention of stopping it. It's an excellent idea. At the very least it will look as though we're doing something about her, and it might even save her. I sent Bernard home, after he reminded me that Lambeth Palace were pressing me for a decision about Bury St Edmunds.

Annie was curious. She asked what he meant.

'I've got to decide who should be appointed to the see.'

'Isn't that a job for the First Lord of the Admiralty?'

'No, Annie,' I explained patiently, 'I'm choosing a bishop.'

She laughed uproariously. 'You?' she gasped eventually. 'That's ridiculous.' She wiped her eyes, weak from laughing.

I couldn't quite see what was so ridiculous about it. I know I'm not religious, but religion manifestly has nothing to do with it. I'm Prime Minister. Annie couldn't see why religion has nothing to do with bishops so I explained to her that they are basically managers in fancy dress.

I showed her the papers from my red box. The Church of England has over 172,000 acres of land, thousands of tenants and leaseholds, and property and investments worth a total of £1.6 billion, comprising industrial, commercial and residential property, and agricultural land and woodland. So, really, the ideal bishop is a corporate executive – a sort of merchant banker, personnel manager and estate agent.

Annie wasn't impressed. 'Speaking as a churchgoer,' she said, 'I'd prefer you to choose a man of God.'

'I was offered one of them,' I explained. 'But he wants to turn the Church of England into a religious movement.'

'I see.'

'The other one, the one they're trying to force on me, is a modernist.'

Annie, being a churchgoer, knew the code. 'You mean a Marxist or an atheist?'

'Both,' I revealed. 'Nobody minds the atheist bit, apparently. But being a Marxist could cause me a lot of trouble when he starts making speeches in the Lords.'

'Can't you reject him?' asked Annie.

'I'd like to. But it will look political.'

Annie was confused. 'But haven't you just been explaining that the Church *is* political?'

I was patient. 'Yes, Annie, but it mustn't look it.'

She considered this for a few moments. 'So why don't you turn him down on religious grounds?'

I couldn't see what she meant exactly. She explained. 'Does he believe in Heaven and Hell?'

'Of course not,' I said.

'The Virgin Birth?' she asked.

'Nope.'

'The Resurrection?' asked Annie.

'Nope.' I was beginning to see what a great idea this was.

'Isn't that enough to be going on with?' she enquired. She's brilliant. Simple common sense. It suddenly became clear to me that I can do what Humphrey suggested and ask for more candidates *without it looking like political discrimination*. Wonderful!

'What I really need,' I said to Annie, 'is a candidate who can get along with everyone.'

'You mean he mustn't have strong views on anything?'

Annie puts it a little cynically, but that is basically right. But there is a proviso. I think it would help if he were *inclined* towards Christianity. That couldn't do any real harm. So what I actually want is a sort of closet Christian.

[*A few days later amid much publicity the Dean of Baillie, the Rev. Christopher Smythe, embarked on his mercy mission to Qumran. When he arrived there he dropped out of sight for three days. Suddenly he re-emerged into the full glare of publicity to announce that he had succeeded in obtaining the release of Fiona McGregor, the young British nurse held there in prison. They were expected back in England the following day. This was thrilling news in Britain, especially in view of the fact that the pound had had another bad day. Sir Richard Wharton, the Permanent Secretary of the Foreign Office, made an entry in his private diary – which was marked 'Private and Strictly Confidential'. The diary was found recently in a basement in Carlton Gardens – Ed.*]*

12 MONDAY
I am profoundly shocked by today's disastrous news. Whose idea was it to send that meddling parson to Qumran? We had the situation comp- under control here. We

PRIVATE and strictly **CONFIDENTIAL**

June 12

I am profoundly shocked by today's disastrous news. Whose idea was it to send that meddling parson to Qumran?

We had the situation completely under control here. We had made our protest, the nurse would have been quietly flogged and stuffed away in some Qumrani jail, and in a couple of weeks the press would have forgotten all about it.

The upshot is that there's terrific damage to the Foreign Office. We had almost got agreement to set up a signals listening post in Qumran. We had told them we wouldn't make any more fuss about the nurse if they signed. Now we have lost our best bargaining counter.

The only good thing to have resulted from this whole silly rescue is that it has got that nurse's ghastly mother off my back. She's been phoning and writing and telling the press we weren't doing enough. And incredibly, the press took her side. They have been going on about how the Foreign Office should be more patriotic. This is nonsense. Our job is to get along with other countries. People have said a lot of unpleasant things about the Foreign Office but no one has *ever* accused us of patriotism.

It is hard to believe that the newspapers have such abject ignorance of diplomatic realities.

Now I foresee that there will be a problem with the PM, because we advised him against letting that clergyman go out there. He will say that we were wrong to tell the Cabinet it was impossible to get the nurse released. But we were right – if they'd left it to the Foreign Office it *would* have been impossible.

226

[The following day Sir Richard received a note from Sir Humphrey Appleby – Ed.]

70 WHITEHALL, LONDON SW1A 2AS

From the Secretary of the Cabinet and Head of the Home Civil Service

13 June

Dear Dick,

    I believe that the F.O. is about to have a P.R. problem.

    The press will say that the church succeeds where the F.O. fails. They may dig out all the old clippings about ambassadors' Rolls Royces, five million pound embassies, school fees at Eton subsidised by the taxpayer, and what does Britain get from it all?

    What do you propose?

SIR BERNARD WOOLLEY RECALLS:[1]

I was summoned to an urgent private meeting with Humphrey, shortly after that nurse was rescued from Qumran.

He knew that the Foreign Office had been against the Dean of Baillie's mercy mission, and he knew that *I* knew.

But in order to forestall hostile press coverage of the FO's passive role in

---

[1] In conversation with the editors.

the proceedings, Sir Richard Wharton had proposed that the FO tell the press that it was Hacker's initiative to send the Dean. The PM would enjoy taking the credit. (And incidentally, there would be no danger of Hacker denying a favourable story just because it was not true.)

Then for the Sunday papers, the Foreign Office would leak the idea that they had suggested this course to the PM when they found the diplomatic channels were blocked. Thus no one would get the blame and everyone would share the credit.

It was a sensible plan. As the PM's Principal Private Secretary my co-operation was needed. I gave it without hesitation.

[*After his meeting with Bernard Woolley, Sir Humphrey received a phone call from the Master of Baillie College. The meeting with Woolley is only referred to* en passant *in the diary, but there are brief notes about the phone call and about a subsequent meeting with Peter Harding, the Appointments Secretary – Ed.*]

Tuesday 13   JUNE

2.30   Successful meeting with B.W. about F.O. press plans.

2.45.   Master of Baillie telephoned, excited that the news of Fiona McGregor's release might help our friend towards preferment.

I was able to inform him that we might not have to wait for a vacancy in another Bishopric. The battle of Bury St Edmunds is not over.

2.30 Successful meeting with BW about FO press plans.

2.45 Master of Baillie telephoned, excited that the news of Fiona McGregor's release might help our friend towards preferment.

I was able to inform him that we might not have a wait for a vacancy in another Bishopric. The battle of Bury St Edmunds is not over. My intention is to get the Dean up to the starting gate as a late entry.

3.00 Peter Harding came to discuss Bury St Edmunds. The Crown Appointments Commission is meeting tomorrow morning.

He was put out that a further candidate has to be submitted to the PM now that he has seen fit to break with tradition by insisting upon a bishop who believes in the Resurrection.

Peter promised me a possible candidate, Stephen Soames. He was regretful because Soames was being saved up for Truro. [*Truro is very remote. It is to the Church what the Vehicle Licensing Centre in Swansea is to the Civil Service – Ed.*]

Soames has been waiting for a bishopric for years. Long time, no See? He is rather a nuisance. He keeps on about his 'duty to God' and that sort of thing. The Church really wants him out of the way. But if the PM wants a religious bishop he is about the only candidate around.

I told Peter that there is a snag. The PM wants *two* more names put up to him. Actually, the PM does not yet know that he wants two more names, but he will realise it as soon as the idea has been put to him. After all, it is only right that the Prime Minister should be given the feeling that he is making a choice.

Therefore, Peter is obliged to put up a second candidate. I encouraged him to find someone plausible but unacceptable. Peter was concerned. He had only till tomorrow morning to think of yet another candidate.

I suggested the Dean of Baillie College. Peter felt he was too implausible even to be suggested, on the grounds that he is unbelievably vain and hopelessly incompetent.

I explained to Peter that the PM doesn't think it's silly to appoint people who are vain and incompetent. Look at the Cabinet. Furthermore, as the Dean has just had some good publicity he must be a plausible second choice.

This made Peter more concerned. This time he was worried at the danger that the Dean might therefore *get* the job.

I was able to smooth ruffled feathers by telling him of the PM's stated view that a devout Christian should be appointed. As the Dean is known to believe only in Islam, the MCC and steam engines, Peter felt relaxed about making him the second name on the list.

I shall have to smooth more ruffled feathers when Hacker recommends the Dean for the bishopric. However, tomorrow is another day.

[*Hacker's diary continues – Ed.*]

June 14th
The morning newspapers were a triumph.

Daily Mail

20p

ANGEL OF MERCY WAS SENT BY PM

By FRANK THOMPKIN

Prime Minister's envoy secures nurse's release

JIM'S DEAN SAVES FIONA FROM LASH

I was given the full credit for it all on the news last night as well. I'm not quite sure why. I suppose it *must* have all been my doing, really. After all, it says so in the papers. I did stop the Foreign Office from stopping the Dean, which comes to the same thing.

Still, it's strange. One normally has such a battle in public life to get the proper credit for anything good one has achieved. Yet here the glory's being handed to me on a plate, when my role in it was peripheral to say the least.

Anyway, there's no point in asking for corrections when the story has come out so thoroughly to my advantage. I suppose I should count my blessings.

I had a final meeting first thing this morning, to discuss the vacant bishopric. Apparently the Palace is now waiting. When Humphrey and Bernard came in, though, I first asked why – in their opinion – the Foreign Office press office gave me the credit for the rescue.

Humphrey took the view that they couldn't take any credit themselves because of their protest. But by giving me the credit, it looks like a government achievement instead of a church achievement.

I suppose that must be it! The first sentence of the Telegraph leader reinforces that view.

16 THE DAILY TELEGRAPH.

The Daily Telegraph

135, FLEET STREET, LONDON EC4P 4BL. TEL: 01-353 4242. TELEX: 22874/5/6

TRAFFORD PARK, MANCHESTER M17 1SL. TEL: 061-872 6838 TELEX: 666991

Imaginative diplomacy

IT DOES the Prime Minister great credit that he has not let himself be bound by the shackles of orthodox diplomacy.

We moved on to the question of the new Bishop of Bury St Edmunds. I was initially in favour of Stephen Soames. Peter likes him too. And although the Dean of Baillie did a pretty good job in Qumran he is said to be fairly eccentric. In fact, I've heard he's barking mad. But when I asked for Humphrey's opinion, his response really frightened me. 'I'm sure Soames is the choice the Crown Commissioners are hoping you'll make, Prime Minister.'

An ominous warning sign. Peter hasn't been levelling with me. I asked Humphrey what the problem is with Soames.

'I've heard it said that he's an extremist.'

What, I wondered, is *extremist* the code word for. 'You mean that he believes in God?' I was groping wildly.

Bernard tried to explain. 'He's *very* religious, Prime Minister.'

I was still groping. 'That's all right for a bishop, isn't it?'

'Well . . . yes and no,' said Humphrey carefully. 'He tends to raise issues that governments often would prefer not to be raised. He is a trenchant critic of abortion, contraception for the under-sixteens, sex education, pornography, Sunday trading, easy divorce and bad language on television.'

Quite a catalogue. This is serious. I don't want some loud-mouth, self-righteous cleric challenging the government on all these subjects.

It wouldn't be so bad if we had a policy about any of them. But they are all matters about which the government is trying to avoid having a policy. Our policy is not to have a policy.

I went over this with Humphrey. 'Quite,' he replied. 'He is against your "no policy" policy.'

Bernard, presumably in the interests of clarity, piped up. 'He would demand that you ban abortion, Sunday trading, contraception for the under-sixteens, sex education . . .'

'Thank you, Bernard, I've got the gist,' I said.

Humphrey said he had more bad news about Soames. 'He's also against oppression and persecution in Africa.'

I saw no problem with that. 'So are we.'

'Yes,' he agreed. 'But Soames is against it when practised by black governments as well as white ones.'

So he's a racist! [*This curious leap in logic is explained by the fact that Hacker had been a* Guardian *reader when in opposition – Ed.*]

I really didn't know what to do. Sympathetically, Humphrey murmured that I could still choose Soames if I wanted to. Obviously I *didn't* want to – but how could I turn down *another* two names?

So we looked again at the Dean of Baillie. I listed the arguments against him. 'He's not really up to it. He's said to be lazy, vain, and totally uninterested in Christianity.'

'Yes,' said Humphrey, 'but he's not *against* it! I think he'd make a thoroughly suitable British bishop – cricket, steam engines, and a complete ignorance of theology. Theology can seriously damage your faith.'

My problem was that he was basically unqualified. The submission said that he has never done a real church job. He's spent his whole life in Oxford. On the other hand, he did very well in Qumran, and so his appointment might be a very popular choice with the voters.

Then Humphrey dropped a bombshell. 'There is a problem,' he said. 'I gather that he is thinking of telling the press that the Qumran visit wasn't your idea. I gather he has a letter from the Bishop of Banbury dated some time before your involvement.'

This was *dreadful* news! It would be an incredible embarrassment. It would look as if I were trying to take the credit for something I didn't do! I can just imagine the headlines. PRIME MINISTER TAKES CREDIT FOR DEAN'S MERCY MISSION. Or JIM DIDN'T FIX IT!

So the question was, how could we stop the Dean from making this embarrassing revelation? It seemed, according to Humphrey's information, that the Dean is peeved because he felt that he hasn't been given enough recognition for his role in Qumran. Or the church hasn't. Or something!

On the face of it, there was an easy answer. I told Bernard to invite the Dean here for drinks this evening. It'll be a very nice photo opportunity for the press, too.

Humphrey, however, said that this would be improper: whilst I am considering two candidates for the vacancy in Bury St Edmunds I can hardly, in his view, invite just one of them here for drinks.

I saw his point. But I had to do *something* to stop him blabbing to the press.

Then Humphrey, thank God, had a brainwave. 'If you had already *given* him the job, then it would be perfectly proper.'

And then, the more I thought about it, the more I began to feel that the Dean might be rather a *good* choice of bishop. After all, he is an enterprising chap. And, as I explained to Bernard, eccentricity can be a virtue: you just call it individualism.

Bernard agreed wholeheartedly. 'It's one of those irregular verbs, isn't it? "I have an independent mind, you are eccentric, he is round the twist?"'

We discussed it further, and agreed that we need people in the House of Lords who understand the Arab world. And cricket. And steam engines. So, after mature consideration, I made the Rev. Christopher Smythe, Dean of Baillie College, Oxford, my choice. I told Bernard to convey my recommendation to the Palace, fast! I wanted the appointment announced by lunchtime, the Dean informed at once, and I wanted him round here for drinks, with a photographer, by six o'clock this evening.

And that's what happened. The crisis was averted. We have a new

Bishop of Bury St Edmunds, the nurse was freed from Qumran, and I got the credit all round.

Humphrey was delighted too. He told me that the appointment of the Dean was an act of wisdom. In fact, he was *so* pleased that I began to wonder why.

I suddenly remembered that Baillie was Humphrey's old college. Perhaps that was why he knew so much about the Dean and why he was so pleased. So I asked him if this was another case of jobs for the boys.

He denied it indignantly. 'On the contrary, Prime Minister. I hardly know him. In fact, I know he dislikes me. You can ask him this evening, if you like. I don't like him much either.'

'So you have nothing to gain from this appointment?'

'How could I have?' he asked.

I couldn't see how. But it all seemed a little coincidental. So while we were having our photos taken by the press in front of the fireplace in the White Sitting Room, I asked the Dean if he liked Humphrey Appleby. 'Can't stand him, quite frankly,' the Dean whispered to me. 'I think he's smug.'

So Humphrey was telling the truth. I am really very grateful to him, for giving me helpful, impartial advice in the best traditions of the Civil Service.

9
One Of Us

June 20th

I had an absolutely sensational Prime Minister's Question Time in the House this afternoon. Members were attacking me from all sides about my controlling expenditure on defence, but I really made mincemeat of them all.

So after I finished work I hurried upstairs to the flat to see the TV News. Annie was watching it, it had started already. I asked her if it was the lead story, but they hadn't mentioned it.

'Typical BBC,' I said.

'It's not the BBC.'

'Typical ITV,' I said.

'It's Channel Four,' she said.

'Oh well,' I said, 'what do you expect?'

I watched what was left of the news, which was entirely devoted to the fate of Benjy, an Old English Sheepdog who has somehow got

Family snapshot.

under the wire and on to a Ministry of Defence artillery range on Salisbury Plain.

According to Channel Four News, Benjy belongs to an eight-year-old orphan called Linda Fletcher. Linda lost both her parents in a car crash last year, a crash that only she and Benjy survived.

The artillery range where Benjy is lost is full of unexploded shells and is highly dangerous except for one fixed road through it. Benjy is a long way from the road. The News showed shots of *Danger* signs, telephoto shots of the dog running around and sitting down, and a tearful little orphan girl looking through the wire fence and being comforted by relatives.

The story finished with the Army expressing their regrets but saying that there is nothing they can do unless the dog comes to the wire of his own accord. It seems inevitable that Benjy will either starve to death or be blown up.

That was the end of the news. I couldn't believe it – there was nothing about me at all! I asked Annie if she could have missed it.

'I watched the whole news,' she said, en route to the kitchen to dish up dinner, 'but you know how it is when one watches it – one sort of mentally tunes out the boring bits.'

'Thanks,' I said, and got myself a Scotch.

She was instantly apologetic. 'No, not you, darling. You're not boring, not to me, even if you are to the rest of the country.' She doesn't mean me *personally*, of course, she just means that some people are bored by politicians.

I was a bit fed up, though. Instead of showing the viewers a significant triumph in the House of Commons they give them a pathetic story about a kid and a dog.

[*Although Hacker regarded the debate in the House as a significant triumph, it is possible that Channel Four News took the view that the debate merely consisted of some juvenile rowdies bickering with each other – Ed.*]

'I thought that the story about the dog was interesting,' said Annie, slicing tomatoes for the salad.

'But it's totally unimportant,' I explained, as I struggled with the tray of ice cubes.

'Why is the story about Parliamentary Question Time more important?' she wanted to know.

'Quite simply,' I said, with all due modesty, 'because it was about me. I am Prime Minister, after all. Doesn't that impress anyone in the media?'

'You seem to be quite impressed enough for all of us,' said Annie. I couldn't understand why she was taking this attitude.

'Annie,' I remonstrated with her, 'the future of Britain's defence was being thrashed out in the great forum of the nation and what do the viewers get offered? Lassie Come Home.'

'But what was decided in the great forum of the nation?'

Annie sometimes asks the stupidest questions. Obviously nothing was decided. You can't leave decisions to MPs. She was just being silly. The real importance of the debate is that *I won it*! And I think that the media should let my people know. [*Hacker was apparently developing a Moses complex after five months in Number Ten – Ed.*] I told her that the media people don't live in the real world, and that I'd like to drop the subject.

But Annie wouldn't let it go. 'I think that a kid losing a dog is much more real than a lot of overgrown schoolboys shouting insults at each other. I think the army ought to rescue that dog.'

Bloody stupid idea! Spend thousands and thousands of pounds in a dog rescue operation when you could replace it for nothing from Battersea Dogs' Home? Kids lose dogs every day. Should the army mount rescue operations for all of them? It's just a television sob story.

Annie told me I don't understand how ordinary people feel.

'I happen to be an ordinary person myself,' I replied loftily.

'Surely not!'

I tried to explain to her that I am in charge of the responsible control of public money. 'It's not for me to spend taxpayers' money to buy a bit of easy popularity.'

'If popularity's so easy' said Annie, hitting straight below the belt, 'how come you're so low in the opinion polls?' She argued that to save the dog would cost a fraction of a penny per taxpayer, they'd all like it done, and that sometimes you have to do things that aren't economic if you live in a civilised humane society.

I told her to write a paper on that and submit it to the Treasury. We don't get a lot of laughs in the Cabinet Economic Committee.

June 23rd
I've had some shocks and surprises during my time in politics, but today I think I had the greatest surprise ever.

The Director-General of MI5 came to see me. Sir Geoffrey Hastings, by name. A tall, shambling St Bernard dog of a man, with mournful brown tired eyes and wobbly droopy jowls.

Bernard showed him in to my study, and I invited them to sit down. Hastings looked pointedly at Bernard. I told him that I always have Bernard present at my meetings.

'Not this time, Prime Minister,' he said gently but firmly.

On reflection, I realise that I don't always have Bernard present at my meetings, and I let him go. After he'd gone I realised that I hadn't been given any papers for the meeting. But Hastings indicated that this was on his instructions. Apparently the meeting was too serious for papers. In other words, there should be no record of it at all. This is almost unheard of in Whitehall, where *everything* is minuted.

I was agog. And my agogness was soon to be rewarded.

'We've just received some information,' murmured Hastings.

I was somewhat perplexed. 'Isn't that what you're supposed to do?'

He nodded. 'You know Sir John Halstead?' I nodded. I never *knew* Halstead personally, but everyone knows he was Head of MI5 in the sixties. And he died last month. 'He left a whole lot of his personal papers to us. We've started to go through them. It's very clear he was passing government secrets to Moscow for several years in the fifties and sixties.'

I found it hard to believe what I was being told. The Head of MI5 a Russian agent? Incredible.

Geoffrey Hastings seemed a little embarrassed to be telling me this at all. I'm not surprised. I asked him why Halstead left the papers to MI5.

'His Will says it's a final act of conscience. But I think he just wanted to do a bit of posthumous gloating. Show us he got away with it. But it's a shattering blow.' And Geoffrey certainly looked shattered. The bags under his eyes extended halfway down his cheeks.

'How much did he tell the Russians?' I asked.

'That hardly matters,' said Geoffrey. 'I mean, what with Burgess and Maclean and Philby and Blake and Fuchs and the Krogers, so many people were telling them things that one more didn't really make much difference.'

'So what is the point?' If it didn't matter about the secrets, I couldn't see *any* reason why it should matter.

How wrong I was! Geoffrey Hastings gazed gloomily at me, his salt and pepper moustache flapping in the breeze. I've hardly ever seen a more lugubrious figure. 'The point is,' said Geoffrey in a voice of profound melancholy, 'he was one of us.'

'One of us?'

He could see that I didn't quite get the full significance. 'He joined

MI5 straight from Oxford. Been in the Civil Service all his life. If this ever gets out, all of us who were recruited by him will be suspects for ever.'

Suddenly I saw the seriousness of it all. 'I see,' I said, and eyed him speculatively. 'And you're not a Russian agent, are you?' Geoffrey stared at me coldly, so I hastened to reassure him. 'Only joking,' I said, 'but you're not, are you?' He remained silent. I realised that, if I ever got an answer out of him I wouldn't know if it were true or not anyway. 'No, of course you're not,' I said, and then told him that, embarrassing or not, in my opinion I ought to make this information public.

He begged me not to. He said there were tremendous security implications. I couldn't see why, if the information itself was unimportant. But Hastings said that it's absolutely vital to keep it secret from our enemy that we can't keep secrets.

'I shouldn't have thought that was much of a secret,' I said with unanswerable logic. After all, it must have been mentioned by Burgess and Maclean and Philby and Blake and the Krogers. But it turned out that the Russians weren't the enemy he had in mind. He was talking about our real enemy – the press.

'We had an internal security investigation into John Halstead in the seventies. There was a lot of media speculation. You remember?'

'Vaguely,' I told him.

'It was all terribly irresponsible and ill-informed,' Geoffrey reminded me bitterly.

'You mean,' I asked, 'the press hinted that Halstead was a spy?'

'Yes.'

'But he *was* a spy.'

Geoffrey sighed impatiently. 'Yes, but they didn't know that! They were being typically ignorant and irresponsible. They just happened to be accurate, that's all. Anyway, the enquiry cleared him. Completely. Clean bill of health. But they missed some rather obvious questions and checks. So obviously that, well . . . one *wonders*.'

This was uttered with tons of significance. He really ladled it on. What does one wonder? I wondered. I couldn't guess, so I had to ask him.

'One wonders about the chaps who cleared him, whether they were . . . you know . . .'

'Stupid, you mean,' I said, then suddenly realised what he was driving at. 'My God . . . you mean, *they could be spies too*??' He nodded,

239

and shrugged helplessly. 'Who headed the inquiry?' I asked.

'Old Lord MacIver. But he was ill most of the time.'

'Ill?' I wanted clarification.

'Well . . . ga-ga, really. So effectively it was the Secretary who conducted it.'

'Who was the Secretary?' I asked.

Geoffrey Hastings gave me a woebegone stare, looked around nervously, and apologetically mumbled, 'Sir Humphrey Appleby, I'm afraid.'

I wasn't sure I'd heard him correctly. 'Humphrey?'

'Yes, Prime Minister.'

'You think he may have been spying for the Russians too?'

'It's a remote possibility, but very unlikely. After all, he's one of us.'

'So was John Halstead,' I pointed out.

He couldn't deny it. 'Well . . . yes. But there's no other evidence at all, not against Humphrey.'

I tried to collect my thoughts. 'Might he have been covering up for one of us . . .' I corrected myself. 'One of *them* . . . er, one of *you*?'

Geoffrey thought that this was a very remote possibility. He actually believes that Humphrey is completely loyal, and that all that Humphrey is guilty of is hideous incompetence.

That's bad enough, though. After all, it's a matter of the highest national security. I asked Hastings what he recommended that I should do about Humphrey.

'It's up to you, Prime Minister. We still haven't got through all the papers. You could set up an inquiry into Sir Humphrey.'

This is rather an enjoyable prospect, I must say. But when I questioned Geoffrey closely it turned out that he didn't really recommend it. 'Not at this stage. Things might get out. We don't want any more irresponsible ill-informed press speculation.'

'Even if it's accurate,' I commented.

'*Especially* if it's accurate,' agreed Geoffrey. 'There's nothing worse than *accurate* irresponsible ill-informed press speculation. But you could send Humphrey off on gardening leave while we examine the rest of the Halstead papers.'

This was also an appealing thought. But Humphrey is fairly useful, in spite of his many faults. And he is the Cabinet Secretary. I felt that I should keep him on unless his loyalty were really in question.

Geoffrey Hastings sees no problem in that. He handed me a file marked TOP SECRET: FOR THE PRIME MINISTER'S EYES ONLY and told me that I could confront Humphrey with all the substantive evidence it contains.

But I didn't really want to interrogate Humphrey. 'If you don't seriously suspect him, shouldn't we just forget it?' I asked.

He looked very doubtful indeed. 'Obviously it's your decision,' he rumbled in a sepulchral tone. 'On the other hand, if you did nothing and it emerged later that Sir Humphrey . . . that he was . . . one of *them* . . . well, it might not look too good. Not to mention the fact that as Cabinet Secretary he co-ordinates all of our security services. There are no secrets from him.'

I was forced to agree. Geoffrey rose from his chair, and straightened his baggy pinstripe suit. 'Personally,' he concluded, 'I find it hard enough to believe that *one* of us was one of them. But if *two* of us were one of them . . .' he realised that this was a logical impossibility and tried to correct himself. '*Two* of them, then all of us could be . . . could be . . .'

He had painted himself into a corner. 'All of them?' I suggested helpfully as I escorted him to the door. 'Thank you, Geoffrey, I've heard enough.'

June 26th

I couldn't talk to Humphrey about Sir John Halstead on Friday. I had appointments all day and so had he. But this morning we had a meeting already pencilled in.

It was to be about the defence cuts that I'm looking for. I decided to have the meeting as planned, and then have a private word with Humphrey afterwards.

I've been trying to find as many small savings in the defence budgets as I can. Defence expenditure in this country is completely out of hand. By the mid-1990's we shall only be able to afford half a frigate. This, I surmise, will be inadequate for our naval defences. The Secretary of State for Defence is getting nowhere so I have decided to take a look myself.

A simple way has emerged of saving three million pounds, for instance, and the Service Chiefs say it can't be done. Humphrey is backing them, of course, with the argument that *any* defence savings can be dangerous.

Ironically, the suggestion being made by the Service Chiefs is to close a hundred miles of coastal Radar Stations. And I know *why* they're suggesting that particular economy: because it *is* dangerous, and therefore they know that I won't agree to it! But *I'm* suggesting

241

that they start eating some of their forty-three years' supply of strawberry jam instead of buying more.

Humphrey couldn't – or wouldn't – see how that would help. 'As I understand it, Prime Minister, the Army haven't got any strawberry jam. It's the Navy that's got it.'

He's right. But the army have seventy-one years' supply of tinned meat. And the RAF, which has no strawberry jam lake and no tinned meat mountain, has fifty-six years' supply of baked beans. So I am trying to get across to Humphrey and the MOD that the Army and the RAF should eat the Navy's strawberry jam, and the Navy and the RAF should eat the Army's tinned meat, and the Army and the Navy should eat the RAF's baked beans. And if they did that with all the other surpluses too we'd save £3 million a year for four years. And I do not believe that the defence of the realm is imperilled by soldiers eating sailors' jam!

Bernard had an objection. 'The RAF's baked beans are in East Anglia and the Army's tinned meat is in Aldershot and the Navy's jam is in Rosyth. So it would mean moving the beans from . . .'

I stopped him there. 'Bernard,' I asked, 'if our armed forces can't move a few tins of baked beans around Britain, how can they intercept guided missiles?'

Bernard seemed perplexed by the question. 'But you don't intercept missiles with baked beans, you have long pointy things which go . . .' I told him to shut his mouth. At which point Humphrey reluctantly agreed that it *could* be done, but added that it would be extremely complicated. 'The administrative costs would outweigh the savings.'

But no one's even worked out the administrative costs. And why? Because there's no need – they *know* that they can make the administrative costs outweigh the savings, if they really put their minds to it.

As the meeting drew uneventfully to a close, a messenger arrived with the latest opinion polls. They contained bad news. I'm down another three points. Not the government – just my personal rating.

I wonder what I'm doing wrong. Humphrey believes it proves that I'm doing things right – politically popular actions, in his view, are usually administrative disasters.

I wonder if it's caused by my failure to get the defence cuts through. Maybe. Though in all honesty I'm not sure that defence cuts are the principal topic of conversation in the supermarkets of Britain. No, the lead story in the newspapers is that bloody lost dog on Salisbury Plain. Perhaps I should forget about my defence policy for the moment and think up a lost dog policy.

Anyway, the meeting was over. And there was nothing for it, I could postpone it no longer: I had to have my private word with Humphrey. I told Bernard that I had to discuss a top secret security matter with Humphrey, and nodded to the door. 'Would you mind, Bernard?'

He went to the door and, suddenly, threw it open! Then he looked up and down the landing to see if anyone was eavesdropping. I realised he had misunderstood me. So I explained that I wished him to leave us alone.

He seemed a little crestfallen. I can see why. That's two meetings in two days that he's been asked to leave. But Geoffrey had no choice, and nor do I – I can hardly let Bernard know that Humphrey, of *all* people, is a security risk at the moment.

After Bernard left us, probably wondering if *he* was considered a security risk all of a sudden, Humphrey and I were left alone. I didn't quite know how to begin, so it was a minute or so before I spoke. Humphrey waited patiently.

'Humphrey,' I began eventually, 'there's something I want to talk about. Something very secret.'

I was stuck. Humphrey leaned forward helpfully. 'Would it be easier if I wasn't here?' he asked.

'It's something very serious,' I replied.

He assumed an appropriately serious expression. 'Very serious and very secret?'

I nodded. 'Humphrey, does the name Sir John Halstead ring a bell?'

'Of course, Prime Minister. He died only three weeks ago. And he was the subject of a security enquiry ten years ago. I had to conduct it myself, virtually. Old MacIver was ga-ga.'

So far so good. I asked Humphrey if he'd found evidence of anything incriminating.

'Of course not.' He smiled confidently.

'Why of course not?' I asked.

'Well, in the first place John Halstead was one of us. We'd been friends for years. In the second place the whole story was got up by the press. And in the third place, the whole object of internal security enquiries is to find no evidence.'

'Even if the security of the realm is at risk?'

He laughed. 'Prime Minister, if you really believe the security of the realm is at risk you call in the Special Branch. Government security enquiries are only used for killing press stories. Their sole purpose is to enable the Prime Minister to stand up in the House and say, 'We have held a full enquiry and there is no evidence to substantiate these charges.'

'But suppose you find something suspicious?'

'Prime Minister, practically everything that happens in government is suspicious. The fact that you asked Bernard to leave us alone together for a secret conversation could be construed as suspicious.'

This surprised me. But it shouldn't have, he's obviously right. Anyway, Humphrey went on to say that the whole story was nonsense, typical Fleet Street sensationalism.

He was so confident that it was inevitable that he would feel really stupid when I revealed what I knew. I was beginning to enjoy myself thoroughly.

'There is *no* possibility,' I asked carefully, 'that Sir John Halstead ever passed any information to Moscow?'

'Impossible,' he asserted. 'Out of the question.'

'You'd stake your reputation on that?'

'Without hesitation.'

I went for the kill. 'Well, Humphrey, I'm afraid I have to tell you that he was spying for Russia for a considerable part of his career.'

Humphrey was silenced. But only for a moment. 'I don't believe it,' he said defiantly. 'Who says so?'

I gave him an apologetic smile. 'He says so himself. He left all his papers to the government with a detailed confession. MI5 says it's absolutely true. It checks out all along the line.'

Humphrey was speechless. This is a sight that I've never seen before, and I must say I thoroughly enjoyed it. He spluttered a bit, and tried to put together a sentence. Finally he said: 'But, good Lord, I mean, well, he was . . .'

'One of us?' I put in helpfully.

'Well . . . yes.' He began to pull himself together. 'Well, that certainly leaves a lot of questions to be asked.'

'Yes,' I agreed, 'and I'm asking you the first one. *Why* didn't you ask him a lot of questions?' Humphrey didn't see what I was getting at. 'Why, Humphrey, did your enquiry exonerate him so quickly?'

He suddenly realised how my questions affected *him*. 'You don't mean . . . surely nobody is suggesting . . .' He went very pale.

So I pointed out to Humphrey that it was all very suspicious. I asked why he hadn't held a proper enquiry. After all, according to the TOP SECRET file, Humphrey had been given evidence of Halstead's surprisingly long stay in Yugoslavia. And shortly after Halstead left Yugoslavia several of our MI5 agents behind the Iron Curtain were rounded up and never seen again.

And there was one specific interpreter with whom Halstead spent a lot of time. I asked Humphrey what he'd found out about this interpreter.

'She turned out to be a Russian agent. We knew that. Most Yugoslav interpreters are Russian agents. Those who aren't in the CIA, that is.'

'But you never followed her up.'

'I had better things to do with my time,' he said defensively.

I stared at him accusingly. 'Three months later she moved to England and settled in Oxford, a hundred and fifty yards from Sir John Halstead's house. They were neighbours for the next eleven years.'

Humphrey was completely demoralised. He tried to defend himself. 'You can't check up on everything. You don't know what you might find out. I mean, if you've got that sort of suspicious mind you ought to . . .'

'Conduct security enquiries.' I finished his sentence for him.

Humphrey's defence, in a nutshell, was that Halstead gave him his word. The word of a gentleman. And you don't go checking up on the word of a gentleman, especially when you were at Oxford together.

I asked him if he'd have checked up on Anthony Blunt. Humphrey said that was totally different. Blunt was at Cambridge.

I listened patiently. Then I was forced to tell him that I had a problem with him.

He was horrified. 'But you don't think . . . you *can't* think . . . I mean, I mean, I don't speak a word of Russian.'

'But you must admit,' I said, 'that it looks as if it must have been incompetence or collusion. Either way . . .'

I left the sentence unfinished. The implications were clear enough. Humphrey was dreadfully upset. 'Collusion? Prime Minister, I give you my word there was no collusion.'

'Is that the word of a gentleman?' I asked ironically.

'Yes. An Oxford gentleman,' he added hastily.

I wasn't really satisfied. 'How's the garden?' I asked.

He relaxed and began to tell me about his roses when he realised the full force of my question. 'No, no, I beseech you, Prime Minister, not gardening leave!'

'Why not?'

'I have my reputation to think of.'

'I thought you'd already staked that on Sir John Halstead's innocence.'

I told Humphrey that I would have to think long and hard about what to do. I indicated that I would talk to Sir Arnold Robinson, his predecessor as Cabinet Secretary, for advice on handling a security enquiry into a Cabinet Secretary. And I cautioned him against speaking to Arnold until after I've spoken to him.

He assured me that he wouldn't dream of it.

[*What possessed Hacker to warn Sir Humphrey that he would be discussing the matter with Sir Arnold? And why did he believe Sir Humphrey's assurance that he would not speak to Sir Arnold himself? These are questions over which historians will ponder for ever. Suffice to say that Sir Humphrey met Sir Arnold for a drink that very evening, at the Athenaeum Club. Sir Arnold's private diary relates what happened in full detail – Ed.*]

Met a flustered and anxious Appleby at the club. After one brandy he revealed the cause of his panic. Apparently the Prime Minister and Geoffrey Hastings of MI5 both think he might be a spy, because he cleared Halstead and Halstead has now confessed all.

Humphrey asked me what he should do. I told him that depends on whether he actually was spying or not. He seemed shocked that I could entertain the suspicion, but I explained that one must keep an open mind.

Humphrey advanced several compelling arguments in his own favour.

1. He was not at Cambridge.
2. He is a married man.
3. He is one of us.
4. He has been in the Civil Service all his life.
5. Unlike John Halstead, he has never believed in things like *causes*. Humphrey argues correctly that he has never believed in anything in his life.
6. He, unlike Halstead, has never had ideas – especially original ideas.

These arguments are all persuasive – but not conclusive.

However, it seemed to me that whether Humphrey Appleby is a spy is immaterial in the short term. I agree with him that, whether he is or isn't, we have to see that it doesn't get out.

Of course, now that I am President of the Campaign for Freedom of Information I am in a very good position to prevent sensitive information from reaching the press. Giving information to Moscow is serious – but giving information to anyone is serious. In fact, giving information to the Cabinet could be more serious than giving it to Moscow.

The key point is that a scandal of this nature could gravely weaken the authority of the Service. This could result in letting the politicians in – as in

America, they might decide to make their party hacks into Permanent Secretaries and Deputy Secretaries. Even Under Secretaries. The top jobs in the Civil Service would be filled with people who would just do what they were asked by the politicians. This would be unthinkable! There are no secrets that anyone could pass to Moscow that would cause one-tenth of the damage that Britain would suffer if it were governed the way the Cabinet wanted. Therefore Humphrey certainly must not confess, even if he is guilty, and I told him so.

He reiterated that he has nothing to confess. Be that as it may, there is still the other possibility. Nevertheless, I asked him to assume, for the sake of argument, that he is innocent.

He thanked me profusely. I repeated that I was making that assumption for the sake of argument only, without prejudice. Unfortunately, however, if he is innocent of espionage, he is plainly guilty of incompetence.

He denied incompetence. He reminded me that I had appointed him Secretary of the Halstead enquiry. And he suggested that I had hinted to him that he was expected to find no evidence against Halstead.

Naturally *I* denied this. He has no written evidence – I made sure of that at the time. And of course I sent him the memorandum that I always sent, the one instructing him to leave no stone unturned, to be no respecter of persons, and to pursue the truth however unpalatable.

In fact, I left a copy of this memorandum in the Cabinet Office files, so there can be no credence given to Humphrey's claim.

Nonetheless, I asked him to assure me that we shall hear no more about my alleged complicity. He gave me that assurance, and we returned to the question of *his* incompetence. I told him that although *we* might both know that he did the job that he was required to do, it would be hard to explain that to the politicians.

He asked me if the politicians have to know. We agreed that it should be avoided, if possible. But the main danger is the Prime Minister: he may want to go around telling people about it all.

Clearly Humphrey must not allow this to happen. It must be stopped. The Prime Minister might tell the Cabinet. They might decide to suspend Humphrey. They might remove him to the Chairmanship of the War Graves Commission!

Humphrey had not considered any of these dire possibilities. He should have. Frankly, I do not mind what happens to Humphrey. He is expendable, and I told him so. He denied it emotionally, but it is true nonetheless.

But even though Humphrey personally is expendable, we dare not allow politicians to establish the principle that Senior Civil Servants can be removed for incompetence. That would be the thin end of the wedge. We could lose dozens of our chaps. Hundreds, maybe. Even thousands!

Therefore I advised Humphrey that he should make himself so valuable to the Prime Minister in the next few days that he cannot be let go. We discussed what the PM is really dead set on at the moment: popularity, of course, which is what all politicians are dead set on all the time.

The biggest current news story is about a lost dog on Salisbury Plain. I advised him to find an angle on this.

[Sir Humphrey's diary makes only a brief reference to the above conversation with Sir Arnold. Perhaps he wished there to be no record of the fact that Sir Arnold considered him expendable, which may have hurt him even more than the suggestion that he might have been a spy. However, Sir Humphrey notes a meeting with Sir Norman Block[1] the following day, at which he made a proposal clearly based on Sir Arnold Robinson's advice – Ed.]

Met Arnold at the club yesterday. He made one or two valuable suggestions, chiefly that I find some way to help the PM increase his ratings in the opinion polls before the end of the week.

The only answer seems to be for Hacker to help the lost dog on Salisbury Plain. Arnold seemed to be suggesting that I should get the Prime Minister to crawl all over Salisbury Plain with a mine detector in one hand and a packet of Winalot in the other. At least it would probably do Britain less harm than anything else he would be likely to be doing.

Today Norman popped in to see me. He was curious as to how his Secretary of State acquitted himself in Cabinet. *[Sir Humphrey Appleby, as Cabinet Secretary, was present at all Cabinet meetings. Other Permanent Secretaries were generally not present unless specially invited, a rare occurrence – Ed.]*

I told Norman that, even though the Cabinet are being resentful, his Secretary of State refused to agree to defence cuts. Norman was very encouraged.

I told him that I needed a favour, on a very sensitive issue. He assumed that I would be referring to Cruise Missiles or chemical warfare, and was surprised when I revealed that I was concerned about the lost dog on Salisbury Plain.

Norman was confident that there were no problems, and that everything was under control. The dog, he predicted, will have starved to death by the weekend. Then the army will recover the body and give it a touching little funeral and bury it just outside the gates. He has made plans for pictures of the guards resting on reversed arms, and to set up a photo session of the Commanding Officer comforting the weeping orphan girl. He says the telly would love it, and there would be pictures in all the Sundays.

I listened carefully, and then proposed that we rescue the dog.

Norman's reaction was explosive. He said it would be highly dangerous. It would take:

a) A squadron of Royal Engineers with mine detectors.
b) A detachment of the Veterinary Corps with stun darts.
c) A helicopter (possibly two helicopters) with winching equipment.
d) A bill for hundreds of thousands of pounds.

All for a dog that could be replaced for a fiver in the local petshop.

I know all this anyway, and I persisted. I asked Norman if the dog *could* be rescued, technically. Norman didn't think twice. He told me that *anything* can be done technically, if you've got the money. But he argued that it would

[1] Permanent Secretary of the MOD.

248

be madness: he is under great pressure from the PM to cut spending, why on earth should he waste hundreds of thousands in full view of the world's press just to save a dog?

Norman was only seeing the *problem*. I flipped it over, and showed him the *opportunity*: if the Prime Minister authorised the rescue, if it were Hacker's initiative, it would make it much harder for him to insist on defence cuts subsequently.

Norman was silenced. Then he smiled a beatific smile. It is clear to me that I have regained my touch. I told Norman the conditions:

1) The real cost of the rescue must not be known to Hacker until after the rescue.
2) The rescue operation should be put on immediate standby, in strict confidence.
3) The PM must get the credit – a Number Ten job.

He agreed instantly.

[*Appleby Papers 28/13/GFBH*]

[*Hacker's diary continues – Ed.*]

June 27th

Sir Arnold Robinson returned to Number Ten today for the first time since his retirement, for a confidential meeting with me about Humphrey. He had been briefed by MI5. He thinks that it was a bad business, an unfortunate business. I went further, and said it was disastrous. Arnold seemed to feel that I was overstating it.

'Not disastrous, surely, Prime Minister. It will never come out.'

'You mean,' I asked, 'things are only disastrous if people find out?'

'Of course.'

Perhaps he's right. If nobody finds out I suppose it's merely an embarrassment rather than a disaster. [*If the Cabinet Secretary were a spy it would be a* grave *political embarrassment – Ed.*]

But happily it turned out that it was not a disaster because new evidence has emerged. Sir Arnold brought with him proof that Sir Humphrey was not a spy.

'MI5 have just come across this document in the Halstead papers. From his private diary.'

He handed it to me, and I read it with a mixture of feelings that I cannot quite describe: relief, joy and glee, perhaps.

> *October 28th.*
>
> *Another session with that prize goof Appleby. Fooled him completely. He never asked any of the difficult questions. Didn't seem to have read the MI5 report. So much wool in his head, its child's play to pull it over his eyes.*

Nothing I have ever read has ever given me so much pleasure.

Arnold assumed that my delight was due to the fact that Humphrey was now exonerated. He wanted to take the Halstead diary back, but I insisted on keeping it.

Arnold then suggested that the matter was closed as there was nothing further to investigate. But I pointed out that the question of incompetence remains.

'We all make mistakes,' said Arnold feebly.

'Not on this scale,' I replied severely. 'Do you think I should sack him?'

Arnold didn't seem to think that this suggestion was even worthy of discussion. Dismissively he replied, 'I hardly think so.'

'Why not?' I asked. 'Do you think Civil Servants should never be sacked?'

Arnold replied with care. 'If they deserve it, of course they should. In principle. But not in practice.'

At first I was sceptical. But he explained that before Humphrey could be sacked there would have to be an enquiry. And all enquiries into the incompetence of civil servants somehow seemed to lead back to mistakes by ministers. However, he offered to chair an impartial enquiry.

I had second thoughts. Since I have been Humphrey's minister for some years I decided that discretion is the better part of valour. I thanked Arnold for his contribution, let him go, and sent for Humphrey.

I put Humphrey out of his misery as soon as he arrived. I told him he had been cleared of spying. Naturally he was extremely relieved, and asked how.

'Something Sir John Halstead wrote,' I told him.

'That's very gratifying,' he said.

I was enjoying myself. '*Isn't* it?' I said. 'I knew you'd be pleased.'

'May one see the document?' he asked.

'Indeed one may, Humphrey. Better still, one can have it read to one.' And one read it aloud to him.

'"October 28th. Another session with that prize goof Appleby. Fooled him completely."'

Humphrey went very pink. 'I see. Thank you, Prime Minister.' And he reached for the diary.

'No, Humphrey, it goes on,' I said. 'Clears you even more. "He never asked any of the difficult questions. Didn't seem to have read the MI5 report. So much wool in his head, it's child's play to pull it over his eyes."' I looked up at Humphrey and beamed at him. 'Isn't that wonderful? You must be *very* happy.'

He pursed his lips. He was visibly seething with indignation. 'I always said John Halstead was a hopeless judge of character,' he snarled.

I pretended to be worried. 'You mean . . . we can't believe it? He's lying?'

Humphrey was cornered. He realised he had no choice but to admit the truth. Very reluctantly he agreed that Halstead's account was absolutely true, but he insisted that Halstead wasn't bright enough to understand Humphrey's subtle questioning techniques. The non-confrontational approach.

I nodded understandingly. 'You were lulling him into a true sense of security,' I remarked.

'Yes,' said Humphrey. 'No,' said Humphrey, as he realised what I meant. 'Anyway,' he added, 'I take it that it's all over now.'

'The collusion charge? Of course,' I said. Humphrey relaxed. 'But we're left with the incompetence.'

He licked his lips nervously. 'Prime Minister, I do urge you . . .'

'Humphrey,' I said. 'Would you condone this sort of incompetence in someone working for you?'

'It was a long time ago,' he pleaded. 'A period of great strain. I had many other onerous duties.'

'You have many other onerous duties now,' I said, threateningly.

But then he redeemed himself. Humphrey with his back to the wall is a valuable man. 'Prime Minister,' he began, 'I have been giving some thought to how you might increase your popularity rating.'

Naturally I was immediately interested. I waited for him to continue.

'A strong government needs a popular Prime Minister.'

How true! I waited for more.

'I think you should do something really popular.'

I was getting impatient. 'Of *course* I should,' I said. 'But what?'

His suggestion was not what I expected. 'I was going to suggest that you intervene personally to save that poor little doggy on Salisbury Plain.'

At first I didn't think he was serious. 'It would certainly be popular, but surely it would also be rather expensive?'

'Surely not?' replied Humphrey.

[*Civil Service watchers will note this skilful reply – not a lie, but hardly revealing the truth – Ed.*]

He told me that time was running out. 'The decision has to be taken right away, this morning, before poor little Benjy starves to death.' I was undecided. Then Humphrey appealed to my emotions. 'There are times when you have to act from the heart. Even as Prime Minister.'

He was right! I gave him the go-ahead. He phoned Sir Norman right away. He told me that he had already put the army on a three-hour standby, and that he was merely waiting for my clearance.

I was delighted. I had just one worry. 'Humphrey, it's not a question of buying cheap popularity, is it?'

'By no means, Prime Minister,' he replied emphatically, and then was put through to Sir Norman at the MOD. 'Norman? Walkies.'

Apparently this was the codeword to begin Operation Lassie Come Home.

June 28th

They saved Benjy today. And I expect to be *very* popular tomorrow.

I watched it all on the Six O'Clock News. It was rather thrilling, feeling like the Commander-in-Chief of a major military operation. I felt like Mrs Thatcher during the Falklands, only more so – almost Churchillian really. The country needs a strong, decisive, tough leader like me.

The operation began on 'B' range early this morning. Four detachments of the Royal Engineers with mine detectors set off from different parts to close in on the area where Benjy was last sighted. It took over an hour to locate him. Then the Royal Veterinary Corps fired a stun dart. We saw him keel over, temporarily unconscious.

The troops couldn't enter the area without detonating shells, which might have injured the dog. So an RAF helicopter was flown in, and an air rescue team lowered a man to pick Benjy up without crossing dangerous ground. He was flown to safety and reunited with his little orphan Linda, who was overjoyed to see him. I think she'd given up hope of ever seeing him again. I was so profoundly moved by my own wisdom and kindness that I cried a little. I'm not ashamed to admit it.

Annie was delighted. I hadn't told her that I'd arranged for them to rescue the dog. When we last spoke about it I'd told her it would be a waste of money.

Her little face was glowing with pleasure and happiness for that child.

I told her that I'd thought again. 'I thought about what *you* said. And I thought "government is about caring".'

'Caring for votes?' she asked.

I was a bit put out. 'That's not very kind, Annie. I thought about that little girl and what the dog must mean to her. Individuals do count – even in a world of budgets and balance sheets. Some people may criticise me for using the army that way, but I don't care. Sometimes, doing the right thing means risking unpopularity.'

I was pleased with the sound of that. I shall use it at question time in the House tomorrow – it's bound to come up.

Annie was totally taken by it. [*It is possible that Hacker said taken 'in' by it, but his words are unclear on the cassette, due to what sounds like an emotional and excitable state of mind – Ed.*]

She gave me a kiss and told me that she *certainly* wouldn't criticise me for it. 'For the first time since we moved into Number Ten, I can see the point of being Prime Minister.' She is weird.

June 29th
The press coverage was wonderful this morning. Even better than I'd hoped.

I showed them to Humphrey. He was delighted as well. Even the leading articles were favourable. '*Today Britain discovered that a real human heart beats inside Number 10 Downing Street.*' I showed it to Bernard. His response was a typical quibble. 'Actually, seventy-four human hearts beat inside Number Ten.' But he was smiling.

I made a slight tactical error with Humphrey. I told him I'd been right and that I have an instinct for what the people want. That's perfectly true, of course – but in this instance it was actually Humphrey who had suggested the rescue, and when he reminded me I graciously gave him full credit. Although, in fact, he mostly has crummy ideas and the credit is *really* due to me for spotting that, for once, his idea was a good one. Still, I let him feel he was responsible for it, as that's always good for morale.

As he had been so helpful on this matter I readily granted the favour that he asked of me. He wanted the question of his incompetence in the Halstead enquiry to be dropped. I agreed at once. Why not? No harm had been done.

Then we moved on to Cabinet Agenda, after we gloated over a few more of the newspaper stories. Wonderful quotes. Linda said: '*My vote goes to Mr Hacker.*' The BBC and ITV reported a flood of phone calls approving my decision to rescue Benjy. And, according to *The Times*, the Leader of the Opposition was not available for comment. I bet he wasn't! He has to choose between supporting me or being in favour of leaving dogs to starve to death! I really got him there!

When we finally turned to the Agenda, Humphrey suggested that we postponed item 3 – the defence cuts. He wanted to refer them to OPD.[1] I couldn't see the sense of this – I wanted a decision at Cabinet, not a sixty-page submission nine months from now.

But then the bombshell hit me. Humphrey revealed that saving Benjy had cost £310,000. It seemed impossible! And yet these were the MOD figures, on a true-cost basis.

My breath was taken away. 'Humphrey,' I said, aghast, 'we must do something!'

'Put the dog back?' suggested Bernard.

On balance, shocked though I was, I still felt it was the right decision – it may have cost £310,000 but I'd won a lot of public support. [*It might have been more accurate for Hacker to say that he had bought a lot of public support. With public money – Ed.*]

But then the full horror dawned on me. At least, it didn't exactly dawn – Humphrey explained it. 'You do not have to postpone the defence cuts, but that would be a very courageous decision.'

My heart sank. 'Courageous? Why?'

'If there are defence cuts, the cost of rescuing the dog is bound to be leaked to the press.'

'Surely not,' I said feebly, but I knew he was right.

He shook his head and smiled a rueful smile. 'Of course, Prime Minister, if you have complete faith in the defence staff's confidentiality and loyalty . . .'

What a ridiculous idea! How could I have? They leak like sieves.

Humphrey rubbed salt into the wound. 'I can see the headlines now. PRIME MINISTER SAVES DOG AT THE EXPENSE OF BRITAIN'S AIR DEFENCES. It would be quite a story.'

'A shaggy dog story,' added Bernard facetiously. Sometimes I'd like to kill Bernard.

I contemplated the situation miserably. For months I've been struggling to make these defence cuts. And now, because of one

---

[1] The Overseas Policy and Defence Committee of the Cabinet.

impulsive, good-hearted decision, I was screwed.

'Of course,' murmured Humphrey, 'it would only come out if . . .' And he gazed at me.

I suddenly wondered if this had been a plot, if Humphrey could have persuaded me to rescue the dog to secure postponement of the defence cuts.

But I quickly realised that this was sheer paranoia. Humphrey is not clever enough for that, nor would he do that to me.

He was simply telling me that somebody in the MOD would inevitably leak the story unless I dropped the defence cuts. He was right. Someone would be sure to see the opportunity to blackmail me.

'I'm not going to be blackmailed,' I told Humphrey firmly.

'I should hope not,' he said. And waited.

And as I thought it all through, I realised I have no choice. So I put the best face on it that I could.

'On the other hand,' I began carefully, 'one can't cut defence too far back. Defence of the Realm, the first duty of government. And there are always unexpected emergencies: Korea, the Falklands, Benjy.'

'Benjy!' echoed Bernard and Humphrey with approval.

'Yes,' I concluded, 'perhaps I have been a bit hasty.' So I told Humphrey that in my considered opinion Item 3 – the Defence Cuts – possibly needs a little more thought. I instructed Humphrey to refer it to committee.

I could see from Humphrey's respectful expression that he thought that I had made a right decision.

'And tell them there's no particular hurry, would you?'

'Yes Prime Minister.'

10
Man Overboard

July 2nd

The Employment Secretary has clearly been thinking hard during Wimbledon. Straight back from the Centre Court he came to me with a fascinating proposal.

In a nutshell, his plan is to relocate many of our armed forces to the north of England. He has come to the realisation that, although we have 420,000 service personnel, only 20,000 of them are stationed in the north. Almost everything and everyone is here in the south. The navy is in Portsmouth and Plymouth. The Royal Air Force is in Bedford and East Anglia, barely north of London. The army is in Aldershot. There are virtually no troops in Britain north of the Wash. And yet – here's the rub – virtually *all* our unemployment is in the north. [*See map overleaf – Ed.*]

Dudley[1] is not concerned about the military personnel themselves. Many of them come from the north anyway. No, what he sees is that if we move two or three hundred thousand servicemen from the south to the north we will create masses of civilian jobs: clerks, suppliers, builders, vehicle maintenance . . . the possibilities are immense, limitless. Three hundred thousand extra pay packets to be spent in the shops.

There is really no good argument against this proposal, and I defy the Civil Service to provide one. [*A rash challenge – Ed.*] They should underestimate me no longer. I'm getting wise to their tricks.

[*Hacker, after eight months in Number Ten Downing Street, was clearly much more intelligently aware of the likely Civil Service response to any alteration in the status quo. Even so, he seems to suffer from overconfidence here, and left the door open for 'a good argument' against this plan. New readers may interpret this attitude as reasonable, moderate and flexible. But those students who are familiar*

---

[1] Dudley Belling, the Secretary of State for Employment.

**MAJOR
MILITARY
ESTABLISHMENTS**

RAF

NAVY/MARINES

ARMY

with Hacker's earlier career will know that Sir Humphrey Appleby could conjure up very good arguments out of thin air. Hacker, unshakeably confident though he was that he was wise to Sir Humphrey's tricks, apparently forgot that he was dealing with a master magician.

As soon as the Employment Secretary's relocation proposal was circulated, an emergency meeting was convened at the MOD.[1] The minutes record total approval for the plan, with a note that minor reservations were expressed about the feasibility of certain peripheral details concerning the actual execution of the proposal. Sir Humphrey's private notes, recently released under the Thirty Year rule, tell a rather different story – Ed.]

Meeting today at the MOD with Alan[2] and Geoffrey.[3]

Geoffrey was late. Not particularly soldierly, I thought, but Alan explained that this proposal by the Employment Secretary has put the whole of the Ministry of Defence into a state of turmoil.

Alan, who's new, was taking it very badly indeed. I tried to explain to him that it was a perfectly reasonable plan, seen from the Prime Minister's point of view. Alan refused to see it from the Prime Minister's point of view, remarking bitterly that this wretched proposal emanated from the Department of Employment, and defence was none of their bloody business. I corrected him: the plan emanated from the Secretary of State for Employment – the Department itself had nothing to do with it.

Furthermore, as I could see civil war between the two Departments looming here, I indicated that all work on the proposal was done by the Employment Secretary's political advisers.

[Sir Humphrey, a circumspect man, probably did not say that the proposal came from the Secretary of State's political advisers. He merely 'indicated' it. He would have been most concerned not to tell lies, even if he was not telling the truth. His distinguished predecessor Sir Arnold Robinson described this process as being 'economical with the truth' on one famous occasion, though he was in turn quoting Edmund Burke – Ed.]

I pointed out to Alan that we should all stay quite calm, and that we were only dealing with a relocation proposal, not a Russian invasion. Alan said: 'I'd be less worried if it were a Russian invasion – the Ministry of Defence is prepared for that.'

We were all more than surprised to hear this. So he clarified the statement: what he meant was that the MOD knows what it would have to do to repel a Russian invasion. I was even more surprised, and asked if we *could*

---

[1] Ministry of Defence.
[2] Sir Alan Guthrie, the Permanent Secretary, Ministry of Defence.
[3] Field Marshal Sir Geoffrey Howard, the Chief of the Defence Staff.

repel it. He said no, of course not, but at least the MOD don't have to do any more *thinking* about it.

It was up to me nominally to defend the Employment Secretary's proposal, since the Prime Minister has publicly supported it, so I reiterated that, although the armed forces contain a lot of men from the north, *they* are not the ones who are unemployed now. And the Employment Secretary's scheme is designed to help those who are currently unemployed.

Alan felt that we were doing quite enough already. Many of our troops from the north *were* unemployed, that's why they joined up. This argument won't wash with the PM, who is concerned about jobs in the north, whereas the troops who have joined up in the north are spending all their money in the south where they now are.

Alan said that this was logically inevitable, since there is nothing to spend it on in the north.

Field Marshal Sir Geoffrey Howard joined us. He went straight on to the attack, informing me that this proposal must be stopped. He told me that you can't just move hundreds of thousands of men around the country like that.

I thought that's what you did with armies. It sounds a feeble argument to me. But upon closer examination it was the permanence of the move to which he objected. Quite reasonably.

He conceded that *some* servicemen could be stationed permanently in the north of England: other ranks perhaps, junior officers possibly. But he made it clear, very properly, that we really cannot ask senior officers to live permanently in the north.

I asked for a list of reasons. He obliged.

1. Their wives wouldn't stand for it.
2. No schools. [*There* were *schools in the north of England at this time, but perhaps Sir Geoffrey meant that suitable fee-paying schools were not accessible – Ed.*]
3. Harrods is not in the north.
4. Nor is Wimbledon.
5. Ditto Ascot.
6. And the Henley Regatta.
7. Not to mention the Army and Navy Club.

In short, he argued that civilisation generally would be completely remote. This sort of sacrifice is acceptable to the forces in time of war but if the move were made in these circumstances, morale would undoubtedly plummet.

I was impatient with these arguments. The matter is to be discussed in Cabinet this afternoon, and more serious arguments are required than senior officers being three hundred miles from the club, however disturbing, however true!

Geoffrey could think of nothing more serious than that. He remarked indignantly that chaps like him and me might have to move up there.

I pressed him for objective reasons against the plan. He insisted that these *were* objective reasons. I decided against showing him the dictionary, and enquired if there are any *strategic* arguments against it.

He said there were. Several. My pencil poised, I asked him to list them. He was unable to do so. He said that he hasn't had time to think about it yet, but that strategic arguments can always be found against anything. He's absolutely correct in that.

So when Alan and Geoffrey have had time to find some strategic arguments, we must ensure that if they cannot stand up to outside scrutiny we will make them top secret. This is in any case customary with all defence matters, and is the way in which we have always managed to keep the defence estimates high. We will make the strategic arguments *For The Prime Minister's Eyes Only*, which certainly means that they will not be subject to expert scrutiny.

However, the strategic arguments might not be sufficient to deflect the Prime Minister from the Employment Secretary's plan. So I proposed that, for additional safety, we play the man instead of the ball. This is always a good technique, and the man in question is – and deserves to be – the Employment Secretary, whose dreadful idea this was.

The plan we devised involves appealing to the Prime Minister's paranoia. All Prime Ministers are paranoid, this one more than most. It should be child's play to suggest to the Prime Minister that the Employment Secretary is plotting against him.

Geoffrey asked if this were true. Soldiers really are awfully simple people. The question is not whether there is a plot (which, so far as I know, there is not) but whether the Prime Minister can be made to believe there is.

Geoffrey asked if there were any chance of getting rid of him completely. At first I thought that he was referring to the PM, and I indicated that it would be an awful pity to get rid of him after all the effort we've put into getting him house-trained.

But it transpired that Geoffrey meant getting rid of the Employment Secretary. The man is dangerous. If he's moved from Employment he might get Industry – in which case he might try to sell the RAF. Or privatise the army. Or float the navy.

In view of the presence of one or two junior MOD officials at the meeting and the consequent risk of ponting,[1] I expressed appropriate horror at Field Marshal Howard's notion that humble civil servants should presume to try and remove a member of Her Majesty's Government from the Cabinet. I explained that it was out of the question, that only a Prime Minister can remove Secretaries of State.

Nonetheless, any Prime Minister would be forced to consider such drastic

[1] See Editor's note overleaf.

action if he were to suspect the loyalty of a member of his cabinet. And since only someone in an advanced state of paranoia would suspect the Employ ment Secretary of a plot . . . we're in with a chance.

Before the meeting broke up we ensured that the minutes reflected our enthusiasm for the Employment Secretary's proposal to relocate substantial numbers of our armed forces, at all levels, in the north of England and Scotland. [*Appleby Papers 36/17/QQX*]

[*Sir Humphrey's comment about the discretion of the junior officials reflects the growing concern about freedom of information at this time. An Assistant Secretary by the name of Ponting was one of those officials who had taken it upon himself to leak information to Members of Parliament and other totally unqualified and unsuitable individuals, in what was claimed to be the public interest. 'Ponting' became the participle from the verb 'to pont' used to describe such leaks, and many junior officials were concerned with the problem of to pont or not to pont, the alternatives being loyalty and discretion in the job or resig- nation from it. 'Ponting' was clearly an attractive temptation, carrying with it the improbability of conviction, the certainty of notoriety and the serialisation of one's memoirs in* The Guardian.

The day following the secret meeting at the MOD, the Employment Secretary's proposal came up for discussion in Cabinet Committee. Hacker's diary continues – Ed.]

July 4th

We discussed Dudley's proposal today in Cabinet Committee and I encountered opposition, just as I expected. Sir Humphrey was present. So were Max[1] and Dudley[2] and several others. Bernard was there too, of course.[3]

Dudley, at my prompting, asked for reactions to his paper.

Max spoke first. He was bound to be against it. 'Well, Prime Minister, I know that on the face of it this plan looks as though it might benefit the employment situation in depressed areas. But this is to be achieved, as I understand it, by relocating most of our defence establishments. I suggest that it affects the Defence Department at least as much as the Department of Employment and I need time to do a feasibility study.'

I looked around the table. Nobody else spoke.

[1] Sir Maxwell Hopkins, Secretary of State for Defence.
[2] Dudley Belling, Secretary of State for Employment.
[3] Bernard Woolley, the Prime Minister's Principal Private Secretary.

'Anyone else have an opinion?' I asked. 'Quickly.' Brian,[1] Eric[2] and Neil[3] all looked rather doubtful.

Brian said: 'Well, I don't really know much about it, but it sounds like a bit of an upheaval.' He's right on both counts.

Eric murmured: 'Rather expensive.'

And Neil commented carefully that it was rather a big move.

Having had my little bit of fun, I gave my opinion. 'I'm thoroughly in favour of the proposal,' I said.

'So am I,' agreed Geoffrey[4] without hesitation.

'Absolutely first-rate,' said Eric, and Neil commented that it was a brilliant scheme. Sometimes being surrounded by yes-men is rather irritating, though it certainly has its compensations. And, after all, since I'm usually right on matters of government strategy it does save a lot of time when they all agree with me right away.

I smiled at my colleagues. 'I think that the Secretary of State for Defence is in a minority of one.'

Max stood up for himself. He was grimly determined. I have to admire that, even though he can't win this one. 'Nonetheless, Prime Minister,' he said, 'I am the responsible Minister and this can't be decided till I've done my feasibility study. The defence of the realm is in question. We must have a further meeting about this, with time allotted for a full discussion.'

A reasonable request. I agreed that we would have a full discussion of it at our next meeting, in two weeks' time, after which we would put it to full Cabinet for approval.

The rest of the Committee agreed with me again. 'Hear hear! *Hear* hear!' they all grunted vociferously.

Dudley added: 'May I request, Prime Minister, that it be noted in the minutes that the Cabinet Committee was in favour of my plan, save for one member?'

I nodded at Humphrey and Bernard, who made notes. But Max refused to accept Dudley's request without comment. 'The one member', he remarked stubbornly, 'is the member whose department would have to be reorganised. It's quite a problem.'

I began to feel impatient with Max. 'May I urge the Secretary of State for Defence to remember that every problem is also an opportunity?'

---

[1] Brian Smithson, Secretary of State for the Environment.
[2] Eric Jeffries, the Chancellor of the Exchequer.
[3] Neil Hitchcock, Secretary of State for Transport.
[4] Geoffrey Pickles, Secretary of State for Trade and Industry.

Humphrey intervened. 'I think, Prime Minister, that the Secretary of State for Defence fears that this plan may create some insoluble opportunities.'

We all laughed. 'Very droll, Humphrey, but not so.' I dismissed them and, as they trooped out obediently, I remained behind to catch up on the details of Dudley's proposal. I hadn't had time to read much of it before the meeting.

'Er . . . Prime Minister.' I looked up. To my surprise, Sir Humphrey had remained behind. I gave him my full attention.

SIR BERNARD WOOLLEY RECALLS:[1]

Not as I recall. And I do recall this conversation very well, as I dined out on it for some months. It went rather like this. Sir Humphrey did indeed say: 'Er . . . Prime Minister.' Thus far Hacker's account is accurate but no further.

'Oh, still here, Humphrey?' said Hacker, reading.

'Yes,' said Humphrey. 'I wanted to have a word with you about the Employment Secretary's scheme.'

Hacker was now engrossed in whatever he was reading. 'Terrific scheme, isn't it?' he replied without looking up.

Humphrey did not think so. 'Well . . . the Service Chiefs weren't entirely happy with it, I gather.'

'Good,' said Hacker cheerfully, then looked up. 'What?' He hadn't heard a word.

Humphrey was getting pretty irritated. He never much cared for the proverbial brush-off unless he held the brush. 'Prime Minister,' he said testily, 'do I have your full attention?'

'Of course you do, Humphrey. I'm just reading these notes.'

'Prime Minister, there's been an earthquake in Haslemere,' remarked Humphrey, by way of a small test.

'Good, good,' murmured Hacker. Then something must have penetrated, albeit slowly, because he looked up. Sir Humphrey, well aware that the Prime Minister had the attention span of a moth, confined himself to repeating with unusual clarity of speech that the Service Chiefs didn't like the plan.

[Hacker's diary continues – Ed.]

Humphrey kept batting on about how the Service Chiefs didn't like the plan. Of course they didn't! One could hardly expect them to appreciate the prospect of moving their wives away from Harrods and Wimbledon.

Sir Humphrey responded snootily to this suggestion. 'Prime

---

[1] In conversation with the Editors.

Minister, that is unworthy. Their personal feelings do not enter into it. Their objections are entirely strategic.'

'Oh yes?' I leaned back in my chair and smiled benevolently. He didn't fool me. Not any more. I spoke with heavy sarcasm. 'Strategic? The Admiralty Ships Division needs a deep-water port so it obviously has to be in Bath – thirty miles inland. The Marines' job is to defend Norway so we station them in Plymouth. Armoured vehicle trials are conducted in Scotland so the military engineering establishment clearly needs to be in Surrey.'

'These are just isolated examples,' replied Humphrey unconvincingly.

'Quite,' I agreed. 'And there's another seven hundred isolated examples in this paper.' And I waved the report at him. He gazed back at me, unsmiling, cold, totally unshakeable, his piercing blue eyes fixed upon me as they stared at me down his patrician nose. I hesitated. [*And we all know what happens to he who hesitates – Ed.*]

'Why are you against it, Humphrey?' I felt I had to understand.

'I, Prime Minister? I assure you, I am not against it. I'm simply trying to furnish you with the appropriate questions. Like the question of cost.'

He has completely missed the point. 'But that's the whole beauty of it, Humphrey. It *makes* money! We sell all those expensive buildings in the south and move into cheap ones in the north. And there would be hundreds of thousands of acres of high-priced land in the Home Counties to sell too.'

'So you think the Employment Secretary has done well?'

'Yes, he's a good chap.'

To my surprise Humphrey agreed wholeheartedly. 'Oh, I do agree with you there. Absolutely brilliant. Outstanding. A superb intellect. Excellent footwork. Strong elbows. A major figure, without doubt.'

I didn't think he was *that* good. In fact, I was rather amazed that Humphrey went overboard for him like that. I said as much.

'But he is a good chap,' insisted Humphrey. 'Wouldn't you say?'

'Yes,' I said. I'd already said it. .

'Yes indeed,' mused Humphrey. 'Very popular, too.'

This was news to me. 'Is he?'

'Oh yes,' Humphrey told me.

I wanted to know more. 'Not *that* popular, is he?'

Humphrey was nodding, eyebrows raised, as if slightly astonished by the extent of Dudley's popularity. 'Oh yes he is. In Whitehall. And with the parliamentary party, I understand.'

I considered this. I suppose he's right. Dudley *is* very popular with. the parliamentary party.

'And with the grass roots, I'm told,' Humphrey added.

'Are you?'

He nodded. I wonder who tells him these things.

'And he seems to have quite a following in the Cabinet too.'

A following in the Cabinet? How is that possible? I'm supposed to be the only one with a following in the Cabinet. 'Tell me more.' I was curious. 'Sit down.'

Humphrey sat opposite me, but seemed unwilling to say more. 'There's nothing to tell, really. It's just that people are beginning to talk about him as the next Prime Minister.'

I was startled. 'What? What do you mean?'

'I mean,' said Humphrey carefully, 'when you decide to retire, of course.'

'But I'm not planning to retire. I only just got here.'

'Exactly,' he replied enigmatically.

I had a little think. 'Why', I asked eventually, 'should people be talking about a next Prime Minister?'

'I'm sure it's just general speculation,' he drawled casually.

It's all right for Humphrey to be sure. But I'm not sure. 'Do you think he wants to be Prime Minister?'

Suddenly Humphrey seemed to be on his guard. 'Even if he does, surely you have no reason to doubt his loyalty? He's not trying to build up a personal following or anything, is he?'

'Isn't he?'

'Is he?'

I thought about it for a few moments. 'He spends a hell of a lot of time going round the country making speeches.'

'Only as a loyal minister.' Why was Humphrey so keen to defend him? 'I'm sure he pays personal tributes to you in all of them.'

We looked at each other. And wondered. 'Does he?' I asked. I'd never thought of checking. I told Bernard to get me copies of Dudley's last six speeches. At once.

We waited in silence. And it occurred to me, once I started thinking about it, that Dudley also spends a considerable amount of time chatting up our backbenchers in the House of Commons tea room.

I mentioned this to Humphrey. He tried to reassure me. 'But you asked ministers to take more trouble to communicate with the party in the House.'

True enough. 'But he has them to dinner parties as well.'

'Oh.' Humphrey looked glum. 'Does he?'

'Yes, he does,' I replied grimly. 'This starts to get worrying.'

There seemed no more to say. Bernard returned and said that Employment had phoned to let us know that we wouldn't be able to get copies of Dudley's speeches till later today or tomorrow. I'll read them as soon as I get them. Meanwhile, I won't worry about it. It's lucky I'm not paranoid. And I'm also fortunate to have someone like Humphrey as my Cabinet Secretary, someone who doesn't shrink from letting me know the truth, even if it is a little upsetting.

July 5th

I couldn't sleep. This business with Dudley is really worrying. I told Annie[1] about it, and she said airily that she's sure there's nothing to worry about. What does *she* know?

Today, first thing, I went through copies of Dudley's six most recent speeches. As I suspected, and feared, there was nothing in them by way of a personal tribute to me. Well, virtually nothing.

I called Humphrey in for a confidential word. Like me, he could hardly believe that Dudley had said nothing suitable about me.

'Surely,' asked Humphrey, evidently puzzled, '*surely* he must have talked about the new Prime Minister bringing a new hope to Britain? *The Dawn of a New Age.* You know, that leaflet you told party headquarters to issue to all MPs and constituencies?'

I shook my head. 'Not a word.'

'That *is* odd.'

'It's more than odd,' I remarked. 'It's suspicious. Very suspicious.'

'Even so, Prime Minister, he surely isn't actively plotting against you?'

I wasn't so sure. 'Isn't he?'

'Is he?'

'How do I know he's not?'

Thoughtfully, he stroked his chin. 'You could always find out.'

'Could I?'

'The Chief Whip would be bound to know.'

Humphrey was right, of course. Why didn't I think of it? I told Bernard to send for the Chief Whip right away. And we were in luck. The Chief Whip was in his office at Number Twelve.[2] We told him to drop everything and come right over.

[1] Mrs Hacker, the Prime Minister's wife.

[2] No. 12 Downing Street, two doors up from the Prime Minister. A half-minute's walk away.

SIR BERNARD WOOLLEY RECALLS:[1]

It was my duty to meet the Chief Whip and show him into the Cabinet Room. So when Sir Humphrey left the Prime Minister, who by now was chewing the Bokhara – figuratively, of course – I hurried out after him. I was anxious for more details of this apparent plot.

I stopped Humphrey in the lobby outside the Cabinet Room, where I could also keep my eye on the front door of Number Ten.

'Sir Humphrey,' I said, 'I'm very troubled by what I've just learned.'

He looked at me with detached amusement, and asked what that was. I explained that I felt that I'd been walking around with my eyes shut. I'd never realised that there was a Cabinet plot against the Prime Minister.

He raised his eyebrows. 'Is there?' he asked. 'How interesting.'

'You said there was,' I said.

He said: 'I said nothing, Bernard. Nothing at all.'

Rapidly, I put my brain into rewind search, and realised that he had indeed said nothing. So . . . what *had* he been saying? Something, certainly, even if it was nothing. But it couldn't have been nothing, or why was he not saying it?

I owed it to Hacker to get to the bottom of this. I decided to ask a straight question. After all, though rare, it was not entirely unknown for Humphrey to give a straight answer. 'So . . . you mean . . . do you know if there is a plot?'

'No.'

This *appeared* to be a straight answer. But no. I sought elucidation.

'No there is a plot or no there isn't?'

'Yes,' replied Humphrey obligingly.

I decided to try a new tack. 'Sir Humphrey,' I said carefully, 'what has the Employment Secretary actually done?'

'Nothing, as yet, Bernard. And we must keep it that way.'

I could see that he was referring to the plan, not the plot. Or non-plot. Then, suddenly, the penny dropped. I had been bemused as to why Sir Humphrey had been so forthcoming about the Employment Secretary's popularity. I now saw that he was playing the man and not the ball.

So I played the ball. 'Isn't the Employment Secretary's plan actually rather a good one?'

'For whom?'

'For the country.'

'Maybe. But that's hardly the point.'

'Why not?'

Humphrey stared at me, irritated. 'Bernard, when you move on from here, where do you plan to go?'

I thought it was one of his threats. Cagey, I replied that I didn't really know.

[1] In conversation with the Editors.

'How would you like to be Deputy Secretary in Charge of Defence Procurement?'

This suggestion surprised me. Dep. Sec. is pretty high. One's K[1] is guaranteed. Dep. Secs are top people, their names are in *Who's Who* and everything. Normally, if Humphrey were trying to threaten me, he'd suggest the War Graves Commission or the Vehicle Licensing Centre in Swansea. So, if he wasn't threatening, what *was* he driving at? I waited.

'You could find yourself doing that job in Sunderland. Or Berwick-on-Tweed. Or Lossiemouth.'

He *was* threatening me. I instantly saw the major drawback to the Employment Secretary's plan. I certainly wouldn't want to leave London for Sunderland or Berwick-on-Tweed. They're up north somewhere!

And I didn't even understand the reference to Lossiemouth. 'Is that a place?' I asked Humphrey.

'What did you think it was?'

'A dogfood.'

Humphrey smirked menacingly. 'If the Employment Secretary has his way you may have a three-year diet of Lossiemouth yourself. You see?'

I saw.

I also saw that the plan cannot possibly be good for the country. It is not possible for a plan to be good for the country and bad for the Civil Service – it's a contradiction in terms. But I still didn't understand why Humphrey had suggested sending for the Chief Whip to confirm a plot that didn't exist.

We were still standing in the lobby of Number Ten, a fairly public place. Humphrey looked around cautiously, to check that we were not being overheard. Then he explained something that I have never before understood.

'The Chief Whip, Bernard, is bound to hedge. He dare not categorically state that there is no plot against the Prime Minister, just in case there *is* one. Even if the Chief Whip has heard nothing, he must say that he has suspicions, to cover himself. He will also say that he has no solid evidence, and he will promise to make urgent enquiries.'

At that moment the Chief Whip himself, Jeffrey Pearson, bustled through the front door like a ship in full sail and surged along the wide corridor towards us. My eyes indicated his presence to Humphrey, who swung round and gave him a warm greeting. 'Ah, good morning, Chief Whip.'

'Good morning, Cabinet Secretary. Good morning, Bernard.'

I asked Pearson to wait in the Private Office.[2] I wanted to be sure that Sir Humphrey and I were now fully in tune.

Humphrey instructed me to go into the meeting with Jeffrey – which, in any case, I would have done – and inform Sir Humphrey of everything that was said – which I may not have done.

---

[1] Knighthood.
[2] The office of the Private Secretary, i.e. Bernard Woolley's office.

'I'm not sure I can do that. It might be confidential.'

Humphrey disagreed. 'The matter at issue concerns the defence of the realm and the stability of government.'

'But you only need to know things on a "need to know" basis.'

Humphrey became impatient. 'Bernard, I need to know everything. How else can I judge whether or not I need to know it?'

I'd never thought of that. Hitherto, I'd thought that others might have been the judge of the Cabinet Secretary's need to know. I decided to get this straight.

'So that means that you need to know things even when you don't need to know them. You need to know them not because you need to know them but because you need to know whether or not you need to know. And if you don't need to know you still need to know so that you know that there was no need to know.'

'Yes,' said Humphrey. A straight answer at last. And he thanked me for helping him clarify the position.

[*Hacker's diary continues – Ed.*]

Jeffrey Pearson, the Chief Whip, was in the Cabinet Room within ten minutes. He was evasive but during the meeting he made it perfectly clear that there is indeed some sort of leadership challenge, either led by Dudley or using Dudley as the figurehead. His problem is a lack of concrete evidence. So he can't make a move to stamp it out.

I was magnanimous. After all, one wants ambitious men in the Cabinet, one *needs* them. Just as long as they don't get *too* ambitious. . . .

I'm grateful to Humphrey for drawing my attention to it. He really is a good man and a loyal servant.

[*Jeffrey Pearson's account of this is somewhat different. We reprint this extract from his stylish memoirs* Suck It And See *– Ed.*]

I had a sudden urgent call from Number Ten. Hacker wanted to see me right away. Bernard Woolley, his Private Secretary, refused to give me a reason.

Naturally I thought I'd done something to upset him. So it was with some caution that I entered the Cabinet Room, with Woolley in attendance. The morning sun shone brightly through the windows, creating patterns of intense light and deep shade.

Hacker sat in the shadows. 'How are things going, Chief Whip?'

Naturally I was cautious, though I had nothing to hide. I told him things were going quite well really, and asked why.

'You mean, you noticed nothing?'

So I was supposed to have noticed something. What, I wondered, had I missed? I couldn't think of anything in particular, though it was a slightly difficult time with a little unrest on the back benches. But then it's always a slightly difficult time with a little unrest on the back benches. Unless, that is, it's a very difficult time with lots of unrest on the back benches.

['A slightly difficult time with a little unrest on the back benches' was what fortune-tellers call a cold reading: something that is always true and always safe to say. A fortune-teller's cold reading might be: 'You went through a slightly difficult time round the age of thirteen.' A doctor's cold reading, if he cannot diagnose an illness, would be: 'I think it might be a good idea for you to give up smoking and lose a little weight' – Ed.]

'Is there anything you haven't told me?' asked the Prime Minister.

I racked my brains furiously. He prompted me. 'A plot? A leadership challenge?'

I hadn't heard a thing. But I couldn't say so, because Hacker obviously had suspicions. Perhaps he even had evidence. I played safe, avoided giving a direct answer, and told him that I had no real evidence of anything.

'But you have suspicions?'

I couldn't say I hadn't . . . and anyway, I always have suspicions of one sort or another. 'It's my job to have suspicions,' I replied carefully.

'Well, what are they?'

This was tricky. 'Jim,' I replied with my frankest manner, 'it wouldn't be right for me to tell you all my suspicions, not unless or until there's something solid to go on.'

'But you know who I'm talking about?'

I had no idea. 'I think I can guess,' I said.

Hacker remained in the shadows. I couldn't quite see his eyes. He heaved a sigh. 'How far has it got?' he asked finally.

I was still searching for a clue as to the identity of the pretender. One thing I knew for sure – it hadn't got very far or I would certainly have known about it. At least, I think I certainly would.

He was waiting for reassurance. I gave it. 'Only to a very early stage. So far as I can tell.' I was still being strictly honest.

'Do you think you ought to have a word with him?' the Prime Minister wanted to know. 'Tell him I know what's going on? I don't want to lose him from the Cabinet. I just want him under control.'

I didn't see how I could possibly have a word with him until I knew who he was. 'Perhaps you should have a word with him yourself,' I replied carefully.

He shook his head. 'No. Not at this stage.'

I waited.

'Who else is involved?'

I saw my chance. 'Apart from . . .?'

The Prime Minister was getting irritable. 'Apart from Dudley, obviously.'

Dudley! Dudley? Incredible! Dudley!!

'Oh, *apart* from Dudley, it's a bit early to say. After all, Prime Minister, there may not be anything to it.'

The Prime Minister stood up. He stared at me over his reading glasses. He looked thin, tired and drawn. This job is taking a toll on him, and he's only been at it less than a year. 'Jeffrey, I'm not taking any risks,' he said quietly.

I could see that he meant business. I left the Cabinet Room, and assigned all the Whips to make some enquiries. Top priority. After all, if there is a plot I need to know its full potential.

[*Jeffrey Pearson certainly wanted and needed to reassure himself that the plot, if plot there was, could be nipped in the bud. If it could not, he would have wanted to reassure himself that it was not too late to change sides.*]

[*Two days later Sir Arnold Robinson, Appleby's predecessor as Secretary of the Cabinet, received a note from Sir Humphrey. It has been found in the archive of the Campaign for Freedom of Information, of which Sir Arnold was the President. Naturally the letter was confidential and has been kept under wraps, but the archive of the Campaign for Freedom of Information was recently made available to historians under the Thirty Year Rule – Ed.*]

Cabinet Office
July 6th

Dear Arnold,

You will have heard on the grapevine about the Employment Secretary's plan to move many of our armed forces' establishments to the north. There are three reasons why the PM is in favour of this plan:

1. It will reduce unemployment.
2. Alternatively, it will look as though he is reducing unemployment.
3. At the very least, it will look as though he is *trying* to reduce unemployment.

The reality is that he is only trying to look as if he is trying to reduce unemployment. This is because he is worried that it does not look as if he is trying to look as if he is trying to reduce unemployment.

Curiously, the P.M. has come to suspect that the plan may be the start of a leadership bid by the Employment Secretary.

This is, of course, a ridiculous notion. But the higher the office, the higher the level of political paranoia. Nonetheless, it is undoubtedly in the national interest that this plan does not proceed, and the Prime Minister's paranoia would undoubtedly be fed (and the Employment Secretary's chances of survival in high office much reduced) if a leak occurred in the press which suggested that this brilliantly imaginative plan by the Employment Secretary was being blocked by the Prime Minister.

We must devoutly hope that no such leak occurs. Have you any thoughts on this matter?

> Yours ever,
> Humphrey

[*A reply was received from Sir Arnold Robinson at the beginning of the next week. A copy was found at the Campaign's headquarters, but we were fortunate enough to find the original among the Appleby Papers – Ed.*]

July 9th

Dear Humphrey,
Thank you for your letter. A leak of the sort you suggest would almost certainly result in man overboard.

I cannot see, however, how such a leak can occur. You as Cabinet Secretary cannot be party to a leak. And although, as President of the Campaign for Freedom of Information, I have an undoubted duty to make certain facts available, I do not see in all conscience how I, as a former Cabinet Secretary, can give confidential information to the press.

> Yours ever,
> Arnold

[*A reply was apparently sent to Sir Arnold Robinson by return – delivered by messenger – Ed.*]

July 10th

Dear Arnold,
I would not dream of suggesting that you give confidential information to the press. It is confidential misinformation to which I refer.

> Yours ever,
> Humphrey

[*Sir Arnold sent a brief and immediate reply – Ed.*]

July 10th

Dear Humphrey,
I shall be happy to oblige.

> Yours ever,
> Arnold

[*The original letters are reproduced on the following pages – Ed.*]

70 WHITEHALL, LONDON SW1A 2AS

From the Secretary of the Cabinet and Head of the Home Civil Service

July 6th

Dear Arnold,

You will have heard on the grapevine about the Employment Secretary's plan to move many of our armed forces' establishments to the north. There are three reasons why the P.M. is in favour of this plan:

1. It will reduce unemployment.

2. Alternatively, it will look as though he is reducing unemployment.

3. At the very least, it will look as though he is <u>trying</u> to reduce unemployment.

The reality is that he is only trying to look as if he is trying to reduce unemployment. This is because he is worried that it does not look as if he is trying to look as if he is trying to reduce unemployment.

Curiously, the P.M. has come to suspect that the plan may

be the start of a leadership bid by the Employment Secretary.

This is, of course, a ridiculous notion. But the higher the office, the higher the level of political paranoia. Nonetheless, it is undoubtedly in the national interest that this plan does not proceed, and the Prime Minister's paranoia would undoubtedly be fed (and the Employment Secretary's chances of survival in high office much reduced) if a leak occurred in the press which suggested that this brilliantly imaginative plan by the Employment Secretary was being blocked by the Prime Minister.

We must devoutly hope that no such leak occurs. Have you any thoughts on this matter?

Yours ever

Humphrey

The Campaign for
Freedom of Information

3 Endsleigh Street, London WC1H ODD
Telephone 01-278 9686

July 9th

Dear Humphrey,

Thank you for your letter. A leak of the sort
you suggest would almost certainly result in man overboard.

I cannot see, however, how such a leak can occur.
You as Cabinet Secretary cannot be party to a leak.
And although, as President of the Campaign for Freedom of
Information, I have an undoubted duty to make certain
facts available, I do not see in all conscience how I,
as a former cabinet secretary, can give confidential
information to the press.

Yours ever,

Arnold.

276

70 WHITEHALL, LONDON SW1A 2AS

From the Secretary of the Cabinet and Head of the Home Civil Service

July 10th

Dear Arnold,

I would not dream of suggesting that you give confidential information to the press. It is confidential misinformation to which I refer.

Yours ever

Humphrey

The Campaign for Freedom of Information

3 Endsleigh Street, London WC1H ODD
Telephone 01-278 9686

July 10th.

Dear Humphrey,

I shall be happy to oblige.

Yours ever,

Arnold.

[*Hacker's diary continues – Ed.*]

July 11th

I am now convinced that a dirty little scheme has been hatched behind my back. It is a disloyal, ungrateful and treacherous plot, and I will not tolerate it.

I spoke to the Chief Whip. He said that he had no real evidence but he had *suspicions*. He said that he would make enquiries! He refused to tell me about them till he had something solid to go on. I regard that as proof positive.

I discussed the matter with Humphrey today. He expressed surprise that Dudley is plotting against me. 'I would have thought all your Cabinet were loyal.' Sometimes I am amazed at how trusting and naive Humphrey reveals himself to be. Loyal? How few people realise what the word loyalty means when spoken by a Cabinet Minister. It only means that his fear of losing his job is stronger than his hope of pinching mine.

'So,' said Humphrey, wide-eyed, 'you believe that the Employment Secretary has his eye on the Prime Ministerial chair?'

'Yes.' I sat back. 'But look what I've got on it.'

Humphrey didn't get my little joke and merely commented that loyalty was a fundamental requirement of collective responsibility.

Hasn't he noticed that collective responsibility has fallen out of fashion? Collective responsibility means that when we do something popular they all leak the fact that it was their idea, and when we do something unpopular they leak the fact that they were against it. This country is governed by the principle of collective irresponsibility.

'You were a Cabinet minister once.' Humphrey seemed to be admonishing me gently.

'That's different,' I reminded him. 'I was loyal.'

'You mean, you were more frightened of losing your job than . . .'

'No, Humphrey,' I interrupted him. 'I was *genuinely* loyal.'

Humphrey asked me why my colleagues want my job so much. The explanation is simple: I'm the only member of the government who can't be sent to Northern Ireland tomorrow.

'Even so,' he remarked, 'I find it hard to believe that the Employment Secretary is actively plotting against you.'

I told him it was obvious. I asked what more proof he would need. He thought for a moment.

'Well . . .' he began, 'this proposal to move Defence establishments to the north is bound to be leaked to the press, isn't it?'

279

'Bound to be,' I agreed. 'I'm surprised it hasn't been already.'

'Well, if it were leaked as the Employment Secretary's plan, I agree that it would confirm your suspicions. But I'm sure it will come out as a government plan.'

He's right. It's a good test. We shall see what we shall see.

July 12th

So much for Humphrey's faith in Dudley's loyalty. *The Standard* today contained the leak we were waiting for. And the proof that that disloyal swine is gunning for me.

THE LONDON EVENING

STANDAR

TONIGHT'S W

THURSDAY, 12 JULY

HACKER HITS

JOBLESS

by Peter Kirkston

SOURCES in Whitehall report that an imaginative plan, an initiative by Dudley Belling, the Secretary of State for Employment, to reduce unemployment in the depressed areas, has been blocked by the Prime Minister.

How dare he? How *dare* he??

It was Humphrey who showed me the newspaper. I was very angry indeed. I told Humphrey how I'd backed Dudley all along, I told him how I fought for that sodding plan of his. I told him how I gave him his first Cabinet post and how I've treated him like a son. And this, I said, is how he thanks me. I was speechless, utterly speechless.

Humphrey nodded sadly. 'How sharper than a serpent's tooth it is to have a thankless Cabinet colleague.'

What can you say? Nothing. 'It's envy,' I said. 'Dudley is consumed with envy.'

'It's one of the seven Dudley sins,' said Bernard, trying to lighten the atmosphere. I quelled him with a glance.

Humphrey, a tower of strength as always, suggested a possible course of action: that we draft my letter accepting his resignation.

But there are several disadvantages to that idea. Dudley will deny that he leaked the story, in which case I've no grounds for sacking him. And if I then sack him anyway, what are the consequences? He'd be even more dangerous on the back benches than in the Cabinet – sacked ministers don't even have to pretend to be loyal.

'So,' enquired Humphrey, 'you intend to go ahead with his plan?'

That option is also closed to me now. Once a story in the press says that I'm blocking it I can't possibly let it go ahead – it will look as though he has defeated me. Regretfully, I must abandon the plan, even though it's good. At least, I think I must.

I told Humphrey my dilemma.

'Prime Minister, you're not being indecisive, are you?'

'No,' I said. He looked at me. He knew I was. 'Yes,' I acknowledged. Then I thought: I'm damned if I'll be indecisive. 'No,' I snarled. Then I realised that I'd already answered the question all too clearly. 'I don't know,' I said weakly, putting my head in my hands. I felt deeply depressed, enervated. All my energy was sapped by the treachery and disloyalty.

He offered to help. I couldn't see how he could. But he produced some papers from a file on his lap. 'Technically I shouldn't show you this.'

'I don't see why not. I'm Prime Minister, aren't I?'

'Yes,' he explained. 'That's why I shouldn't be showing it to you. It's a Ministry of Defence draft internal paper. Top Secret. The Defence Secretary hasn't seen it yet.' He passed it over the desk. 'But as you see, it casts grave doubts on the Employment Secretary's plan.'

This was a paper I was keen to read. It is fascinating. Part One pointed out that many of the 'valuable' army buildings that Dudley quoted cannot be sold. Some are listed.[1] Some are under strict planning controls. Some don't conform to private-sector fire and safety regulations. It all showed that the cost of the move would be prohibitive.

Part Two showed that the move would create massive unemployment in the Home Counties and East Anglia, with far fewer new jobs created in the north-east than would be lost in the south.

And then, in Part Three, which I read in bed tonight, there are pages and pages of objections on grounds of military strategy.

Tomorrow I'll question Humphrey about this further.

July 13th

At a meeting with Humphrey first thing this morning I questioned him closely about the MOD paper. 'Is it quite honest and accurate?'

Humphrey was evasive. He said that everything is a matter of interpretation. And if we were to look at the conclusion of the report we would see that all of the objections to the scheme were known to the Employment Secretary before he produced his plan. He added one other rather telling point: that the whole plan may not be completely unconnected with the fact that Dudley represents a Newcastle constituency.

This had not escaped me either. [*In which case, it is strange that Hacker had never mentioned it – Ed.*].

'The public', I commented, 'has a right to know this.'

Humphrey shook his head. 'It's a top secret document.' I simply stared at him, and waited. 'On the other hand,' he continued, 'the Service Chiefs are notorious for their indiscretion.'

'Notorious,' I agreed.

'It could well find its way into the hands of an irresponsible journalist.'

---

[1] 'Listed' buildings under Section 54(9) of the 1971 Town and Country Planning Act, which was replaced by the Town and Country Planning (Listed Buildings and Buildings in Conservation Areas) Regulations of 1977, which were further amended by the 1986 Act necessitating changes in the Town and Country Planning (Listed Buildings and Buildings in Conservation Areas) Regulations 1987 (S1 1987, No. 349), are buildings which are of special architectural or historic interest listed since 1 July 1948 (when the Town and Country Planning Act of 1947 came into operation) and compiled by the Secretary of State with reference to national criteria, classified into three grades to show their relative importance, namely Grade I, Grade II* and Grade II. It is an offence under Section 107 of the 1971 Act to alter, extend or demolish a listed building unless excepted from control by Section 56, Section 54(9) (see paragraph 73) or Section 56(1)(a) and (b), excluding buildings for ecclesiastical use (see paragraphs 103–105).

'Could it?' I asked hopefully. 'Or several irresponsible journalists?'

Humphrey felt that such an eventuality was not beyond the bounds of possibility.

I made it quite clear, however, that I could not be a party to anything like that, even though it would at least give the public the true facts. Humphrey agreed wholeheartedly that I could not be party to such a leak.

We agreed that we would defer discussion of the plan until an unspecified future date [*i.e. abandon it – Ed.*], and that meanwhile Sir Humphrey would attend to the plumbing.

After he left, Bernard, who lacks subtlety sometimes, turned to me. 'When's he going to leak it?' he asked.

I was shocked. 'Did I ask for a leak?'

'Not in so many . . .' he hesitated. 'No, Prime Minister, you didn't.'

'Indeed not, Bernard,' I replied stiffly. 'I have never leaked. I occasionally give confidential briefings to the press. That is all.'

Bernard smiled. 'That's another of those irregular verbs, isn't it? I give confidential briefings; you leak; he has been charged under Section 2a of the Official Secrets Act.'

July 18th

Everything went like clockwork – until today. Two days ago a story appeared in several newspapers, attributed to various non-attributable sources, effectively torpedoing Dudley's plan.

All the important points were covered – the fact that the MOD can't make a profit on many of the valuable buildings in the London area; the fear of huge unemployment in the south without creating enough new jobs up north; and the military and strategic arguments against the plan. At least two of them ran the story reminding readers that Dudley himself represented a constituency in the north-east.

All of this was picked up by the TV news. [*Television news in the 1980s hardly ever originated a news story – Ed.*]

But today it all came to a head. I was horrified when I saw the front page of *The Guardian* and the cartoon [*see overleaf – Ed.*].

IE GUARDIA

Wednesday 18 July

and Manchester

Dudley Belling alleges conspiracy

Employment secretary denies leaking

By David Tow

Dudley Belling, the Secretary of State for Employment, yesterday denied leaking the details of his plan last week, in which it was revealed that the Government was considering moving some of our military bases to centres of high unemployment.

Mr Belling also claimed that the Cabinet supports his plan, including Prime Minister Jim Hacker. But the leak has caused a succession of other leaks and done considerable damage to his credibility and to his policy. Last night he spoke angrily to reporters and demanded a public enquiry.

The day began with Cabinet Committee, Humphrey and Bernard were waiting for me in the Cabinet Room. They wished me good morning. I told them it was *not* a good morning.

They knew anyway. They'd read the papers.

'Dudley has been answering back to the press about that new leak,' I said.

'Shocking,' said Sir Humphrey.

'He says that he's leaked nothing and that someone's trying to damage him.'

'Shocking.'

'He's demanding a public enquiry!'

'Shocking!!' he murmured again, with real feeling. Bernard was strangely silent.

284

Reprinted by kind permission of The Guardian.

'You'd think he'd know better,' I went on. 'Anyway, leak enquiries never find the true source of the leak.'

'But we know the true source, Prime Minister,' intervened Bernard. 'Just between ourselves. You asked us to . . .'

I quelled him with a look. 'Bernard, you're not saying I authorised this leak, I hope?'

Bernard hesitated. 'No, I . . . that is . . . yes but . . . I mean, I remember now. Sorry.'

I had to be sure. '*What* do you remember, Bernard?'

'Um – whatever you want, Prime Minister.'

'What I want is to show the public that there are no divisions in the Cabinet.'

'But there are divisions,' said Bernard.

'I don't want to multiply them,' I explained.

'Prime Minister, if you multiply divisions you get back to where you started.' I couldn't see what he was driving at. Undeterred, he continued to explain. 'If you divide four by two you get two and then if you multiply it you get back to four again. Unless, of course, you multiply different divisions, in which case . . .'

'Thank you, Bernard,' I said firmly. He is too literal-minded for

285

this job. And we were in a hurry. The members of Committee would be arriving any minute and we had to consider our strategy. I explained my plan.

'Humphrey, I want to keep the Employment Secretary in the Cabinet. *And* the Defence Secretary, Max. But I can't allow this row to go on any longer and I won't allow the Employment Secretary to be seen to defeat me – I can't risk it. Therefore, we must see that his plan is stopped.'

Humphrey gazed thoughtfully at his shoes for a moment, then came up with a three-point plan.

'I suggest you ask the Committee to agree to these three points: First, that they agree to accept Cabinet's collective decision. Second, that there is a cooling-off period with no further discussion. And third, that all further speeches and press statements are cleared with the Cabinet Office.'

Well, that seemed a pretty good plan to me. I instantly understood it. But when the meeting began Dudley immediately challenged the agenda.

'Excuse me, Prime Minister . . . on a point of order, I see that my plan for defence establishments' relocation is not on the agenda.'

I told him that was correct. He asked why. I explained that because of all the leaking that's been going on and the very damaging press consequences, the government looks divided.

'It is divided,' said Dudley.

He's very dense sometimes. 'That's why it mustn't look it,' I explained. I added that it's a very complex issue and that was why I was deferring consideration of it till a later date.

Dudley was baffled. 'I can't understand it. You were in favour of my plan last time.'

I couldn't allow Dudley or anyone to make such a claim, even if it were true. 'No, I wasn't,' I said. Perhaps I should have acknowledged that I *had* been in favour, even though I am now against it. But a simple denial seemed easier.

Dudley stared at me, as if I were lying. [*Hacker was lying – Ed.*]

'You were in favour of it,' he repeated. 'And so was *everyone* except the Secretary of State for Defence.'

'No they weren't,' I said, committed now.

'Yes they were!' Dudley would not let go. 'And you promised further discussion.'

This was perfectly true. I was completely stuck for a suitable reply when Humphrey stepped in. I can't remember what he said, but his gobbledegook interpretation of the minutes of the previous meeting saved the day.

But then we went on to Humphrey's three-point plan and, somehow, I don't know how, I simply can't understand why, we reached a point of no return with Dudley. What I had hoped would be a compromise scheme somehow turned into an ultimatum, and I found myself telling Dudley that he must consider his position. [*This means co-operate or resign – Ed.*]

I fear we'll lose him. I still don't quite know how this happened. Sir Humphrey seemed as baffled as I.

SIR BERNARD WOOLLEY RECALLS:[1]

That meeting was a total triumph for Sir Humphrey's strategy. All along he had been seeking to remove the Employment Secretary from the Cabinet, because he saw this as the only way to save thousands of senior officers and MOD officials from exile in the Siberia north of Birmingham.

Humphrey was not baffled at the outcome, for it had gone exactly to plan. I was not party to his scheme, but I marvelled at the brilliance of both its conception and execution.

Before the meeting he suggested the three-point plan as a compromise, knowing full well that it would be the *coup de grâce*. Hacker's claim that he instantly understood the plan was manifestly false: first, if he had understood it he would have seen the full implications and rejected it outright. Second, he was so confused that he couldn't even remember it. As the members of the Committee were entering the room Hacker was trying to remember it.

'Your three-point plan, Humphrey, remind me.'

'You ask them, Prime Minister, to agree to three points. First, that they agree to accept Cabinet's collective decision. Second, that there is a cooling-off period with no further discussion. Third, that all further speeches and press statements are cleared with the Cabinet Office.'

'Excellent,' said Hacker. 'That should do it. Point one, they cool off and . . . er, no, no further discussion without decision, or decisions without discussions and, what was the second? Collective press statements and . . . sorry, Humphrey, I don't think I've quite got it yet.'

He really was in a frightful state. He could remember nothing. He was flapping around pathetically, the proverbial headless chicken. Humphrey offered to write down the three-point plan for him, and Hacker accepted with gratitude.

Well, the agenda was immediately challenged by Dudley Belling, as Hacker correctly remembered. Dudley reminded the Prime Minister that he

---

[1] In conversation with the Editors.

had supported the proposal last time, and that Hacker had acceded to Dudley's request to discuss the matter again at this meeting.

Hacker was on the ropes when Sir Humphrey intervened.

'There was no such promise,' Sir Humphrey said, being economical with the truth again. 'And the Prime Minister did not support the proposal. If he had it would appear in the minutes. And it doesn't.'

Dudley was floored. 'Doesn't it?' And he glanced hurriedly through the minutes, which we had all agreed – on the nod – to sign as accurate. Careless of him not to have read them more thoroughly.

He looked up, angrier than ever. 'Sir Humphrey, why was my request for a further discussion, and the Prime Minister's reply, not minuted?'

Sir Humphrey was ready for that one. His reply was an object lesson. I recall it perfectly. 'While it is true that the minutes are indeed an authoritative record of the Committee's deliberations, it is nevertheless undeniable that a deliberate attempt at comprehensive delineation of every contribution and interpolation would necessitate an unjustifiable elaboration and wearisome extension of the documentation.'

Hacker stared at him. The Committee stared at him. The Foreign Secretary told me later that he wished he was at the UN where he'd have had the benefit of simultaneous translation. What he had said would have been crystal-clear to most people, but politicians are simple souls.

Finally Hacker said hopefully: 'Does that mean you don't recall the discussion?'

Sir Humphrey's reply was masterly. 'It is characteristic of committee discussions and decisions that every member has a vivid recollection of them and that every member's recollection differs violently from every other member's recollection. Consequently we accept the convention that the official decisions were those and only those which are officially recorded in the minutes by the officials, from which it follows with an elegant inevitability that any decision officially reached will be officially recorded in the minutes and any decision not recorded in the minutes was not officially reached even if one or more members believe that they recollect it, so in this particular case if the decision had been officially reached it would have been officially recorded by the officials in the minutes. And', he finished with triumphant simplicity, 'it isn't so it wasn't.'

There was another pause. Dudley was smouldering. 'It's a fiddle,' he snarled.

Hacker intervened firmly. 'This must stop!'

'Yes it must,' snapped Dudley, though I suspect that they were talking at cross purposes.

Hacker took charge. 'I have drawn up a three-point plan which we must all agree to. Point one . . . er, what did you say, I mean what did I say was point one, Humphrey?'

Humphrey silently unzipped his slimline document case that lay on the floor between the chairs and slid his handwritten, three-point plan a few inches along the Cabinet table till it rested in front of the Prime Minister.

'Thank you,' said Hacker. 'Point one, everyone will accept collective decisions, Dudley.'

'I'm perfectly willing to,' Dudley responded with caution. 'How are they defined?'

He was a good man. He knew the right questions to ask.

'I define them!' said the Prime Minister brusquely. 'Point two, there will be a cooling-off period on the subject of defence relocations. And point three . . .'

He hesitated. We all waited expectantly. Then he leaned towards Sir Humphrey and muttered that he couldn't quite read point three. 'Cleaning what?'

'*Clearing* all speeches . . .' whispered the Cabinet Secretary.

'Ah yes,' said the PM loudly. 'All speeches and press statements must in future be cleared with the Cabinet Office.'

On the face of it point three looked like a sensible way of preventing members of the Cabinet making embarrassingly contradictory statements. But it had one other major virtue – it put Sir Humphrey in charge of all relations with the press.

Dudley spotted it. 'I can't accept point two, we can't cool off discussion on something that hasn't been discussed yet because the officials refused or neglected to minute my request for further discussion – even though it was agreed by you, Prime Minister – and which has consequently been left off the agenda. As for your third point, I cannot in principle accept that anything I say in public must be cleared by him.' He pointed at Sir Humphrey, refusing to dignify him further by mentioning him by name. 'I have no confidence,' Dudley concluded, 'that he will clear what I want to say.'

Hacker was now committed. 'Well, that's my decision and I must ask you to accept it.'

'I don't accept it.' Dudley was implacable.

'Oh,' said Jim. He looked at Humphrey for guidance. Humphrey whispered something to him. Jim nodded sadly, and turned to his Employment Secretary.

'Then, Dudley,' he pronounced solemnly, 'I must ask you to consider your position.'

Everyone present knew that Dudley's career was over.

[*Hacker's diary continues – Ed.*]

July 19th

I was sitting in my study this morning, hoping for the best but expecting the worst. Bernard knocked and entered.

'I have news for you, Prime Minister.'

I looked at him. But I could tell nothing from his face. I waited.

'Do you want the bad news first?' he asked.

I perked up. 'You mean, there's bad news and good news.'

'No, Prime Minister – there's bad news and worse news.'

It was all very predictable. Dudley has resigned. He sent the usual letter, rather more curt than usual. Bernard gave me a draft letter of acceptance to sign. Humphrey and the Press Office were working on a draft press statement for me.

I wanted to have words with Humphrey. I told Bernard to fetch him. But first Bernard told me the worse news: apparently Dudley has made a resignation speech on the steps of the Department of Employment, accusing me of being dictatorial and running a Presidential style of government.

At first I thought Bernard was right to be gloomy. But in fact it's not so bad: I think that Dudley's accusation may do me more good than harm. The people like to feel they have a strong leader. I explained this to Bernard.

He saw the point at once. 'Oh yes indeed. Moreover, strong leadership'll be a new pleasure for them.'

'No it won't,' I replied shortly.

'No it won't,' he agreed without hesitation.

Humphrey arrived at that moment. I did not mince words with him. I reminded him that I had sought to avoid this resignation, and I now realise – too late – that it was his three-point plan which provoked it.

Humphrey had other, surprising news for me. He agreed that the three-point plan had been the last straw. 'But', he added, 'I understand that in any case the Employment Secretary was planning to resign in a couple of months.'

'Was he?' I was astounded. 'Why? When?'

'On the day of the Autumn Budget,' Humphrey revealed. 'On the grounds that the budget is expected to give him insufficient money to deal with unemployment.'

I was shaken. A resignation over the Autumn Budget would have been *really* damaging. And it could have made Dudley extremely popular. In fact, the more I think of it, I've handled this whole crisis pretty well. Brilliantly, in fact. I have forced Dudley to resign on an obscure administrative issue of my choosing instead of an important policy issue of his choosing. No one, either among the voters or the backbenchers, will support him, because no one really understands why he's gone.

I explained all this to Humphrey, who readily agreed that I'd handled the whole affair in a masterly fashion.

[*It is interesting that Jim Hacker never questioned Sir Humphrey Appleby's revelation that the Employment Secretary was planning to resign a few weeks later. Presumably this was because it enabled him to think of his defeat as a victory.*

Bernard Woolley did notice that there was something altogether too convenient about the information and wondered from whence it came.

Later that day he had a private word with Sir Humphrey about it, the gist of which was noted in Appleby's private diary – Ed.]

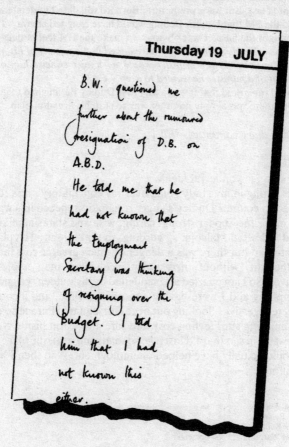

Thursday 19 JULY

B.W. questioned me further about the rumoured resignation of D.B. on A.B.D.

He told me that he had not known that the Employment Secretary was thinking of resigning over the Budget. I told him that I had not known this either.

B.W.[1] questioned me further about the rumoured resignation of D.B.[2] on A.B.D.[3]

He told me that he had not known that the Employment Secretary was thinking of resigning over the Budget. I told him that I had not known this either.

He seemed surprised, and asked me if it was not true.

I attempted to clarify the matter for him. I explained that I had not said it was true. I had said that I *understood* it to be true. The possibility always exists that I could have misunderstood.

BW tried to pin me down. 'So you don't know it's true?'

I explained that, equally, I do not know that it is *not* true. It might be true.

Bernard said that anything might be true. I congratulated him on seeing the point at last. But I was premature: Bernard still didn't understand why I had told the PM that Dudley Belling would have resigned anyway. I should have thought the answer was obvious: to make the PM feel better.

[*And also, Sir Humphrey might have added in the privacy of his personal diary, because the Prime Minister would no longer criticise him over the resignation of a minister he wanted to keep – Ed.*]

Bernard remarked that it was a pity that Dudley Belling had to go. How true! But there was simply no other way to stop his dreadful plan.

[*Hacker's diary continues – Ed.*]

July 20th

Today I had a wonderful idea!

I was sitting in my study going over my conciliatory press release, designed to counter Dudley's angry resignation speech in a way that would make me appear strong, caring, wise and statesmanlike.

I had redrafted Malcolm's[4] wording, so that it read: 'His plan was being studied but there was a danger of much greater cost than was first thought without *necessarily* achieving the employment objectives. So I am puzzled and saddened by his sudden resignation.'

Humphrey and I were having a morning coffee, and a couple of chocolate digestives, looking out over Horseguards Parade sparkling in the morning sun, feeling cosy and safe and warm inside Number Ten. I was still sad that I'd lost a good man, and a terrific plan, a plan that would actually have helped unemployment. And then I had my inspiration!

---

[1] Bernard Woolley.
[2] Dudley Belling.
[3] Autumn Budget Day.
[4] Malcolm Warren, the Press Secretary.

'Humphrey,' I said quietly, 'now that the Employment Secretary's gone we can recreate his plan.'

At first he didn't seem to see the beauty of it. Nor did Bernard. They looked almost horrified, though clearly they must have been as delighted too – I think they just found it galling that I had had the brilliant insight and not them.

'Don't you see?' I explained. 'I can go ahead with it now. It won't look like weakness any more, it'll look like strength.'

'But the whole point was . . .' began Humphrey, and then stopped. He gets confused, poor chap.

'Was what?' I asked. 'It wasn't to stop the relocation plan, was it?'

'No! No, indeed no, it was to, er, was to . . . establish your authority.'

'Exactly!' I said.

He'd figured it out at last. Sometimes he's a bit slow, but he gets there in the end.

So it's all ended perfectly. By reinstating the plan I can *prove* that I wasn't against it. And it will demonstrate to the world that Dudley's resignation was pointless. And having got rid of that bastard who was plotting against me, I've given a warning to others and shown that I can repel boarders with ease. 'Put defence relocation on the agenda for the next Cabinet,' I told Humphrey with quiet confidence.

'Yes Prime Minister,' he replied, staring at me thoughtfully.

11
Official Secrets

July 27th

It's only a week since I was forced to fire Dudley, a man I had always thought of as an old friend and a trusted ally. Imagine my bitterness and pain when Sir Humphrey revealed that he'd been plotting against me.

And now, only one week later, I'm facing another challenge to my authority – and this time it's from an even more unexpected quarter. My predecessor, the former Prime Minister, has submitted the latest chapter of his memoirs for security clearance – and publication *must* be stopped.

First thing this morning, at Cabinet Committee, we were joined by the Solicitor-General,[1] a couple of junior officials from his department, plus Humphrey and Bernard.

[*The Solicitor-General was one of the two senior law officers of the Government, the Attorney-General being the other. Sir Robin was famous, some would say notorious, for adopting a legalistic holier-than-thou attitude towards his political colleagues, and in so doing he acquired the nickname Good 'Evans – Ed.*]

Robin was at his most proper and pious this morning. 'As you know, we have already approved Chapters One to Seven, and I see no grounds for withholding approval of Chapter Eight.'

'Hold on a minute,' I said hastily. 'It seems to me that it contains some highly questionable material.'

Robin looked surprised. 'Such as?'

I'd been up half the night with it. I had all the page references at my fingertips. 'Page 211 for a start.'

I handed the offending page across the Cabinet table to Robin. He stared at the section I'd marked through his half-moon gold-rimmed reading glasses, then stared at me coldly over the top of them. 'It only says that the Minister for Administrative Affairs supported the pro-

[1] Sir Robin Evans.

posal to expand the Sellafield nuclear fuel plant in Cabinet, but spoke out against it in public.'

I was amazed that he couldn't see the problem. 'But that was me! I was the Minister.'

'The point is, Prime Minister, it's not a security leak.'

'The point is,' I responded indignantly, 'it's not true!'

'The documentation is fairly impressive,' he replied dispassionately. ['*Fairly impressive*' is Whitehall code for '*irrefutable*' – Ed.]

His cold blue eyes seemed to twinkle with amusement. But I couldn't see anything funny. 'With respect, Prime Minister,' he continued insultingly, 'if he has libelled you, that's a matter for the courts after publication, not for security clearance before it.'

I disagreed flatly. 'It's not as if the only problem is on page 211. Page 224 has a scurrilous accusation about my stopping that chemical plant project because of a baseless press scare. Then there's an indefensible passage about me on page 231.'

Humphrey took the opportunity to read that bit aloud – needlessly, I now feel. '"Hacker was more interested in votes than principles. He ran for cover at the first whiff of unpopularity. He raised the average age of the Cabinet but lowered the average IQ."'

'Thank you, Humphrey, we've all read it,' I said tartly. I couldn't help feeling that around this table there was more than a little pleasure at my discomfiture.

Robin hesitated, then spoke again. He expressed himself carefully. 'Well, as I say, Prime Minister, I'm not in any way supporting or defending him, but it's not an actual security breach. After all, Chapter Five got leaked to the press and we took no action.'

He'd missed the point. 'Chapter Five was very nice about my getting the Qumran contract,' I explained. 'And about my computer security guidelines.'

'But', Robin persisted, 'it had just as much confidential material. And you never even had a leak enquiry about it.'

They all stared at me. Did they know? 'Anyone could have leaked that chapter to the press,' I remarked, with as much innocence as I could muster.

'Anyone!' agreed Humphrey emphatically.

Chapter Five had been in no way comparable. I turned back to the beginning of the manuscript. 'Look at the *title* of this chapter,' I exclaimed in anguish.

Humphrey read it aloud again. '"The Two Faces of Jim Hacker"?'

'That's not a secret, surely?' Bernard was trying to make me feel better – I think! He caught my eye and fell silent.

I returned to the attack. 'I'm sorry, I think that there *are* security implications. Sellafield is nuclear.'

The Solicitor-General shook his head. 'But the Energy Secretary is responsible for Sellafield, he has seen the chapter, and he says that he has no problems.'

Of course he has no problems. It describes him as the ablest minister in the Cabinet. Which in itself is another slur on me. I pointed this out to Robin, who replied legalistically that he didn't think that it was actionable.

I was tired of all this obstructionism. 'Let's be clear about this. We have the right to refuse publication, don't we?'

Robin nodded. 'We do. But if they ignore us and publish anyway, my legal opinion is that we shall have no hope of stopping it through the courts.'

This was a blow. I suggested that, in that case, we lean on the publishers. The Solicitor-General wanted to know on what grounds. I told him the national interest.

Again he defied me! 'But I've said that there's no grounds . . .'

I cut him off. 'Listen,' I said sharply. 'This is obscene, scurrilous filth. It cannot be in the national interest to publish it and undermine confidence in the leader of the nation. This chapter must not be published. Right?'

They all gazed at me bleakly. The meeting broke up. They hadn't said yes and they hadn't said no. But they know what they have to do.

[*Events moved fast. Only a week later a report appeared in the* Daily Post, *London's newest morning newspaper, that Hacker was trying to suppress a chapter of his predecessor's memoirs. And the story quoted freely from the chapter, printing verbatim the sections that Hacker had found most objectionable.*]

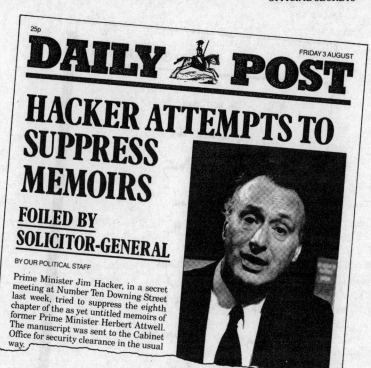

25p

DAILY ⚔ POST

FRIDAY 3 AUGUST

HACKER ATTEMPTS TO SUPPRESS MEMOIRS

FOILED BY SOLICITOR-GENERAL

BY OUR POLITICAL STAFF

Prime Minister Jim Hacker, in a secret meeting at Number Ten Downing Street last week, tried to suppress the eighth chapter of the as yet untitled memoirs of former Prime Minister Herbert Attwell. The manuscript was sent to the Cabinet Office for security clearance in the usual way.

[*An anxious meeting took place in Bernard Woolley's office at 9 a.m. on the morning the story hit the streets. Present were Bernard Woolley, Sir Humphrey Appleby and Malcolm Warren, the Press Secretary at Number Ten Downing Street. A note of the meeting appears in Sir Humphrey Appleby's diary – Ed.*]

Friday 3 AUGUST

B.W., M.W. and I conferred about the story in the Daily Post. We knew that even if the P.M. had not yet read his daily press digest, he would have heard it quoted on the Today show, to which he always listens while he has his breakfast.

B.W. remarked that he had listened too.

B.W., M.W. and I conferred about the story in the *Daily Post*. We knew that even if the P.M. had not yet read his daily press digest, he would have heard it quoted on the *Today* show, to which he always listens while he has his breakfast. B.W. remarked that he had listened too. The presenters had chewed up Hacker for breakfast!

We all regarded it as a somewhat amusing and trivial embarrassment of no particular consequence. The only problem, other than the PM's discomfiture (which was not a problem), was that the leak not only quoted from Chapter Eight but revealed that Hacker tried to suppress it, which means that the leak must have come from someone who was at the meeting.

Malcolm had an immediate problem: half of Britain's press corps were in the press office waiting for Hacker's response, and the other half were on the phone. The foreign press have also picked it up, and there have been interview requests from *Le Monde*, the *Washington Post*, and the *Women's Wear Daily* – which, Malcolm tells me, is an important newspaper across the pond. Thank God *we* do not live in a matriarchy.

[*Appleby Papers 1540/BA/90077*]

[*Hacker's diary continues – Ed.*]

August 3rd

Humphrey, Bernard and Malcolm trooped in as if they were in mourning. Grave faces. Eyes lowered. I stared at them angrily.

'Well?' I asked.

There was a silence.

'Well?' I asked again.

They stared intently at their shoes. 'Say something,' I snarled.

There was a pause. Finally Bernard spoke up. 'Good morning, Prime Minister,' he mumbled.

'Good morning,' the others echoed, apparently grateful to Bernard for having thought of something safe to say.

I banged the *Daily Post*. 'You've read this?'

They all produced copies of it from under their arms or behind their backs.

'You realise what this is?' I asked. I pointed at the story.

'It's the *Daily Post*,' said Bernard unnecessarily.

'It's a catastrophe! *That's* what it is!'

Humphrey cleared his throat. 'With respect, Prime Minister . . .'

I let him get no further. 'With no respect at all, Humphrey.' I was very curt. 'No respect for privacy. No respect for security. No respect for the national interest. No respect for the elected leader of the nation. This is unforgiveable! Who leaked it?'

299

More silence. I waited. 'Who can say?' was Humphrey's eventual and feeble response.

'*You* can say,' I said. 'And you'd *better* say – or else! I want it traced. At once. It must have been somebody at the meeting – I want to know who.'

Humphrey nodded. 'I'll set up a leak enquiry straight away.'

I lost my temper. 'I don't want a bloody leak enquiry!' I shouted. 'Didn't you hear me? I want to know who did it?'

[*Hacker's anger at Humphrey's suggestion was caused by his knowledge that leak enquiries are merely for setting up, not for actually conducting. The purpose of a leak enquiry is to find no evidence. If you really want to find the cause of a leak you call in the Special Branch. Those appointed to a leak enquiry seldom meet, and only report if it is absolutely unavoidable – Ed.*]

'Prime Minister,' said Humphrey gently, apparently in an effort to calm me down, 'when there is a leak, normally one doesn't really want to find out who is responsible, just in case it turns out to have been one of your Cabinet colleagues.'

For once I wasn't worried about that. The Solicitor-General and I were the only ministers left there by then. It can't have been him, he had nothing to gain, and anyway law officers never leak. And I know it wasn't me. Therefore it *must* have been one of the officials. I told Humphrey, then and there, that we would take this right through to the Courts.

Malcolm interrupted. 'I'm sorry, Prime Minister, but I really have to have a statement for the press. They're all waiting. And there are four requests for TV interviews and eleven for radio.'

'Bloody marvellous!' I was decidedly bitter. 'All last week I wanted to go on the air and talk about my successes in achieving détente with the Soviets, and they didn't want to know. Now this happens and they charge in like a herd of vultures.'

'Not heard, Prime Minister,' said Bernard inexplicably.

I told him I'd speak louder. Then I realised I'd misunderstood. 'Herd,' he said, 'not heard. Vultures, I mean, they don't herd, they flock. And they don't charge, they . . .'

'*Yes*? They *what*?' I turned to him, absolutely furious, and waited. More silence. 'Well, what *do* they do, Bernard?'

He could see that he was dicing with death. 'They . . .' he faltered. And he flapped his arms a bit. 'Nothing,' he said, and returned to staring at his shoes again. I have had enough of Bernard's pedantry!

I turned back to Malcolm. 'Don't the press believe in Britain?' I asked rhetorically. 'Why must they always go trouble-seeking and muck-raking? Why can't they write about our successes?'

Malcolm chewed his lower lip. 'Like . . .?'

I stopped to think. 'Like . . . like . . . like my détente with the Russians,' I suggested with relief, thinking of it in the nick of time.

Malcolm considered this idea. 'Well, there are more friendly voices coming from the Kremlin but it hasn't actually led to anything concrete though, has it?'

'It's going to,' I explained. People are *so* picky!

Malcolm glanced at his watch. 'I'm sorry, Prime Minister, but I do have to tell them something about this allegation.'

He was right. We had to say something. I told him to talk to them off the record, attribute his remarks to sources close to the Prime Minister, and be sure to say *nothing* attributable.

He waited, pencil poised.

I began: 'Say that what he says about me is a complete pack of lies.'

Bernard interrupted, worried. 'Um, do you mean, um Prime Minister, about, well, about running for cover and all that sort of thing?' He went pink.

'Yes,' I said. What was his problem?

'Um . . .' Bernard persisted, 'the only problem is, it is the author's opinion. We can't call him a liar for expressing his opinion.'

I didn't see why not, but generously I modified my instructions to Malcolm. 'Well, say it's a pack of lies that I spoke in favour of Sellafield in Cabinet but against it in public.'

'Um . . .!' Bernard appeared to have *another* problem. I narrowed my eyes at him. 'Well, the only thing is, it is sort of true, isn't it?'

'Shut up, Bernard!' I explained.

He wouldn't. 'How do we *say* it's a pack of lies?' he asked with determination.

Malcolm knew. He was already writing it down in the appropriate language. 'The Prime Minister's recollection of events is significantly at variance with his predecessor's.'

Bernard relaxed. 'Oh, I see,' he said, crossed his legs, and sat back in his Chippendale armchair.

'Then say', I told Malcolm, 'that the Cabinet minutes vindicate me completely, but unfortunately under the terms of the Thirty Year Rule they can't be disclosed for another twenty-eight years. Which makes his book deeply unfair as well as totally inaccurate.'

Malcolm got all that. His shorthand is excellent. It's always a good idea to have an ex-journalist as Press Secretary – poacher turned gamekeeper.

'And what about the smears against you personally?' he wanted to know.

'Smear him,' I replied promptly. 'Say the old fool is trying to rewrite history to try to make his premiership look less of a disaster. Imply he's gone ga-ga.'

Malcolm chewed his pencil for a moment. 'Passage of time and separation from official records have perhaps clouded his memory?'

'Fine, as far as it goes. How about the ga-ga bit?'

Malcolm smiled. 'Though no more than one would expect for a man of his age?' he offered.

It seemed all right to me. 'Will that do?' I asked them all.

Malcolm seemed to think so. 'It's okay for refuting what's in the chapter. But what about the story that you tried to prevent publication?'

I could see no problem with that. 'Say that's a pack of lies too.'

Malcolm was perfectly happy. '"A garbled account of a routine meeting. There was never any question of suppression."'

I looked round the table. Humphrey and Bernard were raising no objections. I told Malcolm that I would give no interviews on the subject, and I allowed him to make it a direct quote: 'An insignificant matter of no national importance, typical of the media's trivialisation of politics.'

'Do I attribute that quote to you, Prime Minister?'

'Of course not!' Sometimes I wonder if Malcolm's all there. 'A close Cabinet colleague.'

After Malcolm left we discussed the crisis, and I found that they viewed it far too lightly. My view is that it's a disaster, but Humphrey thinks it's not all that serious.

'Not serious?' I was incredulous. 'Telling the British people they can't trust the word of their own Prime Minister?'

Humphrey was calm and confident. 'They won't believe that,' he asserted. I was tempted to believe him when Bernard piped up.

'They might, you know.' He is *so* discouraging. 'Otherwise, logically, it would mean that they couldn't trust the word of their own *ex*-Prime Minister.'

Humphrey thanked Bernard. [*In other words, Sir Humphrey indicated to Bernard Woolley that he had said enough – Ed.*]

It seemed to me that there was a good chance that, given the choice between my word and my predecessor's, the British public would believe me. They never trusted *him*, that's for sure. Thank goodness I've been able to bring back a little bit of honesty into British political life. [*Hacker's capacity for self-deception was, as with most politicians, one of the essential ingredients of his success. Unless one takes the phrase 'a little bit of honesty' at face value – Ed.*]

We had discussed our rebuttal of the *Daily Post* story for long enough. 'Now,' I said, moving right along, 'about nailing that leak.' [*We have preserved Hacker's mixed metaphors whenever possible, for the insight that they give us into the unusual mind of this great political leader. Bernard Woolley, however, was unable to ignore them – Ed.*]

'I'm sorry to be pedantic, Prime Minister, but if you nail a leak you make another leak.'

I glared at him. He shut up again. 'I want the culprit.' I was implacable.

'Yes, Prime Minister,' replied Humphrey, without argument.

'And I want a conviction.'

Humphrey seemed puzzled. 'Prime Minister, we can try to find the culprit. We can prosecute. But under our current political system there are problems, as I'm sure you must be aware, about the government actually guaranteeing a conviction.'

Of course I knew that. But it's been done often enough, God knows! I suggested a quiet drinkie with the judge.

'Unthinkable!' Sir Humphrey was playing Goody Two-Shoes. It was one of his least convincing performances. 'There is no way, Prime Minister, of putting any pressure on a British judge.'

Who does he think he's kidding? 'So what *do* you do to ensure a conviction?' I enquired.

'Simple,' replied Sir Humphrey promptly. 'You pick a judge who won't need any pressure put upon him.'

I hadn't thought of that. It's always easy when you know how.

'A quiet word with the Lord Chancellor,' continued Humphrey. 'Find a judge who's on the government's side.'

'And who dislikes the *Daily Post*?' I asked.

'They all dislike the *Daily Post*. We need a judge who's hoping to be made a Lord of Appeal. Then we leave justice free to take her own impartial and majestic course.'

I asked if that always does the trick. Humphrey explained that it wasn't foolproof. 'Sometimes they're obviously trying so hard for a conviction that the jury acquits out of sheer bloody-mindedness.'

'So,' I summed up judicially, 'the judge has to have some common sense as well.'

303

He nodded. I can see that it's not so simple as he makes out.

August 6th
Lunch today with Derek Burnham, the editor of the *Daily Post*. It's no pleasure to have lunch with such a person, but he is a representative of the fourth estate and I kept a metaphorical clothes-peg on my nose.

We lunched in the small dining-room at Number Ten. It's a panelled room, a sort of ante-room to the big state dining-room, adjoining the yellow pillared room. It's an impressive place, yet small enough for intimate luncheons. Sometimes I lunch there with Bernard and other officials if Annie's[1] out and I can't be bothered to go upstairs and make lunch for myself.

Burnham is a nondescript, sandy-haired Scotsman of indeterminate middle age, with dandruff liberally scattered across his collar and lapels.

'So what are you asking me to tell my readers?' he asked me over the tomato soup.

'I'm not asking you to tell your readers anything,' I replied carefully, not neglecting to turn on the charm. 'I'm just giving you my side of the story.'

Derek pretended to be puzzled. 'But it's not that important, is it?'

He wouldn't like to have lies written about him in the newspapers! [*Hacker appears to have forgotten that it was* truth *that was written about him in the papers. Or perhaps he did not really forget, for the truth can be even more painful to read than lies – Ed.*]

'Why the big fuss?' persisted Derek.

'Because', I was indignant, 'I do not have two faces, and I didn't try to suppress the chapter.'

'May I quote you?' he asked mischievously.

I was very specific in my reply. I told him that he may not quote me denying that I have two faces.

He grinned. 'It was worth a try.' He slurped his soup. 'But Jim, I really don't know why you're so upset. I agree the chapter doesn't flatter you, but it's just part of the normal rough and tumble of political life, isn't it?'

I told him that I really didn't think that a responsible paper should print that kind of smear. He gave a non-committal nod. So I asked him why he did.

'Because it sold us over a hundred thousand extra copies.'

[1] Mrs Hacker.

'But didn't you see how damaging these accusations are?'

I'd created a trap for myself. 'That's my point exactly,' he grinned. 'Here's this damaging accusation and it's up to you to clear it for publication, and you are asking me to believe that you didn't try to stop it?'

'Of course I didn't.'

'Why not?'

'This is a free country, Derek,' I said grandly. 'Freedom of speech will always be protected while I'm in Number Ten.'

He wouldn't let go. 'But if it's seriously damaging to you . . .'

'It's not all *that* damaging,' I replied irritably.

He sat back and smiled. 'Fine,' he said. 'So what's all this fuss about?'

I could see that it was difficult for me to have it both ways. I tried a new tack. I explained that I didn't care about the damage to me *personally*, it's the damage to Britain that worries me.

He couldn't see, at first, how Britain could be damaged. Patiently I explained that undermining the leadership seriously damages the nation with foreigners. The pound, that sort of thing.

He didn't buy it. Because when I followed up by asking him to retract the story that I'd tried to suppress chapter eight of that damn book, he said that he couldn't.

'*Wouldn't*' I'd understand, but couldn't? I challenged him. 'You're the Editor, aren't you?'

He took a bread roll. Bernard immediately passed him the butter. 'Prime Minister, an Editor isn't like a General commanding an army. He's just the ringmaster of a circus. I can book the acts, but I can't tell the acrobats which way to jump. Nor can I prevent the bareback rider from falling off her horse.'

Cajoling had clearly failed. It was time to try Pressure. 'Derek,' I said carefully as I filled up his glass of Aloxe-Corton (his favourite, according to Malcolm), 'I don't think it would be helpful if you forced us to the conclusion that we couldn't trust you. Obviously we like to co-operate with the press, but you really are making it hard for us.'

Derek was made of sterner stuff. He sniffed the bouquet, swirled the Burgundy around in the glass to let it breathe, and then looked me squarely in the eye. 'I don't think that it would be helpful if you made us think you were hostile to our paper. Obviously we like to co-operate with Number Ten, but if it's war, then . . .'

I let him go no further. I assured him that war was the last thing we wanted, it wouldn't be helpful to either of us. 'I was merely suggesting

. . . merely thinking . . . there could be exclusive interviews and photo opportunities . . .'

'If I retract?' he enquired sharply.

'If you print the truth,' I corrected him.

He sighed. 'Jim, I have to stand by my story until I get hard evidence that it's not true.'

I couldn't think what evidence there could be to disprove the story. [*Perhaps because the story was true – Ed.*]

'Such as?' I asked.

'The minutes of the meeting.'

'I don't see why not, if my integrity is at stake.' I turned to Bernard. 'Bernard, the minutes bear out my account of the meeting, don't they?'

Bernard stammered incoherently. The eyes of all three of us – Derek, Malcolm and myself – were upon him. He said something like 'Well I er um but well er yes but . . .'

'Good,' I said. 'Derek, you may see them.'

Bernard was looking apoplectic. I thought he was about to have a brain seizure. 'But Prime Minister . . .' he spluttered.

I put him at his ease. 'Yes, yes, I know they're usually confidential, but this is a special case.'

Derek was not content with seeing the minutes. 'May I publish them?'

I told him we could talk about that – I haven't seen them myself. I told Bernard to show them to me this afternoon.

[*Bernard's discomfiture had two origins. It is anybody's guess which fear was causing him the greater panic. First, there was the breach of the Official Secrets Act: the idea of showing minutes of a Cabinet Committee to the press was absolutely without precedent. And even if the breach of the Official Secrets Act was made legal by the instructions of the Prime Minister (by no means a certainty), there was the additional problem that Hacker had sworn to prosecute the official who had leaked the discussion about the offending chapter eight – which was undoubtedly less secret than Cabinet minutes.*

But Bernard Woolley had a greater problem still, which he revealed to Sir Humphrey Appleby immediately he was able to get away from the Prime Minister's lunch with Derek Burnham. Sir Humphrey's personal papers contain a detailed report of the ensuing conversation, followed by a rare and valuable insight into his views on political memoirs and the need for secrecy in government – Ed.]

B.W. arrived in my office in a state of advanced dither. His problem appeared to be that the Prime Minister has told the press that the minutes of Cabinet Committee confirm his story that he did not try to suppress chapter eight of the book.

But, Bernard told me, the minutes are not yet written. I felt that this simplified the problem – all he has to do is write them.

Bernard did not feel that this was the answer. He was concerned that, according to his recollection, the Prime Minister *did* try to suppress the book. And he expressed surprise when I expressed surprise at his recollection.

So I explained to him that what I remember is irrelevant. If the minutes do not say that he tried to suppress the book, then he did not.

B.W. went into a greater dither, and said that he didn't see how he could falsify the minutes. He wanted, he said, a clear conscience. I found myself wondering when he acquired this taste for luxuries and how he got into government with it.

Consciences are for politicians. We are humble functionaries whose duty is to implement the commands of our democratically elected representatives. How could we be doing anything wrong if it has been commanded by those who represent the people?

B.W. does not accept that view. 'No man is an island,' he said. I agreed wholeheartedly. 'And therefore never send to know for whom the bell tolls; it tolls for thee, Bernard.'

Apprehensively, he asked for my suggestions, and their rationale. I gave him these thoughts to ponder:

1. Minutes do not record everything that was said at a meeting.
2. People frequently change their minds during a meeting.
3. Minutes, by virtue of the selection process, can never be a true and complete record.
4. Therefore, what is said at a meeting merely constitutes the choice of ingredients for the minutes.
5. The secretary's task is to choose, from a jumble of ill-digested ideas, a version that presents the Prime Minister's views as he would, on reflection, have liked them to emerge.

Later today Bernard returned to my office, still confused. He had considered all I had said and likened the question of ingredients to cooking. A dangerous analogy. It is better not to use the verb 'cook' in connection with either books or minutes.

Once again this raised the question of truth (whatever that may be) and Bernard's erroneous belief that minutes must in some way constitute a true record.

Patiently, I approached the matter from an alternative point of view. I explained the following points as clearly as I could:

1. The purpose of minutes is not to record events.

2. The purpose is to protect people.
3. You do not take notes if the Prime Minister says something he did not mean to say, especially if this contradicts what he has said publicly on an issue.
4. In short, minutes are *constructive*. They are to *improve* what is said, to be tactful, to put in a better order.
5. There is no moral problem. The secretary is the Prime Minister's servant.

In short, the minute is simply a note for the records and a statement of action (if any) that was agreed upon.

So, we turned to the meeting in question. What happened? The Solicitor-General had advised that there were no legal grounds for suppressing chapter eight. The Prime Minister accepted that there were no *legal* grounds for suppression. [*Our italics – Ed.*] That is all that need be minuted.

It is not a lie. It can go in the minutes with a clear conscience. B.W. departed with his conscience feeling less bruised.

These two conversations with Bernard about this storm in a teacup have prompted in me some fundamental thoughts about its origin:

There is no doubt that the real cause of all this trouble is this business of publishing ministerial and Prime Ministerial memoirs.

When I entered the Civil Service in the 1950s it was still possible for a man of intelligence and ingenuity to defend the thesis that politics was an honest and honourable profession. Ministers did not divulge Cabinet proceedings. Leaking to the press was regarded as a breach of confidence, not an instrument of government. And if a Department fell down badly on a job, the minister resigned.

Equally, members of the Civil Service preserved a cloak of anonymity and a tradition of discreet silence which concealed from the rest of the country the fact that they were running it.

Thus Prime Ministerial memoirs and diaries are, I believe, deeply reprehensible. The uninstructed may gain pleasure, and believe that they are being vouchsafed privileged insights, by reading distressingly frank accounts of how politicians reach their main political decisions (or, more frequently, indecisions). Most politicians have a certain lively style, often achieved by those without the reflective profundity to appreciate, or the intellectual apparatus to communicate, those qualifications and modifications which may make their accounts less readable but which could render them reliable.

Leaving aside the poor quality of literature of most ministerial memoirs, the more important *caveat* remains: revelations of this sort should never be published at all.

In such books the old tradition of the responsible minister and his obedient servant is generally misrepresented as a totally misleading portrait of scheming officials manipulating innocent politicians. Although those at the heart of government are aware that this is an absurd travesty, there is a danger that ordinary simple-minded souls may be deceived into believing there may be some truth in it.

The rot began with the Crossman diaries. And once one Minister reveals the secrets of the Cabinet, the others rush in to 'set the record straight', which means, of course, to show themselves in a favourable light.

After reading a succession of descriptions of the same period from opposed ministers of the same government, all of whom were by their own account uniformly honourable in their dealings and right in their judgements, it is hard to see where to lay the responsibility for decades of unprecedented and unrelieved political squalor.

The only scapegoat available must therefore logically be the Civil Servant. This has culminated in a distressing and regrettable change in public opinion, so that the necessary role of the Civil Service in advising caution, taking soundings, consulting colleagues, examining precedents, preparing options and advising ministers on the likely consequences of their proposals if they reached the statute books is perceived as ingrained bureaucratic obstructiveness rather than an attempt to translate narrow political expediency into broad national benefit.

Of course, there is an argument that by maintaining secrecy we would be simply defending the narrow interests of the Civil Service against the greater benefits of more openness about government. Paradoxically, this has not proved to be the case.

When I first attended Cabinet as a Private Secretary in the 1960s, members were irritated at the stultifying boredom of the proceedings and would interrupt with diverting outbursts of truth which would cause much conflict and dissent. Now that I have returned to the Cabinet as Cabinet Secretary over twenty years later, all members of the Cabinet are peacefully occupied making notes for their memoirs and will only make the statements that they want others to record in theirs.

This has been enormously beneficial to the Civil Service, for an interesting reason: the fact is that the movement to 'open up' government, if successful, always achieves a gratifying increase in the level of secrecy. Once a meeting – in Parliament, local council, Cabinet – is opened up to the public, it is used by those attending as a propaganda platform and not as a genuine debating forum. True discussions will then take place privately in smaller informal groups.

In government these smaller groups often contain one or more senior civil servants, so that some element of intelligence and practicability can be built into proposals before they become public and have to be defended with arguments which represent a victory of personal pride over common sense. So the move to greater openness in public affairs has greatly strengthened the level of secrecy and therefore the quality of decision-making in the higher echelons of government.

This is now jeopardised by Hacker's extraordinary, foolish and unprecedented decision to show Cabinet Committee minutes to a newspaper editor, with the consequent risk – nay, certainty – of publication. It is because Bernard and I were present at the meeting that the damage can be contained, and it is for these reasons that Bernard's minutes should take the form that I instructed him to take. [*Appleby Papers PU/12/3/86/NCH*]

[*Bernard Woolley's fears as to the unprecedented release of minutes that he had written were soon to be fully realised. The minutes were indeed published in the* Daily Post *– Ed.*]

MONDAY 13 AUGUST

25p

DAILY 🏇 POST

CABINET COMMITTEE MINUTES PUBLISHED- EXCLUSIVE

The Solicitor-General advised that there were no legal grounds for suppressing chapter eight. The Prime Minister accepted that there were no legal grounds.

BRIEF REFERENCE CONFIRMS HACKER'S CLAIM

BY OUR POLITICAL STAFF

For the first time ever, and with the permission of The Prime Minister, the *Daily Post* publishes an extract from the minutes of a secret cabinet committee. They reveal

SIR BERNARD WOOLLEY RECALLS:[1]

I had lost my cloak of anonymity. For the first time in my life I became a public figure – almost the worst fate that can befall a civil servant, in my view. Other than being sent on gardening leave, of course.

It meant that I myself had to answer questions from the press, questions that I was not free to answer, nor able to – questions that required a degree of prevarication and economy with the truth that I, as a non-politician, was ill-equipped to evade.

The morning those minutes appeared in the *Daily Post* I was accosted in Downing Street on my way to work. Questions were fired at me. My answers were not good enough. No doubt you can find it all by looking up the archives.

No 62,839

THE TIMES

TUESDAY 14 AUGUST

Woolley says Prime Minister is above the law

Official Secrets Act not applicable to Hacker.

By our Chief Political Correspondent.

Bernard Woolley, the Prime Minister's Principal Private Secretary, today admitted that the Official Secrets Act does not apply to the Prime Minister.

His replies turn an interesting light on the unwritten British Constitution.

[*All the newspapers carried essentially the same story. The full verbatim conversation is to be found on the BBC Nine O'Clock News filmed report, and we reprint the transcript overleaf – Ed.*]

[1] In conversation with the Editors.

311

"NINE O'CLOCK NEWS"   "NEWSNIGHT"

TRANSMISSION: AUGUST 14th

ACTUALITY:

SHOT OF BERNARD WOOLLEY APPROACHING THE CAMERA IN
DOWNING STREET

KATE ADAM: Can we have a word with you, Mr Woolley,
about the minutes of Jim Hacker's meeting with the
Solicitor-General which were published in the Daily
Post today?

BERNARD WOOLLEY: Look, I've got to go to work.

ADAM: Just a few questions.

WOOLLEY: I'm sorry, I can't comment.

ADAM: But you'd agree it all looks very suspicious?

WOOLLEY: What?

ADAM: The Prime Minister offered to publish them last
Thursday. Why did it take so long?

WOOLLEY: Well, because they weren't...

    HE HESITATES, AND LOOKS AROUND ANXIOUSLY

ADAM: Weren't cleared? Weren't cleared for publication?
Didn't the Prime Minister clear them last Thursday?

WOOLLEY: Yes, but, well, there's the Official Secrets
Act.

ADAM: That's what we'd like to understand, Mr Woolley.
How <u>can</u> they be cleared for publication if they're
subject to the Official Secrets Act?

- 1 -

WOOLLEY: Well, the Prime Minister can clear anything.

ADAM: So are you saying that the Prime Minister is not subject to the Official Secrets Act?

WOOLLEY: Um, no.

ADAM: No he is or no he isn't?

WOOLLEY: Yes.

ADAM: So when it comes to the Official Secrets Act, the Prime Minister is above the law?

WOOLLEY: Not in theory.

ADAM: But in practice?

WOOLLEY: No comment.

CUT TO:

KATE ADAM TALKING TO CAMERA

ADAM: What Bernard Woolley seems to be saying is that the Prime Minister makes the rules. He would not be drawn further about the content of the minutes, though he denied the rumour that the minutes took four days to appear because Mr Hacker can only type with two fingers.

- 2 -

[*That final comment by Kate Adam resulted in a complaint from Number Ten Downing Street to the Chairman of the Governors of the BBC. The BBC hotly denied that the comment showed any sign of bias against the government.*]

[*Hacker's diary continues – Ed.*]

August 14th
This morning Bernard told me that he had been interviewed by the press. I was not pleased. It is not his job to give interviews.

He explained that he had not meant to do so, but had been trapped into speaking to them.

I asked him what he had said.

'Um . . . Nothing really.'

This answer did not have the ring of truth. If he'd said nothing, he would not have come to confess it. And his eyes were decidedly shifty.

'So what's the problem?' I asked.

'Well . . .' he hesitated, 'they were asking me about you.'

Not very surprising. '*What* about me?'

'About you and the Official Secrets Act, Prime Minister.' [*When Hacker wrote this entry in his diary he had not yet seen the TV news or the morning papers. This conversation with Bernard Woolley took place immediately after he spoke to the press – Ed.*] 'They asked me whether you were bound by the Act.'

'Of course I am,' I confirmed.

'Yes, of course you are,' he agreed.

I waited. Nothing. He stared at the wall unhappily. 'So?' I pressed him.

'Well, it, er, may not come out like that.'

'What do you mean?' I asked with menace in my voice.

'Well, um, thinking back on what I said, and what you said, and what I said you said, or what they may say I said you said, or what they may have thought I said I thought you thought, or they may say I said I thought you said I thought . . .'

He petered out. Grimly, I told him to go on.

He took a deep breath. 'I think I said you thought you were above the law.'

I was aghast! 'You said *that*??'

'Not intentionally. But that's how it seemed to come out. I'm terribly sorry. But they were asking all those questions.'

I couldn't believe it. 'Bernard,' I asked with real curiosity, 'what made you think that, just because someone was asking you questions, you had to answer them?'

He said he didn't know. Nor did I. It was hard to believe. He's never answered *my* questions just because I asked them. I was furious. 'After a lifetime in the Civil Service, an entire career devoted to evading questions, you suddenly decide to answer questions *today*? And from *the Press*?? *You must have flipped your lid, Bernard!*'

He begged me not to shout at him. He was near to tears. He assured me that he wouldn't ever answer any more questions, ever again, ever!

I calmed down. I told him to get Humphrey in at once. And while we waited for Humphrey to arrive, I gave Bernard my eight ways to deal with difficult questions:

1. *Attack The Question*. 'That's a very silly question, how can you justify the use of the words, "above the law"?'

2. *Attack The Questioner*. 'How many years have *you* spent in government?'

3. *Compliment The Question*. 'That's a very good question. I'd like to thank you for asking it. Let me reply by asking you one.'

4. *Unloading The Question*. Most questions are loaded. They are full of assumptions such as 'A lot of people have said that you consider yourself above the law'. There are two possible replies to such loaded questions:

    a) 'Name ten.'

    b) 'Surely in a nation of 56 million people you can find a few people who will say anything, no matter how irrelevant, misguided, or ill-informed.'

5. *Make It All Appear An Act*. This approach only works for live TV interviews: 'You know, I've come to the conclusion that I don't agree with what you suggested I should answer when you asked me that question downstairs before the programme began. The *real* answer is . . .'

6. *Use The Time Factor*. Most interviews are short of time, especially live 'on air' interviews. Reply: 'That's a very interesting question, and there are nine points that I should like to make in answer to it.' The Interviewer will say: 'Perhaps you could make just two of them, briefly.' You say: 'No, it's far too important a question to answer superficially, and if I can't answer it properly I'd rather not trivialise it.'

7. *Invoke Secrecy*. 'There's a very full answer to that question, but it involves matters that are being discussed in confidence. I'm sure you wouldn't want me to break a confidence. So I'm afraid I can't answer for another week or two.'

8. *Take Refuge In a Long Pointless Narrative*. If you can ramble on for long enough, no one will remember the question and therefore no one can tell if you answered it or not.

Bernard listened attentively to this lesson in handling the nosey-parkers from the media. As Humphrey arrived I summed it up for him: if you have nothing to say, say nothing. But better, have something to say and say it, *no matter what they ask*. Pay no attention to the question, make your own statement. If they ask you the same question again, you just say, 'That's not the question' or 'I think the more *important* question is this:' Then you make another statement of your own. Easy-peasy.

When Humphrey arrived I questioned him about the leak enquiry. He was evasive.

'Ah well,' he said, 'the wheels will be turning very soon.'

'I asked for it a week ago,' I said. I reiterated that I wanted it pursued rigorously. And immediately.

Humphrey appeared perplexed. 'Rigorously?'

'And immediately.'

He was still perplexed. 'Immediately.'

'Immediately,' I repeated.

The penny dropped. 'Oh. You mean . . . you *really* want it pursued.'

I told him to watch my lips. 'I-want-you-to-pursue-it-*now*!'

Humphrey remained puzzled, but did not say anything to oppose me. 'If you are serious about it I'll arrange for a genuine arm's-length enquiry – if that's what you *really* want. I'll get Inspector Plod from the Special Branch.' [*Sir Humphrey was speaking figuratively when he spoke of Inspector Plod – Ed.*]

That question settled, I pointed out that we now have to improve our relations with the press. 'These will have worsened today since my esteemed Private Secretary told them that I put myself above the law when it comes to official secrets.'

Humphrey stared at Bernard, deeply shocked. Bernard hung his head.

'Yes, you may well look ashamed, Bernard.' I was not letting him off lightly. I asked Humphrey to let me know the actual constitutional position. He promised to let me have it in writing later in the day.

[Sir Humphrey kept his word. A memo arrived in Hacker's study later that day. We have retrieved a copy of it from the Cabinet Office archives – Ed.]

70 WHITEHALL, LONDON SW1A 2AS

Memorandum

To: The Prime Minister   August 14th

From: The Secretary of the Cabinet

In one sense, Bernard was quite correct. The question you posed, in a nutshell, is what is the difference between a breach of the Official Secrets Act, on the one hand, and, on the other hand, an unattributable off-the-record briefing by a senior official?

The former – the breach – is a criminal offence. The latter – the briefing – is essential to keep the wheels turning.

Is there a real objective difference? Or is it merely a matter of convenience and interpretation? And is it a breach of the Act if there is an unofficial non-attributable off-the-record briefing by an official who is <u>un</u>officially authorised by the Prime Minister?

- 2 -

You could argue that this is not a breach, if it has been authorised by the Prime Minister. Which is Bernard Woolley's position.

You, Prime Minister, will inevitably argue that it is up to you to decide whether it is in the public interest for something to be revealed or not. This would be your justification for claiming that the leak from your meeting with the Solicitor-General, which must have come from an official, <u>is</u> a breach of the Act.

However, this raises some interesting constitutional conundrums.

1. What if the official was officially authorised?

2. What if he was <u>un</u>officially authorised?

3. What if you, Prime Minister, officially disapprove of a breach of the Act but unofficially approve? This would make the breach unofficially official but officially <u>un</u>official.

I hope this is of help to you.

[Hacker's diary continues – Ed.]

August 15th

We reconvened again. [*Tautology is part of Hacker's personal literary style, so we have retained it where possible – Ed.*] We'd all seen Bernard's press and the television interview last night. Bernard was the new hot celebrity. He arrived at the office this morning wearing sunglasses and a big hat, in a typically ineffectual effort to avoid recognition.

The press, strange to say, were immediately drawn to enquire about the strange person who would wear sunglasses and a beaver hat on one of the hottest days of the year.

I thanked Humphrey for his helpful memo – a white lie, I felt – and we discussed how to minimise the week's damage. I suggested having another lunch with a Fleet Street editor – a friendly one this time.

Malcolm Warren had joined us. His comment was that none of them would be awfully friendly at the moment.

'Can't we offer one of them a knighthood in the New Year honours?' I asked.

He was doubtful of the ultimate value. 'Giving them knighthoods is a double-edged sword. It can work for *or* against you. The question is, do you have any control over them once you've given it?'

'I should have thought,' I said, 'that any editor would be rather grateful.'

Malcolm shook his head. 'You see, having got an honour, he may feel free to do and say exactly what he likes. Nothing further to lose.'

I could see his point. You don't get gratitude afterwards. In politics, gratitude is merely a lively expectation of favours to come.

Malcolm thought that, instead of trying to butter up the press, we should distract them. 'Let's give them a story.'

'Such as?' I asked.

'Start a war,' he suggested airily, 'that sort of thing.'

'*Start a war?*' I wasn't sure I'd heard him correctly.

'I was just giving an example of a major distraction.'

'Only a small war,' added Bernard.

They were kidding. They must have been. Humphrey joined in. 'If I may intervene, even a small war would be overkill. But, seriously, why don't you expel seventy-six Soviet diplomats. This has been the practice in the past, when we wished to ensure that the press lose interest in some other matter.'

I was shocked. I rejected the suggestion out of hand.

319

Malcolm persisted. 'It'd be a great headline for you, Prime Minister. "GOVERNMENT CRACKS DOWN ON RED SPY RING." Very patriotic. Goes down excellently with the electorate.'

Humphrey nodded. 'Yes, you see, it must be a story that no one can disprove . . .'

'And which will be believed,' concluded Malcolm, 'even when it's denied.'

'"SOVIET AMBASSADOR'S CHAUFFEUR IS MAJOR-GENERAL IN KGB",' declared Humphrey imaginatively. He was getting quite carried away.

I told them that the whole preposterous notion was completely out of the question. I have been working towards détente for months. It's the only thing that's working for me at the moment.

They all seemed somewhat disappointed. I turned to my Private Secretary. 'What do you think, Bernard?' I enquired ironically. 'You seem to be good at getting things into the papers.'

He blushed. 'Well . . . what about a royal event?' he offered.

I couldn't think what he meant. 'Such as?'

'Well, an engagement . . . pregnancy . . . divorce?'

'You can arrange that?' I asked.

He hadn't thought of that little snag. 'Oh. Well, no, I . . .'

Humphrey had had enough. 'I know,' he said. 'What about "PM'S PRIVATE SECRETARY IN DOLE QUEUE"?'

[*Five days elapsed, and the Leak Enquiry actually reported. The culprit was named. A press officer in the Department of Energy who had been present at the meeting with the Solicitor-General. The Enquiry had no difficulty in finding that he was the source of the leak because (a) there were so few suspects, (b) he owned up immediately. Bernard Woolley and Sir Humphrey Appleby received copies of the Leak Enquiry on the same day. Bernard must have telephoned Sir Humphrey for instructions or advice, because this letter was received from Sir Humphrey dated the day of the report – Ed.*]

70 WHITEHALL, LONDON SW1A 2AS

From the Secretary of the Cabinet and Head of the Home Civil Service

August 20th

Dear Bernard,

Yes, I have read it. This is a potentially difficult situation, as there is no precedent for handling a leak enquiry that actually finds the culprit.

Although the victim is a mere press officer he will undoubtedly be labelled a Senior Civil Servant by the press, simply because he works in Whitehall.

I think we can save him, however.

HA.

A reply from Bernard Woolley:

1O DOWNING STREET

From the Principal Private Secretary

August 20th

Dear Humphrey.
    How can we save him? There's
no doubt he did it.
        Bernard

And a reply from Sir Humphrey:

70 WHITEHALL, LONDON SW1A 2AS

From the Secretary of the Cabinet and Head of the Home Civil Service

August 21st

Dear Bernard,

There will be!

H

[We print the full texts below – Ed.]

August 20th

Dear Bernard,
Yes, I have read it. This is a potentially difficult situation, as there is no precedent for handling a leak enquiry that actually finds the culprit.

Although the victim is a mere press officer he will undoubtedly be labelled a Senior Civil Servant by the press, simply because he works in Whitehall.

I think we can save him, however.
H.A.

A reply from Bernard Woolley:

August 20th

Dear Humphrey,
How can we save him? There's no doubt he did it.
Bernard.

And a reply from Sir Humphrey:

August 21st

Dear Bernard,
There will be!
H.A.

[Hacker's diary continues – Ed.]

August 21st
A difficult meeting this morning – but with the help of my able and loyal staff I was able to snatch victory from the jaws of defeat.

The Leak Enquiry reported yesterday. I read it last night. The Press Officer from the Department of Energy did it. The evidence is irrefutable. And nobody denied it either.

So when we met this morning I asked for the immediate dismissal of the man, and for a prosecution under Section 2 of the Official Secrets Act.

Humphrey was cautious. 'I think not, Prime Minister.'

I mocked him – foolishly, it turned out. 'You think not? Because he's a Civil Servant, I suppose.'

He was not amused. 'Certainly not, Prime Minister. Because it is not in your interest.'

'Not in my interest to punish people for undermining the whole fabric of government?' I enquired icily.

Bernard said: 'Um, you can't undermine a fabric, Prime Minister, because fabric hangs down so if you go underneath you . . .' He tailed off abruptly as I stared him down.

Humphrey, anticipating my every whim, had already consulted the Attorney-General. 'The Attorney-General's advice is that a prosecution will not succeed, because there are no real security implications.'

I said that I didn't care if it succeeded or not. 'At least it will make an example of him,' I added.

Humphrey continued, as if I had not spoken. 'He also advises that if we prosecute we must first undertake a similar Special Branch enquiry into the earlier leak of Chapter Five.'

I didn't like the sound of that at all. Furthermore, I couldn't see why! The leak of Chapter Five was completely different! It was absolutely harmless!

Humphrey took a different view. 'The Attorney-General says that either both leaks were harmless, or neither.' He gazed at me, wide-eyed, innocent. 'So shall I ask the Special Branch to work on the Chapter Five leak?'

He knew perfectly well that only one person who'd read Chapter Five stood to gain anything from leaking it – and I was not about to have myself prosecuted under Section 2.

'On second thoughts, Humphrey,' I told him, 'I think the Attorney-General is right. Forget that prosecution. Just sack the Press Officer concerned.'

Humphrey shook his head sadly. 'That could be difficult. There is some evidence that the Press Officer was not acting on his own initiative.'

I hadn't noticed that bit. 'Meaning?'

'He was carrying out the wishes of his Secretary of State.'

Appalled, I asked for a full explanation. According to Humphrey, the Press Officer had not leaked Chapter Eight out of hostility to me. The truth is that the Secretary of State for Energy was delighted at being described by the former Prime Minister as the ablest man in the Cabinet. He had mentioned to his Press Officer that, so far from suppressing the chapter, he would not mind seeing it in the press at once. Otherwise the public might never get a chance to read it, because of the attempt by Number Ten to censor it.

I asked Humphrey if he were sure of this.

He nodded. 'I'm sure that this will be the Press Officer's explanation when his case comes up for wrongful dismissal before the Industrial Tribunal. He will argue that he was following an implicit instruction, doing what his Secretary of State wanted done.'

I was bitterly disappointed. The upshot is that we have found the leaker, and I can neither prosecute him nor sack him!

Humphrey obligingly offered an alternative. But not a very practical one. 'I'm afraid, Prime Minister, that if you must sack somebody, the only candidate is the Energy Secretary. He is responsible for his Department.'

'But I can't,' I wailed. 'I lost one Cabinet Minister last month. I can't sack another this month.'

'Quite.' He agreed wholeheartedly. 'To lose one minister may be regarded as a misfortune. To lose both looks like carelessness. Furthermore, as the Energy Secretary didn't do the leaking and denies that he asked for it to be done, he might sue for wrongful dismissal as well!'

I couldn't see how to save my neck. The press were clamouring for the result of the enquiry. Humphrey offered up a press release that Malcolm had drafted, but it was hopeless. Phrases like 'Communication breakdown . . . misunderstanding . . . acted in good faith . . . will be dealt with by internal procedures . . .'

'It's a whitewash,' I complained. 'And not even a very effective whitewash.'

'More of a greywash, really,' agreed Bernard.

Humphrey was not of the same opinion. 'It's no whitewash. It shares out the blame equally.'

That's the *last* thing I wanted. It would have made it seem as if I really *did* try to suppress Chapter Eight! [*Which was true – Ed.*]

Humphrey thought for a moment. 'Perhaps . . .' he volunteered cautiously, 'perhaps we should let the story go out – but smother it.'

I saw instantly what he meant.

'You mean . . .?' I asked.

He nodded.

Silence filled the Cabinet Room. We could all see that there was no alternative. After some moments Humphrey put the plan into action.

'I've been meaning to tell you, Prime Minister – there's some very worrying information on the Foreign Office files. About espionage in the Soviet Embassy and Trade Delegation.'

'No!' I said in a horrified voice.

'I'm afraid so. Evidence against a lot of diplomats.'

'How many?' I asked.

'Seventy-six,' he replied.

I wasn't surprised. 'You know, Humphrey, I think the time has come for firm action. After all, the security of the realm is at stake.'

'Precisely.'

So it was done. 'Expel them,' I ordered. 'And we don't want to keep this secret. Tell the press today, at the same time as we tell them the result of the leak enquiry.'

'Yes, Prime Minister,' said Sir Humphrey. 'Good idea,' he added deferentially. We're quite a team!

12
A Diplomatic Incident

September 3rd

Today, the anniversary of the day World War II broke out, was a day with a couple of extraordinarily appropriate developments, a day full of surprises but a day that will one day be seen as a great day, a day on which a new day may dawn for Britain.

[*Hacker occasionally lurched into passages of purple prose. Generally they are meaningless. At best they are insignificant. But they reveal a Churchillian yearning for a meaningful and significant place in the history books which has sadly been denied him by posterity – Ed.*]

The main topic at the first early morning meeting with Humphrey and Bernard after my brief summer hols was the great delay that we are experiencing on the Channel Tunnel.[1] My concern is the big public ceremony to celebrate the start of the work. [*Naturally – Ed.*] For reasons that were unclear to me, the Foreign Office have been stalling again.

Humphrey didn't see the hurry. Nor did Bernard. 'They say the heads of agreement haven't been signed.'

Typical Foreign Office lethargy. 'It's about time they were,' I complained. It should be a terrific ceremony – big gates inaugurated, a foundation stone laid by the Rt Hon. James Hacker, the Prime Minister. I'll do a speech about this historic link, uniting two great sovereign powers. The coverage will be great. The fact that the FO hasn't agreed everything with the French does not, on the face of it, seem a sufficient reason to hold everything up at a time when my opinion-poll ratings have slipped a bit.

So I told Humphrey my decision: to have a summit meeting with the French President and sort it all out myself.

Humphrey was shocked. 'I had no idea that you were considering such a radical approach,' he said, using one of the most vicious adjectives in his vocabulary.

---

[1] A 1980s project for a tunnel under the English Channel, connecting Dover with Calais.

328

'Well, I am.'

Immediately he tried to undermine my self-confidence. 'Prime Minister, do you really believe that you personally are capable of concluding this negotiation with the French?'

I couldn't see why it should be so difficult. 'Yes I do. What are the outstanding points of issue?'

He replied, 'They are mainly concerned with sovereignty. Where do you believe the frontier should be?'

The frontier? I'd never considered it. He meant the frontier between Britain and France, presumably.

[*This entry in the diary tells us all that we need to know about Hacker's thought processes. It is as well to remember the adage: if God had intended politicians to think, he would have given them brains – Ed.*]

I couldn't see a problem. 'What's wrong with it wherever it is now?'

'You mean', enquired Humphrey, 'the three-mile limit? Who would own the middle of the tunnel?'

I had meant the three-mile limit. I'd never considered the middle of the tunnel at all.

[*Undoubtedly so. Hacker had only considered the favourable publicity to be obtained from the opening ceremony – Ed.*]

'You see,' Humphrey explained, 'the British position is that we should own half each. But of course, we could follow your idea, in which case most of the tunnel would be an international zone, administered by the United Nations perhaps? Or the EEC?'

I felt that the Foreign Office had got it right for once – dividing the tunnel in the middle is perfectly fair.

But Humphrey explained that the French *don't* think it is fair. They want an Anglo-French frontier at Dover. A ridiculous notion! 'Perhaps,' Humphrey suggested with a little smile, 'perhaps you would be happy to concede fifty per cent of the French case?'

In the interests of fairness, I told Humphrey, I'm always happy to concede fifty per cent.

'Oh dear,' replied Humphrey with evident satisfaction. 'Since the French have demanded one hundred per cent to start with, they'll end up with seventy-five per cent.'

A trick question. Which explained Humphrey's little smile. He was now looking triumphant, the silly man, because he'd caught me out. Anybody could do that. [*A little unintentional honesty there – Ed.*]

'*Obviously*,' I told him, keeping my temper with difficulty, 'we have to divide the tunnel in the middle. That way we can have sovereignty over half the tunnel, and so can they.'

'And who has sovereignty over the trains?'

I'd never thought of that. Humphrey, who after all has had the benefit of doing some homework on this, threw a barrage of irritating, niggling, pettifogging questions at me.

'If a crime is committed on a French train in the British sector, who should have jurisdiction? The British or the French?'

'The British,' I replied. He stared at me, that irritating little smirk playing around his lips. 'No, the French,' I said. 'No, the British.'

He didn't give me his opinion. He just went on with the questions. 'If a body is pushed out of a British train within the French sector, who has jurisdiction?'

'The French?' I tried. No response. 'No, the British,' I said. No, um . . .'

'If,' said Humphrey relentlessly, 'if a British lorry is loaded on to a French train in the British sector, who has jurisdiction?'

I was pretty confused by now. [*And, indeed, previously – Ed.*]

So was Bernard. 'Could criminal jurisdiction be divided into two legs?' he asked. 'Home and away?'

Humphrey ignored Bernard. 'Should we have a frontier post in the middle of the tunnel, half-way across?'

'Yes,' I said. He stared at me and I lost confidence again. 'No,' I added.

'Or should we have customs and immigration clearance at either end?'

I was beginning to see how complex the whole issue was. 'No,' I decided initially. 'Yes,' I concluded a moment later, having reconsidered.

'Or both ends?' There were limitless possibilities, it seemed.

'Yes,' I agreed.

Sir Humphrey hinted that I was being less than decisive. Very true. But after all, as I pointed out, these were questions for the lawyers in the negotiation.

'Precisely, Prime Minister. But I thought you said you wanted to handle it yourself.'

I was getting irritated. 'I don't want to handle abstruse points of international law, Humphrey, I want to sort out the basic political points at issue.'

'So,' said Humphrey, in a tone of extravagant mock surprise, 'Sovereignty is not political? How interesting.' He's got an endless supply of these cheap shots. He knew what I meant.

[*Hacker was being somewhat optimistic. It is improbable that Sir Humphrey knew what Hacker meant. After years of studying this manuscript we do not know what he meant. At times we are forced to wonder whether Hacker knew what he meant – Ed.*]

'I take it', asked Sir Humphrey, continuing this rather insolent cross-examination, 'that you will agree to the Tunnel being built with the most modern technology?'

'Of course.'

'Then,' replied Humphrey, 'you have just conceded that ninety per cent of the contracts will be placed with French companies. And do you want the signs to be in French first and English second?'

'No!' I was adamant.

'The French do.'

'We don't agree.'

'You can't have your ceremony until we do.'

I suggested a compromise. 'We could have the English first on the signs at the British end. And French first at the French end.'

'What about the trains?'

I was becoming furious. 'For God's *sake*, Humphrey, what does it matter?'

He remained calm. 'It matters to the French,' he explained. 'What about the menus? French or English?'

I looked for a compromise. 'Can't they change the menus halfway?'

He shook his head sadly. 'The French will be adamant. That's why both the British and the French Concorde are spelt the French way – with an E on the end. Of course, if you want to concede all of these points with the French we could have immediate agreement with them. Alternatively – ' he plunged in the knife ' – you can leave it to the Foreign Office to do their best.'

Do their best? It seemed that he did not expect the FO to get a good deal either.

He confirmed that this was his view. 'I'm afraid they won't. But it will be better than you could get, Prime Minister.'

I'm afraid he's right. And yet, it made no sense. 'Humphrey,' I asked, 'do we never get our own way with the French?'

'Sometimes,' he allowed.

'When was the last time?'

'Battle of Waterloo, 1815.' Could he be right? While I pondered this question, delving into my encyclopaedic memory and knowledge of history, Sir Humphrey raised the vexed question of hijacking.

'What if terrorists were to hijack a train? And threaten to blow up the train and the tunnel.'

What a horrific thought that was! 'My God,' I exclaimed. 'Let's give France jurisdiction over the whole thing. Then they'd have to handle it.'

Sir Humphrey smiled a complacant smile. 'You see, Prime Minister?' He was patronising me now. 'If you were handling the negotiations you would have just conceded *everything* to the French. In fact, I believe that the French will come up with some totally underhand ploy to regain the advantage. But no doubt you have anticipated that, Prime Minister.'

The sarcasm was unmistakable. I had to concede that I could not possibly handle the negotiations. With some nations, yes. With the French, never. Also, I could see another, bigger advantage in staying out of it. 'If humiliating concessions are going to be made, I'd like the Foreign Secretary to be in charge.'

'Very wise, Prime Minister.' At last we were in agreement. And we moved on to another matter that has been causing me the most profound ongoing irritation. 'May we now discuss the equally vexed question of your predecessor's memoirs?'

As if we hadn't had enough trouble with Chapter Eight, it seems that he'd now started work on his final chapter, the one that concerns his resignation and my accession to the Premiership. And, to that end, he wanted access to certain government papers.

I asked if we couldn't find *any* way to stop these bloody memoirs before they ruin my career. Little did I know that my wish was about to be granted.

Humphrey shook his head sadly. 'Memoirs, alas, are an occupational hazard.' And he sighed deeply, like Eeyore.

I can't think why he was sighing. I'm the one who's being skewered. And it's not even what he's written that upsets me – it's the betrayal! Until I read the first eight chapters of his book I thought he was a friend of mine!

For instance, in the draft that arrived this morning he'd called me two-faced. I'd shown it to Bernard.

'Very wrong' was Bernard's gratifying comment.

I was grateful for the vote of confidence.

'And unforgiveably indiscreet,' Bernard went on.

'Indiscreet?' I looked at him, surprised.

'And wrong!' Bernard added emphatically.

'How can he tell such lies about me?' I asked rhetorically.

'What lies?' asked Bernard. 'Oh I see,' he said.

Really, Bernard is sometimes remarkably slow on the uptake. How could he have thought I'd changed the subject? But apparently he did.

Why has the former Prime Minister written this garbage? Simply so that he'll increase the sales of the book by inventing stories? I think not. Some people lie not because it is in their interest but because it is in their nature. 'He is a vile, treacherous, malevolent bastard,' I told Bernard, 'and if he's hoping to get any more honours or quangos or Royal Commissions he's got another think coming. He will not get one ounce of official recognition as long as I'm here.'

I regretted this outburst, because at that moment the phone rang. Bernard took the call.

'Yes? . . . look, is this important, because? . . . Oh! . . . Ah! . . . Oh! Dead on arrival? . . . I see.'

Solemnly he replaced the receiver.

'Bad news, Bernard?' I asked.

'Yes and no,' he replied cautiously. 'Your predecessor, the previous Prime Minister of Great Britain and Northern Ireland, has just died of a heart attack.'

'What a tragedy,' I said immediately. I know how to say the right things on such occasions.

'Indeed,' replied Bernard and Humphrey in chorus.

'A great man,' I said, for the record.

'A great man,' they repeated in unison.

'He will be sorely missed,' I said. After all, *someone's* bound to miss him.

'Sorely missed,' echoed the double act on the other side of the Cabinet table.

'And so will his memoirs,' I added.

'Which will never be finished,' said Bernard.

'Alas!' sighed Humphrey.

'Alas!' I said.

'Apparently, Prime Minister,' said Bernard, 'he expressed a hope that he might have a state funeral, just before . . . the end. But in view of your wish to give him no further honours . . .'

Bernard was quite wrong. A funeral was an honour that I was happy to arrange. I told Bernard that he had completely misunderstood me. 'I am sure, Bernard, that a tremendous number of people will want to attend his funeral.'

'To pay him tribute, you mean?'

'Of course,' I said. That was certainly one reason. And to make sure he's dead is another.

[*Working funerals are the best sort of summit meeting. Ostensibly arranged for another purpose, statesmen and diplomats can mingle informally at receptions, churches and gravesides, and achieve more than at ten official 'summits' for which expectations have been aroused. This is presumably why Hacker immediately agreed to a state funeral for his late and unlamented predecessor – Ed.*]

September 4th

A splendid list of acceptances for the funeral already. They're all RSVPing like mad. So far we have seven Commonwealth Prime Ministers, the American Vice-President, the Russian Foreign Minister, and six European Prime Ministers – excellent. And I am the host! I shall be there, among all these great statesmen, at the centre of the world stage. Bearing my grief with dignity and fortitude. Dignified grief goes down terribly well with the voters. Especially when shared with other world leaders. Marvellous thing, death. So uncontroversial.

However, there was one interesting query on the list. The French Prime Minister. I asked Bernard and Humphrey about this when we met to discuss the pleasurable matter of the funeral arrangements.

'I imagine that's what the French Ambassador is coming to see you about tomorrow,' said Humphrey.

I was more immediately concerned with the placing of the TV cameras. 'There will be plenty of room, won't there?' I wanted definite assurances. 'We want them outside Number Ten, along the route, outside the Abbey,[1] inside the Abbey, and one looking straight at my pew.'

Humphrey looked doubtful. 'That would mean putting the camera in the pulpit.'

'Will that be all right?' I checked.

'It won't leave a lot of room for the Archbishop,' said Humphrey.

I understood the problem. 'So where will he preach from?' I asked.

'I think he will need the pulpit.'

This was a bigger problem than I'd thought. 'So where will my camera be?'

Humphrey thought for a few moments. 'Well, there's always the High Altar. But the Archbishop may need that too.'

---

[1] Westminster Abbey.

He'll just have to do without it. [*Apparently the Archbishop was under the impression that the funeral was a religious ceremony. Nobody had told him that it was a Party Political Broadcast – Ed.*]

September 5th

Today I saw the French Ambassador. It's all worse than I thought.

But first I saw Bernard. 'The French Ambassador is on his way. But I know what his news will be: the French Prime Minister isn't coming, the President's coming instead.'

'The President?' I was overjoyed. 'That's wonderful.'

'No, no, Prime Minister. It's terrible!'

Humphrey had heard the news too and, flustered, he hurried in to join us.

I couldn't see the problem – at first. I've not had all that much experience with the French. Bernard could see it all too clearly.

'When the Queen visited France three years ago, Prime Minister, she presented him with a labrador puppy. And now he's bringing one of its puppies to present her with in return.'

Humphrey sank into his chair, aghast. 'No!' he gasped. 'That's what I'd heard! So it's true!'

'I'm afraid so, Sir Humphrey.' Bernard was using his funereal voice.

'I knew it,' said Sir Humphrey, fatally. 'I *knew* they'd do something like this.'

I still couldn't see the problem. 'It seems rather a nice gesture to me.'

'It's a gesture all right.' Humphrey smiled a sour smile. 'But hardly a nice one.'

'Why not?'

'Because Her Majesty will have to refuse it. And there will be . . . repercussions!'

The problem, it seemed, was quarantine! Dogs can't just be imported. This puppy will have to spend six months in quarantine at Heathrow.

It still didn't seem particularly tragic to me. 'The French will understand that, won't they?'

'*Of course* they'll understand it. Privately. That's why they're doing it. But they'll refuse to understand it officially.'

I suddenly saw the problem. The French were creating a diplomatic incident to get their own way over the sovereignty of the Channel Tunnel. I explained this to Humphrey and Bernard, who seemed grateful for the insight. Then, decisively, I sent for Peter Gascoigne,

335

the Foreign Affairs Private Secretary. 'What do we do?' I asked.

'I don't know.' He'd already heard the news and had apparently been struck down by depressive illness as a consequence. He had the look of a desperate man about him.

I hardly expected such a hopeless response. The Civil Service can usually think of *something* to do. 'But you're my Foreign Affairs Secretary,' I informed him. 'I expect some positive suggestions.'

'I'm sorry, Prime Minister, but the Home Office is responsible for quarantine.'

I think he was passing the buck. Or the puppy. I sent for Graham French, the Home Affairs Private Secretary. While we waited for him I explored with Peter the possibility of getting the French to withdraw the gift.

'We've tried everything,' Peter told me desperately. 'We've suggested an oil painting of the puppy. A bronze. A porcelain model. Not a hope.'

'Can't you get them to stuff it?' I asked.

Humphrey intervened. 'There's nothing we'd sooner . . . oh, taxidermy? No chance.'

Graham hurried in. 'Graham,' I said, 'tell your chums at the Home Office that they've got to find a way round these quarantine regulations.'

He reacted rather stiffly. 'I'm afraid that's out of the question, Prime Minister.'

I wasn't expecting to be contradicted. I asked him to explain himself.

'In the first place,' he said, blinking at me nervously, 'we enforce the regulations rigorously with all British citizens and all foreign nationals. Without exception. And in the second place, the Quarantine Act is signed by the Sovereign. She can't be the only one to break her own laws. It would be quite wrong ethically and for health reasons, and is completely out of the question.'

At that moment the intercom buzzed. The French Ambassador had arrived. Things were all happening too fast. Yet nothing can be posponed because the funeral is only three days from now.

So while the Ambassador waited a moment in the little waiting room next to the Cabinet Room[1] I told my staff that we *have* to find a way out of this. I told Peter to get back to the Foreign Office at once and tell them to talk to the Home Office. Graham was to do the same

[1] See Chapter 4, pp. 114ff.

at the Home Office. Both were to keep in touch with Bernard, who would liaise with the Palace. Humphrey was to talk to the law officers in the hope of finding legal loopholes (they all shook their heads firmly at this suggestion), and I told Humphrey he'd be responsible for co-ordinating the whole thing.

'What whole thing?' He seemed confused.

'Whatever whole thing we think up to deal with this French plot,' I explained.

'Oh, that whole thing.' Sometimes Humphrey's a bit slow. 'Certainly, Prime Minister. I'll set up an operations room in the Cabinet Office.'

I seemed to be the only one with any ideas. I asked Humphrey if *he* had any suggestions. He suggested that I didn't keep the French Ambassador waiting any longer. So I sent for him and I asked Humphrey to stay and give me support.

'Do I need any papers?' asked Humphrey, flapping a bit at the thought of the impending confrontation.

'Just a sponge and a towel,' I told him grimly.

The French Ambassador spoke almost perfect English as he slipped elegantly into the room. 'Prime Minister. You are most kind to give me your time.' He is small, slim, and utterly charming.

I told him it was a pleasure.

'I understand you are anxious to finalise the agreement for the Channel Tunnel?'

'Yes, very much so . . .' I began, but out of the corner of my eye I saw Humphrey shaking his head slowly, almost imperceptibly, an unmistakable cautionary signal. I backtracked rapidly. 'But, on the other hand, no *real* hurry,' I said. I'm sure the Ambassador didn't notice.

In fact, he seemed eager to help. 'But it would be nice if we could reach some conclusions, wouldn't it?'

'Nice?' I glanced at Humphrey. He shrugged. 'Nice,' I agreed. 'No question.'

'And', continued the Ambassador, 'my Government feels that if we were to take advantage of the funeral – my condolences, by the way, a tragic loss – '

'Tragic, tragic!' I echoed tragically.

'. . . take advantage of the funeral for you and our President to 'ave a few words . . .'

'Of course, of course,' I interrupted. 'The only thing is, I shall be host to a large number of distinguished guests, and I'm not sure . . .'

His Excellency took umbrage. 'You do not wish to speak to our President?'

'Of course I do.' I smiled reassuringly. 'Yes. No question.' Since my conversation with Humphrey a couple of days ago, I'm well aware of the dangers of my becoming directly involved in negotiating with the French. So I tried to explain that I'd rather simply *speak* than negotiate. I tried to imply that actual negotiations were slightly beneath me.

He understood that kind of arrogance. But he wouldn't let go. 'Don't you think that these little quarrels between friends are best resolved by just talking to each other, face to face?'

'Between *friends*, yes,' I replied. Humphrey blanched.

But the Ambassador was unperturbed. 'I think otherwise our President would be very hurt. Not personally, but as a snurb to France.' I *think* he meant snub. It sounded like 'snurb', but I don't know what a snurb is.

Anyway, I reassured the excellent Excellency that we had no intention of snurbing France, and that I regard the French as *great* friends.

He was pleased. I hoped he'd leave, but no. He had quite a considerable agenda of his own, and we moved on to item two.

He claimed that he was concerned about his Embassy's security during the President's visit. This was rather surprising. I looked at Humphrey. Was there any reason for concern? But no, I could tell from Humphrey's expression that this was just another French ploy. Together, we assured the Ambassador that the Commissioner of the Metropolitan Police has everything absolutely under control.

The Ambassador was not satisfied. 'My Government requests that the French police be permitted to guard our Embassy.'

Humphrey was flashing me the clearest possible warning signals. His look said 'Say no at all costs.' So I told the French Ambassador that it was impossible to grant such a request.

He pretended indignation. 'It is surely not *impossible*.'

I decided to go on to the attack. 'Are you saying that you don't trust the British police?'

'My Government makes no comment on the British police,' he replied carefully. 'But the President would be happier if the French police were in charge.'

I could see that Humphrey was itching to get at him. So I let Humphrey off his leash and sat back in my swivel chair.

'The problem, Excellency,' said Humphrey smoothly, somehow

338

continuing to make the word Excellency sound like an insult, 'is that there are seventy-three Embassies in London. No doubt they would all want their own police. Most would carry machine-guns, given the opportunity. Her Majesty's Government is not convinced that this would make London a safer place.'

The irony went *right* over his head. But he seemed to accept the refusal with diplomatic good grace. 'My Government will be most disappointed. But now I can move on to a happier matter. Our President will be bringing a little present which he will be presenting to Her Majesty.'

I forced a smile. 'How charming.'

'A little puppee,' he explained unnecessarily. Why did he bother, he must have known that we knew? 'She comes from the litter of the very same labrador that Her Majesty graciously presented to Monsieur le Président on her State visit to France.'

I waited. I expressed no pleasure, no thanks. So he continued to the bitter end. 'Perhaps you will let us know the arrangements for the presentation?'

I sighed. 'Your Excellency,' I said patiently. 'It is of course most kind. A charming thought. But as you know it cannot be presented for six months. Our quarantine laws.'

Of course he refused to understand. He told me it was absurd. He reminded me that the Queen presented the dog during her State visit.

I explained that we would be delighted for his President to do the same thing. But the law's the law.

'Surely', enquired the Ambassador, his manner visibly cooling, 'your laws are only to exclude infected animals?'

I concurred.

'But you are not suggesting that the President of France would present the Queen of England with a diseased puppy?'

'No, of course not.'

'Then it's settled.'

'No it is not settled.' I was firm. 'I must ask you to suggest to the President that he find a different gift.'

His Excellency informed me that this would be completely out of the question. 'Were it the President alone, perhaps . . .' He shrugged. 'But the President's wife, our First Lady, has set her heart on it. She is determined.'

A neat move. It now appears that if I now say no, I will be insulting a lady. The first lady.

I told him that we would make every endeavour. But it may not be possible. [*This is the firmest form of refusal known to the language of diplomacy – Ed.*]

The Ambassador rose to his feet. 'Prime Minister, I do not have to tell you the gravity of the affront my Government would feel if Her Majesty were to refuse a request to present a gift in exchange for the one the President accepted from her. I fear it would be interpreted as both a national and a personal insult. To the President *and* his wife.'

I'd had enough of this bullshit. I stood up too. 'Excellency, please ask the President not to bring that bitch with him.'

Humphrey gasped. The Ambassador looked utterly stunned. And I suddenly realised the ambiguity of what I'd said.

'The puppy,' I said hastily. 'I meant the puppy.'

Tonight Annie and I had a quiet evening at home together; in the flat above the shop. [*The top-floor flat in Number Ten Downing Street – Ed.*] We had to go over all *her* arrangements for the funeral. She wanted to know why we had to lay on so many visits for the wives. I explained that the Foreign Office likes it – it keeps them out of the way. They can't be with their husbands, their husbands are busy.

'Only at the funeral itself,' said Annie.

I explained that she'd missed the point of the whole funeral: they're coming for the politics. This is a *working* funeral. As a matter of fact, when we were all at that funeral in Norway a few months ago, the French, the Germans and I were all so busy negotiating EEC farm quotas in the hotel that we forgot to go to the Cathedral.

Annie thought that was very funny. 'Didn't they notice?'

'We got there before it finished. We blamed security. You can blame security for almost anything nowadays.'

In fact, this funeral will be a heaven-sent opportunity. Literally! Much better than a summit, because there are no prior expectations. The public don't expect their leaders to return from a funeral with test ban agreements or farm quota reductions. So we can actually have serious negotiations, whereas a 'summit' is just a public relations circus in which the press never give the politicians a real chance. Journalism wants to find problems. Diplomacy wants to find solutions.

Annie wanted to know if anyone at all would be coming to the funeral to pay tribute to a friend. I laughed. If only his friends came we wouldn't even fill the vestry, let alone the Abbey. No, my illustrious predecessor has undoubtedly done more for the world by dying than he ever did in the whole of his life.

She asked if the service was agreed. Funny old Annie, she's a churchgoer, she cares about these things. I told her that there'd be lots of music, which was all I knew about it.

'That's nice,' she said.

'Yes,' I said. 'That way, we can have useful discussions when the organ's playing. Unfortunately, we have to shut up for the lesson and the prayers.'

Annie smiled. She was getting the point. 'What about the sermon?'

'That's when our guests catch up on jet-lag,' I explained.

Altogether, this funeral has come at exactly the right moment. Apart from the little local problem of squelching those damn memoirs, it will improve my standing in the polls to be seen with all the world leaders and there's lots of things to sort out between NATO and the Warsaw Pact. Also it's a good opportunity to make more friends in the Third World.

'Jim,' asked Annie, 'there's something I've never understood. If we're the First World and the poor are the Third World, then who's the Second?'

'Good question,' I said. 'I've never heard anyone admit to being Second World. We think it's the Soviet bloc, maybe they think it's us – but because no one ever raises the question it's not a problem. Diplomacy, Annie!'

Above all, the Middle East is looking ominous again. I'm sure that, if I could only find the time, I could bring the various warring parties together in peace and harmony. But if we don't sort out some of these problems in the next three days, we'll have to hope that somebody else important dies within the next three months.

September 6th

A variety of suggestions for dealing with the dog crisis poured in from the Foreign Office and the Home Office today, each more foolish than the last.

[*The first came from Sir Ernest Roach, Permanent Secretary at the Home Office, and is reproduced overleaf – Ed.*]

HOME OFFICE
QUEEN ANNE'S GATE
LONDON SW1H 9AT

Memorandum

From: The Permanent Secretary   September 6th

To: Bernard Woolley

Dear Bernard,

    We have two possible approaches to this problem under
discussion:

1. We could pass an enabling Act of Parliament, enabling
    this particular dog to remain in the UK. An enabling
    Act can enable anything.

2. We could turn the whole of Buckingham Palace into a
    dog quarantine zone, thus fulfilling the letter if not
    the spirit of the law.

Please let me have the Prime Minister's reactions.

[Hacker's diary continues – Ed.]

The Home Office's first two proposals are completely cracked. An enabling Act *can* enable anything – in this case it would enable me to lose the next election.

The dog quarantine zone idea leaves one fairly important question unanswered – what would happen to the Queen's other dogs?

The Foreign Office outdid the Home Office. Moments after I'd sent Graham away with a flea in his ear, a memo arrived from King Charles Street.[1]

                                    Foreign and Commonwealth Office

                                        London SW1A 2AH

Memorandum

From: The Permanent Secretary   September 6th

To: Peter Gascoigne

Dear Peter,

      We can only think of one technical way around
this problem: make Buckingham Palace notionally an
extension of the French Embassy. Then the dog could
still be on foreign territory.

      Reactions please.

                        Dick

---

[1] The Foreign Office is situated on the corner of Whitehall and King Charles Street.

[Hacker's diary continues – Ed.]

I gave them my bloody reactions! I told them that, as always, they had revealed themselves to be weak, indecisive and stupid in the face of a genuine emergency. I reminded them that I am currently engaged in a fight for the sovereignty of the Channel Tunnel. What did they suppose I felt about the sovereignty of the Palace?

The Civil Service is usually so frightfully smart and condescending – *especially* the Foreign Office. Life is simple when you have so many precedents to follow; but they're like computers: put them into a *new* crisis, for which they've not been programmed, and their brains short-circuit.

[It must have been very painful for senior Foreign Office officials to be told that they were weak, indecisive and stupid. What would have made it more painful was being told by someone as weak, indecisive and stupid as Hacker. What would have made it most painful was that Hacker was correct – Ed.]

Meanwhile, Number Ten was in a frenzy all day. All the phones were ringing in the Private Office *all* the time.

Bernard was on excellent form. He remembered to phone the Palace and check that Her Majesty was never told *officially* that this gift has been proposed – that way, she cannot be implicated in refusing it.

But even Bernard was at a loss on the matter of this damn dog. All he could suggest was that our Ambassador in Paris tried to 'nobble' it . . . slip it some poison, borrow some umbrella tips from the Bulgarians. *[A reference to the murder in 1978 of Georgi Markov, a Bulgarian dissident working for the BBC's[1] External Services, who was stabbed with a poisoned umbrella tip at a London bus stop – Ed.]*

This sounded like an extremely tricky covert operation, with profoundly embarrassing consequences if discovered. The British voter can stomach rising unemployment, rising inflation, rising taxes, a falling pound, a falling stock exchange – but it would *never* re-elect me if I were thought to be implicated in the demise of a labrador puppy, dispatched to meet its Maker in the Great Kennel in the sky under mysterious circumstances. The British know their priorities!

Meanwhile, in the absence of a solution to the problem with the French, other arrangements continued apace today. We have laid on interpreters for numerous meetings. There were even interpreters

[1] British Broadcasting Corporation.

344

listed for my meeting with the American Vice-President, but I assume that was just a typing error. [*Almost certainly correct. After all, the English-speaking nations can, with a certain generosity of spirit, be said to include the Americans. In fact, it may be thought that the 'special relationship' between us is purely due to the fact that the Americans are no more noticeably multilingual than we are – Ed.*]

The Prime Ministers are flying in tomorrow and Bernard tells me that the Band of the Royal Marines is going crazy – it has to learn to play all the national anthems. There was great relief when we learned the Argentinians weren't coming – not because we defeated them in the Falklands but because the Argentinian national anthem is in three movements and lasts six minutes.[1]

Seating in the Abbey was the big question today. I had to approve it. Incredibly, they had done it alphabetically, which would have resulted in Iran and Iraq sitting next to each other, plus Israel and Jordan in the same pew. We could have started World War III.

Bernard rang through to the Abbey, and was told that it had been noticed that they were all sitting together but that the feeling at the Abbey was that as they were all from the same part of the world they might feel more at home. Bernard was forced to explain that proximity does not equal affinity.

Somebody else pointed out that as Ireland was in the same pew it might make things better. I pointed out that Ireland doesn't make *anything* better. Not for us. Ever!

Peter, my Foreign Affairs Private Secretary, came up to the study to brief me on the various issues we could expect to encounter. Bernard was there too, of course.

'The Spanish Ambassador says his Foreign Secretary will want a word about the unity of nations. And the Italians want a word about the European ideal.'

These were clearly coded messages. I asked what they meant.

Peter translated. 'The Spanish want Gibraltar back and the Italians want to enlarge the EEC wine lakes.' [*When EEC Foreign Ministers returned home after top-level meetings, it would come as a surprise to their governments if they claimed that their time had been spent trying to promote the European ideal. The EEC was just a customs union – politicians won brownie points only by heroically defending their national interest – Ed.*]

---

[1] In fact, the long version lasts for about four minutes (depending on the speed at which it is played) and the shortened form one minute forty-eight seconds. It is interesting to note that Hacker was given this incorrect information by the anti-Argie lobby in the FO.

'The New Zealanders', continued Peter, 'want an *ad hoc* meeting of Commonwealth leaders to discuss alleged British racist support of South Africa.'

I asked why they were raising this again. It was explained to me that there were two possibilities: it was either because of their anger about EEC butter quotas which exclude New Zealand dairy products – or maybe it was a manifestation of the guilt they feel over their about-turn on nuclear policy.

Peter proposed a royal visit for New Zealand. Send the Queen herself if possible. An excellent idea, though rather a long-term solution and no help to the immediate embarrassment unless the offer of the royal visit shuts them up. And Peter warned me that we could expect serious trouble from the South Africans anyway.

'Problems with human rights?' I asked.

'No. They're trying to unload more grapefruit.'

I was briefed about correct modes of address. Apparently the correct mode of address when speaking to a Cypriot Archbishop is not Your Ecstasy, it's Your Beatitude. And if the Papal Envoy says 'We desire to wash our hands' it means he's been caught short.

In the middle of all this Bernard received an urgent call from the Palace. We all held our breath. Had she heard about the puppy and, if so, did she have a view?

But no: the Palace had heard that there was a problem with the red carpets at Heathrow. (Which there was, but had been solved, I know not how.) And Her Majesty was worried that the President of the Ivory Coast wishes – apparently – to award her the Order of the Elephant.

I boiled over. 'Bernard, Peter, for God's sake!' I shouted. 'We can't have another animal. Especially an elephant! The whole of Whitehall, the Foreign Office, the Home Office, the Cabinet Office and the DHSS[1] have been tied up with one puppy for nearly a week. Government has been paralysed. No elephants!!'

But I was mistaken. Apparently it's not a real elephant that the Ivory Coast wants to send – it's a medal. The problem is that the honour is conveyed by a wet kiss.

I'm leaving that one to the FO.

September 7th
Tomorrow is the funeral of my illustrious predecessor. And today we

---

[1] Department of Health and Social Security.

licked the French. I don't know which of these events gives me a greater feeling of satisfaction.

But things did not start auspiciously.

First thing this morning Bernard entered the Cabinet Room with two files – one of them one inch thick, the other six inches thick.

'What on earth is that, Bernard?' I asked.

He indicated the slim file. 'The Channel Tunnel file, Prime Minister.'

'No,' I said. 'The thick one.'

'Oh.' He looked hopeless. 'That's the puppy file.'

'How far have we reached with it?'

'It weighed in at three and a half pounds this morning.'

'The puppy?'

'The file,' he replied seriously.

We had told the French that airport security would regretfully have to impound the puppy and quarantine it at Heathrow. The French had not replied. But in order to make it sound a little better the FO had let the French know that, as Heathrow Airport is en route from Buckingham Palace to Windsor Castle, the Queen will be able to visit it on the way.

I was surprised. 'Can you visit quarantined dogs?'

Bernard didn't know either. 'If she can't,' he replied, tired of the whole business, 'she can sort of wave as she drives down the M4.'

The real question was what measures the French would feel free to take against us, after this alleged and manufactured rebuff. The likelihood was that they would go public over the story if we don't give in to them over the Channel Tunnel.

We were certainly completely unprepared for what happened next. Sir Humphrey burst into the room unceremoniously.

'Prime Minister!' He was quite breathless. 'I have urgent news.'

'Good news?' Hope springs eternal.

'Yes . . . and no.' He was cautious. 'The police have just found a bomb in the grounds of the French Embassy.'

I was horrified. 'Who put it there?'

'We don't know yet. Lots of people could have a motive.'

'Us, for a start!' said Bernard.

'Still,' I said, trying to look on the bright side, 'it's a good job we found it. I suppose.' That must have been the good part of Humphrey's news.

Humphrey had more to say. 'The other news is even worse. The French President isn't flying in for the funeral.'

I couldn't see why that mattered. In fact, it sounded like good news to me. It *still* sounded like goods news (not quite as good, but nearly) when Humphrey said that the President was still coming, but by car – secretly. The plane is a security decoy, a blind.

'That sounds like a good idea,' I said. But I didn't see why it mattered.

'It's a brilliant idea!' said Humphrey, tight-lipped with anger. 'He can bring the bloody puppy in the car!'

Humphrey was right. Was there nothing we could do? 'Are you prepared, Prime Minister, to give instructions for the French President's car to be stopped and searched as he comes here as your invited guest to the funeral?' I had been completely outmanoeuvred. 'Are you prepared to violate their diplomatic immunity and search the diplomatic bag?'

I was confused. 'You can't put a puppy in a bag.'

'It would be a doggy bag,' said Bernard.

'Suppose we did search, and found it?' I was considering my options. 'That would really set the cat among the pigeons.'

'And let the dog out of the bag,' said Bernard.

'But . . . what would be even worse . . . suppose we were wrong?' explained Humphrey. 'Just suppose it wasn't there.'

He was right. I couldn't take the risk. Violating their diplomatic immunity wrongfully? It would be a catastrophe.

'*But*,' said Humphrey, ever the Devil's Advocate, 'if it *is* in the car they will drive it into the French Embassy, and the puppy will be on French territory. Here in the middle of London.'

'Hanging over our heads,' I observed gloomily.

'We'd better pray it's house-trained,' said Bernard.

SIR BERNARD WOOLLEY RECALLS:[1]

That evening we held a diplomatic reception at Number Ten. The evening was full of humour, mostly unintentional.

My role was, of course, to make the Prime Minister's guests welcome. Especially the French. I remember introducing Mrs Hacker to a Monsieur Berenger from UNESCO.[2] He was having a frightfully good time, and informed us both that he thought it was an excellent funeral. The last one he'd been to was Andropov's,[3] which had been awfully gloomy.

I also had the pleasure of introducing him to the Commissioner of the

---

[1] In conversation with the Editors.

[2] United Nations Economic, Social and Cultural Organisation.

[3] Former head of the KGB, then General Secretary of the Communist Party and President of the USSR, then dead.

Metropolitan Police. I explained that Monsieur Berenger was in London as the diplomatic representative of UNESCO. 'Ah yes,' said the bobby, pulling knowledgeably at his little white toothbrush moustache, 'gallant little country.'

[Hacker's diary continues – Ed.]

Star-studded reception at Number Ten – and yours truly wiped the floor with the French. Although in all honesty I must admit that it was a sensational French own goal which brought about my victory.

Everyone was very jolly. No one was at all sad about tomorrow's funeral. The American Vice-President came armed with a new Polish joke which he'd got from Gromyko.[1] 'You've heard the new Polish joke? Jaruzelski!'[2] And he laughed loud and long.

The Vice-President wanted an urgent word about the NATO bases in Germany. It wasn't possible at the party, so we made a deal to discuss them in the Abbey tomorrow. Then he disappeared into the crowd, hopefully searching for some non-aligned countries who would speak to him. [*The definition of a non-aligned country is that it is non-aligned with the United States – Ed.*]

And the Russians were in great form. The Soviet Ambassador sat down next to Sir Humphrey on a Sheraton sofa in the White Drawing-room and reminisced with a gang of us about my predecessor. 'You know, the death of a past Prime Minister is a very sad occasion.'

'Very sad, very sad,' murmured Humphrey dutifully and sipped his white wine.

'But he is no loss to Britain,' continued the Russian. 'You know what his trouble was?'

A leading question. I could think of plenty of answers but I waited for the Soviet viewpoint. 'He had plenty here . . .' the Ambassador pointed to his forehead' . . . and plenty here . . .' he put his hand on his heart. 'But nothing *here*!!' he growled, and made a grab for Sir Humphrey's private parts.

Humphrey squeaked, leapt to his feet and dropped his glass of Macon Villages, while the Russian Ambassador yelled with laughter. I laughed so much that I choked and had to leave the room. And the Russian Ambassador was right, by the way.

I didn't see Humphrey after that for quite a while. He was conspicuous by his absence. I thought he was either recovering his dignity or

[1] The Soviet former Foreign Minister, at the time President of the USSR.
[2] The puppet Prime Minister of Poland.

trying to sponge the wine off his trousers. I'd been looking for him because I wanted the security of his knowledge and advice when I talked to the French President, a conversation that I did not relish and couldn't postpone much longer.

Then Bernard and the Police Commissioner, an unlikely pair, unobtrusively ushered me out of the party in the State rooms, across the panelled lobby and into my study for a private word. Humphrey was waiting there.

'What's all this?' I asked.

'The bomb in the French Embassy garden was planted by the French police,' said the Commissioner.

At first I thought he was joking. But no!

'It was to see if they could catch us out. To prove our security inefficient.'

This was the best news I'd heard for months. They showed me a file of evidence. A matching detonator was found in their hotel. They had confessed.

I was ecstatic. The French cops smuggling explosives into the UK gave me just the opportunity I needed. I told Humphrey to give me a couple of minutes alone with the President, and to interrupt as soon as I pressed the secret buzzer that I have in my desk for that very purpose. [*To contrive apparently chance interruptions – Ed.*]

Well, they showed Monsieur le Président into my study. I apologised to him for dragging him out of the party for a few moments, and indicated that I wished to discuss the Tunnel. But he didn't want to discuss the Tunnel yet. 'First of all, may we clear up a silly misunderstanding? About this little puppy I shall be presenting as a return gift to Her Majesty tomorrow?'

So they *did* smuggle it in! 'Monsieur le Président,' I said, putting my foot down firmly, 'I'm extremely sorry but there is no misunderstanding. I cannot ask the Queen to break the law.'

He smiled. 'I do not want the Queen to break the law, I merely ask the Prime Minister to bend it.'

Again I apologised, formally, and said no. He was haughty, magnificent and deeply hurt. He remarked that if the French people ever learn of this 'rejection' they would take it as a national slap in the face. As if there was any doubt that they would learn of it. Personally I believe that the French people (unlike the British) have infinitely more common sense than their leaders, and would do no such thing.

So we returned to the Tunnel. And now the President pressed home the advantage that he thought he had created. 'As for the

Tunnel, you make it very difficult for me. The French people will not accept a second slap in the face. And you are rejecting our very reasonable proposal for French sovereignty up to but not including Dover. But setting that aside, there is also another question: which shall be the *langue de préférence*?'[1]

I went to my desk, ostensibly to pick up a piece of paper and a pen. I slid my left hand beneath the desktop and pressed the buzzer. He didn't notice. 'Surely,' I said reasonably, 'if half the signs put French first and half English, that would be fair.'

'Fair, yes, but not logical.'

'Does logic matter?' I asked.

'Does the law matter?' he responded.

'Of course it does,' I said. 'Britain is the only European country without rabies.'

Humphrey burst in without knocking. He was carrying the file. 'Monsieur le Président, please forgive me. Prime Minister, I think you should see this urgently.'

I sat at my desk. I opened it. I read it. 'No!' I gasped, and stared penetratingly at M. le Président. He didn't know what it was, of course. I read on, keeping him in suspense. Then I rose accusingly.

'Monsieur le Président, I'm afraid I have to ask you for an explanation.' And I handed him the file full of evidence of the French bomb plot. He read it. His face gave away nothing.

'I hope I do not have to explain the gravity of this,' I said, very much hoping that I *did* have to.

No such luck. He looked up from the file. 'Prime Minister, I am deeply sorry. I must ask you to believe I had no knowledge of this.'

Probably he didn't. But I wasn't letting him off the hook. Nor would he have done, in my position. 'This is an attempt, by guests, to deceive Her Majesty's Government. And there is the serious crime of illegally smuggling explosives into the UK.'

'You must know', he replied reasonably, 'that the French Government never know what French Security are doing.'

'You mean you are not responsible for their actions?'

This was not what he meant. He couldn't deny responsibility. 'No, but . . . if this report is true I must ask you to accept my profound regrets.'

The truth of it was easily confirmed. And then Humphrey went in for the kill. 'You see, it makes it very difficult for the Prime Minister over the Channel Tunnel.'

[1] First language.

I agreed. 'When news of this bomb is published the British people will want to concede very little.'

'They'll wonder if it's safe to go through it!' murmured Humphrey.

'It might be full of official French bombs,' I added.

M. le Président and I stared at each other. He remained silent. The ball was in my court. 'Of course,' I suggested, 'in the interest of Anglo-French friendship we could overlook the crimes of your security men.'

He offered to meet me half-way. Literally! 'I suppose . . . we could agree to sovereignty only half-way across the Channel.'

Humphrey made a note, very ostentatiously.

I said: 'We would like half the signs to place the English language first. And, above all, we want the opening ceremony in two months. In Dover first, and Calais second.'

'I think that is an excellent idea,' he said with a big smile. 'As an expression of the warmth and trust between our two countries.'

We all shook hands.

'Show us a draft communiqué at the funeral tomorrow, would you, Humphrey? And make sure that none of the press find out about the bomb plant. Or the labrador puppy. After all,' I said, looking pointedly at the President, 'if one of the stories gets out, the other is bound to as well, isn't it?'

'Yes, Prime Minister,' he said, permitting himself the slightest trace of a smile. The communiqué would make a wholly successful and utterly joyful day out of what was already a very happy occasion!

13

A Conflict of Interest

October 1st
The newspapers this morning made pretty depressing ·reading. I remarked upon this to Bernard when I met him in my study after breakfast. 'They're all saying that since I've been in office nothing has changed.'

'You must be very proud,' said Bernard.

I explained to him that it was a not a compliment, even though it might appear so from a Civil Service perspective. 'I've read ten of London's morning newspapers,' I admitted, which is surely above and beyond the call of duty, 'and there's not a good word about me in nine of them.'

'But the tenth is better?' queried Bernard, mistaking my implication.

'The tenth is worse!' I explained. 'It doesn't mention me at all.' [*Notoriety is generally preferable to obscurity in the minds of politicians – Ed.*]

All the papers are basically saying the same thing – that I'm a windbag. [*And some of the cartoonists. See overleaf – Ed.*] I showed Bernard. He was as astonished as I. [*Honesty, though doubtless an essential requirement for a successful Private Secretary, must at times be tempered with discretion – Ed.*]

'It is quite extraordinary. The newspapers say that my administration is all rhetoric, that I talk and talk but nothing ever gets done. But it's not true – as I *keep* saying, there are numerous reforms in the pipeline, a great new change of direction is promised, there are great schemes in development, a whole new philosophy of government, and a profound movement in the whole social fabric and geo-political climate of this country.'

Bernard nodded sympathetically. He was in full agreement. 'So what is actually happening, then?' he asked.

'Nothing, obviously! Not yet!' I was impatient. Rightfully so. After all, these things take time. Rome wasn't built in a day.

353

Reproduced by kind permission of Gerald Scarfe.

The truth is that the origin of this latest absurd burst of criticism is that bloody rumour about another big scandal in the City.

So when Humphrey joined us I told him that I had decided to respond to all this press criticism. 'The press are demanding action about the scandals in the City. They shall have it!'

Humphrey looked interested. 'What kind of action?'

'I shall appoint someone,' I said firmly. I was glad he didn't ask me who, or for what, because I haven't yet worked that out. As a matter of fact, I shall eventually need him to help me work that out.

Instead, he asked a question that I didn't expect. 'Prime Minister, when did you make this momentous decision?'

'This morning,' I replied with pride. 'When I read the papers.'

'And when did you first think of it?' He was courteously cross-examining me.

'This morning,' I said, suddenly aware that the suddenness of my decision made me look slightly foolish. 'When I read the papers.'

'For how long, may I ask, did you consider the pros and cons of this decision?' He is sometimes so obvious! He was trying too hard to make me feel that the decision was hasty.

354

'Not long.' I was defiant now. 'I decided to be decisive.'

He could see that my decision, though hasty, was right, for he dropped the subject. [*A fascinating example of the power of the experienced politician to believe what he wanted or needed to believe – Ed.*]

Bernard tried to comfort me. 'Prime Minister, I must say that I think you worry too much about what the papers say.'

I smiled at him. How little he knows. 'Bernard,' I said with a weary smile, 'only a Civil Servant could make that remark. I *have* to worry about them, especially with the Party Conference looming. These rumours of a City scandal won't go away.'

But Humphrey was unflappable. 'Let's not worry about it until there's something more than a rumour. May I show you the Cabinet agenda?'

I wasn't interested. 'Please, Humphrey,' I said. 'The papers are far more important.'

'With respect, Prime Minister,' replied Humphrey impertinently, riled by my refusal to look at his silly agenda, 'they are not. The only way to understand newspapers is to remember that they pander to their readers' prejudices.'

Humphrey knows nothing about newspapers. He's a Civil Servant. I'm a politician, I know all about them. I have to. They can make or break me. I know exactly who reads them. *The Times* is read by the people who run the country. The *Daily Mirror* is read by the people who think they run the country. *The Guardian* is read by the people who think they ought to run the country. The *Morning Star* is read by the people who think the country ought to be run by another country. *The Independent* is read by people who don't know who runs the country but are sure they're doing it wrong. The *Daily Mail* is read by the wives of the people who run the country. The *Financial Times* is read by the people who own the country. The *Daily Express* is read by the people who think the country ought to be run as it used to be run. The *Daily Telegraph* is read by the people who still think it *is* their country. And the *Sun*'s readers don't care who runs the country providing she has big tits.

[*This critique of London's newspapers was found in Number Ten Downing Street shortly after Hacker's eventual departure. Xeroxed copies were found all over the building: the Cabinet Room, the Private Office and, of course, the Press Office.*]

[*Shortly after the conversation about the City reported above, Sir*

Humphrey Appleby met Sir Desmond Glazebrook for lunch at Wheeler's Restaurant in Foster Lane, a well-placed restaurant in the shadow of St Paul's Cathedral, known for the wide spaces between tables, most of which are placed in their own wood-panelled booths. Discreet conversation is therefore possible in this restaurant, which has become a favourite City watering hole.

Sir Desmond Glazebrook was an old acquaintance of Sir Humphrey's. He was at this time still the Chairman of Bartlett's Bank, one of the 'High Street' banks. Sir Humphrey's diary records the menu – Ed.]

Wednesday 3 OCTOBER

Met Sir D. at Wheelers for lunch. Ordered the Dover sole and a couple of bottles of Pouilly Fuissé, Desmond's favourite. As a result he was even more talkative than usual.

I had arranged lunch so that we could discuss the Phillips Berenson business. To my surprise Desmond wanted to talk about it too. He said it didn't

Met Sir D. at Wheelers for lunch. Ordered the Dover sole and a couple of bottles of Pouilly Fuissé, Desmond's favourite. As a result he was even more talkative than usual.

I had arranged lunch so that we could discuss the Phillips Berenson business. To my surprise Desmond wanted to talk about it too. He said it didn't look too good, which is the closest I've ever heard him come to admitting to rampaging fraud and theft among his City friends.

All that the press have said, so far, is that it's a case of another investment bank that's made bad investments. But he implied that it's the tip of the iceberg. Not only have they broken the insider trading regulations, which everyone knows by now though no one can say so yet, they have broken the basic rule of the City. [*The basic rule of the City was that if you are incompetent you have to be honest, and if you are crooked you have to be clever. The reasoning is that, if you are honest, the chaps will rally round and help you if you make a pig's breakfast out of your business dealings. Conversely, if you are crooked, no one will ask questions so long as you are making substantial profits. The ideal City firm was both honest and clever, although these were in short supply – Ed.*]

I tried to find out if Phillips Berenson had been breaking the law. Glazebrook was evasive. He said he wouldn't put it like that. This struck me as virtually conclusive.

I asked specific questions:
(1) Were the Directors of Phillips Berenson siphoning off shareholders' money into their own companies?
(2) Were they operating tax fiddles?
(3) Were there capital transfers to Lichtenstein companies?
(4) Was there bribery?

Desmond's answers were even more evasive, yet crystal clear in their implications. In answer to (1) he acknowledged that this had occurred, although the money might have been intended to be repaid later; nevertheless, this repayment has not yet occurred.

In answer to (2) he agreed that Phillips Berenson had placed their own interpretation on Treasury regulations. It was felt that *someone* had to interpret them, especially as the Treasury's own interpretation didn't seem quite appropriate.

As to (3), capital transfers had occurred 'a bit'. And (4) he did know of undisclosed advance commissions to foreign government officials [*City code for bribery – Ed.*].

And what has brought it all to a head? Phillips Berenson are going to go bust. This is when it matters that they broke the rules – now that the whole story is likely to come out.

Desmond feels passionately that it must be hushed up. This surprised me. He has a big vested interest. I had not realised until today that a huge high street bank like this could be affected by the failure of a small investment bank. But it transpires that Bartletts has been supporting Phillips Berenson in a big way. Glazebrook revealed that they are 'in' for £400 million.

He was rather defensive. It appears that the problem lay with all that Arab money which they had at 11%. They would have looked rather silly if they didn't lend it to somebody at 14%. Trouble was, there weren't all that many people whom you could trust to pay 14%.

Having lent the money at 14% to people who – it turned out – couldn't pay, Bartletts kept putting in more and more money to keep its creditors afloat. And yet they still sank.

Why didn't Bartletts (or Desmond) know that these people were crooks? Why didn't they make enquiries? With hindsight, it's easy to understand: you simply don't make those sort of enquiries in the City. They had seemed like decent chaps, so the *Decent Chap Rule* applied: decent chaps don't check up on decent chaps to see if they're behaving decently. Furthermore, there's no point: if they're honest it's a waste of time – and if they're not honest you don't find out until it's too late anyway.

Then you have two options:
(a) either you blow the whistle on them and you lose all your money, or
(b) you keep quiet and become an accomplice in the crime.

Therefore – and I can quite see why – Desmond Glazebrook chose the third option: namely, to stay ignorant so that the Board of Bartletts Bank could emerge as honourable men who were shamefully deceived by a lot of rotters. Ultimately, the chaps in the City don't mind that. Nor do they really mind people being crooks. What they do mind is people *finding out* that people are crooks. Worse still, people finding out that people *knew* that people were crooks.

But the question remains: the whole mistake has cost Bartletts £400 million. Is ignorance worth paying £400 million for?

Glazebrook felt that it was. Ignorance is safety – at least safety from the law. And, of course, it's not the Bank directors' own money.

So we moved on, over the trifle, to discuss solutions to this thorny problem. Glazebrook felt that there is only one answer: the Bank of England must rescue Phillips Berenson – quietly, with absolutely no publicity. That way we keep it all in the family, and Bartletts Bank would get its money back.

There is one tiny drawback in this scenario: Bartletts gets its money back not from its creditors but from the taxpayer. However, this is not an insuperable problem. Its feasibility will all depend on the new Chairman of the Bank of England – who has not yet been appointed. Unfortunately, the likelihood is that the PM will appoint one Alexander Jameson.

Virtually everyone in the City is against Jameson. It's not simply that he behaves honestly. That, apparently, doesn't matter in itself. It is not seen as a fatal flaw, because smart people can be honest and still succeed. But Jameson goes one step further – he commits the one unforgiveable crime in the City – he moralises [*i.e. he actually tried to stop dishonesty in others – Ed.*]. He conducts search-and-destroy operations. And, as Desmond Glazebrook rightly points out, the world doesn't work like that.

We in Whitehall have also experienced his interference and his moralising. He did a frankly awful report on waste and inefficiency in the Civil Service, containing 209 practical recommendations for reform. It took eighteen months of laborious committee work to whittle them down to three.

Desmond wants Jameson stopped. I agree. But it could be difficult. The appointment of the Chairman of the Bank of England is really a Treasury recommendation. But we cannot let that stand in our way because it's not just the Phillips Berenson case that will be affected if Jameson gets the job and starts all his confounded amateur Sherlock Holmesing. All sorts of other little matters could emerge. He could uncover a major scandal. Followed by collapse of confidence. Sterling crises. The pound could fall through the floor.

It would, of course, be best for all of us if all these City fiddles could be cleared up. But that's just naive optimism, I fully realise. Pie in the sky. The bottom line (as our American cousins like to say) is that the City earns this country £6 billion a year. We can't hazard all that just because a few chaps do a few favours for a few other chaps, who happen to be their friends, without telling the shareholders.

It might be *right* to put a stop to it. But it simply wouldn't be reasonable. The repercussions would be too great. The time is not ripe. [*Appleby Papers RR/2056/LFD*]

[*Hacker's diary continues – Ed.*]

October 5th

Party Conference coming up. I've been working with Dorothy[1] on my speech today, but I'm not happy with it.

She claimed that it's only a first draft, but that isn't the problem. The problem is that it contains no good news. I pointed this out to her and she shrugged. 'We couldn't think of any.'

Feeble! There's always a way. And if there isn't any good news you just have to make the bad news look good.

For instance, I told her, you have to say *something* about the Health Service. Care for old people, mothers and children, that sort of thing. Growing up into a healthy nation.

'Value for money? suggested Dorothy.

'We can't say that,' I pointed out. 'Everyone knows that costs are completely out of control.'

[1] Dorothy Wainwright, Hacker's Chief Political Adviser.

359

Dorothy suggested an alternative: 'We're spending more than ever before to make our Health Service the best in the world.' Excellent!

We turned to Defence. I had meant to talk to Party Conference about defence cuts, but I haven't been able to get the MOD to make any yet. Dorothy had got the idea already. She's very quick on the uptake. 'This government will not put the security of the nation in jeopardy by penny-pinching and false economies.' [*Not that Hacker would have put the nation in jeopardy by, for instance, merging all three music schools of the three armed services. It was a doubtful necessity to have separate music colleges for the Army, Navy and Air Force respectively. There could hardly have been, for instance, a specifically Royal Naval method of playing the bassoon – Ed.*]

We turned to the EEC. A knotty problem. I don't want to attack it because I desperately need the agreement on quota reductions. I can't afford to have all those bloody Europeans ganging up on me again. 'Wholehearted commitment to our friends in Europe' was Dorothy's excellent wording, 'but still vigilant and vigorous in our determination to see that Britain gets a fair deal.'

She's very good. Finally, we turned to the economy, the biggest problem of all. No good news there at all, really. I was plunged into melancholy at the mere thought of having to put a good face on it in public.

Dorothy tried to comfort me. 'We'll find something.'

I asked her if any further bad news was likely to break during the party conference.

'Don't ask me. You're the one who sees the secret Treasury papers.'

'I wasn't really thinking of that, Dorothy.' I sighed heavily. 'I was thinking of the Phillips Berenson business.'

'Ah.' She was non-committal. And looking as lovely as ever – slim, blonde, blue-eyed, cool – a vision of wisdom, beauty and unflappability. She always makes me regret that I'd never had a nanny.

I pressed her. [*Not literally, we think – Ed.*] 'What do you make of it all?'

'I'm suspicious.'

'Why?'

'Because . . .' she replied thoughtfully, 'because of the statements from the Chairman of the Stock Exchange, the Chairman of the Clearing Banks Association, and the Governor of the Bank of England.'

I was puzzled. 'But none of them really said anything.'

She smiled. 'That's why I'm suspicious. If there'd been nothing in these rumours they'd all be falling over themselves to say so.'

Very shrewd. Very wise. She was right, of course – there *must* be more to it than meets the eye. 'Can you find out a bit more about it?'

'I'll try,' she promised.

The whole thing is so *unfair*! City scandals always look bad for the government and it's absolutely nothing to do with me at all! Yet, if the story breaks during Party Conference it could really hurt me.

Dorothy suggested that, to counteract the damage if damage there is, I could announce a wide-ranging review of malpractice. Not a bad idea exactly, but it did sound rather inadequate.

Then I realised that there is one thing I *can* do. I can announce the new Governor of the Bank of England. 'If I choose the right man I can make it look as if no further City scandals will be tolerated.'

Dorothy seemed slightly confused. 'You mean . . . appoint some-one really good?' She was having difficulty in grasping this concept.

I nodded vigorously, stood up, and paced about the study, greatly enthused with the idea. 'Yes!' I was excited. 'Someone vigilant and vigorous.'

She was even more puzzled. 'That'd be a break with tradition,' she observed, and asked me if it were Alexander Jameson I had in mind.

She's no fool. However, I haven't yet made my final decision, and I don't need to yet. I know they'd hate it in the City if I appointed Jameson, and if it turns out there is nothing in this Phillips Berenson affair it may not be necessary.

'If!' said Dorothy.

We continued to work on my speech. We'd reached the economy before we digressed. I couldn't see *what* I could say about that! I mean, if I'd inherited a mess like that from the other party I could blame all the problems on them for the next three years at least. But how do I tell my party that my late, unlamented Right Honourable predecessor had navigated us all up shit creek and then departed with the paddle?

Dorothy tried manfully. 'You could say: "We have come through some difficult times together."'

I didn't dignify such a pathetic offer with a reply. I eyed her balefully. She tried again. '"All the industrial world is facing severe problems."'

I shook my head. 'America and Japan are doing all right.'

'Okay,' she said, not giving up. 'How about "All the European nations are facing severe problems"?'

It was the best we could think of, but not great stuff to lift the party's spirits and send them out happy.

Dorothy needed more information. 'What about output?'

'Down!'

'As far down as last year?'

'No,' I said.

'Great! "We are halting the rate of decline in the nation's output."' Very good. She thought for a few moments. 'Is unemployment coming down at all?'

'Not much,' I replied, but I could see she had a way of dealing with it.

I was right. '"We shall make the attack on unemployment our top priority!",' she offered. Not bad!

'Pay?' she asked.

'It's rising too fast,' I admitted.

'"We cannot afford to pay ourselves more than we earn. The world does not owe us a living."'

True, but not awfully inspiring. Just a bit of Jimmy Carter moralising really. Nobody likes being preached at, especially not by politicians. I wondered if we could turn this section into an attack on greedy unions and spineless managers, thus directing the heat from me and putting the blame fairly and squarely where it belongs.

Dorothy suggested a more diplomatic formulation. '"Both sides of industry must strive to work together in peace and harmony for the sake of Britain."'

One final reference was necessary: to interest rates, which are undoubtedly too high. If *only* they'd come down before Conference it might save my bacon. But I just don't seem to get that kind of luck. We thought about it for hours, but we just couldn't find anything good or positive to say about interest rates.

So we discussed how to finish up. As the whole picture is really a total disaster, the only viable option is to wave the Union Jack. So I'll finish with some rubbish about Britain's unique role on the world stage, and the nation's great destiny.

Dorothy wanted me to say that I'd 'devote every effort to building a peaceful and prosperous world for our children and our children's children'. At least that bit would be honest. It's probably about how long it will take.

SIR BERNARD WOOLLEY RECALLS:[1]

The Prime Minister was indeed exercised about his speech to Party Confer-

[1] In conversation with the Editors.

ence. And he had a considerable problem on his hands. You do need *some* good news if you want to rally the morale of the party faithful.

He made it known to me that he was planning to appoint Alexander Jameson as Governor of the Bank of England. Naturally I reported this to Sir Humphrey Appleby. I must admit to a certain *naïveté*, for I saw this as good news.

Sir Humphrey quickly disabused me. 'It's *appalling* news!' He was so agitated that he rose from his desk and strode angrily about his office, pausing occasionally at the bullet-proof net curtains to stare out over Horse Guards Parade.

At first I couldn't quite see the danger of appointing Jameson, but I readily accepted that Sir Humphrey had greater wisdom or fuller information than I. So I asked him if he were going to try to change the Prime Minister's mind.

He turned and smiled at me, then replied with characteristic precision. 'No, Bernard, I am *going* to change the Prime Minister's mind.'

I couldn't help smiling back, though. I couldn't see how this goal was to be achieved. Jameson was a genuinely good choice, so far as I was aware, and the PM was extremely keen on him – it appeared to be the only hopeful piece of news that he could present to the massed groundlings at Blackpool.

Sir Humphrey found it no deterrent that the PM was keen on Jameson. In fact, he seemed to regard it as a positive bonus. 'That will be my starting point. If you want to suggest that someone is perhaps not the ideal choice [*i.e. rubbish them – Ed.*], the first stage is to express absolute support.'

The reason, as I now understood, is that you must never be on the record saying that somebody is no good. You must be seen as their friend. After all, as Humphrey explained so cogently that morning, it is necessary to get behind someone before you can stab them in the back.

The interesting thing about expressing support for Jameson is that it was indeed the right thing to do. Jameson *was* good. He was extremely honest and efficient. And Sir Humphrey planned to say so. And this is why Sir Humphrey's tactics were so confusing to me at first.

But I should have been patient. He spelled it out.

'*Stage One*: Express absolute support.

'*Stage Two*: List all his praiseworthy qualities, especially those that would make him unsuitable for the job.

'*Stage Three*: Continue to praise those qualities to the point where they become positive vices.

'*Stage Four*: Mention his bad points by defending and excusing them.'

Stage Three is simply done, I learned that day, by oversimplificaton. You *label* someone. If, for instance, someone is a good man he can seriously be damaged by calling him 'Mr Clean'. Strange, but true.

Humphrey had heard that Jameson was a churchgoer, information which I was able to confirm. Indeed, I added, he had once been a lay preacher.

Humphrey's face lit up. His joy was beautiful to behold. 'Splendid news! We can certainly use that against him.'

I asked for an illustration. Sir Humphrey turned to me and spoke as if speaking to the Prime Minister. 'What a charming man. Hasn't an enemy in the world. But is he *really* up to dealing with some of the rogues in the City?'

Ingenious. But I wasn't sure it would wash. For, as I explained to Sir Humphrey, Jameson was in reality a pretty tough customer.

Humphrey remained blissfully unconcerned. 'In that case, we'll go on to Stage Four and say he's *too* tough. For instance, "it probably doesn't matter that he was a conscientious objector, no one has ever *really* questioned his patriotism". Or "I thought the criticisms of him for bankrupting his last company were not entirely fair". That sort of thing.'

It was clear to me that Humphrey would be coming to praise Jameson, not to bury him. Never before had I grasped the lethal possibilities of praise. Humphrey explained that the same principle can be applied to the personal lives of those who cannot be smeared by praise in their professional lives. All you need to do is hint at something that cannot be easily disproved. And if it *is* disproved, you never *said* it anyway, you merely hinted.

The best approach is to hint at a hidden scandal. For instance:

1. If not married – Homosexuality.
2. If married – Adultery, preferably with a lady who is beyond reproach, such as one of the royals or a television newsreader.
3. If happily married – Puritanism or Alcoholism. Or undisclosed Psychiatric Treatment.

The possibilities are most infinite. Careers can be brought to a juddering halt by generously referring to a chap as a great stimulator, a wonderful catalyst, a superb cook, an innovative chess player. As for oversimplification the stages are frightfully easy:

1. Take someone's idea – say, a chap who believes that education subsidies should be funnelled through the parents rather than through the Local Education Authority.
2. Simplify it to the point of absurdity – 'He believes in a complete free for all'.
3. Admit there was some truth in it *once*. 'But we've all realised that there is a less extreme way of solving the problem.'
4. Label him with the idea every time his name is mentioned. 'Ah yes, the educational vouchers man.'

I learned a lot that day that I was able to apply fruitfully as I rose high in the Civil Service. Indeed, I would go so far as to admit that my eventual rise to Head of the Home Civil Service was not wholly unconnected with the techniques that I acquired that morning in Sir Humphrey Appleby's office.

[Hacker's diary continues – Ed.]

October 8th
Dorothy brought me in a new draft of my Party Conference speech. It's marginally better but still pretty uninspiring. And I remain deeply concerned about this Phillips Berenson scandal and its implications for us all.

However, at my morning meeting with Humphrey (and Bernard) my Cabinet Secretary seemed to disagree with me. 'I'm sure it's not that serious' is how he casually dismissed it.

This was like a red rag to a bull to Dorothy. In fact, that's how she always responds to him. I can never make up my mind whether their endless disagreements are highly creative or just a bloody nuisance. But certainly her intention was to defend my position. 'It certainly is serious, Humphrey,' she retorted sharply.

He was patronising. 'No, no, dear lady, I think that the bank over-lent to one big borrower, that's all.'

'There's more to it than that. Some of the Phillips Berenson directors have a slightly shady past, you know.'

He stared at her coldly. 'Can you prove it?'

'No,' she acknowledged honestly. 'It's just my antennae.'

Sir Humphrey chuckled and turned to me. 'I think, Prime Minister, we're in the realms of female intuition.'

Dorothy went white with anger. Tight-lipped, she stood up and smoothed down her tight-fitting black linen skirt. 'We shall see,' she snapped, and headed straight for the door.

'We shall indeed,' murmured Humphrey with a confident smirk.

I wondered why he had such confidence. He gave me no hint. So I told him the good news: that I intended to appoint Alexander Jameson as the new Govenor of the Bank of England.

I wasn't sure what his reaction would be. I was certainly quite unprepared for the great enthusiasm with which he received the news.

'Oh, the Lay Preacher! What a nice chap!'

The Lay Preacher, I thought, must be a nickname. I asked how he got it and was, I must admit, mildly surprised by Humphrey's answer. 'Well, he is one, isn't he?'

I couldn't see how it was particularly relevant, though I'm always a little put off by fanatics of any kind, especially religious ones. But even in these secular days one can hardly hold it against a chap that he believes fervently in God, irrational though that seems to many of us. So I stuck to the point. 'But Humphrey, do you think he's good?'

'Good is *exactly* the word,' replied Humphrey. 'A really *good* man. Did a terribly good job at the White Fish Authority, too.'

The White Fish Authority doesn't sound a totally essential job. Perhaps he spends rather too much time on preaching. '*Where* does he preach?' I wanted to know.

'In church, I suppose. Frightfully religious. Extremely honest. Honest with absolutely everyone.'

Humphrey obviously likes him a lot. And yet . . . there's something about his enthusiasm that worries me. 'It's good, isn't it, to be honest with everyone?' I asked. After all, I was appointing a man to help clean things up.

He was unequivocal. 'Of course it's good. If he finds a scandal anywhere, even here in Number Ten, he'll tell everybody. No doubt about that.'

'You mean . . . he's indiscreet?'

Humphrey looked uneasy. 'Oh dear,' he replied with a sigh, 'that's such a pejorative word. I prefer merely to say that he's obsessively honest.'

I was becoming concerned. I'm all for honesty, God knows, but there's a time and a place for everything. And we are discussing politics. Handling people, that sort of thing. 'Do you think, quite candidly, that he's the right man to bring the City into line?'

'Absolutely,' said Humphrey without hesitation. 'If you want a Saint. Of course, there are those who say he doesn't live in the real world. He *is* extremely puritanical, even for a bible-basher.'

Jameson was beginning to sound like more trouble than he's worth. Or as much trouble, anyway. I indicated to Humphrey that I wanted to hear absolutely all the *cons* as well as the *pros*. Reluctantly he continued. 'Well, I must admit that he is *so* honest that he might not understand their little games. But it probably doesn't matter that the City would run rings round him. And *I* don't think it's true that OPEC[1] would eat him for breakfast.'

He must be a friend of Humphrey's. *Of course* it matters if the City runs rings around him. But would it? I find it very hard to believe. And *who says* OPEC would eat him for breakfast?

I told Humphrey I was confident that he is neither so weak nor so stupid. 'I've heard that he's highly intelligent and very tough.'

Humphrey readily agreed. In fact, I began to see that this may be the root of the problem. 'Very tough, Prime Minister, yes indeed. A bit of an Ayatollah, in fact. The only question is, do you want to risk a Samson who might bring the whole edifice crashing down?'

---

[1] Organisation of Petroleum-Producing Countries.

I couldn't deny that that's a bit of a worry. I fell silent. Humphrey continued to enthuse about him till it began to get on my nerves. 'He certainly is no respecter of persons. He's very stimulating, and a great catalyst. The only thing is that, although treading on toes is sometimes a necessity, he tends to make it a hobby. And of course, he does like everything in the open, he talks very freely to the press – he's not awfully realistic about that.'

I asked Humphrey if he knew anything else at all about Jameson.

'Well . . . one wonders if *anyone* can be *that* moral – I've heard . . .' and then he hesitated.

I was all agog. 'Yes?'

His invariable discretion took over. 'Nothing. Anyway, I'm sure it won't come out.'

'What?' I asked, desperate to know.

'Nothing.' He was trying to reassure me now, but completely without success. 'I'm sure it's nothing, Prime Minister.'

I'm not sure that I can use this man, in spite of Humphrey's enthusiastic recommendation. How little he understands me!

[*News travels fast in Whitehall, and in a matter of hours the rumour reached Sir Frank Gordon, Permanent Secretary of the Treasury, that Sir Humphrey was 'rubbishing' Alexander Jameson. In this situation the Cabinet Secretary and the Permanent Secretary of the Treasury had conflicting needs, opposed ambitions, and different fears.*

The following day Sir Humphrey duly received a particularly friendly note from Sir Frank, which has been fortunately released to us under the Thirty Year Rule and is reproduced overleaf – Ed.]

H M Treasury

Permanent Secretary

October 8

My Dear Humphrey,

You may well have heard that the Treasury would like
Alexander Jameson to be the new Governor of the Bank of England.

We believe that it is about time that the Bank had a
Governor who is known to be both intelligent and competent.
Although an innovation, it should certainly be tried.

The Treasury has endured these City scandals for long
enough. The Chancellor of the Exchequer is quite fed up with
having to defend the indefensible, and so is the Treasury.

Furthermore, we believe that an honest financial sector
cannot damage the national interest. The City is a dunghill
and I propose that we clean it up now. Jameson is our man.

Yours ever,

Frank

[*Sir Humphrey did not hasten to reply. But some days later Sir
Frank received the letter reprinted below – Ed.*]

70 WHITEHALL, LONDON SW1A 2AS

From the Secretary of the Cabinet and Head of the Home Civil Service

12 October

Dear Frank,

Thank you so much for your letter. It is always a
pleasure to hear from you.

I was most amused by your droll remarks about the
Governor-to-be of the Bank of England. I am fully
seized of the need, from the Chancellor's point of
view, for a clean-up in the City. It would indeed
be in the Chancellor's own interest.

But I am sure you will agree that we must all
ensure that the nation's interest is paramount. And
although an honest financial sector cannot damage the
nation in the long term, there would be significant
short-term problems.

An inquiry into the City would undoubtedly
cause a loss of confidence, the pound would plunge,
the share index would plunge – and the Government
would plunge with them.

This would not be in the Chancellor's interest,
nor the Prime Minister's. If I might borrow your
analogy of the City as a dunghill, may I ask what is
left when you clean up a dunghill? Nothing! Except
that the person who cleans it up usually finds themselves covered in dung.

Yours ever,

Humphrey

[*Sir Frank's hostility to the Bank of England embodied a traditional Treasury attitude. Bank of England officials are paid more than Civil Servants, and envy is a factor in the relationship. Further, the Bank is a luxurious institution, serving superb meals in the canteen to its abundantly large quota of staff. The Treasury, on the other hand, is intellectually rigorous and slightly contemptuous of the calibre of those who work at the Bank. The Treasury élite, unlike the Foreign Office élite, are a meritocracy traditionally disdainful of intellectual inadequacy, and even junior officials may express well-reasoned dissent in front of politicians.*

Sir Frank did not apparently let the matter drop. His reply to Sir Humphrey is missing, but it provoked a strong reply from Sir Humphrey which we were fortunate enough to find and which we reprint opposite – Ed.]

70 WHITEHALL, LONDON SW1A 2AS

From the Secretary of the Cabinet and Head of the Home Civil Service

16 October

Dear Frank,

I do not regard this situation as my problem. As you know, sixty per cent of Phillips Berenson's outstanding loans are with a mere three foreigners of dubious repute. The Bank of England was charged with the responsibility of supervising Phillips Berenson, but the supervision was a farce. That is why the Bank of England wants a cover-up - to disguise the undoubted truth that their investigators are a bunch of amateurs.

I understand that you want a clean-up. But I beg you to consider the full implications. The Bank of England may have been responsible for supervising Phillips Berenson, but the Treasury is responsible, in turn, for supervising the Bank of England.

If we have a clean-up, therefore, which would inevitably be a very public affair, the Chancellor might ultimately find that he were held responsible. Then he would be defending the really indefensible this time.

In order to survive the stirring up of this hornets' nest the Chancellor would need considerable support from the P.M. But, strangely, the P.M. isn't all that keen on defending the indefensible.

In fact, the only way that the Chancellor could persuade the P.M. to rescue him would be to convince the P.M. that he (the Chancellor) had been let down by his senior permanent officials.

Think it over, Frank.

Yours ever,

Humphrey Appleby

[*Sir Humphrey's deadly threat won the day. The Treasury stopped pushing for a clean-up and Jameson's chances of becoming Governor of the Bank of England were significantly reduced to almost nil. Sir Humphrey, acting for once in what he believed were Hacker's best interests, had ensured that Sir Frank would now also oppose Jameson if and when it were necessary.*

This development was not, however, known to Hacker. His diary continues – Ed.]

October 17th

I discussed, with Dorothy Wainright and Bernard Woolley, the report I received yesterday on Phillips Berenson.

Dorothy had been absolutely right. It's deeply shocking. Full of irregularities and malpractices. I'm not sure exactly what the difference is by the way, but Phillips Berenson appears to have had an awful lot of malpractices even for a merchant bank. [*'Irregularity' means there's been a crime but you can't prove it. 'Malpractice' means there's been a crime and you can prove it – Ed.*]

It seems that we have got hold of a confidential auditor's report. Actually, it's more than confidential – nobody has seen it. [*In Whitehall, 'confidential' usually means that everyone has seen it – Ed.*]

I asked Dorothy how we got hold of it.

'The Senior Partner at their accountants is a friend of mine.'

'Just friendship?' I wanted to be quite clear about this.

She smiled. 'Apparently he's looking forward to reading the New Year's Honours List.'

That seemed a fair deal. I asked her how we'd do that. In which section?

Bernard leaned forward confidentially. 'How about through the Welsh Office? For services to leaks?' He is irrepressible.

What really suprised me about the whole business is that a High Street clearing bank like Bartletts should be so deeply involved.

But it didn't surprise Dorothy. 'Look at their Chairman – Sir Desmond Glazebrook!'

'You mean, he's a crook too?' I was amazed.

'No,' she explained. 'But he's a bumbling buffoon.'

She's right, of course. I've had dealings with him before.[1]

Dorothy said, 'It's easy to see how he became Chairman. He never has any original ideas, he speaks slowly, and because he doesn't

---

[1] See *The Complete Yes Minister*, Chapters 7 and 13, pp. 152ff. and 297ff.

understand anything he always agrees with whoever he's talking to. So obviously people think he's sound.'

She's dead right. And the trouble is, I've been invited to consult him about appointing the new Governor of the Bank of England. Not that it's necessary to consult anyone – I still intend to get Jameson, even if he is a lay preacher. He's the only chap who could do the thorough clean-up of the City that we need.

'I think you may find', said Dorothy, 'that Sir Desmond doesn't want you to appoint Jameson to do a clean-up.'

'Do I have any alternative?' I asked rhetorically, tapping the Phillips Berenson audited accounts. 'After this!'

She could see the point. 'No . . . not if it gets out.'

'Some of it is bound to get out!'

Dorothy wasn't so sure. 'If it gets to court, all of it will come out. But if the Bank of England does a rescue they can probably keep the worst of it quiet. The bribery and embezzlement, anyway. And the directors investing all the insurance premiums in their private Lichtenstein companies just before the insurance business crashed.'

I wasn't quite clear at first what she was recommending. 'Prime Minister, appoint Jameson right away. Then *you* are protected if it all comes out before he starts. And it's *something* good to announce at Party Conference.'

[*Interestingly, on this rare occasion Dorothy Wainright and Sir Humphrey were both doing all that they could to protect Hacker – and yet their recommendations were totally opposed. She wanted Jameson appointed for Hacker's immediate protection, and he wanted to avoid at all cost the loss of confidence in the economy that would inevitably accompany doing the right thing, i.e. cleaning up the City. She believed, on the other hand, that before you can increase confidence you must first reduce it.*

The crisis festered on, undiscovered by the public, and unreported by the Press for fear of libel actions. Two days later Sir Desmond Glazebrook paid his unwelcome visit to Number Ten – Ed.]

[*Hacker's diary continues – Ed.*]

October 19th
Dorothy and I were again discussing the vexed question of the Governorship of the Bank, when the intercom buzzer rang.

'Who', I asked, 'will Desmond Glazebrook want me to appoint?'

'Sir Desmond Glazebrook,' said Bernard from beside the intercom.

'You're absolutely right, Bernard,' said Dorothy.

He looked blank. 'What about?' he said. It wasn't surprising he was confused, he'd merely been announcing Sir D's imminent arrival. But Dorothy, I realised, was not joking – she meant that Glazebrook would be recommending himself for the job.

I asked if she were serious. She nodded. 'After all, who has the most interest in a cover-up?'

A good point. I took a deep breath and told Bernard to send him in. Bernard reported that Sir Humphrey was with Sir Desmond and that they were both on the way up to the study.

While we waited I asked Dorothy if Sir Humphrey and Sir Desmond knew about the auditors' report on Phillips Berenson. 'Yes,' she said with a warning look. 'But they mustn't know you know. Or you'll have to make the senior partner an Earl.'

When Desmond arrived it was easy to see what made him such a success in the City – tall, distinguished-looking, a full head of white hair, droopy Harold Macmillan eyelids with a moustache to match, casually elegant, the epitome of the English gentleman with all that implies – amateurism, lack of commitment and zero intellectual curiosity. He arranged his impeccable self in my chintz floral armchair and stared at me with his air of baffled amusement. Most people believed that the look of amusement was an act – I knew that the bafflement was as well.

'How good of you to come,' I began. 'As you know, I have to appoint a new Governor of the Bank of England. I'd welcome your views.'

Desmond answered with confidence. 'I certainly think you should appoint one. Bank needs a Governor, you know.'

Humphrey was not unaware that Desmond's confidence was misplaced. 'I think the Prime Minister has more or less decided that. It's a question of who.'

'Ah,' said Desmond wisely, as a little light penetrated into his grey matter. 'Ah,' he said again, processing this information. 'That's tricky,' he went on. 'It's a question of who, is it?' he verified. 'Well,' he concluded, 'it needs to be someone the chaps trust.'

'Yes,' I agreed. 'I feel we need someone really intelligent. Upright. Energetic.'

Desmond looked nervous. 'Well, hold on!'

'You don't agree?' I asked.

He weighed up the question with care. 'Well, of course it's a jolly interesting idea, Prime Minister. But I'm not sure the chaps would trust that sort of chap.'

Dorothy intervened. 'I think the Prime Minister is worried about financial scandals. Are you worried about financial scandals, Sir Desmond?'

'Yes, well, of course we don't want any of those. But if you go for the sort of chap the chaps trust, you can trust him to be the sort of chap to see the chaps don't get involved in any scandals.'

'You mean he'll hush them up?' Dorothy could never resist a provocative question.

Desmond was shocked. 'Good Lord, no! Any hint of suspicion and you hold a full inquiry. Have the chap straight up for lunch. Ask him straight out if there's anything in it.'

'And if he says no?' I asked.

'Well, you've got to trust a chap's word. That's how the City works.'

Perhaps that's how it doesn't work. Moving on, I questioned him about Phillips Berenson. 'What do you know about it?' I asked him.

'What do you know about it?' he countered, cautiously.

'Only what I read in the papers,' I replied.

'Oh. Good.' He seemed highly relieved. 'Well, they're in a bit of trouble, that's all. Lent a bit of money to the wrong chaps. Could happen to anyone.'

'Nothing more?'

'Not as far as I know,' he said carefully.

Dorothy was not satisfied. 'You'd give your word on that?'

Desmond hesitated. His word was important to him. City gents as thick-headed as Desmond know that their reputation for honesty is not to be trifled with – what else have they got? 'I'll look into it for you, if you like.'

Dorothy, a real terrier, just wouldn't let go. 'You haven't heard any rumours?'

'Of course there's always rumours,' he replied, relaxing visibly. That was a full toss and thoroughly deserved to be hit straight to the boundary.

'Rumours,' repeated Dorothy. 'Of embezzlement. Bribery. Mis-appropriation of funds. Insider trading.'

Desmond tried to take the heat out of it. He smiled amicably. 'Come, come, dear lady, those are strong words.'

Dorothy was immune to his charm. 'So it's not true?'

375

'There are different ways of looking at things,' he replied, with a total honesty wholly unconnected to the question he'd been asked.

Dorothy was curious. 'What's a different way of looking at embezzlement?'

'Well, of course, if a chap embezzles you have to do something about it.'

'Have a serious word with him?' I enquired ironically.

Desmond doesn't fully appreciate irony. 'Absolutely,' he replied. 'But usually it's just a chap who gave himself a short-term unauthorised temporary loan from the company's account, and invested it unluckily. You know, horse falls at the first fence. That sort of thing.'

I could see that we were getting nowhere. Obviously Dorothy had been right, Glazebrook did not want me to appoint Jameson. So I asked him who *he* thought should be the Governor.

'Well, Prime Minister, as I say, it's not easy. Not all that many chaps the chaps trust. I mean, it's not for me to say, but if one were to be asked, assuming one were thought to be . . . of course one is committed to one's current job, but if one were to be pressed I dare say one could make oneself available . . . as a duty one owes to, er . . . the nation . . .'

I suddenly realised what he was driving at, and cut through the flannel. 'I was thinking of Alexander Jameson.'

'Ah,' he said, deflated. How could he even *think* that he could be Governor. I'm certainly amazed by the apparently limitless capacity for self-deception that I find in others. [*But never, apparently, in himself – Ed.*]

'What are your views on him?' I asked.

Desmond damned him with faint praise. 'He's a good accountant.'

'Honest?'

'Yes.'

'Energetic?'

'I'm afraid so.'

'So you'd recommend him?'

'No.' Desmond was unequivocal. Not surprising – anybody that interprets the word energetic as a criticism would hardly be on Jameson's side. 'City's a funny place, Prime Minister. You know, if you spill the beans you open up a whole can of worms. I mean, how can you let sleeping dogs lie if you let the cat out of the bag? You bring in a new broom and if you're not very careful you find you've thrown the baby out with the bathwater. Change horses in the middle of the stream, next thing you know you're up the creek without a paddle.'

'And then what happens?' I asked.

'Well! Obviously the balloon goes up. They hit you for six. An own goal, in fact.'

I got the message. Leave things as they are. *Laissez-faire*. Humphrey was nodding in agreement, with feigned admiration, as he sat at the feet of this latter-day Adam Smith.

[*Modern readers may wonder why Sir Desmond Glazebrook wanted to be the Governor of the Bank of England, having already reached the dizzy heights of Chairman of Bartletts Bank. In fact the Governor, though less well paid, was viewed as the top job in the City, with the highest status, influence, trappings and even a little real power. There is something romantic, mysterious and above all* secret *that creates the traditional allure of Threadneedle Street. Furthermore, the Governorship of the Bank can be seen as service to the nation, not merely as enriching oneself further, thus firmly establishing oneself on the list of the Great and the Good to whom further honours, quangos, Royal Commissions and fact-finding missions to sunny climes will be offered upon eventual retirement – Ed.*]

October 24th

This evening I sat in my dressing-room at the Winter Gardens, Blackpool. There was a tatty, grimy old silver star on the door. I didn't feel like a star. I didn't even feel like a sheriff. I felt full of despair.

My walk along the cold and windy sea-front, accompanied by what seemed to be the entire Lancashire constabulary who were clearly out to impress me with their security arrangements, had been wet and bleak. I'd met no one except several dozen cameramen and reporters, all of whom asked me what I was going to say in my speech.

Of course they didn't seriously expect an answer. What worried me was fear that they already knew that I had nothing to say. For, only half an hour before I went on, I was leafing disconsolately through the dog-eared script on my dressing-table and realising – as if I didn't know already – that the speech was *completely* devoid of content.

Of course, that would have made little difference to the reception. I'd have got a standing ovation no matter what! Three and a half minutes. That's if they *didn't* like the speech. Dorothy had made that the minimum; my late unlamented predecessor got three minutes last year so come what may it was to be an extra thirty seconds. All the key people had been issued with stop-watches this morning.

But everyone knew that the ovation was mere window dressing. They would only show a few seconds of that on the news. They'd also show some of my empty phrases, some scattered and half-hearted applause, and then the Political Correspondent would come on and point out that I'd had no good news to offer the party or the country.

Hopelessly I picked up the pencil and stared at the speech once again. 'I need to say something positive,' I said to Dorothy, as make-up was smeared over the bags under my eyes by a pretty girl from our TV consultants.

She leafed through the pages. Nothing came to her mind either, I could tell. 'With the economy in the state it's in, it's the best we can say,' she answered. 'Unless you want to say the tide is turning?'

'There's no evidence,' I complained.

'We don't need evidence – it's a party conference not the Old Bailey. You just need conviction.'

Gloomily I thought that a conviction was what I'd get at the Old Bailey. And my profound melancholy was not lightened when Bernard stuck his head round the door of the dressing-room.

'Prime Minister . . . Sir Humphrey's downstairs with the Burandan High Commissioner. Can they have a word with you?'

I couldn't imagine what about, but I could see no harm in it. While we waited Dorothy said, 'Unemployment is terrible, interest rates are too high, there's not enough investment. What do we do?'

There seemed to be no way out. We couldn't get more investment without cutting interest rates. Yet how could we cut them? There was a case for bringing interest rates down – and a case for keeping them up. Dorothy wanted them brought down in the interests of social justice – but social justice is just another word for inflation.

'Can't you lean on the Chancellor to lean on the Treasury to lean on the Bank of England to lean on the High Street Banks?' she wanted to know.

It seemed rather a tall order to accomplish all that in the remaining twenty minutes before I went on. My option was to announce the appointment of the Lay Preacher, Mr Clean, Alexander Jameson, in the hope of HACKER TAKES NO MORE NONSENSE FROM THE CITY headlines.

[*Hacker's intention to make this announcement even when he was well aware of the risk involved was a result of what is known to the logicians in the Civil Service as the* Politicians' Syllogism:

Step One: *We must do something.*

Step Two: *This is something.*

378

Step Three: Therefore we must do this.
Logically, this is akin to other equally famous syllogisms, such as:
Step One: All dogs have four legs.
Step Two: My cat has four legs.
Step Three: Therefore my dog is a cat.
The Politicians' Syllogism *has been responsible for many of the dis-
asters that befell the United Kingdom in the twentieth century, includ-
ing the Munich Agreement and the Suez Adventure – Ed.*]

There was only one thing puzzling me: Humphrey knew I was
about to deliver my most important speech since my elevation to
Number Ten. Why had he chosen this moment to introduce me to the
Burandan High Commissioner?

I was soon to learn. They bustled into the dressing-room and were
no sooner seated than Humphrey jumped right in at the deep end.

'The High Commissioner', he began, 'is concerned at the rumour
that you intend to appoint Alexander Jameson to the Bank of
England, who will inevitably start an investigation into Phillips
Berenson.'

I couldn't see how this could affect Buranda, and I said so. 'Phillips
Berenson was a shady bank that lent sixty per cent of its money to
three foreigners of dubious repute,' I pointed out.

The High Commissioner spoke. 'Two of those three foreigners
were the President of Buranda and the Chairman of the Buranda
Enterprise Corporation.'

Thank you, Humphrey Appleby, for dropping me in it like that.
'Ah,' I replied thoughtfully.

The High Commissioner did not beat about the bush. 'If you attack
these loans the President of Buranda will have no option but to
interpret this move as a hostile and racist act.'

'*Racist*?' I couldn't believe my ears.

'Of course,' replied the Burandan High Commissioner. He seemed
to have no doubt on the matter.

I tried to explain. 'I . . . I wouldn't dream of attacking your
President *per se*, I would merely . . .'

I was lost for words. Bernard made a suggestion. 'You would
merely say that he was of dubious repute?' I silenced him with a look.

'May I further point out', continued the implacable Burandan,
'that a racist attack on our President would undoubtedly create
solidarity and support from all the other African States.'

'Commonwealth countries, Prime Minister,' Humphrey reminded
me unnecessarily.

379

'We would move to have Britain expelled from the Commonwealth. Our President would be obliged to cancel Her Majesty's State visit next month, and Buranda would immediately sell all the British Government stock that it has brought.'

I turned to Humphrey and whispered, 'Would that cause a run on the pound?'

He nodded gravely. Then he turned invitingly to the High Commissioner. 'Anything else?'

'Isn't that enough?' I snapped at Humphrey. I indicated that the meeting must end because of my imminent appearance on stage. I thanked the High Commissioner, and I promised that I'd give his words the most serious attention.

I kept Humphrey in the room after the African diplomat had gone. I was livid! 'How *dare* you put me in this position?' I shouted.

Stubbornly, he stuck to his guns. 'It's not me, Prime Minister, its Buranda. And the Commonwealth Club is yet another reason for not opening up this can of worms.'

I was furious. 'The President of Buranda is a crook! He doesn't belong to the Commonwealth Club, he should be blackballed.'

'He is already, isn't he?' said a smiling Bernard. 'Sorry,' he added at once, just before I throttled him.

I was angrier with Humphrey than I'd ever been before. 'Humphrey, what are you *playing* at? I don't get it! Why are you so adamant that I should allow another cover-up in the City? What's in it for you?'

Humphrey's reply seemed both desperate and sincere. '*Nothing*, Prime Minister. I assure you. I have no private ulterior motive. I'm trying to save you from yourself. I'm on your side.'

'How can we believe that?' said a sceptical Dorothy, who clearly didn't.

'Because this time it's true,' cried Humphrey revealingly. We stared at him. 'I mean, this time I am *particularly* on your side.'

I had reached the end of my tether. I knew I had to say something good in my speech. I could think of nothing other than announcing that the lay preacher would become Governor of the Bank.

'How about announcing a cut in interest rates?' said Humphrey.

I was about to tell him not to be silly when I realised, from the expression on his face, the he literally had a concrete realistic proposal up his sleeve. [*Not literally, we presume – Ed.*] But I couldn't see how it was to be done. 'Jameson will never agree to a cut in interest rates for political reasons,' I told Humphrey.

'Desmond Glazebrook would,' said Humphrey. 'If you made *him*

380

Governor of the Bank of England, he'd cut Bartlett's Bank interest rates in the morning. You could announce both in your speech.'

'How do you know?'

'He's just told me. He's here. He'll allow you to be first with the good news.'

I was literally torn. [*Hacker had his own non-literal meaning of the word 'literally' – Ed.*] I was genuinely confused about what was right. [*On the contrary, Hacker knew that it would be right for the country if he appointed Jameson. He was perhaps referring to the fact that it would be right for himself, or his party, to choose Glazebrook. And politicians frequently labour under the misapprehension that what is right for them personally is by definition what is right for their country – Ed.*] My problem was that Sir Desmond was such an improbable choice for Governor. He is such a fool. He only talks in clichés. He can talk in clichés till the cows come home.

Dorothy's disapproval was aimed, fair and square, at Humphrey. 'It's jobs for the boys,' she accused him.

He shrugged. He couldn't deny it. But he pointed out that a cut in interest rates would give me a considerable success in my speech.

Dorothy was thinking ahead. 'Won't a cut in interest rates mean that prices will go up?'

She's right, of course, but frankly at that moment I just didn't care, so long as I got a standing inflation. [*We believe that Hacker meant 'ovation', but after serious consideration we elected to print his slip of the tongue because it is so revealing – Ed.*]

Dorothy seemed bitterly disillusioned. 'So you don't want an honest man in charge of the City?'

This struck me as unfair. Desmond Glazebrook's not exactly dishonest. It's just that he's too thick to understand when he's being honest and when he's not. 'The fact remains', I said, as I prepared to walk on stage, 'that the Government simply cannot work without the good will of the City. Can it?'

'No Prime Minister,' said Humphrey.

'And there's no point in upsetting them needlessly, is there?'

'No Prime Minister.'

'Dorothy,' I said, 'fix my speech to announce the cuts in interest rates. Humphrey, get Sir Desmond up here at once.'

'Yes Prime Minister,' they chorused. Within two minutes Desmond had the job, and I was on TV. I got a six-minute ovation. Proof positive that I had made the right decision.

14
Power to the People

October 29th

This morning I had a TV appearance. I hadn't looked forward to it very much. As usual they wanted to interview me about bad news, that's all they're ever interested in. The particular disaster on the agenda today was the ongoing permanent catastrophe of local government, about which I can do practically nothing!

'Almost everybody in Whitehall *and* in Parliament,' I said to Bernard, 'of *whatever* party, agrees that there are a few councils which are run by a bunch of corrupt morons who are too clever by half.'

Bernard didn't disagree. He merely commented that the most that a moron can be is *less* clever by half. He hates to express an opinion on anything that's remotely controversial. But I demanded that he gave me his opinion.

'They're democratically elected,' he remarked cautiously.

'That depends on how you define democracy,' I pointed out. 'Only about twenty-five per cent of the electorate vote in local elections. And all they do is treat it as a popularity poll on the political leaders in Westminster.'

'Nonetheless, they are still representatives.' He's persistent as well as wrong-headed.

'But who do they represent?' I challenged him. 'Nobody knows who their councillor is. And the councillors know that nobody knows who they are. Or what they do. So they spend four totally unaccountable years on a publicly subsidised ego trip, handing out ratepayers' hard-earned income to subsidise lesbian awareness courses and Borough Pet Watch schemes to combat cat theft! They ruin the schools, they let the inner cities fall to bits, they demoralise the police and undermine law and order, and then they blame us.'

'They blame you,' said Bernard punctiliously.

'That's right!' I agreed. '*Me!*'

'Will you say all that?'

382

'I just said it!' I snapped. 'Don't you bloody listen?'

Bernard explained that he'd meant would I say it all on television. What does he think? Of course I wouldn't! It would make me look intolerant. [*It is interesting that Hacker believed that he was not intolerant. Some more ideological politicians might have been proud to be intolerant on this score, and might have felt it would be popular as well. Hacker, however, wanted to be liked, and his greatest problem with these local authorities was that they made him less popular – Ed.*] People assume that I'm responsible because I'm Prime Minister. And now the leader of the Houndsworth Council, that bloody Agnes Moorhouse woman, is threatening to withhold funds from the police, and ban them from council property. If she gets away with it, it'll mean the Government has virtually handed over control of the country to the local councils.

Bernard had looked up the relevant statute. 'She can't do that,' he said. 'Section 5 of the Police Act, 1964, says that Councils have to provide an adequate and efficient police force.'

I'd seen the latest *Guardian* interview with Ms Moorhouse, and I allowed myself to be the devil's advocate for a moment. 'She says that until the police are fifty per cent black they will not be either adequate or efficient.'

'She can't prove that, can she?' Bernard asked.

Who knows? Her current all-white police force is actually the least efficient and most inadequate in the country. Everyone round here is terrified that if we took her to court she'd prove her case.

[*Unfortunately the transcript of Hacker's radio interview that day has not survived, and for that reason we believe that it was not significant. However, the following morning Hacker called a special meeting with Sir Humphrey Appleby to discuss the London Borough of Houndsworth – Ed.*]

October 30th

'Humphrey,' I began, 'it's clear to me that we have to do something about Agnes Moorhouse. Her borough is almost a no-go area.'

He nodded sagely. 'Indeed, Prime Minister.'

'Well . . . what?' I asked.

He gazed hopefully up at the moulded plaster ceiling, and thoughtfully scratched the back of his neck. 'How about a strongly worded letter?'

Not much of a suggestion, in my view. She would simply send us an

383

even more strongly worded letter. Copied to all the newspapers.

Bernard wondered if he might draw her attention to the law, but I don't think that would be much help either. She's a lawyer, getting round the law is what she gets paid for.

In truth, Humphrey and Bernard were rather at a loss. They simply don't understand people who don't play by the rules. It's more or less incomprehensible to them that a strongly worded letter might fail to do the trick. It would certainly bring *them* into line.

Humphrey doodled on his notepad, quietly thinking. Finally he suggested, 'Why not just ignore her?'

I stared at him. 'And have everyone say I've handed over control of the country to the militant loonies? No, Humphrey, someone must have a word with her. And point out the security implications.'

I waited, but the penny didn't drop. 'One of the law officers?' he asked puzzled.

'No,' I said. 'It can't be a political confrontation. It must be an official.' I waited again. Still nothing. 'With security responsibilities,' I hinted.

It dropped at last! 'No! No, Prime Minister, no!' He was desperate not to do it, and I couldn't really blame him. 'Surely it's up to Scotland Yard? The Home Office. MI5. The Special Branch. Lord Chancellor. Department of the Environment . . .'

'White Fish Authority?'

'White Fish Authority!' he repeated in deadly earnest, then realised I was being facetious. 'The point is, not me! It's not fair.'

'The point is, Humphrey,' I explained, 'you are the man who co-ordinates the security services.'

'Yes, but . . .'

'Or should we give that responsibility to someone else?'

My threat was unmistakable. He stopped dead in mid-sentence.

I smiled sympathetically. 'So that's agreed. A quiet word. Reach a gentleman's agreement.'

Humphrey scowled. 'But she's not a gentleman. She's not even a lady!'

'Never mind,' I consoled him. 'I want you to handle her.'

His eyebrows shot up into his hairline. 'Handle her?' Clearly he regarded that as a fate worse than death. I couldn't disagree.

[*Sir Humphrey refers to his gruelling and thought-provoking meeting with Agnes Moorhouse in his private diary – Ed.*]

Wednesday 31 OCTOBER

I met the leader of the
Houndsworth Council today,
at the Prime Minister's
request.

To my intense surprise
Agnes Moorhouse was
a quiet, pleasant,
well-spoken middle-
class lady, apparently
well educated and

I met the leader of the Houndsworth Council today, at the Prime Minister's request.

To my intense surprise Agnes Moorhouse was a quiet, pleasant, well-spoken middle-class lady, apparently well educated and properly brought up. This makes her attitude towards us even more puzzling.

She is extremely hostile, though I must say she has excellent manners. She accepted a cup of tea on her arrival, of course, but she was disdainful of my friendly query as to whether she was Miss or Mrs Moorhouse. I had merely been concerned to address her correctly. But in reply she asked me in a surly fashion if her marital status was any concern of mine.

Of course it's not. Nor have I the faintest interest in it. Meanwhile, she made a clear choice in favour of Orange Pekoe over Typhoo Tea-bags, which demonstrated that she was not wholly uneducated in, or unappreciative of, the better things in life.

385

I enquired with caution if she wished to be called Ms Moorhouse (which is pronounced 'Mis' and seemed wholly appropriate for her). She told me I could call her Agnes. Which, by the way, I had no particular wish to do so. She asked me what she should call me, and I indicated that Sir Humphrey would be quite acceptable.

However, as I was feeling far from first-name terms in this relationship, and being therefore somewhat unwilling to call her Agnes, I opened the conversation by addressing her as 'dear lady'. This mode of address is habitual, and was not intended to carry any resonances of irony. Nor was it intended to be patronising. However, the lovely Agnes told me to 'leave it out' and that she didn't want any 'sexist crap'.

I was now quite confirmed in my first impression of her, namely that this was not awfully likely to be a meeting of minds. But realising that if any progress were to be made we had to get past this interminable problem of how to address each other, I came swiftly to the point. I said that we needed to understand each other and I expressed the hope that we were basically in agreement in that, although she doubtless had her own views as to how Britain should be run, we both agreed that society needs a fundamental base of order and authority.

She claimed that was half true.

'Half true?' I asked.

'You agree, but I don't,' she said. Very droll. An amusing debating point but hardly a serious answer.

In short, she claims that our political system as presently constituted abuses its authority in order to preserve élitist privileges. And that, in so doing, great suffering is caused to the homeless, the unemployed and the aged.

She seemed to feel I was out of touch with ordinary people. I can't imagine where she got such a strange idea. Patiently I explained that I was fully informed about the disadvantaged members of our society, that I'd read all the published papers, seen all the statistics, studied all the official reports. Whereupon she fired a string of irrelevant questions at me: 'What does half a pound of margarine cost? What time do Social Security offices open? How long can you run a one-bar fire for 50 pence in the meter?' and so forth.

Of course I didn't have the foggiest idea of the answers, nor do I see the relevance of the questions. But she seemed to imply that if I had known the answers my attitude to authority would be different.

This is a preposterous notion. We all agree that it would be marvellous if there were no poverty, and we all sympathise with those who are less well off than ourselves. But we simply do not have the resources to achieve an equally high standard of living for everyone. Indeed, the whole notion of 'equality' in an economic sense is a mirage. There will always be somebody who is better off than oneself.

To my astonishment she rose from her chair and started wandering round my office appraising the value of everything she saw, as if she were on a Sunday afternoon outing to Portobello Road. She asked me if my desk was my own. And the portraits. And the porcelain. She knew full well that they were government property, and she estimated that the contents of my office would fetch about 'eighty grand', which I believe is the vernacular for £80,000. 'Enough to keep twenty one-parent families for a year,' she said.

I think that 'eighty grand' is a gross overestimate, but even if she's right she's economically illiterate. I was about to explain to her how depriving the rich does not create any more wealth for the poor in the long term – indeed, the contrary is the case – when she asked me about my salary. I refused to tell her my income but she had looked it up. Is there no privacy any more, no respect? Is nothing sacred?

She had the audacity to propose that I drop my income to £100 per week, leaving £75,000 a year left over for the needy. Once again I tried to explain that my salary is merely part of a complex economic structure. But her mind is closed. She said that when she is in power – God forbid – she will simplify the structure.

All of this I bore in silence. It was my duty. I bit the bullet. But then the damnable woman went too far! She suggested that I was making a profit out of serving my country.

She had done a little research on me, or certainly on my salary. But I too had not been idle in advance of our meeting, and I now asked her a series of questions: for instance, how her policy of banning sexist calendars in council offices helped poverty.

Her answer was most instructive: sexism, she claimed, is 'colonialism against women'. It would have been more correct to describe such calendars as obscene – but the word obscene is now misapplied to describe war, financial fraud or other forms of conduct which may be wrong but are not obscene.

Clearly Agnes thinks colonialism is, by definition, wicked. And by applying the word to sexist calendars the case is proven, without having to be argued further. So I asked her if colonialism against women is reason for Houndsworth's encouragement and approval of the adoption of children by lesbian working single mothers.

'Yes,' she said. 'I am against prejudice in all forms. I do not think that children should be brought up in an atmosphere of irrational prejudice in favour of heterosexuality.' Several more questions begged there, I noted.

Then I asked whether her policy of allowing only free-range eggs to be sold in her borough helped in the fight against heterosexual prejudice, the fight for women's rights, or the fight against poverty.

Her answer: 'Animals have rights too.' Colonialism against chickens, I suppose. But when I laughed she became very emotional. 'A battery chicken's life isn't worth living. Would you want to spend your life unable to breathe fresh air, unable to move, unable to stretch, unable to think, packed in with six hundred other desperate brainless, squawking, smelly creatures?'

Of course I wouldn't. That's why I never stood for Parliament. But the point I was trying to get across to her was that battery hens make eggs more plentiful, and therefore cheaper, and therefore they provide food in her borough for the needy, about whom she professes to care so much.

She refused to concede the point. 'The price of the suffering caused to the chickens is too high.' Funnily enough, I can see her point a little. I prefer to buy free-range eggs – but then, I can afford them. In fact, her concern for the animal kingdom is the reason for her starting a neighbourhood Pet Watch scheme to combat the theft of cats. I indicated that the sum of money might be better spent on the needy – but doubtless she would argue it's being spent on needy cats.

By now I was making Agnes angry. She asked me what I have against our dumb friends. My reply – that I have nothing against them, for I have a great *many* friends in local government – did not amuse her at all.

We bickered for quite a while. Finally, having totally failed to establish any rapport between us, we stopped exchanging slogans and turned to the matter on the agenda: her wish to withhold funds from the police, ban them from council property, sack the Chief Constable, and allow several no-go areas.

I enquired sardonically if she did not even believe in colonialism against criminals, but yet again my little joke fell on stony ground. Agnes believes that people only become criminals because of the unfairness of society. However, this good-natured theory takes no account of heredity, or of the numerous privileged and wealthy criminals whom society has treated extremely well.

She also believes that the police in her borough are insensitive and racist. I'm sure that many of them are the former and some are the latter. But it is still in the interests of all of us, *especially* those ordinary poor people on the high-crime housing estates, to have adequate law enforcement.

This she does not accept either, and this is where I lose all sympathy with her. She acknowledged that she did not mind if those people were in danger of being mugged, raped and bombed by Molotov cocktails.

I tried to explain that it could lead to the overthrow of our whole system of government, our way of life. 'Yours,' she said with a smile, 'not theirs.'

She was, in short, happy to abolish parliament, the courts, the monarchy – everything! I offered her some matches, to burn down my office. But she declined with a smile. I asked her why.

'I might need it,' she said.

[*Hacker's diary continues – Ed.*]

November 3rd

Tonight I sat in my favourite armchair in the flat upstairs, doing my boxes. I thought I'd be alone all evening, but Annie got back early from Birmingham.[1]

I told her that I had told Humphrey to have a meeting with the dreaded Agnes Moorhouse. Annie was amused: 'That sounds like an interesting social experiment.'

Actually Humphrey said the meeting went very well, but I noticed he didn't want to talk about it too much. And Bernard tells me that he had four whiskies in the ten minutes after she left.

Annie said she had her own troubles with local government too, in our constituency. 'It's the Town Hall. They've just cancelled the Old People's Christmas party.'

I was shocked. 'Why?'

'Something about new staff overtime agreements. They said it was all your fault. If you gave them the money, they'd have the party.'

That's exactly what I complain about! It's so unfair. Every piece of stupidity and incompetence in every Town Hall in Britain is supposedly my fault. And yet I have virtually no control over them. I'm going to ask Dorothy to do a 'think' paper on local government for me. Tomorrow!

November 6th

I had a most instructive meeting with Dorothy today. She had plenty to tell me about local government – apparently she's been thinking about it for months, knowing that I'd get round to it sooner or later.

'In a nutshell,' she began, 'there is a sort of gentleman's agreement that the officials won't tell how incompetent the politicians are so long as the politicians don't tell how idle the officials are.'

Just like here at Number Ten, I thought. I asked Dorothy what, if anything, we could do about it.

'Do you really want to know?'

I was surprised by the question. 'Of course I do.'

'It's a Them and Us situation. The Local Authorities ought to be Us.'

I was confused. Did she mean Us the people or Us the government?

'In a democracy', Dorothy pointed out quite reasonably, 'that ought to be the same thing.'

All very well in theory, but we all know that it never is. It turned out that she meant Us the people. 'Local Authorities ought to be running things for Us, they ought to be part of Us . . . but they're not,

[1] Hacker's constituency.

they're running things for Them. For *their* convenience, for *their* benefit.'

I knew that. Everyone knows that. But what was the answer? Fight them?

'No,' said Dorothy, 'turn Them into Us.'

I was confused. I asked for an example.

'Suppose you want to stop a major government project,' she said. 'What do you do?'

'That's easy,' I said. 'Join the Civil Service.'

She laughed. 'No, seriously, if you're an ordinary person?'

'I can't remember what that was like,' I confessed.

She asked me to imagine that I was an ordinary person. That wasn't awfully easy either.

'Imagine that you want to stop a road-widening scheme. Or a new airport being built near your house. What do you do?'

I couldn't think of anything much. 'Write to my MP?' I suggested hopefully.

She wasn't impressed. 'And that does the trick?'

'Of course not,' I admitted. After all, I know *I'd* never take much notice of that. 'But surely that's what ordinary people do, they're stupid.' [*Hacker apparently never considered the personal implications of that remark: the cause and effect relationship of a stupid electorate and his own election – Ed.*]

What Dorothy was driving at was this: what ordinary people do is form a group to fight official plans they don't want. The group represents the local people. The Local Authority, on the other hand, does *not* represent the local people, only the local political *parties*!

'When the local community really cares about an issue it forms a committee,' Dorothy said. 'It makes individual members of that committee responsible for finding the views of a couple of hundred households each. They go round the streets and talk to people, on the doorsteps and in the supermarket; they drum up support and raise money. Now, how is this committee different from the local council?'

'They're decent sensible people,' I said.

'What else?' she asked.

'They *know* the people they represent,' I said.

'That's right,' said Dorothy. 'So they do what the people who voted for them actually *want* done. And the money they raise isn't like rates, because they spend it on what people actually *want* it spent on. Why? Because it's their money. Local councils overspend because they're spending other people's money.'

She's right, of course, for instance, the ordinary people in my neighbourhood at home would love the old folks to have their Christmas party. But the Town Hall would rather spend the money on a new Town Hall, or a fact-finding mission to the Bahamas.

'I see what you mean,' I said. 'Abolish the councils and put everything under the control of Central Government.' [*Hacker had completely missed the point. That would have been Sir Humphrey's solution – Ed.*]

But Dorothy's idea was even more radical. 'The idea is to return power to the ordinary people and take it away from the Town Hall machine. Make local government genuinely accountable.' And she produced this month's edition of *Political Review*. In it there's an article by someone called Professor Marriott. His plan is this:

1. *Create City Villages* – little voting districts with approximately 200 households in each district.
2. *Create Village Councils* – each council elected by the two hundred households.
3. *Give each Village Council money* – a thousand pounds a year, taken out of the rates or local taxes, just to spend on their own little area – a couple of streets, a city village.
4. *The Chairperson of the Village Council becomes the Borough Councillor* – this means that there would be five or six hundred councillors to a borough. Just like Parliament.
5. *Elect an Executive Council for the Borough* – this means that every local authority would have a parliament and a cabinet.

It sounded very appealing, though I wasn't too excited about the idea of a parliament electing a cabinet. That would be carrying participation to a ridiculous extreme and would set a very dangerous precedent. Dorothy insisted that it was the answer to local government. 'The result would be that every councillor would be in door-to-door touch with the people who voted for them.'

She's right. It's brilliant. Who would ever vote for Agnes Moorhouse if they had actually met her? [*More people probably – Ed.*] And the implications are tremendous! This could be like the Great Reform Act of 1832. All of these councils are, in fact, rotten boroughs – with half a dozen people in local parties deciding who shall go to the Town Hall for four years.

If I bring this off I shall be the Great Reformer. I see it now. Hacker's Reform Bill. A place in the history books. I shall present it myself. I immediately had ideas for how to open the debate, which I tried out on Dorothy.

'The strength of Britain does not lie in offices and institutions. It lies in the stout hearts and strong wills of the yeomen . . .'

She interrupted. 'Women have the vote too.'

'And yeowomen . . .' That didn't sound right. 'Yeopeople, yeopersons . . .' I rephrased it. 'The people of our island race. On the broad and wise shoulders . . .'

She interrupted me again. 'Shoulders can't have wisdom.'

I pressed on. 'On their broad shoulders and wise hearts . . . heads, *in* their strong hearts and wise heads lies destiny. We must trust their simple wisdom. We must give back power to the people.' She applauded.

'Dorothy,' I said humbly, 'I'm proud to be the man who will introduce this new system. What shall we call it?'

'Democracy,' she said. And her blue eyes sparkled.

SIR BERNARD WOOLLEY RECALLS:[1]

Whitehall, the most secretive square mile in the world, was paradoxically a sieve. And it was not long before Sir Humphrey Appleby heard that Dorothy Wainwright had recommended Professor Marriott's ideas to the Prime Minister. He asked me in for drinks in his office after work one evening that week.

I too had read Professor Marriott's article but I must confess that, being still slightly green compared with old Humphrey, the wider implications of the theory had not quite sunk in. So when he raised the subject I remarked that in my opinion it was about time that we reformed local government.

The expression on his face told me at once that I should have been slightly more equivocal. So I indicated that I had merely meant that I was not wholly against reforming local government. As his expression remained the same I felt it wise to add that I could see that there might be many convincing, indeed one might say conclusive, arguments *against* reform. I was grateful that he didn't ask me to specify those arguments because, to be quite honest, I didn't see what they could be. More fool me!

Humphrey, of course, had thought it through in his customary meticulous fashion. He explained that if we once create genuinely democratic local communities, it won't stop there. Once they were organised, such communities would insist on more powers, which the politicians will be too frightened to withhold.

The inevitable result would be Regional Government.

This, as every Whitehall chap fully understands, would be very bad news! Let me give you an example: if there is some vacant land in, say, Nottingham, and there are rival proposals for its use – a hospital or an airport, for instance – our *modus operandi* is to set up an interdepartmental committee.

[1] In conversation with the Editors.

That's what we always have done and it's what we always shall do.

This Committee creates months of fruitful work as all the interested Departments liaise: the Department of Health, the Department of Education, the Department of Transport, the Treasury, Environment, and so forth. We all have to see the papers, hold meetings, propose, discuss, revise, report back, and redraft. It's the normal thing.

And why? Because it generally results in a mature and responsible conclusion. But if we had regional government they would decide the whole thing, themselves, in Nottingham. Probably in three or four meetings? How? Because they're amateurs.

You might argue – as I did, that day with Humphrey – that, as it's their city, they should have that right. But I was wrong, and so would you be, for the following reasons:

First: they can't be trusted to know what's right.

Second: there would be so much less work to do in Whitehall that Ministers could almost do it on their own. Therefore we, the Civil Service, would have much less power.

Third: there's nothing wrong with the Civil Service having less power *per se*. Indeed, I personally have always shunned power. [*We remind readers that when Sir Bernard retired he was Head of the Home Civil Service.– Ed.*] But the unfortunate corollary of the Civil Service having less power is that the *wrong people* get more power.

Once Sir Humphrey explained this to me, I quickly saw the error of my ways. At the top of his list of wrong people with power were politicians, local and national.

At first I thought I'd found a flaw in his argument: since the politicians are put there by ordinary voters, I couldn't see how they *could* be the wrong people. Surely, in a democracy, power ought to be vested in the voters?

Sir Humphrey put me right. 'This is a *British* democracy, Bernard. It is different. British democracy recognises that you need a system to protect the important things and keep them out of the hands of the barbarians. Things like the arts, the countryside, the law, and the universities – both of them. And *we* are that system.'

He was right, of course. We, the Civil Service, run a civilised meritocracy, a smoothly-running government machine tempered only by occasional general elections. Ever since 1832 we have been gradually excluding the voters from government. Now we have got to the point where they vote just once every four or five years purely on which bunch of buffoons will try to interfere with our policies.

And I had been happy to see all that thrown away. As Sir Humphrey talked I flushed pink with embarrassment, and hung my head in shame.

'Do you want the Lake District turned into a gigantic caravan site?' he asked me. 'You want to make the Royal Opera House a Bingo Hall and the National Theatre into a carpet sale warehouse?'

'It looks like one, actually,' I replied defensively.

Humphrey was pained. 'We gave the architect a knighthood so that no one would ever say that.' I bit my lip. 'Do you want Radio 3 to broadcast pop music for twenty-four hours a day? And how would you feel if they took all the culture programmes off television?'

I tried to defend myself. 'I don't know. I never watch them.'

'Nor do I,' said Humphrey. 'But it's vital to know that they're *there*.'

Our meeting ended. But I was still confused by one thing. To my certain knowledge Jim Hacker, both before he became Prime Minister and ever since, had always said that he wanted to reform the Civil Service.

Since he was the duly elected, democratically appointed Prime Minister [*depending on your definition of democracy*[1] *– Ed.*], I felt that whether or not we had a duty to reform local government, we *certainly* had a duty to reform the Civil Service. And if local government reform inevitably led to regional government, and therefore civil service reform, perhaps it was our duty to help.

I subsequently plucked up courage and wrote this in a letter to Sir Humphrey. He later told me that he had shredded it. I believe he did so out of kindness, in the knowledge that if my letter had remained on file and ever been seen again it would have fatally damaged any chance I had of reaching the dizzy heights of Permanent Secretary. I shall always be grateful to him for his generosity and foresight.

But I did keep Sir Humphrey's handwritten reply to me [*handwritten, so that there would be no copy in the office – Ed.*] which you may reprint if you wish.

[*Naturally we accepted Sir Bernard's kind offer, and we transcribe this rare personal letter from Sir Humphrey below – Ed.*]

My Dear Bernard,

Whether or not the Prime Minister has said that he wants to reform the Civil Service is completely beside the point. No matter what he has said, it is not what he really wants.

So, you may ask, what *does* he really want? A better Britain? Yes. Better weather? That too. But what is the main objective of all politicians, what is it that obsesses them, day and night, for the whole of their lives? Popularity! Popularity, fame, publicity, their pictures on television, their voices on the radio, their photos in the newspapers. And why? Not just because it gives them a warm glow. Champagne gives them a warm glow, but they're not obsessed with it.

No, the answer is that popularity is essential to them because they want to be re-elected. Government is fame and glory and importance and big offices

---

[1] See Chapter 1.

Cabinet Office
Nov 12th

My Dear Bernard,

Whether or not the Prime Minister has said that he wants to reform the Civil Service is completely beside the point. No matter what he has said,

and chauffeurs and being interviewed by Terry Wogan. Opposition is impotence and insignificance and people at parties asking you if you know Sir Robin Day.

Therefore, the only real job of a government is to get re-elected. And since constituencies of 60,000 voters are far too big for people to know their MP, the electors make up their minds on the basis of television and radio and the press. And then they vote for any idiot that a few dozen people in the constituency party chose as their candidate.

In other words, a politician does *not* really represent the electors. His job is public performance and image-building and generally being famous and popular.

So now we must ask: *what do the politicians REALLY want from the Civil Service?*

1. *Publicity*. They want publicity for all the good things they've done (or think they've done). This is why we have over one thousand press officers in Whitehall. And why we spend so many hours helping them with speeches, articles and photo opportunities.
2. *Secrecy*. They want secrecy about anything that could be used against them. This is why we have the Official Secrets Act. And why we classify every document from the Trident missile specification to the tea ladies' rota.
3. *Words*. They want us to help perpetuate the myth that they were elected democratically. This is why we help them write scripts for various charades, such as parliamentary debates. And we also write papers for Cabinet, so that the Prime Minister can update his colleagues on things that they have have missed in the newspapers.

4. *Government*. They need us to govern the country. This is the most important task of all. The politicians have no training for it, no qualifications, no experience. And no interest in it either.

5. *Pretence*. Finally, they need us to keep up the pretence that they are making all the decisions and we are only carrying out orders. This is why they take a lot of work off our shoulders, such as:
   a) ceremonial banquets;
   b) unveilings;
   c) launchings;
   d) official openings;
   e) foreign delegations, etc.
   They do all of that work and leave us free for what we do best.

Therefore, politicians have no real wish to reform the Civil Service. Under our present political system we do precisely what the system requires of us. We do everything they need. And we do it, if I may say so, brilliantly.

So therefore it must follow as does night the day that if the Prime Minister wants to reform the Civil Service he would have to start by reforming the political system.

But how can he? It is the system that has got him where he is. You do not kick away the ladder you climbed up. Especially when you're still standing on it.

The fact that he proposed this when he was in Opposition all those years ago is completely understandable. Oppositions always want to change the system that is keeping them out of office. But once they are in office they want to keep it. For instance, no one *in office* has ever wanted to change our electoral system to proportional representation. And although every Opposition pledges itself to repeal the Official Secrets Act, no government has ever done so.

In conclusion, Bernard, it is our duty to ensure that the Prime Minister comes to see things this way. It is not for his own good. And we are not without allies: Professor Marriott himself, and Agnes Moorhouse, as you will see.

Yours ever,
H.A.

[*Bernard Woolley kept the letter safely, and it became one of his articles of faith as he strove in later years to help Ministers, and indeed Prime Ministers, understand their proper role.*

While he puzzled long and hard over Sir Humphrey's final paragraph, not understanding how Professor Marriott and Agnes Moorhouse – of all people – could be allies in this situation, Sir Humphrey had a second meeting with Ms Moorhouse. He made a brief note about it in his private diary – Ed.]

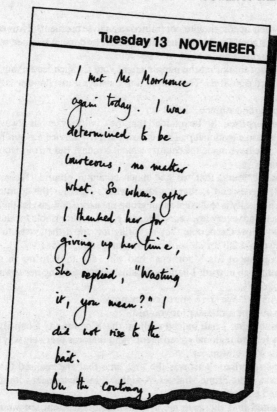

Tuesday 13 NOVEMBER

I met Ms Moorhouse again today. I was determined to be courteous, no matter what. So when, after I thanked her for giving up her time, she replied, "Wasting it, you mean?" I did not rise to the bait.

On the contrary,

I met Ms Moorhouse again today. I was determined to be courteous, no matter what. So when, after I thanked her for giving up her time, she replied, 'Wasting it, you mean?' I did not rise to the bait.

On the contrary, I told her the plain truth: that the Prime Minister is so worried about her attitude to the police that he is proposing a wholesale reform of local government. Namely:

i) street representatives

ii) voting communities of 200 households (average)

iii) selection of local authority candidates by the whole electorate.

I gave her a paper to read which gave the plan in full detail. She was horrified, of course. 'It strikes at the very heart of our democratic social reforms,' she told me.

'By which you mean that the people do not want your policies,' I said.

She denied it. 'Of course they would want our policies if they could understand all the implications. But ordinary voters are simple people, they

397

don't see their needs, they're not trained to analyse problems. How can they know what's good for them? They need proper leadership to guide them the way they ought to go.'

'Do you not think that the people might vote for such leadership?'

She looked doubtful. 'The people don't always understand what's good for them.'

'I do so agree with you,' I told her.

She was surprised. So I explained that the Civil Service has always given such unobtrusive leadership. That is how the Civil Service has survived the centuries. We have made the country what it is today. But no one would ever vote for us.

And so we found that we had much common ground. We are both confident, Agnes and I, that we know what's right for the country. The principal necessity is to have a small group in charge and just let the people have a mass vote every few years. Secondly, it is not advisable for the voters actually to know the people they're voting for, for if they were to talk to them they could fall for all sorts of silly conventional ideas.

At this moment Ms Moorhouse had what she took to be an original insight, although in truth I had been painstakingly leading her towards it.

'Humphrey?'

'Yes, Agnes?' We were quite cosy by now.

'This would be a disaster for you too.'

I explained that I had indeed realised that Community Councils would inevitably lead to regional government. And that was precisely why we had to stop the Prime Minister.

She was surprised. This was the first time that she realised that I too wanted to stop the Prime Minister. And that if I were to meet with success I would need her help.

I requested that she gave me a written assurance that she would stop harassing the Houndsworth police force. She promised to write a letter guaranteeing that the police would not be made more democratically accountable [same thing – Ed.].

Our meeting ended most amicably. She told me that I was a great loss to the militant revolution. I, in turn, expressed my true feeling that she was a great loss to the Civil Service. On this note of mutual respect and regret, we parted.

[Hacker's diary continues – Ed.]

November 14th

A meeting was scheduled this morning with Professor Marriott. Apparently Humphrey arranged it. I didn't know about it.

Bernard offered an explanation. 'I think he feels, Prime Minister, that if you're adopting his scheme it would help to talk to him.'

Dorothy remarked that Humphrey must have an ulterior motive. 'Why?' I asked.

'All Humphrey's motives are ulterior,' she replied simply.

I looked at Bernard. 'Are they? How *does* Sir Humphrey feel about these reforms?'

Bernard's answer was unclear. 'Well, I think, that is, I'm sure, if, if it's, er, if it's what you want, then Sir Humphrey would, er, er . . .'

'As hostile as that?' I asked. 'Get him in here anyway.'

When Humphrey appeared in the Cabinet Room Professor Marriott was conspicuous by his absence.

'Where's the Professor?' I asked.

'He's just outside,' replied Humphrey obligingly. 'Shall I bring him in now?'

'Just one thing,' I said commandingly. 'What's *your* view of this plan to reform local government?'

'I think it's a brilliant way of bringing real democracy into the government of Britain.'

What was he up to? I couldn't work it out. 'You mean you're in favour?'

'That's not what he said,' Dorothy remarked accurately.

He ignored her, as he always does. 'Prime Minister, if you genuinely want full democratic government, you will have my unquestioning support. Would you like to see Professor Marriott now?'

Marriott was a tall, amiable fellow, nervously adjusting his bow tie, rightly overwhelmed at meeting me. We shook hands, exchanged a few pleasantries, and finally Humphrey came to the point.

'Professor Marriott has a sequel to his original article, due to be published next month. Even more exciting than the first one.'

I asked the Professor to tell me more.

'Yes,' encouraged Humphrey, 'tell the Prime Minister about the benefits to Parliament.'

The Professor was only too delighted. 'Well, you see, under this scheme each borough would have its 500 street representatives and the local MP would be able to talk to them all in one hall.'

'So that they'd really be able to get to know each other,' added Humphrey helpfully.

'Exactly,' said the Professor. 'And they'd be able to tell the people in their street all about him. Personal word-of-mouth recommendation for the MP.'

This sounded terrific to me. I glanced at Dorothy, but she was looking decidedly less enthusiastic. She indicated that she wanted to speak.

'Where would the constituency party come in?' she asked pleasantly.

Marriott beamed. 'Well, that's the marvellous thing, you see. The party organisations would be completely bypassed. MPs would become genuinely independent.'

I was aghast.

'You see,' continued Marriott enthusiastically, 'if they were personally known to all their constituents, or to their community representatives, then whether MPs could get re-elected or not would be nothing to do with whether or not the party backed them. It would depend on whether the constituents felt the MP was doing a good job.'

Humphrey smiled at me. 'So if MPs weren't dependent on the party machine they could vote against their own government party and get away with it,' he explained.

'Exactly,' said the Professor again. 'Because there'd be no need for "official" candidates, election would depend on the reputation of each individual MP, not the image of the party leader. It's the end of the party machine. The end of the power of the whips.'

I couldn't begin to grasp how such a system could possibly work. 'So . . . how would the government get its unpopular legislation through if it couldn't twist a few arms? How would it command a majority?'

Marriott's answer was all too clear. 'That's the whole *point*. It couldn't! A government couldn't *command* a majority! It would have to deserve it. Just like in 1832, when an MP's constituency was only about 1200 voters, there could only be legislation if a majority of the MPs were actually in favour of it. And MPs would only favour it if the voters did too. Parliament would be genuinely democratic again.'

I couldn't believe my ears. Who in their right mind could possibly come to the Prime Minister with such a dangerous proposal? Only some damn-fool academic. As far as I was concerned the good professor could return to the ivory tower from whence he came – and pronto!

'That you so much, Professor,' I said with finality. 'Absolutely fascinating.' And I stood up and shook hands.

He was surprised. Beads of sweat broke out on the high dome of his receding forehead. 'Oh, er, thank you, Prime Minister,' he said, and

Bernard whisked him out of the room before his feet could touch the ground.

The heavy panelled door closed with a soft thud. Humphrey smiled at me. 'Isn't that splendid, Prime Minister? Real democracy!' He clapped his hands together and rubbed them with glee.

I ignored him and turned to Dorothy. 'Is he right? Would that happen?'

'I'm afraid it probably would.'

Glassy-eyed, I repeated the dreadful threat aloud. 'MPs free to vote how they like? It's intolerable.'

'Just like the 1832 Reform Act,' Humphrey confirmed.

'But,' I explained to Humphrey, as if he didn't know, 'the whole system depends on our MP's voting the way I tell them. Under this system they could follow the dictates of their constituents.'

'Or their consciences,' agreed Humphrey.

'Exactly!' I said, echoing that bloody Professor. 'Dorothy, this whole scheme's a complete non-starter.'

Dorothy asked what I was going to do, in that case, about Agnes Moorhouse and the police. I was stuck. But to my surprise Humphrey indicated that he had the answer. 'I've had another talk with her, Prime Minister. It's all arranged. I wrote you this memorandum.'

And he handed me a sheet of paper.

[*Fortunately the memorandum in question was found beside the cassette on which this portion of the diary was dictated, and is reproduced overleaf – Ed.*]

70 WHITEHALL, LONDON SW1A 2AS

Memorandum

To: The Prime Minister   14 November

From: The Secretary of the Cabinet

Certain informal discussions have taken place, involving a full
and frank exchange of views, out of which there arose a series
of proposals which on examination proved to indicate certain
promising lines of enquiry which when pursued led to the
realisation that the alternative courses of action might in
fact, in certain circumstances, be susceptible of discreet
modification, in one way or another, leading to a reappraisal
of the original areas of difference and pointing the way to
encouraging possibilities of significant compromise and
co-operation which if bilaterally implemented with appropriate
give and take on both sides could if the climate were right have
a reasonable possibility at the end of the day of leading,
rightly or wrongly, to a mutually satisfactory conclusion.

HA.

[*Hacker's diary continues – Ed.*]

I stared at the sheet of paper, mesmerised. Finally, I looked up at Humphrey. 'Could you summarise this please?' I asked.

He thought hard for a moment. 'We did a deal,' he replied.

He did a deal with Agnes Moorhouse? Splendid! 'How did you fix it?'

He smiled humbly. 'Oh, the old system has its good points, you know. It works things out in its own time.'

I sat back in my chair, relaxed, content to ask no more. 'Yes, it does, doesn't it?' I murmured happily.

'And . . . the Marriott plan?' he asked. He knew what my answer would be.

'I don't think the nation's ready for total democracy, do you?' He shook his head sadly. 'Shall we say next century?'

'You could still be Prime Minister next century,' Dorothy interjected.

'Well, the one after,' I said.

'Yes, Prime Minister,' said Humphrey, quite content. In fact we were all content, Humphrey, Dorothy and me. Friends at last.

15
The Tangled Web

[*The day after Hacker, Dorothy Wainright and Sir Humphrey Appleby agreed to postpone democracy until the twenty-second century, Hacker answered questions in the House of Commons. This was a twice-weekly event: Prime Minister's Question Time. The Prime Minister was likely to be asked about almost anything at all, and was given no notice of the questions. To be more precise, the first question from an MP was likely to be: 'Will the Prime Minister list his official engagements for today?' The supplementary question could be about absolutely anything: e.g. 'Will the Prime Minister find time to consider rising interest rates?' Or 'Will the Prime Minister find time to consider the scandal of Agnes Moorhouse creating no-go areas for the police of the London Borough of Houndsworth?' Or 'Will the Prime Minister find time to consider the scandal whereby 25% of Honours go to less than 1% of the population, most of whom are in government?'*

The Prime Minister can react in a number of ways: honestly, dishonestly, with a mass of figures. He can counter-attack, flatter, or make jokes. The latter is the most dangerous and least recommended response.

Hacker, like all Prime Ministers, would prepare for Prime Minister's Question Time with great care. Bernard Woolley and the Parliamentary Questions Secretary – a Principal from the Private Office – would meet for a briefing from 2.30 to 3.10 p.m. in the Prime Minister's room at the House. They would be armed with a three-volume book which lists what each MP on the Order Paper has asked before, what are that MP's special interests, and – most important – what have been the previous answers.

The Prime Minister is obliged to give an answer to a question about policy. However, if the question demands a purely factual answer, the Prime Minister may be able to give a written reply.

The burden can be lightened by planting some of the questions. Questions come from alternate sides of the House, and a government backbencher hoping for preferment may well inform the Prime

Minister of a potential question – 'I always like to be of service, Prime Minister' – or even offer: 'What would you like me to ask, Prime Minister?'

Furthermore, the job of the Prime Minister's Parliamentary Private Secretary is to 'nobble' an MP: 'The Prime Minister would like you to ask this question.' Nonetheless, the Prime Minister can confidently expect two-thirds to three-quarters of questions to be hostile. And the most awkward questions of all frequently came from the government side – from disappointed, disaffected and sour senior backbenchers who have either been overlooked or sacked from office.

Thus it is that, as a result of Prime Minister's Question Time, a tornado may suddenly appear in what has been a cloudless blue sky – Ed.]

SIR BERNARD WOOLLEY RECALLS:[1]

Jim Hacker had been asked whether he had been tapping MPs' telephones. He had given this excellent answer: 'Much as I respect and value the opinion of this House, I must confess to having no desire to listen to the words of honourable members for any longer than I actually have to,' and he got a big laugh. [*The MPs who laughed would have been largely from his own party, those hoping to be promoted or those afraid of being sacked. This amounts to virtually all of them – Ed.*]

But on our return to Number Ten later that afternoon Sir Humphrey buttonholed me in the narrow twisting corridor that led to the Cabinet Office. He asked me how our great statesman was that afternoon.

'Very cheerful,' I replied. 'He did very well at Question Time this afternoon.'

'Indeed? In whose opinion?'

'His,' I said. In fact I was joking. Everyone had been really impressed with his answer on tapping MPs' phones.

Everyone except Humphrey. Indeed, he seemed so very concerned that I began to fear that there was more to this than met the eye. He ticked me off for not warning him of the question – as Cabinet Secretary, Humphrey co-ordinated all government security. I explained that it was an unforeseen supplementary, but he remarked disagreeably that it was a foreseeable unforeseen supplementary.

It was more than clear from Sir Humphrey's demeanour and agitation that, although the Prime Minister denied that he ever authorised bugging an MP's telephone, this answer was not the truth!

The idea of a British Prime Minister deliberately lying to the House of Commons was deeply shocking to me. It was hard to believe. But Humphrey

[1] In conversation with the Editors.

held a fat file under his arm, and informed me that it contained a mass of incriminating information – including the transcripts.

Humphrey asked to see Hacker immediately. I wondered if we might not leave it a little longer, as the Prime Minister was basking in his success and didn't get many moments of unalloyed pleasure. But Humphrey took the view that Hacker got more pleasures than he deserved, and adamantly insisted upon an immediate meeting.

[*Hacker's diary continues – Ed.*]

November 15th

I gave some brilliant answers in Question Time today. I was on absolutely top form. So I wasn't a bit surprised when Humphrey unexpectedly appeared in the Cabinet Room later that afternoon.

'Prime Minister, I want to talk to you about Prime Minister's Question Time this afternoon.'

'Thank you,' I said, with suitable and becoming modesty. 'I accept your congratulations. Wasn't I brilliant, Bernard?'

Bernard replied without hesitation. 'I believe, Prime Minister, that your replies this afternoon will not be quickly forgotten.'

Humphrey tried to speak but I wouldn't let him. From his manner I might have detected storm clouds on the horizon, but I didn't. Foolishly I insisted on recounting my triumphs. 'Let me tell you what happened, Humphrey,' I crowed. 'The first question was about that Home Office cock-up over the shortage of prison officers. My reply was masterly. "I refer the Honourable Member to the speech I made in this House on April the 26th."'

'Did he remember what you'd said?' Humphrey asked.

'*'Course* he didn't. Nor did I, come to that. But it was the perfect evasive blocking answer, and as he couldn't remember what I'd said any more than I could we went straight on to a question about unemployment and whether the Department of Employment fiddle the figures.'

Bernard corrected me. 'You mean "periodically re-structure the base from which the statistics are derived without drawing public attention to the fact"?'

'Exactly,' I repeated, 'fiddle the figures.'

Humphrey, in spite of himself, was interested. 'Of *course* they do,' he said.

'I know that,' I said. 'But I gave a great answer. I said that I'd found no significant evidence of it.'

Bernard said, 'That's because you haven't been looking.'

'And because we haven't shown you,' Humphrey added.

'I know, Humphrey. Thank you. Well done. So then we went straight on to a googlie about the Department of Energy's looming plans for the disposal of nuclear waste. The question was trying to get me to admit that the Cabinet's divided.'

'It is!' remarked Humphrey.

'I know it is,' I said. 'So I said, "My Cabinet took a unanimous decision."'

Humphrey smiled. 'Only because you threatened to dismiss anyone who wouldn't agree.'

He was right, of course. But it certainly made them agree unanimously. Anyway, by this time my backbenchers were cheering my every word. 'Then there was a question about why, despite all that money we've spent on the new anti-missile missile, it was scrapped as obsolete the day before the first one came off the production line.'

Humphrey was curious as to how I wriggled out of that one.

'This was my master-stroke. I didn't! My reply was sheer genius. I simply said, "Our policy has not been as effective as we'd hoped, and clearly we'd got it wrong."'

Humphrey's mouth fell open. He was profoundly shocked that I'd made such an admission. But it was a brilliant answer. It took the wind right out of their sails. A completely honest answer always gives you the advantage of surprise in the House of Commons.

Bernard was enjoying it in retrospect too. 'There was actually a supplementary, Sir Humphrey. The Prime Minister was asked when he would request the resignation of the responsible Minister.'

That one was too easy. A full toss. I hit it straight to the boundary. '"I will ask for his resignation when he makes a mistake that could have been seen at the time, not with the benefit of hindsight."' My side of the house were on their feet, cheering, stamping, waving their order papers. It was a day to remember!

But unfortunately, it turned out to be a day to remember for other reasons too. Of course I should have detected that something was up from the way in which Sir Humphrey had slunk into the Cabinet Room. I had mistaken his funereal air of impending disaster for simple envy at my brilliance in handling the House so well without any assistance from him. But there was more to it than that.

'I understand', he remarked casually, 'that there was a question about bugging an MP?'

'Stupid question,' I said. 'Why should we bug Hugh Halifax? A

YES PRIME MINISTER

727 *Oral Answers*　15 NOVEMBER　*Oral Answers* 728

Friend the Secretary of State for Education and Science about the nature of the curriculum.

PRIME MINISTER

Engagements

Q1. Mr. Tyler asked the Prime Minister if he will list his official engagements for Thursday 15 November.

The Prime Minister (Mr. James Hacker): This morning I had meetings with ministerial colleagues and others. In addition to my duties in this House, I shall be having further meetings today.

Mr. Tyler: Is the Prime Minister aware of the disgraceful shortage of prison officers caused by the Home Office's present policy?

The Prime Minister: I refer the hon. Gentleman to the speech I made in this House on 26 April last.

Q2. Sir Fred Broadhurst asked the Prime Minister if he will list his official engagements for Thursday 15 November.

The Prime Minister: I refer the hon. Gentleman to the reply that I gave some moments ago.

Sir Fred Broadhurst: Will the Prime Minister assure me that the Department of Employment does not periodically re-structure the base from which unemployment statistics are derived, without drawing public attention to the fact?

The Prime Minister: I am happy to assure the hon. Gentleman that I have found no significant evidence of it.

Q3. Mrs. Huxley asked the Prime Minister if he will list his official engagements for Thursday 15 November.

The Prime Minister: I refer the hon. Lady to the reply that I gave some moments ago.

Mrs. Huxley: Will the Prime Minister confirm that the Cabinet is unable to agree on the Department of Energy's plans for the disposal of nuclear waste?

The Prime Minister: That is not so. My Cabinet took a unanimous decision. [HON. MEMBERS: "Hear, hear."]

Q4. Mr. Allgrove asked the Prime Minister if he will list his official engagements for Thursday 15 November.

The Prime Minister: I refer the hon. Gentleman to the reply that I gave some moments ago.

Mr. Allgrove: Will the Prime Minister find the time today to consider why, despite all the money spent on the new anti-missile missile, it was scrapped as obsolete the day before the first one came off the production line?

The Prime Minister: Our policy has not been as effective as we'd hoped – [*Interruption.*] – as we'd hoped, and clearly we got it wrong. [*Laughter.*]

The Leader of the Opposition (Mr. ~~George~~ Hedley): So when will the Prime Minister request the resignation of the Minister responsible?

The Prime Minister: The right hon. Gentleman well knows that I will ask for my right hon. Friend's resignation when he makes a mistake that could have been seen at the time, not with the benefit of hindsight.

Many Hon. Members *rose and cheered* –

Mr. Speaker: Order.

Mr. Chapman: On a point of order, Mr. Speaker.

Mr. Speaker: I will take points of order in their usual place.

Q5. Mr. Gill asked the Prime Minister if he will list his official engagements for Thursday 15 November.

The Prime Minister: I refer my hon. Friend to the reply that I gave some moments ago.

Mr. Gill: Will my right hon. Friend assure the House that the Government is not and has not been tapping hon. Members' telephones?

The Prime Minister: Much as I respect and value the opinion of this House, I must confess to having no desire to listen to the words of hon. Members for any longer than I actually have to. [*Laughter.*]

The Leader of the Opposition: Is the Prime Minister really saying that the hon. Member for Aintree (Mr. Halifax) has not had his phone – [*Interruption.*] – has not had his

PPS, a member of my own Administration, I can't think where he got such a daft idea.' With hindsight I realised that this reply may sound foolish, but I had no reason at all to suspect the truth. Humphrey tried to interrupt me but I didn't listen. After all, how could I have known that I didn't know?

'Can you imagine?' I said, brushing Humphrey aside, metaphorically that is. 'Why should we want to listen in on an MP? Boring, ignorant, self-opinionated windbags, I do my best *not* to listen to them. And Hugh's only a PPS, I mean, *I* have enough trouble finding out what's going on at the Ministry of Defence, what could *he* know? It's my idea of Hell. That's how God will punish me if I've led a wicked life – he'll make me sit and listen to tapes of MPs talking.'

I must admit I was pretty pleased with myself. Humphrey was not amused. 'So I gather you denied that Mr Halifax has been bugged?'

'Yes,' I said. 'It was the one question today to which I could give a simple, clear, straightforward, honest answer.'

At which point Humphrey ranted for some considerable while. And I simply couldn't understand him, try as I might.

[*Fortunately, Sir Humphrey made a note of his comments in his private diary that very day – Ed.*]

I explained to the Prime Minister that unfortunately, although the answer was indeed simple, clear and straightforward, there was some difficulty in justifiably assigning to it the fourth of the epithets he had applied to the statement [*honest – Ed.*] inasmuch as the precise correlation between the information he had communicated and the facts insofar as they can be determined and demonstrated is such as to cause epistemological problems of sufficient magnitude to lay upon the logical and semantic resources of the English language a heavier burden than they can reasonably be requested to bear. [*Appleby Papers TK/3787/SW*]

Opposite: Prime Minister's Question Time from Hansard.

Thursday 15 NOVEMBER

I explained to the
Prime Minister that
unfortunately, although
the answer was indeed
simple, clear and
straightforward, there
was some difficulty in
justifiably assigning to
it the fourth of the
epithets he had applied
to the statement
inasmuch as the precise
correlation between the
information he had

[*Hacker's diary continues – Ed.*]

I realised that he was wrapping up whatever he was trying to say in the hope that it would be less hurtful or embarrassing or something. But I had to ask for a translation.

He nerved himself up for his reply. He looked at the floor, the ceiling, out of the window – and finally his eyes met mine. 'You told a lie,' he said.

I couldn't believe my ears. 'A lie?'

'A lie,' he repeated.

'What do you mean, a lie?' I simply couldn't understand what he could be referring to.

'I mean, Prime Minister . . .' he hesitated, apparently searching for a way to explain himself, '. . . you . . . lied!'

I didn't know what he was talking about. I stared at him blankly. He tried again. 'Um . . . I know that this is a difficult concept to get across to a politician, but . . . you did not tell the truth.'

Could he mean, I asked myself, that we *are* bugging Hugh Halifax? I didn't know the answer, so I asked him.

He nodded. 'We were.'

'We *were*?' I was appalled. 'When did we stop?'

Humphrey glanced at his wristwatch. 'Seventeen minutes ago.'

I was hurt, and upset that my integrity had been impugned in this manner. 'You can't call that lying,' I complained.

'I see.' Humphrey inclined his head to one side and stared at me hopefully, like a Bearded Collie that is eager to learn. 'What would you call the opposite of telling the truth?'

'There was no intent. I didn't mean to deceive them. I would never knowingly mislead the House.'

[*Hacker, in his state of outraged innocence, had clearly forgotten that he had proudly admitted to misleading the House several times that day. Nonetheless, it is almost certainly true that he would never intentionally have lied to the House, for fear of the consequences. Indeed, for reasons that are quite unclear to the historian, lying appears to be the one offence that the House does not forgive, trivial though it is in comparison to the many great calamities that our politicians inflict upon us – Ed.*]

'Nonetheless,' said Humphrey, 'you did tell them an untruth.'

'But it's not my fault!' He couldn't seem to understand. 'I didn't know he was being bugged.'

Bernard coughed quietly to attract my attention. 'Prime Minister,' he explained sympathetically, 'it's not enough to say you didn't know. You are deemed to have known. You are ultimately responsible.'

Now I was getting angry. 'So why the hell wasn't I told?'

Bernard looked at Humphrey. They were both pretty embarrassed. 'The Home Secretary', mumbled Humphrey, 'might not have felt the need to inform you.'

'Why?'

'Perhaps because he was advised that you didn't need to know.'

This is ludicrous. 'But I *did* need to know,' I pointed out.

At this point *Bernard* took refuge in Civil Service gibberish. He's spending too much time with Humphrey. I haven't the foggiest notion of what he was trying to say.

SIR BERNARD WOOLLEY RECALLS:[1]

I recall what I said only too well. Briefly I explained that the fact that Hacker needed to know was not known at the time that the now known need to know was known and therefore those who needed to advise and inform the Home Secretary perhaps felt that the information that he needed as to whether or not to inform the highest authority of the known information was not yet known and therefore there was no authority for the authority to be informed because the need to know was not at this time known. Or needed.

I should have thought that my explanation was crystal clear but, alas! not to Hacker. Perhaps he couldn't assimilate what I was saying because he was in such a blue funk.

[Hacker's diary continues – Ed.]

I needed a translation. I turned to Humphrey, of all people! He provided it.

'Perhaps the Home Secretary didn't know either. And we assumed that, if you were asked a question in the House, you would stall, or you'd say you had no knowledge, or that you would look into it. We didn't know, we couldn't *possibly* have known, Prime Minister, that you would take the novel step of actually answering a question.'

I could see his point. But I'd evaded and stalled on the previous four questions, I had to give a straight answer to this one. And this seemed safe.

Humphrey was sympathetic. 'Yes, but we couldn't know you'd answer it. And that in the House you would actually deny all bugging.'

'Obviously I would, if I didn't know and I were asked.'

Humphrey said: 'We didn't know you would be asked when you didn't know.'

An idiotic argument. I explained that I was *bound* to be asked when I didn't know if I didn't know. But he didn't seem to understand. Sometimes old Humphrey's a bit slow-witted. It's lucky he's not in politics.

[1] In conversation with the Editors.

Humphrey continued trying to justify his totally unjustifiable position. And in an impatient tone that I did not altogether care for. 'Prime Minister, it was thought it was better for you not to know. Mr Halifax is a member of your government team and as such it was felt that it might be better not to create distrust. We only tell you if you should be aware.'

'When's that?' I asked.

'Well . . . you should *now* be aware because you've just denied it.'

'It would have been somewhat better if I'd been aware *before* I denied it.'

Humphrey didn't see it that way. 'On the contrary, if you'd been aware *before* you denied it, you *wouldn't* have denied it!'

'But', I exclaimed passionately, 'I needed to know!'

'That is not the criterion.' Humphrey was stubbornly insistent that he was right. 'We don't tell you about bugging when you need to know, we only tell you when you *know* you need to know.'

'Or when you need to know that you need to know,' said Bernard.

'Or when *we* know that you need to know,' said Humphrey.

'You see,' added Bernard helpfully, 'at times it is needed for you to need not to know.'

'*That's enough!*' I shouted. Startled, they fell silent at once, staring at me, puzzled. 'Why?' I shouted at Humphrey. 'Why did you decide that I shouldn't know?'

'I didn't,' he said, sounding rather offended.

I was baffled. 'Then who did?'

'Nobody.'

I was getting desperate. 'Then why didn't I know?'

'Because nobody decided to tell you,' Humphrey said.

'That's the same thing, dammit!'

Humphrey had now resorted to his icy-calm-I'm-dealing-with-a-dangerous-lunatic voice. 'No, Prime Minister, it's not. To decide to conceal information from you is a serious burden for any official to shoulder, but to decide not to reveal information to you is routine procedure.'

I told Humphrey that I wanted to know everything.

'Everything, Prime Minister?'

'Everything!'

'Very well.' He consulted one of his files. 'Stationery deliveries this week to the Cabinet Office comprise four gross packets of size two paperclips, 600 reams of A4 cut bank typing paper, nine dozen felt-tipped . . .'

413

He was being silly. 'Important things!' I snarled.

'So who should decide what is important?' he asked with deceptive innocence.

'I should,' I said, and then realised that I was about to be given a list of stationery supplies again. 'No, you should,' I said, and then realised the pitfalls *there*. There seemed to be no answer. Angrily, I asked him to tell me, very simply, how he could possibly excuse this cock-up.

'As you said in the House,' he replied smoothly, 'clearly we got it wrong.'

Imitation is the sincerest form of flattery, but this was flattery that I could do without. 'I got it wrong' is an inadequate excuse for dropping the Prime Minister in the shit.

'I am merely a humble servant,' continued the least humble servant whom I've ever encountered. 'A lowly official. It was the Home Secretary's decision.'

Was it indeed? I might have guessed. He's never liked me. 'Can you think of any reason why I shouldn't ask him to resign?'

Impudently he replied, 'With respect, Prime Minister, perhaps you should not ask him to resign until he makes a mistake that could have been seen at the time, not with the benefit of hindsight. Besides, the trouble today has arisen as a result of your own error of judgement in making this denial.'

I was shocked by his brazen impertinence. 'What?' I said. I was literally speechless. [*We refrain from further comment – Ed.*]

'You should not have denied something about which you were not informed,' he lectured me self-righteously.

I couldn't believe my ears. 'But it's your fault!' I shouted. 'You've just admitted keeping secrets from the Prime Minister.'

Now he was indignant. 'Not at all. The system works perfectly well as long as the Prime Minister tells the Civil Service anything he intends to say before he says it. But if precipitately he says something without first clearing it with his officials he only has himself to blame. You should never say anything in public without clearing it. With respect, Prime Minister, you must learn discretion.'

I've never heard such an incredibly circular argument. 'But I didn't *know*, Humphrey, that there was anything to be discreet *about*!'

'In government, Prime Minister, there is always something to be discreet about.'

A new question suddenly occurred to me. I can't think why I never thought of it before. 'But Humphrey . . . why *were* we bugging Hugh

Halifax? Was he talking to the Russian Embassy?'

'No,' said Humphrey. 'The French Embassy. Which is much more serious.'

'Why?'

'The Russians already know what we're doing,' said Bernard.

But the French are our allies, whatever we think of them – and who doesn't!

[*It is well for the readers to remember that the Foreign Office has three national groups that it loves:*

a) *The Arabs*
b) *The Germans*
c) *The Americans*

And three nationalities that it hates:

a) *The Russians*
b) *The Israelis*
c) *The French*

It hates the French most of all. This is why talking directly to the French is regarded as prima facie an act of treason by the FO[1] *– Ed.*]

'Who authorised it?' I asked. 'Which officials authorised this bugging?'

'The Foreign Office. I just said!' He hadn't just said! And I'd never realised they had the power to authorise buggings. I suppose they can, since they control MI6, but they can't officially authorise surveillance since MI6 does not officially exist. I suppose Foreign Office official officials unofficially authorised MI6's unofficial officials.

Humphrey wanted to bring the discussion to a close. 'Prime Minister, the less said the better, wouldn't you agree?'

I was confused. 'About what?'

'About everything.'

[*Sir Humphrey's wish to say no more about the Hugh Halifax bugging was not to be fulfilled. Shortly afterwards he received a letter from a House of Commons committee, asking him to appear before it to discuss the matter. Sir Humphrey sent the letter to Jim Hacker, with a note asking for Hacker's advice on how to handle it. Hacker sent the following reply, which was released under the Thirty Year Rule – Ed.*]

---

[1] This also explains why the Suez invasion was such a diplomatic trauma for the Foreign Office: the Cabinet sided with the French and Israelis against the Arabs and Americans.

10 DOWNING STREET

THE PRIME MINISTER

November 21

Dear Humphrey,

You can hardly refuse to appear before a Committee of the House. And obviously you must tell them everything that you must tell them.[1] I'm sure you will find something appropriate to say.

yours truly
Jim

---

[1] Sir Humphrey would understand this to mean everything that the Committee could find out from some other source.

SIR BERNARD WOOLLEY RECALLS:[1]

Sir Humphrey called me into his office and showed me the Prime Minister's letter. Of course it offered no answer. Sir Humphrey was concerned with how a loyal public servant should reply if the Committee were to ask him if the Prime Minister had ever authorised the tapping of an MP's telephone. And it was highly likely that the question would indeed be asked.

I suggested that he say it was not a question for him, but for the Prime Minister, the Home Secretary or the Foreign Office.

'Or the British Telecom Service Engineer's Department?' he enquired sardonically.

Clearly I had not given him the answer he wished to hear. So I suggested the usual safety-net catch-all reply: that it's a security matter, and therefore I'm not at liberty to divulge, confirm or deny, et cetera.

Humphrey sighed. 'Bernard, do you think I am unaware of these options?'

Naturally he was aware of them. But he explained that it was a trap: if he dodged the question about the Prime Minister authorising telephone tapping, the follow-up question was bound to be: *Why will you not give the same clear denial that the Prime Minister gave the House yesterday*? To which there was no safe answer.

I made a suggestion to Humphrey: 'You could say that the Prime Minister knows more about it than you do.'

'Then they'd *know* I was lying,' said Humphrey. This was unarguable.

I'm ashamed to admit that, in my eagerness to help, I even suggested that Humphrey simply deny the accusation. Like Hacker had done.

Humphrey, to his credit, was rather shocked. 'You mean lie?'

'No one can prove it's a lie,' I said.

Humphrey appeared to be very disappointed in me. 'So anything is true, so long as one can disprove it? You're talking like a politician, Bernard.'

Indeed I was. And I must tell you that if Humphrey had been *sure* that his statement could not have been disproved, he too would have talked like a politician and denied that the phone had been tapped. My suggestion was bad not because it was misleading but because it was dangerous.

Still, after that reproof from on high I felt disinclined to offer any further suggestions.

At that uncomfortable moment the phone rang. It was the BBC. But it wasn't about the phone tapping. Of all things, they wanted to interview old Humphrey for a Radio 3 documentary on the structure of government. He seemed quite ridiculously pleased. He wanted to accept! Now it was my turn to be shocked. A Civil Servant giving a public interview? How *could* he? And he seemed to have no qualms.

I felt obliged to remind him of the risk. 'They might want you to say things.'

[1] In conversation with the Editors.

417

'That's quite normal on radio.' A facetious, evasive and misleading reply. He knew that it was against all the traditions of the Service to speak on the radio. For a start, one might make a slip and find oneself saying something interesting. Or even controversial.

But times were changing. Civil Servants were beginning to come out of the closet (is that the phrase?). He claimed that he had an obligaton to do it because of his duty to put the record straight. I, for my part, was not aware that the record was crooked.

'It's not for oneself!' He was protesting too much, methinks! 'I have no inclination to become a celebrity. That's just petty vanity. But one can be *too* self-effacing.'

I didn't see how. I told him that my understanding of the Civil Service was that we were supposed to be faceless.

'They don't show your face on radio.'

I was tiring of this self-serving, dishonest claptrap. I could well see how he would fall for such a dangerously seductive offer as a discussion programme on Radio 3, but I really did feel he ought to know better. 'Anonymity,' I reminded him. 'Service. Discretion.'

Embarrassed, he poured himself a glass of Tio Pepe [*It must have been after 6.00 pm – Ed.*]. 'Bernard, they said that if I couldn't do it, Arnold[1] has said that he would.'

'Perhaps that would be better,' I said. Humphrey's eyebrows shot up. But I wasn't being rude. It's just that Sir Arnold was retired, and could therefore not reveal anything much any more, certainly not about current events. Furthermore, he was now President of the Campaign for Freedom of Information and fully committed to opening up government – so long as it was in the national interest!

Humphrey had never got over his jealousy of Arnold, and he yearned for public recognition. But he would rather die than admit it. I'll never forget his lame excuse: 'For myself, Bernard, I'd rather not do this interview, *of course*. But I think one's sense of duty compels one to ensure that Arnold is not held up as an example of a top Civil Servant.'

I pointed out to Humphrey that he would need the Prime Minister's permission. He was momentarily concerned about this. But I took pleasure in adding that in my view there'd be no problem with the Prime Minister because, as it was for Radio 3, no one would be listening anyway.

[*It must have been very galling for Permanent Secretaries at this period of British history. A meritocracy of brilliant men who occupied forty-two of the most powerful jobs in the country, although highly paid and festooned with honours, were nonetheless deeply deserving of sympathy – for by tradition and to their own advantage, they were*

---

[1] Sir Arnold Robinson, Sir Humphrey's predecessor as Secretary of the Cabinet.

virtually unknown. To most British people a Permanent Secretary was the opposite of a 'temp', at best a senior clerical assistant. This is perhaps the reason that Sir Humphrey was quite unable to resist the invitation to speak on the radio, a boost that his ego undoubtedly needed – Ed.]

[Hacker's diary continues – Ed.]

November 26th
Humphrey popped in to see me this morning, looking incredibly tense and nervy. At first I thought some new crisis was about to hit me, but then I remembered it was the day of his radio interview.

I told him not to worry, and he pompously denied that he was anxious. 'I have some experience in dealing with difficult questions.'

'Yes,' I agreed, 'but if you're too evasive or confusing on radio they just edit you out. You actually have to say something.'

He looked blank. 'Say something?' He didn't understand.

'Something simple and interesting,' I explained.

His hand started shaking. 'Simple and interesting,' he repeated, then licked his dry lips. 'Well . . . er, if you have any advice . . . especially if the questions are aggressive.'

I explained that dealing with an aggressive question is like dealing with fast bowling – unless it's deadly accurate you can use its own momentum to help you score. 'The more aggressive the questions are, the better. They'll put the listeners on your side.'

'But nonetheless I may have to answer them.'

'Why?' I asked. 'You've never answered my questions.'

'That's different, Prime Minister,' he replied. 'I may be asked some perceptive questions.'

I glared at him, 'Humphrey,' I asked rhetorically, 'why are you doing this interview? To explain the Civil Service point of view, presumably. So you must do what I do – go in with something to say, and say it. Simply ask yourself whatever question you want to reply to.'

'Fearlessly and honestly,' agreed Bernard encouragingly, who had clearly taken to heart the lessons I'd given him a few months ago.

'Or', I continued, 'if you want more control you say, "That's really two separate questions." Then, fearlessly and honestly, ask yourself *two* questions you want to answer, and answer them.'

Humphrey dried his wet palms on his handkerchief. 'Their researcher mentioned that a lot of people want to know about why so much power is centralised in my hands.'

419

'A lot of people?' I tried not to smile. 'Most people have never heard of you, Humphrey.'

He didn't look awfully encouraged by that insight.

'Perhaps they mean a lot of Radio 3 listeners,' Bernard wondered.

'That's a contradiction in terms,' I said amiably. 'But if they do ask that question, what should he reply, Bernard?'

'Name six of them,' answered Bernard promptly. He's a good student.

'That's right,' I said. 'Because then you've got him. He'll never think of more than two, see?'

Humphrey smiled for the first time. 'I see, Prime Minister. Bernard, how did you know that?'

Bernard said, 'The Prime Minister taught me a few tricks of the trade after my unfortunate talk with those reporters last August – the time I inadvertently said that when it came to official secrets the Prime Minister was above the law.'

'I see.' He turned to me. 'Any other tricks, Prime Minister?'

I turned to Bernard. 'Yes,' he said. 'Attack one word in the question. You know: "*Frequently*? What do you mean, *frequently*?" Or you can attack the interviewer: "You obviously haven't read the White Paper." Or you can ask a question back: "That's a very good question. Now let me ask you one: when did you last visit a decentralised government department, such as the Vehicle Licensing Centre in Swansea?" And if you're desperate you can always use security as an excuse for not answering.'

'Well *done*, Bernard!' I congratulated him. 'You'll go far.'

But something else had just come to Humphrey's mind. 'That reminds me, Prime Minister – I'm afraid that I must appear soon before the Committee to answer questions on the alleged bugging of Hugh Halifax MP.'

I knew that. Bernard had already told me. 'You'll just have to confirm what I said in the House.'

He feigned incomprehension. 'But that would be lying.'

I shrugged. 'No one would know.'

'Oh, what a tangled web we weave . . .' He's so mealy-mouthed!

'Come off it Humphrey,' I snapped.

He had assumed his butter-wouldn't-melt-in-my-mouth choirboy face. 'I'm sorry, Prime Minister, I cannot tell a lie.'

I couldn't believe that he could do this to me. 'But Humphrey!' I found to my horror that I was pleading with him! 'If you don't, it will look as if *I* was lying.'

He pursed his lips and remained silent. Clearly he didn't feel that was his problem. I lost my temper. 'Humphrey!' I thundered. 'You have a loyalty!'

'To the truth,' he agreed primly.

I was up from my chair now, pacing up and down the full length of the Cabinet Room. 'But . . .' I was lost for words. 'But . . . you can't just go in there and shop me in front of all the press and the Opposition. When it wasn't even my fault. You must back me up. You must!'

He refused to meet my eye. 'You make it very hard for me, Prime Minister,' was his totally unsatisfactory response.

'Humphrey,' I said firmly, 'I am ordering you to confirm what I said in the House.'

He stared at me insolently. 'Very well, Prime Minister, I will tell them that you have ordered me to confirm it.'

That was hardly what I meant! 'Humphrey, I order you not to tell them I ordered you.'

He was implacable. 'Then I shall have to tell them you have ordered me not to tell them you ordered me.'

I glowered at him. I was bloody furious. He was icy and superior as only he can be. 'I'm sorry, Prime Minister, I cannot become involved in some shabby cover-up.'

Treacherous, disloyal bastard.

[*Sir Humphrey drove from Number 10 Downing Street directly to Broadcasting House, where he gave his first-ever radio interview. Only one copy of the recording now exists, not at the BBC itself but in Sir Humphrey Appleby's own private archive. With the kind permission of Lady Appleby, his widow, we gained access to the strongroom of the Midland Bank in Haslemere, and we made a transcript of the recording, the relevant portion of which we print below – Ed.*]

Sir Humphrey: Whereas there must inevitably be some element of shared responsibility for the governance of Britain as between the legislators on the one hand and the adminstrators on the other, the precise allocation of cause to consequence, or agency to eventuality, in any particular instance is invariably so complex as to be ultimately invalid, if not irresponsible.

[*It seems that Sir Humphrey was not able to keep his answers either simple or interesting, as Hacker had correctly advised him – Ed.*]

Interviewer: Yes. If I could press you for a more precise answer or a concrete example, how much blame can the Civil Service take for the present level of unemployment?

Sir Humphrey: Well, of course, unemployment is a single name applied by the media to what is in effect a wide range of socio-economic phenomena whose most politically viable manifestation happens to be . . .

Interviewer (interrupting): But to be precise, how much blame . . .?

Sir Humphrey: One moment. Happens to be a current frequency of weekly registrations on the national unemployment register which is deemed to be above what has historically been held to be an acceptable level. But even separating out the component causes, let alone allocating the responsibility for them, is a task of such analytical delicacy as not to be susceptible of compression within the narrow confines of a popular radio programme such as this.

[*Sir Humphrey Appleby's notion that a Radio 3 talks programme was popular suggests a very slight acquaintance with the listening figures. Alternatively, Sir Humphrey may have used the word popular to suggest that it was heard by those outside the top ranks of the Civil Service. One wonders, if that was a popular programme, what an unpopular programme would have been like – Ed.*]

Interviewer: Sir Humphrey Appleby, thank you very much.

[*At this point, when the interview apparently ended, it is possible to hear the bored but polite voice of the Producer – Ed.*]

Producer (over studio intercom): Thank you very much, Sir Humphrey. Absolutely splendid.

[*And now the conversation continues, the tape still running even after the interview is finished – Ed.*]

Sir Humphrey: Was that all right?

Interviewer: Couldn't you have said a little more? At least about unemployment?

Sir Humphrey: Such as?

Interviewer: Well, the truth.

Sir Humphrey laughs.

Interviewer: Why do you laugh?

Sir Humphrey: My dear chap, no one tells the truth about unemployment.

Interviewer: Why not?

Sir Humphrey: Because everyone knows you could halve it in a few weeks.

Interviewer: How?

Sir Humphrey: Cut off all social security to any claimant who refused two job offers. There is genuine unemployment in the north, but the south of England is awash with layabouts, many of them graduates, living off the dole and housing benefit plus quite a lot of cash they pick up without telling anyone.

Interviewer: You mean moonlighting.

Sir Humphrey: Well, it's cheating really. They'd need to earn nearly £200 a week to be better off working full time. But there are thousands upon thousands of unfilled vacancies and most employers tell you they're short-staffed. Offer the unemployed a street-sweeping job and a dishwashing job, and they'd be off the register before you can say 'parasite'. Frankly, this country can have as much unemployment as it's prepared to pay for in social security. And no politicians have the guts to do anything about it.

Interviewer: I wish you'd said that before.

Sir Humphrey: I'm sure you do.

[*The tape ends at this point. Sir Bernard Woolley recalls*[1] *the tape's progress – Ed.*]

The following day Sir Humphrey had asked me to obtain a cassette player, so that he could listen to a cassette that the BBC had sent to him. He was rather excited, because he felt that he had given a thought-provoking, dynamic and thoroughly exciting interview, albeit couched in his usual low-key language.

I had borrowed a ghettoblaster from one of the Garden Room Girls [*the upper-crust members of the typing pool in the basement of Number Ten – Ed.*]. Sir Humphrey had not heard the word ghettoblaster, and enquired if it was used in the demolition industry. How true – the demolition of hearing!

There had been a note attached to the cassette. [*We reproduce it overleaf – Ed.*]

[1] In conversation with the Editors.

Sir Humphrey Appleby
Cabinet Office
70 Whitehall
London SW1   November 27th

Dear Sir Humphrey,

Here is a copy of the off-the-record part of your radio
interview. We found it particularly interesting. I will
contact you shortly.

Yours sincerely,

Crawford James

Crawford James
(Producer, Talks)

The letter struck me as suspicious, for several reasons. Firstly, it seemed to be less than straightforward. What could he mean by 'particularly interesting'? Secondly, I have always had an instinctive distrust of people whose Christian names and surnames are reversible. But when I expressed surprise that his interview could be described as interesting, Sir Humphrey took umbrage – though I don't know why, because his stated intention had been to say nothing, as always.

I had doubted his ability to say nothing on the radio, and the letter had prepared me for a surprise. But not for a surprise of the magnitude that I then encountered. For we switched on the ghettoblaster and I heard a voice that sounded horribly like Humphrey's saying, 'My dear chap, no one tells the truth about unemployment.'

'Why not?' came the question.

'Because', said Humphrey's voice, 'everyone knows you could halve it in a few weeks.'

I looked at Humphrey in horror. He looked at me, poleaxed.

'How?' continued the inexorable tape recording.

'Cut off all social security to any claimant who refused two job offers.'

Humphrey lunged at the ghettoblaster. I think he was trying to switch it off but he pressed *fast forward* by mistake. His voice mickey-moused forward at high speed until he let go of the switch – at which point we heard the fatal words: 'And no politicians have the guts to do anything about it.'

I leaned forward and switched it off myself. We gazed at each other for a long time, in total silence. For the first time I was aware of the distant hum of traffic on the Mall.

Finally I spoke. I had to be sure. 'Sir Humphrey,' I asked quietly, 'that was you, wasn't it?'

'Yes, Bernard.'

'Not Mike Yarwood?'[1]

A faint ray of hope crossed his haggard visage. 'Do you think I could say it was?'

I shook my head gloomily. 'No, they could prove it was you,' I said. I could hardly believe that he had said those things. I asked if there was more. He nodded mutely.

'As damaging as we just heard?'

He nodded again. He seemed unable to speak. But I waited patiently and eventually he croaked, with the voice of a broken man: 'More damaging. I believe I referred to parasites.'

I was incredulous. I asked him how he could have been so indiscreet. He explained pathetically that the interview was over – so he thought! – and that they were just chatting harmlessly. Harmlessly!

'It was off the record,' he said.

'Maybe – but it's on the tape,' I remarked.

[1] A well-known impressionist of the 1980s.

Suddenly, uttering an anguished cry of 'My God!', Humphrey smote his forehead and leapt to his feet. 'Oh my God, oh my God!' he moaned desperately. 'I've just realised. It's blackmail!' And he grasped the letter and shoved it into my hand.

I re-read the ominous document. It certainly looked like blackmail. My suspicions appeared to have been well-founded.

Humphrey stared at me, hollow-eyed, his tie crooked, his hair – usually so immaculately brushed and neatly parted – standing up on end as if he had been awoken at 3.41 am by the ghost of Stanley Baldwin.

'What do they want of me?' he moaned.

I pondered the question carefully. What did the BBC want of Humphrey? What did it want of anyone? This was one of the abiding mysteries of the twentieth century, not to be solved at such short notice by such a one as I.

I tried to think politically, always difficult for someone like myself who has spent a lifetime in the Civil Service. Perhaps, I wondered, the BBC wanted the licence up fifty per cent? Or maybe it was a *private* blackmail by the Producer/Talks, to ensure that the Producer *didn't* talk.

Humphrey was crumbling before my eyes. A piteous sight. He sank into a Chippendale armchair and leaned forward, his head in his hands. 'Doesn't he know I'm a poor man?' he cried.

I wondered. It occurred to me that the Producer/Talks may not have read that Sir Humphrey lived in Haslemere in abject poverty on seventy-five thousand a year.

'What'll I do?' Sir Humphrey, wide-eyed and terrified, was staring ruin in the face.

'Keep your mouth shut in future,' I advised him.

'I mean *now*!' he snapped, staring *me* in the face instead.

I didn't see what he could do, except wait and hope. Wait to see what they demanded. Hope that they hadn't yet distributed cassettes to every national newspaper. I had private visions and horrid imaginings of horrific headlines. CABINET SECRETARY CALLS UNEMPLOYED PARASITES, or GOVERNMENT HAS NO GUTS, SAYS SIR HUMPHREY.

I shared my visions with him. He sat there, stunned, begging me not to breathe a word about it to anyone.

I was perfectly willing not to spread it around Whitehall generally, even though I could have dined out on it for months. But Humphrey's 'anyone' appeared to include the Prime Minister, and I was forced to point out that my duty to him was paramount.

Humphrey tried to regain his authority. He stood up, and faced me squarely. 'Bernard, I am ordering you!'

'Very good, Sir Humphrey,' I replied. 'I shall tell him that you have ordered me not to tell him.'

Hoist by his own petard, he acknowledged defeat, sat down, leaned back and asked the ceiling what he was going to do.

Although he did not appear to be addressing me, hesitantly I offered the only suggestion that I could think of: that he put out a press statement expressing sympathy for the unemployed. After all, he was likely to be joining them at any moment.

[*Hacker's diary continues – Ed.*]

November 28th
I was sitting in the Cabinet Room, all alone, thinking, when Bernard interrupted me.

I asked him what he wanted.

'Excuse me a moment, Prime Minister, but as you don't appear to be doing anything I wondered if I might have a word.'

I gave him an unwelcome stare. 'As a matter of fact,' I replied curtly, 'I am busy. I'm wondering whether to tell the Cabinet about this bugging business. Do I tell them what I told the House, or do I tell them the truth?'

Bernard did not hesitate. 'Prime Minister, may I venture to suggest that perhaps you should behave to the Cabinet as you would expect them to behave to you?'

'You're absolutely right,' I told Bernard. 'I'll tell them what I told the House.'

I returned to the mass of papers on the table and was just starting to read an eighty-page briefing about possible replacements for the anti-missile missile when I heard Bernard cough. He was still there, obviously wanting to get something off his chest.

'What's the matter now, Bernard?'

'Yes, there is a matter, that you need to know.'

Suddenly I was on the alert. 'Need to know?'

I didn't quite gather what he said next. Why is it that both Bernard and Humphrey are pathologically incapable of making themselves clear whenever we're talking about 'need to know' matters? They seem bent on telling me things in such a way that they haven't actually told me at all.

SIR BERNARD WOOLLEY RECALLS:[1]
I was certainly not intending to be oblique in my speech, though I was fairly highly strung. I have looked up my own diaries. All I said was that Hacker needed to know, particularly because Sir Humphrey had particularly asked me to be discreet about the particulars of this particular matter. I reminded

[1] In conversation with the Editors.

427

Hacker that he [Hacker] knew that Humphrey was very particular, particularly about what Hacker needed to know and what Humphrey needed Hacker to know, which he thought he didn't. Need Hacker to know, that is.

I should have thought that was perfectly clear.

[Hacker's diary continues – Ed.]

It appeared that my Private Secretary was talking about Sir Humphrey's radio broadcast. 'Was it boring?'

'Initially, yes,' said Bernard. 'But then it livened up immensely as he became more and more indiscreet.'

I could hardly believe my ears. 'Humphrey? Indiscreet? On the air?'

'Well, he thought the broadcast was over, so he was just chatting. Unofficially. But the tape was still running.'

I began to have a sinking feeling in my stomach. And my heart was literally in my mouth. [*If so, Hacker had a uniquely mobile anatomy – Ed.*] 'He fell for that old dodge?'

Bernard nodded.

'You *always* treat an open microphone as a live one. Doesn't he know that?'

Bernard tried to defend him. 'I don't think he's done a lot of broadcasting, Prime Minister.'

'It sounds as if he's done too much,' I complained. 'Have you heard the tape?'

'A copy, yes.'

'What did he say?'

'Something about it being possible to halve unemployment tomorrow, only the government hasn't got the guts.'

I was so horrified that I wasn't even angry. I just sat and stared.

Bernard tried to explain. 'He didn't know it was being recorded.'

The hideous implications were racing through my head. If the BBC kept the original, which Bernard seemed to believe as they'd sent Humphrey 'a copy', it meant that the story would be all over the papers tomorrow. Yet Bernard didn't seem at all concerned. He simply remarked that Humphrey had not given much thought to the newspapers – yet. He was more worried about the blackmail threat.

Blackmail threat? This was news to me.

'There was an accompanying letter, saying the sender would be in touch shortly. They sent the cassette to Sir Humphrey – which means they have kept the original reel-to-reel tape.'

I had visions of private pirate copies of the tape all over Broadcasting House by tomorrow. 'Bernard!' I said decisively, 'you must do something.'

'Actually, Prime Minister, I've done it already.'

I was not wholly surprised. He was so calm that I'd known that he had it under control somehow.

'I was at Oxford with the producer. When I rang the BBC he reminded me of this. I had not remembered him at all, but it appears that we had mutual friends and he had vivid memories of one of my speeches at the Union – I spoke eloquently in favour of the *status quo* one night. Apparently he was the unobtrusive little chap who used to record the debates. Anyway, it transpires that he never had the slightest intention of releasing the tape. So I got him to give it to me.'

Whereupon Bernard produced a spool of tape from his pocket.

'Is that the original?' Bernard nodded. 'There are no other copies?' He nodded again. 'And does Humphrey know you've got it?' Bernard shook his head. A slow smile of deep content spread across my face. And Bernard's.

'Shall I tell him?' he asked innocently.

'Why?' I enquired.

'I think . . .' Bernard was stepping carefully '. . . that he'd like to know.'

'I'm sure he would,' I countered. 'But does he need to know?'

'Ah,' replied Bernard. There was a gleam in his eye. He thought for a moment. Then he said – and I know because I got him to repeat it – 'You mean *somebody* needs to know, but if you now know then Sir Humphrey doesn't need to know and you need to know Sir Humphrey doesn't know, and he doesn't need to know you know or that you know he doesn't need to know?'

I stared at Bernard, marvelling at the uselessness of an education in logic. 'I couldn't have put it less clearly myself,' I said.

Bernard asked me if I'd like to hear the tape. Of course I was dying to – but then I got a great idea. 'I think it deserves a wider audience, don't you? I think Humphrey should hear it too. Ask him to join us, would you, Bernard?'

He didn't need to be asked twice. He hurried to the phone. 'Tell Sir Humphrey the Prime Minister wants him . . . straight away!'

He hung up and scurried out of the room gleefully to fetch the tape-recorder. On his return, as he threaded the tape from reel to reel, he reminded me that he had told me all this in confidence. It was unnecessary – I always respect confidences.

By now he was grinning from ear to ear. I tried to arrange my face into a solemn expression and told Bernard that this was a very serious matter.

'Yes Prime Minister,' he said, the corners of his mouth twitching.

There was a knock. Humphrey's head appeared round the door. 'You sent for me, Prime Minister?'

'Ah yes. Come in, Humphrey, come in. How did the broadcast go?'

He's not a bad liar. 'Very well. Very well.'

'Good, good,' I murmured amiably. 'Do you remember what you said?'

Sir Humphrey appeared to have only the vaguest recollections. 'Oh, nothing in particular,' he drawled. 'I think I pointed out some of the difficulties in allocating responsibilities as between politicians and civil servants.'

'But were you discreet?'

He cleared his throat. 'Why do you ask?'

'Were you or weren't you?'

A slight pause. 'Yes.'

'Yes you were or yes you weren't?'

'Yes.'

'Humphrey!'

He challenged me. 'Wouldn't you expect me to be discreet?'

'Yes, I would,' I said.

'There you are then,' he retorted, neatly begging the question.

'I see,' I said. 'Then that's all right.' And I treated him to one of my piercing stares.

He wriggled about in his chair, crossed his legs, uncrossed them, and cleared his throat again. 'Why do you ask, Prime Minister?' His voice sounded higher-pitched than usual.

'Because the BBC has just sent me a tape.' He flinched. I showed him the tape-recorder, set up on the table near the door. He hadn't seen it when he came in.

He swallowed. 'A tape? What tape?'

I pretended unconcern. 'Just a tape, Humphrey. Of you. I thought it might be fun for us to listen to your broadcast together.' And I walked towards the tape-recorder.

'No.' He stood up. 'No. No.'

I turned, as if surprised. 'Why not?'

'It . . . it wasn't at all interesting.'

I chuckled. 'Humphrey, you carry modesty and self-effacement too far. Not interesting? The Cabinet Secretary talking to the nation about government?'

His eyes were shifty. 'Well, not very interesting.'

'You mean,' I suggested, 'that you were *too* discreet?'

He was silent. He knew I knew. And I knew he knew I knew. And Bernard knew I knew he knew I knew. [*Hacker was spending too much time with Bernard Woolley – Ed.*] I switched on the tape.

I must say that even I was unprepared for the astounding remarks I heard. Sir Humphrey saying that no one tells the truth, that unemployment could be halved in a few weeks, talk of layabouts, moonlighting, and parasites.

I switched off the tape. And I stared at him in silence.

Never have I seen a more woebegone figure than the Secretary of the Cabinet and the Head of the Home Civil Service. He stared at me, unable – apparently – even to excuse himself. So I just waited. And finally he blurted out: 'Prime Minister, I'm terribly sorry, I had no idea, they didn't tell me. You see, we'd finished the broadcast and . . .'

I held up my hand for silence. 'Humphrey! The irresponsibility! Is there any more?'

'No,' said Humphrey.

'Yes,' said Bernard.

I said, 'We'd better hear it.'

'No,' said Humphrey.

Bernard restarted the tape. 'Frankly,' said Humphrey's cheerful, complacent voice, 'this country can have as much unemployment as it's prepared to pay for in social security. And no politicians have the guts to do anything about it.'

The tape stopped. Silence reigned supreme. I couldn't believe that Humphrey had been foolish enough to talk like that in public, even though *I* knew that it would never be broadcast.

'How could you say that?' I asked finally.

'I . . . I . . . it was Mike Yarwood,' he explained in a strangled voice.

'Was it?' I asked.

'No,' said Bernard.

I wandered from the table over to the window. The afternoon November sky was black and heavy with rain. 'I really don't know how to handle this,' I mused. 'I shall have to take advice.'

'Advice?' whispered Sir Humphrey.

'Yes,' I said, turning the knife in the wound. 'I think I'd better play it to the Cabinet. Get their reaction.'

431

He seemed on the verge of falling to his knees. But 'Oh please' was all he could say.

'Or the Privy Council,' I suggested.

'Oh please,' he begged.

'Or Her Majesty,' I said lightly.

'Oh God!' he groaned, and collapsed into a chair again.

I walked across the room and stood over him. 'Suppose this were to get into the papers? How much damage do you think it would do me? And the government?'

Humphrey, of course, still believed that it *would* get into the papers. 'I shall say I was wrong. That I've checked the figures and it's not true.'

'But it *is* true!' I hissed.

'But I can say it's not. Nobody can prove it. It's never been tried.'

I pretended shock. 'You would deny the truth? In public?'

'Yes Prime Minister. For you!' For me indeed!

He had other ideas. 'We could issue a clarification to the press.'

I indicated the tape. 'I think your views are quite clear.'

'Prime Minister, in government a clarification is not to make things clear, it is put you in the clear.'

'I don't think even a wizard such as yourself could do that here,' I said. 'But I'm touched that you would be willing to lie for me – and I'll take a raincheck on that. And now I've got something to tell you.' And I put him out of his misery. 'Bernard, give Humphrey the tape. Humphrey, this is the original. The master.'

It took him a moment or two to assimilate the news. 'You mean . . .'

'There are no other copies,' I reassured him. 'It has been retrieved from the BBC.'

'How? By whom?'

Bernard flashed a desperate, wide-eyed *remember your promise* look at me. But he needn't have worried.

'Intelligence,' I said calmly.

Bernard visibly relaxed.

'So – you mean it's all right?' asked Humphrey, hopeful but very subdued.

I didn't want to let him right off the hook. I had an important trade-off to offer. 'It depends what you mean by all right,' I said.

'Nobody will ever know?' That's what *he* meant. But I thought about his question, as he waited on tenterhooks.

'I suppose', I answered eventually, 'that depends on whether I choose to tell them. I mean, I could just hand you the tape . . . or I could hold on to it while I consider the security and disciplinary implications. I certainly can't become involved in some shabby cover-up.'

He was waiting for the verdict of the court. So I offered him my deal, casually. 'Oh Humphrey, one other thing. When do you appear before the Committee?'

'Tomorrow, Prime Minister.'

'And have you decided yet what to tell them? About my authorising the tapping of MPs' phones?'

'Oh. Yes. Yes. I've . . . er . . .' he tried to focus on his vague memories of that other problem, the tape recording having temporarily driven all else from his mind. 'I've been thinking about it a lot. Very hard.'

I asked him for his conclusions. They were not wholly surprising. 'I have concluded, Prime Minister, that in the interests of National Security the only honourable course is to support your statement in the House.'

I prompted him. 'You'll say that Hugh Halifax's phone was never bugged?'

'I'll say that I have no evidence that – '

I stopped him mid-sentence. 'No, Humphrey. You'll say that the Government has never authorised any tapping of MPs' phones.'

He breathed deeply. 'And I'll say that the Government has never authorised any tapping of MPs' phones.'

I smiled. He whispered: 'What happens if they ever find out the truth?'

I couldn't even see a problem there. 'You'll have to say that nobody told you. Because you didn't need to know. Agreed?'

He nodded. I handed him the tape. 'Is that settled then?'

'Yes Prime Minister,' he muttered, and clasped the spools of tape close to his heart.

The Patron of the Arts

December 3rd

'Do you think perhaps . . .' asked Bernard hesitantly, 'I mean, would it have been wiser? . . . you know, with hindsight, was it a mistake?'

'Yes Bernard,' I said.

We were discussing the British Theatre Awards, a really unimportant, self-serving, narcissistic gathering, and not one on which the time of the Prime Minister should be wasted.

But Malcolm, my press officer, Bernard and I had spent the best part of an hour wondering how to handle the hideous predicament in which I find myself.

The irony is, I certainly didn't have to agree to present these awards. Malcolm recommended it! He is denying that now, of course. 'With respect, Prime Minister, I didn't actually recommend it. I just said that the British Theatre Awards dinner was being televised live and that as the guest of honour you'd be seen by twelve million people in a context of glamour, fun and entertainment. And that you'd be associated with all the star actors and actresses who give pleasure to millions.'

'And you don't call that a recommendation?' I was incredulous. 'It was worth ten points in the opinion polls, the way you described it.'

Malcolm nodded mournfully. But Bernard was confused. 'Isn't it a bad idea to be associated with actors? I mean, their job is pretending to be what they're not. And if you're seen with them, well, people might realise . . .'

He stopped short. Might *realise*? I stared at him, daring him to continue. 'Go on, Bernard,' I invited him with menace.

He hesitated. 'Er, I mean, not *realise* exactly . . . might suspect, might think that you were . . . I mean, I don't mean they'd think you were *entertaining*, obviously not, I mean, they might see you were pretending . . . Um, what was it you wanted to speak to Malcolm about?' he finished desperately.

The problem would have been clear to anyone except an ivory-tower career Civil Servant like Bernard. Malcolm had assured me that it would be a non-controversial occasion: there would be no other politicians there, and actors and actresses are usually nice to politicians because they live on flattery and some of them dish it out as eagerly as they receive it.

But nobody had thought it through. Accusingly, I tapped the file in front of me. 'What about this?' I asked.

Malcolm was embarrassed. 'I'm sorry, Prime Minister, but we didn't know about that when we accepted the invitation.'

All I can say is, he *should* have known. He should have found out. That's what he's paid for. 'You knew the government was being criticised for not spending enough on the arts?'

He shrugged. 'All governments are always criticised for not spending enough on the arts.'

Bernard hastened to agree. 'It's the standard way for arts journalists to suck up to actors and directors. That's how they get back on speaking terms after they've given them bad reviews.'

'But you knew – or should have known – what the situation would be,' I insisted.

Malcolm stubbornly refused to concede the point. 'No, Prime Minister, we didn't know how small the Arts Council grant increase was going to be. How could we? It was only finalised yesterday.'

He was right. And it was my fault, though I didn't admit it – I had insisted on no leaks. Hoist by my own petard *again*. Yesterday the news broke that there'd be virtually no increase in grant for the National Theatre. And, by a hideous coincidence, the Chief Associate Director of the National Theatre is Chairman of the Awards Dinner, making the speech that introduces me, which will inevitably be full of snide remarks and sarcastic jokes, and which is bound to portray me as a mean-spirited Philistine. Live on TV, in front of twelve million people.

'What about when I make my speech?' I asked hopelessly. 'The audience will be totally hostile. There may even be boos.'

'There's always lots of boos,' said Malcolm. I was appalled. Was he serious? 'But we don't have to pay for it,' he continued reassuringly. I suddenly realised he meant booze, not boos.

'Booo!' I hooted in explanation, and added a 'Ssssss' for good measure.

Bernard was amazed. 'Do actors boo?' he asked, wide-eyed. 'I thought audiences did that.'

'It's an audience full of actors,' I reminded him. 'It's their only chance in the year to do any booing, to get their own back on all the people who boo them.'

Bernard made a suggestion. 'Why don't you go back to the Arts Minister and ask for an increase in the grant? Or, better still, send him along to the dinner instead of you. That way they'll all blame him. That's what junior ministers are for, isn't it?'

On the face of it, it was a smart idea. But on reflection I realised it wouldn't work. 'He'd just blame the Treasury.'

'You could talk to the Treasury,' countered Bernard.

I've been doing that. That's the problem. For six weeks I've been telling them to cut spending!

'It's still better to send the Arts Minister,' insisted Bernard.

'Is it?' I didn't believe it. 'Can't you see the headlines? JIM CHICKENS OUT. PRIME MINISTER RUNS AWAY FROM CRITICS.'

'They wouldn't say that if you had a major crisis to deal with.'

I turned to Malcolm. 'Any major crises coming up, Malcolm?'

Sadly, he shook his head. 'Not really, Prime Minister.'

Incredible, that the lack of a crisis should be bad news for us! I racked my brains, but I couldn't think of one either. 'Any distant crisis we could bring forward?' Malcolm and Bernard shook their heads hopelessly.

I tried to approach the problem positively. 'What sort of crisis would justify cancellation?'

Bernard could think of plenty. 'The pound plunging, small war in the South Atlantic, nuclear power station catching fire . . .'

I stopped him. 'Bernard,' I explained gently, 'I don't think any of those would help improve my image either.'

'No, but they'd justify you staying away,' he said, completely forgetting that the whole idea was – if not to improve my image – at least to prevent it from deteriorating further.

Bernard had a sudden inspiration. 'I know! How about the death of a Cabinet collague.'

'That would certainly do it! Is one imminent?' I asked, trying not to appear too hopeful.

'No,' said Bernard cheerfully, glad to have solved what was, to him, an academic problem. 'But that would justify your absence without damaging your image, wouldn't it?'

Malcolm agreed. 'He's right. But we can hardly hope for that to fall on the right day. At least not by accident,' he added darkly.

Was he hinting? I sincerely hope not. I could see that I really had no option, not at such short notice. 'I'll have to go,' I decided. 'I'll keep a stiff upper lip. Grin and bear it.'

Bernard said, 'You can't actually grin with a stiff upper lip because . . .' And he demonstrated. 'You see, stiff lips won't stretch horizontally . . .'

I might have hit him but he was saved by the bell – the telephone bell. Sir Humphrey was outside, ever anxious to discuss the agenda for Cabinet.

I welcomed him. 'Ah Humphrey, never mind that agenda, I need help.'

'You do!' Instantly I fixed my beady eye on him. 'You do?' I wasn't sure if he was asking or agreeing.

'I've got to make a speech,' I began. 'And I think it could be very embarrassing.'

'Oh Prime Minister, your speeches are nothing like as embarrassing as they used to be. In fact . . .'

These Civil Servants really are appallingly patronising. 'No, Humphrey. I didn't say my speech would be embarrassing, I said the occasion would be.'

'Indeed? Why?'

I explained as impartially as I could. 'It'll be to an audience of hostile, narcissistic, posturing, self-righteous theatrical drunks.'

'The House of Commons, you mean.'

I explained, in words of one syllable, that I meant the British Theatre Awards at the Dorchester.[1] Being the guest of honour is not much of an honour if they don't honour the guest.

Humphrey got the point at once. 'The small Arts Council grant, you mean? Well, it's very hard to influence the Chief Associate Director of the National Theatre, as I know only too well. I'm on the Board of Governors.'

I hadn't realised that. So I asked him what I do about it? How do I make the theatrical community feel that I'm really one of them?

'Surely,' murmured Humphrey acidly, 'you don't want them to see *you* as a narcissistic, posturing, self-righteous theatrical drunk?'

'Not that it would be very difficult,' said Bernard. I suppose he was alluding to my histrionic talents. After all, great statesmen have to be great actors. [*Hacker begs an important question here – Ed.*] Nonetheless, the programme will be live on TV, and I can hardly risk a hostile reception.

[1] Hotel.

437

Humphrey clearly felt that it was inevitable. 'With respect, Prime Minister, if one is going to walk into the lions' den, one should not start by taking away the lions' dinner.'

'So what is your advice?'

'Give them more of their dinner back. Increase the grant to the Arts Council. An extra two million or so would make a significant difference.'

'Two million? That would make it a fairly expensive dinner.'

Humphrey smiled. 'Well, it is the Dorchester.'

This was hardly an impartial recommendation. As a Governor of that subversive body [*The National Theatre, not the Dorchester Hotel – Ed.*] he has a vested interest. And a conflict of interest too! Well, he may want to support that bloody place! But I don't owe them anything. They keep putting on plays attacking me. They set *The Comedy of Errors* in Ten Downing Street. And, I reminded him, they did a modern-dress *Richard II*, making him into a foolish, vainglorious national leader who got booted out for incompetence. 'Don't deny it, Humphrey! I know who they were getting at.'

'I was only going to suggest, Prime Minister, that it was better than setting *Macbeth* in Number Ten.'

A feeble excuse. The truth is, they hate me there. 'They did a whole play attacking our nuclear policy,' I reminded him. 'A farce.'

'The policy?'

'The *play*, Humphrey!' He knew very well what I meant. I asked him why they did it, and why he wasn't concerned.

'It's very healthy, Prime Minister.'

'Healthy?' I couldn't see how.

'Practically nobody goes to political plays.' He sat back and crossed his legs urbanely. 'And half of those that go don't understand them. And half of those who understand them don't agree with them. And the seven who are left would have voted against the government anyway. Meanwhile, it lets people let off steam, and you look like a democratic statesman – with a good sense of humour! – for subsidising your critics.'

I still didn't see that the pros outweighed the cons. 'If they want to criticise me they should pay for it themselves. From the Box Office.'

Humphrey couldn't see that logic. 'Prime Minister, they'd never make enough money. Plays criticising the government make the second most boring theatrical evenings ever invented.'

I was curious. 'What are the most boring?'

'Plays praising the government.'

438

Personally I should have thought that they'd be much more interesting. And I still couldn't see why a theatre should insult me and then expect me to give it more money. But Humphrey explained that this is what artists always do. 'Undignified, isn't it? They advance towards the government on their knees, shaking their fists.'

'And beating me over the head with a begging bowl.'

'Um, Prime Minister,' said Bernard, 'they can't beat you over the head if they're on their knees. Not unless you're on your knees too, or unless they've got very long arms.'

I waited patiently. This pedantic wittering is the price I have to pay for Bernard's undoubted efficiency. Unfortunately it's this obsessive attention to detail that makes him both irritating and essential. I waited till he stopped talking, then I turned back to Malcolm.

'Isn't it true that there are no votes for me in giving money to the Arts?'

'Yes . . . but there's a lot of terrible publicity if you take it away.'

He's right. It's so unfair.

Humphrey spoke up for his vested interest again. 'It's not really unfair, Prime Minister. The arts lobby is part of the educated middle class. It's one of the few ways they can get their income tax back. Mortgage tax relief, university grants for their children, lump-sum pensions . . . and cheap subsidised seats at the theatre, the opera and the concert. You shouldn't begrudge it to them.'

I ticked him off. 'Humphrey, you're getting off the point.'

'Ah,' he replied gravely, 'what was the point?'

Unfortunately I couldn't remember. Bernard had to remind me. 'How to stop the Chief Associate Director of the National Theatre criticising you in his speech on Sunday.'

'That's *right*!' I turned emphatically to Humphrey. 'And since you know him, I suggest you have a quick word with him. You might point out that the knighthood which he might expect in the course of time is within the gift of the Prime Minister.'

Humphrey wasn't impressed with this plan. 'Frankly, Prime Minister, he told me he couldn't care less about a knighthood.'

Humphrey's being silly. Everyone says that about a knighthood until it's actually dangled before them.

[*Sir Humphrey Appleby did indeed have lunch with Simon Monk of the National Theatre. They met in the restaurant front-of-house, where it could be guaranteed that their meeting would be completely discreet and unobserved owing to the unique food offered by that estab-*

lishment. The luncheon is referred to in Simon Monk's best-selling autobiography Sound and Fury – *Ed.*]

We met in the theatre restaurant. Sir Humphrey Appleby had telephoned me previously, wanting to meet in a place where we wouldn't be overheard by people at the next table. Naturally I suggested our restaurant, where it was unlikely that there would be any people at the next table.

Sir Humphrey told me that the Prime Minister was paranoid again, about plays that attacked him. I asked Humphrey to tell Hacker that no one has ever submitted a play defending him, but Humphrey wasn't sure that that would help.

Hacker's in politics. He's fair game. It seemed to me that hostile plays are just one of the crosses he had to bear. To his credit, Humphrey wasn't a bit concerned either. 'He can bear any number of crosses,' he said with a sly grin, 'so long as they're in the right place on the ballot paper.'

Actually, I couldn't have cared less about Hacker's problems. He doesn't spare a thought for mine. All I wanted to know was what that year's Art Council grant was going to be. The Council needed the extra £30 million that it had applied for.

But Humphrey was enigmatic. 'My dear Simon! I couldn't disclose the figure in advance. Least of all to one of the Directors of the National Theatre.'

I didn't expect him to disclose it, not in so many words. So I picked up the bowl of Grissini breadsticks that was on the table and offered them to him. 'Have some of these,' I offered.

Humphrey carefully took three Grissini, and offered them to me.

I was appalled. 'Only *three*?'

I couldn't believe it! But Humphrey nodded gloomily. 'I'm afraid it's the new diet. Three breadsticks is the absolute maximum.'

'Is that gross breadsticks or net breadsticks?' I asked.

'Net breadsticks.'

I had to ask the next question, but I dreaded the answer. 'Then how much are we going to get at the National?'

Solemnly Humphrey broke approximately one quarter off one of the breadsticks and handed it to me.

'Only a quarter? But that's disastrous! How do they expect us to manage on a quarter of a million?' [*It should be noted that the amount in question was a raise of a quarter of a million – Ed.*]

Sir Humphrey looked innocent. 'I don't know where you got that figure from.' He loves playing his little games.

I begged him to help. The problem was serious – and genuine. A quarter of a million was not merely less than we had told the *press* was the absolute minimum to stave off disaster – it was lower even than the *real* minimum required to stave off disaster.

Humphrey said that he could help no further. Even though he's on the Board of the Theatre he explained his first allegiance is to the Government and the Prime Minister. But this turned out to be another of his little games, for he continued: 'Let me make it quite clear that I am here to represent the Prime Minister's interests. Now, certain things would gravely embarrass him. I must urge you on his behalf not to contemplate them.'

I got my notepad out. Things were looking up. 'Good,' I said. 'What are they?'

He smiled. 'Well, you will be making the speech introducing him at the Awards dinner. It would be a courtesy to submit a draft to Number Ten in advance.'

'For approval?' I was surprised.

'Let us say . . . for information.' I saw the point. 'The Prime Minister is extremely anxious that your speech should not refer to the modesty of the grant increase. There are certain words he wants you to avoid: *Miserly, Philistine, Barbarism, Skinflint, Killjoy*.' I was writing as fast as I could. Humphrey speaks fast. 'He also wants you to omit all reference to how much other countries spend on the arts.'

I asked him for the figures. He immediately produced a sheet of paper. 'There you are. To make sure you don't mention them by accident.'

'I certainly won't mention them by accident,' I confirmed.

'Most important of all,' concluded Sir Humphrey, 'the Prime Minister wants absolutely no comparison between the extra money your theatre needs and certain sums the Governent spent last year on certain projects.'

He was being more oblique than usual. I asked him to be more specific.

'Well, suppose the sum you need is four million. Purely as an example, you understand. The Prime Minister earnestly hopes you will not draw attention to the fact that the Government spent five million on radar equipment for a fighter plane that had already been scrapped. Or that the Department of Energy has been able to afford to stockpile a thousand years' supply of filing tabs. Or that another department has stocked up with a millions tins of Vim. Not to mention a billion pounds written off the Nimrod early warning aircraft system.'

'Anything else we can do?' I asked, writing furiously.

'Those are things you can't do,' he reminded me hypocritically. 'What you *could* do is . . . perhaps arrange for the Prime Minister to get an award of some sort? And let him know in advance?'

This was a tall order. An award for Hacker? What on earth for? Philistine of the Year was the only title I could think of. I pointed out that he never even goes to the theatre.

To my surprise, Sir Humphrey defended him. 'He can't really, he's frightened of giving the cartoonists and gossip columnists too much ammunition. He couldn't go to *A Month in the Country* because it would start rumours about a general election, he couldn't go to *The Rivals* because there have been so many Cabinet Ministers after his job, and he couldn't go to *The School for Scandal* for fear of reminding the electorate that the Secretary of State for Education was found in bed with that primary school headmistress.'

I almost felt sorry for Hacker.

'And as for that Ibsen you did, *An Enemy of the People* . . .' I'd got the point. 'So if you could give him some flattering honorary title, that would improve his image and appeal to his sense of self-importance . . .'

What on earth did Humphrey have in mind? Actor of the Year? For the most polished performance, disguising one backstage catastrophe after another? I suggested it.

'Very droll,' chuckled Humphrey. 'No, I think Comic Performance of the Year might be more appropriate.'

I topped him. 'Tragic Performance of the Year!'

'Both!' said Humphrey, and we fell around.

[*Hacker's diary continues – Ed.*]

December 4th

A meeting with Nick Everitt, the Arts Minister. He was in a bit of a state. He's been got at, he's losing his nerve! He was party to the decision about the Arts Council grant – oh no he wasn't, I forgot he's not in the Cabinet, but it's a free country, he could have resigned if he didn't want to support it! Anyway, it's a Government decision, a collective decision, he's part of the Government and he's got to accept it whether it was his decision or not. That's democracy.

'Jim,' he said, 'I think there's going to be terrible trouble when they find out how small the grant increase is.'

'We'll just have to brazen it out,' I said. 'Won't you?'

He didn't look too happy, peering out nervously through his big rectangular glasses. Young, earnest, and a regular visitor to Glyndebourne, he didn't like being accused of Philistinism. 'I do think we'll have to try and find a bit more.'

I told him we'd been through it all before. He shook his head. 'We haven't really taken the employment argument on board.'

I sighed. The employment of actors cannot be allowed to dictate our fiscal policy, however famous and vocal they are. I told Nick that they'd just have to get other jobs, outside the theatre.

'They can't. Actors are unemployable outside the theatre. A lot of them are unemployable in it.'

He's one hundred per cent wrong about that. Annie tells me that half the mini-cab drivers she meets are out-of-work actors.

Nick had a different explanation. 'Most mini-cab drivers *say* they're out of work actors. It's more glamorous than describing yourself as a "moonlighting nightwatchman".'

Bernard raised a forefinger and looked in my direction. Apparently he felt he had a useful contribution to make to the discussion. 'Er, nightwatchmen can't moonlight. It's a moonlight job to start with. If they drove minicabs they'd be sunlighting.'

Nick went through all the arguments that the Treasury had already rejected. 'The theatre brings in tourists,' he declaimed with passion.

'Fine.' I stayed cool. 'Then the British Tourist Authority should subsidise it.'

'But they won't,' he complained. 'That's the trouble. They say they've got better ways of attracting them.'

'So,' I summed up, 'you want us to subsidise a bad way of attracting tourists.' He tried to interrupt. 'No, Nick, we waste too much on the Arts anyway.'

He flinched. Then he tried the old chestnut about how the arts are educational. Maybe – but why should I give public money to people who use it for the very uneducational purposes of attacking me?

'We'd have to spend the money anyway,' said Nick, trying his final ploy. 'It's only a concealed way of preserving old buildings.'

I couldn't see what he meant. 'All those theatres and art galleries and museums and opera houses are listed buildings,' he pleaded. 'We'd have to maintain them anyway. And they're totally useless otherwise. So we put in central heating and a curator and roll it into the grant to make it look as if we're supporting the Arts.'

Half true; but not persuasive enough. I have a simpler solution. We'll sell them.

December 5th

This Arts Council crisis is becoming a bloody nuisance. Tonight we had a drinks and buffet party at Number Ten. A couple of hundred guests, many of them theatricals – we always do this to attract good publicity but tonight's do was organised many weeks ago and, had we known, we would have invited a more respectful bunch: backbench MPs, for instance, who never argue with me on social occasions and usually confine themselves to getting harmlessly pissed. It's a change from Annie's Bar.[1]

As a matter of fact, I've often thought that we should breathalyse

---

[1] One of the many House of Commons bars.

MPs – not when they're driving but when they're legislating. I would guess that well over fifty per cent are over the legal limit by seven pm. Just think of the permanent damage they do to the nation with their impaired judgement and poor reflexes.

Anyway, we had drunken theatricals to contend with tonight. And, which was worse, sober ones! Annie, who didn't realise what was at stake, congratulated me on taking such trouble over all those 'lovely theatre people' even though they're not important.

I explained that they were very important. Not for their votes, which are too few to count, but for their influence.

She was surprised that they have influence.

'Annie,' I explained patiently, 'show business people have a hotline to the media. Once you've drunk a couple of pints in *East-Enders* the press want your opinion on everything: Britain's schools, the Health Service, law and order . . . right through to the European Monetary System. They get far more exposure than my Cabinet.'

There's no sense in it, of course. But editors want people to read their papers, so if an article starts with a picture of Dirty Den[1] they read it. But who is going to read an article because of a photo of the Secretary of State for Trade and Industry?

Annie said, 'So all these actors turn into your supporters after a couple of drinks at Number Ten?'

'Some do,' I told her. 'But not enough. That's why we dish out a couple of CBEs or Knighthoods every year. Keeps them all hoping. And they're less likely to knock the Government next time they're on Wogan.'[2]

[*Simon Monk was, by a fateful chance, one of the guests at this party. His autobiography records his quiet conversation with Sir Humphrey, who had been anxiously waiting at the top of the grand circular staircase, watching out for Monk's arrival – Ed.*]

Sir Humphrey took me aside, into a sort of panelled lobby outside the main state reception rooms. He faced away from a few bystanders and spoke softly in my ear. He wanted me to talk to Hacker that night. In fact, he implied that I'd been invited to the party – several weeks ago – for that very purpose. The date of the grant announcement was known months back.

'But isn't it better to wait till the figure is published?' I asked, not really relishing a confrontation with Hacker that night.

[1] Den Watts. a character in *EastEnders*. a soap opera which had prominence in the latter part of the 20th century.
[2] Well-known TV talk show of the 1980s on which the host. Terry Wogan. talked and the guests listened.

Sir Humphrey was astonished. 'What on earth for?'

'If I try to lobby him before, he won't say anything, will he?'

Sir Humphrey explained. 'Of course he won't say anything. You don't want him to say anything. You want him to *do* something.'

I began to argue. Then I realised that I was getting free advice from the most skilful political operator in the land. 'If you wait,' he muttered into my ear, 'the figure will be published and everyone will be committed to it. They'll have to stick with it to save their faces. It you want to change government decisions you have to do it before anybody knows they're being made.'

It's a good principle. But, I asked, 'isn't that rather difficult in practice?'

'Yes,' Humphrey answered. 'That's what the Civil Service is for.'

'To change Government decisions?' I realised that I was a complete innocent.

'Yes,' he smiled. 'Well, only the bad ones. But that's most of them, of course.'

I asked Sir Humphrey what he wanted me to do. Quite simply, he wanted me to help emphasise to Hacker that a small grant might cause him great embarrassment . . . at the Awards Dinner on Sunday.

SIR BERNARD WOOLLEY RECALLS:[1]

Everyone was politicking furiously. Humphrey got Simon Monk into one corner. And a bunch of actors and actresses got the Prime Minister into another. And Hacker did his utmost to persuade the thespians that he was a theatre lover. Without much success, I fear.

'Do you really believe in the British theatre, Prime Minister?' said a deeply sceptical young actress, whose roots were showing, metaphorically and literally.

'Of course. Absolutely.'

'Why?'

Hacker said something to the effect of 'Well, er, it's, er, it's one of the great glories of England.'

'You mean Shakespeare?' said a smooth old fellow, apparently being helpful.

'Yes,' said Hacker gratefully. 'Absolutely. Shakespeare.'

'Who else?' asked the old smoothie. He had a very plummy voice. I'd seen him at the RSC. Can't remember his name. I liked him though.

'Who *else*?' repeated Hacker, desperately stalling while he gave himself time to think. 'Well, er, Shakespeare of course. And er, er, Sheridan. Oscar Wilde. Bernard Shaw. All great English playwrights.'

'They were all Irish,' said the aggressive young actress.

Hacker tried to charm her with a smile, a fairly hopeless task. 'Yes, I know that, but well, Irish, English, it was all the same thing in those days, wasn't it?'

[1] In conversation with the Editors.

'Bernard Shaw died in 1950,' said a slim young man on the edge of the group, who was apparently studying a Gainsborough on the wall with such intensity that he didn't even turn to look at the Prime Minister.

'Oh I'm so sorry,' replied Hacker inappropriately.

A large middle-aged actress with a beautiful smile and a husky deep voice, born of thirty years of gin and Benson and Hedges, smiled warmly at him and asked if he went to the theatre a lot.

Hacker hedged. 'Well, of course, I'd love to – but you know how it is in this job.'

The plummy old actor spoke up again, quoting the Prime Minister back at himself. 'Don't you think the Prime Minister ought to go. If it's one of the great glories of England?'

The Prime Minister's explanation was less than tactful. 'Oh yes,' he said. 'But the Minister for the Arts goes. His job, really.'

'Why?' asked the plummy actor.

'Well, the Prime Minister can't do everything himself. Have to delegate the work.'

The throaty actress appeared to take offence. 'Going to the theatre is work?'

'Yes. No,' said Hacker indecisively. 'But I don't want to trespass on another minister's territory.'

'Does that mean,' enquired the sceptical young actress with a smile, 'that you can't feel ill without clearing it with the Minister of Health?'

'Exactly,' said Hacker, then realised what he'd said. '*Not* exactly', he added, trying but failing to clarify his position.

The slim young man on the edge of the group turned and asked him if he ever went to the theatre when he'd been in opposition. Hacker started to explain that, even then, it had not been within his purview.

'So when you say you believe in the theatre,' said the young man, 'it's like saying you believe in God. You mean you believe it exists.'

Hacker denied this hotly. I think he should have been wiser to admit the truth, for he was fooling nobody.

'What was the last play you went to?' asked the young actress, contempt written all over her face. These people show no respect at all, you know.

'*Went* to?' repeated the Prime Minister, as if he sat at home all day and *read* plays. 'Last play?' he repeated, panicked, playing for time. 'Ah. Well. Probably *Hamlet*.'

'Whose?' asked the plummy old fellow.

'Shakespeare's,' said the Prime Minister with confidence.

'No, who played Hamlet?' asked the slim young man on the edge of the group. 'Henry Irving?'[1]

'Yes,' said Hacker, 'I think that might have been his name.'

---

[1] Sir Henry Irving was a famous nineteenth-century actor and the first knight of the first nights.

446

The acting fraternity gazed at each other, unable to grasp that the Prime Minister neither knew nor cared what went on in their temples of art and culture.

I saw Sir Humphrey detach himself from Simon Monk. So I detached myself from Hacker and the actors, and took the Cabinet Secretary aside for a private word.

I explained that the Prime Minister was not enjoying himself.

'He's not supposed to,' retorted Humphrey. 'Cocktail parties at Number Ten are just a gruesome duty.'

'But people are asking him questions,' I said.

'He should be used to that.'

'But they weren't tabled in advance. So he isn't briefed.'

'But he's not on the record. Does it matter?'

I explained that all of the people at the party were going to think that he was a Philistine.

'Good Heavens!' said Humphrey.

Joking apart, I emphasised that in my opinion he should be rescued. Humphrey said he would handle it.

As we approached Hacker in the theatrical crowd we passed Annie, the Prime Minister's wife, talking to a very small and dapper musician who'd recently been appointed Principal Guest Conductor of one of the five London symphony orchestras. Annie may have had too much to drink.

'I'm interested in hi-fidelity too,' she said. 'My husband is a high-fidelity husband.'

'That's nice,' said the conductor, who was famous for being exactly the opposite.

'In a way,' she said conspiratorially, and giggled. 'High fidelity but low frequency.'

The conductor, who clearly found Mrs Hacker extremely attractive, seemed unsure how to reply. 'You mean, sort of Bang and Olufsen?'

'Well, Olufsen anyway,' said Mrs Hacker.

[*Hacker's diary continues – Ed.*]

I was doing well with the acting fraternity. To be honest, I really didn't know much about the theatre, but I'm sure they didn't notice, they're all so self-centred.

They all knew the Arts Council grant was to be announced any day now, and of course they all pressured me like hell. But I'm pretty used to being lobbied by vested interests, and I reminded them that there were numerous other calls on the public purse that some people might consider even *more* important.

It is, of course, a basic rule for self-interested pressure groups that you present the case for your own financial gain as if the public interest is all you care about. Teachers present demands for their own pay rises as being for the good of education. Even as they go out on strike their leaders argue that they're doing it for the sake of the children they're sending home. Miners, if we are to believe them, go on strike so that old people can have cheaper coal, Health service workers – from doctors to porters – close down hospitals so as to save the health service for the wretched patients who can't get any treatment in the meantime.

So obviously these very pleasant entertainers, who need the love and applause of thousands of total strangers, and who therefore put on plays because dressing up and showing off in public is fun and makes them feel good, also present their demands for subsidy under the guise of the public interest – education, usually.

So I countered by pointing out that much more money is desperately needed for genuine educational purposes, trusting that they would not mention that I was not in any case giving the money to those with a prior call. Not to mention hospitals, kidney machines . . .

'Tanks and rockets', said one of the actresses, 'is what you spend the money on.'

'H-bombs,' chimed in another.

Perfectly true. But we could hardly defend ourselves from the Russians with a performance of *Henry V*. I said so. They weren't amused.

Humphrey arrived at my side and it was with some relief that I escaped from that little group.

'This isn't a drinks party, it's a siege,' I complained bitterly.

Humphrey merely commented that people are very concerned about the arts. He's wrong. *These* people are very concerned – the nation doesn't give a damn. If they did, they'd spend their own money on the Arts. Why should the Government's money be spent on other people's pleasure, I asked him.

'Nobody could call it pleasure,' said Humphrey rather shocked. He's a true Calvinist at heart. 'The point is that we have a great heritage to support. Pictures hardly anyone wants to see, music hardly anyone wants to hear, plays hardly anyone wants to watch. We can't let them die just because no one's interested.'

I was curious. 'Why not?'

'It's like the Church of England, Prime Minister. People don't go to church, but they feel better because it's there. The Arts are just the same. As long as they're going on you can feel part of a civilised nation.'

All very well in its way, but he's totally unpolitical and unrealistic. 'There are no votes in the Arts,' I reminded him. 'Nobody's *interested*!'

Stubbornly he refused to concede the point. 'Nobody's interested in the Social Science Research Council. Or the Milk Marketing Board. Or the Advisory Committee on Dental Establishments. Or the Dumping At Sea Representation Panel. But Government still pays money to support them.'

'Don't they do a lot of good?' I asked.

'Of course they don't. They hardly do anything at all.'

'Then,' I proposed, 'let's abolish them.'

Now he was panicked. This was not the turn that he had expected the conversation to take. 'No, no, Prime Minister. They are symbols. You don't fund them for doing work. You fund them to show what you approve of. Most government expenditure is symbolic. The Arts Council is a symbol.'

I told him it was no good. My mind was made up. He promptly suggested that I have a word with the Chief Associate Director of the National Theatre, who by chance had also been invited to this drinks do. I didn't want to face another salvo, but Humphrey told me that he's been trying to persuade this fellow Simon Monk to make the right sort of speech at the Awards Dinner.

'That's very good of you, Humphrey' I said gratefully.

'Not at all. But you might have more success than I.' So Humphrey's persuasion had not borne fruit.

Well, before I had time to collect my thoughts I was face to face with this theatrical wizard. He was actually perfectly polite and seemed a little ill at ease. Small, thinning hair and without the beard that I'd so often seen in the newspapers, he could almost have been a politician.

I was ill at ease too. 'So you'll be introducing me at this Awards Dinner thing?' I began.

'That's right,' he replied, and fell silent. We half-smiled nervously at each other for what seemed like an eternity. It became clear that if I didn't speak the conversation might never resume.

'Any idea of the sort of thing you'll be saying?'

'I suppose it all depends really.'

'On – er – on . . .?' I enquired.

'On the size of the grant.'

Just what I'd been warned. And I knew he had no idea what it was to be. [*The Prime Minister was not aware of the discussion with Sir Humphrey about breadsticks in the NT Restaurant – Ed.*] So I told him the grant was still under discussion.

'Of course,' he agreed. 'But if it turns out to be generous it would give me a chance to say something about the way this Government has got its priorities right. Believing in Britain's heritage, and what Britain stands for.'

I hinted that he could say something of that sort anyway, even if I couldn't persuade the Arts Minister to cough up, but he indicated that this would be difficult.

'Surely you wouldn't want to make it a political occasion?' I said in a voice of disapproval.

'Not for myself, no. But I have a duty to the profession.' He's good! 'And to the Arts,' he continued. 'My colleagues would expect me to voice their feelings.'

I tried to make *him* understand about money for inner cities, schools, hospitals, kidney machines. He acknowledged my problem and said he proposed to solve it by making a funny speech about the government.

This was grim news indeed. Humorous attacks are the most difficult to deal with. The one thing I can't afford is to look as though I'm a bad sport or have no sense of humour – the British public never forgive you for that.

[*The following morning the Prime Minister received a letter from Simon Monk. Sir Humphrey Appleby preserved it in the Cabinet Office files, and we reproduce it opposite. It contained a serious threat – Ed.*]

NATIONAL
THEATRE

Patron H'M. The Queen

December 6th

Dear Mr. Hacker,

I enclose a draft of a part of my speech, for your amusement. It will make good television, don't you think, in a
light-hearted way? Of course, I hope I don't have to say all
this, as I would rather not embarrass you. But I do hope you
understand that if we <u>don't</u> get a substantial rise the National
Theatre will collapse - and there will be a huge empty building
on the South Bank, a decaying monument to this country's
barbarism.

Yours sincerely

Simon Monk

enc.

The Olivier Theatre
The Lyttelton Theatre
The Cottesloe Theatre

451

Ladies & gentlemen, I thought that tonight you might be amused by some of the other ways the government has spent your money.

The money it can't afford for the arts.

Did you know that in one year a London borough spent a million pounds on hotels for families while they had 4000 empty council houses?

Did you know that another council spends £100 per week on a toenail cutting administrator? And that one city in the UK was still employing four gas lamp lighters eight years after the last gas lamp was removed? That cost a quarter of a million!

Not to mention the Council that spent £730 to have two square yards of shrubbery weeded. And the government office block that's scheduled for demolition two weeks before it's completed.

And finally, do you know where all the British Local Authorities held their conference on spending cuts? The Café Royal![1]

[1] An expensive and elegant restaurant in Regent Street, London.

[*Hacker's diary continues – Ed.*]

December 6th

I got a vile, threatening letter from that man Monk this morning. Not only was it full of examples of local authority waste, it threatened that the NT would shut down if I didn't hoick the grant up. This would be cataclysmic news for me, the press would kill me!

I called Dorothy to discuss his draft speech. Her view of it was that the TV viewers wouldn't make the distinction between wastage by local or national government – it's all public money, the taxpayer pays the rate-support grant. And therefore they would agree with Monk that if money is wasted like that it would be inexcusable to risk the closure of the NT on financial grounds.

I decided she was right. The fact is, the National Theatre is going to call my bluff.

'What is your bluff?' she asked.

'My bluff is: I'm willing to risk the National Theatre's bluff.'

'What's their bluff?'

'Their bluff is that they think I'm bluffing, whereas . . .'

'Whereas you are!' she said.

I realised that I no longer knew who was bluffing whom. Dorothy thought it was obvious. I couldn't see it. [*Perhaps it was a case of blind man's bluff. Or bland minds' bluff – Ed.*]

My cassette recorder was on the desk, because I was about to dictate some notes for my memoirs and a couple of personal letters. Bernard offered to clarify the situation for me. He then spoke for several minutes but I was none the wiser. So I asked him to repeat his clarification into my cassette.

'Prime Minister,' he said, 'you think that the National Theatre thinks that you are bluffing and the National Theatre thinks that you think that they are bluffing, whereas your bluff is to make the National Theatre think that you are bluffing when you're not bluffing, or if you *are* bluffing, your bluff is to make them think you're *not* bluffing. And their bluff must be that they're bluffing, because if they're not bluffing they're not bluffing.'

I thanked him and resumed the intelligent part of conversation with Dorothy. She asked me what my policy actually *is*? Am I willing to risk their closure if I don't increase the grant?

I replied, flustered. 'I have already stated my policy. I think. All I can do is go on restating it until . . . until . . .'

'Until you know what it is?' Bernard enquired, unhelpfully.

'The point is, this situation is now a real hot potato. If I don't do something it could become a banana skin.'

Bernard intervened. 'Excuse me, Prime Minister, a hot potato can't become a banana skin. If you don't do anything a hot potato merely becomes a cold potato.'

I wonder if Bernard ever realises how close to death he sometimes comes.

December 7th

Dorothy came to me with a plan. Not a good plan, not a great plan – but a plan of sheer genius!

In a nutshell, she recommends calling their bluff. She says I should sell the National Theatre building. And the National Film Theatre. The South Bank is a prime site, overlooking St Paul's and Big Ben.

The site, she proposed, should be sold to a property developer. Her information is that it is worth about £35 million pounds on the market. This money could be put into an Arts Trust Fund, producing – at an average of ten per cent per annum – £3.5 million a year.

This £3.5 million of interest earned from the Trust Fund would finance the National Theatre. Not the theatre *itself*, because we would have sold it, but the company – which is all that matters.

Apparently the current National Theatre *building* absorbs about half of the company's grant, i.e. out of a grant of £7 million about £3.5 million goes into the upkeep of that building. Dorothy contends that this is a waste of money, money that could actually be spent on productions. After all Simon Monk was complaining last week that they shouldn't have to spend their grant that way – 'the theatre is about plays and actors, not bricks and mortar'.

So where would they put on plays? Answer: there are plenty of theatres in London. And all over the country. The National Theatre could rent them, like any other producer.

The scheme is perfect. The company might even have to go on tour and become genuinely national – whereas at the moment it only serves a few Londoners and a lot of tourists. Much more money than ever before could be injected into National Theatre productions while still giving the Government that net profit of thirty million, which could then be invested to produce three million a year for the British Theatre as a whole.

I was exultant. 'No one could accuse me of being a Philistine any more!'

She smiled. 'Not unless they knew you.'

December 9th

The night of the Awards dinner. Confidently I arrived at the Dorchester in my dinner jacket, with Annie on my arm, actively looking forward to the encounter. If there was to be a knock-down drag-out fight tonight, I felt I stood a good chance of emerging as the champ.

Knowing that much of the audience for my speech would be experienced performers, I'd taken some extra trouble. I had rehearsed in front of the mirror. Dorothy had watched my recent TV appearance and had some advice for me.

'Always use full gestures. If you only gesture from the elbow up you look like an Armenian carpet salesman.'

On the whole, it could be better to look like an Armenian carpet salesman than an actor. Or even a politician. But since I now see myself as a statesman, only the most statesmanlike gestures are permitted. Punchy, powerful gestures – but always *preceding* the sentence, Annie tells me, never after! Gestures afterwards look weak and ineffectual.

Of course, before the speech there was the small matter of a final negotiation with Mr Monk. If all went well, I wouldn't have to say anything controversial, which would be the best outcome of all. I always remember the advice given to me by an elderly peer years ago when I first entered the Cabinet: 'If you want to get into the Cabinet, learn how to speak. If you want to stay in the Cabinet, learn how to keep your mouth shut.'

In the ante-room before the dinner Humphrey got me together with Simon Monk. He'd now heard the news about the grant. I gave him a big smile and a sincere handshake [*or was it the other way round? – Ed.*].

He did not smile at me. 'This is very bad news about the grant, Prime Minister.'

'Surely not?' I said innocently. 'It's gone up.'

'Nothing like enough.'

'Enough to make it unnecessary for you to recommend closure, tonight?'

'I'm afraid not.' He was sombre, but confident.

I helped myself to a handful of peanuts. 'Because next year,' I continued indistinctly, 'I think we can really do something significant. You remember you complained that £3 million of your grant goes on the upkeep of the building?'

'Yes?'

'I have a plan that would relieve you of that.'

455

He brightened considerably. 'Really? That would be marvellous.'

'Yes,' I enthused, 'wouldn't it? And it would make the National Theatre really national too.'

Instantly he was on his guard. 'How do you mean?'

'I'm thinking of selling it,' I explained cheerfully.

He was aghast! He stood there, his mouth open, staring at me as though I were Attila the Hun. So I took the opportunity to explain that that's how we save three million on upkeep.

He finally found his voice. 'Prime Minister! That's impossible.'

'No it's not, it's easy.' I assured him. 'We've had a terrific offer for the site.' And we had, too.

Humphrey intervened, apparently shell-shocked. He had been quietly confident that I would submit to Simon's closure bluff. 'But Prime Minister – the National Theatre must have a home.'

I explained that it would have. They could have offices anywhere – Brixton or Toxteth, for instance. Or Middlesbrough.

Simon asked about theatres, about scene-building workshops.

Rent them, I explained, like everyone else. As it is, most of the workshops at the NT are closed down because of bad management and high cost.

'Be like the others,' I exhorted him. 'Perform in the West End. Or the Old Vic. And provincial theatres. Become strolling players again, not Civil Servants. Didn't you once say that the theatre was about plays and actors, not bricks and mortar?'

And, while he was reeling on the ropes, I followed up with the knockout blow. I suggested Dorothy's *second* plan – she came up with it this morning. If anyone complained that the National Theatre needed a *permanent* home, we would designate *all* the regional theatres in the UK the National Theatre. For instance, the Haymarket Theatre in Leicester would become the *National Theatre in Leicester*; the Crucible would be called the *National Theatre in Sheffield*; the Citizens could be subtitled *National Theatre in Glasgow* . . . and so forth. 'You,' I explained to Simon, 'would just run the London branch of the National Theatre.'

It would be a perfectly true description. I reminded him that they are all run exactly the same way, with Artistic Directors and Administrators appointed by local boards of governors, financed by a combination of Arts Council grants, local authority grants and box office income. Why should the London branch of the National Theatre be the only branch entitled to that elevated title? And we could use the £35 million, or the £3 million annual income, to help them all. 'That would be terribly popular with the profession, don't you think?'

Humphrey, who had not heard this plan either, was virtually speechless. His eyes were popping out of his head. 'Prime Minister, it's barbaric!' he gasped.

'Spending money on actors and writers instead of buildings?'

'Yes,' he spluttered. 'No,' he added as, wide-eyed, he realised what he was saying.

'Anyway,' I concluded, 'it's only one of the options. I might decide against it. Or I might not. I could outline it in my speech. It all depends, really.'

Simon spoke at last. 'On what?'

I smiled benignly at him. 'To change the subject completely, Simon, have you decided what to say in your speech yet?'

He was sweating. 'Not finally.' He knew he was beaten.

'You see,' I explained, 'thinking it over, I wasn't sure that those examples of government waste were awfully funny. But of course, it's your decision.' I waited. He eyed me balefully. 'I'm sure you undertand,' I said, and walked away from them both.

Well, either way I was the winner. But I didn't know which way it would go until the last moment. We ate the usual rubber chicken dinner with croquette potatoes – I've never ever eaten croquette potatoes *anywhere* except at formal dinners – I gave the loyal toast, the smokers were told they could smoke, and in no time it was time for the awards. Monk was introduced by the pompous ringing tones of the Toastmaster: 'Prime Minister and Mrs Hacker, My Lords, ladies and gentleman, pray silence for the Chief Associate Director of the National Theatre, Mr Simon Monk.'

He rose to a round of warm applause. 'Ladies and gentlemen,' he said, 'you will have read this morning of the grant to the Arts Council and to the National Theatre. I know that many of us are disappointed by the amount.'

Low hostile murmurs reverberated around the Banqueting Suite. Several 'hear hear's'. Lots of approving bangs on the table-tops. Simon Monk stopped and looked at me. I stared back. Little pink anger spots appeared on his cheeks and he looked back at his speech.

'Of course we would all like it to be larger. But apparently this is a time of national stringency and we all have to think in terms of national needs. There are many calls on the public purse . . .' One of my favourite phrases, that! '. . . Education, inner cities, health, kidney machines.'

I nodded sagely. Another murmur went round the room, this time of disappointment. Simon Monk, it was clear, was not going to attack me. And, in fact, at that moment he removed a couple of pages from his speech and slipped them into his pocket. Very wise. Perhaps he knew the old adage: 'Never speak when you are angry. If you do you'll make the best speech you'll ever regret.'

Simon's speech was unexpectedly brief. All that was left of it was 'I suppose we should be glad that any increase has been possible. And grateful to our Guest of Honour whose personal intervention has made even this small increase possible.'

I beamed at him. The cameras were on me, I knew. 'Ladies and gentlemen,' said Monk, holding up his glass, 'I give you our Guest of Honour, the patron of the arts, the Prime Minister.'

He sat down to a smattering of unenthusiastic applause. Little did his audience know, but he'd made the smart move and the only possible speech.

I let him see me remove the appropriate pages from *my* script. And I whispered to Humphrey: 'Excellent speech, wasn't it?'

He seemed as angry as the theatricals. 'Yes Prime Minister,' he said, through clenched teeth! But then, old Humphrey's always been a bit theatrical himself.

17

The National
Education Service

December 11th

From the arts to education – real education. The party has serious problems with the local authorities and our education system.

But today was fascinating for other reasons. Before I got to the petty problems of British schools I spent the day on the world stage dealing in a statesmanlike way with matters that affect the future, indeed the very existence, of mankind. Or personkind, as some of our more dedicated so-called educationalists would have it.

After Christmas I'm due to visit the USA, which will certainly be good for my standing in the opinion polls. I'm going to try to follow this with a spring trip to Moscow, which will demonstrate to the voters that I'm the man to bring world peace to them.

Of course that may be beyond me in the short term – we will need several more working funerals for that. But it'll still be excellent for the image.

So this morning I was working on my speech for my special appearance at the UN while I'm in New York. My first draft was quite good, I thought. I'd based it on the UN Charter itself. The Foreign Office sent me over a copy, with a note attached explaining that the preamble to the Charter was known as the Unconditional Surrender of the English language.[1]

---

[1] The first sentence of the preamble runs as follows:

WE THE PEOPLES
OF THE UNITED NATIONS
DETERMINED

to save succeeding generations from the scourge of war, which twice in our life-time has brought untold sorrow to mankind, and

to reaffirm faith in fundamental human rights, in the dignity and worth of the human person, in the equal rights of men and women and of nations large and small, and

to establish conditions under which justice and respect for the obligations arising from treaties and other sources of international law can be maintained, and

to promote social progress and better standards of life in larger freedom,

The first draft of my speech referred to the British belief in peace, freedom and justice. It talked of the impossibility of *justice* while the vast majority of member states of the UN have prisoners of conscience; of the impossibility of *freedom* while most of the member states have one-party government (appealing though the idea is if you happen to lead the one party); and of the low chance of world peace when almost everyone votes blindly in special-interest blocks instead of with us. [*It is interesting to note that Hacker, after all this time in government, remained a moralist at heart, even though he was seldom able to see his moral positions through into practical politics – Ed.*]

The FO took one look at my speech. They only got it on Saturday. Today they effectively vetoed it. Dick Wharton[1] phoned me and said that, for God's sake, I mustn't say any of it.

'Because it's wrong?' I asked.

'Because it's right,' he replied.

I told him I didn't want to mouth platitudes or clichés ever again. [*To 'mouth platitudes' is itself a cliché – Ed.*] I reiterated that I wished to say something about peace and freedom. Dick Wharton said that if I insisted I could speak about peace at the UN, but not freedom – it's too controversial. I told him I didn't mind controversy. Controversy gets better headlines.

Over lunch I prepared for PQs[2] in my room at the House. The PQ Secretary expected questions from the anti-nuclear lobby about the rumour in the press today about the latest US missiles. It seems that there's a fear of Soviet infiltration at the place where most of our guided-missile microchips are manufactured.

'Is that California?' I asked Bernard. 'Silicon Valley?'

'Taiwan,' he replied.

I was staggered. 'Taiwan??'

---

[1] Permanent Secretary of the FCO.
[2] Parliamentary Questions.

AND FOR THESE ENDS

   to practice tolerance and live together in peace with one another as good neighbours, and

   to unite our strength to maintain international peace and security, and to ensure, by the acceptance of principles and the institution of methods, that armed force shall not be used, save in the common interest, and

   to employ international machinery for the promotion of the economic and social advancement of all peoples,

HAVE RESOLVED TO COMBINE OUR EFFORTS TO ACCOMPLISH THESE AIMS.

Bernard nodded. 'It appears that we have paid for about fifteen million faulty microchips.'

'What is meant by faulty?' I asked carefully.

He shrugged hopelessly. 'No one knows exactly, Prime Minister. We don't dare ask. Maybe the missiles simply wouldn't work. Maybe they'd blow up in the face of whoever pushes the button.'

'My God!' I said. I was horrified. I asked what else might happen. Bernard shrugged. 'Maybe they'd boomerang. Go all the way round the world and land back on us.'

I stared at him in silence, my boggling mind trying to assimilate the full implications of this horror.

Bernard spoke again. 'Maybe it would be better to avoid full and frank disclosure of this matter.'

Malcolm Warren,[1] whom Bernard had included in the meeting, nodded vigorously, in full agreement.

A sudden thought struck me, a thought even more horrific than that of boomeranging missiles. My mouth went dry with panic. 'When did we buy these?' I asked, petrified.

Bernard reassured me. 'Before you took office, Prime Minister. So there's nothing to worry about.'

Thank God! It's certainly fortunate that I wasn't responsible. But I am now, now that I know! And 'nothing to worry about' is a curious way to talk of guided missiles that might do their own thing. 'Nothing to worry about?' I repeated incredulously.

'No. I mean, nothing to worry about *personally*,' he said. 'Unless they boomerang on Whitehall,' he added pensively.

'And what doesn't?' muttered Malcolm. He's so gloomy!

I asked who was responsible. 'The MOD,'[2] said Bernard. 'And the Pentagon. The issue seems to be lack of control over the defence industries.'

'The issue', said Malcolm, 'appears to be lack of control over the missiles.'

'The issue', *I* said, 'seems to be the low level of imagination in the MOD.'

'Might be better to avoid disclosing that too,' suggested Malcolm.

In the event, the PQs went off smoothly and, as always, I left the Chamber immediately afterwards. The Chief Whip and the Party Chairman were ushered in to my room at the House. I ordered Bernard to stay and listen.

[1] The Press Secretary.
[2] Ministry of Defence.

He was reluctant. 'Isn't this a party matter, Prime Minister? A meeting with the Party Chairman and the Chief Whip?'

'It's also a government matter,' I told him firmly. 'It concerns our education policy.'

Bernard is a stickler for detail. 'The government's? Or the party's?'

'It's the same thing, Bernard!' I was getting testy with him.

Neil, the Party Chairman, who's looking rather overweight and breathless, foolishly interfered. 'With respect, Prime Minister, they're not the same thing.'

Jeffrey[1] joined in. 'That's why we want the meeting.'

Bernard tried to slide out of the room again. 'Well, it seems to be a party matter, so if you'll excuse me . . .'

'Sit!' I commanded him. He sat. He's quite obedient really, and impeccably trained. 'You would try the patience of a saint, Bernard,' I told him. 'Now stay!'

He stayed. I turned to Neil and Jeffrey and asked what the problem was.

'Education,' said Neil succinctly.

I was feeling belligerent. 'What the hell do you think I can do about it?'

'You're the Prime Minister,' said Jeffrey. I knew that already. But so what? The Prime Minister has no direct control over education. I can't control the curriculum, the exams, the appointment of Head Teachers – nothing! But the voters are holding me responsible for everything that's going wrong.

'You do have influence,' said Neil.

'And I'm utterly fed up with it,' I remarked. 'I thought that when I became Prime Minister I'd have power. And what have I got? *Influence*! Bloody influence, that's all! I have no power over the police, the rates, EEC directives, the European Court, the British courts, the judges, NATO, the falling pound . . . What *have* I the power to do?'

Neil eyed me beadily. 'You have the power to lose us the next election.'

'Which you will,' said Jeffrey nodding solemnly. 'Unless we do something about education.'

I wonder if they overstate the seriousness of it. Maybe not. I told them I was listening.

'The voters', said the Party Chairman, beads of sweat appearing on

---

[1] Jeffrey Pearson, the Chief Whip.

his forehead, 'want something done about low academic attainment, the non-competitive ethos . . .'

'You mean the three Rs,' I said, cutting him short. I got the point.

He nodded gloomily. 'Kids are being taught about Marxism, sexism, pacificism, feminism, racism, heterosexism . . .'

Bernard chimed in. 'It's all the isms. They're causing schisms.' I think he was trying to get me to tell him to go. But I wouldn't!

I'd not heard of heterosexism. Neil explained that it's the idea that children are being taught not to be irrationally prejudiced in favour of heterosexuality. 'This has come up before,' I remarked. 'But I see the problem. We don't want prejudice.'

Neil exploded. 'Prejudice!' he shouted. 'You can't describe it as prejudice to teach kids to be normal.' His face had turned a curious mauve colour. I thought he was going to have a heart attack. I wasn't very bothered, to tell you the truth – I was thoroughly fed up at his suggestion that *I* might lose the next election. He's the bloody party chairman, and all he ever does is criticise me. I may be out of a job after the election – but *he* may only have to wait till I reshuffle.

He was still ranting on about 'normal'. I silenced him. 'It all depends, Neil,' I explained, 'on how you define normal. I'm certainly not against homosexual teachers *per se*. And I'm not against sex education. Now calm down.'

He tried. He took a deep breath. 'I'm not against teaching kids the facts of life in the classroom. But not homosexual technique. Nor heterosexual technique, come to that.'

'Where should they learn it then?' I asked curiously.

'Behind the bike sheds,' said Neil firmly. 'Like we did!'

This was a whole new insight into Neil. 'Did you?' I asked with interest.

Jeffrey, our Chief Whip, was not remotely interested in Neil's adolescence. 'Never mind about the sexual technique. Some of our schools are teaching more Hindi than English.'

This was even trickier. Perhaps it's lucky that I have no power over education. *I* agree that English is more important than Hindi. But I can't say it in public – I'll be accused of racism. Only last week, while I was receiving a deputation from the Ethnic Awareness Council, I looked at my watch while a black woman delegate was speaking. I was immediately accused of racist body language. And sexist body language. And I only did it because I was bored rigid!

Still, I'd got their message and I didn't see what I could do. So I asked them to be specific.

'Get Patrick[1] to get a grip on the Education Department.'

'You know it can't be done,' I replied. 'They've got Patrick completely housetrained.'

'Then sack him.'

'I can't have another Cabinet convulsion. Not yet.'

'Then,' said the Party Chairman, 'invite the Leader of the Opposition's wife round to Number Ten.'

'Why? What could she do?' I was puzzled.

Neil's face was a little less puce but no less grim. 'She can start measuring up for carpets and curtains.'

[*Hacker turned to Sir Humphrey Appleby for advice, believing that Sir Humphrey would be a believer in excellence for its own sake. But Sir Humphrey had his own hidden agenda, as this note in his private diary makes clear – Ed.*]

B.W.[2] had a private word with me. He told me the Prime Minister has a problem with Education. I've known that for years. But it's a bit late for him to do anything about that now, especially as he's got to Number 10 without any.

But apparently I was mistaken. The Prime Minister was not concerned about his own education (or lack of it). That would be too much to hope for. No, it was the education *system* that was on his mind – and in my view it's a bit too late to do anything about that either.

He thinks, Bernard told me, that Education is going to lose him the next election. This is indeed a possibility, but it is my view that worse things could befall the nation.

Furthermore, there is nothing to worry about. Our education system does all that most parents require of it. It keeps the children out of mischief while they're at work. Most of them, anyway.

It must be conceded that it does not, as Woolley pointed out, train their minds or prepare them for a working life. But then some of our local authorities would be most unhappy if it did.

When Bernard quoted the Party Chairman's paper, which suggests that the whole comprehensive system is breaking down, I sent him away with a flea in his ear. He's clearly been got at by the enemy – the Prime Minister's Chief Policy Adviser[3] to be precise. I will not put up with Bernard Woolley standing in my office telling me that as comprehensive education was an experiment, it ought to be validated. Of course it should – but on no account should it be invalidated.

[1] Patrick Snodgrass, the Secretary of State for Education.
[2] Bernard Woolley.
[3] Dorothy Wainwright.

Wednesday 12 DECEMBER

B.W. had a private word with me. He told me the Prime Minister has a problem with Education. I've known that for years. But it's a bit late for him to do anything about that now, especially

Comprehensive education was not introduced with the idea of improving educational standards. It was to get rid of class distinction. But the impression has been allowed to develop, quite wrongly, that the intention was to remove class distinction *among children*.

Nobody at the DES,[1] however, ever mentions children. They never have. Comprehensives were introduced so as to get rid of class distinction in the teaching profession. It was to improve the living standards of teachers, not the educational standards of children, and to bring the NUT[2] teachers in primary and secondary-modern schools up to the salary levels of their rivals in the National Association of Schoolmasters who previously taught in the Grammar Schools.

When there is a Labour government the Department's official line is *Comprehensives abolish the class system*. When there is a Conservative government the Department says: *Comprehensives are the cheapest way of providing mass education*. Thus the DES takes the view that selective education is divisive (if you're Labour) or expensive (if you're Conservative).

[1] Department of Education and Science.
[2] National Union of Teachers.

It is in the interest of the Civil Service to preserve this *status quo*. This enables the DES and the Government as a whole to have a happy relationship with the NUT. And it doesn't affect us personally because we educate our children independently.[1]

B.W. stubbornly insisted that the government wants change. Sometimes he is really dense. The teaching unions do not want change – and whereas we only have to cope with any government for four or five years, the teaching unions are there for ever.

Furthermore, Woolley seems to be under the impression that it is our job to get the unions to accept government policy. It is in this very fundamental sense that he has been got at and brainwashed by the enemy. Mrs Wainwright may believe that this course is in the government's interest; she may even have persuaded the Prime Minister; but she is wrong!

Our objectives in the Civil Service are harmony and consistency, conciliation and continuity. Laudable aims, as anybody will agree. And since governments change policy all the time, and the unions never change their policy at all, common sense requires in practice that it is the government that should be brought into line with the unions. And that is what the DES is there for – to get the government to accept the policies of the teachers' unions.

Bernard Woolley remained doubtful, I am sorry to say. He merely reiterated that his master, the Prime Minister, is deeply worried that he is responsible for something he can't change.

I'm sure he is. I call it Responsibility Without Power – the prerogative of the eunuch throughout the ages.

[*Hacker's diary continues – Ed.*]

December 13th

At my usual early morning meeting with Humphrey, right after breakfast, he raised the education question.

'I understand, Prime Minister, that you're worried about the Local Education Authorities?'

'No,' I told him, 'I'm worried about the Department of Education and Science.'

He was visibly surprised. 'In my opinion, the DES does an excellent job.'

He can't possibly believe that! *Nobody* could believe that. 'I don't believe you believe that,' I said.

'You don't?'

'Sorry, no.' Now he was insulted, I realised. I suppose I'd inadver-

[1] Privately.

tently called him a liar. Still, I was committed. 'Don't you believe that I don't believe you believe that?'

He was adamant and emphatic. 'I believe that you don't believe that I believe that, but I must ask you to believe that although you don't believe that I believe it, I believe it.'

I felt I had to accept that, especially as it took me quite a while to work out what he'd said. 'Be that as it may,' I continued, 'look what's happening to education in this country.'

Dorothy had armed me with actual questions from school exam papers. *Which do you prefer – atom bombs or charity*? And a maths question – even maths is becoming political: *If it costs £5 billion a year to maintain Britain's nuclear defences and £75 a year to feed a starving African child, how many African children could be saved from starvation by abandoning nuclear defence*?

Humphrey answered the second question immediately. 'That's easy. None. The MOD would spend it all on conventional weapons. But the question is simply asking for £5 billion divided by £75.'

'Do you deny', I remonstrated with him, 'that kids aren't even being taught basic arithmetic?

'No,' he replied carefully. 'But the LEAs[1] would doubtless argue that they don't need it – the kids all have pocket calculators.'

'But they need to know how it's done,' I reminded him forcefully. 'We all learned basic arithmetic, didn't we?'

Humphrey then asked me a whole bunch of stupid and irrelevant questions designed to prove to me that a strict academic education had no value! Humphrey, of all people! I couldn't believe it. He had the most traditional strict academic upbringing of anyone I've ever met. Anyway, I brushed his smokescreen – for that was what it was – aside.

SIR BERNARD WOOLLEY RECALLS:[2]

I read this portion of Hacker's diary with the greatest amusement. The questions to which he refers were neither stupid nor irrelevant.

When the Prime Minister asserted that we had all learned basic arithmetic Sir Humphrey immediately asked him: 'What is three thousand nine-hundred and fifty-seven divided by seventy-three?'

Hacker prevaricated, then said that he would need a pencil and paper for that. I offered him both but to no one's surprise he refused them, remarking simply that he could certainly have done that sum when he left school.

'And now you'd use a calculator?' enquired Humphrey. The point was

[1] Local Education Authorities.
[2] In conversation with the Editors.

well taken. But Hacker denied that Sir Humphrey had made any useful point at all. Instead, he remarked peevishly that hardly anyone knew any Latin any more either.

'Tempora mutantur, et nos mutamur in illis,' replied Sir Humphrey appropriately.

There was a slight pause as Hacker stared vacantly at him. Finally he was obliged to humiliate himself again by asking him for a translation.

'The times change and we change with the times,' I said.

'Precisely,' said the Prime Minister, as if the quotation proved his point – whereas any fool could see it helped Sir Humphrey's side of the argument.

Humphrey provocatively continued to speak in Latin. 'Si tacuisses, philosophus mansisses,' he said.

Hacker was suspicious. He asked what *that* meant. Sir Humphrey obliged. 'If you'd kept your mouth shut we might have thought you were clever.'

Hacker looked apoplectic. I thought he was going to suffer a coronary then and there. Sir Humphrey hastily explained. 'Not you, Prime Minister. That's the translation.'

Hacker then berated Sir Humphrey for denying the value of an academic education, whereupon Sir Humphrey replied – rather too insultingly in my view – that he could see no use for it if he personally couldn't even use it in conversation with the Prime Minister of Great Britain.

There is no doubt in my mind that Sir Humphrey, with his arrogance and determination to win the argument for its own sake, lost sight of his own policy objectives. By provoking and humiliating Hacker he ensured that Hacker would not drop the matter – a serious miscalculation.

[*Hacker's diary continues – Ed.*]

Humphrey was basically refusing to admit that our educational system was a disaster. I told him: 'Children are being taught subversive nonsense. There is total indiscipline in the classroom.'

Humphrey simply wouldn't acknowledge the truth. He kept making cheap debating points. For instance: 'If there's total indiscipline in the classrooms, they won't even know they're being taught subversive nonsense. And they certainly won't learn any. Anyway, no self-respecting child believes a word the teacher tells him.'

I was getting seriously angry at these facetious and unworthy answers. 'We're supposed to be educating them for a working life and three-quarters of the time they're bored stiff.'

'I should have thought being bored stiff for three-quarters of the time was excellent preparation for working life,' was the flip reply.

'Humphrey,' I said firmly, 'we raised the leaving age to sixteen to enable them to learn more. And they're learning less.'

Suddenly he answered me seriously. 'We didn't raise the leaving age to enable them to learn more. We raised it to keep teenagers off the job market and hold down the unemployment figures.'

He was right. But I didn't want to get into all that. I returned to the rest of the question. I asked him if he was trying to tell me that there's nothing wrong with our educational system.

'Of course I'm not, Prime Minister. It's a joke. It's always been a joke. As long as you leave it in the hands of local councillors it will stay a joke. Half of them are your enemies anyway. And the other half are the sort of friends that make you prefer your enemies.'

I finally saw where he was coming from in this discussion. He believes that education will never get any better so long as it's subject to all that tomfoolery in the town halls. He rightly observed that we'd never leave an important subject like defence to the local authorities – if we gave them £100 million each and told them to defend themselves we could stop worrying about the Russians, we'd have civil war in three weeks.

He claims that that's what we've done with education, that no one thinks education is serious the way defence is serious.

It's certainly true that no one takes *civil* defence seriously, and that's why it's left to the borough councils. But I assured Humphrey that I took education incredibly seriously – it could cost me the next election.

'Ah.' He smiled a superior smile. 'In my naïveté I thought you were concerned about the future of our children.'

Well, I am. These are not contradictory worries. After all, kids get the vote at eighteen.

Humphrey had a simple answer to the education screw-up: Centralise! Take the responsibility away from the local councils and put it under the Department of Education and Science. Then I could do something about it.

I wonder if he's right. It sounds too easy somehow. And yet . . . my hopes were raised.

'Humphrey,' I said, 'do you think I could? Actually grasp the nettle and take the bull by the horns?'

Bernard spoke for the first time. 'Prime Minister, you can't take the bull by the horns if you're grasping the nettle.'

I could hardly believe that this was Bernard's sole contribution to a discussion of such importance. I just sat there and goggled at him. He must have thought I didn't understand him, for he began to explain himself: 'I mean, if you grasped the nettle with one hand, you could

469

take the bull by one horn with the other hand, but not by both horns because your hand wouldn't be big enough, and if you took a bull by only one horn it would be rather dangerous because . . .'

I found my voice. 'Bernard . . .' I said. And he stopped. Perhaps he just can't help it. Attention to detail is all very well, but *really!*

I told Humphrey he'd given me food for thought

'In that case,' he replied complacently, '*bon appétit.*'

December 14th

I'm off on a brief pre-Christmas tour of the North-West tomorrow. Dorothy gave me a schedule, which includes Prime Ministerial visits to factories and hospitals.

'Drumming up votes in the marginal constituencies,' I remarked jovially to Bernard.

'No, Prime Minister,' he said.

I didn't realise what he meant at first.

'I'm coming with you,' he explained carefully, 'so it's a government tour. But if it consists of canvassing in marginals it's a party event and I can't come – and, more to the point, the Treasury can't pay for it all.'

His pedantry can be useful! Dorothy immediately made it clear, for the record, that we are making a government visit to the North-West, and that it is a pure coincidence that all the stops are in marginals. Bernard was satisfied.

I was still preoccupied with education. I asked Dorothy what I could do about it. Quickly!

'Do you mean do, or appear to do?' she wanted to know.

Silly question. 'Appear to do, obviously. There's nothing I *can* do.'

She thought for a moment, then proposed that I made some television appearance associated with something good and successful in education.

I was pleased to hear there *was* such a thing. She delved into her briefcase and handed me a sheet of paper containing details of 'St Margaret's School business enterprise unit'. She thinks I should visit the school on my tour. Apparently it could be squeezed into the schedule.

The school has set up its own manufacturing and trading company. They make cheeseboards, paperweights, toast racks and so on. Then they market and sell them. Furthermore, in their maths and business studies classes they track the whole operation. They involve local businessmen, and parents help too.

It sounds great. And what's more, it costs the DES *nothing* – they make a profit.

I wondered if there was any downside. Bad publicity on the grounds that children are being taught to be grasping? But no – Dorothy tells me they give the money to local charities.

It's obviously a *must* for a North-West trip. I told Dorothy to give it enough time on the schedule for TV cameras to cover it properly. And, I added, 'give me a speech with a snappy twenty-second passage for the TV news. It should all help to win back a few seats.'

Bernard shifted uncomfortably in his chair. He cleared his throat. 'Um, Prime Minister . . .' he reminded me firmly.

'I mean, Bernard,' I said, changing my tone, 'it will give a lead to those responsible for the nation's education.'

'Of course, Prime Minister,' he said with a smile.

[*Hacker's tour of the North-West was a great success, and his visit to St Margaret's School was indeed reported on the national news. The film itself does not survive, but we are fortunate that a transcript was made and we reprint it overleaf, with the kind permission of Independent Television News – Ed.*]

Independent Television News Limited

THE ATTACHED TRANSCRIPT WAS TYPED FROM A RECORDING AND NOT COPIED
FROM AN ORIGINAL SCRIPT. BECAUSE OF THE RISK OF MISHEARING ITN
CANNOT VOUCH FOR ITS COMPLETE ACCURACY

'NEWS AT TEN'

TRANSMISSION: DECEMBER 17TH

ACTUALITY:

NEWSREADER (offscreen): And finally, this morning the Prime Minister
visited St Margaret's School, Widnes, on his north-western tour.

SHOTS OF JIM HACKER, WITH BERNARD WOOLLEY IN THE BACKGROUND,
SURROUNDED BY NUMEROUS PRESS REPORTERS, ENTERING A SCHOOL WOODWORK
SHOP WHERE BOYS AND GIRLS IN NEAT SCHOOL UNIFORMS ARE BUSY.

NEWSREADER (offscreen): The school has set up its own little
manufacturing business where the children make a variety of goods
in the school carpentry shop for sale in the local community.
The children do their own sales and marketing.

CUT TO:
JIM HACKER STANDING WITH A GROUP OF SCHOOLCHILDREN, WATCHING THEM
PACKING, LABELLING AND STACKING BOXES OF GOODS.

NEWSREADER (offscreen): And they use the experience they gain
from the enterprise as a basis for their maths and business
studies.

CUT TO:
WIDE ANGLE - THE SCHOOL HALL. PRIME MINISTER HACKER IS SEEN ON
THE DAIS. A SENIOR GIRL HANDS HIM A THREE-LEGGED STOOL. THEY
SHAKE HANDS. BULBS FLASH FOR PHOTOS.

- 1 -

NEWSREADER (offscreen): The Prime Minister was presented with an example of the school's output.

CUT TO:
MEDIUM CLOSE-UP OF THE PRIME MINISTER, ADDRESSING THE SCHOOL.

HACKER: I must congratulate you all on the hard work, the discipline and the success of your enterprise. You set an example in British education which other schools would do well to follow. We need more schools like St Margaret's. And I shall certainly treasure your present - no Prime Ministers ever lose seats if they can possibly help it.

CUT TO:
WIDE-ANGLE OF AUDIENCE IN SCHOOL HALL. LAUGHTER AND APPLAUSE.

CUT TO:
THE PRIME MINISTER, SMILING AND WAVING AS HE LEAVES THE PLATFORM.

- 2 -

[*Hacker's diary continues – Ed.*]

December 17th

I watched a very satisfying film report of my visit to Widnes on the News at Ten tonight. Annie and Dorothy, who'd stayed for dinner, watched it with me. We all agreed that it had gone pretty well, especially my joke at the end of my little speech.

Actually, Dorothy claimed it was *her* joke. She was being petty. If by *her joke* she meant that she *thought* of it, then I suppose she's right – but that's hardly relevant.

The coverage was much better than it had been on the BBC. The BBC didn't describe it as 'the Prime Minister touring the North-West', they said it was 'Jim Hacker visiting the marginal constituencies'.

Both versions are perfectly true, but in my opinion it shows that the BBC is biased against me. I tried to explain this to Annie, who couldn't see it.

'Why shouldn't they report the facts?' she asked.

I explained that they don't have to report *all* the facts. Furthermore, there's nothing wrong with visiting marginal constituencies, but they imply that there is.

Annie *still* didn't understand. 'You mean, it's all right to report the majority of the facts but not the facts of the majorities?'

That's the kind of smart-alec remark that really makes me angry. The point is, it's all part of a wider picture. The BBC did the same to me earlier on, in the Nine O'Clock News, when they reported our dispute with the French: 'Mr Hacker claimed that the action was permissible, but the French government stated it was a violation of the treaty.'

'Isn't that true?'

'Of course it's true!' I exploded. 'But it makes it sound like me, on my own, being put down by the whole of France. It makes me look as though I'm in the wrong.'

'But the French think you are.'

'That's not the bloody point!' I shouted. 'They could have said: "Monsieur Dubois claimed that the action was a violation of the treaty, but the British Government stated it was permissible." Then it would have sounded – quite correctly – as though all of us were putting some cheeky Frog in his place. But they don't say that! Oh no! They want to get me!'

Annie was apparently undisturbed by the BBC's manifest bias, hatred, intolerance and corruption. 'But what they said was still true,' she reiterated stubbornly.

My jaw seized up with fury and frustration. Through clenched teeth I snarled, 'It's *still* biased to say so!! The other's true too!!'

I didn't want to demean myself by losing my temper in front of Dorothy, who'd so far stayed very quiet. I took several deep breaths, then strolled calmly over to the drinks table and poured myself a very large Scotch.

Annie remained completely calm. 'Jim,' she said, 'I'm not interested in your paranoia, I'm interested in that school.'

Dorothy spoke up, relieved not to have to take sides in a family fight. 'Yes, it must be a good place if parents are queuing up to get their kids into it.'

'What a pity that they can't all get in,' said Annie, and poured coffee for us both. 'Why *can't* more parents send their children there?'

'No room,' I explained.

Dorothy corrected me. 'There is room actually, Jim. School numbers are falling.'

She's right, in one sense. 'But it would be poaching from other schools,' I pointed out.

Annie looked up. 'What's wrong with that?'

'It's obvious. The other schools would then be too short of pupils. They'd have to close.'

'Great,' said Annie. 'So then St Margaret's would take over their buildings.'

I tried to explain to Annie that they couldn't do that. It wouldn't be fair.

'Who to?' she wanted to know.

'To the teachers in the schools that had to close.'

'But the good ones would be taken on by the popular schools. They'd be needed.'

'What about the bad ones?' I argued. 'It wouldn't be fair on them.'

'What about being fair on the kids?' said Annie. 'Or are the bad teachers' jobs more important?'

I sipped my coffee, and put my feet up on the leather footstool. 'It's no good, Annie.' I was tolerant. 'Who's to say which are the bad teachers? It can't be done.'

'Why not?'

I couldn't really think of the reason, but I was sure there was one. Then, to my surprise, Dorothy asked the same question: 'Why not?'

475

This threw me. And to my surprise I found that I was really stuck.

Dorothy took up the argument. 'Suppose schools were like doctors,' she pondered, helping herself to a peppermint cream chocolate. 'After all, under the National Health Service you can go to whichever doctor you like, can't you?'

I nodded.

'And the doctor gets paid per patient,' she continued thoughtfully. 'So why don't we do the same with schools? A National Education Service. Parents choose the school they want, and the school gets paid per pupil.'

'There'd be an outcry,' I replied.

'From parents?' said Dorothy, knowing the answer full well.

'No,' I had to acknowledge. 'From the Department of Education.'

'I see.' And she smiled. Then she asked another question to which she already knew the answer. 'And who has the most votes, parents or the DES?'

That wasn't exactly the point. And she knew it! 'The DES would block it,' I reminded her.

And then she said something so revolutionary, so riveting and so ruthless that it shook me rigid. [*Hacker often displayed a talent, probably subconscious, for alliteration when excited – Ed.*]

'Fine,' said Dorothy. 'Get rid of them!'

It took me a moment to realise what she meant. I think I just stared blankly at her. Get rid of the Department of Education? I didn't really understand.

'Get rid of it!' she repeated. 'Abolish it. Remove it.'

I asked her what she meant, exactly.

'Eliminate it. Expunge it. Eradicate it,' she explained.

I was beginning to understand what she was driving at. But I asked her to explain further.

She looked slightly flummoxed. 'Um . . . I don't quite know how else to . . . well, let me put it this way.' She hesitated for a moment, considering her choice of words carefully. 'What I mean is,' she said finally, 'get rid of it.'

'Get rid of it?' I asked.

She confirmed that she meant that I should get rid of it.

'I couldn't do that,' I said. I was in a daze.

'Why?' she asked. 'What does it do?'

And, suddenly, I realised that I *could* do that! Local Authorities could administer everything that is needed. We could have a Board of National School Inspectors, and give all the rest of the DES's functions to the Department of the Environment. And I could send that house-trained idiot Patrick to the House of Lords.

'Golly!' I wondered in awe. 'What will Humphrey say?'

Dorothy smiled a beatific smile. 'Whatever he says,' she said happily, 'I want to be there when you tell him.'

'And witness a clash between the political will and the administrative will?'

She sat back thoughtfully. 'I think it will be a clash between the political will and the administrative won't.'

December 18th

I called Humphrey in first thing this morning. Dorothy was with me. I tried to disguise my excitement as I casually told him that I wanted to bounce a new idea off him.

The word 'new' usually alerts Humphrey that trouble's in store, but this time he seemed perfectly relaxed and actually chuckled when I told him that I've realised how to reform our education system.

So I let him have it. 'Humphrey, I'm going to let parents take their children away from schools. They will be able to move them to any school they want.'

He was unconcerned. 'You mean, after application, scrutiny, tribunal hearing and appeal procedures?'

It was my turn to chuckle. 'No, Humphrey. They could just move them. Whenever they want.'

'I'm sorry, Prime Minister, I don't follow you.' I could see that he genuinely didn't understand.

Dorothy spelled it out, abrasively. 'The government, Sir Humphrey, is going to let parents decide which school to send their children to.'

Suddenly he understood that we actually meant what we were saying. He exploded into protest. 'Prime Minister, you're not serious?'

I nodded benevolently. 'Yes I am.'

'But that's preposterous!'

'Why?' asked Dorothy.

He ignored her completely. 'You can't let parents make these choices. How on earth would parents know which schools are best?'

Coolly I appraised him. 'What school did you go to, Humphrey?'

'Winchester.'

'Was it good?' I asked politely.

'Excellent, of course.'

'Who chose it?'

'My parents, naturally.' I smiled at him. 'Prime Minister, that's quite different. My parents were discerning people. You can't expect *ordinary* people to know where to send their children.'

Dorothy was manifestly shocked at Humphrey's snobbery and élitism. 'Why on earth not?'

He shrugged. The answer was obvious to him. 'How could they tell?'

Dorothy, a mother herself, found the question only too easy to answer. 'They could tell if their kids could read and write and do sums. They could tell if the neighbours were happy with the school. They could tell if the exam results aren't good.'

Again he studiously ignored her. 'Examinations aren't everything, Prime Minister.'

Dorothy stood up, moved around the Cabinet table and sat down very close to me so that Humphrey could no longer avoid meeting her eyes. 'That is true, Humphrey – and those parents who don't want an academic education for their kids could choose progressive schools.'

I could see that, as far as Humphrey was concerned, Dorothy and I were talking ancient Chinese. He simply didn't understand us. Again he tried to explain his position, and he was becoming quite emotional. 'Parents are not qualified to make these choices. Teachers are the professionals. In fact, parents are the worst people to bring up children, they have no qualifications for it. We don't allow untrained teachers to teach. The same would apply to parents in an ideal world.'

I realised with stunning clarity, and for the very first time, how far Humphrey's dream of an ideal world differed from mine. 'You mean,' I asked slowly and quietly, 'parents should be stopped from having kids until they've been trained?'

He sighed impatiently. Apparently I'd missed the point. 'No, no. Having kids isn't the problem. They've all been trained to *have* kids, sex education classes have been standard for years now.'

'I see,' I said, and turned to Dorothy, who was wide-eyed in patent disbelief at our most senior Civil Servant and advocate of the Orwellian corporate state. 'Perhaps,' I suggested, 'we can improve on the sex education classes? Before people have children we could give them exams. Written and practical. Or both, perhaps? Then we could issue breeding licences.'

Humphrey wasn't a bit amused. He ticked me off. 'There's no need to be facetious, Prime Minister. I'm being serious. It's *looking after* children that parents are not qualified for. That's why they have no idea how to choose schools for them. It couldn't work.'

Dorothy leaned across in front of me, to catch his eye. 'Then how does the Health Service work? People choose their family doctor without having medical qualifications.'

'Ah,' said Humphrey, playing for time. 'Yes,' he said, flummoxed. 'That's different,' he concluded, as if he'd actually said something.

'Why?' asked Dorothy.

'Well, doctors are . . . I mean, patients aren't parents.'

'Really?' Dorothy was laughing openly at him. 'What gives you that idea?'

He was beginning to get extremely ratty. 'I mean, not *as such*. Anyway, as a matter of fact I think letting people choose doctors is a very bad idea. Very messy. Much tidier to allocate people to GPs. Much fairer. We could even cut the numbers in each doctor's practice, and everyone would stand an equal chance of getting the bad doctors.'

I was quietly amazed at Humphrey's – and the Civil Service's – concept of 'fair'.

Humphrey was now in full flow, passionate, emotional, scathing, committed like I have never seen. 'But we're not discussing the Health Service, Prime Minister, we're discussing education. And with respect, Prime Minister, I think you should know that the DES will react with some caution to this rather novel proposal.'

This was the language of war! Humphrey had all guns blazing. I've never heard such abusive language from him.

I stayed calm. 'So you think they'll block it?'

'I mean', he said, tight-lipped and angry,' that they will give it the most serious and urgent consideration, but will insist on a thorough and rigorous examination of all the proposals, allied to a detailed feasibility study and budget analysis before producing a consultative document for consideration by all interested bodies and seeking comments and recommendations to be incorporated in a brief for a series of working parties who will produce individual studies that will form the background for a more wide-ranging document considering whether or not the proposal should be taken forward to the next stage.'

He meant they'd block it! But it will be no problem. No problem at all. Because, as I told him, I have a solution to that. 'So I'll abolish the DES!' I mentioned casually.

He thought he'd mis-heard. 'I'm sorry?'

'We'll abolish it,' I repeated obligingly.

'Abolish it?' He couldn't grasp the meaning of the words.

'Why not?' Dorothy wanted to see if there were any reason.

'Why not?' he said, his voice rising to the pitch of a Basil Fawlty at the end of his tether. 'Abolish Education and Science? It would be the end of civilisation as we know it.'

I shook my head at him. He was quite hysterical. 'No, we'd only be abolishing the Department. Education and science will flourish.'

'Without a government department?' He was staring at us in horror, as though we were certifiably insane. 'Impossible!'

Dorothy seemed almost sorry for him. She tried to explain. 'Humphrey, government departments are tombstones. The Department of Industry marks the grave of industry. The Department of Employment marks the grave of employment. The Department of the Environment marks the grave of the environment. And the Department of Education marks where the corpse of British education is buried.'

He was staring the Goths and the Vandals in the face. He had no reply. So I asked him why we need the DES. What does it do? What's its role?

He tried to calm down and explain. 'I . . . I hardly know where to begin,' he began. 'It lays down guidelines, it centralises and channels money to the Local Education Authorities and the University Grants Committee. It sets standards.'

I asked him a string of questions. 'Does it lay down the curriculum?'

'No, but . . .'

'Does it select and change Head Teachers?'

'No, but . . .'

'Does it maintain school buildings?'

'No, but . . .'

'Does it set and mark exams?'

'No, but . . .'

'Does it select the children?'

'No, but . . .'

'Then *how*', I wanted to know, 'does the Secretary of State affect how *my* child does at *her* school?'

To Humphrey the answer was obvious. 'He supplies sixty per cent of the cash!'

So that's it. We were right. Dorothy pursued the cross-examination. 'Why can't the cash go straight from the Treasury to the schools? And straight to the University Grants Committee? Do we really need 2000 civil servants simply to funnel money from A to B?'

Almost in despair, he shook his head and cried: 'The DES also creates a legislative framework for education.'

What did he mean? There's hardly any legislation at all. What there is, the Department of the Environment could do – Environment deals with other local government matters.

Humphrey was fighting a desperate rearguard action. 'Prime Minister, you *can't* be serious. Who would assess forward planning and staffing variations, variations in pupil population, the density of schooling required in urban and rural areas . . . Who would make sure everything *ran properly*?'

'It doesn't run properly now,' I pointed out. 'Let's see if we can do better without the bureaucracy.'

'But who would plan for the future?'

I laughed. But I didn't just laugh, I laughed uproariously. Laughter overwhelmed me, for the first time since I'd been Prime Minister. Tears were rolling down my cheeks. 'Do you mean?' I finally gasped, breathless, weeping with laughter, 'that education in Britain today is what the Department of Education *planned*?'

'Yes, of course,' said Humphrey, and then went immediately and without hesitation straight into reverse. 'No, certainly not.'

Dorothy was getting bored with the meeting. She stood up. 'Two thousand five hundred private schools seem to solve these planning problems every day,' she commented curtly. 'They just respond to changing circumstances, supply and demand. Easy.'

I wanted to give Humphrey one last chance. 'Is there anything else the DES does?'

His eyes whizzed back and forth, as he thought furiously. 'Um . . . er . . . um.'

I stood up too. 'Fine,' I said. 'That's it. We don't need it, do we? Quod erat demonstrandum.'[1]

[*In her book* The Prime Minister's Ear, *Dorothy Wainwright made an interesting attempt to explain Sir Humphrey Appleby's complex attitude to state education. Her book is now out of print but we reprint a short extract below – Ed.*]

Sir Humphrey Appleby's paternalist attitude may not have been wholly cynical. He apparently believed that more central direction was the answer

[1] QED.

to all the nation's problems. It is probable that he viewed the main purpose of state education as a means of removing children from the undesirable influence of their semi-educated parents. And he doubtless felt that most parents regarded schools as somewhere that they could dump their children during working hours. In short, he truly believed that the man in Whitehall knew best. For at the root of this passionate dispute over education lay the fundamental tribal struggle between the Whitehall Man and Westminster Man.

It is not that Sir Humphrey was against giving the parents what was euphemistically known as a 'voice' in the running of a school. Indeed, he was unconcerned about parent governors because, so long as the parents as a whole were unable to remove their children from a school with which they were unhappy, the parent governors could safely be ignored. If a child was prevented from attending school by a dissatisfied parent, the Attendance Officer was soon on hand to threaten the parent with an appearance in court.

In the end, it was the more affluent middle classes who benefited from the system, the same middle classes who won the lion's share of all the benefits of the welfare state in not only education, but housing and medicine too. Inevitably benefits went to articulate people who could best advance their claims, who could move to the nicest residential areas with the best schools and doctors, who could claim mortgage tax relief, and who enjoyed subsidised art.

Sir Humphrey, however, clung to the only belief that he had left after thirty years in government: that if he had more control, he could make things better. Anything that was wrong with society was evidence, proof indeed, of not enough power. Sadly he remained unshakeably convinced right up till the very day of his death in St Dympna's Home for the Elderly Deranged.

[*The last entry of the year in Sir Humphrey's private diary records a meeting with Sir Arnold Robinson, his predecessor as Secretary of the Cabinet, at their old haunt: the Athenaeum Club – Ed.*]

Met Arnold for lunch at the Club. I told him of the truly appalling meeting with Hacker this morning.

Like me, he thought it was unthinkable. Once they start abolishing whole Departments, the very foundations of civilisation crumble. Indeed he's right. The barbarians are at the gates. This is the return of the Dark Ages.

I asked him if anything so shocking had ever been suggested while he was at 70 Whitehall.[1] Apparently not. Arnold had let them amalgamate Departments, of course, but that's quite a different matter: amalgamation means that you keep all the existing staff and put in an extra layer of co-ordinating management at the top.

[1] The Cabinet Office.

Tuesday 18 DECEMBER

Met Arnold for lunch
at the Club. I told
him of the truly
appalling meeting
with Hacker this morning.

Like me, he thought
it was unthinkable.
Once they start abolishing

But he agreed that, come hell or high water, I have to stop the liquidation of the DES. He asked me if I'd tried discrediting the person who proposed it.

That is impossible in this case, of course. The Wainwright female is the culprit, and therefore Hacker's passing it off as his own idea.

Arnold had a couple of other tired old ideas:
1. *Discrediting the facts its based on*.
   Not possible. It's a political idea, so obviously facts don't come into it.
2. *Massaging the figures*.
   There are no figures involved.

I asked him what he really thought. Shamefully he peered over the side of his leather wing armchair to check that he wasn't being overheard, and then he leaned forward and whispered an appalling admission: that in his opinion it was actually quite a good idea.

I'd never even thought of that: for a mad moment I wondered if we ought to experiment with it, play along with it for the sake of the nation's children.

But this was not Arnold's intention and, seeing that I was wavering, he bolstered me up and gave me courage. 'Never mind about the nation's children! What about our colleagues in the Department of Education?'

I apologised for my lapse. It's just that I've been under great strain.

The fact is that the *only* people who will like this plan are parents and the children. Everyone who counts will be against it, namely:

i) Teachers' Unions
ii) Local Authorities
iii) The Educational press
iv) The DES

We decided upon a temporary holding strategy:

1) The Unions can be counted on to disrupt the schools. And their leaders will go on television to say that it is the government who are causing the disruption.

2) The local authorities will threaten to turn the constituency parties against the government.

3) The DES will delay every stage of the process and leak anything and everything that embarrasses the government. Arnold will be able to help with that, at the Campaign for Freedom of Information.

4) The education press will print any damn fool story we feed them.

We relaxed and ordered a couple more brandies. There was one little problem: we hadn't decided what our argument would be. Arnold suggested that we say that this new proposal will destroy our educational system. But there was a problem: everyone knows it's destroyed already. So we decided that we will say [*by which Sir Arnold meant that the Press will say – Ed.*] that government interference has already destroyed the education system, and that this plan will make things even worse.

I was sceptical. I wondered if that would really do the trick. Arnold assured me that it always has in the past. He's right, of course, but this time the political pressure is much stronger.

We had no answer. Arnold stressed that I must find a *political* weapon with which to fight this battle. It is undoubtedly in the national interest to do so, even though I'd be in conflict with government policy.

'Government policy,' said Arnold thoughtfully, 'is almost always in conflict with the national interest. Our job is to see that the national interest triumphs. Governments are always grateful in the end.'

He may be right. But I have no political weapon in mind, and nor has he. And it's my job. I must somehow prove myself worthy of the high office to which I've been called.

[*But luck was on Sir Humphrey's side. A most unlikely event occurred that changed the course of history. When the Cabinet Secretary arrived at 70 Whitehall the following morning, with leaden step and a heavy heart and no strategy, Bernard Woolley was waiting anxiously to see him. Sir Bernard Woolley recalls*[1] *the momentous*

---

[1] In conversation with the Editors.

events of that morning, the turning point that never was – Ed.]

I was waiting for Sir Humphrey in his oak-panelled office. He was late. The Prime Minister had sent me to find him.

Humphrey asked for the agenda – which was all too simple. The Abolition of the DES.

He commented that it was going to be bloody! I agreed.

And on the way to the Cabinet Room I asked him for some advice on what I thought was an urgent but minor problem.

This was it: St Margaret's School in Widnes, the enterprise school which the Prime Minister had visited at the beginning of the week, where they'd given him that stool, had been in trouble with the law.

It had just come to light that the wood being used in the carpentry shop was stolen. In fact, stolen from the government, from a YTS[1] workshop. It was stolen by the previous year's pupils, who were working there.

Humphrey's reaction astonished me. He stopped dead, in the middle of the long dark corridor, stared at me, and then smiled what I can only describe as an ecstatic smile. 'How shocking!' he beamed. I gave him the file, which showed that the matter had been referred to the DES from the Department of Employment because the theft had come to light in a school. They didn't know whether to prosecute.

I apologised for bothering Sir Humphrey with such a minor matter. Little did I realise the significance of the report at that moment – though only five minutes later it was clear that I'd helped drop an atom bomb on Hacker's educational reforms.

[*Hacker's diary continues – Ed.*]

December 19th

A sad day. My greatest, most fundamental reform had to be abandoned. It's not that the DES is the most significant Department in Whitehall – but to me it had come to represent bureaucracy in its purest, least diluted form – a totally unnecessary Department, one that was not merely irrelevant but which was by its very existence an impediment to reform.

The meeting started well enough. 'Only one item on the agenda – abolition of the DES,' I began cheerfully.

I noticed Humphrey was in much better spirits than I had expected. 'If it's only one item, it's an agen*dum*,' he corrected me arrogantly as he sat down across the table from me.

Bernard leapt to my defence. 'I don't think the Prime Minister got

[1] Youth Training Scheme.

as far as the second declension,' he said. At least, I *think* he was leaping to my defence.

In any case, I felt extremely tolerant, even benign. 'I don't mind you scoring cheap debating points, Humphrey,' I said, 'since you've lost the battle of the DES.' Pride goeth before a fall!

'The DES will be very upset, Prime Minister,' replied Humphrey, who was worryingly relaxed, I noted.

'Does it matter,' I asked, 'since they'll have ceased to exist?'

Humphrey gave me every chance to back out and save face. But he withheld the crucial point of information that had come his way. I knew he was hiding some ace up his sleeve – but I didn't know it was the ace of trumps.

Meanwhile, we sparred. He told me that the process of abolishing the DES would take a year or two, and meanwhile they'd fight tooth and nail.

I asked what they could do to me. He was enigmatic, confining himself to veiled threats, such as 'They are a formidable Department.'

'I'm a formidable Prime Minister,' I retorted.

'Oh indeed,' agreed my Cabinet Secretary, 'but you might still need their co-operation.'

Actually, that idea struck me as intrinsically funny. The idea of the DES co-operating with the Government? Absurd. But as I sat there laughing, the axe fell!

'Fine,' said Humphrey. 'If you don't want their co-operation I'll tell them to go ahead with the prosecution.'

At first I thought I'd misheard. 'Prosecution? What prosecution?' I didn't know what he could mean. I looked at Bernard. Bernard stared intently at his shoelaces. I had no choice but to ask Humphrey what he was talking about?

He smiled again, so I knew I was in deep trouble. 'Well, it's hardly worth bothering you with, but that enterprise school where you were televised this week . . .' He paused, elegantly, to make me suffer.

'Yes?' I said.

'"An example of what's best in education,"' he quoted me saying.

'Yes?' I repeated, my heart in my mouth.

'"A model for other schools to follow."' I began to think he was going to re-enact my entire speech.

'Go on!' I snapped.

'Well . . . it's just that its profits were apparently the proceeds of theft.'

486

I didn't know what he meant. 'What do you mean, theft?'

'I mean', he explained pleasantly, 'removing goods without the knowledge or consent of the owner, with the intent of permanently depriving him of possession.'

'Yes, Humphrey.' I was getting pretty tight-lipped. 'I know what theft means. But what do *you* mean?'

Well, it all boiled down to this: the stool that they gave me in that presentation was made from stolen wood. It was nicked from the local YTS workshop by two of last year's pupils. A *pair* of nickers, as Bernard said, trying unsuccessfully to lighten the atmosphere.

The YTS want to prosecute. And the Department of Education can stop them – by returning the wood and hushing the whole thing up.

Humphrey said that the DES took a different view. Surprise, surprise!

I tried to tough it out. I said that the DES must obviously return the wood and forget the whole thing. It is their duty, I argued – otherwise I'll look ridiculous, having told millions of voters on TV that the school is an example to Britain.

'It is a *sort* of example,' conceded Humphrey maliciously.

'But it's not typical of enterprise schools,' I insisted.

He smiled a malevolent smile. 'It was enterprising.'

'They mustn't prosecute!' I commanded him, cutting the crap.

He looked surprised. 'Is that your instruction?' I nodded. He took a sharp intake of breath. 'Well, I hope that the Department of Education doesn't leak the fact that you're covering up for thieves.'

Blackmail, if ever I heard it. I changed my position immediately. 'You misunderstood, Humphrey,' I said grandly. 'It's *not* my instruction. Just tell them not to prosecute.'

'Ah,' said Humphrey thoughtfully. 'That would need their co-operation.'

Checkmate. Game, set and match. Snookered. I could just imagine the headlines: *PRIME MINISTER OF CRIME*! Or *JIM'S ENTERPRISING PUPILS*.

It was my turn to beg. 'Humphrey,' I said, 'you must persuade them to stop it.'

He was implacable. 'It's *rather* difficult', he drawled, 'to persuade people to co-operate when they're under a death sentence.'

I had no choice but to lie. 'Death sentence?' I queried, in a surprised voice.

'I thought you were about to abolish the Department.'

487

'Abolish it?' I said. 'Oh, *that*!' And I laughed as convincingly as I could. 'No, no, Humphrey, that was just a vague idea. I wasn't really serious. Can't you tell when I'm joking?'

'You're sure?'

'I'm sure I was joking.'

I left myself a loophole. But Humphrey spotted it instantly. 'And you're sure you're not going to abolish the DES?'

'Yes.'

'I have your assurance, Prime Minister?'

I took a deep breath. 'Yes,' I said quietly. My plans were turning to dust. Like all my plans. Suddenly I saw, with a real clarity that I'd never enjoyed before, that although I might win the occasional policy victory, or make some reforms, or be indulged with a few scraps from the table, nothing fundamental was ever *ever* going to change.

Humphrey was now in the best of humour. I heard his voice, as if in the distance. 'Prime Minister? Prime Minister? Are you all right?'

I focused on him. 'Yes.'

'Excellent. Then shall we continue with the agendum?'

'Agendum?' I smiled. All the fight had gone out of me. 'No, Humphrey, we have no agendum any more. Meeting declared closed. All right?'

'Yes Prime Minister.' He smiled at me with sympathy. He could see that at last I understood.